"You are ⸻
aren't you?'

He move⸻
Lady Lucinda. No idea.

Lucinda had to force herself to remain still, hold her ground, and not close the small space that separated her from the duke. What was it about this man that made her act differently? Feel differently? *Want* differently?

Staring into his bottomless eyes, full of mischief before, and now—well, only Lucifer himself could say, Lucinda wondered what made her want to find out. "Is that a challenge, Your Grace?" she asked with light curiosity, her tone matching his.

It was the duke's turn to laugh. "I believe it is, Lady Lucinda. The question is, are you inclined to accept?"

Lucinda's mouth went dry and her mind raced. Surely such questionable banter was beyond acceptable behavior, even for a lady of six-and-twenty.

This was Iron Will. A man with a rake's reputation. A man polite society had deemed wild and unruly. Were it not for his title as the Duke of Clairemont, he might very well have been banned from tonight's ball.

To further the acquaintance would be impossible.

Unthinkable. Madness.

She threw caution to the wind.

"Let the games begin," she answered, her mouth curving into a wicked grin before she offered her hand to the duke.

"Indeed."

The Devil in Disguise

A REGENCY ROGUES NOVEL

Stefanie Sloane

BALLANTINE BOOKS • NEW YORK

A Ballantine Books Mass Market Original

Copyright © 2011 by Stefanie Sloane
Excerpt from *The Angel in My Arms* by Stefanie Sloane copyright © 2011 by Stefanie Sloane

Published in the United States by Ballantine Books, an imprint of The Random House Publishing Group, a division of Random House, Inc., New York.

BALLANTINE and colophon are trademarks of Random House, Inc.

This book contains an excerpt from *The Angel in My Arms* by Stefanie Sloane. This excerpt has been set for this edition only and may not reflect the final content of the forthcoming edition.

ISBN 978-0-345-51739-5
eBook ISBN 978-0-345-51742-5

Cover design: Lynn Andreozzi
Cover illustration: Alan Ayers

Printed in the United States of America

www.ballantinebooks.com

9 8 7 6 5 4 3 2 1

Ballantine Books mass market edition: June 2011

For my mom, Lois Faye Dyer.
I never would have managed to finish this book—
any book, honestly—without your belief that I could.
You are amazing, selfless, strong, and true. In short,
you're my hero.

1

Lady Lucinda Grey had not precisely decided what she would do if the overly eager Matthew Redding, Lord Cuthbert, compared her eyes to the Aegean Sea. Or the most brilliant of sapphire. It had all been said before and—Lucinda admitted with a stab of regret—in much more creative ways than poor Lord Cuthbert could ever dare dream.

"I shall faint, I believe," she said succinctly, straightening the Alençon lace fichu neatly tucked into her jonquille gown.

Lord Cuthbert stopped ogling Lucinda's bosom abruptly, a look of confusion clouding his round face. "I beg your pardon?"

Lucinda realized her earnest suitor clearly felt he'd reached the point in his seduction where she should have been dizzy with anticipation and too caught up in the moment to speak.

"Lord Cuthbert, I do apologize," she offered, taking advantage of the moment to discreetly reclaim her hand from his damp gloved grasp. She slid to the end of the settee, putting two feet of gold damask cushion between them. "Pray continue."

Lucinda felt compelled to see this thing through, despite the temptation to feign what would surely be a spectacular fainting spell. Lord Cuthbert's fumbling attempt at romance was, she realized, not unlike happening upon a carriage accident; be it concern or distasteful fascination, one simply could not look away.

Nor faint away, she acknowledged with a frustrated sigh.

Over the last few weeks, Lucinda had acquired far more experience with this sort of thing than she could have ever imagined or wished to endure. The endless parade of suitors who had found themselves on her doorstep this season had been uninspiring, to say the least.

This was all her dear friend Amelia's fault, of course, Lucinda reflected as Lord Cuthbert droned on. If Amelia hadn't married the Earl of Northrop last year and if the couple had not displayed a love so wide and vast that those observing wondered if they might very well be lost forever . . . well, Lucinda would not be in this predicament.

A fellow ape leader for the last several seasons, Amelia had, until the altogether unexpected appearance of the earl, been a staunch supporter of a woman's right to peace. And quiet. And sanity. In other terms, a woman's right *not* to marry.

"If only Lord Northrop had not worn Amelia down," Lucinda muttered under her breath, causing not even the slightest pause from the windbag before her.

Lord Cuthbert was so completely absorbed in his rehearsed speech, which left her free to return to her contemplation of the events that had led to his presence in her parlor.

Discreetly counting the winged cherubs that inhabited the plaster ceiling in force, Lucinda begrudgingly admitted that Lord Northrup had not precisely worn Amelia down. Not exactly. That was to say, not at all. On the day the two met it was as if the heavens echoed with the cries of angels—and Cupid himself nearly collapsed from the joy of uniting such a pair.

Uncharitable and unkind, Lucinda mentally chided herself. She adored Amelia as though she were her own sister. To be unhappy over her newfound marital bliss would be inexcusable. And in all honesty, Lucinda *was* pleased for her friend. It was just that they had both been so convinced that love was a ruse, invented to keep the poets out of trouble. And now one had only to look upon Amelia and her new husband to know that they'd been utterly wrong.

But the real difficulty was that—London being London—Amelia's blissful state meant that the entirety of polite society assumed Lucinda would follow suit and be felled by love as well.

Frankly, Lucinda found the whole thing somewhat alarming.

And Amelia was no help. Utterly smitten and convinced Lucinda should share her happiness, she had done nothing to defend her friend and dispel the ton's false assumption. On the contrary, she'd worked feverishly to provide every opportunity for Lucinda to achieve an equally sublime level of bliss. And after countless prospects, all of which had been met with what could be politely called mild disappointment on Lucinda's part, Amelia had grown desperate.

Which was how Lucinda had arrived at this moment with Lord Cuthbert, forced by good manners to endure his declaration of undying affection.

Cuthbert's patting of his mud brown hair into place pulled Lucinda from her thoughts. Clearing his throat with theatrical emphasis, he continued his attempts at poetic flattery. "Lady Lucinda, your eyes are, to be sure, the bluest of blues that I've ever encountered. Truly, without a doubt."

She stared at him. She did not know what to say.

He blinked. "Quite blue. Really, truly very blue."

And in that moment, Lucinda realized that there was only so much a lady of reasonable intelligence could be expected to endure.

"My lord," she began, rising from the settee and smoothing the fine lawn skirt of her morning gown, "I fear our time together is at an end."

Cuthbert practically jumped from his seat. He stepped clumsily toward Lucinda, stopping mere inches from her. "Lady Lucinda, are you well?"

It was just the cue she needed. She'd faced much worse from importunate suitors over the last three weeks and hadn't a doubt her dramatic flair would serve her well in this instance. "I seem to . . . that is to say . . ." She hesitated, swaying ever so slightly while raising her hand to her temple. "I must retire. Immediately, if not sooner."

Cuthbert seemed to take this latest development as an opportunity, moving to stand unbearably close. He placed his hand at the small of her back. "My dear lady, you must tell me what you need and I will fetch it at once."

He was determinedly solicitous; Lucinda had to commend him for that. She was going to have to skip to the coup d'etat.

"Lord Cuthbert," she said, pausing to give what she hoped was a convulsive swallow. "I feel obligated to inform you that I fear I shall cast up my accounts at any moment. And I would so hate to ruin your extremely unique puce waistcoat."

Cuthbert nearly shoved Lucinda to the settee in his eagerness to escape the baptism. He bounded across the room to reach a small armchair where Lucinda's maid, Mary, was seated. "Attend to your mistress," he barked. "At once."

"My lady," Mary said quickly, shaking herself from

what clearly had been a pleasant daydream and standing.

Lucinda bit back a smile and focused her gaze on Cuthbert. "Thank you, my lord, you're most kind."

Clearly his fondness for the puce brocade far outweighed his affection for Lucinda. He backed quickly toward the doorway. "Of course, of course. I'll call again at a more convenient time."

Lucinda's butler, Stanford, appeared with such alacrity it was apparent he'd been waiting just outside in the hall.

"My lord," the stony-faced butler intoned His emotionless gaze focused on the gilded mirror just beyond Cuthbert's large head.

Lord Cuthbert bowed again before falling into step behind Stanford.

Mary closed the door quietly behind them.

"He was the worst by far. What on earth could Amelia have been thinking?" Lucinda said, exasperation clear in her voice as she stood.

"That you've refused every eligible man in London under the age of seventy?" Mary answered, her years of service to Lucinda evident in her impertinent answer.

Lucinda laughed, Mary's blunt observance easing the annoyance of the last half hour.

"I do believe Lord Mayborn is actually three-and-seventy." Lucinda said. "And I highly doubt I've made the acquaintance of 'every eligible man' in the entire city. Surely there is at least one or two more for Amelia to proffer up in her quest for my everlasting happiness."

"I've heard Lord Thorp's son is available," Mary answered, peering into the now silent hall before holding the door wide for Lucinda.

Amused, Lucinda arched an eyebrow at her maid's too

innocent expression. "I prefer my men properly attired, which does not include apron strings. And while I do like a good challenge," she added dryly as she crossed the threshold, "I fear the twenty-year gap in our ages would prove to be an obstacle even I could not overcome.

"Hmph," Mary said with unshakable calm as she followed her mistress out of the room. "You've no romance in you, Lady Lucinda. Not at all."

"Well, when it comes to infants, I'd have to agree with you," Lucinda answered over her shoulder as she walked toward the staircase.

Mary hmphed again. "Don't play coy with me, miss."

Lucinda stifled a grin at Mary's curt tone. "Oh, Mary. It's just not true and you know it."

"Really, now?" the servant answered, the sarcasm somewhat lost in her rough Liverpool accent.

Lucinda mounted the carpeted stairs. *"Really,"* she confirmed. And it was the truth. She believed in romance as it pertained to the likes of Anthony and Cleopatra, Henry VIII and Ann Boleyn, Arthur and Guinevere, Amelia and John—though the tragic endings of all but her dear friend's relationship was unsettling, to say the least.

I really must remember to mention this to Amelia, she mentally took note, reaching out to skim the smooth marble balustrade.

The point was, romance was all well and good for others. It simply was not for Lucinda. She did not need a man to make her life complete. Nor did she particularly want one, the emotional upheaval and mercurial behavior that seemed to accompany love something that she neither understood nor desired.

"I'll have to take your word for it, I suppose," Mary answered unconvincingly, then gestured for her lady to continue up the stairs, swatting at her derriere when she did so and eliciting a hoot of laughter from Lucinda.

ʃ

William Randall, the Duke of Clairemont, bent to nip his mistress's breast and licked upward to the vulnerable spot where her pulse pounded at the base of her throat. The woman beneath him twisted, panting, her lush curves slick with sweat where their bodies pressed and slid, bare skin against bare skin.

"Harder, Will." The throaty gasp was half plea, half demand. "Now."

He could see it in her eyes—the heady mixture of heat, passion, and urgent need that told him that a woman was about to come. Never one to deny a lady, he thrust deeply, ruthlessly holding back his own rising need for release.

"Your Grace. If you please . . ."

"No need to be so polite, Beatrice," Will muttered before he realized she hadn't spoken. He bit off a curse and went still, looking over his shoulder.

The ducal bedchamber was cast in gloom, the heavy silken curtains drawn against the afternoon sunshine. Nevertheless, Will instantly recognized his valet's stiffly erect figure, standing just inside the closed door. "What is it, Smithers?"

Lady Beatrice Winn's fingers tightened on Will's forearms, her body stiffening beneath his, and he glanced down at her. Her eyes widened with alarm, chasing away the raging passion of only seconds earlier. Will soothed her concern with a brief, hard kiss. "If you'll excuse me for one moment," he began, lifting off of her, "I'll deliver the sound thrashing that most certainly is in order and return to continue our . . ." he paused, dropping his bare feet to the floor and standing, "discussion of charitable endeavors."

Beatrice discreetly pulled the sheet up to her shoulders, her mouth sulky with frustration. "Think nothing of it, Your Grace. My charity can wait—though do keep in mind that the longer one is kept waiting, the more needy one becomes."

He fully understood Beatrice's warning. She'd proven to be well nigh insatiable in past encounters. "Not to worry. Try to remember where we left off, won't you?"

Satisfied that she was as comfortable as a mistress might be when interrupted by her lover's servant, Will reached for his dressing gown and shrugged into it with quick jerks. He roughly knotted the silk tie and turned to his valet. "Smithers, you have my full attention for precisely two minutes. Shall we?"

Will stalked from the room, waiting until Smithers joined him in the hall and pulled the door closed behind them. "Bloody hell, man, do you have any idea how near I was—"

Smithers quickly gestured toward the stairs. "Lord Carmichael awaits you in your study, Your Grace."

For precisely three seconds, Will held himself silent. And then: "Again you prove yourself unimpeachable, Smithers."

Will quickened his pace and descended the steps two at a time. "Though you could work on your timing, man. One, two minutes, perhaps, could have been spent in quiet contemplation outside my door, if you understand me?"

"Of course, Your Grace, though Lord Carmichael led me to believe his business with you is of importance," Smithers replied from some length behind. "Might I bring you a coat, or perhaps breeches?"

Will couldn't help but grin at Smithers's undying devotion to propriety, even after many years in his employ. "Not necessary, Smithers. But see to Beatrice. Some tea, perhaps?"

"Of course, Your Grace," Smithers said instantly.

Barefooted, Will strode down the hall on the second floor and turned left into his study, slamming the heavy wooden door behind him. Much to his frustration, the sound failed to elicit even the slightest arching of an eyebrow from the man sitting behind his desk.

"You really should have taken Smithers up on the breeches, Clairemont."

Damnation, the man can't be surprised. Will sat down and carefully arranged his dressing gown. "Come now, Carmichael. Clothing can be an impediment in certain situations. If I had known to expect you, then perhaps other arrangements could have been made."

"It's three o'clock in the afternoon. Surely 'other arrangements' could have, and should have, been made with regard to your games above stairs. Won't her husband wonder where she's gone off to?"

Will returned Carmichael's halfhearted reproach with a smile. "You know very well Winn is likely as not foxed by now. And even if he wasn't, he couldn't care less about Beatrice. Which is why she's the ideal woman for me. I really should be thanking the fellow, come to think of it."

Carmichael quirked a brow and said nothing, which Will found highly annoying. "Are we done making comment upon my personal exploits?"

Carmichael looked as if he might smile. "Quite."

"Excellent." Will shifted his position, careful to keep a hand on the disobedient gown. "Now, old man, tell me, are you here on Corinthian business or were you simply anxious to see me?"

Carmichael smiled at the reference to his age, no more than half a dozen years separating the two. "Very well, on to business." He stood, his wiry frame taking little time to unfold. "We've received intelligence from several reliable resources in France regarding a kidnapping plot about to be put in play."

"And the target?" Will leaned forward, instantly focused on the threat, their conversation about his mistress forgotten. "Wellington himself, perhaps?"

"No," Carmichael answered as he started to pace. "No, the goal is money, but this time the target is a wealthy young woman. More specifically, the wealthiest woman in England."

Will frowned as he began a mental check of who that might be. Despite his own family's social significance, he paid little attention to such things, and identifying the chit presented a challenge. "You'll have to give me a clue, here, old man. I'm afraid my years spent cultivating a rake's reputation have hardly left me on intimate terms with the ton's wealthiest debutantes."

"Lady Lucinda Grey," Carmichael answered, stopping just in front of the mullioned window. "Daughter of the late Earl of Sinclair. Or course, the title now belongs to a great uncle. But Lady Lucinda inherited a fortune in unentailed property from her father. Not to mention a townhouse and other bits and baubles from her mother."

Will let out a low whistle of appreciation.

"Do you know her?" Carmichael inquired.

Will relaxed into his chair, stretching his long legs out in front of him and crossing them at the ankles while still managing to remain decently covered by the gown. "Lady Lucinda Grey? Only by reputation Good Lord, from what I've heard of her, the kidnappers should be fearful. Beautiful, charming, and intelligent enough to deny thousands of men the honor of her hand for nearly a decade. Lady Lucinda will have her captors enthralled in no time."

"Perhaps. But I'm afraid we can't count on her charms and ability alone," Carmichael began. "Fortunately for our purposes, she's apparently looking for a husband this season."

Carmichael paused, and he looked at Will as if he ought to know what the hell he was talking about.

"This is where you come in," he finally added.

Will straightened and tried to look into Carmichael's face. But the old man was standing with his back to the window, and his face had been cast into shadow, making it difficult to read his expression.

Will cleared his throat and began carefully, choosing each word with the same precision he reserved for his work. "I'm not sure I understand, especially in light of our conversation a few moments ago. I've spent years cultivating a reputation guaranteed to make the ton believe I'm an irredeemable rake. It's been an excellent cover. I'm the last man anyone would believe to be looking for a wife, never mind the richest, most sought-after woman in all of England."

"Your reputation is an impediment in this instance, I'll admit. But you are, after all, the best actor among all the Corinthians, are you not?"

Will leaned a bit to the right but, much to his frustration, still couldn't see Carmichael's face clearly. "Flattery will get you nowhere, old man. Besides, why not hedge your bets and use someone who actually has a prayer of breathing the same air as Lady Lucinda. Talbot or Wharton would be perfect. They're such, such . . ." He waved a hand, searching for the appropriate term.

"'Gentlemen' is the word I believe you're looking for."

Will shifted to the left but still could not see Carmichael well. "Yes, gentlemen, or in other words, men who would be allowed within ten paces of the woman. Unless it is your intention to terrify the chit. One look at me and she'd succumb to a fit of the vapors."

"Oh, but you have something that no other man in England has," Carmichael said with calm conviction. "And it's something she desperately wants."

Will stood and walked to the fireplace, where he leaned his forearm on the mantel. "What could I possibly have that Lady Lucinda Grey would desire?"

He had a clear view of Carmichael now and easily read the satisfaction on the man's face.

"King Solomon's Mine."

Will was confused. "Why would the richest woman in all of England want my horse? She could buy a stableful of champions."

Carmichael moved around the desk to stand in front of Will. "King Solomon's Mine, as you well know, was bred in Oxfordshire on the Whytham estate, which borders Lady Lucinda's Bampton Manor."

"But why would a woman want a horse merely because he was bred next door?"

"You know women. They're softhearted creatures with minds of steel. And once those minds are made up . . . well," Carmichael shrugged "there's little that can be done to change them. Our intelligence tells us Lady Lucinda was present at King Solomon's Mine's birth and she spent much time thereafter with him. Apparently, she developed a fondness for the colt and considered him her special project. That is, until you won him."

Will had a brief, swift flash of memory. The look of sheer disbelief on Whytham's face when he realized he'd lost the son of Triton's Tyranny had made it a truly unforgettable hand of cards.

"That's all well and good, but what does my owning the horse have to do with Lady Lucinda allowing me into her company?"

"Rumor has it she enjoys a challenge," Carmichael

answered. He glanced at his engraved watch fob and frowned before abruptly tucking it back into his waist-coat pocket. "You're a resourceful man. I'm sure you'll think of something."

Carmichael's tone worried Will. He'd known the man too long to be fooled by his seemingly casual words. "Surely you don't expect me to offer her Sol in a wager of some sort?" He didn't add he'd rather lose a limb than the stallion. The comment would only serve to confirm Carmichael's suspicion that Will had a much softer heart than he would ever admit.

"As I said, you're a resourceful young man."

Will would have pressed further, but the look on Carmichael's face stopped him cold. "There's something you're not telling me. Come now, old man, what is it?"

"It's Garenne."

Will froze. "What do you mean?"

"He's involved."

"No." Will shook his head, refusing to believe it. "That's impossible. He's dead. I saw the body with my own eyes." The night the Corinthians had taken the French assasin down on a nondescript Parisian street was seared into his memory. The organization had breathed a collective sigh of relief with the death of Garenne.

Carmichael cleared his throat. "What was it you called him—the Chameleon?"

"He had a gift for disguises, that much is true," Will said brusquely. "But the man's size, his clothing . . ." He wanted to convince Carmichael, wanted to convince himself. "We received intelligence. It guaranteed that we had the right man."

"We've confirmed sightings of him in Paris," Carmichael said quietly. "And two recent killings of Corinthians involved his calling card."

Will felt his stomach roil at the thought of Garenne's signature. The sadist left each of his victims with a fanciful letter "G" carved into his left breast, the knife strokes revealing the victim's heart, left exposed by the crude cuttings of a madman.

Will flexed his hands before curling them into fists, slamming one and then the other onto the polished top of the massive oak desk.

"He's rumored to be working for Fouché," Carmichael added.

"Napolean must be trying to stick his bloody fingers in every pie on the Continent," Will said tersely.

"I'm afraid keeping up with Joseph Fouché's political loyalties is an exhausting task indeed," Carmichael answered. "No, it seems the man now supports the House of Bourbon. They'll stop at nothing to secure control of the continent—perhaps England as well."

Will looked up at Carmichael, whose brows were knit together in concern. "I suppose you've a starting point for me, then?" he said, carefully resuming his air of insouciance.

Carmichael took a pasteboard card from his breast pocket. "I suggest turning yourself over to Smithers. The Mansfield ball is this evening and we've confirmed that Lady Lucinda will be in attendance." He offered the invitation to Will and walked to the door, pausing to look back. A wry smile tilted his mouth as his gaze flicked to Will's bare toes and back up to his face. "A shave might be in order. She likes her suitors properly turned out. And breeches. Do not forget the breeches."

Will moved to the window and looked out at the garden. The sight of hyacinths, pansies, and a whole host of other flowers that he could not name did little to soothe the growing doubts in his mind. Corinthian business was never a neat and tidy affair. Subterfuge demanded an often skewed view of right and wrong—something that had heretofore suited Will's less than traditional view of life.

It's not as if I've never lied to a woman before, he thought as he turned from the window and rested his shoulder against the heavy velvet curtain. It wasn't something he was proud of, but to live as he did and to be an effective agent for Carmichael often made the truth more dangerous than any lie ever could be.

No, it wasn't the lie that bothered him, but perhaps the intent. To court a woman for the entire ton to see— Will paused mid-thought, nearly shuddering as he steadied himself before crossing to his desk. For a man to engage in a series of activities with the believed goal to be matrimony . . . Well, that was a different animal altogether.

Carmichael had spoken the truth when he reminded Will of his expert acting skills. He picked up a cut-crystal paperweight and addressed it in Hamlet-like fashion. "The woman doesn't stand a chance."

Will knew it. Carmichael knew it. The only individual involved in their scheme who was ignorant of this fact would be Lady Lucinda.

Gently replacing the weight to its proper place, Will straightened his dressing gown and reknotted the silk sash. Could he win the heart of an honorable woman? Could he do so with the knowledge that he would, in the end, break it?

Of course he could. A man in his position couldn't afford a conscience. Why his conscience had chosen this particular moment to come to life, he didn't know.

In truth, to leave the woman to the likes of Garenne

was unthinkable. He'd rather slit his own throat than allow the madman another chance to kill.

"Bloody hell," Will swore, padding across the thick Turkish rug with a newfound resolution. "It's the horse that has me worried," he said to no one in particular as he opened the door. "He really is a fine horse."

2

"Bloody hell, Carmichael."

Will eyed the elegantly dressed throng from his coach window. The crowd ebbed and flowed, moving at an imperceptible pace toward the Mansfield mansion. Traffic slowed to a crawl and then a halt. Horses whinnied and stamped, gentlemen offered their arms to twittering ladies, who—if the overheard snippets of their inane conversations were any indication—had lost their heads over the excitement of the evening ahead.

"And I'm not even in the door yet," he grumbled, pressing his weight against the carriage door and releasing the latch.

His footman leapt down from the back of the coach and scrambled to hold the door. He gave Will a quizzical look. "I beg your pardon, Your Grace?

Will straightened his coat and took a deep breath. "Nothing, Hugh. Nothing at all."

Stepping over a steaming pile of horse dung, he crossed the street and joined the crowd. Almost at once he felt the stares. Then came the whispers, and after that, the urgent conversations clearly concerning him. The crowd parted before him, too stunned to utter a greeting.

"I am apparently Moses," he said under his breath, thinking it was a damned shame he hadn't been able to precede his visit with locusts and flies.

He would, however, draw the line at the death of the firstborn sons. Even he had standards.

With cynical amusement, he made his way into the foyer, eyeing the cluster of ladies and gentlemen climbing the wide marble stairs. With each moment the din from the ballroom seemed to grow in volume, and his annoyance peaked again. Carmichael knew full well what Will thought of polite society—and what they thought of him. His reputation as a hot-tempered man with little interest in propriety was well established. It had served his cover well, as it had his personal life, if he was completely honest. No one bothered to look beneath his gruff exterior, a fact Will acknowledged with both satisfaction and an occasional, but rare, twinge of regret.

And if tonight he actually convinced the fashionable set of his sincere desire to take his rightful place in their midst, what then?

He'd have to live with the ton's smugly satisfied belief that he'd acquiesced to his dead father's wishes and returned, tail between his legs, to assume the mantle of familial responsibility.

Realizing fortification was in order, he abruptly stopped a footman scurrying past with a tray of empty punch cups. "Brandy. Now. I'll wait there." He pointed at the anteroom opening off the foyer.

The young man promptly jumped to the task, tipping the tray as he went, the sound of clanking cups punctuating his progress.

Will had just enough time to enter the room and prop himself against the cream damask wall before the footman returned. He drank the brandy in one swallow and returned the glass to the tray with a decisive click.

"Thank you, my good man."

The liveried servant bowed and departed.

Savoring the slow burn as the brandy snaked its way

to his belly, Will forced himself up the stairs and reached the receiving line.

Lord Mansfield, a portly man whose circumference nearly matched his height, smiled broadly and offered his hand. "Clairemont, welcome. It's been some time since I've had the pleasure of lightening your pockets at Brooks," he said with a wink.

"If memory serves, Mansfield," Will drawled, "I believe I won the last time we played a hand."

"Indeed," Mansfield chuckled wryly.

"Your Grace," Lady Mansfield interrupted, nearly elbowing her husband aside as she inserted herself into the conversation. "You honor us with your presence," she gushed.

"Lady Mansfield." Will inclined his head in an appropriate ducal acknowledgment. "Thank you for your gracious invitation."

"Oh, but no, Your Grace, it is we who are honored that you have joined us this evening," she answered, offering her hand and curtsying to Will before shooting a look of elated satisfaction at the nearby members of the ton.

"Clairemont, my wife, Lady Mansfield." Lord Mansfield met Will's gaze in silent apology. "Priscilla," he muttered, turning to the woman while carefully avoiding the exuberant lavender plumage protruding somewhat her purple turban. "Do behave."

Will tamped down his initial urge, which was to silence her with a cold stare. He thought better of it—for both Mansfield's sake and his own. If ever there was a moment to establish himself as a changed man, this was it.

He took Lady Mansfield's plump, bejeweled fingers in his hand and bowed perfunctorily. "My pleasure, I assure you. In truth, I've been absent far too long from an assembly such as—"

She gripped his hand and gave him a sympathetic look. "Yes, yes, far too long, my dear boy. Why, only last month I happened upon Her Grace while in Bath. She is such a dear woman, your mother. And when I asked after you in passing, I must say that she hastily skirted the subject, offering very little information." She paused for effect, raising an eyebrow at Will and leaning in to murmur conspiratorially. "It was clear she worries after you."

Will froze, hating that he had to remind himself he was playing a part. Hell, hating that he *was* playing a part.

The woman interrupts you when speaking, calls you "dear boy" as though she were your doting aunt from Aberdeen, and has the audacity to assume she knows the private thoughts of your mother. Dear God, he thought, *she's a walking trial by fire. Live through this introduction and the remainder of the evening will be a breeze.*

What was it Carmichael was constantly prattling on about, he wondered? Ah, yes, counting. Count to ten and breathe. Will began his slow ascent to the double digits, his chest expanding and contracting in time.

"Yes, well," he said, finding his equilibrium somewhere around thirteen. Smoothly, he extricated his hand from her clutching fingers. "My mother is an exemplary parent." Will's voice held only a hint of sarcasm as he nodded and stepped back, determined to extricate himself from Lady Mansfield's too sympathetic clutches and make his way into the ballroom.

Laying a restraining hand on his arm, Lady Mansfield began, "Oh, my dear boy, you can be assured that I'll convey your words to her upon our very next meeting and I'm certain . . ."

"My dear, let the poor man go." Lord Mansfield pulled his wife to his side, removing her hand from

Will's sleeve and clearing his way to escape. "Save me a spot at the hazard table, will you?" he asked Will.

Will gave Mansfield a look of thanks and nodded. "A glutton for punishment, I see. Just as well," he continued, smoothly stepping out of Lady Mansfield's reach. "I always enjoy a sound thrashing at the card table—not mine, of course."

He heard Mansfield chuckle behind him as the crowd cleared a path for him. He moved toward the ballroom, the din growing louder as he neared, then paused in the doorway.

The noise hit him first, exaggerated and grating, bits of laughter and feigned interest, colorful gossip and tart reproaches all competing against one another.

The heat was next. The combination of hundreds of candles and even more swirling and animated bodies left little fresh air beneath the glittering chandeliers. The sights were as he had remembered from every other ball he'd attended as a younger man, newly on the town. Jewel-toned dresses interspersed throughout the milder tones of pinks, yellows, and blues. Blondes and brunettes, milky-skinned misses and eager young bucks, aged dowagers and graying lords, some dancing, others conversing, while the wallflowers lined the periphery, valiantly trying not to look desperate.

It was all a gigantic waste of time, as far as he was concerned; too loud to converse on anything of meaning, too hot to do more than wish your clothes were off, and too polite. Far too polite. These people knew nothing of real fun. Wild, free, unadulterated fun was more to Will's liking and often included far more fights and much more drinking. Thank God he'd had the foresight to stop the footman earlier.

"You're glowering."

Years of training meant Will was not caught off guard by the whispered statement just to the left and behind him. "And how would you know, Northrop, considering your inability at the moment to view anything but my posterior?"

John Fitzharding, the Earl of Northrop, came round to stand by Will's side. "I don't need to see your face. It's written all over theirs." He motioned to the crowd beyond, many of whom, judging from their looks of anxious surprise, had taken note of Will's unexpected presence.

"It's your fault, you know. I couldn't possibly come off as anything but terrifying standing next to you." Will raked his friend with an assessing stare. The difference between the two was stark. Will knew his tall, broad frame was all hard angles and rugged features with coal black hair and deep hazel eyes. He was the dark Devil to Northrop's leaner body, angelic golden hair, blue eyes, and gentlemanly appearance.

They'd joined the Young Corinthians around the same time, becoming fast friends despite being different in practically every way. Northrop's calm-and-collected nature complimented Will's wilder tendencies—a fact that had saved Will on more than one occasion in those early years.

"It's more than your muscles and famously short temper that fascinates them," Northrop said, just a hint of amused sarcasm accompanying his smile. "They don't know why you're here. And not to know something is unacceptable to this set. Knowledge is power, after all."

Will met Northrop's half grin with his own. "Bloody hell, can't a man go looking for a bit of entertainment without the entire world wondering what he's up to?"

"Is that it, then?" Northrop asked, one eyebrow lifting in patent disbelief. "You're here for a bit of entertainment?"

Corinthian law forbade discussing a case with fellow members who weren't directly involved. It kept things less complicated. And while Northrop might hint at his suspicions over the reason for Will's appearance, Will could not, would not, reveal his true purpose.

"More than simply entertainment, I suppose," he began. "If you must know," he said, adopting the role of liar as easily as he would throw back his brandy, "my mother has finally succeeded in making me consider the future. It's time I found a wife."

Will watched Northrop take the information in, knowing full well he'd not be able to tell if his friend believed him. As one of the most valuable members of the Corinthians, Northrop would, of course, expertly mask his true thoughts.

The man merely adjusted a cuff. "Well, it's about bloody time we made a gentleman out of you."

Did Northrop believe him? Will couldn't let the thought linger. Besides, it didn't matter much either way. Northrop would help when Will asked, without questions. Slipping a finger between his cravat and neck, Will feigned discomfort. "Let's not get ahead of ourselves. First, the a lady. Any suggestions?"

The two looked about the room, Will with one particular woman in mind. He immediately spotted Lady Northrop, John's wife and reputedly Lady Lucinda's inseparable companion. A circle of men, surrounded Lady Northrop, who stood next to another woman, partially hidden from Will's view by the group. The men appeared to be enthralled by the lady's every word, Will noticed with some cynicism.

"Let's see. There's Madeline Haywood," Northrop began. "Her intellect rivals that of a sack of potatoes, but she's fairly attractive."

The group around Lady Northrop shifted, allowing Will a clearer view of the woman at the center.

Bloody hell. Lady Lucinda Grey was beautiful. Not just pleasing. Not just pretty. Beautiful.

Will felt heat rising from his belly to his chest. A mass of honeyed yellow curls artfully framed her face—and *that face*. The bluest eyes Will had ever seen shone like, well, he wasn't quite sure, not being poetically inclined, but even from his distant vantage point the brilliancy of them could not be denied. Her lips, slightly pink, delicately shifted from question to statement and back again, surely hypnotizing the lot of fools around her.

Don't look down, man. Whatever you do, do not look any farther.

But his eyes seemed to act of their own accord. His gaze lowered from her pert, ridiculously charming chin, and he found himself in forbidden territory. The creamy, milk white expanse of skin that showed above her pale pink evening attire begged to be caressed. As for what came next, even Will felt embarrassed over his reaction. The lady's breasts were, in a word, perfection. Nicely rounded and set high, they appeared to be the ideal size for Will's hands. His palms itched to feel the weight of them.

"If you prefer a touch more intelligence," Northrop said, clearly unaware of Will's distraction, "perhaps Honoria Willett. She's the one in blue, next to her man-of-war-sized and exceptionally opinionated mother, Lady Dandridge." Northrop paused for just a moment, then added, "Come to think of it, I fear your newly re-formed temper may not be ready for Lady Dandridge. What do you think?"

Will couldn't respond. If anyone had told him before tonight that he'd be dumbstruck at the mere sight of a woman, he would have ridiculed them as lackwits.

"Clairemont?" Northrop said. "Clairemont? Are you quite all right?"

Will pulled his gaze from Lady Lucinda and attempted to focus on his friend. "What was that about ships?"

"Keep up, man." Northrop frowned, his sharp gaze

searching Will's face. "Your title and wealth aside, the truth is, you scare the hell out of most men, never mind these naïve misses. You'll need your wits about you to accomplish the task at hand." He looked to the crowd and back. "Now, back to Madeline—"

"And Lady Lucinda Grey. Do I frighten her?"

Northrop looked into Will's eyes more sternly. "You can't be serious. Lady Lucinda Grey? Will, she's not . . . that is to say—"

"The richest woman in all of England. Prim, proper, intelligent, and notoriously particular when it comes to men?" Will interrupted, returning Northrop's look with a seriousness all his own.

"Yes," Northrop countered, lowering his voice before continuing. "But that's not the point, Clairemont. She's a particular friend of Amelia's and because of this I've had the opportunity to further my acquaintance with her. She's a lovely woman. Yes, she's prim and proper and quick-witted. But beyond that, she's loyal and kind and—"

"You sound as though you're describing a favored dog, Northrop. Come now, why, exactly, are you concerned over my possible interest in this woman?" Will press, growing slightly irritated.

Northrop blew out a breath and broke his gaze, looking instead at his wife, standing next to Lady Lucinda. "Listen. This is a woman who has refused every eligible bachelor in England. I'm only trying to save you a wasted effort."

"Will you present me or not?" Will asked, his tone and directness telling Northrop what he couldn't put into words.

Northrop flinched slightly, a sign he had some understanding that this touched on Corinthian business. "All right, then, but Clairemont," he said, placing his hand on Will's shoulder, "have a care, won't you?"

"Have all the rumors about me finally convinced you of my black heart, then?"

"You know I don't give a deuce about what people say. I trust you. It's Lady Lucinda I'm concerned for. She'll not recognize the game you're playing. You're too good at it."

"I need an introduction," Will said simply.

Northrop closed his eyes for a fraction of a second longer than was normal. "I don't want to see her come to harm. However dire the consequences of your assignment, in the end she'll not understand."

Will's eyes met his friend's. "If you do not wish for her to come to harm," he said softly, "you'll make the introduction."

It was the closest he'd ever come to divulging Corinthian business. But Northrop's concern and obvious affection for his wife's friend deserved something more from the situation.

Northrop dropped his arm to his side and motioned Will to follow him across the ballroom.

Will felt the eyes of the entire room on him as he walked toward the women. *Am I that monstrous,* he wondered, nearly tempted to curl his lips and growl at the whole lot. As his father before him, and as far back as anyone cared to remember, the Clairemont men had always possessed a remarkable resemblance to one another. Of course, he'd failed to inherit his father's cold countenance, having been born instead with the Mc-Claine family temper, or so his mother had always told him.

No matter how hard he'd tried to please his father by pretending to be more like him, he always fell short.

Until one day when his father delivered a particularly vile set-down. Will had been only ten, but something in his father's tone and demeanor made him understand full well that the duke loathed not only his son's temperament, but everything else about him.

Northrop made his way to his wife's side and pressed a light kiss to her cheek. "Lady Northrop, have I told you how lovely you look tonight?"

"Only twice in the last hour," she answered, her violet eyes filled with amusement.

The gaggle of young men acknowledged Northrop's presence with brief nods before returning their full attention to Lady Lucinda, who stood transfixed by something behind them.

Confused, all of them turned, then flinched in unison upon seeing the duke.

"Gentlemen," he said, giving each an intense look of warning before returning his gaze to Lady Lucinda.

Mumbling various and assorted excuses, the men hastily said their good-byes to the ladies before scattering to the four corners of the room.

Will stepped closer to the trio and waited for Northrop to make the introduction. He couldn't take his eyes off Lady Lucinda. The low buzz and whirr of the room all but stopped for Will as he rocovered his poise.

"Your Grace, it's been some time since we've had the pleasure of conversing," Lady Northrop said.

It took a moment for Will's addled brain to resume functioning. He looked at Lady Northrop, noticing too late the hint of confusion playing across her features.

Snap out of it, man.

"Lady Northrop, it's been far too long," Will replied, even though he knew full well that, for Lady Northrop, it hadn't been long enough. She'd never been unkind to him, but it had been clear from the beginning of Northrop's courtship she'd been less than ecstatic over her husband's friendship with him. He couldn't blame her. Really, what upstanding young wife would look to

encourage her husband in spending time with a repro-
bate?

He bowed over Lady Northrop's hand, catching sight
of Lady Lucinda's curious look as he did so. She smiled
at being caught and a dimple flashed at the corner of her
mouth. *For the love of all that's holy,* he thought with
bemusement, *how was a man expected to concentrate
with such a creature about?*

He looked at Northrop, who'd been taking in the interaction with keen interest. Leveling a final warning
look, his friend began the introduction. "Lady Lucinda,
may I present to you His Grace, the Duke of Clairemont."

For a moment Will felt time begin to slow again. He
shook off the spell as best he could and forced his lips to
move. "Lady Lucinda, it is indeed a pleasure to make
your acquaintance." He accepted her offered hand and
bowed, covertly taking in the length of her as he did so.

She curtsied low, the graceful movement placing her
breasts directly in his line of sight.

Will fought the urge to linger and looked at her face,
catching an arched eyebrow and, perhaps, the merest
hint of a satisfied smile.

She rose slowly. "Your Grace, it is a great honor to
meet the infamous Iron Will."

It was his face—more specifically, his smile—that
caused Lucinda's heart to skip a beat for the third time
that evening. A young boy caught doing something he
should not, that smile said. Utterly charming and devoid
of any lechery, unlike the myriad men before him, who'd
failed her test.

Amelia had scolded her on a multitude of occasions
for shamelessly using her physical attributes in an attempt to separate out the men looking for more than a
pretty face from the men looking for . . . well, looking.

And, while the Duke of Clairemont was clearly admiring her for something other than her brain, Lucinda couldn't quite muster the indignation to be offended.

Perhaps it was more than his smile. Perhaps it was his fierce stare, which she'd noticed almost immediately from across the crowded ballroom. She'd turned, and her heart had skipped a beat. The man had called to her with that piercing, focused stare; his eyes, as she could now clearly see, were a deep hazel.

She'd tried to ignore him, tried to pretend that her heart had not quickened the moment he'd walked into the room. She had to maintain her composure, converse with her companions with something that at least approximated intelligence.

But it was no use. She kept glancing about, trying to find him again despite her best intentions. She was utterly distracted, a complete ninny. No fewer than three gentlemen had asked if she was overheated.

And then she'd spotted him again, speaking with Lord Northrop in what appeared to be a serious conversation.

Suddenly, without warning, the duke stalked toward her. He moved like a force majeure. Was it his size that made him command such attention, or his demeanor—his gaze never leaving hers, a determined set to his brow that could not be mistaken for anything but purpose.

And then, right next to her, Amelia said with a sigh, "How odd that His Grace would choose to attend Lady Mansfield's ball. Truly, there must be a full moon."

Lucinda took a deep breath then hastily drank her lemonade. She wasn't a mere miss with little or no experience with men. She was, in fact, six-and-twenty and, if one cared to ask any of the grande dames in attendance, painfully past ready for the shelf. No, the ton acknowledged that Lady Lucinda Grey had never, ever, been laid low by a man.

Which was why it was particularly frustrating for Lucinda when her heart missed a beat yet again. *Blast,* she thought to herself as the man in question stopped mere feet from her.

She couldn't look away.

Or was it that she wouldn't?

"Lady Lucinda, may I present to you His Grace, the Duke of Clairemont."

Lucinda started at the sound of Lord Northrop's voice, his words snapping the spell that held her.

The duke made a polite remark and then it was Lucinda's turn to respond. "Your Grace, it is a great honor to meet the infamous Iron Will."

She could hardly believe she'd dared use the man's questionable sobriquet, a sentiment shared by all three of her companions, if their looks of astonishment were any indication.

But slowly, the duke's surprised expression turned to delight, his full lips curving in an amused smile. "Lady Lucinda, I believe I like you already."

A small laugh escaped Lucinda's lips. She considered giving him a vaguely polite response, but the obvious enjoyment in his eyes made her reconsider. "You are something altogether different, Your Grace, aren't you?"

He moved ever so slightly closer. "You've no idea, Lady Lucinda. No idea."

Lucinda had to force herself to remain still, hold her ground, and not close the small space that separated her from the duke. What was it about this man that made her act differently? Feel differently? *Want* differently?

Staring into his bottomless eyes, full of mischief before, and now—well, only Lucifer himself could say, Lucinda wondered what made her want to find out. "Is that a challenge, Your Grace?" she asked with light curiosity, her tone matching his.

It was the duke's turn to laugh. "I believe it is, Lady Lucinda. The question is, are you inclined to accept?"

Lucinda's mouth went dry and her mind raced. Surely such questionable banter was beyond acceptable behavior, even for a lady of six-and-twenty.

This was Iron Will. A man with a rake's reputation. A man polite society had deemed wild and unruly. Were it not for his title as the Duke of Clairemont, he might very well have banned from tonight's ball.

To further the acquaintance would be impossible. Unthinkable. Madness.

She threw caution to the wind.

"Let the games begin," she answered, her mouth curving into a wicked grin before she offered her hand to the duke.

"Indeed."

He was careful to keep his distance, all too aware his failure in this endeavor would mean his death. Not that death itself was a concern. No, not when one lived an existence such as his. But dying would be so inconvenient and, to be quite honest, terribly dull when compared to spending the coin he'd been promised if he succeeded in capturing the wealthy English Woman.

The possibilities for purchases were endless. Whores. The best wine. An exquisite wig made of real human hair that would make the perfect addition to his exhaustive collection of disguises. More whores.

The ballroom was crowded but he adroitly slipped between chattering groups, avoiding collisions. But an inebriated pig of a man staggered, lurching into him and bumping his arm, nearly sending the tray of champagne he carried crashing to the floor.

"*Imbécile,*" he muttered under his breath, cursing his need to masquerade as a servant. Still, the disguise had afforded him entry into the Mansfields' palatial town house and provided access to the target. He'd been un-prepared for the complication presented by the bear of a man conversing with her, however. He'd recognized the man on sight, a familiar foe who'd made appearances in his life unscathed up until this point.

The Duke of Clairemont could well prove a problem if Garenne did not adjust his plans accordingly.

He was a creature of habit with a nearly psychotic need for exactitude. The thought of altering his well-thought-out mission caused Garrene's throat to con-strict, the heat of the room doing little to ease him. Pain stabbed just behind his right eye, only once, but it was followed by the inexorable tightening of an invisible band at his temples. The warning was explicit. He needed to leave the ballroom. Now.

Shortening the time line is of no consequence, he as-sured himself, impatiently stopping to allow a whale of a woman to pass by. *In fact, it will only mean I may re-turn home that much sooner.*

His throat relaxed slowly as he absorbed the im-proved plan. The invisible iron band around his head eased and the pain slowly lessened. *Yes, I'll take the woman tomorrow and be done with this filthy country forever.*

He snaked, nimble and unnoticed, through the crowd as he made his way to the kitchens to refill his tray of champagne glasses.

3

"May I have this dance?" Will asked, bowing before Lady Lucinda with every ounce of gentlemanly grace he could summon.

She slowly extended a gloved hand, her eyes fixed firmly on his.

"Lucinda, dear, I believe your dance card is completely full," Lady Northrop began, the tension in her voice causing the entire party to turn.

"Amelia . . ." Northrop wrapped his arm around his wife's waist and pulled her close. "Let Lucinda be. Surely one dance will not overset the entire evening?"

"No, of course not," Lady Northrop answered quickly. "One dance couldn't possibly be of any consequence. I'll hold back the tide of your suitors," she said, looking directly at Lady Lucinda with an earnest glance, "but do hurry back."

Lucinda released Will's hand and patted Lady Northrop on the arm. "One dance, then, and I'm certain there will be no need for a queue on my behalf. However, I trust you will ask Lady Mansfield to clear the front hall if the need arises, won't you?" she teased, squeezing Lady Northrop's arm with affectionate reassurance.

Lady Northrop relaxed her grip on her husband's arm and gave Lucinda a small private smile. "Of course."

Will turned Lucinda toward the dance floor, surprised

by his determination to have her to himself surprising him.

"Is there a reason we must make haste, Your Grace?" she asked.

He stepped onto the marble floor and gently pulled Lady Lucinda with him. "Only that I cannot resist the waltz," he said, glancing at the musicians as they readied for the next dance.

She followed his gaze, taking note of their preparations before looking back at him. She arched an eyebrow. "Of course," she answered.

Will settled his free hand at her waist, vividly aware the gently rounded slope of her bottom curved just beyond his fingertips. Without conscious intent, his grip firmed and his fingers moved lightly over the soft silk of her gown, testing the heat and supple warmth beneath.

A faint shiver rippled through the woman in his arms and Lady Lucinda eased away from his touch in one swift small step.

Her gaze met his and in the brief moment before her lowered lashes shielded her expression from him, Will thought he glimpsed the same heat and surprise that raced through his veins.

Had she too felt the attraction sparking between them? Did she want to explore the unknown feeling as much as he did?

If she'd only raise her lashes, he could search for answers.

"And you, Lady Lucinda, do you enjoy waltzing?" he asked, after a frustrating moment when she appeared enthralled by his cravat.

His ploy worked. Lucinda's thick lashes swept up and she met his gaze. "It depends upon my partner, I suppose."

Her poise was once more intact. But there was a glimmer of something, though Will could not be sure precisely what it was.

The music began and she followed him gracefully as he swung her into the steps. "Yes, indeed, a skilled partner is truly a necessity," he murmured, rewarded by the barely perceptible tensing of her slim fingers against his palm as he urged her slightly closer.

Satisfied that she wasn't immune to the strange spell he felt binding them together, Will easily led Lady Lucinda in the simple pattern of whirls and twirls.

Will knew the loftier ladies of the ton had termed the waltz the "forbidden dance" due to the proximity required of partners. Privately, he could only wonder at the naïvety of anyone who considered something of such a tame nature "forbidden."

Though, he had to admit, he was finding it hard to focus on his duty with this particular woman in his arms.

Lady Lucinda was the perfect partner—all lightness and grace as the two revolved around the room. The delicate scent of her perfume teased his nostrils with each movement. Although they only touched where her hand lay on his and his hand rested at her waist, the supple flex and sway of her body was pure temptation. Her diamond earbobs caught the candlelight, glittering as the dance pattern repeated and he swung her in smooth turns.

He could have watched her all night. The swift turns and pure enjoyment of the dance heightened her color. Would she turn that same shade of pink in his bed, he wondered. His Groin tightened at the swift mental image of Lady Lucinda stripped of her evening wear and lying underneath him.

"Your Grace?"

He forced the picture from his head and looked down at Lady Lucinda. "Yes?"

"You appear to be woolgathering. Am I that poor a conversationalist?"

Her question made Will realize just how much valuable time he'd spent admiring her. The level of distraction was a startling testament to how unusual his reaction to her had been.

Sparkling diamonds and pink-hued skin be damned. He had to introduce the courtship before the dance ended. Once back in Lady Northrop's company, it was unlikely he would have a second chance.

Will gave her a small smile, the one countless women had told him could melt the coldest of hearts, and deftly steered them around another couple. "On the contrary," he said as they completed the turn. "I was just considering the necessity of having a suitable partner. Such a need goes beyond the dance floor, wouldn't you agree?"

Lady Lucinda stiffened slightly but completed the turn without consequence. "Exactly how far beyond the dance floor were you considering, Your Grace?"

She was direct, he'd give her that. And though the time he'd spent with her was relatively short, he instinctively knew that all the pretty words in the whole of England would only serve to weaken his position.

"The dining room, the library, Lady Lucinda," he murmured, his gaze holding hers. "And, for that matter, every other room to be found under the ridiculously expansive roof of Clairemont Hall."

She followed his lead as they completed the final turn and the music ended. Then she sank into a low curtsy, rising gracefully to survey him.

"Clairemont Hall—your family seat?"

It was clearly a request for clarification. Will nodded abruptly.

"Am I to understand that it is your intent to court me, Your Grace?" She sounded neither disdainful nor dismayed, only slightly puzzled.

He set her hand on his bent arm and led her to the edge of the crowded room. "Yes," he answered simply.

She stopped abruptly, forcing Will to halt mid-stride.

"Your Grace, though we—that is to say, while *I* may have given the impression this evening that we . . ." she began, her voice low, her tone apologetic but resolute. "I cannot allow you to court me. You know this as well as I."

The orchestra began another song, the music blending with the laughter and conversation of the throng that surrounded them.

"Are you afraid of me, then, like all the others?" Will asked, looking at the crowd, then back at Lady Lucinda, surprised that her answer mattered.

She stood a bit straighter, clearly relying on all five feet and four inches of her slender frame to underscore her words. "I am *not* afraid, but I *am* practical. You've no desire to live in my world, nor do I possess an interest in joining yours. Compatibility on the dance floor is hardly a foundation for a lifelong commitment, Your Grace."

Will realized that Lady Lucinda would not be wooed by his questionable charm alone. Dangling King Solomon's Mine as a lure to entice her had to be done. He had to succeed, as he always did. Still, it took a moment to reconcile himself to the task.

Surprisingly enough, he realized that reluctant as he was, the chance of losing his favorite horse, betraying a woman of Lady Lucinda's substantial character was another matter entirely. It didn't sit well.

This bloody well better win me a medal of some sort, he thought, a sharp pang of regret appearing in his heart.

He pushed open the set of French windows leading to the veranda and side garden before responding. "If I cannot convince you with our compatibility in the waltz, Lady Lucinda, then how might you feel about our mutual interest in a horse?"

In truth, Lucinda was far more intrigued at the mention of a horse than she was worried about the duke's having pulled her into the garden. "I'm sorry, I don't quite understand, Your Grace," she answered, allowing him to lead her to a stone bench neatly tucked between two flowering jasmine. "What could a horse possibly have to do with your need of a wife?"

He seated her with inherent politeness before joining her. The bench may have been sufficiently wide for an ordinary man and a lady, but the duke was not an average-sized man. The muscular bulk of his body crowded the seat, his knee brushing hers as he stretched his long legs out in front of him. His shoulder nudged against hers, the powerful muscles of his thigh a scant inch, if that, from her own silk-covered flesh. She felt surrounded by him, the heat of his body enveloping her.

"Do you recall a colt by the name of King Solomon's Mine?"

Shocked, Lucinda's heart leapt, her breath catching on a silent gasp, but she endeavored to mask her surprise. "Yes, I believe so," she managed to say with creditable nonchalance. "He was foaled some four years ago on the Whytham estate. I understood he was lost in a gambling wager, though I never heard to whom."

"To me, Lady Lucinda. I won King Solomon's Mine from Whytham and have owned him ever since." His Grace drew in his legs and turned toward her, the already questionable amount of space between them narrowing with his movement.

A shimmer of sensation began in Lucinda's toes, slowly working its way up through her calves and knees, then her thighs and belly, settling in her breasts, where the tattoo of her pounding heart accelerated ever so slightly. Whether it was caused by news of King Solomon's Mine or her close proximity to the duke, Lucinda couldn't quite discern. Nor could she bring herself to put more, safer distance between them.

"How fortunate for you, Your Grace. He has grown to be a most singular horse, I am sure," Lucinda said, hoping her ridiculously swift beating heart would not betray her. "But I still fail to see how your horse has anything to do with me."

The duke placed one hand on the bench, his fingertips nearly touching the silk gown covering her thigh. "I was led to believe King Solomon's Mine held a special place in your heart. Perhaps I was misinformed?"

"No, not entirely," Lucinda said, distracted as she fought the unacceptable urge to close the distance separating her from His Grace. "That is to say, I *was* present at his birth and he truly is a remarkable horse—or so I assume, having not seen him for some time."

The bench where they sat was in full view of other couples strolling along the garden paths in search of respite from the ballroom's crowds and heat. Nevertheless, Lucinda knew she mustn't lose sight of the potential danger to her reputation by simply being seen with the notorious duke. Her need to appear disinterested in King Solomon's Mine, however, was consuming all her attention. She would simply have to rely on her position in the ton to protect her, she decided. At the moment, it was far more important to deal with the duke's unexpected and intriguing mention of King Solomon's Mine into their conversation.

Did he know about her and her aunts' plans and the importance of the stallion to their success? How could he?

He couldn't, she told herself, because all four women had sworn a vow of secrecy.

"Yes, he is a remarkable horse," the duke agreed, his

words interrupting her frantic thoughts. "And he could be yours."

"Am I to believe that you're offering King Solomon's Mine as inducement to allow you to court me?" she asked, with no attempt to disguise her disbelief. She stared at him, searching his eyes for a clue. Surely, this was a game he played, but to what end, she couldn't discern.

"A wager—a priceless horse for the honor of your company." There was a gruffness to his voice that had not been present only a few moments before and his hazel eyes darkened with unnamed emotion. "If I can't convince you to wed me after, say, three months of courtship, then King Solomon's Mine is yours. And if you consent to be my wife . . ." He shrugged, a wry smile lifting the corner of his mouth. "Then King Solomon's Mine is yours on the day we make our vows. Either way, you win."

"You're mad," she whispered in response. And perhaps she was as well, she thought, for she was sorely tempted.

He rose, inclining his head in a brief, polite bow just short of curt. "You're not the first to make such a claim, nor will you be the last," he said. "But I require an answer, one way or the other."

Lucinda stood, her legs unsteady as she stepped just beyond the duke's reach and turned to face him.

She couldn't possibly allow him to court her. Could she?

She narrowed her eyes at him, forcing her thoughts to move beyond his handsome face and the prized stallion he dangled before her.

The Duke of Clairemont's family possessed all the right connections. And he was wealthy enough.

He was neither as old as Methuselah nor as young as Lord Thorp's boy, whom her maid firmly believed to be next on Amelia's list. No, he measured up in nearly every single category, save for his reputation.

Black.

No, blacker than black, Lucinda thought, eyeing him as he tapped his boot. His conquests were legendary and too numerous to count. From women to fights, drinking to—well, Lucinda could only imagine—the gossips proclaimed Iron Will's appetite for life was voracious, terrifyingly so.

"Have you come to a—" the duke pressed, shifting impatiently.

"A moment more, if you please," Lucinda temporized, plucking a flower from the jasmine before returning to her thoughts.

Of course, she supposed it only made sense that a man of the duke's experience would seek out the one woman in all of England whose reputation could counteract the effect of his own questionable choices.

Really, it made perfect sense, as anyone who bothered to think on it for more than four seconds would see.

And the horse. Well, her aunts could not object to three months spent in the man's company in exchange for King Solomon's Mine.

Surely she would prevail—and her success would change their lives forever.

All Lucinda had to do was allow the man into her presence.

To court her.

It couldn't be too difficult.

Resisting him wouldn't be too difficult, she told herself firmly, absently brushing the velvety soft blossom across her lower lip.

He watched her unblinkingly. In desperation, she looked at the heavens, concentrated, and accurately identified Orion, the Hunter. Ironic though it was, Lucinda congratulated herself for completing a task that required her wits. Given that Lord Clairemont's presence appeared to elicit a physical response she'd never before experienced, she was relieved to learn that the duke held no power over her when held at arm's length.

Which is where he would remain for the entirety of their courtship, she vowed. *If* she agreed to his proposition. She needed more time to consider whether she should do so.

"I will take your proposal under advisement," Lucinda answered, pointing the jasmine at him to underline her decision.

He reached for the flower and took hold of Lucinda's hand. "Of course. Though you should know, I'm not a patient man."

"Patience is a virtue, Your Grace," she said, tugging her hand from his. "And one you'd do well to practice should you wish to go forward with this . . . this . . ." She halted, unwilling to use the word that even now, seemed implausible when applied to herself and the man known as Iron Will.

"Courtship, Lady Lucinda," His Grace finished for her with amusement.

Clearly, she thought with annoyance, the idea of such a connection held no trepidation for him.

And God help me, Lucinda thought as she gave him a curt nod, tilted her chin, and turned toward the ballroom. *God help us all.*

4

A gentle breeze stirred the crimson silk curtain concealing the half-open window in Lucinda's bedroom. Her town house in Grosvener Square was an elegant, beautifully appointed home, and usually Lucinda found it wonderfully comfortable.

Not so tonight.

Unfortunately, the air did little to cool her. She stripped off her diamond earbobs, bracelet, and her long gloves, waiting impatiently as Mary freed the clasp of her glittering necklace. The maid deftly unfastened the pale pink gown, retrieving it when Lucinda stepped out of the crumpled silk. Minutes later, Lucinda was free of her undergarments and dressed in a favorite nightgown of pale blue silk, inset with matching lace.

Mary swiftly plucked the pins from Lucinda's coiffure Lucinda shook her hair free and took the brush, pulling it through the long strands herself as Mary left the room. Normally, she found the rhythmic strokes of brushing soothing, but tonight her nerves wouldn't be calmed. Restless, she quickly braided the thick mane and paced across the room.

Walking didn't ease her.

She still felt overly warm.

She crawled onto her bed and drew up her legs, wrapping her arms around them and resting her chin on her bent knees.

Thoughts of the duke's proposal—and, frustratingly

enough, of the duke himself—sent diminutive flames
flickering across her too sensitive skin. One touch from
him had done more to wreak havoc in her meticulously
ordered life than the fumbling, bumbling, fervent plead-
ings of eligible bachelors from London to Scotland.

And he barely touched me. What have I done?

She vividly remembered the warm weight of his hand
at her waist and wondered whether her vow to keep him
at arm's length was sheer bravado on her part.

"Well, my girl, what news have you of the *ton*?"

Lucinda started at the sound of her aunt's voice and
turned, hand pressed to the silk covering her pounding
heart. "Aunt Bessie, you nearly frightened me to death!"

Elizabeth Bradshaw, the Marchioness of Mowbray,
sauntered barefoot across the plush cream and scarlet
Persian rug toward Lucinda, a delicate Wedgwood plate
piled high with macaroons balanced carefully in her
right hand. She wore a dressing gown of deep rose, the
silk clinging to her curves. It emphasized what Bessie
was perhaps most proud of at fifty-and-some-years of
age—a shapely figure that had inspired awe in the male
gender from the day she'd turned sixteen.

"Hmmm, I suspect that whatever is occupying your
mind at the moment has far more to do with your excitable nerves than my sudden appearance," Bessie answered with her usual shrewd perception, setting the
plate on the bedside table before joining Lucinda down
to a seat beside her on the bed.

Lucinda avoided her aunt's gaze and instead concentrated on tracing her fingertip over the scarlet floral pattern embroidered on her coverlet. "What ever would
make you think such a thing?"

The closed door of her bedchamber burst open with a
clatter.

"Utter one more word without us and we shall never
speak to either of you again!"

Lucinda smiled as her two other aunts, and Bessie's sisters, Victoria and Charlotte, hurried toward the bed.

Encased in yards of white muslin and wrapped in fine cashmere bed shawls, the middle and youngest of the Grey sisters managed to exude an excruciating level of primness that made Bessie's eyes roll nearly to the back of her skull.

"Really, girls," Bessie said, shaking her head. "Are you at such an advanced age that you must cover yourselves from head to toe?" she asked.

Lucinda hid a smile as Bessie, in an automatic move, leaned back slightly so that even Charlotte, whose eyesight was poor at best, could not fail to notice her sister's impressive bosom.

"Once a lady, my dear Bessie, always a lady," Victoria St. Ainsbury, the Duchess of Highbury, answered emphatically with only a touch of sarcasm. She nudged her eldest sister aside with her bony hip to make room for herself next to Lucinda.

Lady Charlotte Grey patted Bessie on the shoulder, took a place at the end of the bed, and eyed Lucinda expectantly. "All right, dear, proceed."

Lucinda took in the sight of her three aunts, "the Furies" as they were known to all. As unlike from one another as anyone could be, the sisters shared one trait in common: sheer, single-minded willfulness. Their differences could always be resolved by their agreement that absolutely nothing should stand in the way of what they wanted. Not men, nor society, and certainly not one another.

"It's King Solomon's Mine," Lucinda began, taking note of the immediate reaction that each sister had to the prize stallion's name. "I've been offered the chance to win him."

"How utterly glorious!" Bessie shrieked, "Rufus will be green with envy. A stallion with the bloodlines of

King Solomon's Mine practically guarantees success. Ours will be the superlative breeding program in all of Britain."

Victoria halted Bessie's rhapsodizing by gently covering her sister's mouth with her palm. "Yes, Bessie, we're all aware of what King Solomon's Mine has to offer," she said before Bessie could interrupt her. She huffed to a halt, drawing a deep breath before continuing. "But do not torture your son with the news just yet. How, exactly, Lucinda, will you go about winning him?"

Lucinda tugged at her long, thick hair. "It's rather simple, really. I've only to allow someone to court me for a specific amount of time. At the end of that time, if I've managed to avoid losing my heart, the horse is mine."

Bessie pulled Victoria's hand away from her mouth and sat up straight. "Considering that you've refused most of the eligible male population of England, this will not be a problem. Now," she continued, reaching for the plate of macaroon. "let us celebrate with a tiny midnight morsel, shall we?"

Charlotte took a treat from the plate and settled back into her cozy spot at the foot of the bed. "Lucinda, dear, I've only one question: Who is he?"

"Yes, who is this man?" Victoria asked, speaking between bites. "I'm afraid I lost track of King Solomon's Mine after that idiot Whytham gambled him away to that infamous Iron Will."

Lucinda discreetly wiped at a bead of perspiration at her temple. "Well," she began, "that is to say . . ." She hesitated and took a hasty bite of her macaroon.

Charlotte gasped, moving closer to the circle of women. "It's him, then, isn't it? The Duke of Clairemont." She looked at her sisters, then back at Lucinda. "It's Iron Will."

Victoria slowly lowered the remainder of her macaroon onto the plate and stared owl-eyed at Lucinda. "Of course not. Lucinda would never entertain the idea—"

"I knew it!" Bessie interrupted. "The open window, your jangled nerves, the telltale perspiration . . . He's captured your fancy! It is Iron Will."

Victoria's eyes were growing wider by the second. "What do you know of such young men? Do act your age, Bessie. Or has your memory failed you yet again. in which Your son, the Duke of Mowbray, is now two-and—"

"Really, Victoria, looking at you is more than enough to underscore our advanced years, thank you very much," Bessie interrupted, tossing her head to shake her glossy, dove gray mass of hair over her shoulder for effect.

Lucinda took advantage of her aunts' sparring to stand and cross the room. She fanned herself with her hand before sitting down at her writing desk, the breeze tickling a tendril of hair at the nape of her neck.

"Ladies, I believe we were speaking of the appropriateness of His Grace as a suitor for Lucinda. Do keep to the subject, won't you?" Charlotte chided gently, pushing her robust frame from the bed. "I knew his parents, of course, but I'm afraid I'm not familiar with the boy. Lucinda, dear, is he a gentleman worthy of your attentions?"

Victoria rose from the bed and marched across the room to where Lucinda sat. "A rake of the first order!" she answered in a severe tone.

"A man of experience, to be sure," Bessie chimed in, rolling over on the soft mattress to lie on her side and smile at Lucinda. "But why that should be seen as an impediment is beyond me."

Victoria frowned and wagged her finger at Lucinda, who had not been able to hide an amused grin. "This is hardly a laughing matter, my dear."

"Yes, quite. Of course, Aunt," Lucinda responded, forcing her lips into a serious line. "Though I would think the news would be cause for some celebration—on your part, in particular, considering your passion for horses."

Lucinda had touched a nerve when she mentioned the one thing in life that had yet to disappoint Victoria. Her marriage at age eighteen to the Duke of Highbury had been a disaster, the duke being far more interested in his many mistresses than he ever was in his wife. Victoria's inability to bear children had broken her heart and driven her further away from her friends and acquaintances, until all she had left were her sisters and Highbury's vast stables.

While the duke understood little about Victoria, he discerned even less about his prize equines. His absence from the day-to-day stable operations left Victoria with free rein to learn all she could. To love as she would, to set free all the passion and caring forbidden her in her marriage.

And she did. Soo every follower of horse racing who ever visited Taltersalls could not get enough of the Highbury horses, whose impressive races were the event to attend.

At first, it was fulfilling for Victoria. But the duke's arrogance over his "influence and guiding hand" caused her mild annoyance with the man to grow to outright hostility, until Victoria could hardly bear to be in the same room as the man.

And then he was killed in a riding accident, his stubborn insistence that his inexperienced mount take a high fence ending tragically for the horse, deservedly for the duke. The lack of an heir meant the estate passed to her nephew, leaving Victoria a very wealthy woman, thanks to her settlement, but without a home.

Her sisters immediately implored Victoria to join

them at Bampton Manor, where they'd resided since the death of Lucinda's parents, the magnificent unentailed estate having been willed to young Lucinda.

Once settled at Bampton Manor, Victoria had enlisted Bessie, Charlotte, and Lucinda's help and begun to build her own breeding program. They created a fictitious male farm manager and, using their ample income, began buying colts and fillies, stallions and mares, and housing them on the estate.

King Solomon's Mine was to be the crown jewel of the stables, a stallion with just the right lineage to guarantee the superiority of their bloodstock for generations to come.

And then Whytham, an irredeemable dolt of a man, had gambled away the key to all of Victoria's dreams.

Charlotte, having watched the play of emotions cross Victoria's face as she considered the situation, cleared her throat.

"To my way of thinking," Charlotte said when she had their attention, "we must ask ourselves two questions. First, is the Grey name sufficiently influential to survive the gossip that will likely ensue if Lucinda allows this 'Iron Will' to court her?"

Bessie rolled over and sat up, tucking her legs beneath her. "Despite his rather questionable qualifications," she began, arching an eyebrow for emphasis, "I would not hesitate to say that the Grey name would weather such a trial in grand fashion."

The women looked at Victoria, whose pinched face and heightened color revealed the struggle between her strict adherence to her moral code and the passionate desire for success.

"Yes, of course," she said finally. "No one would dare question Lucinda's good name should she choose to allow this man the honor of her company."

"We are in agreement, then," Charlotte concurred,

moving closer to Lucinda. Gently, she pushed back a stray curl that had fallen over Lucinda's brow. "Now, dear girl, the second question. I assume you will make your intentions clear to this young man, namely that the horse is your desire, not him."

Lucinda nodded in agreement. "Yes, Aunt, I will."

Bessie left the comfort of the bed and with Victoria joined Charlotte. All three of Lucinda's aunts faced her, concern clearly written across each of their solemn faces.

"Human nature being what it is," Bessie began, "we are somewhat hesitant to release you into the hands of such a formidable foe as this Iron Will appears to be."

"Really, Aunts," Lucinda responded, hoping the instant warmth that flooded her veins at the mere mention of the duke's name wasn't visible on her features, "you've never doubted my resolute will to remain unmarried before. Why now?"

"He clearly made an impression this evening," Bessie began.

"Too true. Her color is heightened, it cannot be denied," Victoria observed.

"Do not forget the perspiration," Bessie hastily added.

Lucinda stood, the heat of the room seeming to grow by the second. "I'm that easily swayed, then? Countless suitors have come before and, may I remind you, been denied. But this one, with a wink and a smile will steal my heart silly?"

It was a question posed to all, including herself.

In a matter of mere minutes the man had somehow appealed to Lucinda's basic needs. Despite all that owning King Solomon's Mine would bring, dare she accept his wager? Could she trust herself with His Grace?

The gentleness of Charlotte's voice calmed Lucinda's

shaken nerves. "My dear, you've only to answer the question and we'll never speak of it again."

"Then do ask, Aunt. Now."

"Are you capable of dealing with the likes of Iron Will?"

Lucinda's mind began to race as images assaulted her senses. The duke's voice, soft as silk, when he repeated her name upon meeting. The feel of his hand at the small of her back when they danced. The look in his eyes when he spoke of the courtship. His fingers tracing the length of hers, branding her with a fire that she swore lingered even to this hour.

But she wanted King Solomon's Mine. And what's more, she realized as she looked at each of her aunts, she wanted what they wanted—the happiness and complete satisfaction to be found in doing something well, doing something that would mean so much for so many.

Lucinda squeezed her eyes shut for a moment and forced from her mind all thoughts of the unsettling affect the duke had on her too susceptible body. "Yes."

The note was delivered just after breakfast. The merest hint of citrus escaped when Will tore open the seal—Lady Lucinda's scent. His training in the Young Corinthians had ensured he could discern a staggering number of details about an individual in a relatively short period of time. Along with her height and approximate size, he'd already committed to memory her voice and any number of physical characteristics that might be useful during the course of keeping her safe. Or bedding her, though he was fairly sure that both Carmichael and Northrop would have him castrated on the spot.

Another agent had guarded Lady Lucinda when she'd left the ball, and then yet another agent, this one masquerading as a footman, had been installed in her household. Assured she was well protected, Will had gone straight from the glitter of the Mansfields' ballroom to Carmichael's office. The exclusive group of men gathered there were committed to capturing Garenne. Will joined them, spending the next hours poring over documents and maps, discussing and hammering out a detailed plan. When they disbursed to their homes just before dawn, he was satisfied that their scheme to protect Lady Lucinda was seamless.

He'd managed perhaps an hour of sleep before receiving her note, and there'd been little point in trying for more after reading her reply. Smithers had been too enthusiastic for Will's taste at such an ungodly hour, but he couldn't have done without his valet's help. Arranging his wardrobe fell just below learning to play the pianoforte on Will's list of things one must master before dying, though he had to admit that Smithers's choice for the day was quite . . . well, gentlemanly. Snug, fawn-colored breeches were tucked into his Hessians, which were polished to a high shine. A pale green waistcoat beneath a dark blue coat of superfine cloth completed with an intricately tied cravat.

The damn neckcloth was the one thing Will could barely tolerate. Brummell should have been hung by a length of his own neckcloth, as far as Will was concerned. The strips of starched linen would see far better use in bandaging a wound or tying a woman to the bedpost.

Depending on one's situation, of course.

Will had endured Smithers's fussing for a good hour before the valet pronounced him fit to leave the house. For his part, Will had thought himself remarkably patient, but he couldn't help but wonder if Lady Lucinda would be suitably appreciative.

With expert maneuvering and a firm hand on the reins of his matched bays, he threaded his high-perch through traffic. He nodded at an acquaintance who hailed him from the walk but did not slow for a more substantive greeting.

He couldn't shake memories of Lady Lucinda.

The blasted woman dancing, smiling as she turned so easily in his arms, nearly coming undone at his touch. His imagination took flight. He wondered if she dabbed the faint lemon scent on her slender wrists, the soft skin just behind her knees, and lastly, between her breasts.

Will grimaced, frowning. Height, weight—these were familiar factors to remember in his line of work. But the feel of her as they danced, conjuring up a vision of her unclothed? Will couldn't quite convince himself as to the relevance of such things.

This was not beginning well. He needed emotional distance from his charge—anything less could result in a slip in his concentration and thus danger to Lady Lucinda.

True, he thought, narrowing his eyes against the midmorning sun, never before had a woman been so intimately involved in Corinthian business, at least not to his knowledge.

Also true, his fondness for the fairer sex was no secret. News of his liaisons had found their way into the gossip rags, the legend of Iron Will growing with each report.

But this was different. Lady Lucinda was different. And it had to stop. It was distracting and, even worse, dangerous.

Will slowed the bays and brought them to a dancing stop, noting the movement of the sun behind the stone façade of de Bohun House. Carmichael had mentioned on more than one occasion that Will's mental strength was rivaled only by his physical prowess. He would test that theory thoroughly with this mission, his wits sure to be put to the test by both Garenee and Lady Lucinda.

He would perform his duty to the best of his ability.

But his fascination with this woman would end at her doorstep.

It would not be simple, but it would be done.

His tiger leapt down from his perch and ran to the bays, grasping a halter strap with both small hands.

Will stepped down, handed the reins to a waiting groom, and strode up the steps to the front door.

"Where the devil did he disappear to?" Bessie asked, attempting to discreetly poke her head around the gold damask curtains and peer out the spotless windowpane at the street below.

"Remove yourself from view at once," Victoria hissed. She rapped her sister's arm with her fan, the audible thwack earning a startled squeak from Bessie.

Charlotte tsked gently, sighing as Victoria nearly toppled over as she leaned toward Bessie in an attempt to peer outside. "Really, ladies, do you think your curiosity will hasten the gentleman to our door?"

"He has lovely dark hair, that much I saw before he disappeared," Bessie continued dramatically, ignoring Charlotte's mild chastening.

"Are you speaking of the horse or the man?" Victoria asked. And she was so utterly serious that the rest of them could not help but giggle.

"His Grace, The Duke of Clairemont is in the foyer and wishes to join you, my lady," Stanford interrupted in a flat voice.

The aunts immediately ceased their laughter, but not Lucinda. She couldn't stop giggling, no matter how long she looked at Stanford's morose visage.

"Lucinda, dear, are you quite all right?" Charlotte asked.

She nodded at her aunt and smoothed the skirt of her manila brown morning dress. In truth, she'd been asking herself that same question since waking. A night spent tossing and turning was never a good thing, but when the restlessness was caused by dreams the likes of Lucinda's, well, it was a wonder she'd managed to appear for breakfast. The dreams had started out respectably enough, with Lucinda and the duke hammering out the details of their courtship. But it had ended with his mouth seeking hers in a breathtaking kiss, then an embrace and the loss of clothing and . . . Lucinda would not think on what came next.

Knowing she would see him today had done little to calm her nerves over breakfast. If the man had invaded her dreams and sent her into such a state, what would happen once he was within arm's reach?

"Enough!" Lucinda ground out, belatedly realizing that all three of her aunts and Stanford were staring at her, confusion clearly written upon each of their faces.

These women were the reason she'd agreed to the courtship, she reminded herself. Her aunts meant the world to her. All three had happily stepped in to care for her upon her parents' death—to teach her, love her, nurture her in a way that only family could. So really, allowing His Grace to court her was nothing in comparison. Easy. Beyond easy.

Or at least it should be.

Lucinda steeled herself with newfound resolution. "Enough," she repeated firmly, anxious to show all that she was perfectly in control. "Aunts, do choose a seat. And Stanford, please show the duke in."

"Yes, my lady." The butler bowed and departed.

Lucinda tucked an errant curl into place, pinched her cheeks for color, and sat in a patterned armchair.

"A chair? Really, Lucinda, after your years of experience in society and dealing with men, surely you know better!" Bessie exclaimed in a hushed tone, rising from the window seat. She pattered quickly across the room and tugged Lucinda to her feet.

"The settee, at once," she demanded, pointing to the cream silk sofa that, in theory, fit two full-grown individuals.

In reality, Lucinda had always thought it was best suited to duos of considerably smaller stature than the average couple.

"Aunt Bessie, the man is a giant," she protested. "I'm not sure that he alone would fit on that particular piece of furniture, and certainly not the two of us."

Victoria plied her fan in a most vigorous manner. "What, exactly, is wrong with the chair?"

"This is a courtship, not a trial. I'm sure even you remember the purpose of such meetings—to converse, to flirt, to establish a connection of a physical—"

Victoria's fan moved faster, her grip threatening to snap the delicate, hand-painted sticks. "This is not at all about conversing or flirting or . . . or . . ."

"I believe her words were 'establishing a physical—'" Charlotte offered with the merest hint of a smile quirking her lips.

"Stop!" Victoria hissed vehemently, clearly not enjoying the joke at her expense. "A horse," she reminded them sternly. "We are here to gain a horse. Now, do sit down before Stanford returns."

Bessie pulled a chair nearer and quickly sat, adjusting her skirts.

Heavy footsteps sounded in the hallway just outside the room. Lucinda could not allow the duke to see her ill of ease. The courtship must begin on her terms, and must remain entirely within her control.

In a decidedly unladylike but necessary move, Lucinda gained a few precious moments by nimbly hopping over the footstool in her path and throwing herself onto the nearest seat—the slight settee.

"Brava," Bessie whispered loudly.

"Hush, he'll hear you," Charlotte warned from her

corner of the room, giving Lucinda a small smile of reassurance before schooling her features into a proper expression of serenity.

Lucinda smoothed her skirts and took a deep breath just as the door opened.

"His Grace, the Duke of Clairemont."

5

Will had lied, cheated, stolen, maimed, and killed in the line of duty. In turn, he'd been shot at, pummeled within an inch of his life, stabbed repeatedly, and nearly drowned—all for King and Country.

One look at the women ensconced within the beautifully appointed sitting room and Will knew, beyond a shadow of a doubt, that it had all been child's play up to this point.

By the time the introductions were made, he had shrewdly assessed and identified which sister would most willingly be finessed (the brazen one), which one would prefer to see him run down by wild horses rather than extend him one ounce of graciousness (the dower one), and finally, which one was clearly undecided, her quiet demeanor showing nothing of her leanings (the reasonable).

"Do sit down, over there," the brazen one had urged, pointing to the ridiculously tiny settee where Lady Lucinda was seated.

He'd complied, having to practically fold himself in half to fit. Being so near Lady Lucinda was hardly in keeping with his plan to remain cool and detached, but Will knew better than to argue with a determined aunt.

"I hope the morning finds you well," Will said to Lady Lucinda, aware her aunts were listening to each word. He had to twist his neck in a wholly unnatural way to look at her, due to the damned doll-sized seat.

"Where are the flowers?"

Will turned to the dower one. Her pinched mouth looked as if the effort of speaking to him was leaving a sour taste on her tongue.

"Flowers?"

She rolled her eyes, obviously finding him lacking, and pressed on. "Yes, the flowers. Perhaps you're unaware of the workings of a respectable courtship, Your Grace. It is customary to bring a bouquet when calling upon a young woman."

"Aunt Victoria," Lady Lucinda protested, clearly uncomfortable with the woman's bluntness.

Will had never cared a farthing for what people thought of his actions and he wasn't about to start now. Nevertheless, the woman was Lady Lucinda's aunt. "My apologies. I had forgotten."

"If I find myself in need of flowers all I've to do is walk into the back garden," Lady Lucinda answered with calm practicality. "And there I'll find more than twenty varieties—"

Will pried himself from the settee and strode toward the door. "A moment," he said, then exited the room, finding his way quickly to the rear of the town house. He walked the length of it, peering into each room before finding a set of doors that led to the small garden.

He let himself out onto the neat flagstone terrace, the surrounding flower beds fragrant in the sunshine.

And he began to pick one of each flower he could find, until there were an even twenty blooms with long stems neatly tucked into the crook of his arm.

He returned to the drawing room, and the ladies gasped in unison.

"With my sincere apologies, Lady Lucinda," he said, offering the flowers to her with a deep bow.

Her smile nearly had Will searching for a seat on the far side of the room. Her blue eyes glowed with delight.

She was clearly surprised, which was charming enough, but also pleased, which made Will's chest tighten with . . . with what? Pride? Joy? He couldn't quite name it, but whatever the emotion was, it wasn't good.

The sour aunt who had brought up his lack of flowers apparently thought he'd acted to mock her. Her fan beat an annoyed tattoo on the arm of the Windsor chair where she sat.

In truth, he'd forgotten the custom. His last visit to a woman that could have in any way been considered proper had been too long ago. The women he associated with wanted neither flowers nor ridiculous little gifts. They wanted an occasional very expensive gift—but mostly, they wanted him.

This would take some getting used to, this gentleman business, he realized. The problem was, he didn't have time to relearn his manners. Garenne was somewhere out there, close at hand, and he wasn't a patient man.

Will made a mental note to question Smithers regarding the requirements of a gentleman before turning to sit.

He'd only just settled himself on the settee when the sour one barked at him yet again.

"And the horse, Your Grace. Just where *is* King Solomon's Mine?"

Will was inclined to answer "In my pocket, my dear, along with a suit of armor and the crown jewels, of course," but thought better of it. "He should be taking a mid-morning rest in preparation for our afternoon ride."

"A mid-morning rest? Really, Your Grace, what sort of training regimen do you have for this horse that allows a mid-morning—"

"I assure you that he is—"

"An afternoon ride, how delightful!" the brazen one

said with a gleam in her eye, successfully cutting off both her sister and Will.

"Yes, I prefer an afternoon ride, though—"

"I believe it's time for tea," the reasonable one interrupted Will, crossing to tug the bellpull.

Will didn't bother to address her concerning the tea. He felt a headache coming on. He hated tea. And he'd yet to get a word in edgewise, so best to sit back and plan at this point. He'd be damned if he'd let three unruly women get the best of him, even ones referred to as "the Furies"—though now that he'd spent some time in their company, the title made much more sense.

Lady Lucinda leaned toward him. "I suppose I should have warned you to gird your loins prior to dancing attendance on me," she whispered, a wry smile accompanying her comment.

Will suppressed a laugh but returned the smile, her dimple wreaking havoc on his concentration. "I'm not a regular at Gentleman John Jackson's boxing academy for the masculine company alone. Your aunts may think they have the upper hand, but just you wait."

Lady Lucinda arched an eyebrow, her eyes twinkling. "Now this I must see," she said conspiratorially.

A footman appeared with the tea, placing it on the table then disappearing.

"Milk, Your Grace?" the reasonable one asked.

"No, thank you."

"Sugar?"

"No, thank you. The blacker, the better," Will answered.

He stretched to take cup and saucer from her and his thigh brushed Lady Lucinda's. He murmured a polite thank you for the tea and tried to remember what they'd been discussing before he'd been distracted. *Ah, yes— King Solomon's Mine.*

"Despite his prowess, Sol is a sensitive soul, which is

why he's allowed the luxury of a mid-morning rest," he said before downing his tea.

The dower one's lips pursed as if she'd just bit into something tart. "Really, Your Grace, a horse of his lineage, sensitive?"

"How kind of you, Your Grace," the reasonable one interrupted, "your attentiveness is truly inspiring."

"Oh, now really, Bessie. 'Inspiring'? Do you take the man—"

"I was just pondering a walk in the park," the brazen one began in a completely different direction. "Though walking by oneself is lonely, wouldn't you agree?" she finished, batting her eyelashes at Will.

"Why yes, as a matter of fact I'm in complete agreement," Will answered, still not quite sure of what the aging coquette was playing at.

"Excellent. Lucinda, do don your pelisse, my dear."

"But—" the dower one began.

The brazen one rose from her chair and walked toward the pair. "Oh, did I fail to mention that I'd been thinking on a walk not for myself, but for Lucinda? Silly me."

"But—" the dower one said more loudly.

"A bit of fresh air would be most welcome," Lady Lucinda swiftly responded, taking Will's hand and standing.

"Well, I . . . that is to say . . ." the dower one protested, her fan at the ready.

"Dearest Victoria, we'll send Mary along with her cape and gloves to chaperone," the brazen one said soothingly.

Will didn't dare look in "dearest" Victoria's direction. Instead, he stood aside to let Lady Lucinda walk ahead of him, then bowing to the remaining ladies, hastily gave his thanks, and followed her out of the room.

He attempted to shut the door but encountered resistance.

The brazen one stuck her head out and eyed Will with a hawklike stare. "I believe I see in you what others do not, Your Grace. Please, do not prove me wrong."

And with that, she disappeared behind the door and firmly shut it.

Lucinda was rather proud of herself. She'd made it nearly across the street before letting out the laugh that had been bubbling in her throat for the last five minutes.

The duke had no more handled her aunts than had anyone else in the history of the world.

His smug smile of success all but melted away at the sound of Lucinda's laughter. "Lady Lucinda, I can't imagine what you find so amusing," he said with mock affront, the flash of amusement in his eyes belying his tone.

Lucinda couldn't help but find him charming. He was so large, yet so like an adorable little boy at times. She very nearly reached out to caress his cheek, but thought better of it.

"Come now, Your Grace. It really wasn't that bad." Despite her best efforts to remain solemn, she couldn't prevent a smile from curving her lips. "It was your first meeting with them, after all, and there were three of them and only one of you. Perhaps a few more sessions at Gentleman John Jackson's and you'll be ready for another round?"

"Impertinent chit," the duke said under his breath, taking care to escort Lucinda into the central garden area of Grosvenor Square.

Lucinda glanced over her shoulder. Mary had settled into a leisurely pace behind them, slow enough to allow a comfortable conversation, yet fast enough to insure that the duke would not pull Lucinda into the bushes and have his way with her. Or dash behind a tree with her in tow and steal a kiss. Or anything of the kind. Which Lucinda most certainly did not want to happen. Ever. At least not today.

Well, she was fairly certain anyway.

Why had she not refused when Bessie had suggested a stroll? Because she'd been caught up in his charm, in his smile, in his eyes, which changed from cool hazel to heated green depending upon what he was thinking. What he was feeling.

And just what *was* he feeling, Lucinda found herself wondering, not for the first time.

Drat! This was not like her at all. If this were any other man—Lord Cuthbert, for example—she would not be strolling with him. Nor would she have spent one moment wondering whether he'd enjoyed his tea, never mind suffering curiosity as to his thoughts about her.

This was ludicrous. This was madness.

"Lady Lucinda," the duke said for what was clearly the second or perhaps even third time.

"Hmmm," Lucinda said belatedly, still struggling to marshal her thoughts.

"I've commented on the weather," he said. "Twice."

Lucinda abruptly stopped and stepped to one side of the path. She beckoned him closer. "Your Grace."

"Yes?"

"I've something to ask you."

He leaned in a bit, his broad shoulders blocking her. "In relation to the weather?"

Lucinda huffed out a breath. "No, not exactly. That is to say, not at all."

"I see. Well, let me gather my wits first," he responded, squeezing his eyes shut, visibly bracing himself before opening his eyes. "All right, I believe I am ready."

Annoyed, Lucinda frowned at him. "This is a serious matter."

"I can see that," he said. "I apologize. Now, the question," he finished, the twinkle in his eyes nearly stopping Lucinda from speaking.

"What are your intentions?" she asked plainly.

She could see that she'd taken him by surprise, all of the humor disappearing from his face.

"With regards to?"

"Me. That is to say," Lucinda began, somewhat nervously, "us. You and me, and this, this . . ."

The duke looked amused. "'Courtship,' I believe is the word you're searching for."

"Yes, precisely," she said, somewhat relieved that he appeared to be blunt as well. "I understand that you've nothing to lose—"

"What of King Solomon's Mine?" he interrupted.

"Oh, well, of course. But I mean of a more personal nature, such as your reputation or, well, your heart, if I may be so bold," she answered, vaguely shocked by her honesty. Though at this point, she thought, really— what was the point in speaking in circles when she'd broached such a forbidden topic?

He didn't respond, only stared, his eyes deepening in hue as they searched hers.

"I've offended you, haven't I?" she asked, feeling oddly shy. She looked at the ground, unable to meet the intensity of his gaze as he appeared to consider her question.

"No, not in the least," he said at last, his deep voice strangely soft. His hand was warm when he cupped her chin, tipping her face up so that she was looking at him once more. "I prefer honesty, but I've found it to be a rare quality in a woman."

She exhaled, unaware that she'd been holding her breath, awaiting his reply.

That his opinion should matter so much made her uncomfortable. It was also unsettling that his disregard for society's rules governing male behavior seemed to coax her into behaving in ways she could only term improper.

Before this, only Amelia had been aware of Lucinda's "occasionally unruly nature". Even as a child, Lucinda had instinctively hidden that part of herself from the world. And though she enjoyed much of her life as Lady Lucinda Grey, she was always aware that beneath the silks, satins, and jewels she wore, there smoldered a hidden desire to be more than the proper lady the world expected.

Amelia would turn pale and quite possibly faint if she were privy to the conversation taking place between Lucinda and Iron Will.

The proper gentlemen of her acquaintance expected her to be above reproach, the perfect lady. What was she to do with a man who expected her to be only herself?

"Now, to answer your question, my intentions are entirely honorable," he said, lowering his hand and taking her arm to turn her back onto the path.

The duke tucked her hand into the crook of his arm, lessening the distance between their bodies as they walked. "It's no secret that every eldest male Clairemont throughout history has been expected to marry and continue the ducal line."

He looked out over the well-groomed park, his profile turned to her as he took in the shrubs that lined the walkways, the expanses of clipped grass, the strolling couples and nursemaids with their charges.

"And I like you, Lady Lucinda," he continued after a long moment. "You have a mind and you use it. You make me laugh, which I enjoy immensely. And though I feel sure that you've heard it a thousand times before, you are beautiful."

He turned his head to look down at her, pinning her with an intense glance. Lucinda couldn't look away. Tension spun between them, heightening with each moment. The unfamiliar feeling of vulnerability surfaced up yet again.

"I've no intent to court you for sport," he resumed, pulling her from her thoughts. "I may be voracious and varied in my many appetites, Lady Lucinda, but in this I am single-minded and focused. You have my word."

She knew to the core of her being that she trusted him. After all, his line of reasoning did make perfect sense; a duke must marry, must have a son to carry on the family line. But beyond that, she sensed that William Randall, the Duke of Clairemont, meant what he said.

And though her intent was to walk away with only King Solomon's Mine after their time together, somehow knowing that he liked her—truly liked her, despite her candor and intelligence—made all the difference.

Lucinda relaxed and allowed herself to enjoy the fine spring day. It was early yet, too early, really, for the more sophisticated set to be out and about, which made their walk even more enjoyable. In truth, when in residence at her country estate, Lucinda often walked for miles in the morning, the stillness of a world that had yet to completely awaken providing a stark contrast to her usual routine of social events and obligations.

Though she'd never admitted it to anyone but Amelia, at times Lucinda chafed from all that went with her place in society. She was far too practical a person to suppose that she would be happy as a squire's wife, but the lure of somehow being free of all of society's expectations that accompanied being titled, rich, and well-bred could be oh so intoxicating.

Perhaps this, in part, was what she liked so well in the duke. His utter disdain for the ton's stricture and society in general was—well, to be quite honest, most refreshing. It was something Lucinda secretly admired.

Regardless, she knew that if even a modicum of

proper behavior was to be maintained, it clearly would be her place to set the standards.

If she could.

She eased away from His Grace, putting several more inches of space between them—and instantly missed his warmth.

"Now I've offended you," he said in a low tone before tipping his hat and rumbling a greeting to Lady Foxbury as her carriage rolled by in the street. The matron's eyes widened with shock as she returned the polite gesture.

Lucinda nodded to Lady Foxbury, quickening her pace when her polite greeting was returned. "Not precisely, no," she answered. "You've surprised me, certainly. But this way of speaking one's mind plainly is something I'm beginning to enjoy."

And something I could easily become accustomed to, she thought.

"In that case," the duke returned, pulling her closer yet again, "let me be perfectly frank and tell you that I much prefer you by my side than several steps distant."

Lucinda laughed, knowing her rebellious body also enjoyed the nearness of his much taller, broader frame. "Your Grace, though I understand you've been out of polite society for some time, I suspect you recall what is considered appropriate behavior while courting a lady. This," she said, motioning to the distance she was currently putting between them, "is acceptable. I will not have my reputation sullied for the sake of a horse."

His disgruntled growl should have frightened Lucinda, but she found herself amused and charmed, even when he frowned at her.

"So it's the horse alone that convinced you to allow me to court you?" he asked.

Lucinda chided herself for the delight she seemed to be finding in every tiny detail about this very large man. Why on earth was she amused when he voiced his displeasure? Why did she not feel threatened by his obvious irritation instead of noticing that his eyes appeared more green than hazel when he wore a green waistcoat?

She shrugged mentally. Surely what she was feeling was a normal reaction to a very handsome man.

"It is King Solomon's Mine that holds my heart, Your Grace," she answered, then added, "his is, after all, quite a horse."

"Quite a horse indeed," Will muttered, landing a punishing blow on his sparring partner's jaw and sending him to the mat.

"My apologies, Dinsford." He pulled the man to his feet and propped him up in the corner.

The young man massaged his jaw and grinned at Will. "It's me own fault. Shouldn't'a taught ya the right hook."

Will smiled, taking a towel hanging on a peg in the wall. He wiped the sweat from his arms and bare chest, the pounding exchange of the last hour beginning to make itself felt.

"Something on your mind?"

Will turned slowly and saw Carmichael seated in the shadows against the wall. "I was just about to ask you the same question, old man." He bent to shake his wet hair before rubbing his head with the damp towel. "You've been sitting there for nearly an hour without a word. That's quite an accomplishment for you," he finished, grinning.

Carmichael merely wiped at a bead of moisture that had somehow made its way to his immaculate breeches and stood. "Buy me a drink and I'll tell you."

"I hope the ale is to your liking." Will motioned for his superior to follow him.

Carmichael sidestepped a burly man lifting what

looked to be two sacks full of grain tied to a long pole, before answering, "I suppose it will have to."

The two men moved toward the edge of the shadowy room, where a table was simply laid with pitchers of ale and tin tankards.

"I see the aristocracy has invaded your pugilistic paradise," Carmichael began, filling a tankard for himself.

Will let out a growl of disgust. "Every ham-fisted idiot with all his teeth wants to lose a few of them here. What was wrong with a bucket and ladle, I'll never know."

He filled his tankard and took a swig, swishing it about in his mouth then spitting into the empty pitcher, the ale tinged with his blood.

"You might want to hold on to some of that."

Will set the container back on the table and joined Carmichael on the raised plank seating built to afford an unobstructed view of where the men boxed. "Didn't you kow? I've an endless supply of blood."

Carmichael quirked a brow then unobtrusively took in their surroundings, his gaze sharp. Apparently satisfied that they wouldn't be overheard, he looked at Will. "I understand congratulations are in order."

"Does anything happen in London that you are not instantly aware of?" Will asked sarcastically.

"No. That's the whole point. Now brief me on Lady Lucinda."

Will waited until the pugilists in the ring resumed their match. The cheers of the men seated on the benches farther down the room, combined with the thuds from fists hitting muscle and grunts of pain provided cover for his answer. "Against her better judgment, she's agreed to let me court her."

"I told you she'd fall for your brawny charm."

Will gave Carmichael a piercing look before taking a drink. "Think again, old man. I had to offer King Solomon's Mine."

Will could swear he heard Carmichael chortle, though not a hint of a smile spoiled his solemn demeanor.

"I am sorry for that."

"No more sorry than I." It was true that Will prized the stallion, but he'd been a Corinthian long enough to know that no horse was worth the life of a lady. He'd done his job to the fullest, securing a legitimate reason to spend time with Lady Lucinda so he could protect her. But he'd done vastly more than was necessary. He'd shamelessly flirted with the woman. He'd gone out of his way to impress her.

And the aunts. He'd held his tongue and smiled and did the pretty when he'd wanted to run from the room and break as many items in his wake as possible.

"Bloody hell," Will growled. "I don't know that I'm the right man for this."

Carmichael watched the fighters resume their match, their rough dance gaining speed. "Clairemont, you know as well as I that there is no going back now. If it's the horse—"

"It's not the horse, it's the woman. I want to—"

Carmichael applauded a particularly skillful blow. "Bed her? That's nothing to be concerned about."

"Of course I want to bed her," Will said impatiently. "A man would have to be dead and buried not to. No," he said, his frustration growing, "I want to talk to her. I like talking to her. Dammit, the bedding part is natural. Wanting to spend time with her outside the bedchamber is not."

Carmichael turned to look at Will, understanding written across his face. "I see."

"Then you'll find someone else—"

"Just because I understand the situation does not mean that I've any more options than before. You're the man for this assignment." Carmichael turned back to the sparring match. "You've already made the initial contact. To send in another agent at this point would cause suspicion."

Will suppressed the desire to slam his fist through the planked seating and instead unleashed his anger on the tankard, nearly denting the tin. "You don't understand; I fear that my preoccupation may put the mission at risk."

"I trained you myself. I know what you're capable of," Carmichael answered, his tone slightly altered, the earlier understanding replaced with steel. "Are we in agreement?"

Will carefully set the tankard on the wooden bench. He knew better than to press Carmichael further. The man had the temperament of a bulldog, no matter how elegantly he dressed. Once his mind was made up, he was unswerving in his determination. Besides, Will knew that Carmichael was right; to bring in another agent at this stage of the game would be dangerous. In truth, his feelings for Lady Lucinda would only strengthen his resolve to keep her safe from Garenne.

Perhaps that was the answer, then: focus on his hatred for Garenne and let all other emotions go.

"Yes, we're in agreement," he finally responded, settling his elbows on his knees and massaging his temples.

"Good. Now, about Lady Lucinda. It seems she enjoys early morning rides—alone."

Will dropped his hands and turned to Carmichael. "You mean accompanied only by servants, yes?"

"No, by 'alone' I mean just that. She's adamantly opposed to having an escort, despite the best efforts of the Furies."

"Good God, man, you must have been misinformed. Those women control all they survey. Not even Lady Lucinda would dare cross them."

Carmichael rose. "As you've said, she's a most remarkable woman."

* * *

Lucinda wanted to scream with joy. The wind had pulled the pins from her hair and the thick braid blew free, whipping like a banner as she raced Tristan, her dapple gray gelding, through Hyde Park. The sun had only just come up, setting the birds to singing on what promised to be a fine day.

She slowed the gelding with a gentle tug on the reins and crossed to follow her favorite path. Lucinda lived for her morning rides, free of everyone, even the servants, and the expectations that normally followed her wherever she went.

It hadn't been easy, but she'd managed to convince her aunts of the need for such a thing. Actually, in truth she'd blackmailed each of them into submission. And while reading to Charlotte each evening from the Bible, writing Bessie's frightfully colorful dictation to her many admirers, and sneaking Victoria's favorite brandy past the entire household on a monthly basis was not how Lucinda would ideally spend her time, it was worth it all the same.

She suspected that somewhere, amongst the groves of oak trees, near the eastern gate by which Lucinda arrived and left, a groom lingered for what must have been, at times, a miserably cold and dreary two hours.

Halting the gelding next to a large rock she'd used to dismount many times in the past, she gathered the skirt of her green riding habit and slid from the saddle. Tristan turned his head, ears pricking forward with interest at the sight of the lugh, green grass. Lucinda drew the reins over the gray's head then allowed him to graze.

She gratefully sat down near him, dropping the reins to rest in the spring grass. She'd tossed and turned most of the night, nervous energy coursing through her veins and keeping her from soundly sleeping. Even with a pillow over her head. "Even with two," she solemnly told

Tristan, who simply paused for a moment, then continued to chew the flavorful grass.

The conversation with the duke plagued her conscience. "He is, after all, quite a horse," she scoffed, wondering at the boldness with which she'd so easily responded. Really, the entire conversation had been altogether too bold, as Amelia would undoubtedly point out had she known of it.

But she didn't. Not yet anyway. A twinge of guilt flickered. She'd not sought out her dearest friend's company since the ball—or, if she were completely honest, since meeting the duke.

Lucinda pulled a daisy free and began to tear the white petals from the flower, one by one. She knew what Amelia would say of the scheme—even worse, what she would think of Lucinda's obvious attraction to him.

And worst of all? Amelia would be right. Lucinda was treading on dangerous ground, which only made it all the more exciting. Actually, it rather shook the earth, if the current vibration of the ground beneath her had anything to do with it.

Puzzled, Lucinda looked up. A massive, coal black horse and its equally large rider were quickly approaching.

She jumped to her feet, holding tight to Tristan's reins. For his part, the gray thought little of their impending guests, affording them only a slow glance before setting his sights on a patch of succulent overgrown blades.

The black horse was eating up the earth with his powerful strides, the rider sitting easily in the saddle despite the speed. Lucinda didn't know whether to be thrilled or terrified by the sight and wondered for a moment at the curious relationship between the two emotions.

She couldn't identify the horse and rider, for the morning sun hazed their figures. Her eyes narrowed in an attempt to make out the man.

With nary a second to spare, the rider reined in the big black and the horse immediately responded, slowing to a canter, then a trot, and finally a walk.

Lucinda gathered her wits about her and prepared to unleash a particularly pungent verbal set-down. She shaded her eyes from the sun in order to see the pair more closely.

"Fancy meeting you here."

Despite having met him only mere days before, Lucinda would have known that voice anywhere. The husky tone sent a shiver down her spine and all the way to the tips of her riding boots. She relished the sensation for a moment then remembered what she had been about to do. "Your Grace, how nice of you to join me. Oh, and I do thank you for refraining from running your overgrown mount over the top of—"

Her reference to the horse had been smartly punctuated with a sweeping gesture and sarcastic look in the horse's direction. That was the moment Lucinda realized the identity of the horse.

"King Solomon's Mine," she breathed, dropping Tristan's reins to rush to his side.

She stroked his head, pressing her own cheek to his before kissing his velvety nose. "It's been so long since I last saw him," she said, tears misting her eyes.

The duke dismounted and joined her. "Has Sol grown that much, then?" he asked playfully.

Lucinda rolled her eyes at him before turning back to the horse. "Oh, no, not at all. It's the forelock," she began, reaching for the long, glossy length of hair that fell just between King Solomon's ears. "He used to wear it to the side much like the other young bucks about town. This is far superior, though, I must say," she finished, giving him one more loving pat on the neck before stepping back to reclaim Tristan.

The duke led the stallion past Lucinda to where Tristan was happily grazing. He gestured toward a bench neatly tucked into a copse of trees nearby. "May I join you, or would sharing a seat be too scandalous an act for the proper Lady Lucinda?"

Lucinda knew from the amused half smile accompanying his question that the duke was simply quizzing her, but she desperately wanted to prove the blasted man wrong. "By all means," she replied, failing to add that they were, in fact, not alone, if her suspicion was correct that a groom followed close behind.

She strode to the bench and primly sat down, taking care to arrange her riding havit and reaching to adjust her black beaver hat. She felt the loose braid at her neck and nearly yelped. What must he think? She was unaccompanied, in the middle of Hyde Park, and with her hair nearly falling in her face.

She looked up just in time to catch the duke tossing his crop, hat, and gloves on the ground before pulling at his somewhat wrinkled neckcloth. His hair had been tousled by the wind, the long dark locks escaping what looked to have at some point been a neatly combed style. The once severely pressed wool of his dark blue waistcoat was now creased across the shoulders, whether from the ride itself or simply from accommodating his massive muscles Lucinda could not say. His leather riding breeches were in fairly good condition, though they did mold to his legs in such a way that Lucinda found it troubling.

He looks good enough to eat, Lucinda thought to herself, realizing that His Grace most likely would not give a fig whether her hair was finely coiffed or not.

He sat down next to her, running a hand through his thick hair, then turning his gaze to hers. "Good morning."

Lucinda slicked her tongue over her suddenly dry lips before answering. "And good morning to you. What brings you to Hyde Park at such an early hour, Your Grace?"

He looked tired to Lucinda, his eyes still soft from sleep and his jaw rough with hair. Something in her begged to reach out and run her gloved finger over the light beard. Would it be soft, as surely his deep black hair was, or coarse? She wouldn't—no, couldn't—find out.

"What wouldn't bring me, Lady Lucinda? The fine weather. A healthful ride. You," he answered, resting one booted foot on the opposing knee.

His leg now touched hers, the fitted breeches and her bright green merino riding costume all that separated their skin. Her fingers tingled and she instinctively moved to touch him. With effort, she restrained herself, clenched her fingers, and tucked her hands beneath her skirts. She offered a small smile to the duke. "I find my hands in need of warmth just now. I am chilled—that is to say, my hands are, and I fear these York gloves are doing little to help."

He looked slightly puzzled at Lucinda's stammering, then understanding dawned. "Let me be of service," he said, pulling one hand into his and then other, cupping both and gently rubbing back and forth with his own.

This is what I get for playing with fire, Lucinda mused silently, the rhythm of his ministrations lulling her into a pleasant fog.

"Are we quite alone?" he asked, his tone gruff but not angry.

Lucinda sensed that she should rouse herself, but the feel of his hands on hers was overwhelming. "Yes."

His hands stopped and tightened around hers. "The women I choose to court are not allowed to cavort through the woods like fairies, unattended and in a state of some dishabille."

Now he sounded angry, the flecks of green in his eyes

clouding to a deep moss. Lucinda bit her lower lip in response, her own eyes unable to hold his absorbing glance.

Lucinda very nearly felt embarrassed and apologetic.

Very nearly.

Her initial response shifted into something altogether different, something akin to outrage and sheer, hot fury. She pried her hands from his and took a deep breath. "You have absolutely no right to speak to me in such a superior tone," she ground out, her hands balling into fists.

The duke was looking just past Lucinda's head at the copse of trees behind them. His eyes were practically black, the pupils dilated with rage. Lucinda began to reconsider her words, though her anger at his ridiculous remark was warranted, on that whe would not budge.

And all at once, he grabbed her by the shoulders and heaved their combined weight against the back of the bench, upending the seat until they were delivered to the soft ground below. "You impertinent, impossible woman," he bit out, just before he pulled Lucinda to him and kissed her.

Oh, God, this is madness, Lucinda thought, wondering whether she'd hit her head and was now imagining the duke's surprisingly soft yet firm lips on hers, his tongue as it nimbly attacked her own, his hands as they freed her buttons, revealing her thin white habit shirt beneath.

Lucinda's leg hitched over his hip, confirming what she'd feared: This was not the product of a particularly nasty spill and she'd no hope of saying no, as her body clearly had other plans.

The duke growled low into Lucinda's mouth, obviously pleased with her counterattack. He heatedly untied the bow at her neck, then pulled his mouth from

hers, his lips traveling the length of her neck before setting to work on her shirt buttons.

Lucinda's body pulsed with diminutive fireworks
bursting into vivid colors with each button he released.

She ran her hand through his hair, stopping at the
nape to entwine a lock between her fingers. She'd intended on pushing him away, but somehow the need
growing inside of her wouldn't let her. She squeezed her
eyes shut, a pleasurable sense of dizziness pushing her
toward something that both thrilled and terrified her.

"Are you quite sure that it is Sol who holds your heart
entirely, my lady?"

He moved swiftly, silently down the wooded trail.
Pain stabbed his skull in a series of knife-sharp jabs. He
swung his head to the right, then left to assure he was
alone, and brilliant comets of light flared on the edges of
his peripheral vision. He narrowed his eyes against the
resulting disorientation and snarled silently as his throat
constricted, making it difficult to swallow.

He should have followed Clairemont home from the
ball last night and killed him when he'd had the chance.

How the man had sensed his presence among the
park's trees was beyond comprehension. But the duke
had, looking directly at Garenne before throwing the
woman to the ground. There'd barely been enough time
to control his rage, to stop himself from throwing his
knife directly into the bastard's neck.

It would be maddening to the average man, but
Garenne knew himself to be exceptional. It was not his
fault that Clairemont's presence at the ball had forced
the attempt. Nor was it a lack of skill that had led to the
failure. Clairemont was to blame and, in time, Garenne
would make him pay. But for now, he knew that all of
his focus must be on the woman.

Pressure built inside his skull, rage exacerbating the inevitable reactions brought on by frustration.

He came across a hare, frozen with fright in the middle of the path. Garenne threw the knife with expertise, landing its tip in the animal's left ear and pinning it to the ground.

He walked to where the rabbit lay, wounded and terrified. He bent down to retrieve his knife with one hand, the other coming to encircle the rabbit's neck. He squeezed hard, then flung the limp animal into the foliage.

The pain eased and the lights impacting his vision ceased flashing. Once again, he could consider the situation dispassionately.

"Clearly, I will require assistance. A few choice operatives should accomplish the desired goal.

"Soon. Very soon," he whispered to himself before making his way from the park.

7

"Perhaps the blue?" Lucinda held up a length of deep-hued sapphire ribbon, the satiny end trailing from her gloved fingers. The bright blue gleamed against the rose pink bodice of her walking dress.

Pomeroy Milliners sold the finest ribbons in the whole of London, their countless offerings varied enough to satisfy even Lady Hertford, the Prince Regent's notoriously discriminating mistress. And while Lucinda knew full well that this particular shade of blue suited her perfectly, she welcomed the opportunity to distract Amelia from her current line of questioning.

"Your skill at evading inquiries is impressive, but hardly a match for me. I know you too well." Amelia slipped the ribbon from Lucinda's fingers and returned it to the glass-topped counter case. "Now, please explain how allowing the Duke of Clairemont to court you is in any way advantageous."

"Shhh." Lucinda lowered her lashes and her gaze flicked over the shop. Across the room, ladies and their maids crowded around a table where a new shipment of ribbons was decoratively displayed with a rainbow of matching gloves and lace-trimmed handkerchiefs. Their chattering filled the air, conveniently covering her murmured conversation with Amelia.

Nearer at hand, however, the narrow-faced clerk behind the counter had sidled closer. Lucinda was sure the woman's apparent absorption in rearranging spools of purple and blue ribbons was wholly feigned.

Convinced the clerk had heard Amelia's question, Lucinda smiled sweetly when the woman glanced sideways, her cheeks flushing as she met Lucinda's gaze.

"I believe I would like to see something in red," Lucinda said, politely but firmly.

She waited until the clerk had disappeared behind the heavy curtain that separated the storage area from the remainder of the shop before she answered Amelia. "How could it *not* be to my advantage?" she asked, turning to stroll between the tables heavily laden with ribbon. The move took them farther away from the counter and, in an excess of caution, also put more space between them and the other shoppers. Gossip spread through the ton with amazing speed; Lucinda refused to aid it by being carelessly overheard.

Amelia hurried after her, took a firm hold on the skirt of her pelisse, and tugged.

Pulled off stride, Lucinda halted abruptly and turned to look at her friend. "Was that truly necessary?" she asked mildly.

Amelia let out an exasperated sigh and slipped her arm through Lucinda's, steering them toward a settee, comfortably upholstered in gold and white striped silk and situated conveniently along the opposite wall.

"Sit," she commanded, and waited for Lucinda to do so before settling beside her. She tugged off her right glove and touched her palm to Lucinda's forehead. "Are you feeling well?"

Lucinda's swift gurgle of laughter had her glancing quickly at the crowd of ladies crowding the shop's aisles before answering, "Yes, quite well, thank—"

"Have you been imbibing? Running wild through the heath by the light of a full moon?" Amelia's eyes grew rounder as she whispered, "Did the Devil himself visit you in a dream?"

Lucinda couldn't help herself; she tilted her head back and let out a most unladylike laugh. The trio of dower ladies examining the selection of velvet ribbon two aisles away turned as one to gape at her. The eldest frowned, her gray brows lowering over dark eyes that snapped with disapproval.

"I beg your pardon, but my friend possesses quite an imagination and took me by surprise," Lucinda said in apology. The older woman sniffed, but she and her companions nodded and returned to perusing the selection.

"Amelia, what on earth would lead you to believe that any of those outrageous claims would be true?"

The look of concern disappeared from Amelia's face, replaced by a glint of mischief. "How else would one explain your sudden lapse in judgment? 'How could it *not* be?'" she repeated in a gently mocking tone. "How *could* the duke's courtship be advantageous to you, a woman who has always declared that marriage holds no interest for you whatso—"

"Of all people, Amelia, you're the one I would expect to be happy for me," Lucinda interrupted. "Wasn't it you who told me: 'Your one true love is out there, just waiting for the day you'll find him.'"

Amelia rolled her eyes in response. "Of course, but I wasn't speaking of His Grace, Lucinda."

"But why? He's wealthy, handsome—"

"And a hedonist," Amelia continued in an urgent whisper. "Rumored to have coaxed a woman out of her clothes with merely one word. Is this your one true love?"

"Impossible," Lucinda balked, and then couldn't resist adding, "Who was the woman?"

"Lady Swindon," Amelia answered dramatically. "And she's only one of many."

Lucinda's mind raced back to the park bench, when the duke's lips had been on hers. He'd completely undone her in less than five minutes. Lady Swindon was clearly either weaker or wiser than she.

"I am no Lady Swindon, as you are well aware," Lucinda said, desperately trying to harness her thoughts before they betrayed her.

The lanky clerk appeared through the curtained doorway and came toward them, her arms laden with ribbons in every shade of red.

"Are you absolutely certain this is all you have?" Lucinda asked, desperate to secure their privacy once more.

"I'll look again, my lady," the clerk answered before disappearing back into the storeroom.

"Exactly my point," Amelia shot back in a hushed tone. "You are a woman of discriminating sensibility with no inclination to take a husband. So why are you engaged in this ill-conceived association with Clairemont?"

To disappoint Amelia was unthinkable; to lie to her, impossible. Lucinda took her friend's hand in hers and squeezed. "If I confide in you, you must promise to tell no one, not even your husband," she said earnestly, all amusement gone.

"Is that quite necessary? I share my deepest, most private thoughts with John—"

"Not even John," Lucinda insisted.

Amelia narrowed her eyes consideringly. "Very well. I promise. But only because I am sure you wouldn't ask this of me were it not absolutely necessary."

Lucinda leaned closer until there wasn't a hairsbreadth between their skirts on the settee. "I've come to an agreement with the duke regarding King Solomon's Mine," she whispered.

A look of confusion clouded Amelia's face. "What on

earth does a horse have to do with you finding your one true love?"

"Nothing, actually. I've not changed my opinion in regards to marriage, Amelia. I am and will always be deliriously happy for you and your John, but it simply isn't something I want." Lucinda paused, glancing about to ensure no one was listening. "Clairemont has acquiesced to his mother's wishes for an heir—which requires him to find a bride."

Amelia sat back and absorbed this piece of the puzzle, clearly still befuddled. "Well, I'm delighted he has agreed to marry, but I fail to see how this has anything to do with the horse."

"We've come to an understanding. I allow him to court me. If, at the end of the allotted time, I've fallen for his innumerable charms, we marry. If not, I win King Solomon's Mine and secure the stallion for our breeding program."

Amelia's mouth curved into an O of comprehension as the last piece fell into place. "Lady Lucinda Grey, you know that I hold every confidence in your ability to do anything you set your mind to, but this is no ordinary man you're dealing with."

"Oh, Amelia, I'm fully aware of that. But I've declined proposals from nearly every eligible bachelor in London. Surely I have one more refusal left in me." The heat that had flared when the duke traced her bare skin with his fingertips lingered on Lucinda's body and flared anew with the mere mention of him. Her awareness of just how unordinary the man was could not be denied but she wouldn't, couldn't, confess her weakness to Amelia.

Amelia squeezed Lucinda's hand. "And the Furies, what do they have to say about your ambitious scheme?"

"They had their reservations," Lucinda began, a wry

smile curving her lips. "That is, until I told them that the duke is a particular friend of your husband's."

Amelia's eyes flew wide with alarm. "You didn't!"

Lucinda chuckled. "Really, they're not that terrifying, are they?"

"You have to ask?"

Lucinda patted Amelia's hand and stood, pulling her friend after her. "I'm only having a bit of fun, though Lord Northrop's friendship with the duke may be of some help to me."

Amelia flashed a wicked grin. "Leave it to me," she said knowingly, then stopped. "But Lucinda, you will take care, won't you? I've never considered fighting a duel, but to save you from the clutches of Iron Will, I would do so without question."

Lucinda knew that despite Amelia's light tone, her friend's concerns were real. They matched the very ones taking shape in her own heart, and for the first time in her life Lucinda wondered whether she'd taken an irrevocable misstep.

"I know, and I would do the same for you without hesitation," she answered. "But first . . ." She looked toward the counter where the exhausted clerk had arranged what was surely every last red ribbon in the shop's inventory for their review. "I believe we have need of many red ribbons."

How women could spend such a vast amount of time doing what amounted to child's play was beyond Will. Lady Lucinda and Lday Northrophad been occupied in Pomeroy's for nearly an hour, leaving Will to loiter on New Bond Street like some young buck desperate for attention. "Purveyors of the finest ladies millinery, ribbons, and bows," Will quoted, reading from the gilded scrollwork on the wooden sign above the shop's entry.

He bit out a curse, muttering under his breath.

If someone had told him a fortnight ago that he would find himself within ten miles of such a ridiculous shop, Will would have laughed. And then, most likely, hit the man for having the temerity to suggest he'd dangle after a woman while she trolled the shops for fripperies.

But the incident in the park had been too near a thing for Will's liking. Garenne wouldn't take the failure lightly. Will's unorthodox method of thwarting the Frenchman would likely fuel his determination to complete the mission.

Will planned to keep Lucinda under Young Corinthian guard day and night until the Frenchman was in custody and her safety assured. Which was why he found himself outside Pomeroy's, wishing to God that Lady Lucinda had opted to spend her time at home in her parlor.

Still, the crowded avenue offered many shops in which a man of Will's social and financial position could claim an interest. "Haberdasher, tailor, fanciful snuff boxes," he recited as he surveyed the shops surrounding Pomeroy's.

"Unfortunately," Will muttered under his breath, "I couldn't give a bloody damn about any of it."

Still, anyone seeing him would have to agree it was plausible that he would be found at one time or another on New Bond Street, a fact that would not be lost on Lady Lucinda.

Lady Lucinda. The taste of her lingered on his tongue. Her sweet surrender in the park had been as surprising as it was unforgettable. He ached at the memory of her—the lush curves of her body lifting against him, her skin flushed with desire.

But the park had been the wrong place, the wrong time. Just plain wrong. Will had come to know Garenne's habits too well to have lingered in the grass with Lucinda. Though the Frenchman wouldn't allow himself to be drawn out, he was no less dangerous. He would waste no time before attacking again.

Will had alerted Carmichael and his fellow Corinthians about the foiled attempt, arranging for more men to be assigned to the case. He knew that he did not *need* to be here, watching her, but he felt a certain sense of duty to the case. She required looking after. And he was the right man for the job.

A gaggle of fresh-faced young misses approached, giggling and eyeing him with interest as they walked by. Will ignored them and looked past the group to the tall, impeccably dressed gentleman strolling toward him, a few yards behind the chattering girls.

"I never would have pegged you for a dandy," Lord Marcus MacInnes, the Earl of Weston, drawled as he neared Will, coming to stand next to him. "Yet here you are, Clairemont, shopping. On New Bond Street. Will wonders never cease?"

Will eyed Weston, relieved to have the seasoned Corinthian on the case. The Scotsman's fashionable appearance and devil-may-care attitude had proven to be the perfect cover for Corinthian business in the past, and Will had high hopes it would serve their efforts well now.

"You've caught me, then," Will responded sarcastically. "Though one has to wonder just what you're doing here."

Weston grinned. "Well played, Clairemont."

The door to Pomeroy's opened suddenly and Lady Lucinda and Lady Northrop stepped over the threshold, followed by their maids, who carried several wrapped parcels. The sight put an abrupt halt to their conversation.

"Drop back and follow us," Will said in a low tone, keeping his facial expression relaxed and uninterested.

Weston clapped Will on the back and laughed. "Of

course," he replied, his jovial action belying the true nature of their interaction.

Will moved quickly, easing behind a passing tall, elderly gentleman escorting a very rotund lady gowned in black. He used the couple as concealment until they were close to Lady Lucinda's party. Then he slowed, letting space lengthen between himself and the elderly couple.

"Lady Lucinda, Lady Northrop." He approached the two women and their maids.

He held back a smile at the surprise and, if he wasn't mistaken, pleasure that appeared on Lucinda's face.

"Your Grace," Lady Northrop began, her expression markedly less cheerful than Lady Lucinda's. "I must admit to some surprise at finding you here," she said.

Will bowed, smiling at Lady Lucinda before turning to Lady Northrop, a look of bewilderment clouding his face. "Indeed? I cannot imagine why."

Lady Northrop's ears turned scarlet at the tips as they almost always did whenever they met. "Surely I am not the only one to marvel at the sight of Iron Will strolling down New Bond Street. Or would you have us believe you've suddenly become obsessed with the cut of your waistcoat?"

Will spread his hands, palms out, in a plea for mercy from Lady Northrop. "Ah, you've caught me out. In truth, I could not have cared less for any of this." He paused, gesturing at the surrounding shops. The fashionable set thronged the walkways and street, to see and be seen. "But of late I've found myself quite taken with the notion of self-improvement."

He looked at Lday Lucinda, lifting an eyebrow in a silent request for confirmation. "Lady Lucinda, have I not demonstrated a marked desire to prove myself a gentleman in every way?"

He dared her to answer truthfully. The narrowing of

her eyes told him she knew he was referring to their interlude in the park.

"I wouldn't dream of judging you, Your Grace, though your 'marked desire' is most convincing." She finished off the sentence with a serene smile, and he half expected her to drop into a polite curtsy.

"Be that as it may," Lady Northrop cut in, "I pray you will remember that a well-cut coat alone does not make the man. A true gentleman is one in both manners and heart."

"Time spent with you is always edifying, Lady Northrop," Will assured her solemnly. He offered an arm to each lady. "Would you care to instruct me further while enjoying ices? We're nearly to Gunter's"

Lady Northrop looked confused for a moment, clearly searching for the words to refuse him without violating the code of manners drilled into all genteel young girls long before they entered society.

"That would be most gentlemanly of you," Lady Lucinda responded, taking Will's arm.

Lady Northrop's mouth opened and closed in a vaguely fishlike fashion as the two waited patiently for her response. Finally, she settled her gloved fingers on Will's coat sleeve. "It would be rude of me to deny your request at this juncture, would it not?"

"Yes," Will and Lady Lucinda said in unison.

"Very well." Lady Northrop glanced over her shoulder before catching Lady Lucinda's eye. "Perhaps we should have your Mary tell the coachman we'll be a bit longer and then send our maids home?"

Lady Lucinda agreed, and moments later Will escorted the two women down the street toward Gunter's.

The three walked in silence the short distance to Berkeley Square, curious looks from fellow pedestrian meeting their every step.

Will leaned toward Lady Northrop, dropping his

voice to a murmur as he asked, "Lady Northrop, have you engaged in some sort of scandalous behavior that I should be aware of?"

Lady Northrop's eyebrows shot up and she gaped at him.

"Everyone is looking at us," he explained, all innocence.

Her eyes narrowed, and her mouth opened, but she lost her opportunity to reply when Will drew them to a stop.

"Ladies," Will said, holding open the door and stepping back to gesture them inside.

The fashionable crowd inside turned to see who was entering, their heads swiveling almost as one and then nodding in the expected polite greeting to both Lady Lucinda and Lady Northrop.

Their expressions of surprise, shock, and utter dismay when they recognized Will were laughable. He fought back the urge to bare his teeth at them, simply for the amusement of hearing them all gasp, and instead intercepted a waiter. "A table for three," he said gruffly.

The waiter jumped to attention, motioning to a fellow server to make room in the already crowded parlor for the trio. A table and three chairs were brought out and set near the window; the waiter bowed to Will's party and gestured for them to follow.

Will could have sworn he heard a unified intake of breath as they made their way to the table, utensils full of fanciful sweets stopping just short of gaping mouths.

"Lady Northrop, I beg your pardon," he said, settling his frame into his chair after assuring the ladies were comfortably seated.

"What for?" Lady Northrop asked suspiciously.

"Clearly it is Lady Lucinda who has inspired such interest," Will said sardonically.

Lady Lucinda responded by arching a brow at him in amusement. Lady Northrop sniffed her disbelief and the two turned to question the hovering server about the cakes available.

No sooner had the trio ordered than the tinkling of bells signaled a newcomer. The door swung wide and a footman appeared, dressed head to toe in scarlet livery, his gold buttons and embroidery bright enough to reflect and perhaps substitute for the midday sun. The man swept the room with a supercilious gaze, stepping back with a low bow to usher in a woman.

Her spectacular mane of auburn curls was fashionably bound beneath a charming deep forest green hat. Her matching pelisse clung to the curve of her shoulders, draping expertly over the gown beneath. The woman surveyed the shop's occupants, her emerald green eyes reflecting the pleasure she felt at such attention.

She walked across the room to join a group of women clustered at a table, the hum of whispers beginning anew.

"Lady Swindon certainly does know how to make an entrance." Lady Lucinda commented.

Lady Northrop rolled her eyes in response and unfolded a linen napkin. "That is one way of looking at it," she confirmed, arranging the snowy white square over her lap.

Will kept his eyes on the window, hopeful that the two were finished.

"Are you acquainted with Lady Swindon, Your Grace?" Lucinda asked.

Will's instinct was to growl a particularly fervent oath, but even he knew that such a response was beyond the outer bounds of propriety. Fortunately, the waiter arrived with the requested ice, tea and plate of cakes before he could speak. The brief interruption allowed him time to manage a politer reply. "Yes, we are acquainted."

"Would you be so kind as to introduce me?"

Will turned to Lady Lucinda, not quite sure he'd heard her correctly. "I'm sorry?"

Lucinda dabbed at her mouth, looking up at him through her lashes. "I'm not acquainted with Lady Swindon, though I have heard a great deal about her. I find her interesting, and would like to meet her."

Will slowly continued to spoon the cold ice into his mouth. When he'd reached the bottom of the bowl, he looked at Lady Northrop, whose bland stare told him she wasn't about to offer help in any way. He turned his attention to Lady Lucinda, who eyed him expectantly.

He wondered how long he would have to pretend he hadn't heard her before she released the request.

Lady Lucinda smiled sweetly. "I do wonder, Your Grace, if you would introduce us?"

A great deal longer than this, apparently.

"Bloody hell," he muttered under his breath before dropping his spoon on the table with a clatter. "She is not like you, Lady Lucinda, not in any way."

Lady Lucinda looked into his eyes, her brows furrowing. "Whatever do you mean, Your Grace?" she asked softly.

"She may have a title, but she does not possess any of the qualities that someone in her position should."

"Not unlike you, Your Hrace," Lady Lucinda responded. "And yet, look at how well we are managing."

"Oh, my," Lady Northrop whispered, her gaze focused just beyond Will's shoulder.

Will and Lady Lucinda turned to see what had upset Lady Northrop, only to find Lady Swindon herself approaching.

Will's last encounter with the woman had not gone well. She'd convinced a footman to allow her entry to his town house and Will had found her disrobed and wild-eyed in his bed, begging him to take her back.

She'd been reasonable enough in the beginning, joining in long nights of lusty sex with unabashed enthusiasm and no expectations beyond the carnal. Which was exactly what Will had hoped for from the young, beautiful widow.

But then she'd married the aging Lord Swindon, turning her from a widow to the wife of a respected acquaintance. He'd ended the affair as gently as he could, but the woman clearly still held a grudge, if the expression on her face was any indication.

"Lady Swindon." Will said politely, standing. "You're looking well."

She acknowledged the compliment with a gracious nod, her emerald eyes taking in the trio. "Your Grace, how kind of you to say so," she responded coolly before turning to Lucinda. Her frosty gaze examined Lady Lucinda's face as if committing it to memory. "Lady Lucinda, your reputation precedes you."

Will shifted, resting one hand on the back of Lady Lucinda's chair. The implied intimacy of the act was duly noted by the redhead and her eyes narrowed.

"Lady Swindon." Lady Lucinda nodded, a sincere smile on her lips.

Lady Swindon's creamy complexion pinkened as she glared at Will. "Really, Your Grace. She is charming. So very charming," she murmured in a tone that could cut glass, before turning her attention back to Lady Lucinda. "You'll have quite a time of it taming this one, Lady Lucinda."

"We shall see," Lady Lucinda replied resolutely, then glanced at Will and Lady Northrop. "Your Grace, I do believe it is time for us to be off." She turned back to Lady Swindon, inclining her head in a gracious nod. "Good day."

Lady Swindon forced a smile before returning to her seat.

"Lady Lucinda," Will murmured as they rose and she took his arm, "I believe I underestimated you."

Lucinda looked up into Will's face. "Do not let it happen again, Your Grace."

8

The Young Corinthians Gentlemen's Club was not the most exclusive club in the city. Its membership boasted titles from baron to duke, but these barons and dukes (and quite everything in between) were not always of spotless reputation and respectability, which was why so many of them held the club in such affection. They darkened its doors at all hours of the day and night, comfortable in the knowledge that their fellow patrons could not afford to be judgmental, and, therefore, would not be.

The men enjoyed the comfortable armchairs and daily newspapers, complimentary bottles of sherry, and a limited selection of well-cooked English dishes. The brandy was a touch above good and the gambling opportunities plentiful. The Corinthians Club was what every gentlemen's club should be: an escape from the daily duties that men in such a position endured.

It neither stood above the other clubs nor fell beneath, but rather maintained a constant level of comfort that its members had come to expect.

In all ways but one very important, and very clandestine, exception. For within the walls of the club the Young Corinthians conducted their business, perfectly hidden within the normal daily rhythms of catering to London aristocrats.

Staffed entirely by Corinthians and with a sufficient number of secret passageways, concealed entryways, and meeting rooms to satisfy even Carmichael himself, the club, it could be said, was an indispensable member of the Corinthian team.

To Will, it was simply home. He'd never really felt comfortable in the ducal mansion. The specter of his father cast a shadow so dark and wide it was well nigh impossible to escape the late duke's influence without walking out the door.

And so Will had—walked out the door, that was, hastening to the Corinthians Club at every available opportunity, business or not. He'd spent more birthdays there than he cared to admit and celebrated the successful conclusion of countless missions. In many ways, the club afforded Will a life he'd never known outside of its walls. The enduring relationships and satisfying work he'd found in Carmichael's organization were far more meaningful for him than anything his family offered.

Little else outside the Young Corinthians held a place in Will's heart.

Until now.

He appeared to be obsessed with Lady Lucinda.

Clearly this had come about because her life was in grave danger. Any man, or at least any man trained by the Young Corinthians, would find it difficult to ignore a woman in such straits.

It had nothing to do with her beauty.

Or her sense of adventure.

Or her intelligence.

Or her—

He stopped. He literally stopped moving. He had, in theory at least, been reaching for his glass of brandy. But he had stopped, because it seemed to be the only way to force his bloody brain to stop as well.

Of all the things he needed in his life, a mental catalog of the many attributes of Lady Lucinda Grey was not among them.

"Are you planning on drinking that brandy or have you decided to perform a magic rite for its continued safety and good health?"

Will looked at Carmichael, then looked at his arm, still frozen in space, hovering over the table.

He looked like a damn fool.

"Sit," Will said, motioning to the chair near him.

"What were you doing?" Carmichael inquired, settling in.

Will lifted the heavy crystal glass to his lips and swallowed, the liquor burning pleasantly down his throat. "Thinking, Carmichael. I can't recommend it highly enough."

Carmichael lifted a brow. "Work or pleasure?"

"Both, actually," Will replied, then half heartedly retrieved the day's paper from the mahogany side table next to his chair.

"I trust you're not mixing the two."

Will took the paper in both hands and opened it wide.

Carmichael called to a footman to bring him a brandy. "You don't read the paper, Will."

"I do," Will replied gruffly.

The liveried servant set Carmichael's drink on the table and disappeared.

"Give me a moment," Carmichael said, then took a hearty sip of his brandy, swallowed, paused to consider, and shook his head decisively. "No, you still do not."

"Bloody hell."

"You know where we stand on such things. Personal interest has no place in Corinthian business."

Will dropped the *Times* in his lap and reached for Carmichael's brandy. "Just a moment, won't you," he said before throwing his head back and draining the glass. "Yes, I still do. Now, shall we talk about something else?"

"As you wish."

Will appreciated Carmichael's concern, but he could not bring himself to discuss the problem that was Lady Lucinda. Not only would Carmichael likely tell him in great detail why Will's interest in her was forbidden to an agent, but Will feared he would be disappointed in him. To engage in anything other than what the mission demanded with any asset—which clearly defined Lady Lucinda—was forbidden, but to contemplate relinquishing one's position in the Corinthians for a woman? The mere thought of surrendering his significant role within the brotherhood for something as inconsequential as love was simply too ridiculous for words. Such things had always mystified Will.

Northrop's choice of Amelia over his field position was beginning to make some sort of odd sense to Will—and this scared the hell out of him.

Regardless, he knew his duty and all that he owed to the Corinthians, and to Carmichael. To fall short in the eyes of his mentor was too much to risk.

Will roughly folded the paper and leaned forward, resting his elbows on his knees. "The incident in the park, then."

"Anything of particular interest?" Carmichael asked.

"No, though he's doing what I'd expected of him, I'll give him that," Will answered. "One attempt and nothing more. Garenne can't abide failure of any kind."

Carmichael nodded in acknowledgment. "His next move?"

"He prefers to work alone. He won't want to hire associates, but considering the mark, he may have to." Will paused to rub his temples. "Kidnapping a well-protected, prominent member of society is a far different proposition than assassinating an agent in the field. If he chooses to hire assistants, depending upon their number and skill, he could strike at any time. And my guess would be that he'll choose somewhere less public."

Carmichael toyed with his gold watch, the engraved head of a lion catching the candle's light. "You're comfortable with the number of our men assigned to the situation?"

"He's not human, old man, so no, not even a thousand agents would put my mind at ease," Will answered. "But we'll catch him, that I know for sure."

"Alive, Will," Carmichael's low murmur cautioned. "He's no good to us dead."

Will resisted the urge to argue the point, methodically rubbing his temples once more in an attempt to dispel vivid thoughts of just what he would do to Garenne if given half the chance. "Yes, alive. If possible." He dropped his hand, fixing Carmichael with a hard stare. "If I have to kill him to save Lady Lucinda, I will."

Carmichael shrugged. "Of course."

A sudden burst of laughter erupted from the gaming room, the volume and intensity signaling the late hour.

"Now come with me," Carmichael said in a lighter tone. "I believe there's a five pound note I've need to win back."

Will stood up from his chair and stretched. "Ever the optimist, Carmichael."

"Hardly. But I know a thing or two about odds, and you're bound to hit upon a losing streak one day," Carmichael answered, making his way to the gaming room just beyond.

"As I said, ever the optimist."

Lucinda had never dreamed that he would accept her invitation. Iron Will agreeing to attend an assembly at Almack's? Inconceivable.

But he had. Lucinda now stood with the duke just inside the assembly's upper rooms within the King Street building that housed Almack's. They faced Lady Jersey, as she eyed him skeptically from head to toe. No visitors to Almack's would be admitted tonight without Lady Jersey's approval.

Lucinda offered the woman a sweet smile when the patroness flicked her a sharp glance before returning her narrowed gaze to the duke. Clearly her perusal was an attempt to find fault with His Grace's appearance. In truth, his reputation alone should have barred him from the assembly.

But he was obviously escorting Lucinda, a fact that Lady Jersey could not overlook. Lucinda also knew Aunt Victoria had tortured the woman's mother for years with a particularly juicy bit of gossip involving the countess and an Italian opera singer from their youth. So Lucinda was not terribly surprised that the woman was having a difficult time of it.

Still, Lucinda had demanded that he play by the rules. Which meant he had to comply with the sartorial regulations, which had led to him donning the knee breeches that he currently wore. Trousers would never do at Almack's and she was beginning to understand why. The cream breeches molded to his legs in a most appealing way, *to say nothing of his—*

"Lady Lucinda?"

Lucinda pulled her thoughts from such an inappropriate path and focused on Lady Jersey. "I do beg your pardon, Lady Jersey. Would you be so kind as to repeat your question?"

"I said," the birdlike woman began, flicking her fingers dismissively in a distinct air of irritation, "that the duke is granted a Stranger's Ticket for the evening."

The duke offered Lady Jersey a dazzling smile and bowed. "Lady Jersey, always a pleasure."

"Hmph," the woman replied, gesturing for the two to remove themselves.

Lucinda curtsied with just the right mix of deference and serene confidence, then allowed the duke to escort her into the main assembly room, crowded with the cream of society.

"Was it the breeches?" he whispered in her ear. "I'm told I look especially fetching in breeches." His warm breath brushed her neck as he spoke and her skin prickled, her pulse racing.

Lucinda reined in her shivering nerves, relieved to spot her aunts not far away. She seized the distraction, lifting her fan to gain their attention. "I warn you, Your Grace," she said as she drew him with her through the throng, "you'd do well to be on your best behavior within the hallowed halls of Almack's."

He flashed her a wicked grin. "Must I? Even as pertains to you, Lady Lucinda?"

Her mouth formed an O of surprise. The shocking and, to be perfectly honest, delicious nature of his comment was outrageously pleasing. "Your Grace . . ." she whispered repressively, trying to restrain the rush of excited curiosity as to his meaning.

"I do adore the way you say that," he replied huskily, pasting a bored look on his face as they came to stand with her aunts.

"Well, well, Lady Jersey is wiser than I believed her to be," Victoria said in greeting, eyeing the duke with amusement. "And you, Your Grace, polish up quite well, I must say."

Will bowed before the aunts then flashed a charming smile. "High praise, indeed, especially from you."

"Do not become too used to it," Victoria replied, slyly winking at Lucinda before turning to her sisters. "Ladies, tepid lemonade and abysmal cake first, or straight to the tables?"

Charlotte gave Victoria a chiding look before answering. "The tables, I believe. Bessie, do you have a preference?"

Bessie was far too engrossed in admiring the duke's

breeches to hear Charlotte's query. The slight smile of appreciation on her face made Lucinda swallow her laughter. She knew just how her aunt felt.

"Aunt Bessie," Lucinda said a bit more loudly, waving her fan as unobtrusively as possible to gain her aunt's attention. "Shall we," she asked, holding out her arm for her aunt.

Bessie pulled her gaze from the duke and took Lucinda's arm, the entire group moving towards the card room with its gaming tables. "Yes, quite," she said, then added, "I'm sorry, where are we going?"

"To the tables," Lucinda replied, then whispered, "Do try to keep up, Aunt."

"It's hardly my fault, dear. You are the one that insisted he wear those breeches," Bessie answered in a hushed tone, the smile returning to her lips.

"Fair enough."

They were, in a word, dangerous. Will now knew what the Furies did to pass the time. No sewing or needlepoint, painting or reading for this trio. No, clearly the three habitually played cards well into the wee hours, if their current individual winning streaks were any indication. Will looked out at his fellow five-card loo players and sighed. "Poor bastards," he said under his breath, watching the Marquess of Billingham accept his loss and Charlotte's latest win with as much grace as he could muster.

"Did you say something?" Lady Lucinda asked softly, her eyebrow arched in a most attractive way.

"You knew, and yet you did not warn me," he murmured, bending his head toward her, the intoxicating scent of her skin mingling with the heated air.

She merely smiled in response. Will existed in a simmering state of arousal in her presence and the wicked curve of her lips badly threatened his control.

"You brought me here for this very reason, didn't you?" he asked, leaning in closer. He was much taller than she was, and seated this close, the sight of her breasts as they rose and fell more rapidly in time with her quickened breathing did little to ease his current state. The faster flutter of her pulse beating at the base of her throat only heightened his desire. "It wasn't enough to watch poor Billingham fall to the Furies. You wanted to embarrass Iron Will."

Across the table, Billingham's wife tapped him on the shoulder and the marquess reluctantly stood, vacating his chair to stroll off with his spouse.

Lady Lucinda gently blew out a breath, then folded her hands in her lap. "Come now, it's all in good fun," she responded, her teasing tone laced with desire.

"Is it fun you're after, then?" Will asked softly, resting his hand on the curve of her knee beneath cover of the table. "Be careful what you wish for."

She turned toward him and licked her lips before speaking, the sight of her tongue urging Will on. "Are you warning me?"

"Good evening, all."

Will turned abruptly to see Lady Northrop slipping into the marquess's abandoned chair, Northrop standing just behind.

Lady Lucinda smiled in welcome and greeted her friend. "Amelia, Lord Northrop, how lovely to see you this evening."

Will nodded to Northrop, rolling his eyes when his fellow Corinthian asked whether this was the duke's first trip to Almack's. "Surprisingly, yes," he answered sarcastically.

"Better late than never, I always say," came a sultry voice behind Will, the look of distaste on Lady Northrop's face telling him what he already knew.

"Lady Swindon," he replied before pushing back his

chair and standing. "I hardly expected to see you here this evening."

She adjusted a glove slowly, eyeing Will with a predatory stare. "You're not the only one with friends in high places, Your Grace," she answered, peering down at Lucinda with a disingenuous smile. "Lady Lucinda, you look lovely this evening. I do adore the country influence we're seeing this year."

Lady Lucinda acknowledged the thinly veiled insult with a cool glance and brief smile. "You are too kind, Lady Swindon."

"Oh, I don't know about that." She turned her attention to Will, her catlike eyes gleaming with malicious enjoyment. "Perhaps we should query the duke on such matters. We are, after all, particular friends, are we not, Your Grace?"

"Lady Swindon," Will's voice was lethal. "I believe it's time for you to go." He took hold of her arm and turned her around. "I'll just deliver Lady Swindon to her carriage and return directly."

Lady Lucinda nodded in agreement, her face devoid of emotion. "Of course. Good evening, Lady Swindon."

Will did not bother allowing time for the woman to respond. Arm in arm, he moved her inexorably toward the edge of the room and the exit beyond. "Just what do you think you're up to, Sarah?" he growled.

She pressed her shoulder against him and leaned in. "Perhaps I should be asking you the same question. Lady Lucinda Grey, really? She's hardly a match for your particular tastes."

He marched her down the hall toward the exit, the gilt-edged mirrors lining the walls reflecting their forms. "I hardly think it's any of your concern."

She stopped abruptly, taking him by surprise as she yanked him into an alcove, nearly toppling a potted palm in her haste. "You are wrong on that point, Clairemont. And I shall prove it." Her lips pressed hard against his, her hands reaching beneath his coat to clutch, gripping his waistcoat.

He heard a gasp of dismay just as he savagely wrenched his mouth from hers and pushed Lady Swindon away from him. He turned and nearly cursed aloud.

Lady Lucinda stood in the empty hall, only feet away, her mouth covered with her hand, her eyes filled with emotion.

"Lady Lucinda, this is not what it seems."

Lady Swindon's low, satisfied chuckle sent Lady Lucinda running down the hall, toward the other end of the building.

"I'll deal with you later," Will growled to Lady Swindon. "Leave. You won't like what happens if you disobey."

He saw her eyes widen in sudden fear. Assured she'd not linger, he hastened to catch up with Lady Lucinda. He saw her approach the staircase leading to the upper floor and hesitated, hoping she would slow if she thought he was not in pursuit.

Unfortunately, she only quickened her pace, lifting her narrow skirts and taking the stairs as quickly as she could. He followed, reaching the top floor in time to see her disappear through a large oak doorway. He surveyed the empty, silent hall, making sure there was no one about, then let himself into the room, closing the door and locking it quietly.

It was a storage room of sorts, tables and chairs filling nearly the entire space. Lady Lucinda stood across the room, looking out the window at the dark night.

"Lady Lucinda," he began, walking slowly toward her, his movements muffled by a worn carpet.

She turned to look at him, anger practically rising in visible waves off her body. "I do not wish to speak with you," she said succinctly.

Will pulled a flask from the inner pocket of his coat and took a drink. "Bloody hell," he growled, coming to stand next to her.

"How dare you use such words in my presence," she began, eyeing the flask. "And you know very well that spirits are not allowed here."

"And you must know that Lady Swindon means nothing to me. If I wanted her back I would have taken her weeks ago."

Lady Lucinda pressed a hand against the cold windowpane. "She is brash. And bold. She would think nothing of doing this," she ground out, reaching for Will's flask and taking a long drink.

"Lady Swindon is everything I am not," she finished, her voice cracking, the words husky from the brandy.

"Precisely," Will answered, reaching unsuccessfully for the flask. "My time with Lady Swindon came to an end the moment she married. An end, Lucinda, and of my own doing."

She took another long drink, the burn of the alcohol reflected in her pained expression. "But you were lovers—"

"Lady Lucinda," he interrupted, reaching out again. "This is not who you are."

"Perhaps not now, but I could learn."

Will closed the gap between them. "Do not make such ridiculous statements—"

"If you'll only be patient, I am confident—"

He reached out and cradled her face in his hands. "Lady Lucinda, do not say such things. Hell, don't even think . . ." He paused, collecting his temper. "You are everything a man could ever want and more."

She covered his hands with her own and looked up into his eyes. "Show me."

*   *   *

Lucinda did not know if it was the effects of the brandy or simply her heart winning out over her head, but she needed the duke in a way that she'd never felt before.

Happening upon him with Lady Swindon in the alcove had been torture, rage and jealousy filling her entire being until she'd had to run away or risk making a fool of herself.

"Lady Lucinda," he said, his voice low and husky.

She gently urged him closer. It did not matter that she knew little of what she was doing. Nor did she weigh the consequences that would surely come with such a bold move. Lucinda abandoned all that she knew of what she *should* do, and instead let her heart lead her astray.

She went up on tiptoe to reach him and pressed her lips against his, pouring all of the torrent of emotion she was feeling into the embrace.

His body tensed, muscles going hard with seemingly iron control as he hesitated, pulling his mouth from hers and looking deep into her eyes. "You do not want this," he ground out, his breathing labored.

"You're wrong." She rested her cheek on his, her lips nearly touching his ear. "I want this. But more importantly, I want you."

"You do not know what you ask of me," he growled, his hold on her arms tightening.

"Please."

He took her mouth with such seductive force Lucinda nearly wept. His tongue sought out hers, leaving her breathless with anticipation. She was barely aware he released her arms, but then his hands moved to her waist, rough caresses causing fresh sparks of need to ignite in her veins.

She ran her hand through his hair, stopping at the nape to entwine a lock between her fingers. She squeezed her eyes shut, a pleasurable sense of dizziness pushing her toward something that both thrilled and terrified her.

His mouth left hers and his lips trailed a slow assault down her neck, kisses so sweet yet so seductive Lucinda thought they would surely drive her mad. She was vaguely aware that he walked her backwards before urging her gently to the floor and onto the soft, thick pile of a Persian carpet.

She opened her eyes and watched as his head bent toward her, sighing as his mouth moved over her throat, then lower, to the slope of her breasts above the gown. He tugged the bodice lower. He sucked at first, then licked the shape of her entire breast before moving on to the other one.

"Yes," she urgently whispered, every inch of exposed skin screaming for his attention. "More."

His hands stroked down the length of her, over the inward curve of waist and the outer curve of hip and thigh. She shivered beneath the pleasure of clever hands before he reached the hem of her pale blue evening gown and slowly pushed it up, first to her knees, and then her thighs, stopping just below her waist. He lifted away from her, just far enough to take in the sight of her, and his eyes hazed with desire. His gaze seared her skin and her heart beat faster.

Desperate for release, she caught his hand in hers and kissed the palm. She took one finger in her mouth, sucking lightly at first, then harder, the salty taste of his skin surely the most intoxicating flavor she'd ever encountered.

"Bloody hell," he growled.

Lucinda opened her eyes at the sound, seeing the duke pull at his neckcloth and rip it from around his neck. He pulled his finger from her mouth, caressing first her top lip, then the bottom before tracing a path between her breasts and down to her belly and beyond, coming to rest just below her corset.

He towered over her, supporting himself on his knees while one hand reached for her breasts, gently tugging at a nipple then releasing, drawing a circular pattern in and out, heightening the desire.

The sensations pulsing through Lucinda's body and mind surged in waves, higher and higher, the unfamiliar pleasure coursing through her veins nearly impossible to contain.

She felt the sudden brush of cooler air between her thighs. The duke placed his finger where only moments before her chemise had been, rubbing gently, the exquisite friction coaxing Lucinda to new heights.

Somewhere in her mind reason screamed for her to stop, but she could not. She wanted this—wanted him—more than she'd ever wanted anything before in her life.

"Please," she sobbed, looking into the duke's eyes.

His fingers quickened their pace, driving Lucinda's tension higher, and bent to kiss her mouth, the flick of his tongue stirring the sudden explosion of Lucinda's entire being.

Pleasure radiated from the juncture of her thighs outward, pulsing through her body. The sensation seemed to build on itself, wave after wave of intense emotion assaulting her anew.

She threw her arms around him pulling him down on top of her. Stars burst before her heavy lids as she kissed him with every last ounce of energy she had within her, moaning under the pulsating pleasure.

Long moments later, he dragged his mouth from hers, dropping his head to rest below her breasts. "What have I done?" he asked, the low timbre of his voice vibrating against Lucinda's sated body.

"Nothing that I did not ask for," Lucinda responded, slowly sitting up and urging him to do the same. "I needed something in a way I'd never experienced . . ." she began, hesitating in an attempt to find the right words. "I needed you, and I will not, cannot, apologize for it. Neither should you, unless you—"

Lucinda stopped, doubt suddenly filling her. Had he only taken pity on her? Obliged her out of lust and some twisted sense of duty rather than any real feeling for her?

"Do not, for a moment, think I do not want you, Lady Lucinda."

Lucinda couldn't think beyond this moment, the ramifications of what had just transpired too numerous and earthshaking to entertain. When at last his lips left hers, she rested her head on his shoulder and sighed contentedly. "In that case, I do believe it's time you called me Lucinda."

9

Nearly eighteen hours had passed, but Will could still smell her on his skin, taste the salt of her sweat in his mouth, hear her panting in his ear.

She'd caught him off guard, the need so achingly apparent in her eyes that even Iron Will could not say no. He could take some relief in the fact that he'd left her maidenhead intact. "Cold comfort," he growled, rolling the cue ball with such force that it crashed into the remaining balls, sending them careening across the baize surface to bounce off the sides of the billiard table.

Will stalked to the sideboard near the fireplace in Clairemont Hall. He hastily poured two fingers of brandy into a cut-crystal glass and tossed half of it down, returning the decanter to the silver tray before dropping into the leather chair angled next to the hearth.

"Christ," he whispered, nearly unable to believe his reaction to her. He'd wanted to bury himself so deeply inside of her that their mingled cries could be heard in heaven itself.

But more than that, his own need for connection matched hers, his heart and soul echoing what he saw in her eyes.

He stood abruptly and savagely threw the crystal glass into the fireplace. A thousand tiny shards rained down over the flickering flames, pinging against brick and stone.

"This cannot be." He turned toward the door, halting abruptly to drop to his knees. *This cannot be!*

Desperate for something, anything, to release his anger upon , he roughly took up a nearby billiard cue and snapped it in half, flinging both pieces to crash against the wall. He sat back on his haunches and covered his face with his hands, the dawning recognition of such unfamiliar emotions washing over him anew.

What was happening to him?

Love, you giant damned fool. Love, he thought, unable to even speak the words out loud.

He raked his hands through his hair before standing. "And danger." Dangerous for him for so many reasons. But worse, dangerous for Lucinda.

Will could not be the man she wanted, that was certain. His faults could fill a thousand books. His father had been right about one thing: Will could never be what a duke should be.

But more than that, he could not be the agent he must be with such feelings hammering away at his heart.

Or could he? Will propped himself against the billiard table and looked deep into the fire. Perhaps it was those very feelings that made him the perfect man for the job. After all, what other man would have a more vital reason for keeping her safe than he?

He gripped the edge of the table with both hands, his knuckles turning white from the effort. This was madness. Lunacy. He'd steeled himself from such involvement countless times before, flirtations and physical encounters serving to fill the void that years of emptiness had created.

And when it hadn't been enough? Will had found comfort in the Young Corinthians, the endless hours of intelligence work numbing him beyond the ability to feel.

And yet, somehow, some way, he could not let Lucinda go. With every single detail he discovered, he only yearned to know more of her.

To give in to the madness could be his salvation, a new life, where love filled his soul rather than loathing and rage. But what of his old life? His debt to the Young Corinthians could not be repaid from behind a desk.

He unclenched his grip, leaving the table to walk across the deep red and taupe patterned carpet, stopping in front of the window that looked out on St. James's Square. He caught his reflection in the glass. Hair mussed, his neckcloth missing, his jaw in desperate need of a shave. And those eyes. "Nearly as dark as the hell from which you came," his father would say.

"She couldn't love you, you fool," he gruffly whispered, looking past his image to the square below. Streetlights were just being lit, the dusk silently settling into the deepening expanse of night.

He'd tortured himself for naught, he realized. A woman such as Lucinda would not, could not, love a man such as he.

A carriage rolled to a slow stop in front of the house, The Clairemont crest barely visible in the waning light. "Bloody hell," he growled, watching the footman jump down from his perch to open the door. "As if I am in need of further distraction." His brother, Michael, emerged first, fingering his neckcloth and smoothing back his meticulously groomed hair before offering his hand to the remaining occupant.

A dainty gloved hand appeared, then one slim arm draped in a scarlet wool shawl. Finally the remainder of Will's mother came into view as she stepped down onto the pavement bricks. Her hair was just as it had always been, though silver locks now glimmered among the ebony tresses visible beneath her bonnet. She'd aged somewhat since he'd last seen her, and yet one could not deny that the duchess was still a striking woman, even at the advanced age of five-and-fifty.

She paused to smooth her skirts, looking up at the house with a mixture of emotions playing across her face.

Will turned away from the window and moved across the room slowly, reluctant to meet his unexpected guests. He knew how difficult it was for his mother to be here; the memories of life with his father were extremely painful ones. But the strain of entertaining his family was more than he cared to take on at the moment.

He met Smithers in the hallway, the man's dismay punctuated by the grim set of his mouth.

"Your Grace," Smithers began, stepping in time with Will, "your family—"

Will chuckled, despite Smithers's obvious discomfort. At least he could always count on him to behave exactly the same, every day. It was oddly comforting to Will and he clapped the man on the back. "My family, yes, I know. Thank you, Smithers—though this can all be left to Peterson, you know."

"If I may be so bold, the duchess and Lord Michael require special consideration, which is not Peterson's forte, Your Grace," he replied, a slight hint of irritation apparent in his tone.

Will laughed out loud this time. "No, Smithers, I suppose it is not."

The natural order of things put right, Smithers cleared his throat and picked up the pace. "Might I suggest the rose room for your mother and the—"

"Do as you see fit, Smithers," Will interrupted.

"Excellent, sir," the valet responded, then nearly ran down the hall to the stairs.

If only Smithers could manage the whole of my life, Will thought to himself, hesitating in the hall for a moment before making his way to the foyer.

*   *   *

When Will's father was alive, dinner demanded military precision. The candles were lit to cast a warm glow over the entire room. The food was prepared to entice and delight, every course agonized over by the staff until no fault could be found in their offerings. The crystal and china shone like jewels, the silver sparkled, and the table linens were pressed to hard-edged perfection.

Or else.

Will had detested every meal in the ornate room, the painted pastoral scene circling the four corners only serving to irritate him further.

One of the first dictates he had given upon assuming the title had been to never eat another meal in the formal dining room. He'd seen to the packing up of the room himself, taking great delight in swathing his father's chair in Holland cloth and distributing the ornate silver to a collection of street urchins he found down near the docks. They'd given him looks of disbelief when he'd approached with the rough sack of treasure, but quickly changed their minds when he began to dole out what would surely be a year's worth of meals for each of them.

It would have killed his father to see such a thing, which was exactly why he did it.

Though he had to admit, observing his brother and mother's attempt at normal behavior as they sat around the table in the morning room, he'd not considered the effect on the rest of his family.

"If I had known you were coming, Smithers would have seen to the airing of the dining room," he said, cutting a large bite of mutton in half before forking it into his mouth.

The duchess took a demure sip of her wine and gave him a small smile. "What is good enough for you is good enough for us, William," she answered quietly.

"And that is precisely the problem," Will countered, dropping his knife and fork to the table with an audible thwack.

"It truly is tiresome to have the exact argument over and over again, wouldn't you agree?" Lord Michael Randall pointed out, his face—the spitting image of Will's—a tight mask of frustration.

Will glared at his younger brother, the urge to throttle him tempered only by his love for the young man. They'd been inseparable as children, their boyish pranks proving too much for nearly every nursemaid south of Hadrian's Wall. And then their father's hatred for everything familial intensified, causing Will to distance himself from Michael in an attempt to spare the boy from the ugliness.

It had worked, though Michael had not understood his older brother's behavior, taking his cold treatment for dislike and betrayal rather than what it truly was.

Will had saved his brother's life, and sacrificed his love in the process.

The loss of his brother's respect had hit hard, but the realization that his mother would do nothing on his behalf hurt the most. No matter how cold his father's treatment, the magnitude of his insults, or the viciousness of his behavior, she sat idly by, absorbing the damage in quiet pain.

He'd often wondered as a child about his parents' relationship. His mother, so capable and assured with him and his brother, would be reduced to tears by his overbearing father. It was a transformation he could not understand—and one he came to detest.

"How long will you be in town?" Will asked abruptly, ignoring his brother's statement.

The crease between the duchess's eyebrows softened, the change in topic settling her. "Well, I suppose that depends entirely on you."

Will drained his glass of wine and motioned for a servant to take his plate. "You know me, Mother, ever the amiable host. Stay as long as you like. The old pile of bricks is as much yours as it is—"

"No," Her Grace smoothly interrupted. "You've misunderstood me. We received news of your courtship of Lady Lucinda Grey and had hoped our presence would be required in the not-so-distant future."

"Bloody hell."

"William—manners, please," his mother chided, falling into the parental role much too easily for Will's taste.

"My sentiments exactly," Michael muttered, spearing an artichoke from his nearly empty plate.

Will propped his elbows on the table and leaned forward. "You mean to tell me that the gossipmongers took the time to spread such drivel all the way to Derbyshire?"

"I don't know why you're upset, William. It is wonderful news, is it not?" his mother answered. "Besides, Derbyshire is not as far from London as you make it out to be. And those gossipmongers you refer to are some of my closest friends, so I would thank you to be a bit more respectful when speaking of them. If it were not for them, we may not have heard for some time, which would have been more embarrassment than I could have withstood."

The look on his mother's face spoke clearly of the pain he'd caused in allowing her to find out such personal family news from anyone but him. The knowledge needled at Will's heart.

He ran a hand through his hair and looked at Michael, who simply stared back at him, his face now expressionless. "A fat lot of good you are, then?" he said dryly.

"Oh, I've talked myself blue in the face, but the

woman will hear nothing of it," his brother said. "For some reason Mother is inclined to believe persons whose comments suggest you may be less than concerned over familial ties, though I can't imagine why. And Lord knows I'm mmore than happy to continue performing the ducal duties—without the title, of course—so you're able to . . . I'm sorry, Will, what is it that you do?"

"Michael, please," the duchess said, the muscles in her jaw tightening. "We are here, together, as a family. That is what is important."

Will could not take any more, especially in light of the day he'd endured. "I apologize. Can we be done with it?"

"Of course," his mother answered quietly.

Michael nodded, the movement abrupt.

The duchess paused to let a servant clear her plate, then leaned slightly forward, a twinkle visible in her hazel eyes. "Now, when might we meet Lady Lucinda?"

"Bloody hell."

"Lucinda, even King Solomon's Mine could win against you today," Victoria chided.

Lucinda pulled herself from her thoughts in time to see Charlotte stifling a small laugh.

She winked at Charlotte before turning her attention to the cards in her hands. "I'm sorry. I'm afraid I've been woolgathering, Aunt Victoria." She played the four of hearts, wincing slightly at the headache pounding behind her eyes.

Victoria let out a "harrumph" of displeasure before adding her card to the table. "Woolgathering indeed. And over that Iron Will, I suppose. Tell me, is it absolutely necessary for you to meet his family?"

"Surely there is no need to be quite so cold, Victoria," Charlotte protested, an audible "tsk, tsk" punctuating her words. "The dowager and I came out the same year, you know. She was something, quite out of the ordinary, until . . ."

Charlotte looked down at the book in her hand, fingering the pages slowly.

"Until . . . ?" Lucinda asked, suddenly desperate to learn all that she could of Will, though equally anxious to keep such feelings from her aunts.

Charlotte reached for a length of moss green ribbon and placed it in her book before closing it. "Until she married the duke."

"And then?"

"And then that man drained her of everything that made her who she was," Victoria said bluntly, eyeing the cards on the table before looking up at her sisters and niece, all three frozen with looks of horror on their faces. "Well, he did, did he not? I didn't know her personally but according to the endless supply of gossip, the woman was the most vibrant of beings before marrying Clairemont and a miserable captive after."

Lucinda turned to Charlotte. "Is this true?"

"I'm afraid so. Despite having the attention of every eligible bachelor that year, she fell in love with Clairemont." Charlotte set the book on the small side table and adjusted the soft woolen throw. "No one could blame her. He was a duke, after all, and terribly handsome."

"And charming," Bessie added, her head tilted and eyes hazed over ever so slightly as she thought back to her younger days. "Oh, so charming."

"Yes, well, he was all of these things and more. Unfortunately, beneath the smiles and handsome façade, there beat a heart as black as the moors on a December night. No one believed his dalliances with other women would stop once he was married."

"No one except the duchess," Victoria interrupted, her voice softening. "She fell for the roué despite all the rumors of debauchery, and lived to pay the price. Poor woman."

Lucinda set a card on the table without looking at it. "He did not stop, then?"

"Oh, the exact opposite, I'm afraid. If the gossipmongers were to be believed, the duke tortured his wife not only with his affairs but with verbal thrashings, and, on occasion, physical violence, too."

"She could do nothing," Charlotte said. "His Grace threatened to take everything from her, even the children, if she dared to disobey him."

Lucinda fanned her cards out on the table, her brows knitting together. "She was trapped. And he knew it."

"Exactly so. I think it's fair to say that the day the duke dropped dead in his mistress's bed was, perhaps, the happiest day of Her Grace's life."

"And the boys?" Lucinda wondered aloud.

The three aunts looked at one another for a time, Charlotte finally speaking. "Dear, we would not want you . . . that is to say—"

"Regardless of their father's treatment, they are grown men, fully capable of making their own decisions, good or bad," Victoria interrupted, leaning across the card table to take Lucinda's hand. "We would not want to sway your regard for the duke based on the sins of his father."

"The boys?" Lucinda pressed, knowing the answer but needing to hear it regardless.

"There were rumors; servants and staff who shared stories with other servants and staff, who passed the information on to their employers. Your Iron Will took the brunt of it—out of choice, if memory serves. He adored his younger brother, by all accounts, and purposefully set himself between the father and the boy."

Could this be why he's strayed so far outside society?

Lucinda wondered to herself, pieces beginning to fall into place before her eyes.

Victoria squeezed Lucinda's hand with her own, then leaned back against the mahogany parlor chair. "This revelation should not be calculated into your dealings with the duke," she said her firm tone in place once more. "No matter his history, he is who he is, and that, my dear, does not change."

Despite the lack of candlelight, Lucinda's eyes had adjusted to the darkness of her room. Moonlight filtered in around the curtains, throwing shadows here and there. She'd long since abandoned her games, naming this shadow a minotaur, and that one a lamb, all in an attempt to hasten sleep.

Slumber had not come, yet Lucinda could not bring herself to leave the bed, the warmth of her cashmere coverlet creating a cozy nest that provided some comfort in the absence of rest.

The invitation to attend the opera with Will and his family lay next to her pillow, the fine linen paper creased from her repeated readings. The day had been long and hard, in no small part due to the brandy she'd so foolishly imbibed the night before. But she knew she could not pin the entirety of her current state on the liquor.

No matter how many times she examined her feelings, replayed the events of the last days, or imagined any number of possible outcomes, Lucinda could not deny one truth: William Randall, the Duke of Clairemont, had conquered her heart.

"I love him," she said into her pillow, the sound of her voice ringing unfamiliar to her own ears.

The revelations earlier in the evening concerning Will's childhood had not, as her aunts had feared, swayed her. Not completely, that is. Their interlude at Almack's had started her mind racing, the intimacy of the encounter still overwhelming her, even now. They were not suited; all of the ton—including her three aunts—were in agreement that such a match would be unthinkable. Impossible.

Insanity.

Lucinda fidgeted with the cream ribbon at her bedgown's neckline. "Do you truly love Will?"

She looped the ribbon around her forefinger, tightening it as she went. "I do."

He might be just as his father was, utterly charming yet a monster underneath. He could ruin her reputation with hardly any effort, leaving her without the comfort of family and friends. He could simply not love her—the thought surprisingly painful, yet altogether possible.

He could change everything she'd expected for her life, something Lucinda found most frightening of all.

She released the ribbon and gently massaged her finger, slightly numb from the pressure of the binding.

Her feelings for Will were simple. They were pure. This was everything Lucinda had been missing without even being aware that something was lacking.

"I love him."

But could he love her in return?

10

It was decided that Charlotte would act as Lucinda's chaperone for the evening, though it had taken some time for the four women to reach an understanding. Lucinda had done her best to remain impartial, but she'd secretly hoped that it would be Charlotte who accompanied her. Bessie would have tried to seduce Will's brother, and Victoria may have used the opportunity to suggest the duke abandon the courtship all together and simply hand over the horse.

Charlotte's previous acquaintance with the duchess had been the deciding factor, and the other two had reluctantly complied, leaving Lucinda free to fret over her dress and hair, her jewels and slippers.

She looked from the blush silk to the capucine silk in Mary's arms, feigning interest for the sake of holding off what would surely be a litany of questions from Mary regarding the duke.

Lucinda couldn't have cared less what she wore. Her feelings for Will made clothing seem a trivial matter that held little importance to her at the moment.

She'd not seen Will since attending Almack's. She blushed at the memory of her appearance, her cries of delight at the storm of emotions and pleasure he'd coaxed from her. Her body heated at the thought, small patches of perspiration forming in the most delicate of places.

"The capucine, my dear," Charlotte said from the doorway.

Lucinda turned, smiling at her aunt. "Do you think so?" she asked, posing a question in order to earn a few moments to compose herself.

Charlotte stepped into the room, her matronly rose-hued gown making the slightest of swishing sounds as she did so. "Does the capucine not suit your tastes?"

"No, not at all. It's just, well, that is to say," Lucinda began, and suddenly realized she'd run out of time. "No, not at all. It's lovely."

Mary dropped the rejected blush silk on the bed and carefully held up the burnished orange with both hands. "This one it is, then."

Charlotte motioned for the servant to hand her the dress. "Thank you, Mary, I'll assist Lucinda in dressing this evening."

Mary released the dress and swiftly curtsyed before leaving the room. "Careful of her hair," she said over her shoulder, then smoothly closed the door.

Charlotte turned to look at Lucinda. "My dear, what ever is the matter?"

"I'm sorry?" Lucinda said, distracted, as she rose from the edge of her bed and crossed to the window. "With the dress, you mean?"

The swish of Charlotte's gown once more signaled her progress across the floor. "Not with the dress, my dear. With you. You seem quite distracted. Is it the prospect of meeting Lord Clairemont's family?"

Lucinda wanted nothing more than to tell her aunt the truth. She needed the counsel of a trusted confidant, but her dear, kind aunt could not be responsible for carrying such a secret.

Lucinda turned from the window and loosened her dressing gown, letting it fall to the floor. "No, it is not that, Aunt Charlotte. I'm simply tired, that's all. The last few weeks have found me in situations I am not accustomed to and I fear I am much more a creature of habit than I ever would have cared to admit."

She finished with a practiced, bright smile then raised her arms in preparation to receive the dress. "Do not forget the hair. Mary will scold both of us, you know," she finished teasingly.

"Oh, I know all too well, my dear. All too well."

It had been some time since Will's last appearance at the theater, even longer since he'd arrived with his family. The Grecian-inspired Royal Opera House stood proudly in front of them, four large, fluted columns supporting a portico under which a large number of society's elite congregated.

Michael held out his arm for their mother as she exited the carriage. "Prinny himself laid the foundation stone apparently," he remarked, assisting his mother to the bricked pavement.

"Hardly a ringing endorsement, brother," Will said, stepping out to join them. "Come, it's beginning to rain."

Large, fat drops of water chased their progress as they made their way through the crowd. The glances and sly stares began almost immediately, the hum of low voices acting as the trio's own personal accompaniment.

Michael assessed the crowd around them as they mounted the stairs, then looked at Will. "Are you always so popular?"

Will nodded to a Young Corinthian as they crossed paths. "Well, I am, after all, Iron Will. Though I would think your presence here this evening, as well as Mother's, is a particularly juicy tidbit for these imbeciles. How long has it been since you were last in town? Four months? Perhaps six?"

"We were here for the Yuletide, as you well know,

which was barely four months ago. And our presence here was entirely thanks to you, if I remember correctly." Michael paused, meticulously wiping the rain from his coat. "You could not be torn away from town, requiring Mother to travel in the century's most severe snowstorm—"

Will shook his head, holding lightly to his mother's elbow as they ascended the stairs. "Is there something you wish to discuss, Michael? Or are you merely making conversation?"

"This Grimaldi, is he as good as they say?" the duchess asked, cutting through the impending argument with quiet, practiced skill.

Will's sharp gaze located a Corinthian agent stationed near the landing and he nodded discreetly, receiving a brief nod of recognition in reply. "Better. I had the pleasure of attending a private performance by Grimaldi. He is a comic genius, to be sure." He paused. slowing his pace, "Although I fear you may disapprove of his antics, Mother."

The duchess allowed Will to steer her toward the entrance to the Clairemont box. "Do you truly, or are you merely being polite?"

"You wound me, Mother," Will replied, clutching at his chest as though a death blow had been delivered to his heart.

His mother's light laughter made bystanders turn their heads as the three walked through the parted red velvet curtains and reached their seats.

"And you would do quite well out there," she said, gesturing with her hand toward the stage. "I enjoy a good laugh just as well as the next person."

Will looked at her with mock disbelief. "Really?"

"Yes, William, I do," she answered in an altered tone, the teasing quality of her voice having vanished.

"As do I," a feminine voice came from the back of the box.

The three turned to see Lady Charlotte Grey enter the box with Lucinda following behind.

"Mother," Will began, "Michael, may I present Lady Charlotte Grey and her niece, Lady Lucinda Grey."

The duchess smiled endearingly. "Charlotte, it has been far too long since we last met." She moved toward Lady Charlotte, both hands outstretched.

"I could not agree more," Lady Charlotte replied with feeling, moving to take Will's mother's hands in hers. "You look as lovely as the first time we met."

The duchess quietly clucked her tongue. "You are too kind, Lady Charlotte," she said, then turned her gaze to Lucinda, "And you, my dear, are just as I'd hoped."

Lucinda graciously smiled and came to stand next to her aunt. "Your Grace, now I fear you are the one who is too kind."

The three ladies softly laughed, looking from one to the other with instant affection. The low lighting from the candles reflected off their dresses—Lucinda's dress perfectly complemented by the soft rose of Lady Charlotte's and the deep brown of his mother's. It was as if Thomas Lawrence himself were readying to paint the trio, their ease with one another as pleasing to the eye as it was to the soul.

Will didn't know whether to be elated or terrified, the conflicting emotions discomforting. "Do not forget my little brother, ladies," he said, oddly compelled to dispel the heartwarming scene.

"Lady Charlotte." Michael bowed. "And Lady Lucinda."

"Lord Michael," Lady Charlotte replied, dipping her head in unconsciously regal acknowledgment.

Lucinda stepped forward and curtsied with easy grace. "Lord Michael, I am most happy to make your acquaintance." She rose, offered her hand to Michael, and smiled brightly.

He bent to kiss her hand, a smile to match Lucinda's. "My mother was correct, you are lovely indeed." He waited just a moment too long for Will's comfort before he released her hand.

"And you, Lord Michael, are very much His Grace's brother," she answered in kind, the slightly teasing nature of her words vexing Will further.

The sound of the gong from the stage signaled the call for the audience to find their seats, putting an end to the party's friendly conversation.

"About bloody time," Will muttered under his breath, escorting Lady Charlotte the few steps to her seat then returning to Lucinda. "Lady Lucinda," he said, offering her his arm.

She smiled in warm response and linked her arm through his, allowing him to guide her to the front of the box. He waited for her to sit, then dropped into the miniature seat next to her.

"Oh, my . . ." she murmured. Will immediately wondered whether in the process of attempting to settle his frame comfortably in the ridiculously small seat he'd managed to tread on her gown.

About to apologize, he belatedly noticed Lucinda wasn't looking in his direction, but rather out at the theater. He followed her gaze and realized what had caused her unease.

It appeared the entire audience was not buzzing with anticipation over the impending performance, as they should be.

No, their attention was concentrated on the Clairemont box, every set of opera glasses in the whole of the Royal Opera House trained on them. The sight brought to mind countless curious owls avidly eyeing a particularly delectable mouse.

"Lean ever so slightly to your right," Will whispered to Lucinda, who, despite clearly being confused, did as he asked.

He leaned in the same direction and the two watched every last owl do the same, following them with marked determination.

Lucinda muffled a laugh and centered herself in her seat before turning to Will. "This could prove to be quite amusing," she said, a wicked grin curving her lips.

"Oh, yes. The stupidity of the ton is an endless source of entertainment, particularly when you are as popular as I am." Will winked at her.

She laughed out loud, causing all three of their box mates to turn.

"I . . . that is to say . . ." Lucinda began, desperately trying to piece together a proper explanation. "I simply cannot bear the anticipation! Everyone of my acquaintance talks endlessly of the great Grimaldi. Are you not all as excited as I to be here tonight?"

It was clear from their faces that the three were skeptical of her comment, but they smiled politely and returned to their conversation.

"You really do need to practice your prevarications, Lucinda," Will whispered, keeping his eyes on the audience. "It is a skill that can be quite useful, especially for those in my social circle."

"You called me by my first name."

His gut told him to look at her but his brain demanded he keep his eyes on the stage.

"I like a man who can follow directions," she continued smoothly.

The massive red and gold curtain that divided the stage from the audience slowly began to open and the crowd hushed, preventing Will's response.

What was the enchanting woman playing at? Will's body was literally humming from the effort of sitting still next to her. He'd spent almost the entire day attempting to decide upon a course of action. His past relationships with women were of no help, intimate displays of affection being merely an expected part of the equation there.

But Lucinda was different for so many reasons. Or was she? Perhaps he'd been wrong in assuming she would be affected by their interlude.

He glanced at her discreetly. She looked to be perfectly comfortable despite the fact that he'd pleasured her in the storage room above Almack's.

The entire audience erupted with laughter, as did Lucinda, Lady Charlotte, his mother, and Michael, giving Will the opportunity to look at her directly.

She turned and gave him a dazzling smile, her eyes dancing with merriment. "He is wonderfully wild, is he not?"

"Indeed," Will answered, his light tone failing to betray his thoughts.

He gripped the spindly arms of the chair, loosening his hold when they audibly creaked in protest.

If Lucinda had deeper feelings for him, there would have been telltale signs, Will was sure. The woman wasn't practiced in the ways of deception. He'd witnessed her face flush with color over lesser things; her eyes shielded by her lashes when she wished to conceal the truth; her searching for words that would hide what she was thinking.

No, that small sliver of hope for something he couldn't quite explain had been in vain. *Be thankful, you fool,* he thought to himself, releasing the chair and folding his arms across his chest. *She's doing you a favor.*

The audience erupted with laughter again, and this time Will joined in. He, unlike Lucinda, was well versed in the art of deception, and he'd be damned if he would let something as trivial as his emotions compromise the quality of his work.

"Are you enjoying yourself?" he asked Lucinda.

She leaned in conspiratorially, her shoulder connecting with his. "Immensely."

"In that case," he replied, turning to look at her. "Perhaps you'll do me a favor. After all, Grimaldi is quite the most difficult ticket to obtain in town."

She turned to face him, her eyebrows furrowing. "What might that be, Your Grace?"

"Assure me that we've come to an agreement concerning your morning rides."

She pulled back, the absence of her shoulder leaving Will cold. "I thought I made myself clear."

Will smiled charmingly. "Really, because I'm quite sure that I made myself clear as well. It is neither safe nor appropriate. And, as your suitor, I do have some say in the matter."

The color began to rise from her chest, slowly creeping its way up to settle in her cheeks. "I do so appreciate your concern. But let us remember, you are not my husband, Your Grace."

"Not yet," he growled. Why was she being so disagreeable? He was doing his bloody best to play by the ton's rules—and if that meant he would not have to rise at an ungodly hour in order to keep her alive, well, all the better.

"Are you expressly forbidding me from my morning ride?" she furiously whispered, her face turned toward the stage.

Will took a deep breath, his cravat suddenly tight. "I am."

Her jaw clenched. "And if I do not obey?"

"Lucinda," he began, itching to rip the bloody cloth from his neck. "Is it even necessary for me to answer?"

"We shall see."

THE WILY WOLF TAVERN
CHARING CROSS, LONDON

Will lifted his tankard and drank deeply, realizing belatedly that claiming a need for ale as an excuse for taking his leave from his mother and brother had not entirely been a ruse.

After receiving word of Garenne from a Young Corinthian at Covent Garden, he'd escorted a chilly Lucinda and her aunt to their carriage, then accompanied his mother and brother home, only to excuse himself and immediately head out into the dark night.

He set the pewter tankard on the rough-hewn, scarred tabletop and took in his surroundings. He'd heard of the Wily Wolf, a popular gathering place for London's criminally inclined, and he had to admit, it lived up to its reputation.

Scant light threw ominous shadows around the interior. Smoke from the tallow candles hovered in a thick cloud against the ceiling and hazed the room, preventing clients from getting more than a minimal view of their fellow drinkers.

It was a sizeable room, though Will had counted a total of only twelve tables and a large bar that ran along the back wall; hardly surprising in such an establishment, where privacy was a necessity.

Will gestured for the serving girl to bring him another ale and eased back onto the hard wooden bench. He allowed his eyelids to droop, the half-hooded appearance affording him the opportunity to observe while appearing uninterested.

He knew most of the cutthroats present; his Young Corinthian duties had brought him into contact with many of them. One-Eyed Jack, named for the eyeball he'd lost to the knife of a business associate, slumped over a plate of alehouse food in the back. His stringy gray hair fell across his face, nearly covering the large black patch concealing his empty socket.

The man sitting opposite One-Eyed Jack had his back to Will, but from his size and build it could only be Monty Milburn, or "The Mountain" as he was called by friend and foe alike. Monty often worked with Jack, hitting the respectable neighborhoods of London with a ragtag army of street urchins. From bank notes to valuable jewelry, the two made a living off the ton, a fact that made Will smile quietly.

Jack and Monty were harmless enough. The two sitting across the room from them were not.

Owner of the brothel Giselle's, Clive Baskers was a ruthless, moneygrubbing bastard who, by all accounts, enjoyed killing far too much. Rumor had it that more than one man had gone missing from the rooms above his gambling hell. Since the dead men were always from the lower class, Baskers had no need to worry that the authorities would bother with the matter.

Will watched the brothel owner for a moment. His gaunt frame rattled each time he coughed and spat into a worn handkerchief in his hand. But tonight, Will was more interested in the man who accompanied Baskers. Philip Gaston, a Frenchman of questionable lineage who owned a stake in the brothel. Gaston had sworn allegiance to no one, offering up information to the highest bidder regardless of their loyalties.

He'd frequently provided intelligence to the Young Corinthians through a network of communication that ensured he was kept at arm's length and never given the opportunity to guess the true identities of the agents.

Despite his belief that the Corinthians net of secrecy held fast, Will was thankful for the rough workman's clothing Smithers had provided him in the carriage. A secret compartment beneath the cushioned seat contained everything Will might need in the line of duty.

g, assorted weapons, money, and a number of
er items occupied the compartment, all magically re-
plenished by Smithers when necessary.

Will fingered the lapel of the nondescript coat he was
currently wearing, absentmindedly noting the difference
between the coarse wool and the smooth quality of the
evening attire he'd donned for the theater earlier in the
evening.

He would not be so stupid as to entertain thoughts of
Lucinda outside of the confines of Corinthian business
again, he brooded, tracking a pair of drunken seamen as
they staggered toward the long bar. Her mercurial mood
had left Will confused and frustrated—a far cry from
what he'd been hoping for.

But he would not allow a woman, not even Lucinda,
to distract him in such a way ever again.

The serving wench came toward his table, her tray
heavy with full tankards. She set one in front of him on
the table. "Can I offer you anything else?" she asked,
leaning over to show her impressive breasts.

"No, thank you, love," Will replied, reaching for the
tankard.

"'Ave it your way," she answered in her thick Cock-
ney accent, then lowered her voice. "You're needed out
back, I'm to tell you. By a man with the breath of a
dragon. He dinnat give a name, just said you'd know
'im."

Will reached inside his coat and pulled out several
coins. He tossed enough for the two ales on the table,
then added another. "Thank you."

The wench eyed the money greedily. "Anytime. Anytime," she replied, scooping up the coins and dropping
them into her ample cleavage.

Will took one last swig of ale before sliding out of the
booth. He tugged the brim of his hat lower over his
brow and made his way toward the door, careful to not

move too quickly. The last thing he needed was for one of these men to become curious.

Garenne pushed his stew about, forking a chunk of mutton into his mouth and chewing. His beard itched as did the snarled wig atop his head, but he hardly noticed as he swallowed the gristley meat. Watching Clairemont from across the tavern had proven enjoyable for any number of reasons, not the least of which was the fact that the giant knew nothing of his presence. "*Idiot,*" he muttered to himself, nearly choking on the inferior cut of meat.

It galled Garenne to admit that such a man had kept him from success, but he would not have to suffer at the hands of the duke for long. The man had made a disastrous mistake interfering with plans for Lady Lucinda Grey, but he would pay. Slowly, methodically, and, with any luck, painfully. The duke would pay.

It was a pity that Garenne himself would not be the one to deliver the death blow, but there were details to decide upon and he would not leave one out of place.

Garenne tossed a coin onto the planked table and moved toward the door. No, everything would be in order and the woman would be caught. Or else.

Once the tavern's heavy door slammed shut, the dark night shrouded Will. The moonlight was faint, thick clouds nearly concealing the pale curve. Will picked his way around the decrepit building, dodging refuse and a trio of scavenging, half-starved dogs along the way. The rear of the tavern was cast in shadow, the meager light glimmering from two dirty windows above the establishment not enough for Will's liking.

The hair on his neck stood up, a sign he had learned to trust years before. He spun, backing up against the wall, and pulled a knife from a sheath sewn inside his coat.

"Gaston, I trust you know better than to screw with me," he said sternly, quickly assessing his surroundings and calculating his escape routes.

A flash of silver caught the light. Will braced himself as a dark figure flew out of the blackness at the back of the alley, followed closely by a second and third. Will pressed against the wall and waited, dropping to his knees at the last second.

The first man missed Will and hit the wall hard, the sound of his face connecting with brick filling the air. He crumpled on the ground to Will's right, moaning.

Will drove forward, slamming his fist into the second man's groin and sending him flying backwards into a massive pile of rubbish. But before Will could spin to face the third, he attacked from behind, slashing a knife across Will's back and slicing deep before grabbing his shoulder and dragging him around to face him.

He kicked Will's knife from his hand, a second vicious kick catching Will's chin. Will dropped to the ground, stars whirling as his sight dimmed, and before he could recover, the man straddled him.

The attacker's lips curled in an evil grin, his bared teeth gritting with exertion as he struggled to hold Will down.

"He said you'd put up a fight," he spat out, gloating as his fingers closed on Will's throat and he raised the knife. "You gentry coves are all the same."

A potent mixture of anger and bitterness raced through Will's veins.

He roared, startling the man sitting on his chest just enough to make him slacken his grip. Will grabbed a thick piece of firewood on the ground beside him and swung.

The savage blow clubbed the man on the side of his

head, sending him flying backwards. Will shoved upright and hit him in the rib cage, then the leg. The attacker screamed.

"We are not all the same, you useless bastard," Will panted, leaning over the man.

He readied himself to deliver the death blow, his arm arching over his head with the wood in hand.

At the last moment Will lowered the weapon and stood back. "You're not worth the effort."

He moved toward the alley, cutting across two streets to where a hackney waited. "The Young Corinthians," he told the driver, slamming the door himself.

The cab came to life, the pull of the horse throwing Will back against the seat. He cried out in pain, his injuries just starting to make themselves known.

Sheer force of will was keeping him conscious despite the blackness that threatened, beckoning just at the edge of his vision. He began to count, this time starting at one hundred.

"You're bleeding," Weston observed as he helped Will into the back parlor of the Corinthian Club. "Profusely, actually."

Will winced with pain when Weston's arm pressed against the wound on his back. "I'm well aware of that," he ground out, allowing the man to aide him as they mounted the stairs.

He'd managed to drag his battered and bruised body to a hackney, sheer will keeping him conscious despite the blackness that threatened, beckoning just at the edge of his vision. The ride from the Wily Wolf to his waiting carriage had seemed an eternity, the wound across his upper back burning with pain.

By the time they reached the lower floor and the two made their way to a bookcase, third from center of the shelves lining both sides of the hallway, Will was leaning heavily on Weston's strength. Without comment, Weston reached for the slim volume of Shakespeare's sonnets. He pulled hard on the false book, triggering a hidden mechanism, and the section of the wall swung out, revealing a second hallway, lit by Argand lamps.

"Shall I carry you from here?" Weston asked, winking at Will.

Will fought off the urge to punch the man, knowing he'd only injure himself further if he did so. "Do and you'll live to regret it."

They entered the last room on the right in silence. Carmichael and the Corinthian's physician met them at the door.

"On the table, Your Grace."

Will followed the physician's orders and awkwardly eased facedown onto the table, unable to silence a small grunt of pain. Wordlessly, the men took out knives and cut his shirt off.

"Hmm," the physician muttered deep in his throat, then reached for a cloth, dipping it into a basin of water.

Will flinched when he began to clean the wound, a sharp wave of pain nearly knocking him unconscious.

Carmichael handed Will a silver flask. "Drink this."

"All of it," the physician added, finishing with the cloth.

Will turned his head to the side and swallowed the contents of the flask, the brandy slowly warming him from the inside out.

"How did this happen?" Carmichael asked, the anger in his voice barely contained.

Will lowered the empty flask to the tabletop, next to his face. "The usual way. A knife. A stiletto, if I'm not mistaken."

His flip response met with clear disapproval, Carmichael's mouth tightening to a grim, thin line. "More importantly, perhaps, *why* did this happen?"

"I've been told that meetings with Gaston are usually quite predictable," Will began, flinching as the physician began to stitch his flesh back together. "I had no reason to believe this one would be any different."

"Need I remind you that Garenne is here, in London?"

"Of course not," Will growled in response.

Weston pulled a slim flask from his coat and offered it to Will. "Gaston is a right bastard, but he's never betrayed us before."

"Well, now he has," Carmichael hissed, turning his back to the trio.

Will emptied the second flask and handed it to Weston. "We'll take further precautions, old man. You have my word."

Carmichael turned back, his eyes shuttered once more. "Let us hope you live long enough to make good on that."

11

"I want him to come," Lucinda spoke out loud, ripping the petal off an errant wildflower that she'd pilfered from Tristan's shaggy mane. "I do not want him to come," she continued, another poor petal meeting its untimely demise.

It was a dreary, gray morning, the lovely spring flowers in the fields that bordered Lover's Walk in Hyde Park doing little to lift Lucinda's spirits.

She looked up at the sky, noting the full clouds that threatened rain at any moment. She slowed Tristan to a plodding walk and allowed him to wander off the path and drop his head to the green grass.

She'd barely slept the night before, the evening spent with Will and his family occupying her thoughts entirely. Lucinda could not say what she'd expected from the duke, but it was certainly not what had transpired.

He'd been the perfect gentleman—charming, polite, and utterly devoid of any sign of a connection beyond what was expected. Then his demeanor had changed drastically, his assumption that he held any real power over her as a suitor irritating at best.

She'd struggled to keep from whispering her feelings in his ear the moment Grimaldi had taken the stage, Will's use of her given name pure music to her ears. And then he'd transformed into what, she couldn't quite tell. It was all quite upsetting.

Tristan abruptly stopped grazing and raised his head,

his ears pricking forward at the sound of someone approaching.

Lucinda tossed the flower to the ground and reached for the reins. Tamping down her nervousness, she blew out a breath and sat straight in her saddle. A raindrop landed on her nose sigh. "Perfect," she muttered, tucking a lock of stray hair behind her ear.

To her surprise, the horse cantering toward her was not the majestic King Solomon's Mine. The mount was a stout chestnut, his rider's build not as bulky as Will's and the man was fairer in coloring. Lucinda narrowed her eyes in an effort to make out the man's identity but could not, and resigned herself to turn Tristan about in order to face the oncoming rider.

The stranger pulled the chestnut to a walk and slowly approached. "Lady Lucinda Grey?"

"Yes," Lucinda answered hesitantly.

The man smiled, his handsome face lighting with apparent pleasure. "You've nothing to fear, Lady Lucinda, though I suppose I have the look of a beastie this early in the morning. I am Marcus MacInnes, the Earl of Weston." He tipped his hat, managing an elegant bow while seated, his sun-streaked golden hair falling into his face. "Clairemont sent me to see to your safety."

Lucinda relaxed back into her saddle, not sure if her relief was due to Lord Weston's legitimacy or the absence of Will. "Safety, Lord Weston? From what exactly? The beasties you made reference to?"

His green eyes flashed with amusement. "Oh, yes, there's the beasties and any other number of woodland sprites, Lady Lucinda. Don't tell me you've yet to see one in this fair park?"

"I don't recall such a sighting, Lord Weston, though I suppose it is entirely possible I did come across one of your sprites and simply did not recognize it for what it was," Lucinda replied, allowing the whimsical tone of their conversation to ease her mind.

"Impossible," he said with a laugh. "When you meet a sprite, you'll know it. Now, shall we get you home before the weather turns?"

It was Lucinda's turn to laugh as she glanced at the darkening skies. "Lord Weston, has the weather not turned enough for your liking, or would you prefer snow before returning to the comfort of your town house?"

Lord Weston walked the chestnut behind Tristan and reined him alongside Lucinda's mount. "I spent a fair amount of my youth in Scotland, Lady Lucinda. This," he waved negligently at the menacing sky, "is nothing compared to the ferocity of a Highland storm. But I've no doubt Clairemont would have my head on a pike were I to let you catch a cold, so shall we?" He smiled, gesturing for Lucinda to take the lead.

She clucked at Tristan, lifting the reins and turning him back onto the path. "How is it you know the duke?"

"Doesn't everyone know Iron Will?" he countered, joining her.

"That, Lord Weston, is not what I asked."

Lord Weston laughed again, the melodious deep baritone falling easily on Lucinda's ears. "He said you were a woman with a quick wit and sharp tongue. Will and I met at Eton, or to be more precise, we met in the headmaster's office at Eton, on a regular basis, as it were."

"Partners in crime, then," Lucinda confirmed.

He grinned and winked at her. "Not exactly, no. It took some time, and much blood, before we recognized our shared goals."

"Which were?"

"To beat the life out of anyone we could," he said matter-of-factly. "We were good at it too," he added, giving her a knowing look. "The moniker Iron Will isn't handed down lightly."

A giggle flew from Lucinda's mouth.

"Are you laughing at me, Lady Lucinda?" Lord Weston asked, wiggling his thick blond eyebrows up and down.

Lucinda forced a frown. "Of course not, my lord. That would be . . ." She hesitated, searching for just the right word.

"Heartless? Cruel? Unspeakably unkind?" he offered helpfully.

"You are very kind, Lord Weston," she said simply.

"And you are too generous," he answered, underscoring his sincerity with a smile. "Though I am not surprised. Will said as much."

Lucinda figeted with her reins. "The duke is quite chatty, is he not?"

"Not usually. But when it comes to you, he's a veritable font of knowledge."

"It does makes one wonder, then, why he could not summon the interest required to rise and meet me this morning."

"Oh, well, Will *is* a busy man," Lord Weston began, "what with being a duke and all."

The chestnut nosed at Tristan, blowing out a huff of air when he failed to receive a response. "That's a handsome horse ye have there. Thoroughbred?" Lord Weston asked.

"Yes," she replied, almost certain that he'd changed the subject on purpose. He did not want to divulge anything more about Will, although Lucinda did not know why. And there seemed little point in trying to question him further.

"Yes, he is. And yours? He's a beauty. Reminds me quite a bit of Sebastian's Fury."

Lord Weston's expressive face registered surprise. "Fury was Pokey's sire. You know horses?"

"Pokey?"

He leaned forward, covering the chestnut's ear with his palm. "Shhhh," he cautioned in a loud whisper. "Poor Pokey did not inherit his sire's gift for speed. He's sensitive, though, so I try to spare his feelings when I can."

"Ah, I see," Lucinda murmured before raising her voice. "Well, my lord, Sir Pokey is, without a doubt, the most gorgeous chestnut I've seen of late. Such strength, such character—he truly is one of a kind."

Lucinda could have sworn the horse's ears pricked up at the lengthy compliment and his stride took on a prouder attitude. She smiled with delight.

Lord Weston mouthed "Thank you" as he stroked Pokey's neck. "He is indeed, and we thank you kindly for your generous words."

The rain began to pour in earnest and the wind picked up, ruffling the skirt of Lucinda's blue velvet riding habit. "Shall we, Lord Weston?"

"We shall," he returned, settling his hat more firmly as he pulled the brim lower on his brow.

They urged their mounts into a faster trot and made haste for home.

"My dear, we leave for Clairemont House soon," Charlotte called from the drawing room.

Lucinda slowed her steps, her bedraggled riding habit dripping water on the marble foyer floor, and stopped just beyond the threshold to the room. Somehow, Lucinda had convinced herself that if she forced all thoughts of Her Grace's kind invitation for tea from her mind, perhaps Charlotte would forget as well.

Clearly, that had been wishful thinking.

"Do we have an engagement?" She stood in the doorway, feigning confusion. Attempting to tuck-up her rain-soaked hair was a useless effort, as was smoothing her sodden, wrinkled skirt. Her efforts did little to right the ruined garment.

Charlotte looked up from her needlepoint, her shock at Lucinda's appearance quickly giving way to concern. "Good heavens, Lucinda, you're soaked through to the skin." She hastily rose from the settee and crossed the room, yanking at the bellpull.

Mary appeared instantly, taking one look at Lucinda's soggy state before urging her upstairs.

"We must get you out of those clothes, my lady," she instructed, pausing mid-flight to stop a footman and demand that hot water be brought up.

Lucinda lifted her sodden skirt as she trudged up the stairs, Mary urging her from three treads above as Charlotte huffed from behind.

The moment they entered the bedchamber, Mary undressed Lucinda then went to supervise the filling of the tub. Once it was full, she summoned Lucinda and waited to leave until her lady was safely emerged in the steaming hot water.

Charlotte came to stand next to the tub. "You soak every last ounce of rainwater off of you, young lady. I need to see how the gardener is managing my rosebushes this morning, but I will come and check on you shortly. I want you warm and dry by the time I return."

"You enjoyed your time with Lady Clairemont," Lucinda said, not making it clear whether her words were a statement or a question.

Or had it been an accusation?

Charlotte paused dropping her gaze to look at Lucinda. "I did, very much so." She turned her gaze back to the doorway and began walking, stopping just short of the hallway. "It is as if she is experiencing life for the first time, now that her husband has died."

"She has her freedom," Lucinda answered quietly.

"Exactly."

Charlotte disappeared around the corner, leaving Lucinda to stare at her toes.

Her aunts had extolled the value of a woman's independence since she was a child, until it had become her credo. Freedom was more than most women could hope to attain.

The pursuit of absolute freedom had been the impetus for her involvement with Will, King Solomon's Mine being the key. With the stallion they would not only establish a credible reputation within the male dominated equine world, but they would improve upon it, breeding quality horses and providing for the studs into their retirement years. Will could not give her what the prized stallion surely would.

"That is it, then," she said out loud, letting the water trickle through her fingers. "You choose a horse over a man."

In some measure, the choice had been made for her, since Will's feelings clearly did not match her own. But she took some small comfort in uttering the words nonetheless.

She reached for the perfumed soap, a new feeling of resolve blooming in her breast. She would have tea. She would, before this charade had run its course, have danced, flirted, made polite conversation, and demurely deflected countless empty compliments.

"It is a small price for freedom," she said, quietly but firmly, then began to scrub in earnest.

Clairemont House overlooked St. James's Square and was surrounded by sumptuous homes that only the cream of the ton could call their own. Hidden from the street by a sizeable iron gate, the short drive curved in a graceful arc, affording guests the opportunity to view the house and extensive grounds as they approached. Despite the dazzling quality of its fellow structures, Clairemont House stood out. The façade was entirely of Portland stone, the architecture fashioned in the neo-classical style, complete with eight massive columns and as many windows framed in ornamental carvings.

"Don't gape, dear," Charlotte said to Lucinda, straightening her own bonnet ribbons as the carriage came to a stop.

Lucinda pursed her lips, taking in the house before her. "Aunt Charlotte, I am not one given to gaping, but this . . ." She blinked, gesturing to the view beyond the carriage door. "It is—"

"Impressive? Yes, I know. I still remember my first ball here. Such grandeur, such opulence." Charlotte's features turned wistful for a moment before she returned to her practical self. "It's as breathtaking inside as it is on the outside, so I suggest you take a moment before we disembark to collect and prepare yourself."

Lucinda sat back against the wheat-colored squabs and took a deep breath, then expelled it with all the force she could muster.

"Better?" Charlotte inquired.

"Yes, thank you," Lucinda answered, though a question niggled at her. "You spoke of attending a ball here, yet I have never heard of any events being held here. Why is that?"

Charlotte looked to the house again. "It's my understanding that the duchess refused to host parties of any kind once the boys were sent off to school."

"Good for her," Lucinda said, following Charlotte's gaze.

"Yes, I would have to agree," her aunt said with a firm nod. "Are we ready, then?"

As ready as I will ever be, Lucinda thought to herself. "Yes, of course. A cup of tea would be most welcome."

Charlotte's fist thumped the ceiling of the carriage twice. The liveried footman jumped down immediately, lowered the step, and opened the door. Charlotte descended first, taking the driver's arm and allowing him to assist her safely to the ground.

Lucinda took one last, deep breath and stepped out onto the graveled forecourt to join Charlotte. Together, they strolled to the impressive front door, where the beautifully carved knocker announced to the world that the duke was in residence.

A house footman held open the massive oak door, bowing to usher them over the threshold. An anxious-faced butler waited just inside, his build and demeanor reminding Lucinda of a nervous bird she'd once seen at the Kew Botanical Gardens.

"Madam," he said, bowing to each of them in turn with quick, efficient bobs of deference. "This way, if you please."

He led them through the sumptuous foyer, their slipper heels tapping lightly on the black and white marble floor. Lucinda tilted her head back to better admire the Doric frieze that adorned the ceiling high above. They reached the impressive staircase, a wonder of engineering in stone that possessed a gorgeous balustrade done in trompe l'oeil.

The butler slowed, stepping aside when they reached the stairs. He gestured for them to ascend, then followed. Charlotte gripped the ornate iron baluster, while Lucinda counted the steps.

"Sixty-two," she said under her breath as they reached the first floor.

"Pardon? Did you say something?" Charlotte asked somewhat breathlessly, though to her credit she did not faint on the spot.

"No, nothing. Nothing at all," Lucinda replied, bending her head to conceal her gaze from Charlotte. She tightened her grip on her rose print skirt, lifting it to clear the toes of her slippers as she climbed, and attempted to hide her fatigue.

She rather suspected that she hadn't managed a single good night's rest since meeting Will. She tossed and turned, trying to remember every word they'd spoken, and then worse, thinking on each one until she was dizzy. And if she managed to finish that, she spent the next hour berating herself for being unable to sleep.

It was madness, and it had to stop, but for once in her life, she could not make her feelings bend to her will.

They reached the top of the stairs and followed the butler down a long hall lined with Grecian busts, stopping midway. Lucinda paused to allow her aunt to enter the room first.

"Lady Charlotte Grey and her niece, Lady Lucinda Grey, Your Grace," the butler announced.

Lucinda looked to the end of the room, where a massive fireplace took up nearly the entirety of one wall. Graceful wood furniture was arranged before it, The duchess seated in a chair nearest the window. Lord Michael rose.

Lucinda's gaze swept the length of the room from one end to the other, frowning when she didn't find Will.

"I'm afraid you'll have to excuse my brother," Lord Michael said, strolling toward them. "He's been detained by business and will not be able to join us."

He met them halfway down the long room and escorted them to join his mother. Both Charlotte and Lucinda dipped a curtsy to the duchess before taking seats, side by side, on the embroidered, blue silk cushions of the settee.

"I hope the duke's business matters aren't of serious concern for him," Lucinda said, unable to contain her disappointment—and, if she was being completely honest, a healthy dose of irritation. How was she to stop loving him if she was never given the opportunity to observe what she assumed were his many shortcomings?

Her Grace smiled politely. "No, no, nothing is amiss. Simply a matter that required his strict attention, that is all."

Two footmen and the butler entered the room. One held a large tray with a gleaming silver tea service while the other two brought forth a variety of sandwiches, tea cakes, and other delecacies.

The duchess waited until they had deposited the trays and departed the room, then sat forward in her seat and saw to the tea, pouring with consummate ease as she made polite conversation.

Lucinda participated in the discussion of the latest on dits, though her mind couldn't help but wander. What business could be keeping Will? To the best of her knowledge he was not in the least committed to the duties a duke would normally shoulder.

She accepted from Her Grace a delicate china plate holding a cucumber sandwich and nibbled. Was it possible he had simply grown tired of their game? A sense of indignation washed over her. If that was the case, she would refuse to release him from their agreement, and King Solomon's Mine would be hers.

"Lady Lucinda?"

Was he avoiding her?

"Lady Lucinda?"

Lucinda looked up to discover Will's brother addressing her. She swallowed her bite of sandwich quickly and smiled. "I'm sorry, Lord Michael. You were saying?"

Amusement tugged at the corners of his mouth. "Would you join me in a stroll about the room?"

Lucinda arched an eyebrow and tilted her chin. She might have pleaded a reluctance to leave the conversation, but was curious to know what Lord Michael wanted. So she gave him a small nod of acceptance and rose.

He tucked her gloved hand through the crook of his arm and led her toward the far end of the room, beginning a clockwise circuit.

"A shilling for your thoughts," he said in a low tone.

Lucinda glanced out the window, desperate to keep the discouragement of Will's absence to herself. "And just what would lead you to believe I am thinking on anything in particular?"

Lord Michael let out a low chuckle. "Come now, Lady Lucinda, you and I have no need to play games."

She turned back to face him. "You've your brother's laugh."

"And you lack the talent for subterfuge."

"Fair enough."

The two remained silent as they passed Charlotte and Her Grace, though they needn't have bothered. The ladies had their heads together and were giggling like two young girls.

"Now then," Lord Michael continued. "Where were we?"

"You were prying, I believe," Lucinda answered succinctly.

"Yes. Do continue. You were going to tell me what thoughts absorbed your attention so completely."

Lucinda drew a deep breath, holding it for a moment before expelling it in a heavy sigh. "I suppose there would be no harm in sharing my dilemma with you. It's just that . . . well . . ." she began, hesitating as she leaned in to murmur privately, "the Foster masquerade ball is nearly upon us and I have yet to decide on a costume."

Lord Michael's serious expression turned to confusion and then amusement. "That is a dilemma. A much larger one than I'd first assumed."

"Yes, well, not being a woman, how could you have

known the paramount importance of choosing just the right attire?"

"A gown is a much larger dilemma, indeed, than my brother could ever be."

Lucinda, to her credit, did not break her stride, though the mention of Will made her heartbeat stutter. "I do not believe we were speaking of the duke."

"Indeed we were not." He paused. "But now we are."

Lucinda narrowed her eyes at Lord Michael. "In addition to his laugh, you clearly share the duke's ability to manipulate a conversation to your advantage."

"I will take that as the compliment I'm sure it was meant to be," he replied. "But I believe we were speaking of His Grace."

Lucinda came to a complete stop, forcing Lord Michael to follow suit. "I am at a loss for words."

"Then allow me to help you," he murmured, looking out over the extensive gardens at the back of the house. "Do you intend to marry my brother?"

Lucinda let out a squeak of surprise, though thankfully they were far enough away from Charlotte and the duchess not to draw their attention. "Lord Michael, I do not believe we have known each other long enough to speak with such frankness."

"Come now, Lady Lucinda." He eyed her consideringly. "Avoidance is hardly attractive in an intelligent woman such as yourself."

She raised her chin and met his stare. "I believe, Lord Michael, that you must address your questions to your brother."

"Forgive me, Lady Lucinda. Perhaps I should have asked, if the offer is made, will you accept?"

Lucinda's heart raced, the tattoo it beat out faster than she would have preferred. In a desperate attempt to end the questioning, she purposely turned to the garden view framed by the window. "Your gardens are beautiful. And the beds of tulips and daffodils are exceptionally fine—they are truly lovely this time of year."

"Yes, quite," Lord Michael answered impatiently. "Lady Lucinda, allow me to apologize. I do not usually act in such a forward manner, but when it comes to my brother, time is of the essence. Despite his assumptions to the contrary, the duchess cares very deeply for him and would like nothing more than to see him happily settled."

Lucinda nearly nodded her head in agreement. It was exactly how her aunts had described it, and after meeting Will's mother, she now shared their opinion.

Lord Michael continued. "You are the first woman His Grace has shown any real interest in. Some indication that the courtship is progressing toward the desired outcome would be most welcome."

"The natural outcome of most serious courtships in our social strata is marriage," she began, looking back at the duchess and Charlotte. The two women were now unabashedly watching her and Lord Michael brother converse. She managed a brief smile before turning back to her escort. "But, as you know, nothing can be assumed when dealing with the duke. What I can confirm is that, for my part, the courtship is progressing as expected."

Lucinda congratulated herself for providing such a vague, yet perfectly polite answer. Lord Michael's questions clearly indicated he wasn't privy to the details of her and Will's agreement. And if Will had not shared the truth, she certainly was not prepared to do so.

Lucinda released Lord Michael's arm, turning to look up at him when they were still several yards from Her Grace and Charlotte, but far enough removed to allow private conversation. "Is that the information you hoped to gain, my lord?"

"Hardly," he answered. "It appears I must question my brother on the topic."

"And you're brave too," Lucinda exclaimed lightly. "I marvel you've not married."

He chuckled, the low, gruff quality sounding so much like Will that Lucinda's heart caught.

"I suspect it's not bravery on my part," he replied. "You mentioned that I am like my brother in many ways. Pigheadedness, I'm afraid, is one of those qualities we seem to share."

He turned toward her, and she smiled, thinking that he was ready to allow the conversation to drift toward less personal waters. But then his eyes met hers, and there was something so stark and raw in his expression.

She wanted to cry. She had no idea where it came from, this sudden burst of emotion, but it was all she could do to hold it back, to cling on to some semblance of her dignity.

"I suppose," he said, his voice catching slightly on his words, "that despite my brother's oft-demonstrated dislike for all things familial, I cannot help but want the best for him."

"He loves you, you know. Deeply," she blurted out in a soft murmur, her hand flying to her mouth as soon as the revealing words were uttered. As much as she wanted to tell him of all that her aunts had shared concerning the duke's painstaking efforts to keep his brother safe, she dared not speak another word.

"Michael, Lady Lucinda—do rejoin us before we eat the remainder of the pastries," the duchess called. Charlotte's good-natured harrumph of confirmation regarding the disappearing confections made Lucinda laugh despite the tears that hovered on her lashes.

"I should not have said that," she murmured, brushing her fingertips across her lashes. "Please accept my most sincere apologies. It's not my place to speak of such intimate matters."

"Do you lie?" he asked simply, his face devoid of any emotion other than polite interest, though a rough urgency ran beneath his words.

"No. Why would I, my lord?" Lucinda answered, then turned to rejoin the two women.

"I don't know," Lucinda heard him mutter.

She did not turn back, despite her deepest desire to do so.

It hadn't been the best of days, Will reflected grimly, wincing as he shifted beneath the sheets on the massive ducal bed.

After being stitched and dosed with brandy, Weston had accompanied him home and dragged him to his bedchamber, aided by Smithers. The brandy had made the wound more bearable, but it had done its work on his wits as well. His dissection of the evening's events with Carmichael would have to wait.

He'd woken with a pounding headache and enough bandages wrapped about his chest and back to rival those of an Egyptian mummy. Those at least he could hide, even if the wound hurt like the very devil.

The problem was his face. His right eye was ringed in black bruises and swollen half-shut. And his jaw didn't look much better.

He wouldn't have been averse to using the box of stage paints packed away in the armoire across the room. He'd made use of the charcoal and pots of paint a time or two in Corinthian dealings. But on those occasions, he'd had the cover of night to help conceal what would surely be detected in the brightness of day.

And the wounds were far too fresh to offer any believable explanation for their appearance. If he could avoid Lucinda for a day or two more, he could pass it off as a boxing injury. But any sooner and she'd never believe him.

Much as he disliked it, there seemed no other option than to remain in his room until he looked a little less battered.

"I'm assuming from the looks of things that the lion won?"

Will sat up, wincing when the movement pulled the stitches and stretched the wound on his back. Gingerly turning his head, he saw his brother standing in the open doorway, one shoulder propped against the door-jamb.

"Hardly." Will fingered his jaw and winced. "Though he did land a few good blows."

Michael strolled into the room and walked to the glowing fireplace, taking stock of the pewter candle-sticks poised at each end of the stone slab mantel before dropping into a leather armchair facing the bed. "Is this the business that so desperately needed your attention?"

"And if it is?" Will countered. He threw back the sheet and swung his legs over the edge of the bed, grunt-ing at the protest of torn skin and muscle. His head swam and he sat without moving, fighting the sensation.

Michael stretched out his legs, crossed his booted feet, and propped his elbows on the arms of the chair. He templed his fingers just below his chin and contemplated Will. "Far be it for me to advise you in the ways of women, but . . ."

"But?" Will pushed, the slightest hint of irritation pre-sent in his voice.

"I don't think Lady Lucinda would take it well if she knew you'd returned to your old ways."

"Bloody hell," Will bit out, standing too quickly. His body clenched with pain and his vision danced with tiny black motes. He steadied himself with one hand on the bedpost and waited for the burning sensation on his back to subside. "Don't involve yourself in my dealings with Lady Lucinda," he snarled.

Michael rubbed at his lower lip with his forefinger, clearly restraining himself from responding in kind. "Mother wants to see you happily settled," he said, then, in a quieter voice added, "As do I."

Will gripped the bedpost tighter. Michael's words carried a weight and sincerity he'd rather ignore.

"You care for Lady Lucinda, do you not?" Michael asked, breaking the heavy silence.

Will was unsure how to answer him. His brother's words revealed genuine interest; his demeanor held a depth of emotion Will had not witnessed in him for too many years.

He released the bedpost and slowly walked across the floor, the fine wool carpet providing little warmth against his bare feet. He came to stand in front of the fire, his back to Michael. "I do."

"Then for once in your life, do what is right for you— for your heart. Do not endanger what will make you happy."

Will was glad he'd turned toward the fire; his face surely revealed far more than he wanted to express at the moment. Why had his brother's feelings for him changed, turning from contempt to care overnight?

But this sudden change of heart? Will searched for a rational explanation, but his exhausted brain failed to find one. He simply could not comprehend the emotion brought on by Michael's words, so he beat it down as best he could and forged on.

"Very poetically put, little brother." He turned away from the fireplace and winced when the flames heated his wound. "Clearly tea with the ladies was most beneficial."

Disappointment flickered on Michael's face briefly before the boredom and mild irritation that Will knew so well returned. "Yes, well, I'd venture to say even the most hardened of hearts would melt in Lady Lucinda's presence."

Will nodded in response.

"Oh, wait, that's already been proven, hasn't it?" Michael continued, crossing his legs, the leather chair absorbing the movement.

"Michael," Will began, his tone one of warning.

"I do wonder, though, what she sees in the likes of you. Because, let us be completely honest: The woman could have any man she wanted. And yet, she has chosen you, his brother added."

Will knew when he was being baited. Michael was, without a doubt, doing his damndest to upset him. The question was, *why*.

"Yes, well, it is the mysteries in life that make it all so interesting, wouldn't you agree?" he replied, his tone deceptively light.

"Quite," Michael replied. "Though, I do think that I should make one thing perfectly clear: I find Lady Lucinda delightful—a fact I shared with her today during our walk about the room—"

"Michael," Will interrupted, coming to tower over his brother.

"She was quite thankful for my proposal."

Will raked a hand through his hair, then folded both arms over his chest as he counted to ten. "And what offer might that be?"

Michael uncrossed his legs and stood, their eyes meeting. "Well, I think we all know what will come of this *courtship*," he said, disdain dripping from his tone. "I wanted her to know that I would not abandon her, though the entirety of the ton surely will once you're finished."

Will stretched to his full height, barely a hairsbreadth above his brother's. "Enough!" he yelled, grabbing at

Michael's arms and holding him in a vicelike grip. "I would rather die than do Lucinda harm."

"Your very presence in her life harms her more than—"

"Do not speak of things you know nothing about!" Will hissed, his hands tightening about Michael's arms.

The grim set of Michael's mouth slid into a satisfied smirk. "I lie. No such proposal was made to Lady Lucinda," he said smoothly, "though it is encouraging to see that you are in possession of a heart after all."

Will wanted to hit him—lay him out flat on the floor of the ducal chamber and be done with it. But it was not so simple. It never was when it came to his family.

"I am in possession of a temper, little brother," Will replied, belatedly releasing Michael's arms. "And I am tired. I do believe I'll go to bed. You'll have to wait a bit to get the best of me."

"I wouldn't be so sure of that," Michael said, his voice barely above a whisper.

Will watched Michael's back as he walked from the room, the uneasy feeling that he should stop him weighing heavily on his heart.

12

"Are you quite done with the preserves or would you rather eat them straight from the serving dish, my dear?"

Lucinda looked to her plate, where her toast was now swimming in strawberry preserves, and set her knife down. "It is wonderful jam, Aunt Victoria."

"But hardly a meal in itself," Victoria countered, beckoning for the serving dish.

Lucinda took a bite of toast and began to chew, hesitating for just a moment before passing the jam to Victoria.

"Impertinent little chit," Victoria said, taking up her own knife and spreading a minute portion of the sweet preserves on her toast.

Lucinda offered a small smile in response, the disappointment of Will's absence yesterday lingering.

"Ha!" Bessie yelled, then clapped the table with her hand, holding Bell's Weekly Messenger in the other. "It appears our Lucinda has gained the attention of the society pages."

"Gossip rags, you mean?" Victoria replied, rolling her eyes in Bessie's general direction before taking a bite.

Bessie ignored Victoria's remark and continued on. "Your outing to the opera with the duke caused quite a stir."

She turned the paper so that the rest of the table might see the story and accompanying illustration.

Charlotte lowered a forkful of eggs back to her plate untouched and squinted at the drawing. "Is that meant to be Lucinda and the duke?"

"He resembles an ape of some sort," Victoria commented dryly, "though perhaps the most attractive ape I have ever seen."

Lucinda gestured for Bessie to pass her the paper, the excitement exhibited by her aunts hard to ignore. "Aunt Victoria is correct. The sketch of the duke bears a striking likeness to a very large ape," she confirmed, taking another bite of toast while she studied the picture. "I must say, the artist made me look rather fetching, though the discrepancy in our height is rather severe, wouldn't you agree?"

Stanford came through the door, a silver tray in his hands piled high with the day's mail piled high. He set the tray down near Charlotte, removed a letter from the top, and rounded the table to Lucinda. "My lady, a rider delivered this just a moment ago and asked that it be given to you directly."

Lucinda set down the paper and took the missive from the servant. "Thank you, Stanford."

The man bowed and took himself off, leaving the four women alone.

"More regrets from the duke, I suppose," she said quietly.

She broke the wax seal and unfolded the note. The black handwriting was not Will's—the small, blocklike quality very unlike Will's large, firm strokes.

"Oh, no." She barely breathed the words, unaware she'd spoken them aloud as she read. Her heart slammed, her lungs seized with fear as Lucinda gripped the missive tightly.

In unison, her aunts jumped from their chairs and hurried to cluster around her.

"Whatever is the matter?" Charlotte asked as all three bent nearer to read over Lucinda's shoulder.

"It's from Perkins. Something is terribly wrong with Winnie," she answered, holding back tears.

Lady Winifred, or Winnie to those who adored her, was perhaps the single most valuable mare in the family stable. She was bred to the county's top stallion and due to foal any day.

Samuel Perkins was in charge of the horses' care at Bampton Manor, overseeing everything from their food to their exercise schedule. His diagnosis of a complication involving the unborn foal was extremely worrisome.

The stable manager was a capable, calm man and not given to flights of fancy or worry without cause. That he'd felt compelled to inform Lucinda of Winnie's illness spoke volumes about the depth of his concern.

"I must go at once," Lucinda said in a panic, dropping the letter to the table and pushing back her chair to stand. "Should I write to the duke? We were to attend— the Whitney musicale this evening."

Victoria retrieved the note from the table and tucked it into her sleeve. "No, my dear. We will see to everything. Now go."

"No, you're right. Of course," Lucinda replied tearily.

The three aunts stood back and made room for Lucinda, who ran from the room in haste.

"I will accompany her," Charlotte said to the other two. "Please, alert the servants. We will leave the moment we're packed."

"What, in God's name, is in Bampton?"

Will's man in the Grey household gave him a weary look from across the ducal bedchamber. "A horse. A sick horse, to be more precise."

Will leapt from bed, wincing at the fresh flash of pain

from his wound. "And Lady Lucinda is the only person in all of England who can cure this equine?" He stalked across the room to where the man stood.

The agent took two steps back. "It is a mare of some importance to her apparently."

"Smithers!" Will yelled viciously, his eyes remaining on the man. "Apparently," he repeated, his tone lethal.

"Your Grace," Smithers said breathlessly as he entered the room. "A note from Lady Charlotte has arrived."

Will grabbed the offered note and ripped it open, reading the contents quickly.

He crumpled the correspondence in his fist then tossed it to the floor. "You," he said gruffly to the waiting agent, "Lady Lucinda is traveling to her home in Oxfordshire. Take two men and follow her."

The man nodded firmly and turned to go.

"Smithers, my clothing."

The vague feeling of light-headedness he'd experienced last night returned; only this time it was punctuated by a loud gasp from Smithers.

"Your Grace, you seem to be bleeding."

Will cocked his head in an attempt to view his back; the little he could see was covered in white bandages, a crimson stain spreading rapidly.

"I'll summon the doctor at once—"

"There is no time for such trivialities!" Will said angrily. "You'll find fresh dressings in the bathroom."

A frantic Smithers ran for the bandages, returning to stand in front of Will. "My lord?"

"Blast, Smithers," Will growled, reaching around for the soaked fabric and pulling. He grazed the edge of the wound, spitting out an expletive in reply.

"All right, then," Smithers said quietly, his composure returning though his face remained deathly pale. "Do turn around, Your Grace."

Will was finding it hard to stand upright, Smithers's hesitation doing little to help. "Now, man!"

All at once, Smithers ripped the bandages from Will's back, the pain causing him to see stars. He steadied himself with one hand on the wall and took a deep breath. "Good man. Now fetch me that brandy," he said, gesturing toward the decanter on the far table.

Smithers did as he was told, walking as fast as he could to retrieve the brandy then returning.

In one swift move Will uncorked the crystal decanter and poured the liquid over his shoulder, the burning sensation dropping him to his knees and ripping a deep, guttural grunt from his throat.

"Your Grace," Smithers gasped, leaning over to offer his aide. "The stitches have been upset."

"The bandages. Now," he demanded through clenched teeth, ignoring the valet's concern.

Smithers set about reapplying the bandages quickly and efficiently. "I've done all that I can, Your Grace," he said, offering Will his arm. "I do think that a doctor—"

Will waved off the help and awkwardly rose. "We've wasted enough time as it is. Bring me my clothing."

To his credit, Smithers did not argue, choosing to retrieve a shirt, breeches, boots, and neckcloth in silence.

Will took the proffered clothing and dressed as quickly as he could, affording minimum care with his wounds. "Give my mother and brother my apologies," he ordered the valet, then walked to the door.

"Your Grace, I have not packed your things. You cannot leave without—"

Will continued to walk, savagely pulling open the door and sending it crashing into the wall. "Send them along after me," he shouted, his fatigued body barely able to keep up with his agitated state. "Or do not. I don't bloody well care either way."

* * *

Antoine Garenne was many things. Patient was not one of them. He took a drink of the abysmal red wine and pursed his lips in distaste. He must wrap up his business in this godforsaken country and return to France—if for no other reason than to get his hands on a decent bottle of wine.

He'd killed the fools who had failed to take care of Clairemont—a charitable act, really, considering the damage the giant had done to them.

But the lady's unexpected trip to the country was, quite simply, more than a man could take.

He paused to look out the dingy window of his rented room. On the narrow street below, a trio of prostitutes called out to passing men, their lewd and explicit invitations to potential customers rising on the damp spring air.

The band of pain around his head, reduced by a bout of vigorous coupling, gained strength, cinching tighter. His grip on the wineglass tightened and anger roiled in his gut.

He'd use the days that Lady Lucinda was absent from London to refine details for two potential kidnap schemes. And if the Duke of Clairemont died during either of them, so much the better.

He tipped the glass up and swallowed with difficulty, his throat constricted by rage.

"Lovie."

Garenne pushed himself away from the scarred table and stood, crossing to the rumpled bed, where a nude prostitute lay. "It's a bit cold without you," she said coyly, her garishly painted face only serving to make her more disgusting to Garenne.

"We would not want you to be cold," he replied, leaning one knee on the sagging bed and reaching for a pillow.

leaning one knee on the sagging bed and reaching for a pillow.

The filthy whore had eased some of the pain, but not all. He required more of her.

The woman smiled lewdly at him as he brought the pillow nearer. And when he brought it down hard over her face she complied, the many twisted demands she'd endured in the past hour telling her that he meant no harm.

But when he failed to release her, she began to struggle, her arms flailing in an attempt to free herself, her legs kicking out at the air. Her response pleased Garenne. After all, without a struggle there was no thrill, no satisfaction. No pleasure.

Her legs stilled, then her arms, signaling the arrival of death. Garenne waited a moment, then lifted the pillow away from the woman's face and threw it across the room. He took in the frozen look of terror on her face and smiled, the irritation of the mission easing slightly.

He stood and walked to the window. Squinting through the dirt and grime, he eyed the women across the street. Standing within the pool of light cast by the newly lit lantern, the small group included a round, buxom redhead, a tall blonde, and a petite black-haired one, all more than willing and expertly able.

"I'll bury myself in the black-haired whore. Or perhaps the blonde tonight?" A slow smile curved his thick lips. "All three it is."

"Bloody British rain," Will cursed, tugging his hat brim lower on his forehead. Sol pinned his ears back and snorted, clearly in agreement with his master.

"You've no one but your beloved Lucinda to blame for this," Will said to the stallion, brushing water from his mane. Given that the horse was soaked, the action did little good and was more a rough gesture of affection. "Well, Lucinda and a mare named Winnie."

He'd ridden at breakneck speed, not stopping until he reached the Rosemont Inn despite the dizziness that threatened to unseat him. He was terribly tired and the pain from his wound unbearable, the countless hours spent astride only having adding to his misery.

The rain quickened, accompanied by a tepid wind from the north. Will turned up the collar of his greatcoat just as the dim light from the Rosemont's muddy yard came into view.

He turned Sol into the yard and slid from the saddle, nearly falling to his knees in the dank mud. A young man approached and Will handed him the reins.

He reached in his pocket and pulled out several coins. "Has a Lady Lucinda Grey taken a room for the evening?" he asked pointedly, dropping half a crown into the flat of the man's palm.

The man stared at the coins in Will's hand, scratching his head in earnest. "There's only one lady of quality that's taken a room for the night. Blonde, blue eyes, traveling with a companion—an older woman."

Will dropped the remaining coins into the man's hand. "Thank you. Take care of my horse and there will be more where that came from."

"Yes, sir!"

Will thumped Sol on the rump and walked toward the inn. *Strange candles, those, that they would dim as one drew near.* He squinted at the lights that flanked the front door, blinked once, then again, but they continued to dim.

Before Will knew what was happening, the night sky had engulfed him and he was falling, though there didn't seem to be a damn thing he could do about it.

*   *   *

Lucinda stared up at the darkened eaves of her room in the Rosemont Inn, restless and weary.

The trip to Bampton Manor always felt endlessly long, and today's journey was no exception. Lucinda had wanted to travel straight through, stopping only to secure fresh horses. But Charlotte had objected, insisting Lucinda would be of no use to Winnie if she arrived exhausted and addle-brained from lack of sleep.

"Shouldn't the patrons be abed by now?" Charlotte asked, stifling a yawn.

Lucinda rolled to face her aunt, tucking one hand under her feather pillow. "I highly doubt that anyone is thinking on what they *should* do, Aunt."

The Rosemont's tavern was exceedingly popular, though it had nothing to do with the quality of the establishment. On one of her many trips between London and Oxfordshire, Lucinda had discovered that the Rosemont was the only watering hole for some twenty miles.

The carousing had started innocently enough with a snort of laughter floating up here and there through the floorboards. But in the last hour the intensity of the evening had taken a turn for the worse.

"Too true, dear girl," Charlotte answered. "Too true."

The bed dipped slightly as Charlotte rolled from her back to her side. "I suppose absolute silence would fail you as well with all that must be on your mind."

"Winnie, you mean?" Lucinda asked apprehensively, fingering the rough bed linens.

"Yes, my dear. Who else would I be referring to?"

Lucinda chewed her bottom lip. "Precisely."

"Although," Charlotte began, "there is the duke."

Lucinda froze, thankful for the darkness that filled the room. "The courtship is proceeding as planned," she lied, squeezing her eyes shut. "Sol will be ours by summer."

"Perhaps you did not hear me, my dear. I mentioned the duke, not the horse."

Lucinda turned her face into the pillow, frightened that she might cry. "The duke? Well, he is . . ." She swallowed, urging the lump in her throat to move lower. "That is to say—"

"My lady!"

The sound of their coachman's voice was punctuated by three loud raps upon the wooden door.

"Rogers?" Lucinda and Charlotte said in unison, the bed nearly breaking in two from the force of their combined exodus. They fumbled about in the dark for their dressing gowns, Lucinda finding hers first, then dashing toward the door.

She unlocked the door and swung it open. "Rogers, what is it?"

"I am sorry to disturb you both, but the innkeeper has need of you," he said, averting his eyes. "Seems there's a gentleman that's fainted and they don't know who he is."

Charlotte knotted the robe's sash about her waist and came to stand next to Lucinda. "Rogers, I don't mean to be obtuse, but how on earth might we be of assistance? In all likelihood there are several individuals passed out below-stairs."

"Beg your pardon, my lady. This gentleman didn't drink himself to sleep. He's injured. But he asked after Lady Lucinda before planting himself facedown in the yard."

Both women gasped in horror.

Charlotte reached for Lucinda's arm. "Who on earth could it be?"

Lucinda patted her aunt's hand reassuringly despite the macabre curiosity she felt. "I can't imagine. But surely there is a reasonable explanation."

Rogers continued to stare at the door. "Er, will you go and see him?"

"Oh, of course," Lucinda replied, taking Rogers's offered candlestick. "We'll be but a moment."

Charlotte closed the door firmly and turned to where her things were. "Have you any idea—"

"None at all," Lucinda interrupted, struggling to pull her nightgown over her head.

"Come, let me help you," Charlotte said, walking to where Lucinda stood by the rumpled bed and reaching to pull at the gown. As soon as they were both dressed, Lucinda hurried toward the door, readying to open it.

"My dear, a moment," Charlotte said, prompting her to turn back.

"Yes," Lucinda replied, her brows knitting together.

"I know that it has been a trying time for you, what with Winnie and . . ." she paused, taking Lucinda's hands in hers. "Well, I do worry that the sight of a grievously injured man may be that proverbial straw."

Lucinda tried to smile. "Are you calling me a camel?"

"Lucinda!" Charlotte attempted *not* to smile. "What I am trying to say is, there's a limit to the number of misfortunes one person can endure."

Lucinda gripped her aunt's hands tightly as if to keep herself from falling. "Aunt Charlotte," she began, looking down at their joined hands. "Sometimes in life, the only option one has is to continue on. Would you not agree?"

"Wholeheartedly," Charlotte confirmed, freeing her hand and reaching to caress Lucinda's cheek. "When did you become so wise, my dear?"

"Precisely fifteen seconds ago," Lucinda answered, offering her aunt a lopsided smile. "Shall we?"

"We shall."

The two walked to the door, opening it slowly.

Rogers stood in the hallway. "Come with me, then, ladies."

They followed him down the dimly lit corridor, the sounds from below having quieted somewhat.

"Here we are," Rogers said, gesturing to the last door on the right. He opened it and stepped aside, allowing Lucinda and Charlotte to enter. "I'll be in the hallway if you need me."

The women nodded at the coachman, then stepped across the threshold. A man in dark traveling clothes stood with his back to the door, obscuring the bed just beyond.

He turned at the sound of their entry. "Splendid. One of you is Lady Lucinda Grey, I presume?"

"I am she," Lucinda answered hesitantly.

"Well, come along, then," he urged impatiently. When Lucinda failed to obey him immediately, he let out a rather loud harrumph of displeasure. "Ladies, I am a man of science and, as such, social graces are not my forte. Please, forgive me," he said, quickly bowing. "Dr. Elijah Forrester at your service."

Lucinda and Charlotte bowed and made to properly complete the introduction. "Lad—"

"All right, then. Who might this man be?" Dr. Forrester interrupted. "I've a patient in Dunsford who requires my attention."

Lucinda stepped past the doctor and turned to look upon the man, the flickering candlelight casting him in shadows, though the hideous bruising on his face was readily apparent even in the dim light.

She gasped and stepped forward, her hand flying to her mouth. "Will?!"

Charlotte rushed to the bed. "Good Lord," she uttered with horror, steadying herself against the doctor.

Forrester propped Charlotte upright and cleared his throat. "You know this man, then?"

"He is the Duke of Clairemont," Lucinda said halt-
ingly.

The doctor gaped at her. "The . . . who?"

Lucinda brushed past him, blinking rapidly in the
hopes that Will's injuries were nothing more than a trick
of light. "Who did this to him?"

The doctor reached for his kit on the side table and
began to rummage through it. "We might never know."

"Surely you're not implying that he . . ." Lucinda
paused, her voice shaking with the effort. "That he will
not wake?"

"Well, one never can tell in these sorts of situations,"
he replied simply. "Only time will tell."

Lucinda reached to stroke Will's hand, noting the
smudges of dirt and blood on his hands and face. "Is
there nothing that we can do?"

Dr. Forrester produced a small leather pouch from his
kit and gestured toward Will. "Actually, yes, there is."

He handed Lucinda the pouch then reached for Will's
shoulders, pulling him to a seated position. "Now, if
you'll hold him thusly I will stitch up his back."

Charlotte reached for Lucinda's arm. "My dear, the
duke is undressed—"

"Aunt Charlotte," Lucinda pleaded in a low tone.
"The doctor needs my assistance."

Charlotte's brows knit together as she considered her
options. "All right."

Both Lucinda and Charlotte leaned forward in order
to see the wound, the amount of coagulated blood encircling the gash making them gasp.

"Why was this not seen to immediately?" Charlotte
demanded, fanning herself vigorously with her hanky.

The doctor gestured for Lucinda's help. "No one
could identify the man. How was I to know if he could
afford my services?"

Lucinda bent down and exchanged places with the

doctor, the substantial weight of Will's debilitated body coming to rest against her as she faced him.

"He is the Duke of Clairemont," Charlotte said angrily. "He could very well die and you would be held—"

"Please," Lucinda cried, halting her aunt's indictment. "It is of no consequence now." She looked up at the doctor and swallowed. "Just do what needs to be done."

The room fell silent as the doctor prepared the needle and set to work.

She held Will about the waist with the greatest of care, the feel of his bare, sweaty skin on hers oddly comforting.

Resting her chin on his shoulder, she breathed in his familiar scent and tried to will him awake. She watched the doctor draw the thread through the wound over and again, panic rising in her stomach with every stitch.

You cannot die, she screamed in her head, tightening her grip about his waist. *Please, hold on. There's so much I need to say.*

"That should do it," the doctor said, dropping his instrument on the side table and picking up a length of linen. He bandaged the wound and pulled Will from Lucinda, the absence of his body leaving her bereft.

Charlotte put her hand on Lucinda's shoulder and squeezed. "What signs are we to look for, Doctor?" she asked worriedly.

"Well, if the duke does not wake up, then we've a real problem," he answered, swiping at his needle with a cloth then returning it to his kit.

"He will," Lucinda whispered. "He has to."

Dr. Forrester held his palm to Will's forehead. "I do hope you're right," he said.

But he was shaking his head as he said it.

A heavy hand on his aching forehead forced Will to awaken, and then the pain began in earnest.

"Christ," he blew out, struggling to sit up, then wishing he hadn't, the pain from the tortuous wound on his back multiplying in intensity.

He opened his eyes to find three hazy forms leaning over him. He squinted, bringing his view into focus— one stranger, Charlotte, and *Lucinda*.

And that was when he found his voice. "What in the name of all that is most holy is going on?"

"Dr. Elijah Forrester, Your Grace," the man said, reaching to press on Will's jaw. "You were found in the yard. Luckily, Lady Lucinda was able to identify you."

"Lucinda, I am eternally indebted to you," Will replied through gritted teeth, the man's probing fingers doing little to ease his discomfort.

"I am assuming those bruises on your face and the mighty gash on your back were not the result of your fall in the yard."

Will ran his hands through his hair. *Well, now. Collapsing has never proven to be quite so convenient.* "A band of highwaymen, Doctor. Some two miles back. I trust you'll find a few strewn about in the bushes."

The women gasped, Lucinda's hand moving to cover her heart. "Your Grace, how you can you be so cavalier when you—" She broke off, gathering her composure. "You could have been mortally wounded."

Will was enjoying this far more than he should. "But I am not mortally wounded, correct?" he asked, looking to the doctor.

"No, not mortally," the doctor replied, turning to his kit and pulling two bottles from the bag.

"The blood loss from the wound on your back is what caused you to faint. Odd thing that gash," he began, giving Will a questioning look before setting the bottles down on the side table.

Will eyed the doctor with a superior glare. "I've incurred my share of injuries in the boxing arena and beyond. This latest round of scrapes hardly signify, I assure you."

"Very well, then," the doctor answered succinctly, any questions he may have had concerning the wound having conveniently disappeared. "Ladies, if you'll follow me below we'll see to the instructions for the duke's care."

Lucinda whispered something in Charlotte's ear, to which her aunt answered firmly, "No." A second bout of whispering began, the request being granted, though with conditions.

"Rogers will be right outside. The door will be open at all times. Do I make myself clear, dear?"

"Yes," Lucinda answered quietly. "Of course. You have my word."

Charlotte looked to be rethinking her decision, but the doctor's prodding won out, the aunt shuffling from the room while Lucinda stayed behind.

"Lucinda, to say that I'm shocked would be an understatement," Will teased, wincing with pain as he attempted to sit up.

She moved to adjust his pillows, the smell of her filling Will's nose.

"Why are you here?"

"In this bed—"

"You know what I am asking of you," she interrupted, pushing her long, golden hair from her face.

Will settled into the fluffed pillows. "I would hardly be a proper suitor if I allowed you to gallivant across the countryside alone."

"You knew that Aunt Charlotte accompanied me—"

"And how would she have fared against the highwaymen, hmm?" he asked accusingly.

She massaged her temples, the fatigue plain on her face. "Will."

"Yes?"

She situated herself on the edge of the bed, careful to not touch him. "I cannot do this."

A sudden sense of dread filled the pit of Will's stomach. "Lucinda?"

"You told me once that you admired my honesty, did you not?"

Will thought back to their first walk in the park when he'd paid her the compliment. "I did."

She folded her hands in her lap and took a deep breath, her gaze suddenly fixed on his. "I have not been honest with you of late. I have tried to be someone that I am not. Played at games that I knew nothing about. Inspired feelings in you for false reasons. And none of it has turned out as I planned."

Will reached out, placing his palm on the small of her back. "I am sorry."

"You've nothing to apologize for. Reacting to my many moods and attempts to manipulate your feelings must have been exhausting," she pressed, her eyes filling with tears. "I am the one who is sorry."

He would do anything to make her pain go away. *Anything but tell her the truth, you loathsome cad.* God, to sit there was torture, the knowledge that he was the one who'd manipulated her from the start burning a hole through his heart. "Lucinda, please, there's no need to apologize. You are tired and overwrought with concern for your horse—"

"Will, let me finish before I lose my courage," she urged quietly.

Will tensed, anxious to hear the words he'd been sure he never would, but terrified as well.

She laid a hand on his cheek gently, the soulfulness in her eyes nearly making Will weep. "I ask nothing of you—only, know that I care for you deeply. And, I think I always will."

Will could not find enough air to fill his lungs, the

weight of her declaration nearly knocking him back into unconsciousness. "Lucinda, I . . ." he began, choosing his words carefully.

"Lucinda dear," Charlotte called out from the hall. "The duke needs his rest now. Do come to bed."

Lucinda stood up and Will reached for her gown, but he missed it.

"Please, don't—"

"Do I need to fetch you myself?" Charlotte said, peeking around the door.

"Rest well, Your Grace," Lucinda said, offering him a wistful smile then turning to go, the door shutting quietly behind her.

Will groaned with frustration. "Not bloody likely."

The next morning came too early for Lucinda, the deep sleep she'd fallen into after speaking with Will not something she was eager to leave behind.

But she had, with much poking and prodding from Charlotte, and the two had readied themselves for the day, taking a light meal in their room, then meeting Will in the yard.

Will had used every argument he could to keep from riding in the carriage with Lucinda and her aunt to Bampton Manor, but Charlotte had insisted. And when a Fury insisted, well, not even the Duke of Clairemont could say no.

Sol's reins were tied to the carriage and the three set off for Oxfordshire, Lucinda on one seat, with Will and Charlotte opposite.

Lucinda had tried in earnest to keep up with the steady stream of conversation, but she'd failed miserably, nodding off just after Charlotte made mention of the returning rain and not waking until they'd pulled into the circular drive of Bampton Manor.

She'd seen to their guest, instructing the servants to escort Will to a suitable room, then insisted that her aunt rest, before taking her leave and running as fast as she could to the stables.

In the past, the familiar smell of hay and horses had always been a comfort to Lucinda. But not today. The rain beat down outside, drumming a military tattoo on the roof.

She stood in Winnie's stall, watching the mare as she attempted to shift her cumbersome weight. She'd arrived to find Perkins watching closely as the veterinary-surgeon examined her. Though she was due to foal, she was not acting in a manner that led anyone to believe this would be an uneventful birth.

The mare ignored her oats and ambled awkwardly nearer to stand with her head next to Lucinda's. She stroked the chestnut's silky flaxen mane and kissed her irresistibly soft nose. "Whatever is the matter, Winnie?"

The mare nuzzled Lucinda's face, chin, cheek, and temple, huffing warm breath that stirred Lucinda's hair above her ear, then dropped her head low, her right eyelid drooping.

Will appeared, propping his elbows on Winnie's gate and gently clucking to the mare. "How is she?"

Lucinda gave Will a look of disappointment. "I instructed the servants to lock you in your room."

"I escaped."

"Why does that not surprise me?" she said wryly.

"Because you know me too well," he answered. "Now, how fares Lady Winifred?"

Lucinda took a long worrisome look at the mare before answering Will. "We can't be sure, but we believe it may be related to the foal. It's something to do with her right side. She'd not able to move as she should."

Will slowly reached for Winnie, the mare allowing him to rub her forelock. "And you? Are you all right?"

Now I am, Lucinda thought. "As well as can be expected."

She yawned unexpectedly, her hand coming to cover her mouth. "I'm so sorry," she offered, meeting his gaze.

Will stepped closer. "You need your rest. I'll stay with the mare."

"I was not attacked by highwaymen mere hours ago nor can I currently lay claim to several spectacular bruises and one hideous wound on—"

Will placed his index finger on Lucinda's mouth. "Have you eaten dinner?"

She nodded a "no."

"Slept in a comfortable bed since leaving town?"

She begrudgingly blew out a breath.

Will lifted his finger and replaced it with a gentle kiss. "Four hours. That is all that I ask."

"But if she worsens—"

He moved toward the gate and let free the latch, swinging the door wide enough for Lucinda. "I send come for you at once."

Lucinda readied to argue, but Will came up behind her, kneading her shoulders with his powerful hands. "Go."

"Do I have your word?" she asked, leaning into the feel of his touch.

"Of course, Lucinda. If the mare worsens and there is something to be done, I will send for you immediately."

He dropped his hands and pushed her gently forward, closing the gate behind her.

Lucinda lingered, watching the mare wearily. "What do you mean 'something to be done'?"

"If Winnie's condition worsens and there is *nothing* that can be done for her," Will said gently, reaching at and caressing her shoulder, "would you want me to fetch you, though it would mean leaving her side?"

"Of course not," she answered immediately. "I would not have her without the comfort."

"Then we are in agreeement. Now go. You will be of no use to Winnie unless you take care of yourself" he said simply.

She could not argue with his logic nor the exhaustion that inhabited every last bone in her body.

She reached for Winnie once more, lovingly patting her soft head then turning to go.

Will kickied his chamber's door shut and removed his sodden coat, revealing the white shirt beneath, now soaked in blood.

Winnie had remained stable for some time after Lucinda had gone, making Will hopeful that she would fully recover. And then she'd staggered toward the gate of her stall and collapsed against it. Will had yelled for Perkins, but the few moments it took the man to run the length of the barn aisle to Winnie's stall were too many. The mare was gone, the only thing left to do being to save the foal.

Perkins had disappeared into the tack room and returned with the necessary tools. When it came time, Will pulled the sleek chestnut-colored foal free without injury. Perkins had left Will with the foal momentarily, returning shortly with a mare whose own foal was nearly weaned. The little one had curiously sniffed the mare as she did him, the two falling into a companionable silence before the foal nosed his way to suckle at her teat.

It was so beautiful, and yet Will could not appreciate it fully, knowing the pain to foal's beginnings would bring to Lucinda.

A soft knock at the door interrupted Will's thoughts. He crossed the room and quietly cracked open the door.

"She's in the library, Your Grace." One of his men

stood just outside, the light from a slim candlestick he carried illuminating his face.

Will nodded his thanks and turned from the door. He crossed the chamber and picked up his discarded shirt from earlier in the day. He dressed quickly then stepped out into the hall.

The waiting agent handed the candlestick to Will. He opened the door carefully, and the two moved silently down the hall.

They didn't encounter anyone on their way to the library, the lateness of the hour shrouding the household in sleep and darkness.

But not Lucinda, Will thought to himself with dread as he silently padded his way down the long gallery where her long-dead ancestors eyed him from their gilded-framed portraits lining the walls.

The two men descended the mahogany staircase and crossed the entry hall, avoiding a massive stone sculpture of a horse in the process. They stopped in front of the library's closed door and Will handed the candlestick to the agent. He opened the door and stepped in, searching the room for Lucinda. He could not see the glow of candlelight anywhere. The room was huge, with tall bookcases standing at right angles to the walls and creating aisles down the carpeted length to the cluster of chairs grouped in front of a fireplace at the far end.

A faint sound caught his attention. The soft crinkling noise came again and he followed it, silently crossing to the opposite corner. He reached the last of the bookshelves and saw a spill of soft candlelight gleaming on leather book spines. Inching silently closer, Will leaned to his right to see beyond the rows of books.

The source of the sound was immediately apparent. It came again as Lucinda turned a page of the large book lying open on her lap.

Will stepped out into the light, clearing his throat as he did so.

Lucinda looked up in surprise. "Will?"

"I'm sorry to disturb you," he said in response, the agony of the news he must share weighing heavily on his heart.

"Is it Winnie?" she asked anxiously, moving to sit on the very edge of the leather-bound chair. "I'm sure you're disappointed that I did not sleep longer, but I do believe I've discovered what's troubling her," she continued, opening a large leather-bound book in her hands. "It has to do with the foal's placement in relation to her stomach and the—"

"Lucinda," Will interrupted, stepping forward farther into the candlelight then leaning down on one knee, reaching to take Lucinda's small hand in his. "Lucinda," he began, his throat thick. "She was gone in an instant. I wante you there—but I could not leave her alone."

Lucinda's eyes pooled with tears and she let out a wail of protest.

"No, please tell me it's not true." She stopped abruptly, her voice cracking with emotion. "Not Winnie," She stood from the settee, her embroidered wrapper parting to reveal a nearly translucent white cotton nightrail.

He couldn't bear to see her like this, hurt and in pain. "My God, Lucinda, you don't know what I would do to make it a lie," he began, standing again to meet her gaze. "But it's the truth."

"No. Not Winnie," she whispered, then fell silent as emotion clearly overwhelmed her. She closed her eyes tightly and wrapped her arms about herself, looking as though she thought to block the world from her battered heart.

"Lucinda," Will uttered quietly, not sure of what else to do.

She began to cry, soft whimpers of distress escaping her mouth.

"Lucinda."

"Say my name again," she pleaded, her eyes opening to meet his.

"Lucinda."

She edged closer to him and reached out, her arms coming to encircle his waist.

Will enfolded her in his warmth and bent his head to gently kiss the top of her head, her silken hair smelling of spring. He uttered words of comfort into the soft shell of her ear, eager to end her suffering.

She raised her head to his and looked into his eyes, a wealth of pain and sorrow, questions and something Will could not quite guess at reflected in her own. Slowly, she rose on tiptoe, then placed her lips on his tentatively.

He hesitated, pulling his mouth from hers and looking deep into her eyes. "You do not want this," he said in earnest, his breathing labored.

"You're wrong," she began, resting her cheek on his, her lips nearly touching his ear. "I want this. But more importantly, I need you."

Lucinda wrapped her arms around him, pressing the length of her body against him. She returned his bruising kisses with unbridled enthusiasm, her tongue first retreating, then darting out to meet his, learning the sensuous rhythm with an eagerness that drove Will beyond rational thought.

Her fingers pulled at his shirt and Will's blood burned. He broke the kiss and yanked the garment up and over his head to toss it behind him to the floor, the pain from his wound lessening with each second.

Her hand reached for his, moving it to the ribbon at her neck. He tugged and the ribbons fell loose, releasing the front of her wrapper. The garment fell open, exposing an expanse of creamy skin. He caught the hem of her wrapper and nightrail in both hands. With her gaze locked on his, she raised her arms and he pulled her nightclothes up and off. He closed his fists, bunching the fabric, and bent his head, breathing in her scent before he looked at Lucinda.

She had slender legs and sleek thighs, hips that cradled the flat curve of stomach where the small indentation of her belly button seemed flagrantly female. And her breasts were perfect, high and firm, the nipples a deep dusky pink.

She touched him, her fingers shyly caressing his upper chest before trailing lower. She pulled at the buttons on his breeches before finally freeing them one by one.

He backed her up against the bookcase, muscles tense as he hesitated, though he could hardly bear to do so. "There is no going back after this. Once we join, nothing will ever be the same for either of us."

Lucinda gave him a pleading look. "I've no desire to go back, Will. Now come to me."

The reasons for avoiding involvement with Lucinda disappeared, practical logic overthrown by what Will could not deny in his heart. He wanted Lucinda more than any other woman he had ever encountered. But beyond the lust, he loved her. He'd never given her the words, but he needed to show her now with his mind, body, and spirit—their lovemaking a testament to his true feelings.

He lifted her up, hooking her legs around his waist before piercing her damp core with his cock. Her sudden, sharp intake of breath was quickly followed by panting as each thrust sent her pleasure higher.

"Yes, yes, yes," she moaned, clutching at Will's shoulders. Her nails bit into his skin with each rhythmic stroke, the pain only heightening the erotic play.

Will covered her breast with his right hand, toying

lightly with the nipple, then kneading, tugging, and finally pinching it between his forefinger and thumb. He moved to the other breast, roughly fondling it until Lucinda uttered a breathless "Please!"

She moved restlessly beneath him, instinctively spreading her legs farther before her body went rigid, her cry of surrender signaling her climax.

Will released her nipple and slowed his pace, savoring the flavor that was uniquely Lucinda before raising his head.

"I love you," she whispered.

Lucinda could not have known what those words meant to him, the thought of ever surrendering himself so completely to one person simply not possible only weeks before.

He quickened his pace, grinding against her. She tilted her hips, moving in time as if they'd done this dance before.

Will could no longer wait. He drove deep inside her, his cock pulsing as he surrendered to the pounding lust and need.

He blanketed her with his body, his face buried in her silken hair. "Lucinda," he said simply, repeating her name again and again.

She said nothing in response, only enfolded him in her arms and held on tightly.

13

As Will and the handful of Corinthians waited for the remaining two agents to arrive, the words "no rest for the wicked" felt tailored just for him.

He'd helped Lucinda into her nightrail and wrapper after their lovemaking, and walked her back to her bedchamber. He hadn't wanted to leave her, but he'd resisted the temptation to linger in the interest of duty. He'd made his way through the darkened house and across the grounds to the barn. He'd not been the first to arrive at the prearranged meeting, but he'd not been the last, either—a testament to his superior strength if ever there was one.

A young barn cat wound around Will's legs, purring loudly. He bent to pick it up and sat down on an upturned bucket, tucking the warm fuzzy calico on his lap.

Superior strength, my arse, he thought.

He should not, under any circumstances, have allowed himself to make love to Lucinda. Never, in all of his time spent with the Corinthians, had he made such a fatal mistake. He knew damn well that the sight of her alone in the library, wearing little more than a few scraps of fabric, had tested his will beyond measure.

But he could have resisted that. It would have been hard. Hell, he would have been hard. For days, most likely. But he could have done it. He'd have stopped before he took her virginity. He could have done it. He knew he could have done it.

The cat jumped from Will's lap and trotted across the hay-strewn floor, pausing to tilt its head and sniff the wind before heading off toward the tack room.

Will let out a long breath, watching the cat as it disappeared around the corner, its tail giving one final flick of farewell. Around him, the Corinthians continued to gather, but Will couldn't seem to take his eyes off the last spot where the cat had been.

Staring. Still staring. But seeing nothing.

Thank God he'd had the sense not to tell Lucinda that he loved her too. At least not in so many words. His body had communicated what his brain could not, and he knew, even if she perhaps did not, that the intimate joining of their bodies had been a silent testament to his feelings for her.

Even now, the concept defied comprehension. Despite any long-buried, secret desires that hid deep within his heart, Will had long ago given up on the likelihood that anyone could ever love him. If a man's own father was unable to feel affection for his son, then what hope was there?

And then Lucinda had declared her feelings in no uncertain terms, completely destroying what Will had settled long ago. But more than that, the tender feelings she inspired in him were in direct contrast to the single-minded, cold focus he needed to do his job. Spying was not for those inclined to softness or fancy. It was a dangerous vocation that demanded unwavering concentration, the ability to make the right decision no matter how difficult, and a deep conviction to do what was right—even if lives were lost along the way.

Cold, calculating, demanding, dangerous. The words described exactly who Will was—or rather, they were the qualities that had made him the most valued of all Corinthian agents.

Until now.

The last of the summoned agents entered the barn and joined the group illuminated in the low circle of light.

"I know you're all tired, so we'll make this as brief as possible," Will began. "Weston, what news of Garenne?"

Weston stepped forward, his right eye ringed with ugly black, blue, and livid red bruises. "Our sources confirm what we suspected: The Frenchman made inquiries several months ago in the area concerning Lady Lucinda, including the details of her estate grounds."

"Any sightings recently?"

"None that we can discern," Weston replied, "though the local frogs have been active of late. None of our sources are willing to give the bastard up—at least, not yet."

Will paused to take the information in. Garenne had not lured Lucinda from London with false tales, that much was clear. But it didn't mean that he wasn't lurking in the shadows even now. "I assume that whomever blackened your eye has been taken care of?"

"You know me better than to ask such a thing, Clairemont," Weston replied, a smile spreading over his tanned face.

"Good," Will said with satisfaction. "Now, Parsons, your report on the surveillance efforts."

The meeting, true to Will's promise, was quick and efficient, the necessary information shared, plans for the morning reviewed, and the men sent back to their various posts to resume their duties.

Will slipped quietly back into the manor and made an unsuccessful attempt at sleep, only to be awakened two hours later when sounds from below signaled the house staff was up and readying for a new day.

Dressing quickly, he escaped the manor undetected and made haste for the stables, saddling Sol and leaving the property at a hard gallop.

He was glad for the forethought he'd shown when he'd left Lucinda at her chamber door and told her he would be gone this day due to business in the district. It would allow him the opportunity to interrogate informants who had yet to yield to his fellow Corinthians' wishes—always an activity that proved useful in ridding oneself of excess anger and frustration. And, more importantly, it would remove Lucinda from his sight, giving him the distance needed to make a decision he knew to be absolutely necessary.

But he dreaded it, all the same.

Weston appeared not far up the road at the agreed upon meeting site, his gelding's ears pricking with interest at Sol's approach.

Will didn't slacken the stallion's speed and Weston kneed his mount into motion, joining Will on the road as the two horses raced neck and neck toward town.

There were certain obligations that came with country life, and chief among them was replying in the affirmative when one's closest neighbor issued an invitation for supper. In Lucinda's case, this meant that when the Earl of Rowton, upon learning of her unexpected arrival at Bampton Manor, arranged for a meal in her honor, she had to say yes.

She was not quite certain how Lord Rowton had heard that she was in residence, but it didn't really matter. Her aunts had brought her up to be a good neighbor, and a good neighbor she would be.

And so here she was, climbing the steps to Rowton Manor, Charlotte at her side, trying desperately not to wince as she moved.

She was sore. Really sore. How was it possible that her regular riding schedule had not better prepared her limbs for the physical exertion of lovemaking?

"Where is His Grace?" Charlotte asked once she'd

surveyed the room and taken note of those attending. "He agreed to come, did he not?"

"Yes, of course," Lucinda assured her. He hadn't been particularly pleased about it, but she'd eventually wrenched a yes from his lips. It was what a proper suitor would do, she had said sweetly. That had been met with a scowl.

They *were* courting, weren't they?

His scowl gave way to grumbling.

So she'd launched into her good neighbor speech, sounding to her ear remarkably like her aunts.

He had acquiesced immediately.

He had said that he'd some business in town, although what she could not imagine, but he'd promised that he'd be there.

"I'm sure he'll arrive shortly," Lucinda told her aunt. "He mentioned that he might be delayed by some sort of ducal business."

"Here?"

Lucinda shrugged. As far as she knew, Will had no property in Oxfordshire, but the dukedom's holdings were vast, and she was quite certain she did not know the extent of it.

"Do you see Rowton?" Charlotte murmured in her ear.

Lucinda shook her head. She had known Lord Rowton for years. He was ten years her senior and had made no secret of his desire to join their properties. His father had suggested the match at her birth, and Rowton had taken up the cause as soon as Lucinda had reached a marriageable age.

She had not mentioned this to Will. It did not seem relevant, at least not while she was trying to convince him to accompany her.

"Ouch!" Lucinda looked over at Charlotte with some irritation. "What was that for?"

Charlotte retracted her elbow, which was presently dug into Lucinda's ribs. "Rowton, my dear," she murmured without moving her lips.

Lucinda's gaze followed Charlotte's. "Oh," she said under her breath.

Each pasted a smile on her face and prepared to greet their host.

There was nothing precisely wrong about Lord Rowton. He was an avid horseman, which was certainly a point in his favor, and he did not bore Lucinda with recitations of parliamentary proceedings while implying they were beyond her understanding.

In truth, Lucinda had to suppose that Lord Rowton had been the best of her suitors, or if not that, certainly the most convenient.

But that had been before Will. And with the memory of his body on hers still burned into her memory . . .

"Lucinda!"

She turned to Charlotte. "What?"

"You moaned."

"I did not," Lucinda shot back, horrified.

"Oh, you did. I assure you my hearing is—Lord Rowton! How nice to see you again."

Their host stood before them, smiling down at both. "Lady Charlotte," he began, nodding, bowing, and grasping her hand to kiss the air just above her fingers.

Charlotte had barely murmured a brief response before he turned to Lucinda, the look of adoration plain for all to see. "And Lady Lucinda. It has been far too long since our last meeting."

"Lord Rowton," Lucinda began, reluctantly offering her hand, "you are too kind."

His lips barely brushed her fingers, though they lingered too long for Lucinda's comfort.

She gently pulled back, not wanting to create a scene

but desirous to retrieve her hand all the same. "This looks to be quite a happy gathering, I must say."

"Indeed," he replied, gesturing for the ladies to accompany him into the room. "I was surprised to find you in residence at this time of year."

Lucinda eyed Charlotte wearily, her heart not quite prepared to speak of Winnie with the indifference necessary for such settings. "An ill horse, I'm afraid."

Charlotte cleared her throat. "Thank you for asking, Lord Rowton."

"And will you be staying on?" he pressed. "It really seems a shame to come all this way only to stay for a few short days."

Lucinda smiled sincerely. It was difficult not to admire his determination. "Aunt Charlotte wishes to stay on for the remainder of the week, and so we will."

"I'm *very* glad to hear as much," Rowton replied enthusiastically.

The three walked toward the pianoforte, where a plump, brown-haired woman was busily playing Mozart. She ended the piece with a dramatic tinkle of two keys and smilingly received the polite round of applause.

"Miss Winstead, you play beautifully," Lucinda said to the woman, her compliment failing to draw the round young woman's chocolate brown gaze away from Lord Rowton.

"Thank you, Lady Lucinda," she replied, her attention focused unwaveringly on Lord Rowton.

This could work to my advantage, Lucinda thought to herself, winking at Charlotte before proceeding. "Would you not agree, Lord Rowton?" she asked.

"I'm sorry?" The earl replied, his glass of wine halfway to his lips.

"I was just commenting on Miss Winstead's skillful playing."

"Oh, that. Well—"

"I could not agree more." The deep, masculine comment came from somewhere behind Lucinda.

The fine hairs on her nape stood up, her body coming to life as if he'd commanded it to do so.

She showed restraint though, waiting to turn until her companions did. "Your Grace," she began, not wanting to appear overly eager. "Do join us. I very much would like to introduce you."

He walked purposefully toward them, failing to acknowledge the buzz of surprise and excited whispers that were taking place about the room.

He joined them, standing between Charlotte and the seated Miss Winstead, whose seemed to have removed her attention from Lord Rowton and refixed it firmly on Will.

Lord Rowton cleared his throat, and everyone turned to look at him. Lucinda thought he resembled a yearling she'd once owned. The young horse's reaction to castration had been to stand at the fence that separated him and the other geldings from the resident stallion and watch with quiet and decidedly bitter resignation as the virile Thoroughbred pranced about, displaying his undeniably large and functional manhood for all the world to see.

"I do beg your forgiveness, Lord Rowton," Lucinda began, pausing to push the thought of the defeated gelding from her mind. "Do you know His Grace, the Duke of Clairemont? He arrived in Oxfordshire most unexpectedly."

"Of course," Rowton replied, with remarkably little inflection.

Lucinda acknowledged his comment with a smile and a nod. "I assured His Grace that Aunt Charlotte and I would do everything in our power to show him all that we have to offer. An introduction to what makes our little corner of the country so special would not be complete without attending one of your soirées, would you not agree?"

"Welcome to my home," Lord Rowton said, nodding at Will. He did not appear terribly excited to have a duke in his midst, but he was nothing if not polite, and he added, "Any friend of Lady Charlotte and Lady Lucinda's is, without a doubt, a friend of mine."

"It's a pleasure to meet a close family friend of the Greys," Will replied with a polite, ducal nod.

Lord Rowton returned the pleasantry with a perfunctory bow. "If you will excuse me, I must tell my staff we'll be one more for dinner." He gave the group a vague smile, ventured one last, lonely glance at Lucinda, and took his leave.

"Well, I suppose that leaves you, Miss Winstead," Will said.

The young woman's eyes grew wide as saucers. "I'm sorry, Your Grace?"

Will gave her a devastating smile. "Forgive me. It's most improper to speak before being introduced, but I simply could not wait any longer."

Lucinda took pity on the blushing girl. "Miss Winstead, may I introduce His Grace, the Duke of Clairemont."

Will bowed over her hand.

"Your grace . . ." Miss Winstead began as she rose from her bench, her voice trailing off into confused silence when Will refused to release her hand.

"I am a most devoted student of all things musical. And you," he said, gesturing for her to be seated once again, "are a truly talented musician. Please, gift us with another piece. Do not deny the world your talent."

Miss Winstead giggled and succumbed with blushes and an agreeing nod. She retrieved her hand from Will and thumbed through the sheet music, uttering an "Aha" when she found just the one.

Will left her, returning to stand between Charlotte and Lucinda. The three clapped softly as Miss Winstead readied herself.

"Just what are you playing at?" Lucinda asked Will from behind her fan.

Miss Winstead boldly began a piece by Handel, her pleasure at being singled out by a duke evident in the particular enthusiasm with which she played.

"Your Miss Winstead is a more accomplished player than most young women of her acquaintance," Will murmured. "If Rowton is ever to take notice of the chit, she'll need to make use of any assets at her disposal. I'm simply helping her along."

"How sweet—and quite clever of you, to boot," Aunt Charlotte commented. "If I did not know better, I'd say you're a bit of a romantic, Your Grace."

"You overestimate my capacity for kindness, Lady Charlotte."

A servant entered the room, tapping a small metal gong with a padded mallet. "Dinner is served."

"I think not, Your Grace," Charlotte said, her lips curving into a knowing smile. "My estimation of my fellow man, or woman, is rarely wrong." With that, she tucked her arm into the crook of Will's and allowed him to lead her away.

Will escorted Lady Charlotte to her seat, then looked about for his own, the many-armed epergne placed strategically in the middle of the table making it a rather more difficult task than it should have been.

"I do apologize, Your Grace," Lord Rowton began from his place at the head of the table, "but the servants were hard-pressed to rearrange the placement on such short notice."

Will walked to where Rowton sat, nodding in understanding. "Of course, Lord Rowton, think nothing of
it." He continued on, pausing to stand over Lucinda.

He leaned in slightly so that Rowton would not over-
hear. "Now, where do you think I might find my seat?"

Lucinda's expression, only just a moment before one
of happiness, turned serious as she gestured for Will to
move closer. "About that," she began. "You're seated
next to Lady Shipley, at the end of the table."

Will schooled his features to match Lucinda's. "Is this
information meant to inspire fear in my heart?"

"Well . . . That is to say . . ."

"Lucinda," Will urged gently.

"Do be kind to her, please," she asked solemnly.

Will raised his eyebrows in mock outrage. "You
wound me, Lady Lucinda. Truly," he replied.

"Oh, and do remember to speak directly into the
trumpet. And the louder, the better," she whispered urgently.

Will looked at her quizzically, but thought it best to
end their conversation before any more mysterious odd-
ities were introduced.

"If you'll excuse me, I must join my fellow dining
companions in what I can only assume is the northern
wing, if I am to judge by distance."

Lucinda laughed, then mouthed "Thank you" as Will
left her side and walked to his seat.

Lady Shipley enthusiastically swung the brass trumpet
about and raised it to her ear in anticipation of a conversation.

"Lady Shipley, how delightful to find myself sitting
next to you," Will offered, smiling at the woman as if
she were the only person in the room.

Confusion crossed the older woman's face. "You must
speak into the trumpet," she yelled, pointing at the ap-

paratus as if Will might confuse it with another ear trumpet in the room.

"Bloody hell." *This is going to be far more difficult than I'd anticipated.*

"What was that?" Lady Shipley yelled again.

"I could not agree more," a raspy voice offered from the seat at the very end of the table.

Will turned to take in the man. Slight of build with wispy tufts of white hair and a nose that was far too large for his face, the elderly man stared back at Will with a look of boredom.

"Shipley," the man said, then gestured toward his wife. "And you've met Lady Shipley."

"Alistair, you know it vexes me so when you leave me out of the conversation."

"Precisely," the baron answered, though his wife could not hear.

Will arched an eyebrow in response. "I am Clairemont."

"Ah, the man who has stolen Lady Lucinda away, then."

"I don't know that I would put our courtship in such terms—"

"No need to be polite on my behalf. Rowton had every opportunity to land the woman. Tactically, his campaign was an unmitigated disaster."

"Gentlemen," Lady Shipley pleaded, her voice quivering with curiosity. "Do tell me what you're speaking about."

The baron rolled his eyes then leaned forward toward the trumpet. "This is Clairemont, the 'devil of a duke,' if I recall your words, who's attempting to steal Lucinda away," he yelled, the polite conversations at their end of the table coming to a sudden halt, all eyes turning toward the baron.

Will could feel Lady Shipley shiver next to him, her

ample bosom shaking the table as she threatened to expire on the spot.

"Your Grace," she said in a shrill whisper. Rowton's wolfhound let out a pained whine from the corner of the room.

Will turned to the woman, offering her a sympathetic smile. "Lady Shipley, I have been called far worse, and, I might add, by far less charming individuals. And in truth, I am courting Lady Lucinda, though," he paused, looking down the length of the table with a possessive gaze to where Lucinda sat, "it remains to be seen whether or not the lady's heart will be won."

Lucinda's eyebrows shot shockingly close to the crown of her head while every other woman in the room sighed with sentimental enthusiasm. The men simply took the opportunity to begin eating.

"Ah, the soup," the baron said, a servant having appeared silently at his elbow with a silver tureen. Another servant carefully ladled a portion of the white soup into his bowl, then moved to fill Lady Shipley's.

Will waited patiently while his own bowl was seen to, then brought a spoonful of the fragrant soup to his lips, the scent of chicken broth and a hint of peppercorn filling his nostrils. "Tell me, Lady Shipley," he began, shouting into her trumpet. "Have you always resided in Oxfordshire?"

"Glutton for punishment," the baron said under his breath, then quietly slurped up a spoonful of soup.

Will acknowledged the man's comment with a perfunctory glance then turned his attention back to Lady Shipley.

"*That* is a fascinating story, Your Grace," she replied, her eyes bright with excitement.

The courses flew by in a blur of savory and sweet until the end of the meal was at hand. Will popped a walnut into his mouth and smiled at Lady Shipley.

He would have been hard-pressed to repeat most of what she'd shared, the pace at which she narrated simply too swift to follow. But one thing he knew without a doubt: He'd enjoyed himself, because *she* had.

Good God, what is becoming of me?

The women began to stir, Rowton's great-aunt being the first to rise from her chair and the others following suit.

"I do hope Miss Winstead will honor us with a song," Lady Shipley announced, nodding to her husband and standing.

Will rose and gave Lady Shipley a charming smile. "It was truly a pleasure, Lady Shipley."

"Oh, Your Grace, I dominated the entire conversation," she replied, color heating her cheeks.

Will could not argue. But more troubling, he didn't want to.

"When I remember Oxfordshire, it will be with great fondness. Do you know why?" he asked, speaking into the trumpet.

"The white soup?" she replied, clearly pleased with her cleverness.

"No, not the soup. You, Lady Shipley."

He bowed politely to the baroness, noticing as he rose that Lucinda was watching him. The smile on her face indicated she'd been doing so for some time.

He returned her smile, though the emotions playing across her face jangled his nerves.

Was he unsettled because he'd so thoroughly enjoyed an evening spent in the company of a woman such as Lady Shipley? Or unsettled because Lucinda had so thoroughly enjoyed his enjoyment?

Or maybe—

Ah, hell. The night was too fine to pick apart one's feelings.

"Come, Your Grace, do sit down," Shipley instructed.

The port will appear any moment. Rowton's port is the best in the county—and the reason I allow myself to be dragged to these dinners at all."

Port is just the thing, Will thought to himself, then obeyed Shipley's command and reclaimed his chair.

14

"Our country air appears to have failed you," Lady Charlotte said, approaching the bench where Will sat in the morning sun.

The gravel path ran throughout the large kitchen garden just off the north end of the Bampton Manor. He'd chosen this particular place to sit because he was sure no one would find him there.

He shaded his eyes with his hand in an attempt to block out the bright sunlight. "And how is that, Lady Charlotte?"

She joined him on the stone bench. "The country is known for its restorative qualities. And you, Your Grace, look anything but restored." She settled herself on the bench, neatly smoothing out the fabric of her bishop's blue morning dress before folding her hands in her lap. "Did you attempt to rest in a tree?"

"I must say, Lady Charlotte," Will propped his elbows on his knees and grinned at her with honest amusement, "you are the most surprising of all the Furies."

"How dare you say such a thing!" she exclaimed, pretending irritation. Unfortunately, the smile tugging at the corners of her mouth gave her away.

"How dare I what? Make reference to society's affectionate name for the three of you?"

"No, not that," Lady Charlotte answered. "I no longer take notice of such silliness after all of these many years. No, I speak of your inference that I am the least colorful of the group."

Will ran his hands over his face, beard stubble rough against his palms. "With all due respect, Lady Charlotte, is that not a good thing?"

Lady Charlotte paused to consider, frowning at the rows of green herbs that neatly unfolded before them. "Mmmm, you may have a point, Your Grace."

The two sat in companionable silence for a short while, entertained by a honeybee that buzzed busily around a tuft of daffodils.

Will would have preferred not to have to speak, but he liked Lady Charlotte too well to be rude.

"Will Lady Lucinda be joining us?" he asked, looking at the manor.

The bee completed his business and flew off, his route cutting between the two humans.

"No, not this morning," Lady Charlotte said, flinching slightly when the bee came close to her shoulder. "Lady Thornton, a dear friend of Lucinda's from childhood, invited her to call."

Will already knew Lucinda's whereabouts; the report of her invitation from Lady Thornton had been relayed by Weston during their morning ride. Still, Will kept up the charade, pretending not to know Lucinda's plans rather than risk the elderly woman's suspicions.

Lady Charlotte squinted at Will, her assessing gaze traveling over his face. "You look exactly like your father, you know."

The muscles in Will's jaw contracted, his teeth clenching of their own accord. "So I've been told," he responded, his voice flat, unengaged.

"I meant that as a compliment," Lady Charlotte said quietly, returning her gaze to the rows of green shoots before her. "He was the most handsome man I had ever seen," she continued, her countenance softening. "Every single woman that season wanted him as a husband."

"Even you?" Will asked, surprise punctuating his question.

"Even me," she said. "But it was not to be. He had designs on your mother from the very beginning. No other woman compared."

Will laughed, a short, hard sound. "No, I'm sure they didn't. It is difficult to imagine any other woman being quite so perfect a victim for the Duke of Clairemont."

Lady Charlotte's gaze turned abruptly to Will, her eyes flashing with anger. "You'll do well to remember we speak of your mother."

Will stood swiftly, forcing down the urge to reach out and break something. "Pardon me, Lady Charlotte," he said tightly, "but it's not something I'm likely to forget."

Much as he'd tried.

His father may have been a monster, but his mother had been something much worse.

She had been . . . She'd been . . .

Nothing.

She had been nothing. She had watched when his father had beaten him, and then— No, she hadn't even done that. She had turned away. She had allowed it all to happen, never once lifting her voice in his defense.

He was alone in this world. The message had been clear. If he sought comfort, if he sought protection, he was on his own.

"I was lucky enough to count her as a dear friend," Lady Charlotte said quietly. "A force to be reckoned with, Her Grace was. Did you know that?"

Will began to count backwards in his mind from ten to one. "Is that so?" he asked in response, hardly aware that he'd done so.

Charlotte stood and joined him. "She really was extraordinary, which is why, I would imagine, the duke chose her."

"She could have said no."

"You know as well as I that to refuse him would have been unthinkable. He was a duke. Never mind the fact that she loved him."

Having reached the number one, Will began to count again. "More fool her."

Lady Charlotte's fingers closed over his coat sleeve. "No one knew what existed beneath your father's charming exterior. He drew people to him like moths to a flame. She loved him and assumed he felt the same. We all did. It was not until after the marriage that he showed himself for what he really was."

"I've no need to hear this, Lady Charlotte," Will interrupted, looking down at the elderly woman. "I do not mean to offend, but I know only too well what kind of man my father was."

Lady Charlotte rearranged her shawl, holding it tighter as a slight breeze picked up from the north. "That may be true, Your Grace, but your mother is a mystery to you, clearly."

He came so close to telling her, in scathing terms, just why he was the only one who truly knew what went on in the house with his father and mother.

But her eyes as she peered up earnestly stopped him. They were so like Lucinda's in color and shape, yet uniquely her own.

"Your father was a tyrant, that much you know," Lady Charlotte began. "The demands he placed on your mother were . . ."

She hesitated, the distress such memories caused clearly written across her face. "Well, the duchess did everything she could to preserve herself, but it was pointless. He drained her of life, of confidence, of love—

of everything that she was, until there was not a recognizable trace of the vibrant girl she'd once been."

Will looked hard at the woman as she spoke. He concentrated on the information as if it were part of an assignment, the thought of the impact such revelations could make on an unguarded heart pushing him to focus.

"He seemed to take pleasure in robbing her of joy, and when you were born—"

"Stop."

Lady Charlotte grasped his hand in hers. "I do not mean to distress you, Your Grace," she said in a gentle tone, "but I feel it is important that you know the truth, no matter how painful."

Clearly, she was going to force him to hear her confidences through to the end. He wanted to run. Hell, he wanted to hide. But there was no escape. Funny how a unassuming old woman could manage what the most hardened of criminals could not.

Reluctantly, he accepted his fate and nodded for her to continue.

Lady Charlotte acknowledged his acquiescence and continued. "When you were born, your father used your existence against her, threatening to take you away from your mother if she didn't do exactly as he asked." She patted his hand then gestured for him to walk along the path with her. "She knew all too well what he was capable of and she could not risk losing you. And so she agreed, and lost herself in the hellish bargain."

Will felt numb; the anger he'd suffered for so many years over his mother's indifference wasn't easily defeated. He wanted to argue with Lady Charlotte. Couldn't his mother have escaped? Taken him to live with her parents? Hidden on the Continent somewhere?

But with brutal honesty, he had to acknowledge that these scenarios would have been impossible. His father had the power, and the legal right, to track her down like a common criminal and do with her—and the boys—whatever he wished.

"The duchess worked very hard to protect you, and all on her own, I might add," Lady Charlotte said, interrupting Will's thoughts. "He forced her to cut ties with all those she held dear, including me. Despite this, she spent every waking hour doing what she could to ensure your safety and that of your brother. It broke her heart to refrain from showing her love for you boys, but she knew your father's temper would only be more vicious if she had."

Will closed his eyes momentarily, the spring sunshine warming on his face. Lady Charlotte's determined championship of his mother and blunt condemnation of his father was almost more than he could absorb. He'd made assumptions about his mother's reasons for her actions. Could he have been so completely wrong?

"Why didn't she tell me?"

"Would you have believed her?"

Will knew the answer without even stopping to think: no.

"You do not strike me as a man who dwells on the past, Your Grace."

"Meaning?"

"Meaning," the elderly woman began, "that while there is nothing to be done about what has transpired, there is always ground to be gained in the future."

Will smiled wryly at Lady Charlotte. "Am I to understand you see a heartwarming reconciliation in my future?"

"What you do with this information is, of course, solely your decision, but I would think a man of your intelligence would hardly let such an opportunity pass without some deliberation."

She tugged gently on Will's arm and turned toward

the house. "There is so much to be learned from your parents' actions, would you not agree?"

Will nodded absentmindedly, still trying to make sense of all he'd heard during the last few moments.

"A woman such as your mother, so intelligent and capable, is still vulnerable when it comes to affairs of the heart. Most women are."

"Yes, quite," he replied, then stopped. "Lady Charlotte, have you something else to say?"

She urged him into motion once again, continuing their stroll along the graveled path. "I'm certain you must realize how deeply my sisters and I care for Lucinda."

"Of course."

"You are in a unique position, Your Grace," Lady Charlotte said, pausing to snap a sprig of mint from a raised herb bed. She twirled it between her forefinger and thumb. "Do not let what happened to your mother happen again."

Will stiffened. Of course she would be concerned for Lucinda. Her beloved niece was being courted by the Duke of Clairemont, whose own father had destroyed a woman. Despite the logic of her concern, however, he felt only outrage and violent rejection of the possibility that he would harm Lucinda. "You think highly of me, then?" he answered coolly.

She looked directly at him. "Do not misunderstand me, Your Grace. You are not your father. But . . ." She hesitated, weighing her words carefully. "I have watched the two of you together. Lucinda cares for you—something she has not allowed herself to do with any other man."

She held the sprig of mint to her nose, her hand visibly shaking. "I should not be speaking to you of this, and normally I would never presume to invade your or Lucinda's privacy. But though I know you to be an honorable man—and I do, without a doubt," she continued, tossing the bit of greenery back into the garden bed, "a woman in love is a fragile thing, Your Grace, a very fragile thing indeed."

Will's heart could stand no more. He wanted nothing more than to ride straight to Gentleman John Jackson's and lose himself in the battering and blows until the physical pain was all he felt.

"Promise me you'll take care with her," Lady Charlotte said in a low tone, nearly pleading.

Will had always operated with the assured confidence of one who knew the difference between right and wrong. Truth and falsities. And now? All was in tatters and Will did not know how to put his world back together.

He relied on the only weapon left in his exhausted arsenal and answered the woman with convincing assuredness.

"You have my word."

A bar of bright sunlight marked the open doors at the end of the aisle between the stalls, but the stable's hay-scented interior was shaded and cool. Lucinda stood in Cleopatra's stall, braiding the rough silk of the mare's black tail as Winnie's foal watched her curiously from where he hid.

Cleopatra stood patiently, reaching out to nuzzle the foal now and again.

"Winnie would be proud, Cleo," Lucinda commented, the weight of such a loss slightly lessened by the lanky foal at Cleo's side.

The mare swished her tail lightly, twitching it from Lucinda's grasp.

"Now look what you've done," Lucinda scolded.

She caught up the thick length of hair and started

over, secretly pleased that her time with Cleopatra was extended.

"How is the colt today?"

Lucinda looked up. Will leaned lazily against the stall gate, his amused half grin making her want to kiss him right where his lips curved upward.

She smiled in response. "He is exceedingly handsome, is he not?"

He slid the lock free and pushed the wooden gate open, strolling inside the stall with its deep layer of bedding straw. He slowly approached the colt, extending a hand toward him. The colt looked ready to bolt, then sniffed Will and decided against it, his pink tongue darting out to lick at Will's palm. All at once the colt relaxed, moving toward Will until he threatened to climb into his lap.

"You've an admirer," Lucinda laughed.

Cleo pinned her ears and glared at Will, hardly happy about her new ward's enthusiasm.

Will backed up and allowed the mare to nose the colt closer to her side.

"Do not take offense," Lucinda offered, finishing the braid. "Cleopatra is only doing as any good mother should."

"Cleopatra?" Will lifted an eyebrow. "Surely not the same Cleopatra who bested an entire pack of stallions—in both the Ascot and the Doncaster Cup?"

Lucinda smiled, delighted he'd recognized Cleopatra, and gestured for him to hand her the length of red ribbon looped over the gate.

"The one and only," Lucinda replied, taking the ribbon from Will's hand and securing the end of the mare's braid. "Though, with any luck, that distinction will be short-lived," she added. "In due time, she'll be foaling champions."

"And the sire?"

Lucinda smiled. "King Solomon's Mine, of course."

"Bloody hell."

Lucinda's smile widened. "Really, Your Grace."

"Call me Will, you silly chit." He covered her hand with his much larger one, capturing it against the mare's warm hide. "The surprising bit here is not my interest in horse breeding, but yours."

"Does it make me less appealing? That I have a brain and choose to employ it for such a masculine pursuit?"

"You know damn well it only makes you more irresistible to me," he answered in a gruff tone, his eyes heating. "Or have you not learned all there is to know about the infamous Iron Will?"

Cleopatra shifted her weight and a loud gurgling sound echoed through her belly.

Distracted, Lucinda didn't answer Will; instead, she slipped her hand from under his and circled the horse, stopping on the far side of the mare. She frowned, worry creasing her brow as she examined her beloved mare's mid-section.

"Lucinda, it's nothing more than her digestive tract," Will said in an assuring tone. "Cleopatra is not Winnie."

She bent low to scan the mare's stomach. "But what if it is the grass? Or perhaps the oats. All of the horses receive the exact same oats."

As she rose, from the corner of her eye she glimpsed Cleopatra's braided tail, slowly rising.

"Oh—!"

Too late. The cloud of noxious gas that exited noisily from Cleopatra's posterior slowly filled the stall with a decidedly horsey smell.

"I suppose this means we've identified the stomach ailment?" Will said, his face solemn, though his eyes laughed at Lucinda over Cleopatra's wide back.

Lucinda felt her cheeks grow hot as she struggled to find an appropriate response. "Well . . ." she began, then burst out laughing, the worry she'd felt only moments before dissipating with each giggle.

Will cocked an eyebrow, feigning disappointment, and attempted to maintain an unmoving expression. He failed miserably, his deep, throaty laughter joining hers.

"You," he told her when their mirth subsided, "are a bad influence for a man struggling to act like a gentleman."

"You would be hard-pressed to find anyone who would disagree with you on that point, were they made aware of the last few moments."

Somehow, Cleopatra's impolite emission had put Lucinda at ease. Throughout the day, she'd been unable to focus on anything other than thoughts of Will. Could she expect intimacy would now play a regular role in their relationship? Because, God help her, she certainly did hope so. And most importantly, what happened next?

In all honesty, Lucinda had failed to entertain the possibility that she might fall in love with Will, so there had never been the need to think beyond a brief courtship and the eventual claiming of King Solomon's Mine before they parted ways.

But she had fallen in love. Fallen so completely, in fact, that she barely recognized herself now, the need for him akin to her requirement for air or food.

"Will," she began, finding the courage to look into his dark eyes, "what are we meant to do now?"

"First, I suggest removing ourselves from the stall before Cleopatra relieves herself again." His voice held a smile.

"That is not what I meant, and you know it."

He ducked under Cleopatra's neck and joined Lucinda, settling his hands on each side of her waist. "I believe you know what comes next. I've taken your virginity," he murmured, mindful of the presence of stablehands on the far side of the barn. "For a man and woman in our social circle, more than a simple thank you is required."

He backed her against the wall, his hard frame pressing hers from chest to thigh. He cupped her face in one palm and traced her lower lip with his thumb, his hooded gaze intent on her mouth.

"Then you would marry me out of obligation?" she asked, trying desperately to ease the dread constricting her chest.

He muttered something she couldn't understand and replaced his thumb with his mouth, kissing her tenderly at first, then coaxing her mouth open with the glide of his tongue over the seam of her lips.

Lucinda couldn't stop her response, despite the unanswered question. She slid her arms around his neck and pulled him closer, the tips of her breasts pressed against his chest. The sensation was sweet torture and she shivered, her body quivering with anticipation.

He lifted his head to look at her.

"It would be an honor, my dear Lucinda. Never an obligation," he whispered. "Do not doubt my feelings for you. Ever."

She sighed as he took her mouth again, their mutual need growing hotter by the second.

The rattling of wheels, accompanied by piercing, tuneless whistling shattered the spell that held them. Will's arms tightened, his head lifted, and then he dropped to the stall floor, taking Lucinda with him. He rolled, putting her against the wall with himself between her and the horses.

The loud noises stopped in front of Cleopatra's stall,

followed by the sound of hay being shifted. "'Ello, my beauty, how we doing today, luv?"

A large forkful of fine grass hay landed in the feeder just above Will's head, bits of dried green leaves and stalks sifting over the two hiding behind the mare and foal. In her enthusiasm to get at the hay, Cleopatra nearly stepped on Will. He didn't move for fear of being seen by the man outside the stall.

"'Ere you go, then," the stablehand whispered, "don't go tellin' the other horses, now. I always save the best for you." The sound of Cleopatra biting and crunching an apple made Lucinda smile despite her perilous position.

The rolling sound started up again, accompanied by the off-key whistling, and signaled the man's movement toward the large stable doors.

The two hiding in the stall waited until they heard the familiar thud of the doors being pushed shut.

Will rose and helped Lucinda to her feet, bending to brush at the hay clinging to her dress. "I can honestly say I've never been in a fix quite like this one," he said, finishing with her dress and turning his attention to her hair.

"Nor I," Lucinda replied, the ridiculousness of her answer causing Will to smile.

With a few quick swipes he knocked the hay from his own attire and shook his head to free his hair of smaller pieces. "Come," he said, taking her hand and leading her around Cleopatra and the colt. He opened the stall door noiselessly and poked his head out to look up and down the aisle.

"It's clear." He pulled her out and gestured for her to follow the stablehand's route. "I'll give you plenty of time to reach the house before I follow."

Lucinda hesitated, torn, wanting desperately for him to pull her back into the stall and continue where they'd left off when the stablehand interrupted them. But she knew how risky such a thing would be.

So instead, she went up on her toes and kissed him, reveling in the heat of his body pressed to hers for just one more moment before leaving him.

15

Lucinda was exhausted, but weariness had been unavoidable. Despite drooping eyelids and tired muscles, she smiled with joy as she gazed out the carriage window at the spring greenery rolling by. She'd awakened early in order to spend as much time as possible with Winnie's foal before leaving.

The little colt had already stolen her heart, his resemblance to Winnie remarkable. He had her color and her kind eye, but more than that, he possessed her sweet and inquisitive nature, making him everything Lucinda had hoped he would be.

"Thinking on the foal?" Charlotte asked from across the carriage.

Lucinda met her gaze. "Indeed. Such a strong little one he is," she replied, leaning back against the squabs. The deep blue velvet cushions were soft and comfortable.

Charlotte took up her knitting, the needles clicking as she expertly set stitches in sunshine yellow yarn. "Does he look to be a racer?"

"I can't say for sure at this point, but he certainly has the conformation needed. We'll just have to wait and see what sort of passion for racing he has."

Lucinda glanced out the coach window, where King Solomon's Mine trotted beside the carriage. Will controlled the powerful stallion with ease, despite his injuries. His long-limbed body balanced in the saddle with an athleticism and competence born of long practice.

He wasn't wearing a hat. His thick black hair perfectly suited his untamed nature and was utterly, sinfully sensuous as it lifted and blew back from his brow in the light breeze. He wore a many-caped greatcoat, his shoulders strong and straight. She had a swift, unbidden mental image of candlelight gleaming over his bare shoulders, the muscles flexing as he held himself over her . . .

"Now, that's a different smile altogether."

Distracted, Lucinda frowned in confusion. "I'm sorry, Aunt, what did you ask?"

Charlotte ceased knitting, threaded the long needles into the bright yarn, and tucked them into the basket on the seat next to her. "I didn't ask a thing. I simply made an observation concerning the smile that until quite recently resided on your lovely face."

"Oh," Lucinda continued, still recovering from the vivid image of Will imprinted in her mind. "I'm just so happy about the foal."

"You do not fool me for a moment."

Lucinda's brows furrowed, the likelihood that they would return to their rightful place anytime soon becoming slimmer by the moment. "I'm afraid I've no idea what you're talking about, Aunt Charlotte."

"That," Charlotte leaned forward to point out the window, "is what I am talking about."

"King Solomon's Mine?"

Charlotte rolled her eyes, reminding Lucinda of herself. "My dear girl, I would think after all these years you would realize you cannot hide things from me."

Lucinda flushed under her aunt's knowing gaze, the carriage growing warmer. The coziness of her cashmere shawl, so welcome moments before, now threatened to overheat her. "You're very cryptic." She pulled the shawl from her shoulders and laid it on the seat beside her with meticulous care.

"I concede that cozening your aunt Bessie doesn't take much effort, what with her head being constantly occupied by some drama or another, making it fairly simple to conceal an assortment of truths," Charlotte replied, ticking off on her fingers the points she intended to make clear. "Victoria presents more of a challenge, I suppose, but in the end she admires the sound of her voice to such a degree that even Prinny himself could convince the woman of his need to gain weight, if given enough of a chance. I love my sisters but there is no point in beating about the bush."

Lucinda peeled off her gloves, since removing her shawl had not provided a sufficiently cooling effect.

Charlotte folded her hands in her lap and pinned Lucinda with a direct, unswerving gaze. "I, on the other hand, listen when spoken to—and, quite honestly, oftentimes when I am not. And you, my dear Lucinda, are in love with the duke."

A fine line of perspiration dotted Lucinda's upper lip, but she resisted the urge to wipe it away. The look in Charlotte's eyes told her that denying her feelings for Will would be pointless. She'd never witnessed her aunt in such form, the usual calmness of her demeanor infused with a blunt, straightforward assurance that surprised her.

Lucinda opened her mouth to reply, then shut it, realizing belatedly that she wasn't sure of what she should say. "Aunt Charlotte, you surprise me."

"In what way, dear?"

"Well," Lucinda began somewhat nervously, "I would have expected such a conversation to have been initiated by Aunt Victoria, her abrupt nature seems made for such things. Or even Bessie, whose love of the dramatic you so expertly noted earlier. But you?"

Lucinda paused, not wanting to offend her aunt, though eager to be honest. "I've always assumed that your quiet, calm exterior applied to your character in general. I felt sure any currents running beneath your even demeanor would be anything but fierce. Clearly, I was wrong."

Charlotte leaned forward and patted Lucinda on the knee. "Think nothing of it, my dear. Society's assumption that I am a shy, retiring flower is of great use to me. You've no idea what people venture to say in my presence!"

The two women laughed together, putting Lucinda a bit more at ease.

"But as to your duke—that's very deep play," Charlotte said, returning to her earlier line of conversation without preamble.

"But what of King Solomon's Mine—"

"You would risk your heart for a horse?" her aunt countered, the disbelief in her voice communicating to Lucinda exactly what Charlotte thought of such a thing.

"It is not as if I planned for any of this to happen," she protested.

Charlotte twitched her skirts, straightening the Devonshire traveling dress with precise movements. "Well, of course not. No woman ever does."

"Is it such a bad thing, to fall in love?"

"Then you do admit that you love him?" Charlotte pressed, the concern in her words echoing the worry in her eyes.

Lucinda blinked as tears welled, the relief of unburdening herself nearly overcoming her. "I do."

Charlotte took a deep breath and looked out the window at Will. "And does he return your affection?"

"Yes," Lucinda responded in a resolute tone. There was no need to tell her aunt that he'd yet to say those three words to her. His actions had communicated everything she needed to know regarding his feelings.

Charlotte returned her troubled gaze to Lucinda. "Do you plan to marry him?"

Lucinda squared her shoulders and sat back. "He's given every indication that he intends to propose. It is simply a matter of timing. There are strict social rules to be followed, after all, not to mention a trio of protective aunts to be convinced."

"You know his heart, then, my dear."

"I wonder if any woman has ever known a man's heart more," she answered simply, looking out at Will with a longing she could not bother to deny.

Charlotte reached for Lucinda's hand and took it in her own, squeezing gently. "I cannot say I give you my blessing without some hesitation, my dear. I believe the duke to be an honorable man, and I hope for your sake he is," she said, squeezing Lucinda's hand once more before releasing it and settling back against the cushions. "Now, on to the matter of convincing Bessie and Victoria."

"I'd quite hoped you would puzzle that bit out."

"Impudent girl," Charlotte cried, winking at Lucinda with delight.

The return trip to London had been uneventful, just as Will and his fellow Corinthians had hoped it would be. He'd kept his distance from Lucinda as best he could, riding alongside the carriage. When they'd stopped for the night, he'd convinced the Rosemont Inn's keeper to place Lucinda and her aunt in the same room, in order to keep them safe.

After, he'd seen the two women to their home before returning to Clairemont House, the greeting he received from his mother and brother awkward at best. Lady Charlotte's revelations concerning his parents had sunk in for the most part, no small feat considering the havoc they'd wreaked on his heart, but Will had yet to come to terms with his newfound feelings.

As for Michael, their heated discussion in the ducal bedchamber had been the last they'd spoken before he'd left for Bampton, and the tension returned the moment Will walked into the family residence.

Will literally jumped at the chance to leave when news of Lucinda's impending shopping trip reached his ears. Poor Sol hardly had the time for a proper meal before Will pulled him from his stall and urged him on toward New Bond Street.

Will watched, amazed, while Lucinda and her maid walk along the fashionable location. She'd been absent from London less than a week, but somehow the woman apparently found it necessary to empty the shops. The multiple packages Mary carried appeared ready to topple the outspoken maid at any moment.

Gravity being what it was, the round hatbox nestled just beneath Mary's chin wobbled, then fell to the ground, a prim pink bonnet coming to land squarely in the street. The women giggled then made haste to recover the hat along with the remaining boxes that had fallen as well. Two large men appeared out of nowhere, their fine yet ill-fitting clothes causing the hair to stand up on Will's neck. "Bloody hell," he said under his breath, pushing away from the wall he'd been leaning against. He walked swiftly toward the two women.

He quickened his pace, using his size to his advantage as he forced his way through the afternoon crowd. The men approached the two from behind, surprising Mary and causing her to drop several of the packages she'd managed to retrieve. They looked to be making their apologies and offering assistance as the women gestured down the street to where their carriage waited.

Will stepped out into the street and began to jog

toward the group, the oncoming coaches easier to dodge than the current flow of shoppers on the walkway. One abruptly took hold of Lucinda's arm, the other Mary's, and forced the women into an unfamiliar carriage, then disappeared into the crowd.

"Christ," he gasped, breaking into a run and narrowly dodging a curricle as it careened down New Bond Street. The hot breath of a matched pair of horses blew past his cheek, their sharp hooves barely clearing his shoulder. He righted himself and took off again, dread growing in his gut.

He darted toward the carriage. The driver looked up, his eyes widening when he saw Will. He cracked his whip and the bays harnessed to the carriage leapt to life, taking off as if the very fires of hell licked at their hooves.

Despite his strength and speed, Will knew without a doubt that he could not single-handedly stop the oncoming carriage; his options ran out as the horses bore down on him. He lunged out of their way at the last second and went airborne as he launched himself. He grabbed the decorative wooden lip circling the carriage roof with both hands. The conveyance swayed dangerously, rocking under his sudden weight.

He pulled himself up, kicking at the stairs until they fell.

"Get off, damn ye." The driver turned his whip on Will, slashing at the knuckles of one hand until his hold broke. He slammed back against the carriage door and the sound of Mary's terrified screams reached his ears.

He pulled himself up one-handed, his body hitting the carriage with aggravated force. Ignoring the pain coarsing through his wounds, Will stretched to reach the ornamental lip, his right hand closed once more over the carved wood. This time, his feet found the lowered steps before the driver's whip could hammer him. One-handed, he yanked the door open.

A man waited just inside, a knife at the ready. His soulless eyes held no fear when they met Will's.

Will recognized the professional calm of a seasoned criminal and did not waste any time. His balance on the steps was precarious, the swaying of the coach threatening to shake him loose at any moment. He caught the thug off guard, knocking his knife from his hand with one swift blow to his wrist. Before the criminal could recover, Will grabbed a fistful of his hair and yanked, pulling him toward the doorway and out of the carriage. Will saw the man hit the ground, and glimpsed Weston pounding toward them on his gelding, four more riders close on his heels.

Will dismissed the man, knowing the agents behind him would deal with him. He swung his body through the open carriage door, bracing himself against the rocking, unsteady carriage floor. Lucinda was pressed against the far wall, her hair flowing about her in wild curls, the sleeve of her gown ripped. Mary was clinging to her mistress's side, her eyes wild with fright.

"Lucinda," Will said, gesturing for her to come to him.

The terror on her pale face eased; she slid across the seat, reaching for him. "Who are these men?" she cried.

"I'll explain later," he answered. "We must go at once."

Lucinda looked at Will as if he were mad. "But we're moving."

"Yes." He glanced out the swinging carriage door. Weston raced beside them, keeping pace with the coach. His gaze met Will's and he nodded.

"Surely you're not suggesting that we—"

He didn't have time to explain. Will thought it best to

take Lucinda by surprise. He spun her around, her back to his chest, and wrapped his free arm around her waist.

"Weston will catch you," he told her. "Watch out for the carriage door."

Before she had time to protest, he swept her off her feet and moved them outside the coach. He ignored her muffled shriek of terror, balancing on the steps as he passed her to Weston, one-armed, the other anchoring them with his grip on the edge of the carriage roof.

The moment he felt Weston take her weight, he returned for Mary, pulling the now screaming maid from the carriage and depositing her into the arms of a second mounted Corinthian.

Will yelled an obscenity at the driver, then leapt out and away from the carriage, tucking his body as he hit the ground, rolling across the brick street.

The wheel of an overturned drayman's cart stopped him, his body jolting against the load of spilled vegetables. He braced his hands on the ground and pushed himself upright. The pain he felt all over his body seemed manageable enough for now, which probably meant he hadn't broken any bones.

He swung his head, searching the street. Several yards away, he found Lucinda, standing near Mary and Weston. Relief that she was in one piece washed over him, making him light-headed for one unsteady moment. Three agents joined the three and Weston left them to set off on a dead run toward Will, the reins of his gelding in his hands. He slowed as he neared but Will waved him on, determined the carriage driver be caught. Weston swung aboard the gelding and quickly disappeared around a corner.

Steadier now, Will walked toward Lucinda. More Corinthians had joined her, clearly unnerving her further. Her expression lightened when Will reached the small group and she stepped closer to him.

"You two." Will gestured to Hopkins and Newell.
"Assist Weston and the others." The men climbed
aboard their mounts and set off at once, leaving Lucinda
and Will with the three remaining Corinthians. "Thomas,
I've need of your horse. You three take Lady Lucinda
and Mary to the nearest safe house and stay with them
until I return." He caught Lucinda's hand in his.
"You're safe now. Go with my men and do as they ask.
I'll return as soon as I can." He kissed her fingers, the
only outward show of affection he was allowed, and
leapt aboard Thomas's horse.

She was silent; standing there in the street, covered in
dust and bruises, she looked up at him with a face full of
confusion and tears.

He could not delay, no matter how much he wanted to
comfort her and tell her everything would be all right.

He nodded at the officers then kicked the horse into a
run, urging him on with grim determination.

"Can you tell me . . ." Lucinda paused, unsure precisely what she wanted to ask. The last hour had left her
stunned and bewildered. Her mind continued to race,
trying to make sense of it all.

"About the men who brought you here?" the woman
prompted. She dipped a clean cloth in a bowl of warm
water and gently, carefully, washed the dirt from Lucinda's cheek.

Lucinda grimaced as she sat still on the settee, the
sting telling her that a scrape existed beneath the grime.
"Yes. To begin with anyway."

"Unfortunately, no, I cannot. But I can tell you that
you're perfectly safe. There's not a man among them
who would harm you."

Dressed in a silk wrapper and matching nightrail of
deep emerald green, the woman's lush form was volup-
tuously curved. Her thick sable hair was piled atop her

head, held in place by emerald ribbons woven artfully through the loose curls. There was no denying she was attractive, her full rouged lips, almond-shaped eyes, and milky complexion only adding to her appeal. But even distracted as Lucinda was, she sensed something faintly sad in her demeanor.

"May I speak freely?" Lucinda asked as the woman eased the damp cloth over her scraped cheek once more.

"I know no other way, my lady," she replied. "I am Minerva."

The woman stroked the cloth over Lucinda's fore-head, frowning in apology when Lucinda winced. "I'm sorry. If we don't clean the dirt from your cuts, they won't heal properly." She turned away to rinse the cloth in the basin of water. "Now, what would you like to know? I will answer as much as I can."

"Is this . . ." Lucinda peered around the room, searching for the best way to phrase her question. "That is to say, are you . . ."

"A kept woman?" Minerva interrupted, amused. "What gave it away?" She looked about her. "The garish colors, perhaps? An overabundance of pillows, lace, and ribbons?" She paused, looking down at her ample bosom in the seductive silk. "Did my clothing tell you this isn't Mayfair?"

Lucinda swept the room with an assessing gaze before treating Minerva to the same considering look. "All of the above, actually."

Minerva laughed, setting the bowl aside and handing Lucinda a fresh linen cloth. "He said you were a smart one. He never mentioned that you were funny as well."

"He?" Lucinda queried, though intuition and the queasy roll of her stomach told her she already knew the answer.

"You are correct in your assumption," Minerva answered, ignoring Lucinda's second query, and instead addressing her surroundings. "This," she said, standing and turning with a graceful flourish of one slim hand and arm, "belongs to a very wealthy and powerful gentleman, though I often wonder at the power of a man who would give me all of this for what I give him in return."

Lucinda decided against pressing for an answer regarding the man who had spoken of her intelligence.

Instead, she smiled at the woman, quietly applauding her performance, and followed her lead. "Well, he sounds very much like all of the wealthy and powerful men of my acquaintance, I'm afraid."

Minerva's eyes widened in surprise, then lit with amusement. "I like you," she said and rejoined Lucinda at the settee, next to the folded green gown and shawl. "You'll want to change out of your gown, I imagine."

Lucinda looked down, surprised by the damage she saw. The once lovely yellow muslin was stained and smeared with mud, the diminutive ivy-print background of the fabric scarcely visible beneath the grime. One sleeve was completely gone, the other holding on by mere threads, and the stocking on her right leg was torn below the knee.

Disconcerted, she felt she really should be embarrassed by her appearance, but given the events of the afternoon, she simply couldn't muster the energy.

"Would you like some help?" Minerva asked matter-of-factly, making it clear she thought none the less of Lucinda for her current state of disarray.

"Thank you, but I can manage."

Minerva ignored Lucinda and instead pulled her to rise and spun her around. "I've seen worse," she said, loosening the gown down the back with nimble fingers. "Remember where you are; there's no need for you to feel anything but superior. It's simply the way of the world."

Minerva urged Lucinda to raise her arms, then gently guided the torn material over her head. She deftly unlaced the corset beneath and left Lucinda to remove soft half boots, garters, and torn stockings.

Lucinda dropped the ruined silk stockings atop her boots on the floor next to the settee.

"Lift your arms," Minerva commanded, and when Lucinda complied, the other woman slipped the green gown over her head.

Lucinda's view of Minerva was briefly interrupted by the gown. She pushed her arms into the sleeves and the fabric fell down her body, covering her to her toes. She twitched it into place, surprised by the simple cut of the soft cotton gown. There was nothing overtly seductive about it; in fact, it reminded her of her own gowns. She glanced up and found Minerva watching her.

"We do not always dress to seduce," she explained, reaching for a shawl and offering it to Lucinda. While she adjusted the length of cashmere around her shoulders, Minerva stood back and surveyed her work. A quick satisfied nod of her head said she was pleased with the results. "Much better."

A firm knock rattled the door.

"That will be *him*," Minerva said knowingly. "Take care, my lady." She crossed the room and pulled open the door.

"Your Grace," Minerva said, moving aside to allow him entrance. She gestured for him to come closer and went up on tiptoe to whisper in his ear before stepping into the hall, closing the door firmly behind her.

Will stalked toward Lucinda, the grim set of his features frightening her. "Will?" Relief that he was here, his body whole and safe from harm, flooded her and tears threatened.

Will reached her and wrapped around her. "Are you all right?" he asked, his voice hoarse with emotion.

She breathed in the scent of his skin and was instantly comforted. "Yes, I am now." She brought her arms around his waist and pressed closer. "Are you?"

He kissed the top of her head. "Of course. Am I not Iron Will?"

"Don't tease, Will," Lucinda said, leaning back to look up at him. "What happened in the carriage? Who were those men? Where is Mary?"

"Mary is safe. Weston saw to that himself?"

"What is going on?" she pressed, her heart beating faster. The hard planes of his face were unreadable.

"Did Minerva tell you anything?" His voice was desparate, demanding she answer.

"No, nothing of consequence," Lucinda got out. "What, exactly, happened in that carriage? Why am I here, and what does all of this have to do with you?"

His eyes darkened but he didn't speak.

"I have a right to know," she insisted. "Please," she begged.

Will's arms slipped from her and he pulled her down to sit next to him on the settee. He took her hands in his. "First, you must promise me that you'll tell no one what I'm about to share."

Lucinda felt the room begin to spin. What was going on? Could Will's legendary indiscretions have left him and those close to him vulnerable to such attacks?

"Will—"

"Do you agree?" Will interrupted firmly, though it clearly pained him to do so.

"Yes, of course," Lucinda replied anxiously.

"Your life is in danger."

The words hung in the air between them, Lucinda unable to take them in.

"A man by the name of Gareene has been hired to kidnap you. He is the man behind today's attempt," Will continued, his grip on her hands tightening.

"I . . . But . . ." Lucinda tried in vain to speak, but could not absorb what he'd said. "This can't possibly be true."

"I would never lie about such things," he replied, rubbing the pads of his thumbs over her trembling hands.

She pulled away and stared at him. "It cannot be. Why would anyone want to kidnap me?"

"I know that this is hard fo your to hear," he began gently. "The particulars are not important now, but in short, it's your money they're after."

Lucinda looked away from Will, the pieces of this unfathomable puzzle slowly coming together. "Who are you?" she asked quietly, not entirely sure she wanted a reply, but knowing that she needed one.

He reached to reclaim her hands, swearing under his breath when she resisted. "Please, Lucinda. This is difficult enough."

"Who are you?" she repeated, turning to look him in the eye.

"I am a member of the Young Corintheans, a select group sworn to serve England in matters here and abroad."

"What sort of matters?" Lucinda interrupted as she attempted to make sense of his words.

Will scrubbed at his jaw with one hand. "The details are of no consequence. Lucinda—"

"You're a spy, then?" she asked hesitantly.

"Yes," he answered simply.

More pieces fell into place. Their meeting at the Mansfield ball had been so deliciously unexpected. The interlude in the park an awakening, their lovemaking in the library a rebirth.

And all of it was a lie, done out of duty—out of obligation.

"You're wrong, you know," Lucinda began, her eyes

lowering to fix on her folded hands in her lap. "Details have everything to do with you and me."

She could hear it, the sound of her heart breaking. But she would not let herself cry. And slowly, the numbness of realization and regret settled into her, until she could feel nothing.

"Lucinda, please, let me explain," Will begged, dropping to his knees and covering her hands with his in her lap.

"Do you love me?" she asked, her voice sounding eerily detached, even to her.

"Do not demand this of me, Lucinda," he answered, his voice barely above a whisper.

A pounding at the door was followed immediately by the sound of it opening. "Sir, beg your pardon, but we need to take Lady Lucinda home now."

Lucinda looked across the room. The man standing in the open doorway was the one who had escorted her here earlier in the day. He'd been so kind, so comforting as he'd concealed her in a heavy, hooded cloak and hastened her through the city streets. But it made no difference to her, all that had come before this moment now meaningless.

"Of course," she answered. On some level, she was vaguely surprised that her legs supported her as she stood.

"We aren't through, Lucinda." Will's voice was a harsh murmur beside her and she realized he'd stood, looming next to her. For the first time since they met, her body didn't sing with awareness. She felt frozen.

"Oh, but we are," she said. "I have my answer—and you, your duty."

She bent to retrieve her boots, not bothering to put them back on. "I am ready," she replied to the waiting Corinthian, and turned to go, not once looking back.

* * *

Lucinda refused Will's arm as they made their way down the stairs and outside to the waiting carriage. She awkwardly climbed inside, gently tossing her boots and torn stockings to land on the cushioned bench, then delicately sitting down.

Will climbed in after her and slammed the door behind him, taking a seat on the bench opposite Lucinda's.

The carriage rolled to a slow start, the clip-clop of the horse hooves on the bricks marking each second that passed.

Lucinda reached to part the curtains that hung in the window, a sliver of the setting sun appearing before Will brusquely slid the material back into place.

She looked as if she would argue, then dropped her hands into her lap, her gaze following suit.

"It's for your own safety," he tried to explain, becoming irritated when she failed to look up.

"Lucinda. Please, say something. Say *anything*," Will pleaded, sitting forward on the bench. "Curse me. Tell me to go to hell. Swear that you'll never love me again— I just need a starting place. When you hear what I have to say—"

"I'll forgive you, is that it?" she asked quietly, her face tipping up to meet his gaze.

He reached across for her hands but she hastily folded her arms across her chest.

"I need a chance. Please, give me a chance, Lucinda."

"The Mansfield ball. Hyde Park. The Rosemont Inn— the library . . ." She paused, her face crumpling with distress. "All an elaborate ruse," she finished, shakily inhaling a breath with care.

Will grabbed at the bench on either side of Lucinda's hips, his hands digging into the velvet cushion. "No, you do not understand," he began, the disappointment in her eyes more than he could take.

"Have I misunderstood, then? Has it not been your duty to protect me these last weeks?" she pressed, bitterness lacing her words.

He dropped to his knees in front of her, roughly laying his head in her lap. "Yes, in the beginning, but you have to know that what I feel now has so little to do with duty and so much to do with you."

She pushed him to the floor and slid to the corner of the carriage. "That's not enough, Will," she said through her tears. "And you know it as well as I."

He savagely punched the cushioned back before reclaiming his seat on the opposite bench. "You do not know what you ask of me, Lucinda."

"Are you unable to give to me what I so freely and foolishly gave to you?" she whispered.

"Goddammit, Lucinda, do not do this," he pleaded, sensing defeat. "Ask for my protection, for my loyalty—hell, for my horse. But do not ask for my heart."

"The rest is of no use to me without it."

"Lucinda," he begged, hating himself for denying her.

"Stop!" she screamed, her hands flying to cover her ears. "Not another word. You've no right."

He reached across the space between them and attempted to pull her in.

"You broke my heart," she cried out, her arms unfolding to strike at Will, landing a stinging smack on his cheek.

Will dropped his elbows to his knees, his fingers coming to angrily thread through his hair. He couldn't move. Couldn't feel anything beyond the shame that threatened to eat him alive.

The carriage came to an abrupt stop, throwing Lucinda backwards. "Where are we?" she asked, her voice hoarse with emotion as she righted herself.

"Your town house," Will replied hollowly, lifting his head to meet her gaze.

He watched her as she determinedly altered her countenance, straightening her dress, then her hair, and her face, wiping at her eyes with the back of her hand. She set to work on the ruined boots with deftness, forgoing the stockings altogether.

She was slipping away from him, right before his eyes, and there was nothing he could do.

The driver opened the carriage door and reached for Lucinda's hand. "My lady."

"Thank you," she replied graciously, taking his hand and stepping down, leaving Will all alone with nothing but regrets for comfort.

16

Will's formal attire was bloody uncomfortable. The neckcloth chafed his throat, and the fine wool of his dark blue coat was too warm.

He surveyed the drawing room of Lansdowne House, noting with irritation that every other male in attendance looked perfectly comfortable. He, however, wished for nothing more than to strip down to his shirtsleeves and forgo the formal dinner in favor of billiards and an endless supply of brandy.

But duty demanded him entirely tonight. Lucinda had agreed reluctantly to continue on with the fictitious courtship, the need to keep Garenne in the dark as much as was possible a top priority at this point in the game.

A portly baron whose name Will could not remember bowed with polite civility as he passed by, an equally portly, horse-faced woman on his arm.

Will returned the greeting and forced himself to start counting backwards from ten. God knew he had a perfectly good excuse for being in such a foul mood. He'd broken Lucinda's heart, and in turn, his own. The consequences of his actions were more painful than all of the disappointment and heartache up to this point in his life put together and multiplied a thousandfold.

"William?"

He looked to see his mother at his side, her eyes filled with concern. "Yes?"

"Are you quite all right?"

For the first time that he could recall, he wanted to answer her honestly, but knew he could not. To confess even a small piece of the truth might put her in danger. "Of course. Why do you ask?"

"Well . . ." She touched her nape, smoothing the tendrils there with a gloved hand, "Lady Lucinda and her aunts arrived some time ago and you've yet to join them."

His gaze followed Her Grace's and found the four women in question standing together—conversing with Lady Swindon.

"Bloody hell," Will growled, his neckcloth growing tighter with each breath.

He looked apologetically at the duchess. "Forgive me, Mother."

"No need, William. Though I spend my days in the country, I am as aware of Lady Swindon as anyone else. Do you plan on rescuing Lucinda," she queried, her gaze returning to the group. "Or shall I?"

Will gave his mother an appreciative look then made his way across the large room. Though no crystal had been thrown, nor did any of the Furies appear to be threatening to pummel Lady Swindon within an inch of her life, Will knew immediate action was necessary.

"Ladies," he drawled, joining the group and standing next to Lucinda. His arm brushed hers and he felt the swift tensing of her slim body.

There was an awkward pause, the Furies acknowledging his presence with notable discomfort, while Lady Swindon simply smiled, clearly enjoying the entire episode.

"Your Grace," Lucinda replied in a clear, controlled tone, laying her hand on Will's arm. "You just missed Lady Swindon's nearly encyclopedic recounting of Iron Will's adventures."

Will looked at Lady Swindon. Perhaps he should have

left her to the Furies. "You cannot believe everything you hear," he commented.

"Oh, Your Grace, modesty does not become you." Lady Swindon's voice was a sultry innuendo, her gaze blatantly traveling the length of him.

The audacity and inappropriateness of her appraisal wasn't lost on the Furies. Their eyes collectively widened before narrowing with affront.

The Duchess of Highbury stepped toward Lady Swindon, her demeanor taking on a decidedly terrier menace. "Lady Swindon, let me tell you exactly—"

"Dinner is served."

Never in his life had Will been more thankful for the readiness of a meal. "Let us adjourn to the dining room," he interrupted Lucinda's aunt before she had an opportunity to elaborate.

The group split up, Will leading the way with Lucinda on his arm.

He bent toward her, the tantalizing citrus scent of her hair teasing his nostrils. "I apologize."

"I'm afraid you'll need to be more specific, Your Grace," she murmured, the placid nature of her smile in direct contrast to her biting tone. "There are so many things for which you should feel remorse."

Will had expected her to reject his apology, though he'd underestimated the strength of the stab of pain her icy tone inflicted.

"Understand this," she continued, lowering her voice further as they neared the dining room. "You've taken nearly everything from me. But you'll not steal my reputation." She released his arm and demurely clasped her hands at her waist. "I'll continue this charade, but in the end it is you who will bear the blame. Not I."

"Of course." Somehow, he managed to keep his tone light and his expression mild as the room filled with chattering dinner guests.

Lucinda took note of those around her with a gracious smile, then turned back to Will. "The stage is yours, Your Grace."

"I will carve him up and put him in a stew."

Lucinda, Charlotte, and Bessie all looked up from their open books and eyed Victoria, their expressions reflecting equal parts surprise and horror at such a statement.

"I beg your pardon?" Charlotte said.

Victoria closed her book with an audible thwack and drummed her fingers on the table. "Clairemont. I believe he'd do best in a stew, though I suppose it's possible that he'd suit a shepherd's pie as well."

They were gathered, as they frequently were, in the library, all four of them seated around the large, square table they'd brought with them from the country. It had been built according to the women's specifications; thus, its width and length was more than large enough to accommodate all four of them as well as any number of books, writing instruments, paper, and—more often than not—various and assorted tea cups and china plates.

It was their favorite spot, and this afternoon should have seemed like any other afternoon, and indeed it would have done were it not for the stony-faced Young Corinthian standing just to the right of the entryway.

Lucinda could not help but glance his way before turning back to her aunt. "Aunt Victoria, do lower your voice. Please."

"Pish-posh." Victoria glared at the agent. "I am quite sure worse has been said of the man—and in much more colorful language, to boot!"

"Yes, let us all be thankful that you've shown a modicum of restraint," Bessie said sarcastically. "After all, you just as easily could have suggested we fillet the man or stuff an apple in his mouth and roast him whole."

"Excellent idea!" Victoria countered, her expression brightening.

"Really?" Bessie said with interest. "I thought the pig suggestion to be slightly de trop."

"Ladies," Charlotte interrupted, sipping her tea before setting the delicate Wedgwood cup down. "Can we all agree that the carving up and cooking of the duke would hardly be productive—or polite?"

Her two sisters pondered Charlotte's request, then begrudgingly nodded their agreement.

"Thank you," Lucinda said with relief, turning her attention back to Gerald Hobson's dry but comprehensive *Timing and Rate of Skeletal Maturation in Horses*. While Lucinda normally approached such topics with unabashed interest, she had to admit that she was having difficulty mustering the enthusiasm for equine anatomy today.

Of course, it didn't help matters that nearly all of Lucinda's energy had been tapped for more personal reasons, chief among them keeping herself from collapsing in tears in front of her aunts.

She'd known this would be hard. From the moment Will had told her the truth, she'd known. But somehow she'd thought it would just be when she saw him, that when she was not in the same room with him, it would be different. She'd thought . . . She didn't know what she'd thought, just that if she was going to cry, it wouldn't be in public. It wouldn't be anywhere but in her own room, with her own pillow muffling the sound.

But now, every time one of her aunts looked at her, her insides began to shake, and she had to look away, or claim she was about to sneeze.

It was awful. It was exhausting. She'd half expected to not wake this morning.

And the night before—dear God, that had been the worst. Why she ever thought she could manage the dinner party at Landsdowne House, she would never know. Lucinda and her aunts had barely entered the drawing room before Lady Swindon swooped down on them like a perfectly groomed vulture. It had been an astounding violation of polite rules, and nearly enough to undo Lucinda.

And then there was Will. Lucinda had not been so hen-witted to think she could avoid him the entire evening, but when he'd come to her rescue, it had somehow made everything even worse.

He wasn't supposed to be her hero. Damm it, he wasn't *allowed* to be her hero, not after what he'd done to her.

It had been a harrowing few days. Learning her life was in danger was terrifying enough on its own, but when paired with Will's betrayal? It was more than any woman could be expected to bear. Her heart absolutely ached with fear and sorrow.

And now she had to pretend as if nothing had happened. She'd had no choice in the matter; the Corinthians had made it clear that her cooperation was vital to the successful completion of the mission. Her aunts' too. Until this Frenchman—le Comte de Gareene was his name—was captured, none of them could safely go on with their lives.

Lucinda had agreed that her courtship with Will would continue on, exactly as it had prior to the kidnapping attempt. All of their social engagements and outings would remain on the calendar. From the outside, everything would look precisely the same.

But Lucinda could not have been more aware that her life had changed completely, the army of Corinthians assigned to her safety hardly allowing for privacy of any kind.

And through it all, she could not stop blaming herself. It was easier, and far more satisfying, to insist that this was all Will's fault, that he had used her and lied to her, and that she had been an innocent victim.

But she knew that she too was culpable. Despite everything her aunts had taught her, she had made the mistake of listening to her untried heart. She had trusted too soon, been far too quick to believe her own day-dreams. She never should have entertained such roman-tic notions, let alone acted on them. And though it was cold comfort that she was hardly the first woman to fall for Iron Will, the knowledge did provide some small measure of relief.

"Lucinda?"

She looked up, blinking. Victoria was regarding her with a quizzical expression, and Lucinda did not want to guess at how many times her aunt had called out her name.

"Did you find the answer?" Victoria asked.

Lucinda shook her head. "I'm still looking," she mumbled. On the same page. She'd been on the same page for forty minutes. She looked back down and tried to read.

Special care must be given to syndromes of the patella.

She was pretty sure she'd read that already.

Bloody . . . stupid . . . If one of her horses had to be put down because of a knee injury, she was blaming Will. It was his fault she couldn't concentrate on the text.

Will.

He was an awful man.

Truly, truly awful.

And he'd never said that he loved her.

Should she have suspected something sooner? Had she been a fool to believe he simply could not put into words what he felt for her?

Well, yes, obviously.

She'd been a complete fool, but worse than that, she'd expressed her love for him, a man who was simply doing his job and nothing more.

It would be so easy to lose herself in anger, to blame him for taking advantage of her. To hate him for the emotions she'd believed he'd shared with her, all the while he was aware he was only playing a role.

But Lucinda was never one for taking the easy route. She preferred to do something right or not at all.

Years from now, she would look back on this as a lesson learned, she vowed. And for now, she would do what was necessary to keep herself and her family safe, even if it meant pretending that she was the woman she'd been before.

"Lucinda, dear," Charlotte said sweetly. "Are you well this morning?"

Her question pulled Lucinda from her thoughts and she looked up. All three of her aunts watched her with varying expressions of concern, the expanse of the cluttered library table separating them.

Lucinda forced a smile. She and Charlotte had decided to keep the truth of Lucinda's feelings for Will a secret from both Victoria and Bessie. The two had been so angry over being kept in the dark by the Corinthians that the revelation of Lucinda's broken heart would surely have forced them over the edge.

"Yes," Lucinda said, giving the beloved trio a reassuring smile. "Of course."

It was not so hard, after all, to lie, Lucinda realized, turning back to her book.

Garenne would not leave anything to chance this time. The extreme discomfort he found in failure was a new and unappealing sensation and one not easily quelled. Even slitting the throat of a street urchin who had dared to cross his path that evening had done little to abate the vicelike grip that the pain currently held on his skull.

"Do you have any questions?" he asked the petite blonde sitting across from him, her cold green eyes taking in their surroundings with catlike precision.

"No," she said simply, her beautiful face devoid of emotion.

He drained his tankard of ale and gestured for the serving girl. "Good." He preferred to keep their conversation minimal. "You will succeed," he told her. "Or you will die."

She didn't flinch only reached across the table and picked up the soft leather pouch, tucking it into a hidden pocket in her cape, then nodding. "You've no need for concern."

And with that she was gone, silently making her way to the tavern's door and disappearing into the night.

Garenne felt the pressure of the note in his breast pocket. Fouché was growing impatient, even going so far as to question Garenne's abilities. The imbecile was lucky he was safely in France, with the width of the English Channel between him and death.

The woman came highly recommended.

She would succeed, or he would kill her himself.

17

A horse race of some importance, the Queen's Cup took place in late April of every year. The ton made their way annually along the King's Road to Camden, only a few miles outside London. The queen in question had been Anne, who had, upon delightedly discovering a large parcel of flat land during one of her riding expeditions, purchased the hundred acres in order to establish the yearly event.

The popularity of the race had grown over the years, and now the crowds nearly overflowed the grounds.

Will surveyed the noisy gathering from his station near the starting post and grimaced. He'd protested until he was hoarse with the effort, but Lucinda would not yield: She would attend the Queen's Cup with or without him. Her love of horses, once endearing, was becoming downright irritating.

"You really must work on a less ferocious facial expression," Northrop drawled, reining his bay gelding next to Sol and Will.

"But this one works so well in keeping *most* away," Will said sarcastically to his friend.

The two observed the scene in silence. Excited Thoroughbreds pranced and snorted in anticipation, their owners preening over the prized equines while jockeys prepared themselves mentally for the race. The crowd milled about, enjoying the sun and festive frivolity.

"Utter chaos," Northrop remarked.

Will nodded in agreement.

"You should have told me."

Will gave him a quizzical look. "You've attended the Queen's Cup before, surely."

"Not about the race, Clairemont," his friend replied, "about Lady Lucinda."

Will scowled. Carmichael had enlisted Northrop's help despite Will's protests, making the already complicated situation even more so.

"You didn't really believe I'd reformed, did you?" Will kept his tone light, careless.

"You should have told me."

"You know very well I couldn't, so there's no point in belaboring the point, is there?" Will shot back, but he could hear his voice changing, his carelessness unraveling to reveal a darker emotion.

Northrop heeded the warning and broke their stare, turning to look over his shoulder at his wife, who stood chatting with Lucinda and her aunts. "Amelia fears that Lady Lucinda has a tendre for you."

Will kept his eyes fixed on a spot in the distance. "What good does it do to discuss this?"

"And you? Do you love her?"

Will stiffened, hands tightening on the reins. Sol shifted uneasily; he tossed his head and whinnied. "I have a duty to perform, and it doesn't include love."

A chorus of horns signaled the imminent beginning of the race.

Northrop turned his mount toward the women, pausing to look once more at Will. "I wasn't aware that with one you couldn't have the other."

Will reined in Sol and they fell into step next to Northrop and his gelding, the two picking their way across the flattened grass and churned-up ground to join the ladies.

Amelia greeted Northrop with such love in her eyes that Will felt a sudden stab of jealousy slice mercilessly through his already fractured heart.

Lucinda's look was pleasant enough, but the stark contrast between the two left Will cold.

The Furies, however, quickly brought him back to reality. The duchess pinned him with a vengeful glare, while the marchioness haughtily turned away with a huff. Lady Charlotte maintained an air of politeness, acknowledging him with a nod of her head. "Your Grace, a lovely day for a race, wouldn't you agree?"

Will dismounted, Sol's reins held loosely in his hand. "Indeed, Lady Charlotte, it is."

"One might wonder how you could possibly enjoy the race, burdened with what must surely be an unbearably heavy conscience," the dower duchess interjected, walking around to face Sol.

The entire group turned to stare at her, their eyes wide with shock.

She returned their stares with composure.

"Surely I'm not the only one to question the sanity of a man who would keep a horse such as King Solomon's Mine from his destiny?" the woman queried, stroking Sol's silky mane.

"Why would one assume Sol wants to race simply because he is fast?" Will countered, barely maintaining his composure.

"He is a Thoroughbred, Your Grace." She shot Will a look of utter disgust. "And not just any Thoroughbred, but the son of Triton's Tyranny. Racing is in his blood. It is what he was bred and born to do."

Will had to admit that Sol's quickness had everything to do with why Will found him invaluable. The stallion's speed was absolutely essential to Will's success as a Corinthian. Still, he could hardly point out such a thing, not with Lady Northrop present.

"He appears perfectly happy to me," Will answered, standing back to eye Sol critically.

Lucinda joined her aunt, her affection and admiration for the horse obvious as she reached out to caress his velvety nose. "Look in his eyes, Your Grace."

Will walked forward and stared directly into the large, black eyes. They flickered with curiosity and excitement. He'd heard tell of a horse having a kind eye, the relaxed, open nature of the expression speaking to the horse's state of mind. But this was something different. Sol exhibited an eagerness that was nearly palpable as he looked away from Will and chose instead to watch the ebb and flow of the noisy crowd and the horses.

"Do you see it?" Lucinda asked quietly.

"Bloody hell," Will said under his breath, stepping back. Did Sol have the same fire in his eyes when racing through the streets of London on Corinthian business?

"Never fear, Your Grace," the dower duchess said, lovingly patting Sol on the neck. "You may have denied him his first love, but I would bet my carriage and matching grays that he'll take to his new job with even greater enthusiasm."

His new job? What the devil was she talking about? Will opened his mouth to ask her what she meant, but just then, the crowd around them roared to life as the racehorses lined up at the starting post. The Furies joined the crush of humans, pushing their way through with well-aimed pokes of umbrellas. Northrop took his wife's arm and guided her safely on toward a spot midway down the circular track.

Sol pawed at the ground with his front hooves, his knicker of excitement growing louder. Head up, hooves dancing, ears pricked forward.

"He's too excitable," Will told Lucinda as he tightened his grip on the reins. "I can't allow him any closer to the crowd. If you like, Weston or Talbot would happily escort you to a more suitable viewing spot."

Lucinda didn't answer. Instead, she reached up and clasped the saddle. "Lift me up," she demanded.

"I'm sorry?"

"I've not come all this way to miss the race," she answered, irritation growing in her voice. "The ideal spot for viewing is on the back of this horse. Now, assist me or I shall be forced to ask one of your men."

Will reluctantly placed his hands about Lucinda's waist and lifted her into the saddle. He waited to release her until she found her balance in the seat, sitting sideways in a man's saddle no easy feat. She straightened her pelisse and held out her hand for the reins, silently demanding he give them to her. "Absolutely not," Will said in no uncertain terms.

Lucinda stared at him with a stony gaze before she shrugged, conceding. "Very well."

Horns trumpeted and the race began. The ground rumbled beneath the pounding of fifteen sets of thundering hooves. Will felt the rhythm reverberating through his boots and on up through his body. He looked at Lucinda atop Sol and found her focused on the race, shading her eyes with one gloved hand to take in the progress.

"Do you have a favorite?" he called to her over the shouts from the crowd.

"Number four, Braveheart," she replied, her head turning as she followed the horses.

Will surveyed the pack of five horses that led the way and located Braveheart, a giant chestnut with amazing speed. "He's fast." He watched as Braveheart broke from the pack, his long, powerful stride eating up the dirt track. "And if I'm not mistaken, it looks as though he's about to win."

Lucinda let out an unladylike shriek of approval. "Run, Braveheart, run!" she yelled, belatedly checking her unabashed enthusiasm with a palm over her mouth.

Will was riveted by Lucinda as she followed the race, her breath quickening with each stride the giant chestnut took, her arms rising in the air, her hands clenched into fists. Her enthusiasm was infectious, and he found himself smiling despite the realization that this time with her, when he was allowed to see her for who she truly was, would be short indeed.

He longed to place his hands around Garenne's neck and put an end to his threat. But Will knew that day would be the last he'd spend in Lucinda's company. There would be censure following their broken courtship. But he could bear that. Being blackened in polite society was nothing new to him.

But to be denied the pleasure of Lucinda's company? That, he did not know how he would survive.

Will stared at Lucinda's profile as she braced her hands on the saddle leather and stretched taller, her head turning to follow the horses as they rounded the last turn. Will watched the final furlong, Braveheart crossing the finish line some three strides in front of the other horses. The crowd erupted with cheers, men slapping one another on the back and women hopping up and down with joy.

"My first Queen's Cup win!" Lucinda exclaimed, sliding down from her perch atop Sol.

"I'm sorry?" Will queried. He couldn't have heard her correctly. His lips tightened as he looked down at her, annoyed that she hadn't waited for his assistance.

Lucinda straightened her pelisse and gown, brushing Sol's black hairs off her skirt. "There is a certain confidentiality between you agents and their assigned protectees, is there not?"

"Of course," he replied, still not entirely sure what Lucinda was getting at.

"Excellent. Then there is no danger in sharing our plans with you." She finished brushing her gown and turned to await the arrival of the rest of their party. "For some time now, my aunts and I have been building a breeding stable. Braveheart is the sire of Winnie's foal." She looked up, smiling brilliantly at the approaching party. "And now that he's won the right to race in the Ascot, that foal is substantially more valuable."

Will began to piece together tidbits of conversations he'd overheard while in Brampton. The odd comment by Lucinda's aunt concerning Sol's impending enthusiasm for an unnamed employment putting everything into focus.

"You see, Your Grace," Lucinda said, her voice crisp and clear, "my heart may have momentarily gotten in the way of my goal, but this was always about King Solomon's Mine."

She smiled as her aunts' "huzzah!" reached her ears. "And in the end, I'll have gotten what I wanted all along," she added.

Will struggled to reply. "You cannot mean—"

"Your Grace, I do not think even your King Solomon's Mine could have outrun Braveheart today," Victoria interrupted, exuberant as the group came to stand next to Lucinda and Will.

He nodded, the weight of not being able to address Lucinda's painful revelation leaving him speechless.

The inner parlor at the rear of Madame Beaufont's salon was small, to be sure, but the amenities and comfort of the surroundings more than made up for what it lacked in size. Divided from the front of the store by a luxurious length of the palest of pink velvets, the exclusive enclave was reserved for Madame's best clients.

Those ensconced within its fashionably papered walls were treated to a dish of Twinings best pekoe tea, the most delicate of patisseries, and the melodious efforts of a single female harpist tucked neatly into one corner of the cozy room.

Madame Beaufont, whose colorful history rivaled that of any member of the royal family, stood before Lucinda and Amelia, scrutinizing the sleeve of the deep purple taffeta gown being held up by one of her assistants.

Her lips pursed as she fingered a rosette. "*Non*, this will not do."

She waved the girl away and turned to gather up a stack of illustrations. "Why a woman of her age insists on such frivolous touches, I will never know."

Amelia leaned forward. "Yes, that would be Lady . . . er, her name escapes me . . ."

Lucinda shot her friend a look. Her attempt at ferreting out the owner of the purple creation was hardly subtle.

Madame Beaufont sat in the chair facing Amelia and Lucinda, fluffing the pink and cream striped pillow to accommodate her petite size. "Lady Northrop, such tricks will not work with me." She sighed dramatically. "Though, if one were to take note of a gown just that shade on Lady Swindon at the Foster masquerade ball, well . . ." Her shoulders lifted in a very Gallic shrug as she shuffled through her lapful of drawings. "It would hardly be my fault."

Amelia bit into an almond biscuit, the smile on her lips bringing to mind a cat who had just swallowed a parakeet. "I knew it," she said smugly after finishing her bite.

"Tsk, tsk," Madame Beaufont remonstrated, while clearly enjoying the gossip as much as Amelia. "Now, ladies, we must choose a design for your masquerade gowns immediately or I fear they will not be completed in time."

Lucinda nibbled at her petite four. Conversations between Madame Beaufont and Amelia always followed the same pattern, Amelia drawing out as much information as she could manage, while Madame Beaufont groaned over the impossibility of finishing her unique creations within the allotted time. Week in, week out, Amelia walked away from the shop with five to seven new tidbits of gossip, and Madame Beaufont always finished the gowns on time.

Their lively interaction was predictable, something that, Lucinda suddenly realized, was truly comforting. With all that had happened—all that continued to swirl around her—Lucinda was more than content to sit comfortably in Madame Beaufont's parlor and watch a scenario play out that she'd witnessed countless times before.

The petite Frenchwoman dramatically whisked an illustration from the stack in her hands and held it aloft. "Lady Northrop, the design for this gown came to me in a dream."

Amelia's mouth formed a delicate O of delight as she took in the drawing of the evening gown, a frothy confection of pomona green. "It is truly exquisite, Madame Beaufont," she exclaimed, poring over the lovely illustration.

"Yes," Madame agreed as she happily eyed the creation. "One of my best, I believe."

The mousy shop girl returned, bending to whisper in Madame Beaufont's ear.

The designer scowled, then furiously nodded at the girl. "Ladies, I will return in a moment," she said apologetically, setting the illustration down and gracefully rising in a rustle and swirl of skirts. She disappeared through the pink curtain, leaving Lucinda and Amelia alone with the harpist.

Amelia peered after her and the moment the curtain settled, she reached for the drawings, only to have her hand rapped with Lucinda's fan.

"Ouch!" Amelia squeaked, quickly rubbing her knuckles. "Was that entirely necessary?"

Lucinda arched her eyebrows. "It was either that or allow you to bear the brunt of Madame Beaufont's wrath when she discovered you'd had the audacity to peek," she answered with a smile.

Amelia returned the expression. "You are a true friend."

"The truest," Lucinda agreed, taking a sip of her tea and contemplating eating an almond biscuit.

"Do you love him?"

Startled, Lucinda gasped and choked, nearly dropping the delicate bone china cup into her lap. "I'm sorry," she sputtered, allowing Amelia to take the cup and dabbing at the few drops on her skirt.

"Am I to take that as a yes?" Amelia teased, pouring a fresh cup of tea for Lucinda.

Lucinda accepted it and sipped, the hot, sweet liquid soothing her throat, though it could do little for her nerves. She had agreed not to tell Amelia about Garenne or the Corinthians. And there was no way to explain how she felt about Will without divulging this information.

But she *longed* to talk to Amelia.

"You're referring to the duke," Lucinda said, maintaining her calm composure by carefully not looking directly at Amelia.

Amelia huffed and sat back. "Well, of course I'm speaking of the duke, unless there is another suitor whom I am not aware of."

Lucinda answered with a shrug and set the fragile

china cup and saucer on the table, next to Madame Beaufont's illustrations. "What do you think?"

Amelia didn't say anything for several seconds. "Is he aware of your feelings?" she finally asked, her voice gentle.

"Yes," Lucinda answered simply. "He knows." She swallowed, afraid of how Amelia would respond.

She was immediately enveloped in her friend's arms. "And does he return your feelings?" Amelia asked, releasing Lucinda to sit back, the better to see her face.

The relief Lucinda felt at telling Amelia about Will was overwhelming. She shook her head, tears joining the three tiny tea stains that marred her peach gown.

Amelia produced a lace-edged handkerchief from her reticule and wiped the dampness from Lucinda's cheeks. "Shhhh," she soothed.

"You warned me," Lucinda murmured, her words nearly lost beneath the dulcet tones of the harp.

"It does not matter now," Amelia assured her, taking Lucinda's hands in her own. "I have watched Clairemont in your presence, and he clearly feels affection for you," she said earnestly, pausing to tuck the now damp scrap of fabric into her reticule. "Where there is affection, there is always the possibility that love will grow in time."

Lucinda tried to smile, but Amelia did not know the whole truth. If she had, her dear friend would never have suggested such a thing.

"You are right, of course," Lucinda said, squeezing Amelia's hand, "and I am a behaving like, well, very much as one who has more hair than wit."

"You are a woman in love," Amelia stated matter-of-factly, "and therefore have no need to apologize for your behavior."

"Is this what you wanted for me? All of those suitors you encouraged in the hopes that I would choose one, fall desperately in love, and lose all hope of retaining any semblance of the intelligent, eminently reasonable individual I once was?"

Amelia reached for an almond biscuit, gave it to Lucinda, then selected a second one for herself. "Er, well . . . yes."

The two looked at each other as they nibbled the biscuits, then laughed.

"Lucinda," Amelia said, once their laughter had subsided, "love embellishes your soul, it does not detract. Do you understand?"

Oh, how she wanted to see the sense in Amelia's statement. The idea of love's ability to open up her world rather than destroy all she'd carefully built was nearly irresistible. But it was too late for such flights of fancy.

"Am I to understand you approve of my feelings for the duke?" she teased, hoping to move the conversation toward a lighter tone.

"He is handsome enough, I'll give the man that," Amelia countered.

Lucinda mindlessly bit into the biscuit and chewed slowly. "Yes, well, he's not the only attractive man in London. There will be others."

"Oh no there won't."

Lucinda stopped, a sudden sense of unease settling into her stomach. "Come now, your list of eligible bachelors rivals any of the most determined of matchmaking mamas. You'll find another one soon enough for me."

Amelia bit into the biscuit and crunched, her eyes taking on the look of a seasoned general. "The duke simply needs the right opportunity to avail you of his true feelings," she began, squinting her eyes as she visually laid out her plan. "And we shall give him that opportunity."

Lucinda's mind raced to catch up with what had just transpired. "I don't think that such a plan is—"

"Vauxhall!" Amelia nearly screamed, the harpist tripping over her note in response.

"Amelia, I—"

"It's perfect!" her friend interrupted excitedly. "In fact, that is where John and I first . . ." She paused, checking herself. "Well, that is another story for another time."

Madame Beaufont's distinctive voice called to one of her clerks, just beyond the doorway.

Amelia placed the remainder of the biscuit in her mouth and chewed quickly.

Lucinda did the same, swallowing just before Madame pulled back the curtain and announced, "Now, ladies, where were we?"

"Are you all right?" Will asked, bending down to look at his opponent. The man was sprawled awkwardly on the floor of the ring, one eye swollen shut. A crimson trickle ran from his nose toward his mouth.

"I'll live, but I'm going to need some help here."

Will stood to the side while two attendents picked the man up, one taking him at the shoulders abd the other holding tight to his feet.

"I hope it helped."

Will tensed at Carmichael's voice but awkwardly patted the battered man once on his shoulder and wished him better luck next time, before turning. "You'll have to be more specific."

"Pounding a succession of opponents," Carmichael clarified. "I hope it helped."

Will joined his superior. "Immensely," Will said sarcastically, then motioned for Carmichael to follow.

The two made their way in silence across the club to an anteroom just off the entrance. The room was sparsely but comfortably furnished. Will doubted the proprietor would approve of his sweat-soaked body coming in contact with the elegant furniture, but he hardly cared. The room was empty and would afford the privacy the two men needed.

He pulled a chair out for Carmichael and dropped into the one opposite, mopping at his face with a rough linen towel.

"We've run out of time."

Will stopped and looked at Carmichael, his body tightening at the older man's grim expression. "Time for what?"

"Simply put," Carmichael began, crossing his legs and assuming a casual appearance should anyone happen in, "we can no longer afford to wait for Garenne to make his move. We must lure him out of hiding."

Will gripped the arms of his chair. "What do you mean we can no longer afford to wait? I don't see how we could afford not to."

Carmichael fingered his signet ring, turning it once, twice, as he pondered his response. "We have limited resources, Will. And much as I would prefer to tell you our assistance is not needed elsewhere, it is. Nearly half of our agents are working this case. It cannot continue."

Will ran his hands through his hair before propping his elbows on his knees. "What do you propose?"

"You won't like it," Carmichael replied, "but we've no choice."

"You know I have no qualms about putting myself in harm's way."

Carmichael stared at Will, his face unreadable.

"Bloody hell, man, out with it already," Will said impatiently.

"It's not you we need to use, Will. It's Lady Lucinda."

Will's vision turned hazy as he absorbed Carmichael's words. "You cannot be serious."

"Deadly so," Carmichael responded, the lines at each side of his mouth deepening as he grimaced.

"This is Garenne we're speaking of, not some pickpocket from London's stews." Will's voice remained level, but anger swelled and grew within him. "Lady Lucinda cannot be expected to hold her own against such a man."

"We have no other options—"

"He's a bloody monster, you fool," Will roared, shoving out of his chair to stalk a handful of steps toward the door, then returning, coming to stand in front of the man.

Carmichael's eyes flared, betraying his surprise at Will's outburst. "You forget yourself, Clairemont." The admonition was given in the same calm, cool voice he always used, but a thread of steely warning underlay the words and cut through Will's haze of rage as nothing else could have.

"I apologize," he bit out. He turned abruptly away and reached for the first object he could find. The small side table broke as though it were kindling when Will threw it against the wall.

"I warned you not to get involved with Lady Lucinda," Carmichael said quietly. "You cannot do what we must—see what we see—and expect to maintain any sort of normalcy in your life, especially not with someone so intimately involved in Corinthian business."

Will wiped his arm across his forehead, removing the beads of sweat, and leaned his back against the wall. He knew Carmichael was right, a realization that only added to his pain. Nothing was as it should be, every last relationship in his life was turned upside down. So much so that Will hardly knew how to go about righting them—or if repair was even possible at this point.

"Give me more time," he growled, unable to look Carmichael in the eye.

"I can hold off for three days. No more."

"Fair enough," Will replied, then stalked from the room.

18

"Are there to be fireworks?" Amelia asked Lord Northrop, nearly bouncing with excitement as the group's boat floated along the Thames. Lucinda smiled at her dear friend, whose enthusiasm for fireworks was second only to her love of Cook's strawberry tarts.

Amelia sighed contentedly as she rested her head on her husband's shoulder. Seeing her expression of utter happiness, Lucinda had to admit that perhaps something else had surpassed both fireworks and strawberries in Amelia's heart.

Lucinda found herself sighing as well, though for a vastly different reason than Amelia's. An evening at Vauxhall Gardens was never a restful affair, the sheer magnitude of the spectacle enough to overwhelm the most enthusiastic of attendees. But for Lucinda, tonight presented special challenges.

Although, she thought, glancing down at her dress, she could not have been any better outfitted for the evening.

The dress itself, a fetching gown in the Grecian style, was truly lovely, the golden silk warming Lucinda's skin, while the cut and drape accentuated her curves. The trouble was, there was far too little of the gown for Lucinda's taste. The neckline dipped low in the front, revealing and displaying Lucinda's cleavage, while the sleeves were practically nonexistent.

Madame Beaufont insisted that in light of Lucinda's

involvement with the duke, it behooved her to dress more daringly.

Lucinda sighed again, recalling Madame's air of conspiracy when she carefully placed the wrapped package containing the finished gown in her hands. "Forgive me," she whispered. "But I made a few alterations to the gown." The woman's eyes had positively flashed with delight.

"You should have known better," Lucinda said under her breath, then shivered in response to the light breeze coming off the river. She pulled her shawl higher over her shoulders in a vain attempt at warmth.

"Would you like my coat?" Will asked, his brows furrowing with concern.

No matter how long Lucinda lived she would never forget his voice and the troubling sensations it sent pulsing throughout her body. The deep, husky tone ignited a fire in her belly, little flames licking their way toward every limb until she wondered if she would simply burst. She fought the urge to lean into his warmth, then felt his breath on her bare nape and closed her eyes. She opened them a moment later to see the cool, icy stares from all three of her aunts. The sight immediately strengthened her resolve.

"No, thank you," she said coolly, bracing herself as the boat came to a slow stop, bumping against the landing. Northrop and Will stepped out first, then aided the ladies in debarking, the entire party making their way finally to the Vauxhall Stairs. After showing their season tickets, they were escorted through the crowd toward the Grove, where revelers gathered in groups or inside supper boxes, mingling and enjoying the music wafting from the Orchestra building.

"Much could be said of Vauxhall," Northrop commented over his shoulder, as he led Amelia up the steps toward their supper box, followed by the Furies, Lucinda, and Will. "Though I doubt very much that the word 'subtle' could be used."

Lucinda saw Amelia playfully swat her husband's sleeve with her fan.

She allowed Will to accompany her into the box and to a seat on a deep green cushioned bench, avoiding his gaze by pretending to be absorbed in the scene below them.

It would be tempting to forget Will's betrayal. So easy to allow herself to be caught up in the spirit of the evening, the knowing glances, intimate whispers— the romance that Vauxhall's proprietors inspired with the heady mixture of sights and sounds all wrapped up with a gaily colorful bow.

Lucinda tried unsuccessfully to cover her expanse of skin with the silk shawl. She glanced up as Will sat down, his worried gaze causing her breath to catch.

He looked away, responding to a question from Northrop.

The dull ache in her heart that she'd grown accustom to over the last few days only increased when Will was near.

She had been blind with anger, his betrayal cutting to her very core. The intimacy she'd believed to be an expression of their love had suddenly been made cheap and meaningless by the revelation of his ties to the Young Corinthians. But one thought niggled at the back of her mind night and day: There had been more to their lovemaking. She'd seen it in his eyes, heard it in his voice. Felt it in his touch.

She was sure he felt more than duty toward her. She was sure of it, but how could she convince him to admit such a thing?

Lucinda prayed that Amelia had been correct when she suggested that the duke would be more inclined to reveal such close-held feelings if given proper physical inducements.

Will turned his attention back to her. "Have you need of anything, Lady Lucinda?" he inquired, his eagerness threatening her resolve.

"No, thank you," she responded politely, though her nerves were now dancing.

Amelia had promised she would secure a certain amount of privacy for the two to be alone. Her dear friend had assured Lucinda that their plan would work.

Half of her wanted desperately to prove Amelia right. And the other? The other was afraid that even with the dress and the practiced seduction, Lucinda would only succeed in proving her wrong!

The group listened to the music for some time, sipping wine and dining on Vauxhall hame. They visited with friends who strolled by or stopped to visit and enjoyed the antics of the crowd.

The orchestra ceased playing and polite applause filled the air as the musicians left the stand. Amelia stood and gestured for Lord Northrop to do the same. "I suggest we take a stroll before dinner is served," she said to the group.

"I cannot see from down there," Victoria protested. "And Lord Humphrey is about to make a complete fool of himself. I don't want to miss it."

Bessie leaned in toward Victoria and focused her opera glasses on the crowd. "Where?"

"There," Victoria answered impatiently, discreetly pointing toward a tall bald man in evening dress waving his hands wildly as he addressed his wife. "Near the statue of Handel."

"Oh," Bessie began, only to follow with a scandalized gasp when the man in question managed to slosh Madeira down the front of poor Lady Humphrey's gown.

Charlotte adopted a look of disinterest, though she slyly moved nearer to the railing, where the view of Lord Humphrey's antics could be more easily seen. "You go ahead," she said, "do take care not to dally, though." Her gaze rested briefly, meaningfully, on Lucinda, her point made clear.

"Oh, look!" Bessie squeaked, causing Charlotte to turn toward the crowd.

Amelia quickly took Lucinda's hand in hers and pulled her to the stairs, the men following behind. "All right, then," she said over her shoulder as they descended the steps.

The men escorted them into the crowd.

"I haven't walked the Downs for some time," Amelia said to the others. "Lucinda?"

Lucinda hesitated, nervously fingering her shawl. If she agreed with her friend, the four would walk amongst shrubs and trees that allowed for more intimate conversations. And if she declined, they would take the Grand Walk, the more populated of the two, with nary a private spot in sight. One direction took courage, the other offered safety. Lucinda had been taught by the Furies to never refuse a challenge.

"Yes, the Downs it is."

"Bloody hell," Will growled under his breath as he escorted Lucinda toward the shadowy paths of the Downs. Lady Northrop had suggested the ramble and is friend had heartily agreed, leaving Will and Lucinda to follow.

Will tugged at his neckcloth as they walked, his fingers itching to rip the cursed material free. Lucinda had politely allowed him to escort her to the gardens for the evening. And she had politely smiled at his conversation. She'd politely declined his coat when the wind picked up. And she had politely taken his arm as they set off after Northrop and his wife.

Will had just about had it with all of the bloody politeness.

The rage Will felt at Carmichael's threat of using her for bait continued to burn in his chest. Allowing Lucinda to act as a decoy would be tantamount to signing her death sentence, plain and simple. After far too much brandy and far too little sleep, Will's heart had given in and surrendered the hopes and dreams that Lucinda's love had offered. Her life was far more important than his happiness.

But dammit all, did the woman have to test him on every front? He discreetly looked out the corner of his eye and assessed her dress. The bodice was cut so low that he could, from his considerable height, peer down at the creamy, white expanse of her breasts, the pink-hued nipples barely hidden from him.

His groin tightened. The scrap of fabric that clung so artfully to Lucinda's luscious curves tortured him. Surely God Himself was testing Will, the Downs yet another obstacle in his elaborate plan.

If it were not for the army of Corinthian agents fanned out about the grounds, Will would have objected to the route. But as it was, not a single suspect individual would be allowed within two yards of Lucinda. All agents had been instructed to attack first, ask questions later.

Lucinda edged closer to Will, pressing the curve of her breast against his arm. "I fear the chill is getting the better of me this evening."

Will flicked a glance over the path ahead of them, noting with displeasure that Northrop and his wife had stopped to admire the life-sized lead statue of Milton. "Here," he offered, slipping his arm around her shoulders, sheltering her next to his body. "Though the Furies would faint from the scandal of it, I fear your freezing to death would be equally distressing."

Will could just make out Lucinda's hesitant smile in the fading light.

"Well, we do, after all, need to keep up appearances if we've any hope of succeeding at this game."

Will nodded in agreement. "And what would mean success to you?" he asked, his voice low and rough.

"I suppose continuing to exist would be rather nice," Lucinda began, steering Will toward a small turnout in the path where a fountain quietly gurgled. "And securing your heart for myself would be most welcome."

Will froze for a moment, certain he'd misheard her.

Lucinda slipped out from under his arm and stood in front of him, bare inches separating them. She let her shawl fall from her shoulders and took his hand in both of hers, pressing it against the thin silk bodice of her gown. His palm cupped the lush upper curve of her breast. "My heart is yours, Will. All you have to do is take it."

He could feel it beating, pounding fast beneath his palm, the increased speed belying her calm.

She stepped closer, rising on her toes to his face. "Take it," she whispered. "Take me."

Her mouth met his, the lush lower lip and curved upper parting.

Will instinctively returned the kiss, pulling her against him, her soft curves accommodating the harder angles of his body.

"Say you love me, Will."

Her fervent plea pulled Will from the mindless fog of lust and desire that held him. She offered him everything. What could he possibly give in return?

He forced his arms to release her and his unwilling legs to step back. "Lucinda, I'm sorry."

She faced him proudly, hands clenched, her chin lifted

bravely. "I love you, but I'll not allow you to have such a hold on me if my feelings are not returned."

"You've no idea how sorry I am—"

"Do you love me?" she asked plainly, her eyes welling with tears.

He would not lie to her, and so Will said nothing, though it killed him inside to remain silent.

"Very well," she said in a hushed tone, retrieving her shawl and wrapping it about her shoulders. "I wish to return to the supper box."

"What can I say?" Will asked, his voice betraying his anguish.

"Nothing." She moved to step around him, wincing when Will grabbed for her wrist and held tight. "You've my heart already, do you really need my dignity as well?" she choked out.

"Lucinda," he pressed, the shock of her words taking his breath.

"Let me go," she pleaded, pulling away.

He dropped his hand from her wrist and followed her onto the path, keeping a safe distance behind her as she retraced their steps back to the crowd.

"But I can't," he whispered to himself, "and therein lies the problem."

It had been easy enough to satisfy Amelia's need for details. Lucinda's vague answers had supplied her hopeful friend with enough encouragement to ensure that she assumed the courtship was continuing on a decidedly more romantic path.

Lucinda was determined to sever her connection with Will, however, and that meant she had to find a way to end her need for protection by the Corinthians.

Securing an audience with Will's superior had been far more complicated than convincing Amelia that her plan had worked. Lucinda had seen little of the duke for the past two days, the time they were forced to spend in each other's company proving both awkward and draining.

"Come with me." Lord Weston held out his arm to steady Lucinda as she alighted from the coach in front of a stone town house, its details hardly distinguishable in the darkness of night. Lucinda spied mullioned windows and a row of tidy hedges before Lord Weston instructed her to watch her step as they entered the building.

She held tight to his arm and allowed him to lead her in, the interior of the building hardly more revealing than the outside had been.

Sparse candlelight illuminated a long hall at the end of which stood two large men—Corinthian agents, Lucinda was sure, though none she had ever seen.

Lord Weston gestured for Lucinda to follow him.

She took a deep breath then walked quickly, casting quick glances at the landscape paintings and portraits that occupied the walls.

"Gents," Lord Weston said with a brief nod, though neither of the two acknowledged his presence. "Social interaction is not their forte," he whispered to Lucinda, then rapped his knuckles on the door.

"Come in," a man's voice called from within.

Lord Weston nodded for Lucinda to proceed. "I'll wait out here with the opera dancers," he said, then winked.

Lucinda managed a wary smile in return, then pushed the door open and entered.

She could see the profile of the man as he sat at a large desk, his hands busily rifling through a sheaf of papers. He stopped when Lucinda approached, pushing his chair back as he stood.

"Lady Lucinda."

"Lord Carmichael," Lucinda replied with as much confidence as she could.

He gestured for Lucinda to sit, then did the same. "I trust that Lord Weston was a satisfactory escort."

Lucinda took the offered chair, thinking back on Weston's role in tonight's meeting. When she'd threatened to expose the Corinthians if he did not arrange the introduction, he'd agreed, though many colorfully voiced misgivings had accompanied his promise.

"Of course," she answered with conviction.

Lord Carmichael settled back in his chair and propped his elbows on the arms. "Lady Lucinda, please know that we had no other choice but to proceed in such an aggressive fashion."

Lucinda had not come for an apology. While the Corinthians' presence was bothersome, at the moment, they were most comforting as well. All except one.

"Thank you, Lord Carmichael," Lucinda said, pausing to clear her exceedingly parched throat. "But that is not why I'm here. I wish to speak to you about the Duke of Clairemont."

Lord Carmichael fixed his sharp blue eyes on Lucinda. "Clairemont is the best man I have, though his involvement with you beyond a professional level is—"

"With all due respect," she broke in, the heat traveling to her cheeks only humiliating her more. "I do not wish to discuss the personal nature of my relationship with the duke."

Lord Carmichael looked confused at Lucinda's words. "I'm sorry, Lady Lucinda. Then I'm afraid I do not understand the purpose of this conversation," he said gently.

"I would like him to be removed from my situation," Lucinda said plainly.

"That is impossible."

His tone was resolute, his answer immediate.

Lucinda's heart dropped. "Nothing is impossible, Lord Carmichael," she replied desperately. "Surely not for the Young Corinthians."

"Lady Lucinda—"

"Please, my lord," she interrupted, loosening the strings of her cape. "Do not tell me what you cannot do, but rather what you can."

Lord Carmichael rose from his chair and walked to the heavy door, murmuring to the men outside before closing it firmly. "Lady Lucinda," he began, coming to sit on the edge of his desk across from Lucinda. "Your life is in danger. To remove Clairemont from the situation would guarantee your death."

He toyed with the large signet ring on his right hand, the engraved band of gold twisting round and round. "I am sorry for the discomfort that his presence causes you," he paused, his gaze enigmatic as it met hers, "but I cannot endanger you further by making such a tactical error. It is out of the question."

It was clear from Carmichael's tone that he would not change his mind, which meant that there would be no relief from the emotional onslaught that Will brought on with his nearness. His very voice made Lucinda want to weep; his touch when he took her arm in the interest of appearance caused her heart to break all over again.

"I will die either way," she said quietly, hardly aware that she'd uttered the words out loud.

"There is something."

Lucinda looked up slowly at Carmichael, the hesitancy in his eyes giving her pause. "Lord Carmichael?"

He was struggling with how to proceed, that was clear. "May I speak plainly, Lady Lucinda?"

"I insist."

"What I am about to propose to you," he began, pausing to clear his throat. "It will enrage Clairemont.

In all honesty, it might cause him to quit the Corinthians."

"The proposition, Lord Carmichael," Lucinda pressed, her anxiety growing.

"If we were able to draw Garenne out into the open, our considerable forces would most assuredly capture him, bringing what has been an impossible situation for both you and His Grace to an end."

"And how would we go about doing such a thing?" Lucinda asked, her heartbeat quickening.

Carmichael grimly gazed at Lucinda before answering. "With bait, Lady Lucinda."

19

"The kitchen exit?"

"You've already asked after that one, Will," Weston said smoothly, the two surveying the Foster masquerade with expert eyes. "Twice, actually."

"Humor me," Will replied in a barely restrained growl.

Weston winked at a group of giggling young misses in Grecian costumes and golden masks as they strolled past with their mamas in tow. "Four men at the kitchen exit, eight at the main entrance, another four near the doors that—"

"Thank you," Will interrupted, fidgeting with his cuff.

"Try to relax," Weston urged, stopping a servant and taking two flutes of sparkling wine from his tray.

Will accepted a glass and sipped, but his eyes continued to scan the Foster's grand ballroom for signs of danger.

The news that Lucinda had agreed to be used as bait had enraged Will. He'd all but quit the Corinthians, his argument with Carmichael both savage and futile. He'd said such cruel and vicious things to his superior that Will was sure the man would never forgive. His threats of physical harm had failed to affect the man, Carmichael merely standing his ground and urging Will to do what he felt was needed.

Something in Will had wanted Carmichael to fight

back, a physical encounter preferable to his superior's steady implacability. But Carmichael had coolly refused, choosing instead to recount the reasons why the plan was the only option left. Will's rants had fallen on deaf ears, and eventually he'd stopped yelling long enough to listen.

"Her Grace, the Duchess of Clairemont, and Lord Michael Randall."

The announcement of the arrival of Will's family pulled him from his brooding. The two made their way toward him.

"William," his brother said, briefly nodding in greeting.

Will returned the gesture and turned to the duchess. "Mother, you look lovely this evening."

Her Grace smiled at the words, clearly pleased. "Thank you," she replied, leaning in to offer Will her cheek. She smoothed the skirt of her rose-colored gown, the silver spangles sewn into the bodice shimmering with her movement.

"The Duchess of Highbury, the Marchioness of Mowbray, Lady Charlotte Grey, and Lady Lucinda Grey," the majordomo announced.

"But nowhere near as fetching as Lady Lucinda," the duchess replied, turning to watch Lucinda and the Furies enter the ballroom.

Will had been informed of Lucinda's costume ahead of time, though the description had hardly done the dress justice. She moved gracefully toward him, her head held high and a smile on her face. Her deep blue gown floated about her, the silk shimmering in the candlelight. Rows of beadwork in hues of green, purple, and blue danced about the dress in a fanciful design that echoed the peacock feathers adorning her cleverly designed mask. Her golden hair fell over her shoulders and down her back in a waterfall of soft curls.

Will felt the world stop as she approached.

He loved her. She'd captured him, heart and soul, and now, as he drank in the sight of her, he knew he would never recover.

She swept toward him, coming to stand next to his mother. "Your Grace," she said to the duchess executing a perfect curtsy, then turning to Will and the rest of the party. "Your Grace, Lord Weston, Lord Michael. How perfectly delightful to see you this evening."

"Lady Lucinda, you look stunning. Is Madame Beaufont the one we must thank for creating such a beautiful costume?" the duchess responded, kissing Lucinda's cheek in a warm greeting.

"Yes," the Duchess of Highbury answered succinctly as the Furies joined the group. "Madame Beaufont's cup of inspiration overflows, as you can see." She gestured to herself and her sisters, whose dresses exactly matched the hues found in Lucinda's mask and gown. Each woman wore a peacock feather neatly tucked into her coiffed hair and a mask that matched her gown.

Will grimaced at the woman's poorly hidden indignation, knowing full well that her ire was aimed at him. The ladies had been instructed to wear the matching gowns so that they were clearly visible among the throng, a precaution that, despite their misgivings, the Furies had not been able to refuse.

"It is quite original, each of you complementing Lucinda's gown," Her Grace reassured the Furies.

"Well, that is one way of looking at things," the dower duchess said acerbically. "Though I have to question whether Madame—"

"Is that a waltz I hear?" Will interrupted, eager to stop her before she continued.

The orchestra had played the opening notes of the next dance and couples moved smoothly to the floor.

"Lady Lucinda," he said, offering her his arm. "I believe this waltz is mine."

"Of course, Your Grace." Her hesitation was so brief as to be barely noticeable by any onlooker. She took his arm and addressed the Furies. "I'll return shortly," she said reassuringly.

Will led Lucinda to the dance floor, a reluctance in her step that belied her agreeable expression. He didn't allow her to tarry for long when stopped by a friend or admirer, a glare from Iron Will proving sufficient to clear the path before them.

They reached the far end of the room. The musicians were situated on a dais at the edge of the polished marble dance floor. Potted palms and tall baskets of flowers were arranged about the perimeter and a multitude of candelabras added their glow to the chandeliers suspended high over the room.

Will turned to face Lucinda and took her in his arms. The music began, and he expertly swept her into the dance steps, encircling the floor before he spoke.

"Why have you refused me entry into your home this past week?" Will asked simply, the frustration over being kept on duty *outside* the town house—and having to hear of Lucinda's demand from Weston—still lingering in his gut.

Lucinda smiled and nodded at a passing couple before looking at Will. "I did not want to see you."

Her honesty stung. "And your role tonight? Was that an effort to end our acquaintance as well?"

"I certainly have no desire to pit myself against a notorious French assassin, if that is what you are thinking," she replied caustically, turning lightly at his lead.

"You must know that I adamantly opposed your involvement tonight," Will growled, the feel of her in his arms straining his control.

Lucinda stiffened at his words, her mouth thinning to

a firm line. "And you must know that you've no right to feel anything beyond professional concern in this matter, Your Grace."

He wanted to kiss away the anger and hurt that had filled her eyes—tell her he'd been a fool to deny his love for her, and beg her forgiveness. He wanted to forget every last reason that had kept him from following his heart.

"Lucinda, please," he began, his voice harsh and strained with emotion. "You're a woman who deserves much more . . . More than I could ever provide."

She faltered and he caught her, easing her back into the rhythm. "I've no need to hear your excuses," she replied bitterly.

Will knew what she needed to hear.

I love you. God help me, I always will.

"Lucinda . . ." He looked away from her, the pain in her eyes clawing at his heart. His gaze was caught by Weston, who stood propped against the wall just to the left of the orchestra. He gave Will the signal to follow, then started walking.

"Yes?" Lucinda asked, her tone taut.

He stopped abruptly and caught her hand, drawing her with him to the other end of the ballroom. "I'm sorry," he said, his body tightening with grave foreboding. "Something requires my attention at the moment. I'll return you to your aunts."

"Do not touch me," she whispered angrily, tugging her hand from his.

"Lucinda, please—" He reached for her arm.

She recoiled at his touch. Belatedly remembering their audience, she pasted a small smile on her face. "Release me," she said through her teeth.

"I cannot leave you alone."

She glanced behind them to where a hall led to the ladies' retiring room. Two Corinthian agents stood near, pretending to be deep in conversation. "I need a moment to myself, Your Grace," she answered testily, though there was a pleading quality to her tone. "As you can see, I will not be alone."

Will's gaze flicked over the two agents and down the hall. He could not follow her into the retiring room. The need to play this evening perfectly if they were to catch Garenne made it absolutely necessary that everything appear as it should.

"Very well," he agreed reluctantly, but caught Lucinda's elbow as she turned to go. "Do be careful."

"Of course, Your Grace," she said hotly, the fresh tears that showed on her cheeks just below her feathered mask betraying her.

Will watched as she walked down the hall and disappeared into the room, his heart in her hands, though she did not know it.

He vowed then and there that when Garenne had been captured he would tell Lucinda that he loved her. And then he would never let her go.

Lucinda waited until Ladies Turner and Hightower had exited the retiring room before dissolving onto the settee in a puddle of blue silk and hot tears. She yanked off her feathered mask and dropped it into her lap, then savagely tore her gloves off.

She was not a stupid woman. She'd managed to avoid marriage to countless men. She owned a portion of what would surely become the most successful breeding stable in the whole of England. She'd survived despite the deadly threat of a maniacal Frenchman.

No, she was not stupid in the least. Yet she'd bared her heart to Will and asked for his in return—no, begged. And he'd refused.

She breathed deeply in an effort to regain her composure, opening her eyes at the sound of someone in the room.

Hastily, she wiped her tears, embarrassed to be found crying. A woman walked out from behind the curtained area at the end of the room. Lucinda blinked with disbelief at the sight of her.

"Lady Lucinda, I presume," the woman said.

Lucinda had the oddest feeling that she was peering into a mirror. The woman standing before her was the image of herself from head to foot. Same hair, same dress, same voice. It was uncanny, and altogether unsettling.

"Who are you?" Lucinda asked, rising from the settee.

A small malicious smile lifted the woman's lips. She stepped nearer. "That is not important."

"I dare say it is," Lucinda responded with asperity, the hairs rising on the back of her neck.

"There's hardly time to argue, Lady Lucinda." A man emerged from behind the curtain, his tall, wiry form coming to stand directly in front of her. "You've been most uncooperative these past weeks," he said in a low, lethal tone, his black eyes narrowing with cruel, maniacal determination.

"Garenne," Lucinda whispered in grim recognition. She backed away awkwardly, her legs bumping into the settee. She took him in, her mind trying to reconcile what her eyes saw. He was beautiful—almost too beautiful, his pale complexion, aquiline nose, and full lips more suited to an archangel than the devil she knew him to be.

She looked toward the door, her lungs constricting with fear. "I've only to scream and two Corinthian agents will pounce," she threatened, her voice trembling.

The Frenchman squeezed his eyes shut and dropped

his angular chin, reaching to massage his temples. "Your faith in the duke is really quite heartwarming," he remarked snidely, opening his eyes and smoothing back a lock of his dark brown hair. "But I fear I've reached the end of my patience."

He lunged at Lucinda with such speed she didn't have time to scream. He grabbed her and slapped a rough cotton cloth over her mouth and nose. It smelled awful, the noxious fumes nauseating.

Lucinda lashed out, her arms and legs thrashing as she tried to free herself from Garenne's grasp. She clawed at the devil, her nails cutting into the skin of his hand.

"Stupid chienne!" he uttered, pressing harder on the cloth.

"Delay as long as you can," she heard him say, his thick accent slurring. "Do not let—"

All at once, Lucinda's limbs felt too heavy to move, her arms and legs slowing to a stop. She struggled to speak but her words dissolved into an inaudible whisper.

And then the world went black.

She was taking too long.

"Would you not agree, Your Grace?" Lady Mansfield asked.

"Oh, yes, quite," Will replied, though he had no idea what he'd just agreed to. The woman had accosted him the moment Lucinda had fled and he'd been trapped ever since.

Lady Mansfield pushed her ridiculous checkered mask back into place and smiled widely at Will. "Excellent."

Bloody hell. Will pinned Weston with an angry stare that told him to hurry along.

Weston smiled, clearly enjoying Will's pain as he joined the two.

"Lady Mansfield," Weston began. "I'm afraid I've

need of the duke—quite a serious matter, I assure you," he said smoothly, winking at the woman as he extricated Will from her grasp.

"Oh, well, of course," she replied, somewhat reluctantly.

"Thank you," Weston mouthed at Lady Mansfield, wriggling his eyebrows.

The woman turned to rejoin a group of friends near the refreshments.

"Yes?" Will asked expectantly, the sight of Lucinda emerging from the retiring room slightly easing his anxiety.

"A man of interest was found in an upper room. He's been detained in the library," Weston answered, his serious tone belying his lazy demeanor.

Will listened with keen interest to Weston's report, though his eyes remained fixed on Lucinda as she walked down the hall.

She hesitated for a moment when her gaze met Will's, offering him a small smile before threading her way through the crowded ballroom.

"Come with me," he ordered Weston. Instinct had him moving to follow her before he realized what he was doing. As he purposefully made his way through the throngs of revelers, he noticed her hair color, just a shade off from his vivid memory of her lying back in the library, her golden hair fanning out about her beautiful face.

His eyes narrowed, his gaze lowering to the woman's shoulders as she picked up her pace. He'd never forget the exactitude with which Lucinda's slender shoulders fit into his embrace, as if they were made only for each other. This woman's shoulder span was slightly wider than Lucinda's, though Will doubted anyone other than he would have noticed.

He was nearly upon her now, his alert senses all but

confirming what he suspected. He caught hold of her arm just as she turned to leave. Pulling her around to face him, he looked at her mouth. Her lips lacked the lush fullness and unique hue of pink that Lucinda's possessed. Nor was her nose a complete match, though Will mentally congratulated Garenne on finding such a passable double. Dread filled his heart as he pulled the feathered mask from the imposter's face.

He spared but a moment to look at her before gesturing for Weston to take her away. And then he ran, screams of surprise erupting from those he pushed aside as he urgently made his way toward the retiring room. He raced down the hall with two Corinthian agents close behind and kicked in the door.

A swift search verified Will's worst fears—they found no one.

"Your Grace." Agent Chilson drew Will's attention to an open window.

Will strode across the room and peered out, noting the distance to the ground. It would have been risky, but Garenne could have accomplished such a task if he'd lowered Lucinda to someone waiting below.

He gripped the window frame with both hands, his lungs struggling to fill with air. "Chilson, have Weston bring the woman to the library. You," he said to the two other agents, "search the grounds."

He released the frame and stood, willing himself to remain calm. He would find her. There was no other option.

20

Lucinda awoke with a pounding headache, disoriented and terrified. She felt about in the pitch black, reaching blindly for anything that might tell her where she was. Her knuckles suddenly scraped against a cold brass knob. She turned it and pushed gently, but the door would not open.

She put her eye to the keyhole and peered out. The outer room was lit, blinding her for a moment.

She squinted until her vision adjusted, then looked again. The room beyond was dingy, its dirty windows shabbily hung with torn curtains. Sagging furniture was arranged haphazardly. And Garenne bent over a large desk, humming a haunting tune while busily writing.

Lucinda pressed her hand tightly over her mouth to hold back a scream. She had no memory beyond the attack in the retiring room that ended with the foul-smelling handkerchief over her nose. Clearly he'd managed to spirit her away. But to where?

The musty smell of her prison wasn't that of a salt-encrusted sailing vessel, so she felt sure the Frenchman hadn't brought her aboard a ship. The reassurance that she was still on English soil gave her reason to believe that Will would come for her. But she could hardly sit and wait for his arrival, the little she'd been told of Garenne having indicated that he was not to be underestimated.

She reached for the hem of her dress and lifted it, fingers searching her inner thigh for the small knife that she'd strapped there when dressing for the ball.

The sounds of Garenne's approaching footsteps startled her, nearly causing her to drop the knife. She caught the weapon with her other hand and quickly jammed it into the keyhole.

"Lady Lucinda," Garenne called in a disturbingly calm voice. "It is time to rise and meet your destiny."

Lucinda tightened her grip on the knife and held her breath.

He put the key in the hole and turned the knob, jiggling it forcefully in rapid succession. "Come now, do you really think that a wooden door will keep you safe?" He let go of the knob and threw his body toward the door, the wooden slats absorbing the blows with audible cracks. "You stupid chienne. You've tried my patience for the very last time."

Lucinda bit the inside of her cheek, panic rising in her throat. He rammed the door again and a horrified scream escaped from her lips.

"Come out, Garenne. You're surrounded."

The booming voice from outside the house startled Lucinda, sending her jerking back and away from the door. She landed against the far wall with a thud and dropped the knife. She scrambled forward on her hands and knees, desperately searching for the weapon. Her fingers closed over the haft and she gasped with relief. Clutching the knife, she looked out the keyhole, searching for Garenne. He was back at the desk once again, hastily stuffing papers into a leather satchel.

"Do not be concerned, Lady Lucinda," he said over his shoulder, the malevolence in his voice making Lucinda's blood run cold. "We will be leaving here together. Whether you will be alive or dead, well"—he closed the clasp on the bag and turning to cross the room—"that is up to your duke."

Another shout from outside was followed by a loud crack. Garenne's footsteps stopped and Lucinda held her breath, waiting.

The sound of Garenne's retreating footsteps and the low creak of stairs reached Lucinda's ears. She knelt and peered out the keyhole. He was nowhere to be seen, the dingy room empty once more. Fearing what the French madman planned for those who waited outside, she set to work on the lock and prayed that she would escape in time to warn them.

Carmichael had offered Garenne's decoy passage to Canada if she gave them the Frenchman's location. She'd acquiesced, the loyalty between thieves and murderers was evidently as expendable as their consciences.

The late night ride had been pure torture, images of Garenne with his hands on Lucinda flashing in Will's head. He'd urged Sol on at breakneck speed, the entire contingent of Corinthian agents hard on the stallion's heels. They'd slowed to a walk once the hovel had been spied, Will using hand signals to tell his men where to deploy.

He'd taken the lead position, dropping from Sol's back and picking his way through the heavy brush that surrounded the cottage. He walked the perimeter of the house, crouching down at each window to carefully conceal his presence. When Weston signaled that the men were in place, Will had pounded on the door and demanded that Garenne give himself up.

Silence greeted him. Will was hardly surprised, but what little patience he possessed had been used up long ago. He pounded on the door again and yelled for the Frenchman to come out, punctuating his request with a savage kick that left the door split near the bottom.

He was readying himself to kick it in when one of his men shouted for him to stand clear. Will spun, assuming the threat came from behind, but instead he found himself pinned to the ground under Garenne, the man's pistol poised at Will's temple.

"Your Grace, we meet again."

It took all of Lucinda's remaining mental fortitude to hold fear at bay while she picked the lock. She grunted with relief as the lock gave and opened the door slowly, not entirely sure of what she might find on the other side. She narrowed her eyes and glanced quickly around the room. Male voices shouted just beyond the front door.

Frantically, she peered through the darkness, looking for another door. Finding one at the back of the cottage, she pulled on it, prying it open a crack so she could peer out.

Suddenly, the doorknob was yanked from her grip as someone pushed the door wide. Hands grabbed her and pulled her roughly outside; a man rolled with her onto the ground. The scream building in her throat was stopped by a large hand clapped over her mouth. She kicked and struggled against the heavy weight on top of her. He rolled her onto her back with one swift motion. Lucinda flailed her arms and desperately wished for her knife, but it had been knocked free from her in the melee.

"Lucinda?" Lord Chilson whispered gruffly, taking his hand from her mouth and looking at her as if attempting to memorize her face. "Is that you?"

Lucinda nodded her head frantically. "Where is Will?"

Chilson climbed off of Lucinda and stood, offering his hand to her. "Are you all right?" he demanded.

"Garenne is loose, we must find him." Lucinda pushed her tangled hair out of her eyes. *"Now,"* she implored, though Chilson only looked to the other Corinthians, standing behind her.

"Why are you not moving?" she demanded, her entire body shaking.

Chilson took her by the arm and pulled her toward a grassy outcropping where King Solomon's Mine stood, pushing her down onto a large boulder. "Garenne captured Clairemont near the front of the cottage. You must wait here—where it's safe."

His words froze Lucinda's heart, seizing her breath. She could not lose Will, not now.

She wasn't about to sit idly by and allow him to be killed, even if it meant defying the Corinthians. She scrambled to a standing position on the boulder and grabbed Sol's reins, hoisting herself onto his back in one smooth motion. She kicked her leg over and settled into the large saddle, yanking the voluminous skirts of her gown free to allow her to sit astride.

Too late, Chilson realized what she was doing and lunged for the horse. His hand just missed the Thoroughbred's hindquarters as Lucinda kneed King-Solomon into motion. She trotted him to the corner of the house, stopping at the sight of several Corinthian officers.

Garenne and Will stood with their backs to her, the Frenchman's pistol cocked and held at Will's temple while he shouted his demands to Lord Weston.

Fear gripped Lucinda as she took in the sight. She would have only one chance to save Will. She looked to Lord Weston and captured his attention with a wave. Swiftly gesturing with her hands and indicating her plan of attack, she shook off his clear refusal. He looked back to the two men, gesturing to Will to be ready.

Lucinda gripped Sol's reins with one hand and wound her other into his mane. Then she kicked her heels hard into his ribs and the Thoroughbred exploded, moving forward in a blur of speed. Despite her scream and the thunder of hooves, Garenne had only just turned when Solomon reached him.

Cursing, he lifted his pistol and aimed at the horse. Will grabbed his arm and the gun went off. King Sol reared, whinnying with fear at the sound of the shot. Will savagely lashed out at Garenne, landing a blow to his jaw that sent the man to the ground. Sol reared again, this time crushing Garenne beneath the force of his massive, slicing hooves as he came back down to earth.

Lucinda's hold on his reins and mane was jolted loose. She threw her arms around the stallion's neck, hanging on desperately as he bolted toward the edge of the clearing. It took seconds to catch the reins and pull herself upright, tugging Sol to a stop. He stood, shuddering and wild-eyed as she slid off his back. She looped the reins around a tree branchthen ran back to Will.

She threw herself into his arms, burying her face in his neck.

"What the bloody hell did you think you were doing?" he began, pushing her to stand at arm's length. "You could have been killed!" he yelled, then pulled her back in, crushing her lips with a soul-searing kiss.

He broke the kiss abruptly and stared down into her eyes. "You saved my life," he said, his voice hoarse.

"And you saved mine," Lucinda replied, her hands reaching to cup his face. "You brave, bloody fool!"

"You are the brave one, Lucinda, you," he began, looking at her with such love and devotion. "I was a coward. I couldn't see my way clear—I was afraid of what I felt, afraid of what it would mean to admit such a thing—"

He stopped abruptly and swallowed hard. "I love you, Lucinda. I have all along."

Lucinda's heart felt ready to burst with joy as she

pulled his face to hers, their lips nearly touching. "It is about time, Your Grace."

He closed the distance between them and kissed her again, a tender lingering touch that filled Lucinda's heart with hope anew.

"Promise me you will never attempt such a dangerous act again," he said as he gathered her more closely to himself.

All around them was chaos, Corinthians descending on Garenne's body while others tended to the nervously dancing King Solomon's Mine. Carmichael aided Lord Weston, who had been grazed in the leg by Garenne's haphazardly fired bullet.

But here, with Will by her side, all was quiet, the world finally as it should be.

"You'll need to make an honest woman of me to earn such a promise, Your Grace."

"Bloody hell, woman, is that all?"

"Hardly."

"Good," he replied, a crooked smile capturing his mouth. "I would hate to think that love had softened your self-possession."

Lucinda laughed knowingly as she looked up into the dark canopy of trees overhead, the moonlit sky peeking through here and there. "Oh, Your Grace. You've no idea. No idea at all.

Epilogue

CASTLE CLAIREMONT
DERBYSHIRE
1812

Will rubbed Lucinda's lower back gently, causing his beautiful wife to emit small sighs of relief. "Shall I fetch a chair?" he asked, looking with concern at her sizeable belly where it just skimmed the wood fencing.

Lucinda raised a hand to her brow, shadowing her eyes from the bright sun in order to see the new stallion as he romped in the pasture. "Will, I'm perfectly fine," she answered reassuringly. "Now tell me, what do you think of Thor?"

Will's gaze followed Lucinda's, catching sight of the majestic bay Thoroughbred as he pranced about in the lush green field. The horse had arrived only the day before, yet he'd settled in with ease. "I think my opinion is of no consequence. It's what you see that matters."

"Smart man," Lucinda confirmed, turning to Will and smiling beatifically. "His legs are as straight as they come and his eyes—oh, so kind, yet the sheer, unadulterated pleasure in them when he runs? Yes, I think he'll serve your mares well."

"Better than Sol, then?" Will asked wistfully.

Lucinda reached out and cupped his face in her hands. "I miss him as much as you, my love. But I fear Cleopatra would perish if we were to separate the two—never mind my aunts."

Will knew she was right, of course, the aunts having taken control of the Grey breeding program with iron—and quite expert—fists. In little more than a year the first of Sol's offspring would race, and anyone worth his spurs was sure that it would be *the* moment to see. He would not stir up trouble between Lucinda and her aunts simply because he missed his horse.

He couldn't.

He wouldn't.

Will turned his attention back to his wife, her growing belly making him smile once more. So much had happened in the last year that Will wondered at times if it was all a dream. He'd allowed himself to love and be loved, something he thought was not possible. And surprisingly enough, his world had not ended, but rather expanded in a way that he could have never imagined.

His involvement with the Corinthians had changed drastically, which had surprisingly suited Will perfectly. His life was so full now that he was no longer the angry Iron Will of old, who'd run from his demons while lacking a true path.

He'd found that true path, and blessed peace, at Lucinda's side.

His wife dropped her hands to her hips and breathed deeply.

"Are you quite sure you wouldn't like a chair?" Will pressed.

"No," Lucinda replied, turning back to watch Thor. "Your mother and Lord Pinehurst are due to arrive any moment. I hardly want to be found dusty and smelling of horses when they do."

It had taken time. A lot of time, actually, but Will and

his mother were slowly reclaiming the love that had been lost between them. Will could not say that he'd let go of the past entirely, but he'd made a start. They'd made a start, together.

"Will they marry?"

Lucinda eyed Will hesitantly. "Do you want them to?"

"I do, actually," Will replied, rather surprised at his answer. "Do not misunderstand me. All this family needs is another pigheaded male. But they do seem to care for each other. Quite a bit, from what I've seen—though I'm hardly a judge of such things."

"You have the softest of hearts—"

"Speaking of pigheaded men," Will interrupted, sure that his wife would dissolve into a puddle of tears if he did not, "where is that brother of mine?"

"Practicing his proposal on Serendipity."

Will came to stand next to Lucinda at the fence line, capturing her with an unabashedly confused stare. "What could my prized mare have to do with a proposal? And, more importantly, what could Michael have to do with either?"

"He's intent on asking Lady Mariah for her hand—but not before he's spoken to you first," Lucinda replied, her eyes glistening. "He'll leave for London straightaway after the baby is born, so please, do make yourself available. You've been so caught up in the harvest I fear he hasn't had the opportunity to broach the topic."

"Why on earth would the man want to talk to me? What do I know about proper courtship and proposals?"

Lucinda looked at him full in the face and Will knew they'd not escape the day without one more good cry. "Because you're his brother—a true and proper one, now that you've taken back the ducal responsibilities."

"Don't cry, Lucinda. I'll talk to Mich—"

"It's just that I'm so proud of all you've done. For Michael, and for your mother. But especially for your-self," she said, the tears slowly beginning to slide down her full cheeks.

Lucinda turned to look at Thor, who had stretched his long neck over the fence and was now nudging his nose up against Lucinda's belly. "Tell me that you're as happy as I am, my love."

Will reached out and patted the giant horse softly on the head. "Indeed. And more, my love. So much more."

Acknowledgments

They say that it take a village to raise a child. Oddly enough, I found the same to be true of writing and producing a book.

Randall. You are mine, andI am yours. I'm pretty sure that I got the better end of the bargain, but I'll take it. Thank you for loving me far better than I could ever love myself.

The Girls. You challenge me to be a better person every single day. No, really. Every. Single. Day. And I love you all the more for it. XO to infinity.

Wallace Dyer Jr. Thank you for Bob Dylan and Diet Sprite, for Christmas trees and deliciously crude humor. You left us too soon.

Michael Dyer. You rolled me down a hill in a box when we were young and told me whatever didn't kill me would make me stronger. You were right.

Julie Pottinger. You picked me up and brushed me off when I needed you to, laughed and cried with me, and convinced me that the impossible *was* possible if tackled one step at a time. Thank you for walking the road with me.

Jennifer Schober. One. Awesome. Agent. Thank you for reminnding me that it's all in the journeey, not the destination.

Junessa Viloria. Best. Editor. Ever. Your professional-ism, editorial skills, and keen reader's eye made this book what it is. It's that simple.

Jennifer McCord. You shared your expertise and in-sight at no cost, encouraged me to follow my heart, and became a dear friend. For all of this and more, I thank you.

Franzeca Drouin. I've said it before and I'll say it again: Your brain, it is an impressive thing. Thank you for your mad research skills, ability to meet ridiculous deadlines, and coolness in general.

Read on for an exciting sneak peek at

The Angel in My Arms

Stefanie Sloane's next Regency Rogues novel

Coming from Ballantine Books
Available wherever books are sold

SUMMER; DORSET
1811

Marcus MacInnes, the Earl of Weston, looked out over Lulworth Cove and chuckled. "Well now, Sully, you've seen it for yourself. Aye, it's my own personal Jericho. Wouldn't you agree?"

The valet's swarthy face remained unreadable, the lines around his eyes deepening as he squinted, his gaze focused on what lay below them. The cove's blue water lapped at the hulls of fishing boats. On the shore, the village dozed sleepily in the warm sunshine.

Exactly the sort of spot a gentleman might just be sent to rusticate after a gunshot wound. Especially if the gentleman happened to be a spy.

Sully turned to look directly at his master. "It looks quiet enough, I'll give you that."

Marcus smiled wryly before turning his horse back onto the leafy path. "Indeed."

Sully followed suit, kneeing his bay gelding next to Marcus's chestnut Thoroughbred. "There *could* be smugglers."

Marcus slowed his mount just long enough to give him a dubious look.

"Or not," Sully admitted somewhat dejectedly.

Marcus ducked his head to dodge a low-hanging limb and the green leaves of one of the massive whitebeam trees that lined the trail. "What a waste of time."

But there was nothing he could do about it. He'd been given an order, and he'd bloody well follow it.

Marcus was a Corinthian, and that meant something. Damn it.

He and Sully continued on in silence. Their horses, Marcus thought absently, seemed thankful for the slower pace after the three-day ride from London to Lulworth.

The shaded lane curved, and ahead of the two riders rose Lulworth Castle, Marcus's home. Originally built as a hunting lodge, the impressive structure had been expanded over the years until it was the largest home in the district.

The unentailed castle belonged to Marcus, due to his mother having been an only child. Yes, it was all his. And it was undeniably magnificent. But it was not where he wanted to be.

Marcus was a member of the Young Corinthians, a clandestine spy organization led by Henry Prescott, Viscount Carmichael. There was an unwritten rule among the Corinthians never to question an assignment. The life of a spy demanded complete loyalty and unswerving belief in your superior's judgment—a fact Marcus found tiresome at the moment.

When a bullet found its way into his leg during a mission this past spring, Marcus had known that his role within the elite organization would change dramatically. Until his injury fully healed, he was more of a liability than an asset in the field.

Nevertheless, when Lord Carmichael suggested that Marcus investigate recent smuggling activity near his ancestral home in Dorset, Marcus nearly abandoned his well-practiced charm and informed his superior just what he thought of the ridiculous assignment.

Finding yourself with a bullet in your leg was one thing. Having your superior send you off on a fool's errand was quite another.

He couldn't deny that in all likelihood he'd made himself somewhat of a nuisance to Carmichael as he impatiently waited for his blasted wound to heal.

And if he admitted that much, then he really could not blame Carmichael for dispatching him to the Dorset countryside when news of a possible connection between radical revolutionaries and local smugglers had the prince Regent's drawers in a twist.

As Carmichael had informed him over plates of roast beef at their club, a string of recent robberies in London were believed to be related to the suspicious activities in Lulworth—and both were somehow tied to Napoleon's supporters.

Marcus had only stared at Carmichael in disbelief, a heavy goblet of brandy poised halfway to his mouth. Really, it was too much to be believed.

But still, Marcus now reluctantly realized, if he was to be completely honest, his irritation with the assignment had as much to do with the location as with the smuggling investigation itself.

During his boyhood, when not in Inverness at his father's estate, the family had split their time between London and Lulworth. At least in London he'd been able to lose himself amidst the constant thrum of social and sporting events. But the same could not be said for Lulworth. The hamlet's inhabitants had never got over his Scottish father's stealing away the fairest of their English roses. It hadn't helped that the elder Lord Weston embraced his role as the brutish Highlander with particular relish. His habit of donning a tartan and broadsword whenever his family visited the castle had only made things worse.

The locals hadn't liked the father, and as a result, they didn't like the son. And Marcus had known, from a painfully early age, that he simply did not fit in. Not in Lulworth, where everyone from the baker's son to the solicitor's daughter saw him as nothing more than the son of a thief. Not in Inverness either, where the blue English blood in his veins meant he'd never be a true Highlander.

"I've sorely missed Cook's pheasant," Sully said, pulling Marcus from his thoughts.

The stone castle stood before them with all the welcoming warmth of a mid-winter snowfall.

"You're an accomplished liar, Sully, I'll give you that." Marcus's amiable tone belied his recent grim thoughts. "But I know you too well. It's Cook that you've been looking forward to, not her creamed peas."

"Pheasant," Sully corrected him. "And it's quite a succulent bird that she cooks," he protested. "Though her creamed peas are quite delicious as well."

Marcus reined in his horse and raised a hand. "Far be it from me to intrude upon the ways of love," he said sardonically, prompting a harrumph from his valet.

With a noticeable lack of his usual ease, Marcus awkwardly swung a leg over the saddle and lowered himself to the ground, an instant stab of pain shooting up from the healing wound in his thigh. He ground his teeth together until the sensation subsided, then drew the soft leather reins over Pokey's head and handed them to Sully. "I'm going to walk off this stiffness. I'll be along shortly."

Sully gave Marcus a considering look then leaned from the saddle to take the reins. "Are you up to it?"

"Awa' an' bile yer heid!" Marcus growled, though the valet's thoughtfulness made him smile.

"Oh," Sully began, turning the two horses toward the stables, "I'll be missing that burr of yours while we're here. Can't be playing Lord of the Manor like onee of them Jacobites, now, can we?" he teased. "I'll be in the kitchen, then."

"Oh, that's a given," Marcus shot back, sounding like the perfect London swell. For as long as he could remember, he had made it a habit to hide his burr from everyone but Sully and the Scottish side of his family. There was simply no good reason to remind people of his ancestry.

"I'll send the hounds out if you've not limped your way home by dark."

"That's terribly thoughtful of you, old friend."

"Don't mention it—"

"And I do mean *old*," Marcus added with a gleam in his eye.

He could just make out another harrumph as Sully clucked to his horse and rode on, his pace quickening as he disappeared into the copse of trees that separated the expansive lawn of Lulworth from the rest of the grounds.

Marcus stretched, trying to ease the aches in his travel-weary muscles without irritating his wound. He turned and strolled, limping slightly, toward the wood, his destination undecided. The tension that had gripped his gut when he'd first spied the castle slowly dissipated as he moved farther into the trees. He tugged at his carefully tied cravat, a low sigh escaping his lips as he yanked the length of white linen free of its intricate knot and unwound it from his throat. He mopped his brow with the dust-covered cloth before dropping it into the pocket of his deep brown riding jacket.

The shade from the green-leafed canopy of oak trees provided some relief, but Marcus needed more. He stopped to orient himself, looking north, then east. Realizing that he wasn't far from the lake where he'd fished as a child, he set off at a faster clip.

A refreshing swim was precisely what he needed. The water would cool his body, clear his head, and, hopefully, tire him to the point that he no longer cared about where he was.

A high-pitched scream shattered the quiet and stopped Marcus in his tracks. A second scream followed and Marcus ran, willing his wounded leg to keep pace with the rest of his body as he crashed through a bank of quickthorn bushes.

He fought his way through the thicket, the branches lashing his arms and legs until he broke into the open. The castle lake lay before him, sparkling in the sunlight.

He examined the water's surface, then the shore from left to right, but failed to find the source of the screams. Something moved suddenly in his peripheral vision. He narrowed his eyes and once more searched the lake. Water rippled in a circle too large to have been caused by a jumping trout.

He stripped off his coat and prepared to dive in. Just then two figures broke the surface of the water. A peal of feminine laughter filled the air.

"You promised!" a young male voice whined indignantly.

Marcus squinted against the sun and made out a boy, sodden hair plastered to his skull.

"I never promised, Nigel," a woman's voice answered teasingly, "and it's very poor form of you to lie."

Marcus shielded his eyes with one hand to see the woman better. She bobbed up and down in the water, clearly amused with whatever had transpired between her and the boy.

Suddenly she looked straight at him, her eyes widening in surprise.

And then she smiled. A brilliant, wide smile that

seemed to light up the entire world. She was soaking wet, auburn curls in damp corkscrews atop her head and hanging to her shoulders. Her ivory skin flushed under the hot sun, a trailing frond of green water weed peeking out above the neckline of her dress.

Marcus could not imagine a more bonny sight.

She seemed about to speak to him when her gaze shifted past him and over his shoulder. Shock and dismay filled her expression. "No, Titus!" she cried out. "No!"

Marcus turned his head just in time to make out a massive dog galloping toward him. The fawn-colored animal launched itself into the air, toppling Marcus backward onto the clay earth of the lake bank.

The weight of the beast's body settled on Marcus's chest and it planted a dinner-plate-sized paw on either side of Marcus's head. Then the dog lowered its massive face, the drool from its sharp-fanged mouth threatening to drop at any moment.

Marcus held himself completely still, knowing full well the animal had the upper hand. The dog sniffed carefully, its noxious breath hitting Marcus's nostrils with pungent force.

"Titus, get off that gentleman now. This! Very! Instant!"

The dog offered Marcus a sheepish, apologetic look before swiping its lolling tongue in friendly salute across Marcus's face.

"Now! Get off him. You bad, bad boy!"

Another apologetic look and the dog rose, allowing Marcus to sit up.

The woman leaned down to peer anxiously into Marcus's face.

"I must apologize for my dog's behavior," she said earnestly, now leaning so close that Marcus felt tiny droplets of lake water hit his skin when she moved.

"He is—"

"A menace to society?" the young boy at her side offered, giving Marcus a toothy grin.

"He is an enthusiastic participant in life." The woman rose to her feet to glare at the boy. "Titus is simply in need of proper instruction in manners."

"That is one way of looking at him," the boy countered, pointing at the dog, who was now a few feet away and busily tearing holes in Marcus's castoff coat.

"Titus!" The woman protested, dashing toward the Shetland pony–sized dog. She tripped on a tree root and landed awkwardly on all fours, her nicely rounded derriere sticking up in the air.

Marcus stood with difficulty, wincing, his leg throbbing like the devil. He brushed without much success at the dirt stains on his buff-colored breeches and white linen shirt.

"Who is she?" he asked, failing to hide his stunned reaction.

The boy, whose features exactly matched the young woman's, chuckled. "Oh, no one of consequence, I assure you." He offered his hand to Marcus and shook enthusiastically. "I, on the other hand, am Nigel Edward Tisdale."

She was now engaged in a heated game of tug-of-war with the dog, her petite frame hardly a match for the big dog's superior strength.

"Marcus MacInnes, Earl of Weston," Marcus replied, hiding his brogburrue with practiced ease. His gaze returned to the woman. "I wonder, should we assist Miss—"

"Not *the* Errant Earl?" the boy asked in wonder.

Marcus turned and looked at the lad, assuming that he had misheard. "I'm sorry, what was that you said?"

"Surely you know what people in these parts call you? I'd rather poke myself in the eye with a sharpened stick than listen to my mother and her friends gossip, but even I've heard the talk, and it's—what the word I'm looking for?" Young Nigel paused and drummed his fingers against his lips as he thought.

"Unfavorable," Marcus offered helpfully.

"Well, I was going to say 'downright nasty,' but yes 'unfavorable' will do."

Clearly, while the world about it continuously moved forward, the village of Lulworth stalwartly cleaved to unfounded and exaggerated assumptions. Marcus assumed that he should be offended, but honestly, he had neither the energy nor the interest at the moment.

He looked back to the woman, who was desperately attempting to maintain her foothold. "Shouldn't we . . ." he began, gesturing toward the pair.

"Oh, no, that would irritate Sarah to no end," the boy answered, watching the scene with marked delight as he wrung out his sodden shirt. "And trust me, you don't want to irritate my sister."

Marcus couldn't help but picture the woman irritated—enraged, really, as he sensed it would take very little to make her so. Her auburn hair flying about her like a fiery halo, her skin heated to a delicious pink hue.

Marcus shook his head from left to right, wondering if the dog had indeed done some sort of damage to his mental faculties.

The two males watched for a moment more as the woman dug in her heels and seemed to be gaining the upper hand. But then the dog began to drag her forward, pulling her lower and closer to the ground until she collapsed with an audible expulsion of breath, facedown in the dirt.

"Sarah?" the boy queried in a mischievous tone. "Have you rescued Lord Weston's coat?"

The woman froze. Then slowly she released the torn

coat and pulled herself upright, brushing lightly at the front of her wet, mud-stained gown.

"I beg your pardon, Nigel. Did you say 'Lord Weston'?"

The dog galloped to a stop beside her and dropped the coat at her feet.

"Bad dog!" she whispered vehemently, bending to snatch up the torn garment.

The boy elbowed Marcus in the ribs. "Why yes, Sarah," he said, drawing her attention back to her question. "The coat belongs to *Lord Weston.*"

The lady's demeanor changed instantly. She leveled a cool glance at her brother, her chin tilting slightly higher. Her diminutive shoulders squared and she attempted to unobtrusively peel the clingy gown from her fair skin.

Marcus stifled a laugh. She was covered from head to toe in dirt and God only knew what else. Any woman in her right mind would have fainted from the embarrassment of the situation. And, he realized, any man would have politely excused himself by now.

Yet, here he was.

"I do apologize for my dog's behavior, Lord Weston," she said agreeably. The trailing bit of bracken at her hemline did little to aid her dignity as she walked toward him. "And I will, of course, pay for the damages to your coat."

She thrust the ruined article of clothing toward him, avoiding his gaze.

"Mother is going to be apoplectic when she hears about this!" Nigel said with glee.

She caught Nigel's arm with some force, if the boy's pained expression was any indication. "Nigel, make yourself useful and properly introduce us, please."

"She'll be abed for days with this one—"

"Nigel!" the young woman remonstrated, maintaining a polite, if strained smile.

"Very well," Nigel begrudgingly agreed. "Sarah Elizabet Tisdale, my I present Marcus MacInnes, the Earl of Weston."

The Bizarre quality of the moment was not lost on Marcus. Here he stood, clothing torn and mauled by what was clearly the result of a misguided romantic encounter between a canine and a large bear. The female standing in front of him was in absolute and, not to put too fine a point on it, scandalous disarray. And a devilish sprite was performing polite introductions in the middle of the wood.

It was of Shakespearian proportions, a farce, to be sure.

He should be appalled. Any man of his standing would be.

But he was delighted.

And he couldn't remember a time that he'd been so thankful for the ache in his leg and the need of a walk.

"Miss Tisdale," he said, offering a respectful bow in her direction.

She offered an awkward curtsy. "Lord Weston, I'm delighted to make your acquaintance."

Marcus found it oddly amusing, their mutual adherence to the proprieties despite the clearly improper circumstances of this encounter. "And I yours."

She looked at him then, a blush settling on her ivory skin. "We were not aware you were in residence at the castle."

"Do you only make use of the lake in my absence?" he asked teasingly, his charm returning.

"I can assure you, sir, that we do not make a habit of trespassing on your—"

"We most certainly do," Nigel interrupted indignantly. "It's the best fishing in the county."

Miss Tisdale looked as if she might spontaneously combust. The flush of heat traveling from her neck upward would most certainly erupt in flames upon reaching her fiery auburn curls.

She took a deep breath, an impish grin coming to rest on her lips. "Oh, all right, then. We do. Now, Nigel," she paused, looking about as if searching for something, and then whistling in a most unladylike fashion, "do secure Titus's leash."

The earth shook as the huge dog ran toward them. Marcus braced himself as Titus came to a sliding stop mere inches from his legs.

Nigel retrieved a leather lead, coiled in a serpentine pile near the bank. "I don't know why we bother with this. It would hardly keep him—"

Miss Tisdale daintily cleared her throat and shot Nigel a murderous look. "The lead, Nigel."

No sooner had the boy obeyed than Titus lifted his massive head and caught the scent of something on the wind. He bounded off with Nigel in tow, leaving Marcus and Miss Tisdale quite alone.

She watched as Titus dragged her brother along, a small smile forming on her mouth. "Serves him right," she said under her breath.

Marcus pretended not to hear her, as it was the polite thing to do. Still, he smiled.

He could not look away. The sun had begun to dry her mass of auburn hair so that it gleamed in the sun, threads of gold catching the light in a dizzying array. He wanted to reach out and touch it, to measure the weight of it in his hands.

Her profile enthralled him. Her pert nose—sprinkled with freckles, no less—was the perfect accompaniment to her high cheekbones and that damnably kissable mouth.

"I apologize, Lord Weston," she offered quietly, without looking at him.

Marcus abruptly ended his cataloging of her features. "For trespassing or for Titus?" he quipped.

"Both, actually," she answered, turning to look at him, a charming smirk lighting up her face. "And the mud. I'm really quite sorry for the mud."

And just like that, she ran from the lake bank and disappeared into the shrubbery, her long auburn hair swaying behind her as she went.

"What in bloody hell just happened?" Marcus said aloud, not sure what to do next.

BLUE WARRIOR

MIKE MADEN

BERKLEY BOOKS
NEW YORK

BERKLEY

An imprint of Penguin Random House LLC
375 Hudson Street, New York, New York 10014

BLUE WARRIOR

A Berkley Book / published by arrangement with the author

ISBN: 978-0-425-27806-2

PUBLISHING HISTORY
G. P. Putnam's Sons hardcover edition / October 2014
Berkley premium edition / October 2015

PRINTED IN THE UNITED STATES OF AMERICA

10 9 8 7 6 5 4 3 2 1

Interior map copyright © 2014 by Jeffrey L. Ward.
Cover design by Richard Hasselberger.

Penguin
Random
House

For Angela, my wife.
Always.
Everything.

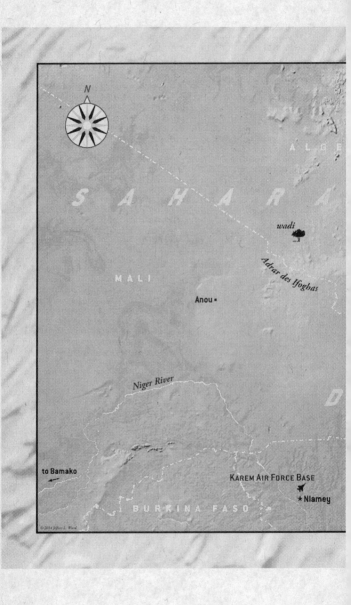

↑ to Malta

Tassili du Hoggar

AÉROPOSTALE STATION 11

• MAERSK OIL
PUMPING STATION

BASE AÉRIENNE ARLIT

• Arlit

E S E R T

NIGER

0 Miles   100   200
0 Kilometers   200

NIGERIA

Knowledge is more than equivalent to force.

—SAMUEL JOHNSON, *The History of Rasselas,*
Prince of Abissinia, ch. xiii

2015

= 1 =

Maputo International Airport
Maputo, Mozambique
1 May

The gusting wind battered Troy Pearce's bearded face. He didn't care. It kept the humidity low and the stink of jet fuel at bay while he and Johnny Paloma finished loading up the last of the gear into a rented 2008 Toyota Land Cruiser pickup. They had two drone contracts to fulfill this trip.

Johnny hardly said a word. Unusual for the former SWAT officer.

"Something on your mind?" Pearce asked. A pair of dark aviators hid his world-weary blue eyes.

"Been meaning to ask you something."

"So why haven't you?"

"Seems like the last couple of weeks you haven't been yourself."

More like a couple of months, Pearce thought. He didn't think it showed.

Even though Pearce was the CEO of his global contracting firm, he liked getting his hands dirty out in the field. Didn't believe in leading from behind. He slammed the truck gate shut. "So ask."

"How about I run this first training consult by myself?"

Pearce liked Johnny a lot. He was street smart and fearless, a real door buster. Proved his worth last year in the ops they ran against the Mexicans and Iranians. Since then, Johnny had picked up on the basic technical aspects of drone operations and proved himself a decent small unmanned aerial systems (sUAS) operator.

Pearce Systems specialized in drone operations. Their first gig this week was an sUAS delivery and training consult with Sandra Gallez and the World Wildlife Alliance. Four days from now, they would deliver a security package to the South African special forces training center at Fort Scorpio.

For the first time in a while, Pearce smiled. "You want that Gallez woman all to yourself."

"She's a friend, that's all. I just think I'm ready to lead the training. Don't need you to wet-nurse me."

Sandra Gallez had flown up to Addis to sign the WWA contract three months before. The two of them obviously hit it off.

"I call bullshit." Pearce saw the way he looked at her when she came into their office.

"We've stayed in touch." Johnny grinned. "By phone, mostly."

Pearce couldn't blame him. The Belgian wildlife conservationist was a real looker, and bright. It was a good match.

"Maybe it is time you took point." Pearce tossed him the truck keys. "No point in wasting that picnic basket, either." He'd seen Johnny sneak it into the pickup that morning. "Unless you packed it for me."

Johnny smiled. "Not exactly."

"I'll secure the Aviocar."

Pearce was glad to let Johnny do the training. Their destination today was the Great Limpopo Transfrontier Park, but Lake Massingir bordered the wilderness reserve. Pearce had fished all of his life, all over the world. He thought he wouldn't get a chance to bait a hook this trip, but now Johnny made that possible. Maybe things were looking up after all.

He headed back into the rented hangar. Pearce and Johnny had arrived with Dr. Rao's shipment last night from Addis in the Pearce Systems C-212 Aviocar, a boxy, top-winged, twin-propped STOL cargo plane. Pearce was doing most of his own flying these days now that his personal pilot, Judy Hopper, was gone.

The South African equipment was stowed away in a secret, locked compartment under the deck. Pearce shut and locked the plane's cargo door, then shut and locked the hangar doors. Determined thieves could still break in, but he hired an armed security service to keep an eye on things while they were in the field.

Pearce climbed into the truck cab on the passenger side. The a/c was blowing good and cold.

Johnny checked the map on his satellite phone. Didn't look at Pearce.

"You see those two jokers in the silver Mercedes G-Class, by the fence?"

"They picked us up back at the hotel an hour ago," Pearce said.

"You could've said something."

"How'd you manage to survive in LA with eyes like yours?"

"High-capacity magazines." Johnny chambered a round into his Glock 19 pistol. "Any idea who they are?"

"SVR. Russian intelligence service."

"What do you think they want?"

"My head." Pearce had killed Ambassador Britnev for masterminding the plot that murdered President Myers's son last year and nearly drew the United States into a shooting war with the Russians.

"I thought you got away clean on that one."

"So did I."

"What do you want to do?"

"They had a clear shot at me. So taking me out isn't the objective."

"An exfil back to the Motherland? They must be really pissed."

"Britnev was a douche bag, but he was their douche bag."

"Two against two. We can take them."

"Too risky."

"Got a better idea?"

"I always liked the G-Class. Reminds me of a Tonka truck." Pearce pulled out his smartphone. "Let's roll."

Johnny pulled away from the hangar and through the fence gate, heading for the road exiting the airport. The boxy German SUV sat tight as Johnny passed by their parking place, just as Pearce instructed.

By the time Johnny cleared the airport, the Mercedes was in his rearview mirror, keeping a discreet distance.

"The driver's good," Johnny said.

Pearce tapped keys on his phone screen. "The SVR only sends the best. They won't try anything until we've cleared the city."

Thirty minutes outside of Maputo, traffic disappeared. The highway was an empty straight line for miles. The silver Mercedes glinted in Johnny's rearview mirror a mile back. Couldn't miss it.

"That G-Class AMG is a sweet ride," Johnny said. "Hundred thirty grand plus, just to drive it off the lot."

"It's an amazing piece of technology. All the latest bells and whistles."

"Ready?" Pearce asked.

Johnny smiled. "Say the word."

"Red-line it," Pearce said.

"God, I love this job." Johnny mashed the gas pedal to the floorboard.

The Toyota rocketed forward, but the straight-six engine was topping out at 180 kph. Not good enough.

Pearce glanced in the side mirror. "He's coming on, fast."

The Mercedes's thundering 5.5-liter turbocharged V-8 was still accelerating. They were just a quarter mile back.

Shooting distance.

Pearce tapped his phone screen, capturing the Mercedes Distronic Plus radar-controlled cruise control. Ran his finger along a slider. Told the radar unit that an object was just one inch away from the Mercedes's front bumper.

The power disc brakes locked. Pads and rotors screamed.

The big Mercedes tumbled end over end on the asphalt, glass flying, steel crunching, doors exploding. On the third rotation, a body flew out, cartwheeling on the asphalt. Four more devastating rotations, and the crumpled Mercedes finally landed in a shattered heap on the side of the road.

"How'd you manage that?" Johnny asked. He pulled his foot off of the gas pedal, dropping back down to the legal speed limit.

"Pirated his Bluetooth back at the parking lot."

Johnny chuckled. "Technology's a bitch."

Pearce powered down his smartphone. "Let's go find your girl."

= 2 =

S he was there at the beginning, when the U.S. government first weaponized the Internet. In fact, she had loaded some of the first rounds into the cylinder and cocked the hammer.

Jasmine Bath was twenty-four years old when she earned her M.S. in computer science from UC Berkeley. The striking Afro-Asian woman was one of the first recruits into the NSA's Office of Tailored Access Operations (TAO) program. They started her at Fort Meade but moved her around, grooming her for bigger things. She was a software specialist but became familiar with hardware operations, too. She helped write some of the first coding for the NSA's pervasive XKEYSCORE surveillance software before moving up into senior development positions within TAO's aggressive counterintelligence ANT program. Her coding fingerprints were all over persistent software implants like JETPLOW (firewall firmware), HEADWATER (software backdoors), and SOMBERKNAVE (wireless Internet traffic rerouting). Those successes earned her multiple commendations and promotions, leading to training and supervisory positions in newly developed TAO sites in Hawaii, Texas, Colorado, and even the Dagger Complex in Germany.

That meant the vast resources of the NSA were entirely at her disposal. She now had access to TAO's shadow networks of servers and routers, used for covertly hijacking or herding unsuspecting Internet traffic through them. It was the Internet equivalent of the CIA opening up a cell phone store in Abbottabad and secretly selling supposedly untraceable burner phones to al-Qaeda terrorists.

With the help of the CIA, FBI, and other national security agencies, TAO also planted hardware and software bugs and malware in electronic devices manufactured around the globe—including memory chips, hard drives, motherboards and cell phone cameras, to name just a few—to gain access to their data.

TAO also remotely implanted software bugs and malware into network firewalls and security software programs, allowing the NSA to back-door more malware into, and harvest data out of, entire computer networks or individual computers, tablets, and phones. They even had their own manufacturing facilities, producing compromised keyboards, monitors, routers, and connector cables that secretly transmitted user data. The NSA also operated mirrored cell phone base stations that acted like legitimate cell phone towers, secretly capturing entire networks of cell phone users without their knowledge.

In short, nearly every kind of commercially produced electronic device had been compromised, infected, and harnessed to TAO purposes, allowing them to hear, see, or read virtually any data-capable device on the planet without the knowledge of either the users or manufacturers. Best of all, these devices, once installed, remained in place, continuously harvesting data for future NSA use—data that Bath still had access to as well.

But that wasn't all.

The NSA and its sister agencies successfully compromised nearly every social networking site on the planet. They even penetrated the "Dark Web," where criminal and terrorist activity supposedly occurred without public knowledge or government interference.

The NSA also created hundreds of fake jihadist, anarchist, and terrorist websites, blogs, and Twitter accounts in order to gather data from incautious users, identify new suspects, compromise dangerous individuals and organizations, and plant false data into hostile communities. They operated cybercafés around the world, offering free Internet access to unsuspecting customers, not unlike the CIA conducting fake vaccination campaigns to harvest DNA data on terror suspects. Conservative politicians who supported intrusive surveillance activities never realized that certain security agencies had also created virtual "Honey Pot" websites in order to draw out the most extremist elements within Tea Party, nationalist, constitutionalist, and "prepper" circles.

Jasmine Bath had access to all of these fake portals as well.

With all of these weapons in hand, Jasmine Bath could find out just about anything about anybody, or plant credible false evidence against any person. That gave her the kind of power that state security agencies had sought since the time of the pharaohs but could only dream of.

And that's when she quit.

Bath's extensive experience and exposure gave her a big-picture overview of the NSA's far-reaching capabilities and boundless resources. It also allowed her to secretly pocket a number of tools she would later use to pick the locks at her former employer in order to form her new company, CIOS. In effect, she used the NSA's resources against them in order to exploit the NSA as her own spying agency. Who watches the watchers? Jasmine Bath does, she'd joke. She spied on the spies—or, more accurately, spied through the spies—without their even knowing it.

With her top-security clearances, impeccable credentials, and agency contacts, she acquired several legitimate NSA contracts for CIOS just hours after tendering her resignation. But the real money to be made had nothing to do with honest work. She knew her unparalleled ability to find or fake information on virtually anybody, anywhere, would pry open the deepest wallets in Washington.

She felt no guilt. She lost count of the number of "false flag" operations governments around the world—

including her own—had used to start wars in the last forty years, or the lies told by politicians, bureaucrats, and advocacy groups to justify radically new domestic policy agendas. Venerable science journals and prestigious research institutions were plagued with falsified data in the scramble for federal grants and venture-capital investments. Bath just wanted her piece of the pie.

All she lacked was the funding to launch the venture. But she didn't have long to wait. A silent investor approached her and offered her unfettered control of her company. In exchange for no-strings-attached financing came his quid pro quo of no questions asked, and in turn, she was to be available when called upon, which would be both rare and remunerative.

The silent investor's name, she would discover much later after proving herself to him, was startling. One of the true power brokers in Washington. His connections provided her with all the cover she would ever need should her formidable defenses ever fail. Owing to his preeminence in her corporate life, she always referred to him as The Angel.

= 3 =

P earce scratched his beard with his free hand, wild and woolly the way he wore it back in the war, except now it was flecked with gray, just like his long black hair. The crow's-feet around his eyes had deepened.

He reached into the bucket for another bottle of Sagres Preta, a local Portuguese dark lager, and worked the black cap off with a knife edge. He'd been drinking too much for the past few months, and his gut showed it. He never drank at work, only after hours, and never got too drunk. Just numb.

Mostly.

The locals told him bloody chicken livers were the next best thing to live bait if he wanted to catch one of the razor-toothed tiger fish lurking in the deep water, a hundred silvery pounds of thrashing mouth full of vicious teeth as long as sixteen-penny nails. They told him to keep the hooks small unless he wanted to catch one of the really big monsters, but then he'd have the fight of his life on his hands—literally.

He went with the big hooks.

The choppy water chucked against the hull of the small wooden boat. His fishing line hadn't budged in hours in the gray water. Sunset wasn't too far off. If something didn't strike the bait soon, he'd start rowing back. He flexed his blistered hands. In this wind, he was in for a long haul back to shore.

He'd rejoin Johnny tomorrow, back in the park after Johnny finished up his training consultation with Sandra.

Troy took a sip of beer.

He thought about his old man a lot lately, a Vietnam vet killed by the war years after it ended. Wondered if the same fate awaited him.

Growing up, he and his dad had fought their own private little war, scratching out a living in the mountains of Wyoming. The old man would laugh at him now, for sure. Wasn't he becoming all the things he said he hated about him?

Probably for the same reasons, too.

His dad didn't talk much about the war. Didn't have to. Wore it in his brooding face, the scars in his flesh. If he had regrets, he didn't say. He just drank.

Pearce had no regrets. Was proud of his CIA combat service. In SAD/SOG, he engaged the enemy wherever he found them. Righteous kills, each one. But the War on Terror had taken too many of the people he cared about, sacrificed on the altar of political ambition. So he quit. He missed them all.

Especially Annie.

Pearce still loved his country but hated politics. He formed Pearce Systems because he could pick and choose his operations with a certain moral clarity. And it paid well. More important, deploying remotely piloted vehicles kept his friends out of harm's way even when the bullets were flying.

So what was his problem?

He was an angry man. Always had been, bar brawling all the way back in high school. Stanford took some of the edge off. Practically civilized him. Then he joined the CIA. They honed his angry edge into a fine killing blade, but under control.

Maybe he was losing control.

His anger had deepened the last few months, for sure. So had the depression. Didn't make sense. His company had never been more prosperous, or done better work.

After last year, he focused Pearce Systems on the commercial uses of drone technologies. More opportunities, more money. And little chance of his people getting killed. The South African delivery was a favor for an old friend, and probably the last military system he would ever deliver.

But bitter disappointment still ate at him. The United States had cut and run out of Iraq and Afghanistan. Now both were sliding back into chaos and radicalism. Tens of thousands of brave Americans bled and died to free those nations, but the jihadi shits they fought remained, which meant they won.

His government had broken faith; now Pearce felt like he had lost his.

Serving President Myers last year rekindled it briefly. She was the one politician he could believe in, because she put the national interest ahead of her own. He trusted Myers completely. But she resigned, falling on her sword to keep the nation safe.

He and his team proudly fought the Mexican cartels and the Iranian terrorists. He was grateful Myers secured blanket immunity for them all after it was over. But he didn't need a law degree to know that only criminals need immunity.

Heroes got medals, not pardons.

President Greyhill and Vice President Diele were in charge now. Exactly the kind of politicians he loathed.

He was done with it.

Pearce took a long pull on his beer. His line still didn't budge. He hoped Johnny was having more luck than he was in trying to land his own pretty fish.

Great Limpopo Transfrontier Park
Mozambique

Johnny Paloma pretended to stare at the solar-powered drone in Sandra Gallez's hands, but he couldn't take his eyes off of her face, confident and curious.

"Like this?" she asked. The Belgian beauty held the

Silent Falcon's carbon-fiber fuselage forward with one
hand while the other supported the tail structure. The
six-bladed prop spun almost silently, but the electric
motor threw enough torque into the blades even at this
low speed to blow her dark, curly hair away from her
cheeks. Working undercover in L.A., Johnny encountered plenty of hot women in the clubs and on the
beaches. He even worked a few side jobs as a bodyguard
for some of the best-looking women in film. But Sandra's
natural, unadorned beauty enthralled him.

"Yes, about forty-five degrees. Just like a Raven,"
Johnny said. He held the Nintendo-style controller in his
hands. The auto launch toggle was selected. This would
automatically take the Silent Falcon to an altitude of five
hundred feet and circle it until it received further commands. Onboard sensors and software avoided obstruc-
tions in its flight path or possible collisions with other
aircraft.

"Now?"

"Now!" He laughed.

She threw it. Despite its seven-foot wingspan, the
lightweight sUAS lifted effortlessly into the bright
morning sky.

This portion of the park was mostly flat grassland,
populated by a smattering of acacia trees. Perfect for
small drone operations, especially landings by rookies.
It was elephant country. Rhinos, too.

Sandra jogged back over to Johnny, standing behind
the brand-new green Land Rover Defender utility wagon.
The famous World Wildlife Alliance white rhino logo was

painted on the hood and the rear door. Pearce Systems fitted out the wagon with all of the necessary drone operations gear. The talented young conservationist was in charge of the WWA's most advanced research project.

"Now put the goggles on," Johnny said.

Sandra picked up the wireless Fat Shark Dominator HD video goggles and slipped them over her eyes. They were lightweight but huge, like a telephone handset attached to her face. Of course, she couldn't "see" out of them—they didn't have any lenses. The Fat Shark was a video projection system—a wearable digital theater.

"Now take this." Johnny handed her the flight controller.

"Fantastique!"

"Quite the view, eh?"

"Like a bird. I can see everything."

Sandra's entire field of view was filled with a perfect HD first-person video (FPV) image on the screen, which was also simultaneously recorded on a hard drive in the Rover. The forward-looking bird's-eye POV through the spinning propeller was mesmerizing. She tapped another toggle and a real-time map of Limpopo Park appeared on her video screen. A blue dot indicated the GPS location of the Silent Falcon, and a red dot indicated the position of a recently GPS-tagged rhino, part of the last herd in Mozambique, about five kilometers away.

"Now rotate the camera," he said. "The god's-eye view is even cooler." The Silent Falcon was equipped with a rotating gimbal that housed the optical and infrared cameras, along with a laser pointer.

"This is perfection, Johnny!" Sandra rotated the camera through its entire range of motion, like she'd done on simulated practice sessions before, but this was her first real-time flight with the Silent Falcon.

The WWA recently made arrangements with Mozambique's Wildlife Department to take over rhino observation-and-research duties. The cash-strapped, ill-equipped bureaucracy had become rather lax in its conservation responsibilities in the last few years, particularly in regard to the endangered rhino population, now perilously small and reduced to just a dozen adults. The sad truth was that some of the poorly paid Mozambican park rangers were known in the past to have colluded with poachers to gather up the rhino horns so prized by wealthy Chinese for their supposed powers as aphrodisiacs and medicinals. But even the honest park police were increasingly tasked with counterterror duties, and wildlife considerations took a backseat to the new security priorities set in Maputo.

The quiet exchange of cash to the appropriate government ministers gave Sandra's privately funded NGO the chance to get into the GLTP and begin monitoring the rhinos. Fortunately, poachers hadn't been seen on the Mozambique side of the Limpopo in over a year, so the human threat to those magnificent animals wasn't her main concern.

Tracking rhino migration patterns and feeding grounds was the primary focus of Sandra's research. Her dream was to introduce more rhinos into the local population and restore the herds that once roamed freely here.

The joy in her face at that moment was palpable, and Johnny had just handed her the high-tech key to her dream. He had no idea it was possible to be this happy for someone else.

Pearce Systems' research director, Dr. Kirin Rao, selected the solar-powered sUAS because it had a fourteen-hour flight time and a nearly silent propulsion system, both features that made it a perfect platform for wildlife observation. Rao paired up the hand-launched surveillance drone to a control station and a video camera system with an editing suite installed in the cargo area of the oversize Land Rover, but the Silent Falcon could also be easily flown with the handheld controller that Pearce Systems provided. With detachable wings, the Silent Falcon could be quickly disassembled for transport, and just as easily reassembled in the field. Along with spare parts, extra batteries, a charging station, and all the other equipment needed to operate it, the solar-powered drone system was completely contained in the self-sufficient Land Rover. Dr. Rao hoped that this new unit would be the test bed for a whole range of new wildlife applications.

"Oh! Johnny! I see them!"

Johnny glanced into the back of the Land Rover. In the corner he'd stashed a small picnic basket with avocado and tomato sandwiches and a bottle of vintage Portuguese wine, and even a blanket, all courtesy of the hotel concierge. The river wasn't far from here. It was going to be a damn good day. Maybe one of the best days of his life.

= 4 =

China National Petroleum Headquarters
Beijing, China
1 May

Zhao Yi watched the automatic window blinds blot out the smog-choked sky. He sat in a crowded conference room on the top floor of one of the three glass-and-steel monoliths of CNPC headquarters, buildings that were as gray and uninspiring as Beijing's nearly unbreathable atmosphere. His morning runs in the park the last few days had burned his lungs and stung his eyes. Unfortunately, he was in for more of the same in here. The older executives seated around the long mahogany table lit up cigarettes after tea and coffee had been served by the waitstaff, and now the air in the conference room was clogged with acrid smoke.

As the recently appointed vice president of business affairs of the newly formed Sino-Sahara Oil Corporation, Zhao was expected to spend more time in Beijing, which technically was his birthplace but hardly his home. The grandson of an original Politburo Member and the son of a princeling on the ruling Standing Committee, Zhao was as close to royalty as a communist regime would allow. This gave him unprecedented freedoms, powers, and privileges, but equally binding responsibilities both to his family and his nation. Responsibilities that the handsome and athletic forty-year-old took quite seriously despite his famously hedonistic lifestyle.

Zhao believed he could best fulfill those responsibilities by remaining out in the field and Skyping meetings like this one rather than sitting in a sealed conference room. But when Zhao's uncle, the chairman of CNPC, summoned him back to company headquarters, Zhao was compelled to obey both as a dutiful nephew and as an up-and-coming executive in the state-owned enterprise through which his family had amassed a three-billion-dollar fortune during the last four decades.

But Zhao's meteoric rise was due primarily to his outstanding performance in the field, not his family connections. He'd just outmaneuvered a European energy consortium and brokered a lucrative new oil contract with the Azerbaijani government, still reeling from the Russian invasion nearly two years before. Zhao's latest promotion was just another rung up on the lofty ladder of his ambition. He had already climbed high, and swiftly, but he had much farther to go. He also knew that one false step from this great height would be fatal to his career, if not his life.

Zhao sat bolt upright in his leather chair and wore the

standard gray business suit so common among his peers. However, his suit was an elegant English, hand-tailored affair, perfectly cut to his broad shoulders and accented with a stunning light blue Italian silk tie and pocket square. The effect was bold, even brash, but not rebellious. Zhao was completely committed to serving the cause of China, but equally committed to serving it with style.

The analyst presenting today's briefing was a member of the Ministry of State Security. Zhao knew him well. They had risen through the ranks of the MSS together, though Zhao's membership in his nation's foreign intelligence service was itself a closely guarded state secret.

Zhao's government properly understood that economic development was itself a weapon in the war against the West, and resource acquisition was key to furthering China's blistering economic growth. The Western nations still waved the flag of "free enterprise," but its most successful corporations long ago abandoned pure capitalism in exchange for securing favors with their respective ruling classes by guaranteeing the politicians' perpetual reelection in exchange for favorable tax and regulatory policies that guaranteed the "too big to fail" corporations hegemonic dominance in their markets.

Zhao constantly marveled at America's repudiation of its own past greatness. During his university days, Zhao met more committed communists on the campuses of UCLA and Harvard than he ever had in Beijing. The running joke among the ruling class in China these days was that if you wanted your child to study socialism, send them to an American Ivy League school, but if you wanted them to learn about capitalism, send them to Shanghai. Not only was China a more capitalist nation than the United States these days, it vigorously applied the lessons of American economic development that the Americans themselves had long forgotten. In a short period of time, aggressive, mercantilist trade policies catapulted a newly independent nineteenth-century America into the ranks of the wealthiest nations of Old Europe. Now America ran half-trillion-dollar annual trade deficits, exporting both wealth and jobs as quickly as it was accumulating debt from the same nations with which it ran trade deficits, particularly mercantilist China.

America was in rapid decline, even as its few ruling elites and their "too big to jail" client corporations accumulated ever-more-egregious amounts of wealth and political power. China understood, in fact, that it was because American elites enriched themselves without responsibility to their society that the United States was in an economic and political death spiral. China believed that capitalism should serve the interests of the state. American political elites apparently believed in crony capitalism where the state served the interests of the capitalist masters. The twenty-first century would soon decide which of the two systems was most viable.

The lights dimmed and a 4K HD digital projector lit up a massive screen on the far wall. Images of various African nations, Chinese corporations, and specific industrial enterprises—particularly oil and other natural resources—flashed on the screen as the analyst spoke. No recording devices, tablets, or even paper and pencils were allowed in the room. Today's meeting was top secret, and the security services feared the Western intelligence agencies and their vast cybersurveillance efforts. CNPC was a known target, particularly of the CIA. The purpose of the briefing was for policy orientation only.

"Today, there are over eight hundred Chinese corporations operating in nearly every nation on the African continent," the analyst began. "Many of them are engaged in resource extraction to meet the growing demand of our rapidly expanding industrial and manufacturing sectors." Icons matching African resources and Chinese industries flashed in sequence. "Every day, new resource potentials are being discovered and developed across the continent, but none so important as the recent location of new uranium and, amazingly, massive rare-earth-element deposits here in the Saharan desert, in the far reaches of Mali. In fact, Mali may have the world's single greatest known deposit of lanthanum."

The screen zoomed in on an image of northeastern Mali to emphasize its importance. The executives gathered around the table whispered excitedly. Lanthanum was critical for the manufacture of batteries. Hybrid cars like the Toyota Prius required more than ten kilograms of the mineral per vehicle, and more hybrids were being brought to the market every day. China itself was now the world's largest car market, and hybrids were key to the expansion of that market. The startling new REE discovery in Mali was obviously the reason why this top secret emergency meeting had been called.

"As you are all well aware, China is the world's largest producer of rare earth elements, giving us nearly monopolistic control over their use. This allows us to minimize their costs for ourselves but also deny their use to our biggest competitors." From an earlier briefing, Zhao knew that the seventeen chemical elements on the periodic table known as REEs weren't, technically, "rare" so much as widely dispersed throughout the earth's crust—but seldom in harvestable amounts. Those elements were critical in other key new technological products like wind turbines, lasers, and cell phones. China was the country with the greatest concentration of REE deposits and was currently mining between 80 and 90 percent of all REEs today. That near monopoly provided China with a significant competitive advantage it had no intention of relinquishing. That competitive advantage was one of the reasons why Los Angeles Metro had purchased its first all-electric buses from the Chinese corporation BYD.

"Fortunately," the analyst continued, "Mali has recently signed new contracts with the Sino-Sahara Oil Corporation, which includes provisions for all other forms of underground resource acquisition. Unfortunately, Mali, like most other African nations, might soon be tempted to reconsider the terms of the very generous contracts we have signed with them. They also have an indigenous population problem in the area."

"You mean the Tuaregs," Zhao said. Prior to his new appointment, Zhao had thrown himself into research of the Sahara region. The vast desert occupied significant portions of Mali, Algeria, Niger, and Libya, which also happened to be the most important resource states in the area. Nomadic Tuareg warrior clans had freely roamed the vast Sahara since the fifth century before Christ.

"The Mali government has already begun operations to nullify the Tuareg problem," the analyst said. "They are fractured and disorganized."

"Are you referring to the Africans or the Tuaregs?" one of the executives blurted out. The room exploded with laughter. Even the stoic chairman grinned.

"The Tuaregs have been restless for quite some time," Zhao interrupted. "Are you confident the government in Bamako is on top of this?"

The analyst smiled. "I believe the term *Tuareg* in Arabic means 'abandoned by God.' So, yes, unless God shows up, President Kouyaté should be able to quell them soon enough."

"You just can't trust a damn African," a voice in the dark muttered. It was the vice president of one of the civil engineering firms building new highways in the rapidly expanding northern corridor. Murmurs rumbled around the table as graying heads nodded in agreement. "The Kenyans canceled one of our contracts for the new high-way expansion project between Mombasa and Nairobi last week. They claimed there were environmental concerns, but all they really were concerned about was more money." The middle-aged executive slowly rubbed his open palm for emphasis.

Zhao knew what the engineer said was true, but it was only a small piece of the picture. China's decades-old policy of "noninterference" in the domestic affairs of other nations meant his government would gladly do business with the tyrants and despots that the West shunned on humanitarian grounds. Chinese government and business officials also freely issued "soft" development funds and loans—financial transactions unencumbered by human rights provisions or even basic accounting principles. These aid packages were giant pots of money from which greedy, cruel African elites could dip freely for their personal use so long as Chinese interests were also served in the process.

Chinese firms were also quick to provide arms, ammunition, and other contraband items denied to dictatorial regimes by the moralizing Western powers. Security treaties and Chinese military bases soon followed. By such means, China swiftly gained lucrative footholds across the continent.

But the other reality, Zhao knew, was that Chinese firms wreaked terrible environmental damage all over Africa in recent years—just as they had in their own country for decades. Over eight million acres of arable Chinese land were now so polluted they could never be used for food production. Arable land had decreased in China even as industrialization exploded. Africa, on the other hand, possessed the world's largest supply of arable land and could amply serve as China's new food basket if exploited properly.

Chinese companies also imported their own labor, even low-skilled positions, and dominated local economies. They were as rapacious and colonizing as the

Great Powers had been in the nineteenth century, lacking only the missionary zeal of "the white man's burden" to justify their efforts. The Chinese government no longer had any vested interest in spreading the gospel of communism, as it once had in the sixties—such quaint sentiments were bad for business. Freshly minted Third World communist revolutionaries tended to nationalize key industries, and Chinese businessmen held no interest in that. Neither did Zhao. He fully appreciated the Africans' concerns, but he didn't care about them. Like his own government, Zhao was a supreme pragmatist. Economic development always came at a high price, and every great nation had to pay it at one time or another. If Africa wanted to develop with China's help, Zhao reasoned, it should have to do so on China's terms.

The bottom line for African governments, even the despotic ones, was that they were beginning to count the true costs of doing business with a predatory partner like China and found the transactions wanting. They were changing up the rules of the Chinese game with the help of the opportunistic West. It was a worrying proposition for the Politburo. The general secretary himself had visited the African continent on his first official overseas tour abroad to underscore China's interest in the region, and its concerns.

"Thank you for the excellent presentation, Mr. Li," the chairman said as the lights went up. The MSS analyst bowed gratefully and took his seat. The chairman continued. "The Standing Committee has decided to draw a line in the sand in Mali. We want to create a new model of *secure* cooperation and development for our other African partners. The future of China depends upon it. That is why I am calling upon the resolute Mr. Zhao Yi to represent us in the Malian venture." The chairman waved a hand at his nephew, who stood, beaming with confidence. All eyes turned to him.

"Thank you, Mr. Chairman. I won't let China down." He bowed respectfully to his uncle, then the room.

The chairman himself led the others in a round of applause.

= 5 =

The village of Anou
Kidal Region, Northeastern Mali
1 May

The village slept this time of day. No one would come to the shop until later. The relentless heat blanketed everything. But Ibrahim couldn't sleep. The curse of advancing age, he supposed.

The shopkeeper felt the gentle breeze of the old GE oscillating fan on his back. The aluminum blades were bent, rattling the little wire cage enclosing them. Ibrahim didn't care. The rattling sound comforted him. So did the heat and the sun. He liked familiar things these days, even the unpleasant ones.

He glanced out of his doorway into the little village square. A half dozen mud-brick buildings just like his faced the old well, but his was the only shop. One hundred and seven people last count, mostly women, children, and old

men like him. That made him the village elder, in deed if
not in title. He wore that responsibility like the black
tagelmust wrapped around his head and face. All of the
young men were gone, shepherding their flocks or driving
trucks in the south.

Or riding with Mossa Ag Alla.

If he was a young man, he'd be in the hills with Mossa,
too. Both he and Mossa were Kel Tamasheq, were they
not? People of the Tamasheq tongue? Not Tuaregs, as the
outsiders called his people. Different classes, yes. Mossa
of the Ihaggaren nobility, and warriors; Ibrahim of the
vassal Imrad—traders and shepherds. But Chief Mossa
cared not for such distinctions. Only his people. Imohar.
Free people. It was the new way, and Ibrahim agreed with
it. The world was changing, and it was the better way.
Especially now with all of the troubles.

Ibrahim's anxiety spiked. The *misbaha* prayer beads
in his right hand sped faster through his callused fingertips as he touched an amulet unconsciously with his
left. He detested the jihadist Ansar Dine, his own people, or so they claimed. But they cared for Mali more
than the rights of the Imohar. The al-Qaeda Salafists
cared for neither Mali nor the Kel Tamasheq. Indeed,
they detested even the prayer beads. Ibrahim was glad
the French had driven them out, and glad the French,
too, had left again. All of them had come and now all
had left, and that was a fine thing, he thought.

He stepped back from the doorway and glanced at
the far wall. A yellowed French military map was pinned
neatly to it, the ancient folds forming a grid. In the

bottom right-hand corner in minuscule numbers and letters his dimming eyes could no longer read it gave its origin: *Le Département du Armée de Terre, 1937.*

Thirty years before, his wife had drawn a small red X on the map where she thought the village was located, in case a traveler ever wanted to know where he was standing. Ibrahim had laughed at her. Only Imohar and other nomads who knew of the well ever bothered to come here to water their camels and flocks, so they would already know where it was, he insisted. They yelled at each other for an hour over that one. But the X stayed, and so did the map. Ibrahim smiled. But that was a long time ago. At least the map was still here, and so was the X, and so was the village.

I brahim lit another cigarette and glanced at the clock-faced thermometer. The red hand pointed at 41c/107f. Not unusual for the desert this time of year, especially in this part of the region. The hottest time of the day. Soon it would cool again, as it should. A man couldn't sleep when it was too hot. He glanced around the shop—really, just the front room of a three-room building where he and his grandson lived. Not like a real shop he'd once seen in Timbuktu, before the troubles. He wondered if it was still intact. He heard rumors that many shops in that fabled city had been burned to the ground by the AQS if they sold what was *haraam.*

The three wooden shelves screwed into the adobe wall were full. Toothpaste, razors, gum, canned goods—meat, milk, fruit. Even a red-and-white carton of Lucky Strikes, the brand the Chinese requested when they passed through two months ago. Ibrahim paid hard cash in Kidal for the expensive American brand, but the Chinese hadn't returned. That was unfortunate. The Chinese had paid too much for the poor ones he had in the shop, and they didn't bargain, which was a blessing. Just paid his price. He thought again about opening the carton and selling the cigarettes one at a time, the only way his friends could afford them. But perhaps the Chinese would return soon. *Inshallah.*

His grandson would be home soon from the government school in the next village. Eight years old and already doing higher math. Ibrahim was proud of him. The boy would someday make a fine shopkeeper. Tonight he would feed him, then send him to the widow's house with her cell phone. It was on the shop floor connected to the car battery, charging. It wasn't much money for the service, but every little coin still helped fill the purse. The cell phone couldn't make a signal here near the well, but it could a half kilometer east outside of the village. The widow could still walk that far and back, and tomorrow was her regular day to take a call from her son working in Bamako and she wanted her phone fully charged. Life was good in Bamako, her son said. Many Chinese, and much money to be made. And peace.

Peace is better than money, Ibrahim thought. Like cold water from that well in the square.

He spun his beads, waiting for the boy.

Great Limpopo Transfrontier Park
Mozambique

"I've lost it, Johnny."

"Lost what?"

"The video image." Sandra pulled the Fat Shark goggles off. "It just went blank."

Shit. There goes the picnic, Johnny thought. "Let's check the control station." Johnny and Sandra climbed into the back of the Rover. She was right. The video image was gone.

"We lost the video signal." Johnny realized how stupidly obvious he sounded.

"Now what?"

Good question. The Solar Falcon was preprogrammed to automatically return to base when it sensed either low battery or signal disruption of any sort. Johnny checked the monitors. At least the Solar Falcon was still broadcasting a GPS signal. The drone was turning a lazy figure eight, but not returning to station.

"That's weird," Sandra said. "Why is it doing that?"

Johnny shrugged. "Something wrong with the motherboard, I guess."

"I thought you said these things are reliable. We paid a lot of money for it."

"The Solar Falcon is as reliable as they get. But it's still just a machine. Things happen."

Something caught Sandra's eye. She leaned over. Glasses tinked. "What's this?"

"Nothing."

"There's a picnic basket back here. Looks like some good stuff."

"The hotel concierge pulled it together for me," Johnny confessed. "The basket, too."

She smiled mischievously. "So that's why Pearce isn't here today."

Johnny frowned, worried about his friend. "Not exactly."

Sandra pointed at the GPS monitor again. "So what should we do?"

"We jump in the Rover and go find us a Falcon."

The small herd of white rhinos chuffed and snorted contentedly as they fed on the grass beneath their heavy feet. Two calves brayed as they chased each other in circles around a big female, her ear tagged with a great yellow tab marked "WWA." A nearby bull swung his heavy head with its menacing long horn in their direction, just checking to make sure no threats had startled the bellowing calves.

A thousand feet above the herd, Sandra's Silent Falcon drone was still making a lazy figure eight, its camera still pointing at the big female. Had the rhinos any inclination to gaze skyward, their famously poor eyesight wouldn't have allowed them to notice the aircraft at its current height, but even their excellent hearing couldn't have picked up its whisper-quiet motors at that altitude.

But a four-wheel-drive ground vehicle? That caught the herd's attention, though nobody stopped feeding.

Heavy, tube-shaped ears perked up and rotated in unison in the direction of the engine rumbling toward them from a distance. As the sound edged nearer, heads lifted warily. The big bull grunted, then turned and trotted heavily for a nearby stand of acacia trees for shelter. The others followed swiftly behind him, the trumpeting calves falling in line behind their mothers. The female with the yellow tag took the rear and felt the bee as it zipped past.

Only, it wasn't a bee.

It was a bullet. Then a hundred.

The air roared with gunfire.

Men shouted.

The bull had led them all into a trap.

The tagged female ran. Her flanks suddenly stung with heat. Her sides ached as if tree branches were thrust into her ribs. She bellowed in pain.

They were all bellowing.

Except the babies. They cawed like birds, high-pitched and keening.

The tagged female dropped to her knees. Saw the flash of metal in her dim eye. Searing pain exploded in her snout as the machete blade *thwock*ed into the bone just above the horn.

Two dozen men. Black, like shadows, swarmed the herd. Rhinos down. The men circled them. Arms swinging, blades chopping. Blood and skin and bone flecked into the air with each strike. Men pulling hard on the horns while others chopped at the roots. Panicked eyes rolled white in shock as blood seeped into the grass.

And then the big bull roared.

He was on his knees but still swinging that giant horn and roaring, knocking a shadow man to the ground.

More gunfire. The bull's guts spilled into the grass.

And the last baby screamed.

The Land Rover bounced over the uneven terrain, but Johnny kept the pedal floored. He kept one eye on the GPS locator on the dashboard and one on the windshield.

Sandra pointed at a thick stand of acacia trees looming in the distance. Bright red burning bush creepers flowered brightly in the tree branches. "They must be in there." Sandra had lost visual contact with the herd when the video feed was cut but the falcon was still tracking them, apparently. A handheld tablet monitor was in her lap now.

Johnny yanked the wheel hard to avoid a fallen log, then pointed the Land Rover toward the acacia stand. A path of beaten-down grass wound around toward the back. "Looks like our rhinos were here after all," Sandra said, nodding at the grass track.

The Rover sped around the bend and past the first tree. Johnny slammed the brakes.

The man standing in his way was Chinese, tall, broadshouldered. His face was edged and hard, but creased with a smile. He was focused intently on the dark gray Silent Falcon fuselage high above doing loops, guided by the radio transmitter in his hands. He didn't budge despite the Rover's skidding stop just ten feet from him. He wore green camo without insignia, but his bearing was pure military. An operator, Johnny guessed. Special forces. They all looked the same, no matter where they came from. A combat knife was strapped to the man's leg.

"Who is that?" Sandra asked, pushing open the door.

Johnny grabbed her wrist. "No, stay here."

"I'm coming with you," she said.

"You wait here. I'll check it out. This is my rice bowl, remember?"

"Careful, Johnny. Please."

"I'm a cop. I'm always careful." He flashed her a smile.

Johnny shut the door behind him and approached the lone Chinese. Johnny's Glock 19 was in his waistband at the small of his back. The smiling man finally turned his gaze toward him.

"An expensive toy," Guo Jun said, nodding at the sky.

"Not a toy. A camera, watching everything you do."

"And recording it, too, I'm certain," he said. "I should like to see the pretty pictures."

"Then buy your own."

"Why should I? I have yours now." Guo looked back up at the Silent Falcon.

"Because it doesn't belong to you. It belongs to the World Wildlife Alliance." He threw a thumb over his shoulder. "To that lady in the truck."

"She won't be needing it anytime soon, Johnny."

Johnny startled at the sound of his name but hid it. "If you're going to say my name, say it correctly."

"And how is that?"

"For dickheads like you, it's Mr. Paloma."

"Too bad your name isn't Troy Pearce. I was hoping to play a game with him today." Guo's eyes were still fixed on the plane.

"What game?" Johnny slipped his gun hand toward his back.

Guo tossed the transmitter at Johnny.

Instinctively, Johnny caught it, worried about crashing the drone overhead. A steel fist punched his chest, knocking the wind out of him. He dropped the transmitter into the grass. Looked down.

Saw the carbon blade wedged in his chest up to the hilt.

Johnny grabbed the blade as he crumbled to his knees, gasping for air. His darkening eyes saw the smiling Chinese still crouched in a throwing stance, throwing arm extended, fingers pointing at him like an accusation. A swarm of Africans burst out of the trees behind Guo, flashing long blades.

Sandra called his name, but her muffled screams seemed far away.

= 6 =

Lake Massingir
Mozambique
1 May

Pearce tossed the last empty bottle of Preta by the neck like a potato masher grenade. It whistled through the air until it finally splashed into the water. It joined a half dozen other empty bottles bobbing around the lake like forlorn sailors lost on a dismal sea.

Pearce sighed. The wind wasn't letting up, the fish still weren't biting, and now he was out of beer.

A truly shitty day.

His ears perked up at the sound of distant thunder, mechanical and regular. Chopper blades hammered low on the eastern, treeless horizon.

Pearce watched the diving speck racing toward him, barely ten feet above the deck, like a strafing run. Within moments the helicopter took shape; a Bell JetRanger, if memory served. Nose down, full throttle, the single rotor kicked up a pair of misty wingtip vortices off of the lake surface that melted away in the gusting wind.

Thirty seconds later, the helicopter flared, rotated ninety degrees, and hovered a hundred feet away from Pearce. The rotor's downwash battered Pearce even from this distance, and he fought to hold on to his boonie hat. Bright yellow letters on the black and white zebra-striped fuselage shouted *Air Safari!* as the passenger door slid open. The pilot was clearly fighting the crosswinds on the lake as the bird struggled to hold position.

The man in the passenger seat wore a light blue linen suit without a tie. He waved a cell phone in the air, then tapped on the screen. Seconds later, Pearce's cell phone signaled a text message: "Pearce?"

Pearce glanced back at the helicopter and nodded heavily. His phone chimed again.

"DIGNAM, US EMBASSY."

Great Limpopo Transfrontier Park
Mozambique

The *Air Safari!* copter cycled down as Pearce and Dignam hunched beneath the blades, racing toward the burned-up Land Rover. Dignam briefed Pearce on what little he knew on the flight over. The CIA station chief, Jack Hawkins, had remained on scene, afraid to leave before Pearce arrived. Six Mozambique park rangers in floppy hats and faded green fatigues stood in a loose perimeter scanning the horizon, clearly skittish, rifles high.

So much blood.

Hawkins worried that if he left the scene, the rangers might have bolted, too. Whoever had done this could still be around, and it was only an hour until sunset. But the rangers' dignity, such as it was in their disheveled uniforms and battered assault rifles, wouldn't allow them to leave if the American had the balls to stand fast. Especially an African-American like him.

Pearce marched up to Hawkins.

"Troy. I'm so sorry." Hawkins shouted above the helicopter turbine still winding down. He extended his hand.

Pearce stared at Hawkins's hand for a moment, trying to clear away his rage, then reluctantly took it. Hawkins wasn't to blame, that was for damn certain. Pearce leaned in close so he didn't have to shout. "Thanks for holding down the fort, Jack." Hawkins nodded. Pearce and Hawkins briefly met years before in D.C. When Pearce and Johnny had checked into the embassy a few days before, Hawkins was there to brief them over rum and Cokes.

"Dignam gave you all of the particulars. There's not much more to add, but I wanted you to be able to get a look-see before this place got picked clean by the locals." Hawkins defined "locals" by nodding at the park rangers nervously fingering their rifles.

"Show me what you've found," Pearce said.

Dignam jogged back to the chopper while Hawkins walked Pearce to the back of the Land Rover. The windows were busted out from the intense heat that had melted away all of the plastics, tires, and paint. "Bodies?" Pearce asked.

"Not here."

Pearce forced open the back door of the utility wagon, the spare tire melted off of the rim. The hinges creaked with stiff resistance as if rusted shut. Clearly, everything inside was destroyed.

"Gear's missing," Pearce said.

"Burned up?"

"No. The bays are empty." Pearce pulled out his smartphone, pulled up a locator app. No GPS signal from the Silent Falcon. "Shit."

"You lose any classified stuff?"

"Not exactly. But it's not the kind of equipment you want to hand over to your worst enemies, either."

Pearce glanced back over at the park rangers. "What do you think?" Park rangers all over Africa had a mixed reputation, especially the armed ones.

"No. Bishop and I were here first, before those boys showed up. He's an ex-pat and a drinking buddy. He was flying the park when he saw the bodies and the busted-up Rover. Figured they might be Americans or Europeans, called it in to me, then flew me out here. I recognized Johnny from our meet and greet the other day. Thought I'd better find you."

"Where is he?"

Hawkins knew Troy's record. A real tough customer. Figured Pearce could handle seeing his friend.

Doubted he'd seen worse, though.

"Follow me."

They trudged over to the stand of acacia trees. The park rangers spread out a little further to give Pearce and Hawkins privacy. With the helicopter rotor finally shut down, the air filled up again with the sickly stench of death.

Johnny was just inside the tree line, lying in the dirt in a crumpled heap, like a bag of bloody laundry that had fallen off the back of a speeding truck.

"Jesus."

Pearce kneeled down. Johnny's jaw had been sheered away by some kind of jagged blade. The rest of Johnny looked worse. He'd been hacked viciously by dozens of blows. Machetes, judging by the width of the cuts. A chunk of scalp was missing. So was the left cheek, now covered in clotted, black blood. They even cut off his nose all the way down to the bone, leaving a gaping hole. The cut was too neat, though. That was done with a sharper, smaller blade. A message? Heavy black flies buzzed around Johnny's face, darting in and out of the gaping sinus cavity. Pearce batted them away.

"Fucking savages," Hawkins said. He wasn't thinking about race, obviously. But if the ambassador had heard him say that, she would've written him up on the spot.

The underside of Johnny's broken forearms were shredded with blade cuts, too. "He tried to put up a fight," Pearce said. "That must have freaked them out. Most people drop at the first hit."

"So they frenzied."

"Maybe." Pearce knelt closer. Saw something. Unbuttoned Johnny's shirt. "Look at that wound in his chest."

"What about it?"

"Knife wound."

"I don't understand."

"One knife wound, the rest machete strikes."

"What does it mean?"

"I don't know." Pearce stood. "Where's the girl?"

"Not far. She have a name?"

"Gallez. Sandra. World Wildlife Alliance. A Belgian national."

"I'll have Dignam call that in to their embassy. That's the same Alliance project you told me about, right? It's why you guys were here?"

"Yeah."

"Nothing else? I mean, off the books?"

"No. Straight up."

"I've heard . . . rumors." Hawkins was sympathetic, but he had a job to do, too.

Pearce glared at him. "I'm giving you the straight dope."

"Why no security? This is Indian country out here."

"Johnny was the security. He was a good gunfighter."

So are you, Hawkins wanted to say but didn't. "And you went fishing?"

"Johnny wanted to make his play on the girl. Didn't need a third wheel to cramp his style. You know how it is."

"Yeah."

"I'm just surprised anyone got the drop on him. This is all close in. No bullet casings? Nine mil?" Pearce was thinking about Johnny's Glock.

"Not around here."

"The girl?"

Hawkins pointed up ahead. "Over there." He led Pearce twenty feet farther in and pointed to a female form splayed under a camouflaged rain poncho borrowed from one of the park rangers. Pearce pulled back the poncho. She was stripped naked except for the pink sock still on her left foot. She must've fought, too. Her fair skin was tattooed with welts, scratches, bite marks. Her broken jaw was purpled and swollen. The perineum was a red ruin, the blood turning to a sticky black in the heat.

"Extensive bruising around her neck. No bullet wounds. I'm no CSI, but I'd say they'd strangled her to death," Hawkins said. "If she was lucky."

Pearce knelt down beside her. Closed the lifeless green eyes still staring into the faces that had killed her.

"She was a smart girl. Johnny was sweet on her."

Dignam approached cautiously with a couple of neatly folded body bags.

"You need to see anything else?" Hawkins asked Pearce.

Pearce shook his head.

Hawkins nodded at Dignam, who signaled a couple of park rangers for help.

"What's that god-awful smell?" Pearce asked. But he knew.

"You haven't seen the worst of it," Hawkins said. "At least in terms of pure savagery."

Hawkins led the way past the outer ring of trees and into a tree-canopied clearing. The air roared with thousands of buzzing flies.

Pearce stopped dead in his tracks. "Oh my God."

A dozen adult rhinos lay on the ground, all dead. Two calves, too. All of them had had their horns hacked off, leaving gaping wounds of exposed bone and broken flesh. Each lay in a puddle of its own blood.

"Poachers aren't exactly surgeons, are they?" Hawkins pointed at the massive spill of intestines in the grass around one of the big females. "Some of these weren't even dead when they butchered them."

Pearce spat in the grass. "All of this because some old Asian dirt bags can't get a hard-on."

"Your friends must have stumbled upon the slaughter in progress. The butchers didn't want to leave any witnesses behind."

A park ranger screamed. Pearce and Hawkins whipped around as a rhino crashed out of the tree line, eyes crazed, bellowing. Blood soaked its snout, a gaping hole where the horn used to be. It loped toward the ranger, three thousand pounds of deadweight lunging on three wobbly legs, the fourth leg shot to hell.

A yellow tag pinned to its ear.

The ranger tossed his battered rifle and bolted away, shouting for help in his tribal tongue as the other rangers opened fire. Dozens of steel-jacketed 7.62mm slugs slapped into the thick gray hide. Hawkins hit the dirt at the first shot, but Pearce stood firm, mesmerized. The animal's front legs gave out first and its heavy, ruined head hit the dirt with a grunt, followed by the rest of the shredded torso. The rhino corpse kneeled there for a second before it crashed over on its side. The rangers finally stopped firing. The gunfire echoed into the distance, then finally faded away. The air still buzzed with flies.

Hawkins stood and dusted himself off.

"Congratulations," Hawkins said. "You just witnessed the killing of the last rhino in Limpopo Park. Hell, in the whole damn country."

Pearce turned around and watched Dignam and the other park rangers gently lift the body bags.

"I should've been here," Pearce said. He glanced at Hawkins.

Hawkins's pitying eyes agreed.

Pearce snatched off his hat and crushed it in his hand as he trudged behind the corpse of his friend back to the helicopter, its turbine slowly spinning up.

= 7 =

To Zhao's dismay, much of the new construction in the capital city was in the current pseudo-modernist style now in vogue throughout the Middle East. Zhao found the sharply angled cement and reflective glass structures to be distinctly childish and unsophisticated, if not pathetic. But this was the trend all over the developing world, including the new Sino-Sahara Oil Corporation building rising up on the bank of the Niger River.

Zhao witnessed the rise of such monstrosities in the pleasure capitals of Dubai and Doha. He'd even stood on the heli-deck of the soaring Burj Khalifa, soon to be the not-tallest building in the world thanks to the towering ambition of his own proud nation. Pounded by

ninety-kilometer-per-hour winds and clutching his
safety helmet, Zhao had struggled even more with the
blustering of the emir's nephew, who proclaimed with
wild gesticulations the Burj as proof of a new Arab
renaissance. Zhao bit his tongue to keep from laughing
in the young fool's face. Didn't he realize the soaring
Burj was designed by Americans and constructed by
Koreans using cheap imported Indian labor? The only
thing "Arab" about the building was its location. Even
the money that paid for it was Western, technically, from
oil discovered, exploited, refined, and shipped by the
Western powers themselves.

So when Zhao was given the choice, he located his
personal residence in Bamako in one of the city's old
quartiers, in a refurbished French colonial compound.
The pink and white nineteenth-century Beaux Arts building and its furnishings were perfectly anachronistic and,
like him, sophisticated, refined, and decadent. As the vice
president of Sino-Sahara Oil Corporation, he was expected
to entertain prominent officials, none more important
than the minister of internal security, General Abdel Tolo,
second only to the Chinese-installed president himself.
Tonight's debauch was in General Tolo's honor.

The heads of the ministries of mines, natural resources,
energy, and trade were also in attendance, along with a
wide selection of the finest Thai and Ukrainian whores
that Zhao kept under contract. For appearances' sake,
Zhao invited the Chinese ambassador to the evening's
event, but dismissed him immediately after dinner. The
prudish and inefficient party bureaucrat frowned on

Zhao's famously lavish sex-and-drugs style of diplomacy and, no doubt, would have reported the abundant presence of prostitutes and cocaine in Zhao's residence had he remained for the festivities. An even greater liability, as far as Zhao was concerned, was the fact that the ambassador possessed the complexion and deportment of a small toad wearing an ill-fitted suit.

Zhao and Tolo had retired to his private study and indulged in snifters of Martel X.O. cognac and Cuban cigars. The corpulent African was clearly enjoying the *cohiba* he was puffing with relish. Zhao lifted the distinctive arch-shaped bottle and refilled Tolo's glass. Heavy techno beats thundered on the other side of the thick wooden doors.

"Thank you, Zhao," the general said. "You are a gracious host." He lifted the glass to his round face, admired the copper-colored liquor, then took another sip, followed by another long drag on his cigar. Zhao studied the general's medal-clad dress uniform. He wondered if any other armchair general in history had ever acquired so many pieces of spangled baubles in just one lifetime. "I am a humble guest in your country, General, and your servant."

The African roared with laughter. Blue smoke billowed out of his wide mouth. "Bullshit! Don't pull that 'Mandarin servile' act with me." The general pointed the smoldering cigar at him. "I know you, Zhao. I've even seen you with your pants down around your ankles."

"Indeed, you have." Zhao first met Tolo at a military trade show in Paris the year before. Zhao not only threw an infamously raucous bacchanal that week but participated vigorously in the festivities. "So you also know why I'm here."

"We have everything under control in the Kidal," Tolo said, referring to the region of Mali where the REE deposits had been discovered earlier.

"I should hope so, now that your security forces have been amply resupplied by my government."

"It's not guns that matter. It's guts," the general harrumphed. He tapped his temple with a thick thumb, the smoldering cigar dangerously close to his bald scalp. "And brains."

"Yes, of course," Zhao said. He leaned forward and lifted his snifter toward Tolo. "To guts and brains."

Tolo smiled and gulped down his cognac. Zhao sniffed his, savoring the aroma.

"My company is concerned about the safety of its workers," Zhao said. "There are rumors of Tuaregs in rebellion all over the Sahara."

"Rumors only. The 'godforsaken' are like dried grass. A small puff of wind and—" The general pursed his lips and blew. "They disappear."

"We have a saying, too. When a little grass catches fire, the whole village is in danger."

The African belly-laughed again. "You Chinese and your proverbs! Enough. The Tuaregs are easily dealt with."

"The Tuaregs have traversed the Sahara for nearly three millennia. They are superlative desert fighters. No one has ever found them easily dealt with. I've read recent reports that they are rising up again in Niger."

"Yes, around the uranium mines you Chinese are operating there. And do you know why? Your operations are draining away all of the scarce water in the region, robbing the Tuaregs of grasses to feed their precious camels, sheep, and goats. You're polluting the land, and worse, you import cheap labor, so you don't even give those poor bastards jobs in those filthy mines while you're starving and killing them." Tolo set his snifter down.

Zhao nodded. It was true. His countrymen were often worse colonialists than the British and French they had displaced. But then again, Zhao reflected, these were only Africans they were talking about. If Africans weren't meant to be skinned by the Chinese people, then history would not have made them rabbits.

"Mistakes have been made, and they are being corrected. I assure you no such abuses will occur among your people," Zhao said.

Tolo shook his massive head. "We both know you are making promises you can't keep. But what do I care for such things? Eggs must be broken in order to be eaten. Still, if you were to bring jobs to the Kidal, this would be a good thing for you."

"But we can't bring jobs until operations begin, and we can't begin operations until the Tuareg problem is settled." Zhao stabbed out the butt of his cigar in a crystal ashtray. "How do you plan on doing that?"

Tolo glanced at his empty glass. Zhao unstoppered the bottle and refilled it.

"The Tuareg problem now is simple. Always these 'godforsaken' have been restless and rebellious, but the desert grows hotter and they grow fewer. They are divided by clans and tribes, often fighting among themselves, at least until now."

Zhao emptied the last of the Martel into the snifter. Tolo nodded his thanks. *"Merci."*

"De rien," Zhao said. "What is different now?"

"The whole of the Tuareg nation now looks to one man. He is called 'The Blue Warrior' by his people. His name is Mossa Ag Alla."

"'The Blue Warrior'?" Zhao sat back and let the image of a blue-turbaned desert warrior roll around in his mind for a moment, admiring its mythical possibilities. "Yes, that makes perfect sense. The Kel Tamasheq men are famous for wearing the indigo blue headdress and veil."

Zhao had done his homework. Unlike other Middle Eastern cultures, it was the Tuareg men who wore veils, not the women. Often living as fugitives, the Tuareg *tagelmust* was the way the Tuareg fighters hid their identities as well as protected them from the violent sun and heat of the desert. The long garment that was used to wrap their heads and hide everything but their eyes was also considered a protection against the *djinn* of the desert, and when they sweated, the indigo dye bled onto their unbathed skin. The ultimate symbol of the Tuareg warrior was his blue *tagelmust*.

Tolo shrugged his sloping shoulders. "He is but a man, and the Tuaregs a plague. We'll kill him, and that will be the end of the affair."

"But how will you find him?" Zhao asked. The Tuareg were virtual ghosts when hiding in the desert.

"We don't have to," Tolo said. "He will come to us, like a fish to the net."

"Why would he do that?"

"We will smash the Tuareg villages, one by one. And he shall hear of it, and he will come out of his lair and strike, and then we will spear him!" Tolo laughed. His people had fished the Niger River for five hundred years.

Zhao began to say something but held his tongue. The Malian's confidence was evident. Perhaps it was best to give him a chance to handle this problem. There was a gentle knock on the door.

Zhao smiled. "I believe my token of appreciation has arrived for you, General."

Tolo chuckled, and set down his snifter and cigar. He turned heavily in his chair toward the door.

"Come," Zhao said in a language Tolo didn't recognize.

The heavy door swung open. Three Thai girls with tall drinks and short silk dresses entered, giggling.

Tolo turned back toward Zhao, white teeth grinning. "You are a good man, Zhao!"

"I knew you were a confident man, General." He winked, and pointed at the three women. "Let's see how far that confidence goes."

"Trust me, Zhao. I won't disappoint them—or you." He laughed again. So did Zhao. If the fat man failed, Zhao would be the one still laughing when he put a bullet between those bulging white eyes. But that would be little consolation. It would be his neck on the chopping block if this mission failed.

"If you'll excuse me, General. I have some business to attend to." Zhao excused himself with a wink and headed for his secure communications room to contact Dr. Weng. He'd give the general a chance to complete the mission, but that didn't mean he couldn't call in reinforcements, just in case.

= 8 =

Captain Naddah rode in the old Baptist missionary bus with the new recruits, still in civilian clothes. He worried they might lose heart as they neared the village. Two weeks' training was just enough to teach them to use their rifles and follow basic orders. But this was their first mission. In Allah's sense of humor, he had chosen the right bus for them after all. The Toyotas carried his most trusted militia fighters, men with blood on their hands, like his.

Naddah was a captain in name only. He didn't belong to the Mali army, though they supplied his militia with weapons, food, and an abandoned camp for training. When the foreign jihadists and Tuareg separatists rose up to seize cities in the north, Naddah quit his job in the repair shop and joined Ganda Koy, and when the Tuareg jihadists Ansar Dine declared sharia law in Gao and began destroying his people's sacred shrines, Naddah volunteered to fight them.

It surprised Naddah how much he enjoyed killing the whites and the foreigners and how much skill he had in doing it, at first with only a machete and then a gun after he had taken one from a man he had killed.

They gave him this mission because he had proven himself loyal to Mali and his people, but also because he could follow orders and even read a little.

The faded letters of the *akafar* Christians on the side of the bus were blacked out and *Ganda Koy*—"Masters of the Land"—painted over them. The Songhai Empire was the greatest of all African empires five hundred years ago, but invasions by foreigners had robbed his people of their land, wealth, and dignity for centuries. Black Africans like the Songhai were reclaiming their rightful place under the sun, and Ganda Koy was the tip of the spear in Mali.

The windows were up but fine dust and sand somehow still creeped into the bus, and the overhead fans only blew the hot air and dust around. The recruits didn't seem to mind. They had sung a few patriotic songs earlier and now sang Songhai folk songs, shouting over the roaring bus engine. His number two was his morale officer, a short, powerful woman from Gao like himself, though he never knew her until now. She had recruited seven women for this mission, three of them her nieces. All had been raped by Tuaregs in the past and all wanted bloody revenge. Number Two and her recruits would lead the rape gang, house to house, after first killing whatever men or boys they found.

Naddah checked his watch, then stood. Number Two stopped singing and the recruits quieted down. Their earnest faces dripped with sweat, black skin glistening in the heat.

"We are only ten minutes away. Squad leaders, do you remember your orders?"

"Yes, sir!"

"And the rest of you? Are you ready to cleanse our land of the Tuareg filth that has covered it?"

"Yes, sir!"

"Do you hate the arrogant Tuaregs as much as I do?"

"Yes, sir!"

"Their white skin?"

"YES, SIR!" Now their faces broke into smiles. Some of them stood, shouting and throwing their fists.

Number Two shouted, "Mali for Africans! Mali for Songhai!" The bus rocked violently.

"Mali for Africans! Mali for Songhai!" they echoed. Naddah pumped his fists in the air and shouted with them.

Number Two shouted louder, "MALI FOR AFRICANS! MALI FOR SONGHAI!"

"GANDA KOY! GANDA KOY! GANDA KOY! GANDA KOY!"

———

The boy drank the ice-cold Coke greedily, sweat still pouring down his small, handsome face. Ibrahim loved that small face. It reminded him so much of his daughter, long since dead.

Ibrahim laughed. "Not so fast, you'll get cramps." He owned one of the few small refrigerators in the village, along with one of the few kerosene-burning generators to power it. He loved that boy with all of his heart. Everything he had was his, in time.

The boy drained the last dark bubbles from the bottle, then grimaced. "Wee-ya!" He laughed, eyes watering with the Coke burn in the back of his throat.

Ibrahim roared and clapped his old, dark hands. He was tempted to offer him another. But the sound of the whooshing air brakes outside and the squeak of heavy leaf springs invaded the magical moment. Was it a truck? What would a truck be doing here?

Ibrahim and his grandson exchanged a glance, each asking the same questions with their eyes.

Ibrahim stepped over to the doorway, his grandson at his side. Ibrahim saw an old bus, faded white. Saw the black words painted on the side. Words that nearly stopped his heart. His worst fear.

Ganda Koy.

The bus's front door snapped open with a clang. A dozen black men with rifles and machetes poured out. The rear emergency gate burst open next and still more men with guns and machetes leaped into the dirt. Women with guns, too. Strange, he thought, his feet frozen in terror.

A wild-eyed Songhai man in a faded military uniform pointed and shouted at Ibrahim. Three men in mismatched camouflage pants and soccer shirts put rifles to their shoulders.

"Run!" Ibrahim grabbed his grandson by his shirt and dragged him away from the door as the rifles exploded behind them.

"The phone!" Ibrahim pointed at the cell phone charging on the car battery, but his grandson didn't need the direction. He snatched the phone up on a dead run, snapping the charging cable in half. No matter now.

The rifles opened up again. Bullets splattered the canned goods on the shelves in a spray of peaches and milk, then stitched the wall above their heads as they dashed past it, shards of mud brick stinging their faces. His grandson yelped but kept running toward the back of their little house. They spoke often of escape plans should such a day arrive. Ibrahim had put a door in the back of the kitchen for access to the little courtyard and outhouse, but also as an escape route. His grandson bolted for the door and yanked it open as Ibrahim reached into a drawer.

"Run! Find Mossa!"

"No! Not without you!"

"RUN!" Ibrahim flung the skinny young body out the heavy wooden door and slammed it shut. He turned as heavy feet pounded through his front doorway, an ancient French army revolver now in his trembling hands.

He pointed it at the doorway, pulling the trigger as fast as he could at the screaming faces spilling through, guns blazing. Fists of molten lead slammed him against the door, clawing his chest open like a hoe turning wet earth after a storm. His body tumbled into the dirt, blocking the exit, the boy's name on his lips like a prayer.

Maputo International Airport
Maputo, Mozambique

Pearce and Hawkins stood by the tall glass window of the new Chinese-built international terminal. Pearce watched Johnny's aluminum shipping coffin scissor-lifted up to the cargo bay of the Boeing 737. He had booked the first commercial flight out he could get for Johnny, a thirty-hour transshipment from Maputo to London, then LAX. The family had enough to deal with without having to wait another week for the next available flight. He would have flown Johnny home on one of the big jets in the Pearce Systems fleet, but they were all deployed on other missions. Like everything else on this trip, bad timing was kicking his ass.

"His sister asked me to thank you, by the way," Hawkins said.

"For what? Getting him killed?"

"For making all of the arrangements. Paying for the flight. She was grateful. Nice woman."

"I wish I could've done more." Pearce still felt guilty about his friend's death. Sandra's, too.

"I know."

The two men watched the ground crew shut the cargo bay door and secure it.

"Still no leads?" Pearce asked.

Hawkins shook his head. "The locals are running the investigation now. Told us to stand down. I wouldn't hold my breath if I were you."

The scissor lift began descending as the ground crew disconnected the fuel line.

"What's next for you?" Hawkins asked. He turned to Pearce.

But he was gone.

= 9 =

The village of Anou
Kidal Region, Northeastern Mali
4 May

Captain Naddah leaned in the doorway of Ibrahim's shop and took a long pull on the Lucky Strike, draining the last of the sweet American tobacco smoke into his lungs. He held his breath, then exhaled slowly, through his nose, savoring the aroma.

Naddah checked his watch. It was just after two in the morning. He had finished his turn in the rape house about an hour ago, then made his rounds in the village, checking on the sentries. He found them all awake at their posts, eager to get another go with the Tuareg whores before they pulled out at dawn. His new orders targeted a village thirty kilometers to the north.

How long can those women keep wailing? Naddah's men had been raping them for hours, each man taking his turn. Naddah's favorite was the young girl with the long, angular face and pale brown eyes that spit fire at him.

Naddah started to pull another Lucky Strike out of a crumpled packet but changed his mind. His throat was dry. Instead, he popped the can of cold Coke open and took a long swig.

He crossed back over to the doorway and stood there, staring at the house on the left, hearing the cries. He checked his watch. Time enough to go back to the house before dawn. He would like one more turn with the girl with the pale brown eyes and—

Naddah's left kidney exploded with fire. He dropped the Coke as he screamed, but nothing came out of his mouth. His throat was clamped shut by a powerful hand that pulled his entire body backward, deepening the knife thrust.

Naddah's legs buckled, but the powerful hand gripping his throat kept him standing long enough for the blade to be pulled out and thrust again into his lower back, severing the spinal column. His bowels gave way and he felt the shame of that. The hand let go.

Naddah fell. His skull cracked on the hard dirt floor, eyes exploding with light.

Naddah drew his last breath, a whimper.

Because he knew.

There is no paradise for a man covered in his own shit.

Northwest Polytechnical University (NPU)
Xi'an, China

Xi'an was a city with a long memory and an even longer history. Home of the fabled terra-cotta warriors, the ancient city at the headwaters of the Silk Road was the wealthy capital of more than a dozen Chinese empires in antiquity. Commerce between East and West flowed along the courses of the Silk Road, but equally important, so did technology. Europe acquired many Chinese inventions over the centuries thanks to the Silk Road. It was only fitting that the flow had now changed directions.

Beijing was the nation's capital today, but Xi'an considered itself to be the intellectual and cultural soul of the Middle Kingdom, as it had been for centuries. Hundreds of Western corporations recently established themselves in the thriving metropolis. Some of China's leading military, security, and space research facilities were also located there, as were fourteen universities, including NPU, one of the most prominent in the nation.

Dr. Weng Litong was officially listed as an adjunct faculty member in the electrical engineering department, but in reality she was the head of the Expert Working Group for Robotics Weapons Systems, which was under the direction of the PLA's General Armament Department, which itself was under the authority of the Central Military Commission of the Communist Party of China. She was, in fact, the most powerful person on the university campus and, arguably, in the entire province of Shaanxi. The Central Commission recently turned its focus to unmanned weapons systems, particularly LARs—lethal autonomous robotics—which they now considered to be the future of warfare.

Weng was the daughter of a prominent PLA Air Force general who sat on the Central Military Commission, and her mother was an active Party functionary and a noted economist in her own right. But Weng's brilliant mind and ruthless cunning had won her the honors and responsibilities she now enjoyed, including her top-floor office towering over the tree-lined boulevard.

Weng earned her first engineering doctorate at the age of eighteen at the prestigious Tsinghua University, where she was first recruited by the General Armaments Department into their "Flying Doves" program, sending tens of thousands of talented young Chinese students abroad for espionage and intelligence-gathering activities. Weng was provided a new identity and legend and sent to MIT, where she earned a second doctorate in robotics and electrical engineering.

The specially selected "doves" were expected to demonstrate the mythical qualities of the favored bird: fierce loyalty and fecundity. Weng exhibited both qualities admirably. Besides distinguishing herself as an engineering student, the young spy recruited and ran eleven Chinese expats and Chinese-American doctoral students, who all went on to significant positions within the American national security establishment. The homely but winsome young graduate student easily won over her American colleagues with her gracious and unassuming demeanor, even as she arranged for the arrest and execution of Chinese nationals whom she identified as having betrayed the Revolution while studying abroad.

Weng's nationalistic zeal and engineering brilliance,

however, didn't blind her to the reality that China was badly losing the drone arms race to the United States. Her Expert Working Group set up over a dozen RPV labs around the nation, each focusing on specific applications— land, sea, and air—and each had achieved some measure of success.

Bio-bots were proving to be one of the most promising developments. Animals were nature's perfect machines, engineered by evolution to run, crawl, fly, and swim for survival. They also had the advantage of nature-engineered intelligence, still far superior to China's feeble attempts at AI. During World War II, the Americans hired the behaviorist B. F. Skinner to train homing pigeons as autonomous guidance systems for bombs, and the Soviets deployed trained bomb-carrying dogs as autonomous antitank weapons against the Germans.

But as exciting as some of her bio-bot breakthroughs were, none was as startling or decisive as the drone technologies the Americans already deployed. This led her inexorably to the logical solution: steal everything the Americans made.

She accomplished this task through the vast network of international student and faculty exchanges—functions that NPU was famous for arranging—as well as planting vast quantities of Chinese-manufactured computer chips and processors with "back door" apps that were commonly installed in American systems. Hacking, of course, was another primary source—and the primary reason why so many Chinese weapons systems, manned or unmanned, bore such an uncanny resemblance to their American counterparts. Capturing or stealing platforms in the field, however, allowed Weng and her teams to reverse-engineer actual working systems, and no one was better at acquiring them than Guo Jun, her best operative. Thanks to him, she now possessed her first working model of a Silent Falcon.

But she had a problem.

She glanced out of her top-story window. It offered a 180-degree view of the sprawling campus, most of it ancient. But her glass-and-steel tower was in the new section. Construction cranes were raising four more towers nearby, all funded with PLA money. But her eyes focused on the famous statue down below. Even this high up, the white limestone torso of the warrior statue was gargantuan. It was one of the most famous sculptures on campus. Famous, but in the wrong location. So she had it moved to where she could see it daily. The giant warrior's bowed head nearly touched the grass, his muscular back and shoulders exposed to the sky. In front of his head, two massive stone hands thrust up out of the grass holding a great stone sword parallel to the earth in obeisance to an unseen master. It was the image of the victorious, all-powerful warrior humbled before its master.

Guo was such a warrior. Perhaps the greatest in China's military. Guo and his handpicked operators, posing as an elite police unit, had won the international Warrior Competition in Jordan two years before, besting more than thirty other SOF teams from around the world. Guo had won the individual sniper competition as well.

But for all of his skills, Guo lacked humility.

It was the reason she would eventually have to execute him.

She picked up her secured phone and dialed.

PLA Safe House
Johannesburg, South Africa

Guo and his team returned to their secured residence in South Africa's largest city, melting back into the largest population of ethnic Chinese on the continent. His secure satellite phone rang. Only Dr. Weng had his number. He clenched his jaw, answered.

"You violated your orders," Weng said.

"My orders allow me to kill when it is necessary to protect the identities of my team members."

"How were your identities compromised?"

"The two *guǐlǎo*s possessed advanced surveillance and intelligence capabilities. It was highly unlikely but still possible that we had been under their surveillance with the Silent Falcon. When they arrived at the scene in the surveillance vehicle, I assumed we had been compromised."

"Ridiculous. We hacked the World Wildlife Association cloud server. The Silent Falcon in their possession was meant only for animal research purposes. That's how we knew to send you there to retrieve it in the first place."

"Things aren't always as they appear. Perhaps they were undercover."

"Spies? Impossible. But even if it were so, it would have been better to capture them and bring them here," Weng said. Still, there was some nagging doubt. The Belgian's identity was confirmed with the documents recovered by Guo. Just another feckless Westerner "chasing her bliss." But the American was a member of Pearce Systems with known ties to the American government. The woman's death was truly of no consequence. But killing the American robbed Weng of valuable insight. "Why didn't you capture them instead of killing them?"

"I had intended to. But the African gangsters I employed overreacted. Short of killing the Africans on the spot, there was no way to stop the carnage."

"But you did kill the Africans?"

"Of course, but later. They were drug addicts and criminals. They were a liability, so they were eliminated."

"Why did you employ such unreliable elements?"

Guo hesitated before answering. When Weng recruited him into her organization, she'd promised him the chance to win glory for himself in battle. His greatest desire was to prove to himself he was the world's best warrior. His loyalty to China was an accident of fate. Had he been born an Israeli, he would have gladly joined the Sayeret Matkal; born an American, he would have joined the SEAL teams. All that mattered to him was to be the best. That was hard to do as an errand boy.

"My extra assignment for the general was to secure rhino horn for him while I was on this mission. I have no such expertise, so it was necessary to employ locals who could fulfill the task."

"And why are you so resentful? Were you not adequately compensated for both missions?" Weng asked. "Paid fully in gold?"

"It was an inappropriate use of resources, in my opinion. I am a soldier. Not a delivery service."

"Are you referring to the Silent Falcon or the rhino horn?"

"Both."

Weng was silent.

Guo stood a head taller than the older woman, but he feared her greatly. She could easily order the other members of his team to kill him, and they would obey her without question. Or at least try to. But Guo feared anonymity even more than death. Death was eventual for everyone, and it was final. Only a man's fame could live on forever, and few ever achieved it.

"Killing that American was a mistake," Weng finally said.

"I've killed Americans before."

"In Afghanistan, as a sniper, secretly assigned with other Hunting Leopards. Not like this."

"It won't happen again."

"I know your desire to prove yourself in combat, particularly against Americans. You will soon have that chance again, but only under my authority."

Guo allowed himself the least possible smile. "Where?"

"Mali. I have a target for you to eliminate. A desert warrior. Quite dangerous. Your contact there will provide the details. You will proceed there directly. I am sending some equipment there for your use."

"Will Americans be there as well?"

"Perhaps. Until then, remain focused on the task at hand. Drones are the future of warfare and China must have them, but our nation still needs soldiers like you to acquire them. Don't disappointment me again."

"I won't."

= 10 =

The elephant stared at him.

"Hold?"

The baritone voice slapped Pearce's fogged mind back to reality. His bleary eyes switched from the dusty elephant head looming over the polished mahogany bar to the man in front of him. Thousand-dollar suit. Million-watt smile. Forty-five caliber, short-barreled chrome pistol in a shoulder holster. Not that the Australian needed it. He outweighed Pearce by fifty pounds, all muscle, straining against the fine Italian silk suit.

Peace glanced at his cards again. Hard to focus after three days of drinking. After loading Johnny's coffin on a commercial flight home, he headed for a familiar dive in the old port district, a crumbling relic in the part of town where tourists and police both feared to tread.

Hammered as he now was, he still couldn't dull the image of Johnny's slaughtered corpse in his mind.

Or the guilt.

"C'mon, Pearce. Quit playing the stunned mullet."

Pearce tossed three cards on the felt. "Hit me."

Pearce scanned the room as the Australian dealt. The two Iraqi bodyguards were slumped in their chairs, suits crumpled and stained, bored out of their minds. The ancient barkeep was stocking liquor. No other patrons.

"Well?" The Australian nodded at the three dealt cards on the felt.

Pearce picked them up. Glanced at the pile of cash on the table, along with a large leather pouch and his own holstered pistol. He was all in now.

Yup. Everything.

Pearce squinted at the blurry numbers on the cards.

"Don't like what you see?" The giant Aussie smiled.

"Hey, boss." A familiar voice.

A soft hand fell on Pearce's shoulder. He turned around.

"What are you doing here?" Pearce asked.

Judy Hopper smiled softly, lowered her voice as if she were speaking to a dim-witted child. "You haven't picked up your phone for days."

Pearce set his cards on the table and patted himself down, face screwed with confusion. "Guess I lost it." He glanced back up at her. "How'd you find me, anyway?"

"Ian."

Like every other Pearce employee, Troy had a proprietary tracker installed in his body. Judy was already in Africa a few borders away, which meant she was closest to him on the ground. That wasn't saying much. Traveling in Africa was always difficult. Ian explained the situation, sent her the coordinates. She came as fast as she could.

The bodyguards eyed Judy, but not for weapons. She wore her mouse-brown hair in a ponytail and no makeup on her plain, tired face, but she was easy on the eyes, especially at this hour.

"Not your first card game, is it?" Judy asked. "Or your first stop."

"I thought you quit," Pearce said. "You said you quit."

"Miss, we're in the middle of a hand. If you don't mind—" The Australian's deep voice was kinder than she'd expected.

"Just a moment, I promise," she said with a polite, earnest smile. She stepped closer to Pearce. One of the bodyguards sat up, the chair scraping on the old stained floor.

"I didn't quit. I took a leave of absence. That's different."

"How?"

"You're still paying me."

Pearce shrugged. "But you still quit on me."

"I didn't quit on you. I just needed time away. Spent it with some friends in Kenya."

"A vacation. Sounds nice."

"Miss?" The Australian's tone sharpened.

"It was a refugee camp. No canoes or S'mores, if that's what you're thinking. I'll tell you about it some other time."

"Looks like you quit them, too."

Judy wanted to cry. Or scream. She'd never seen Pearce this wasted before. "Yeah, to find you, you . . . drunkard."

BAM! The Australian's hand slapped the table. "Are we going to finish this game or not?"

"WE'LL FINISH THE FUCKING GAME!" Pearce roared.

"Whoa. What's this?" Judy picked up the leather pouch on the cash pile. Unbuttoned it. Rifled through the neatly folded documents. She found the title to the Pearce Systems Aviocar, still parked at the airport. "You're betting my plane?"

"Your plane?" Pearce asked.

"Why am I arguing with a lush? What time is it?" Judy asked.

Pearce checked his wrist. Nothing.

The Australian pulled back his suit sleeve. Shoved the military-style watch in Pearce's face. Pearce's watch. The one Annie gave him years ago.

"Two . . . eighteen?" Pearce finally said, squinting.

Judy pointed the pouch at Pearce. "You can't bet the Aviocar."

"Sure I can."

"Of course he can. He did." The Australian pointed a thick finger at the pouch. "Put it back. Please."

"We're gonna need that plane," Judy said to Pearce.

"I don't need it anymore. And you quit, remember?"

"Well, I'm here now. We've got to go." Judy tucked the pouch under her arm and grabbed Pearce's shirt collar.

The Australian whipped out his chromed .45 pistol and held it to Pearce's temple. Both bodyguards were on their feet now, pistols drawn.

"Pick up your damn cards and play your hand." He waved the gun barrel at Judy. "And put those papers back."

Judy sighed, frustrated. Tossed the pouch back on the table.

The Australian pointed his pistol at Pearce's chest. "Mr. Pearce, last warning."

"Sure. No problem."

"Boss—"

"Shhh!" Pearce held a finger to his lips to quiet her. "The man just wants to play a hand of cards. No harm in that." He glanced at the Australian. "Right? Everybody calmed down now?"

Pearce tossed off a glass of vodka in a single throw and slammed it back on the table. "Now, where were we?"

"Cards!" the Australian blurted.

"Boss, it's important. Really important."

"Then you should've called sooner," Pearce said.

"I did. Like, a hundred times," Judy said. "So did she."

"PLAY, God damn you!"

"She?" Pearce asked.

"Yeah. An old friend has been trying to reach you." Judy punched a speed-dial button on her smartphone.

"I don't have any old friends." Troy laid his cards down in a crooked fan.

The Australian leaned forward to look at them. He howled with laughter. Fanned his own cards on the table.

"Sorry, Mr. Pearce, but three of a kind beats none of a kind." He reached for the pile.

Judy handed Pearce her phone. "It's for you."

He frowned. Took the phone. "Pearce."

"Troy, it's me. Margaret Myers."

The Australian stacked the bills on the table, smiling and counting. Pearce listened intently.

"Right away." He tossed the phone back to Judy. Stood. The bodyguards rose, too. Pulled their guns.

Pearce pointed at the pile of winnings. "Gonna need that plane after all, friendo."

= 11 =

The American and Texas flags snapped in the crisp noon breeze.

The small plaza was a favorite hangout for locals and tourists who came to watch airplanes from all over the world make their north–south landing approach. It was a gift to the public by DFW Airport, the scene of last year's murderous mortar attack by Iranian and Mexican cartel terrorists.

A small crowd had gathered for today's announcement. A news van from a local ABC affiliate was there to broadcast the live event. The camera operator checked her sound levels against the aircraft noise while the on-air reporter checked her makeup.

"How's my hair look?" the young reporter asked, worried about the wind.

"We're live in three, two, one."

David Lane (D–24th District, Texas) approached the music stand serving as his podium. Forty-four years old, boyishly handsome, and tall, Lane had the confident, well-earned swagger of a former Air Force MC-130 Talon pilot who flew SOF operators in and out of hot spots all over the world. Lane's chief of staff, his wife and three kids, and his parents stood beside him. He carried no notes.

"My name is David Lane and I have proudly served the 24th district for three terms, working on both the Homeland Security and Veterans' Affairs committees, sitting on a variety of subcommittees, including Border and Maritime Security, Intelligence, and Counterterrorism. It has been an honor and a privilege serving my constituents and the nation on these committees.

"As I promised when I ran six years ago, I would limit my service in Congress to just three terms. I will therefore not be seeking reelection to a fourth term next year. In this current era of mistrust of government, it is especially important for elected officials to keep their word. I also want to set an example for my three young children, who are watching me like hawks."

Lane turned and smiled at his twin first-grade daughters and pre-K son, who was squirming in his mother's grip.

"At the urging of friends, family, and constituents, I am also here to announce my candidacy for the Democratic presidential nomination in 2016.

"I'm making this announcement today despite the reality that I have very little chance of winning. Money dominates every aspect of government today, including election cycles. The fact that it will be hard for me to win is the reason why I need to run. Our system of government is broken. I intend to fix it.

"Today we live in an entitlement society, where everybody wants all of the privileges but none of the responsibilities of citizenship. Too many Americans who want to work or start a business are thwarted by federal policies from both parties that favor Wall Street at the expense of Main Street. Worst of all, to remain in office decade after decade, our career politicians keep giving away benefits we can't afford to supporters who haven't earned them by borrowing money we don't have from children who haven't been born yet. That's a recipe for disaster. It's also just plain wrong.

"Most people in my district probably don't even know my name. Even fewer in the state know who I am, and I'm hardly a blip on the national radar. If you want to know who I am and what I stand for, I guess the best way to describe me is as a Kennedy Democrat, just like my father, a combat-wounded Vietnam veteran, and my mother, a retired schoolteacher.

"I'll be posting all of my policy positions on my website, but all of my ideas for future legislation and policy initiatives can be summarized in the great words of President Kennedy: 'Ask not what your country can do for you, ask what you can do for your country.' It's not an original campaign theme, but it's the most necessary one I can think of. It applies to every American citizen, but it should apply to our politicians, too. Me most of all.

"Thank you, and God bless America."

Lane's mother whooped with pride, and the rest of his family clapped.

"Better go grab that interview," the camera operator said to the reporter. "He's leaving."

The reporter rolled her eyes and whispered, "Boring."

The camera operator shrugged. "I kinda like what he said. He's right, though. He hasn't got a chance in hell."

U.S. Senate Select Committee on Intelligence
Hart Senate Office Building, Room 412, Washington, D.C.

Senator Barbara Fiero was neither the chairman nor the highest-ranking majority member of the Senate's intelligence committee, but she had arranged for this closed-door, classified intelligence briefing on al-Qaeda in Africa. She did it for her own personal benefit, but not her knowledge—she could've given the briefing herself to her octogenarian colleagues. What mattered is how she performed during the briefing and the relationships she could further cultivate afterward. How the meeting came to be scheduled, and others canceled or rearranged to accommodate this one, would never be discovered by the chairman or his staff, only that it had magically appeared on the digital calendars that dictated everyone's schedule both on Capitol Hill and over at Langley these days.

Fiero always had objectives in mind when she attended these briefings. Today she had three.

Fiero always arrived early and left late for the closed-door meetings just for the chitchat. She'd found over the years that it was in those small, human moments that unsuspecting minds were changed and alliances formed. Just this morning she had stood in the soaring sunlit atrium of the Hart Building, exchanging pleasantries with today's CIA briefing analyst, when she learned that his daughter was struggling to get into NYU's graduate film school. "My husband is a member of the Dean's Council for Tisch. I'm certain he can make a call on her behalf."

"You'd do that for her?"

"It's nothing, really." And just like that, she turned a disbelieving smile into another indebted ally. Her life was seemingly filled with such coincidences.

Amazing coincidences. Almost unbelievable.

And those coincidences could always be turned into favors, favors Fiero collected like buffalo-head nickels, never to be spent, but always traded up when something more valuable came along.

Fiero was also funny and personable in a disarming way; the self-deprecating charm and razor-sharp intelligence behind her bright, alluring eyes attracted most men, even ones half her age. Not that her age mattered. She was fifty years old but had the body of a much younger woman, thanks to exercise, nutrition, and cosmetic surgery. Like most beautiful older women, she practiced the simple secrets of looking younger. The first, of course, was having the right parents—DNA went a long way. But perfect, blazingly white teeth (Lumineers), regular professional hair coloring to keep out the gray, and a simple but modern fashion sense made all the difference. At five-eleven she was strikingly tall, but she never used her size for intimidation. She was a master of the comforting touch and the firm but not-too-confident handshake, both equally necessary in the world of fragile male egos.

Fiero also carried an intoxicating aroma about her, the most aphrodisiacal scent of all: money. She was the richest woman in the Senate, with an officially self-disclosed net worth of between $7 and $180 million, thanks largely to her husband's consortium of international investors. In reality, if one ignored the accounting gimmicks but included the deferred-compensation packages and offshore assets, she and her husband were worth triple the latter figure.

That kind of cash left a scented pheromone trail all over Wall Street and Washington that drew insatiable suitors to the queen's hive, where deals, votes, and alliances were fervently consummated.

The irony, of course, was that wealthy people like Fiero never had to spend their own money. It was the lesser people desperately seeking their favor who wound up spending their own cash to win her patronage. People all over town were desperate to get into a relationship with Barbara Fiero, who everybody knew would win her party's presidential nomination the following year.

"AQ in Africa has been relegated to the villages and

hinterlands," the CIA analyst summarized. "Particularly in Mali, where French and ECOWAS troops were able to push back rebel groups, including the MNLA, Ansar Dine, and AQ Sahara last year."

"Weren't those rebel groups fighting each other as well?" Fiero asked. Despite their mutual hatred of the corrupt Mali national government, the rebel groups were bitterly divided among themselves over political aims, ethnic rivalries, and religious doctrines.

"Yes they were, but in that struggle, each was also occupying strategic villages and towns in the resource-rich areas of the north which threatened the sovereignty of the weak national government. It was necessary for West African and French forces to intervene in order to stabilize the new government by pushing al-Qaeda Sahara out."

"By 'new government' you mean the one which had overthrown the previous government because it couldn't contain the Tuareg uprising, correct?" Fiero asked. She smiled coyly at her new CIA friend.

"Exactly, Senator. You certainly know your African politics."

"Oh my gosh, the teacher's pet is showing off again." The old man harrumphing was Senator Wallis Smith, a staunch Republican ally of President Greyhill, which naturally made him an enemy of Fiero. The room ignored the snarky comment, but Fiero didn't. She'd just been called out as smart by the ranking Republican in the room.

First objective accomplished.

"And how would you characterize the new Bamako government? I mean, the one that just replaced the one that replaced the one just before it." She said it in such a comical, offhanded way that the entire room chuckled, even Smith. What Fiero was referring to was the messy succession of incompetent, corrupt Malian governments. The thoroughly corrupt Touré regime had been overthrown by a military junta in 2012 led by an unremarkable American-trained army officer who, in turn, relinquished his temporary government to a French-approved civilian who, in turn, stepped down six months ago in favor of the new president, Ali Kouyaté, who had known ties to the Chinese government.

"I would characterize the Kouyaté regime as somewhat more competent and somewhat less corrupt than all previous administrations, and therefore, probably the brightest hope for Malian stability over the next few years."

"Why the brightest hope?"

"The French are exhausted, politically and economically. They have vested interests in the uranium mines in Niger, but little in Mali. They're pulling back everywhere they can in Africa right now to consolidate their diminishing resources, including Mali. China, however, recently took an interest in Mali, and President Kouyaté enjoys Beijing's favor, along with Beijing's considerable resources."

"That would seem to pose a problem, wouldn't it?" Fiero said. "We don't want China gaining another foothold in Africa."

"Why not?" Smith interrupted. "Let the goddamn Chi-coms wrestle with that mess for a while. We could use some consolidating of our own."

"They're already all over Africa, Barbara. Maybe they're too spread out. Let them get swallowed up in that godforsaken hellhole. No point in us jumping in after them." Senator Anne Coates was a Democrat from Ohio. Her state had lost tens of thousands of manufacturing jobs to the Chinese over the last two decades. She was a commonsense moderate, not an ideologue, but she could always be counted on to vote the straight Democratic party line when it mattered.

"I'm not certain why the Greyhill administration wants to cede vast portions of the globe to our biggest geopolitical competitor, particularly when it comes to strategic, resource-rich areas like the Sahara," Fiero insisted. The heads of the chairman and the other neocons around the table nodded in agreement with her.

Second objective accomplished.

"What invaluable resources are you referring to? Sand? Who the hell needs sand?" The skin around Smith's jowly neck flared red. Like his ally, President Greyhill, Smith was committed to the Myers Doctrine: no new American boots on the ground anywhere until America's fiscal house was put back in order.

"Not just sand, Senator," the CIA analyst said. He was actually the CIA's Africa strategic-resource specialist, which was why Fiero wanted him to brief the committee. "We know there are significant uranium deposits in the region, particularly Niger, which both the French and Chinese have exploited, particularly the French in support of their extensive domestic nuclear reactor program. Unlike the Germans, who have committed to dismantling all of their nuclear reactors, the French remain committed to their nuclear industry. It not only produces seventy-five percent of their domestic electricity supply, but France is also a net exporter of electricity, which earns them over three billion euros per year."

"We don't need any Malian uranium, that's for sure, or Niger yellowcake, for that matter." Senator Bolt was a staunch antinuclear activist. His home state of Washington became alarmingly concerned about nuclear catastrophe after the Fukushima disaster. Environmental activists up and down the Pacific Coast were monitoring Fukushima's Texas-sized debris field floating toward California, and feverishly testing local habitats for cesium and other fatal contaminants. Locals carried Geiger counters and posted their findings on YouTube. Officially, the federal government wasn't concerned. Privately, Bolt was losing sleep over it. He was a leading member of a bipartisan antinuclear power caucus in Congress that had gained an upper hand after the Japanese catastrophe.

"No, but we do need REEs, and we've just learned that a Chinese mining outfit recently discovered a vast new deposit of them, particularly of lanthanum," the analyst said. "By the way, that information is for your ears only. Highly classified."

"The whole damn meeting's classified," Bolt complained. The old Vietnam antiwar protestor turned environmentalist had long argued against all closed-door government meetings, particularly of the intelligence committees. He'd first come to Capitol Hill as a staffer for Frank Church during his famous CIA hearings.

He'd heard firsthand what kind of havoc was wrought by too much governmental secrecy.

"REEs?" Smith asked, incredulous. In the old cowboy's mouth, the "EEs" was drawn out like a long pull of saltwater taffy. "What the hell are R . . . E . . . Es?" Smith turned in his chair and glowered at Fiero. "I suppose *you* know?"

Fiero smiled. The CIA analyst had just confirmed what she needed to know. Or, more accurately, what she already knew. Her secret source had informed her about the massive new REE deposit two days before.

Third objective accomplished.

"Rare earth elements, I believe," Fiero said. "But I'm no expert." She smiled at the analyst, her signal to him to fill in the details.

Fiero pretended to pay attention while the analyst droned on about REEs. She was already plotting her next move. Greyhill had no political incentive to invade Mali. She would have to give him one.

= 12 =

Thanks to a phone call from Judy earlier, the Aviocar was fueled and prepped at the Maputo airport and waiting outside of its hangar when Pearce and Judy braked in a screeching halt in front of it. Fifteen minutes later, they were cleared by the tower and in the air. After leveling off at cruising altitude, Judy patched Pearce through to Margaret Myers at her home in Colorado.

"Troy? It's Margaret. Can you hear me?"

"Loud and clear," he said, wincing. He rubbed his aching head. He and Myers hadn't spoken since the day she'd resigned the presidency the year before. She had resumed her duties as CEO of her software company, and he assumed she was too busy to reach out to him.

Pearce had been busy, too, but that wasn't the reason he never tried to contact her.

Judy listened in on the conversation through her headphones.

"I'm sorry to have chased you down, but I didn't know who else to turn to. I tried to pull some strings for Mike on my end, but I couldn't make it work. I knew I could count on you."

"What's his status?" Pearce asked.

"He's reported as wounded and in serious but stable condition. He needs immediate evacuation."

"Who made the report?"

"Female, unknown. But I'm working on it."

"Then how do you know this is the real deal?"

"Only two people in the world have my private cell number. Mike is one of them." She didn't need to remind Pearce that he was the other person with that number, even if he never used it.

"Could be a trap," Pearce said. "Targeting you. Maybe they tortured him for the info. Maybe he's already dead."

"Maybe. You willing to let it go?"

"No."

"Me neither. But I'm not the one putting my butt on the line. It's not as if they would've expected me to personally fly in there. And they wouldn't know who I'd send in to do the job—maybe the Marines. They made no demands, gave no conditions. Just said 'Hurry.' Doesn't sound like much of a trap to me."

"We're not talking about brain surgeons. If some joker is looking to create an international incident, they've got the perfect megaphone with someone like you involved."

"Even if it is a setup, I'm still willing to stick my neck out on this thing," Myers said. "Obviously, so are you."

"It's Mikey we're talking about. God knows how many times he pulled my bacon out of the fire."

"I'm glad you're the one on the ground out there, Troy. And I heard about your man Johnny."

Troy hesitated, pushing away the memories. Didn't want to talk about it. "You have a plan, I take it?"

"Pulling some things together for you now. Everything should be in place by the time you land in Niamey."

"Mikey's in Niger?" Pearce asked.

"Mali. But Niamey's your jump-off point. It's the best I can do on short notice."

"What's Early doing in Mali?"

"Not sure. The GPS coordinates on the cell phone that made the call came from the Kidal region. That's Tuareg country."

"The 2012 Mali civil war was about them, wasn't it?" Pearce asked.

"It's complicated, but yes. What time is it now on your end?"

Pearce lifted his bruised wrist to check his watch. His fists still ached from the fight in the bar. He wiped the dried blood off of the watch face. He just couldn't leave it behind. It was the only thing he had left of Annie. Something she'd touched. Never should have bet it.

"Zero-three-zero-five, local."

Judy tapped in Niamey, Niger, into the GPS navigator.

"About fifteen, maybe sixteen hours flight time. Three refueling stops, too. Better add another three hours, minimum."

Pearce frowned. Not good. That was a long time for a wounded man to wait for an exfil. But there was nothing to be done at this point. He hoped Early really was in stable condition.

"I'll call you as things firm up on my end," Myers said. "Good luck to both of you."

In the air

Northwestern Zambia

Six hours and twelve hundred miles later, Judy tapped the fuel gauge. "Know any good gas stations around here?"

Pearce shook his aching head. Sober, but hungover now. "No, but I have a Shell card if you find one." He glanced out the window. The morning sun behind them bathed the savannah below in a sweet, golden light. "Postcard Africa," Judy called it. A small town hugged the Zambezi River in the bottom of their windscreen.

"That's Mwinilunga. Nice little place."

"You know it?"

"I grew up in this part of the world, remember?"

"They got a Starbucks?"

"No, but I have a friend who lives about five miles north of here. He has an airstrip we can use. And by 'airstrip' I mean a stretch of flat ground and not too many trees nearby."

"McDonald's has pretty good coffee. Or Hardee's. And they've got biscuits. Either of those will do."

"Whit will have coffee, for sure. Probably a batch of antelope stew, too."

"Sounds like a winner. I don't suppose he has any fuel?"

"Whit runs the Aviation Mission Fellowship station. He should have plenty."

"You know everybody around these parts," Pearce said.

"The missionary community is pretty tight-knit, and missionary aviators even tighter."

"You ever think about going back to that life?"

Judy ignored the question. "I checked your manifest. You've got a delivery to Fort Scorpio due in about an hour. What do you want to do about it?"

The Aviocar still contained the special-delivery packages for the "Recces," the South African special forces. Johnny was supposed to run that training, too.

"Gonna have to disappoint them."

"Buckle up. We're heading down."

Minutes later, Judy flared the nose and wings as she landed the boxy airplane. The Aviocar's fixed tricycle landing gear absorbed the grassy field with hardly a bump. She taxied over to the hangar. Three ancient Cessna 172 Skyhawks were parked neatly in a row on the far side of the building. They were all painted in the mission's famous Florida-orange paint scheme. Their old logo—a cross, a Bible, and a dove—had since been painted over and replaced with a simple *AMF* in black letters. It wasn't just a marketing gimmick. Too many

Islamic extremists had taken potshots at "infidel" planes in the last year to ignore the problem.

"Interesting paint jobs," Pearce said.

"They paint them bright orange so that when they crash we can find the bodies more easily and send them back home." She flashed a smile. Soldiers weren't the only people with guts.

A big man in stained coveralls and a crew cut ambled heavily out of the open hangar door, like a bear walking on two legs. He stuffed an oily rag into a rear pocket as he approached the plane.

Judy and Pearce stepped out of the cargo door, stretching out their tired muscles.

"Judy!" The big man dashed over, surprisingly fast for his size. They hugged. Judy nearly disappeared in his massive embrace.

"So good to see you, Whit."

"You, too, sister. Who's this?" Whit's green eyes beamed through a pair of rimless glasses. His hair was so blond it was nearly white, and the bristles in the crew cut were as thick and stiff as a shoe brush.

"Whit, this is Troy Pearce. Troy, this is the Reverend Whit Bissell. He runs the AMF division in central and west Africa."

Whit thrust out a meaty paw. "Great to meet you, Mr. Pearce. And call me Whit."

Troy took it. The man's hand was a vise. "Name's Troy. Mr. Pearce was my father."

"I just put on a pot of coffee back at the house. Should be ready in a jiff. You two want to clean up while we wait?"

"We need to fuel up and get going, Padre. We have an emergency."

"What kind of emergency?"

"A friend in trouble. We need to go get him," Judy said.

"What kind of trouble?" Whit asked. He frowned with pastoral concern.

"Not the kind of trouble you can help with," Troy said. "Unless you're handy with a—"

"We can use your prayers, Whit, that's for sure," Judy interrupted, throwing Pearce a nasty glance. "And a refuel."

"I can pray, but I'm not sure how much fuel I can spare. How far are you going?"

"Heading up north. Cameroon," Judy said, lying by omission. "We're bone-dry and we need a full tank to get there."

"How much is a full tank?"

"Five hundred and twenty-eight gallons," Judy said. "And 80/87 avgas is fine. We don't need the fancy stuff."

"Sorry, but I can't spare it."

Pearce pointed at an old GMC fuel truck parked a hundred yards away on the far side of the airstrip. "Is that thing full?"

"Half."

"That must be, what, fifteen-hundred-, two-thousand-gallon capacity?"

"Two thousand."

"So we take five, we leave you five. What's the problem?" Pearce asked.

"We're glad to pay for it," Judy said.

"It's not that, though we could surely use the donation.

The problem is, we need the gas. We do a lot of medical missions and emergency transport. Just got back from one yesterday, as a matter of fact. And I'm the fueling hub for two other agencies. Avgas is hard to come by in this part of the world. When the refinery has it, I have to make a six-hundred-mile round-trip to go get it, and they say it will be another four to six months before I can restock. I'm sorry, but I can't do it."

"Our friend is in trouble, Whit. We really need that fuel." Judy laid a hand on his forearm.

Whit shrugged. "I understand, but I'm sorry."

"I think Jesus wants us to have that gas, Padre."

The missionary's broad back stiffened. "I don't take kindly to blasphemy, Mr. Pearce."

"I'm not blaspheming. I'm quoting scripture."

"Excuse me?"

"Sermon on the Mount. 'Give to every man that asketh of thee; and of him that taketh away thy goods ask them not again.' So I'm just askin'—can we please have that fuel?"

"No. I'm sorry. There are too many other lives at stake."

"Our friend's life is at stake, too," Judy said.

"Then I'll pray for him."

Pearce stepped closer. "There's another verse, Padre. Something like, if a man strikes your face—"

"*Troy.*" Judy's eyes flared.

Whit didn't back down. "You'd rob a mission? We're doing the Lord's work here."

"Didn't David eat the Bread of the Presence from the tabernacle?"

"The Devil can cite chapter and verse, too."

"Then pray for us sinners, Padre, but only after you help me get that damn fuel loaded."

Whit tugged on his ear, then laughed. "You might be a horse's ass, Mr. Pearce, but somebody's darn blessed to have you as a friend."

= 13 =

Zhao residence
Bamako, Mali
6 May

The Malian boxer was ten centimeters taller and at least ten kilos heavier than Zhao, but it was his face and not Zhao's that was drenched in sweat and bleeding heavily over the left eye.

Both men were shirtless and ripped. The black man kept his gloved hands up by his face, one hand carefully guarding the eye now swelling shut. He kept driving cautiously toward Zhao, who was springing on the balls of his feet, dancing half circles around the squeaking parquet dance floor, first left, then right, then back again, a smile plastered on his handsome face, his bare hands loose and bouncing in front of his broad chest.

Guo stood at parade rest. The boxing ring was in Zhao's colonial mansion. Previously it was a ballroom with a giant crystal-and-gold chandelier dangling overhead. Guo disapproved of the entire house and its furnishings— a garish historical anachronism. Everything about the house screamed excess and self-indulgence. Guo preferred the sleek linearity of his modern high-rise apartment in Beijing, or the spartan efficiency of a military barracks, to this European monstrosity.

It was an honor for Zhao to personally request Guo's services. Zhao was the kind of man the Party groomed for leadership. If Zhao's star continued to rise, he would inevitably reach the Standing Committee, perhaps even the presidency. Weng emphasized the importance of this mission to Zhao's career, which meant, of course, his own. Their fates were now intertwined. The two men were practically mirror images of each other: ambitious, intelligent, powerfully built, and ruthless. They were even the same height. The primary difference was that Zhao fought in boardrooms, Guo on battlefields. Politics versus blood. In Chinese history, the two were often commingled.

"You read the files I sent you, Guo?"

"Yes, sir."

The Malian threw a lightning left jab into the space where Zhao's head had been a nanosecond earlier. Threw a second. Missed again. Zhao laughed.

"What did you learn?"

"Mossa Ag Alla is a dangerous opponent, that he is to be killed upon contact, and that I am to conduct operations without revealing my identity or location while in country."

Zhao danced right, then left. "Correct on all counts.

And secrecy is vital. The Mali government would be outraged if they knew you and your team were here."

The chiseled Malian charged again, throwing a vicious right cross, lowering his left hand just a few centimeters.

Zhao saw the punch coming in the man's eyes even before he threw it. As the African swung his enormous right fist, Zhao spun on the ball of his right foot and launched a devastating roundhouse kick. His heel crashed into the boxer's left temple, just behind the swollen left eye. The African boxer grunted as his brain short-circuited. His upper body still twisted on a right axis, following the centripetal weight of the failed right cross, and the strike from Zhao's heel into his skull accelerated the spin. The big Malian pirouetted on his right leg, then tumbled to the floor like a bag of wet meat slapping wood. He didn't move.

Zhao sauntered over to a gilded table and pulled a bottle of water from a champagne bucket brimming with ice. He tossed it over his shoulder at Guo, who caught it in one hand. Zhao cracked one open for himself, pointed it at Guo. *"Gānbēi."*

"Gānbēi"

Mali was hot. Guo was glad for the cold water. He drained it.

But Zhao sipped his water, Guo noticed. The man also wasn't breathing hard, and didn't seem to be sweating much, if at all.

"So tell me, Guo," Zhao said, smiling. He nodded at the unconscious African. "What should we do about him?"

"What do you mean, sir?"

"You said that you were to conduct your mission without revealing your identity or location while you were here. And yet you revealed both in front of this man."

"I assumed he was in your employ, sir. Otherwise, you would not have summoned me in his presence nor inquired about my mission."

"Not an unreasonable assumption. He does work for me, but he is an African. Where do you think his loyalties are?" Zhao knelt down next to the boxer, felt for his pulse.

Guo flushed with humiliation. It had been a test, and he'd failed. He drew his combat knife. "I'll take care of him now."

"No need. I already solved your problem." Zhao stood, held out his hand for Guo's knife.

Guo turned the blade in his hand and extended the handle to Zhao. His mission was over before it began.

"I was told you were the best," Zhao said. He drained the last of the water and let the bottle tumble to the floor.

"I am the best."

"That's disappointing." He lifted the heavy combat knife in his hand. "Nice weight. Well balanced. Is it a good thrower?"

"Yes, sir. It is."

Zhao glared into Guo's emotionless eyes. Raised the razor-sharp blade behind his ear to throw it.

Guo didn't flinch. How one died mattered even more than how one lived.

The blade launched from Zhao's hand. It thudded heavily between the shoulder blades of a naked young

French woman combing her long red hair. The carbon steel blade buried itself into the plaster wall behind the old oil painting.

"Never really cared for Degas," Zhao said. "You?"

"I don't have an opinion, sir."

"Be sure to keep your blade sharp. And don't make me clean up your mess again."

"No, sir."

Zhao picked up his shirt and pulled it on. "My bartender makes a fantastic Rusty Nail. We'll drink a few and talk some more about your mission. I especially want to hear more about this Pearce fellow you are supposed to capture, if you have the time."

"Yes, sir."

Of course Guo had the time. He had all the time in the world now.

CIOS Corporate Offices
Rockville, Maryland

CIOS wasn't unique. American defense and intelligence agencies like the NSA contracted with thousands of private, nongovernmental companies to handle their enormous workloads. CIOS was just one of hundreds of contractors like Booz Allen Hamilton, the infamous former employer of NSA whistle-blower Edward Snowden.

As an authorized NSA contractor, Jasmine Bath had either legal access to NSA resources or the knowledge to gain access to those resources, and the ability to cover her tracks while doing so in either case. She had been subjected to the pervasive scrutiny of security-clearing authorities, not only before she was initially hired by the NSA, but also during and after her government employment, then reexamined again when she applied for her contractor authorization. Those investigations themselves were conducted by a private contractor, National Investigative Services. Bath easily penetrated the NIS mainframe and wrote her own glowing clearances.

She was also well aware that her bank accounts, e-mails, and all other data footprints were subject to constant, randomized checks to ensure her continued loyalty and fidelity. But since the day she entered Berkeley, Jasmine had been prescient enough to sanitize her own records and to create the necessary fictions to maintain the illusion of purity.

As far as she was concerned, it didn't matter that her job was to violate the privacy of other people in the name of national security. It was no one's damn business but her own to know whom she slept with, which nineteenth-century German transcendentalists she read on her Kindle, or how often she ordered Kao Pad Poo at the Smiling Panda.

It also didn't bother her one whit to dig wherever she was told to dig, especially by The Angel. What did it matter to her that she generated lists for him of Dark Web porn downloads, offshore painkiller prescriptions, or secret organ-donor purchases of certain committee chairmen, Treasury Department undersecretaries, and Senate staffers? Politics was a game of sharp elbows and vicious cross-checks. Bath wasn't playing the game. She wasn't even keeping score. She was just supplying the sticks and blades for a hefty fee.

That morning she had received a new research request from The Angel. "Lane, David M." She knew the name. Had watched his pathetic announcement a few days earlier. The congressman seemed earnest and sincere in his speech, but those qualities in politics were about as useful as a floppy drive on a MacBook Air, so she dismissed him out of hand as a loser.

So why the research query from The Angel?

Hers not to reason why, only to cash the checks. She ran her searches, a digital colonoscopy. But Lane came up clean.

As in, nothing. As in, not doctored or laundered or sanitized, or even a fictional legend concocted for some CIA spook needing a cover. Nope. Nothing.

"You're sure?"

"Positive."

"Then you need to create some catastrophic filth. Put it out there in a credible way, the way you do better than anybody else."

"No problemo."

"Get started on that right away, but don't let it out. Yet."

"You got it."

"I'll be in touch."

Lane, David M. Sincere, earnest . . . lame.

Like Justice Tanner. Tanner killed himself, sure. Jasmine looted the coroner's hard drive. Saw the crime-scene photos. A bloody mess. Jasmine hated that. But it wasn't her fault. She didn't put the gun in his mouth, did she? Or pull the trigger? No. But maybe she supplied the bullets, metaphorically speaking.

Screw the metaphors.

Screw Tanner. And David Lane.

Not her problem.

Her problem was Margaret Myers. The former president was a software engineer in her own right and owned her own software company. The truth was, the two of them had a lot in common. In another reality, or a J. J. Abrams parallel universe, the two of them could've been friends.

But Myers wasn't her friend. Myers had been sniffing around the Tanner suicide for weeks. The initial queries had been clumsy, almost like a drunk walking into a plate-glass door he had trouble seeing. But Myers came back, slowly, cautiously, and from new directions, using bots, mostly, tapping into a wide variety of public databases, then breaking through passworded accounts and, finally, private nets, all unaware of Jasmine's presence monitoring her searches. Or, at least, so Jasmine hoped. What was clear to Jasmine, however, was that Myers was assembling the right data set. But just to be sure, Jasmine broke into Myers's toy box and took a look around. Then there was no question.

Myers knew, or at least was on the verge of knowing.

Jasmine informed The Angel. Now Myers was his problem.

"Are you sure?" he asked.

"The only way to be metaphysically sure is when the feds come rolling up to your driveway in a fleet of those big black Suburbans."

"Can't you steal her database? Drop a virus into the network?"

"If she has any brains—and she does, believe me— she's got hard copies of everything, or cloud backup, or both. But even if she didn't, once I broke in there and stole everything, she'd know that we know, so you'd alert her and she might be forced to act or go deeper. I think it makes more sense for me to sit tight and watch what she does. If she alerts the black-Suburban boys I can let you know, but there are a whole lot of intermediary steps she'll be taking before she gets to that point, and right now I'm completely invisible to her."

"Sounds like a plan, so long as you're sure you're invisible to her."

"Guaranteed," Jasmine wrote. "Trust me."

= 14 =

Vin Tanner was the first U.S. Supreme Court Justice to commit suicide while in office. That's how he would always be remembered in the history books. Myers chose to remember him only as her friend.

She'd known Tanner for twenty years before she nominated him to the Supreme Court. Knew his wife and kids well. Their two skiing families vacationed together in Vail several times. Justice Tanner sent her a handwritten note when her son had been killed, and enclosed an old Polaroid of their two young boys in soccer jerseys, skinny arms draped over each other's shoulders, gap-toothed smiles and sweaty foreheads, best friends forever.

But Myers didn't nominate Tanner because they were friends. He was a brilliant jurist, but more important, a thoughtful and prudent political theorist. Small government, small businesses, and small farms were his Jeffersonian mantra. Her opponents on the Senate Judiciary Committee hung the libertarian label on him at the televised hearing, thinking that the old canards about legalized prostitution and disbanding the FDA would scuttle his chances, but his effortless, irrefutable defense of limited constitutional government silenced his critics. His confirmation sailed through with only two dissenting votes.

Myers was certain at the time that Tanner's appointment would be one of the highlights of her presidency. She hoped it would be the beginning of the end of the "tyranny of black robes." She believed Tanner would cast a number of crucial swing votes that would finally begin to push back the overwhelming encroachments of federal legislation and administrative decrees that now impinged upon nearly every facet of American life. But to her chagrin, he cast the deciding vote in favor of upholding sweeping new regulations promulgated by Senator Fiero's finance committee, regulations that would only serve to further empower the largest banks and enlarge yet again the role and opacity of the Federal Reserve.

His decision deeply troubled her. The nation had nearly seven thousand banks, but just six of them controlled sixty-seven percent of all banking assets. Those "too big to fail, too big to jail" bankers were largely responsible for the 2008 crash and the long Great Recession still ravaging the nation and much of the globe. The last thing Wall Street and the Big Banks needed was more power and more regulatory protection in the guise of banking reform. If any Supreme Court Justice could have been expected to vote against the Fiero legislation, it was Tanner. Instead, he wrote the majority opinion. As any student of the Court knows, justices have a funny habit of changing after their appointments—and disappointing their champions. Myers and Tanner would be in the footnotes, too, but for a grislier reason.

She reflected on her decision to visit Tanner two weeks prior. Myers may have resigned the presidency but she still felt responsible for his disastrous decision. She had the right to know why he made it. God knows he'd been pilloried in the media, crucified on both the left and the right for his inexplicable vote. She had known that if the media got wind of her visit, it would only make his bad situation worse. But she had needed to see him face-to-face, look him straight in the eye.

She arrived at his Georgetown brownstone late in the cool evening, unannounced. That way she could avoid the press, and Tanner couldn't avoid her. She knocked.

Tanner's dark, sleepless eyes narrowed when he saw her that night. He reluctantly waved her into his study.

"I'm surprised it took you so long." He lit a cigarette. "Where's your Secret Service detail?"

"I discharged them. I'm no longer the president, so why should the public have to pay for them? Only pimps need an entourage like that."

"The world's a dangerous place, Margaret. You need to be more careful."

"Where's *your* security detail?"

"Gave them the night off." He led them into his study. Offered her a chair. Floor-to-ceiling built-in shelves were crammed with books.

"How are Michelle and the kids?"

"They're fine. Visiting her parents." He took a long drag. "Kind of late for a social visit."

"I'm just a concerned citizen calling on an old friend. You look awful, by the way."

"There's nothing to talk about. What's done is done. And I don't owe you anything."

"I'm not a debt collector. I just wanted to know why."

"It's all in the majority opinion."

"I think it's all in your face."

"What's that supposed to mean?" He stabbed the cigarette out in a crystal ashtray full of butts.

"You're one of the most principled men I've ever known, and yet you've obviously made a decision you regret. You regret it so much it's tearing you up. The Vin Tanner I know would never make a decision that violated his principles, but something compelled you to do so."

Tanner's face blanched. "I'll have to ask you to leave. Now."

"Is there anything you want to talk about?"

"No."

"Is there anything I can do?"

He rose to his feet. "Yes, leave. This minute." His shoulders slumped. "Please."

"I'm sorry I've upset you."

She left.

Three hours later, Tanner put a revolver in his mouth and pulled the trigger.

Myers blamed herself, of course. The timing of Tanner's death couldn't have been coincidental. That meant she played a part in it. The guilt had eaten her alive since that day. But something else was wrong. Her intuition told her she was being followed. She couldn't prove it. But the more she thought about it, the more she realized she probably was under surveillance. She made herself a target the minute she knocked on Tanner's door. Stupid.

There was a knock on her door.

"Come in."

The service technician. He'd left twenty minutes before, after a service call. Her TV signal had been experiencing irregular glitches the last few days. She had called for service and the tech arrived today, to replace one of the circuit boards on the satellite dish.

"Forget something?"

"No, ma'am. Found this about a mile up the road." He handed her an electronic device about the size of a tablet.

"What is it?"

"Not sure, ma'am. But it's generating a radar signal. And it was pointed in the direction of your house."

"I don't understand."

"I'm retired Navy. I just do this job to keep from

getting bored. Radar is kind of a hobby of mine. I carry a homemade rig in my truck, picks up all kinds of radar signatures, especially wide-spectrum. About a mile north of here, my rig alarmed. It wasn't one of the police bandwidths, for sure. So I pulled over. Looked around with my handheld. Found an all-weather box strapped to a tree. Kind of unusual, to say the least. Found that inside. Just thought you should know."

She flipped the device over. No markings. "What do you think it was doing?"

"Can't be sure, but I'd guess it's some kind of surveillance function. You need to run it by your people, just to be sure."

Her security chief, Roy Fox, was scheduled to stop by after lunch. She'd ask him then.

"Thank you for taking all of the time and effort to bring me this."

He shrugged. "Glad to do it." Then he added, "If you don't mind my saying, ma'am, you were a damn fine president. I hated like hell to see you go."

Roy Fox arrived on schedule after lunch. He was former FBI, a specialist within the communications exploitation section (CXS) of the bureau's Counterterrorism Division. Fox easily identified the tablet-sized device in his hands as one of the next-generation PHOTOANGLO radar units.

"This isn't good."

"What's the problem?"

He explained. Myers agreed. This wasn't good at all. The presence of a PHOTOANGLO unit meant

LOUDAUTO passive room bugs, or their equivalents, were planted in her house. The LOUDAUTO units were nearly impossible to find, either by electronic detection or physical inspection, if they were properly inserted. The miniature microphones turned room audio like human voices into analogue electrical signals that were picked up by the PHOTOANGLO radar unit, rebroadcast to a relay station, then reconverted to audio files for analysis.

Fox went on to explain that similar passive bugs could record keyboard strokes, printer outputs, and even video cable signals.

"God only knows how long they've been in place." His face flushed. "I'll tender my resignation immediately, of course."

Myers didn't know what to think. She had hired Fox to protect her security. He'd obviously failed. But whoever had deployed these devices was world-class. Maybe she was at fault for not taking her security more seriously.

"Well, at least we know now." She pointed a finger at an invisible room bug. "And so do they."

"I just hope there isn't another PHOTOANGLO out there still picking up this conversation."

"Why don't you and your team conduct a sweep. Yank out everything you can find."

Fox pulled out his cell phone, scrolling for numbers. "I've got a few favors I can call in. I'll get a team here right away. I won't let you down again."

He bolted out of the room with the phone in his ear.

Myers didn't know what to do next. She knew that all of this equipment was standard NSA ANT spy craft—the kind of technology they deployed to spy on the European Union, the UN, and sometimes even hostile governments in its DROPMIRE program. Not that any of these devices were stamped *NSA*. But she herself had approved of their deployment when national security was at stake. At least, that's what she believed at the time.

Now that she was being targeted by the very same technology, she began to doubt the wisdom of her previous decisions. She felt horribly exposed, even violated. She understood that sometimes people were targeted in order to eliminate them as suspects. Didn't matter. Her privacy had been stolen from her, and no matter the reason, she resented it. Now she understood the rage of people like Chancellor Angela Merkel, who had been similarly bugged by her American "friends." Was it possible that spying on allies caused more damage than it prevented? Spying, by definition, was illegal. Spying on allies violated trust, and alliances were built on trust.

Myers knew these surveillance units were also available to other federal agencies, and even state and local investigative units, including some of the larger metropolitan police departments. Undoubtedly, other national governments had access to similar technology as well. There was really no way to determine who might be behind these incursions. But she hadn't committed any crimes. This couldn't be an official investigation. This was a private affair—undoubtedly, the same people connected to Tanner's death.

Her visit with Tanner had been unofficial, off the books. She hadn't called him in advance or sent an e-mail. She'd known that if he was home he'd let her in, so why give him the chance to wave her off beforehand? Myers thought it wise to not volunteer any information about her visit that night, and neither the district police nor federal authorities had ever contacted her after his death. She didn't attend his funeral, probably the reason she had never gained closure with his death.

Why had he killed himself? Even if he had made a ruling he'd regretted, it could have been addressed, either by later rulings or in off-the-record interviews. Unless he couldn't do either. That meant some kind of pressure had been applied to him, didn't it?

Whoever had pressured him was now coming after her. If that person could break Vin Tanner, they could break her. And now they had the gall to come after her. That made her angry. It also scared her. Whom could she trust?

A horrible thought crossed her mind. What if her own security chief had been part of this? He probably wasn't—she'd known him for years—but now she had doubts. Was he really unable to find those devices? Or was he hiding them? Once again, the very existence of the technology had poisoned the well. Could she really trust him? Now she wasn't certain.

She wanted to call Troy. But if her phone was compromised like her computer, she'd only put him in danger, too. She may already have. He was too busy on Early's rescue mission to help her anyway. What was she thinking?

She needed to find a way to securely contact Ian

McTavish, Troy's computer genius. Troy gave her permission last year to contact anyone at Pearce Systems for any reason. Finding Tanner's blackmailers seemed like a good reason to her. Not getting killed by them was even better. The brilliant Scot could help on both counts. She'd already worked with him to make arrangements for Troy's rescue of Mike Early. Now she was the one who needed a little rescuing.

She made a decision. Purse, keys, cash.

Time to run.

═ 15 ═

Karem Air Force Base
Niamey, Niger
6 May

Guess we'll have to play it by ear," Pearce said.

"Is that before or after we're shot down?" Judy was nervous flying toward an American military base without the proper clearances or emergency call signs. The Aviocar they flew in was strictly commercial and broadcasting the proper IFF signal, but her alarms indicated they'd been lit up with antiaircraft radar and laser range finders.

"We have our orders. Let's stick to them and see what happens next."

"Sure. What's the worst that can happen?"

Pearce was concerned, but not for himself. Myers had called back late yesterday and instructed them to arrive at the American air facility precisely at 2100 local, and promised to call back with details about the plan but never did. Pearce tried to reach her but couldn't. Either she was in trouble or running from it.

"Bet you wish you hadn't threatened to beat up a missionary right about now, eh?" Judy grinned.

"Maybe we should've let the padre keep the gas after all."

"Bravo Two-Four, Bravo Two-Four, do you copy?" A woman's voice crackled in their headsets. The Air Force air controller.

"Guess they got the message. That's our call sign," Judy said to Pearce. She radioed back, "This is Bravo Two-Four. Copy."

"Bravo Two-Four, this is Tower Control. You are cleared to land. Come to two-seven-zero heading. Over."

"Copy that, Tower Control. Coming to header two-seven-zero. Over."

"Here goes nothing." Judy gently pushed the rudder pedals and turned the yoke to the new heading until the long black strip of illuminated asphalt was centered in her windscreen, one of three on the small air base. A granite-gray, push prop aircraft with a twenty-meter wingspan stood on one of the runways.

"Reaper drone," Pearce said. "Night ops."

"No wonder they built their own little base out here." The U.S. Air Force located the facility five miles north and west of the city, not far from the N24 roadway, which they repaved and widened to accommodate larger military vehicles. Diori Hamani International Airport was about two miles south and east of Naimey's outermost boundaries. Diori Hamani had too much civilian traffic and security problems for a sensitive military operation to have to deal with.

Just five hundred feet off the ground they could make out a series of low-lit prefab buildings and trailers: hangars, offices, quarters. At least one of those trailers was the ground control station (GCS) for the Reaper and its crew. Pearce watched the Reaper roll down its runway and gently angle into the brilliant night sky pregnant with stars. He lost sight of it as soon as it cleared the runway lights, but he could discern its deadly shadow blotting out a swath of starlight.

M oments later, Judy landed with practiced perfection. She taxied as directed by the tower toward an available hangar, an airman first class marshaling her into position with red-lighted batons. She was a young Hispanic, probably no more than twenty, Pearce guessed, with a pair of orange safety earphones nearly as large as her head. Did the recruiter tell her she'd wind up at a super-secret drone base in Africa when he visited her high school back in El Paso or Denver or Sacramento? The young face was earnest and confident in the blinding landing lights as she crossed the batons over her head, signaling a stop. Judy pressed the brake pedals. The marshal dropped her arms back sharply to her sides, then snapped the right baton to her throat, parallel to the ground, signaling Judy to cut her engines. Pearce threw the young woman a mock salute, and she allowed herself a small smile before turning on her boot heels and heading back into the hangar.

"Now what?" Judy asked.

Pearce pointed out the window. "There's our ticket, I'm guessing."

A black Chevy Suburban with tinted windows raced toward them.

Judy and Pearce went through the shutdown procedure, powering down and securing the aircraft. By the time they opened the cargo door, the big Chevy SUV had pulled to a stop and two doors had swung open. The man in the front passenger seat made a beeline for Pearce and Judy, buttoning his suit coat as he marched toward them. He was followed closely behind by a harried young Air Force captain in her camouflaged ABUs and carrying a clipboard. Her name tag read SOTERO in block letters. The driver, a private, remained behind the wheel, but a square-jawed AF Security Forces sergeant named Wolfit stood watchfully by the vehicle, eyes boring a hole in Pearce. An M4 carbine with an HK grenade launcher and high-end optics was slung across his broad chest.

"Troy Pearce, Judy Hopper, it's a pleasure to see you both again. You probably don't remember me, but I'm Bert Holliday. We met at the HIV/AIDS conference in Nairobi last year." He shook Pearce's hand warmly.

"Bert, of course. Great to see you again, too." Pearce had no idea who he was.

"Mr. Holliday," Judy offered, shaking his hand without conviction.

"I'm sure you're both surprised to see me out here. I was recently reassigned to this mission, and with Ambassador Ray just called away yesterday, I'm now the acting chargé d'affaires." Holliday wore his smile as easily as his neatly tailored suit, no tie, and custom-made cobalt-blue oxford shirt. He pointed to the captain. "And this is Captain Eva Sotero, the officer in charge this evening. Captain, this is Troy Pearce and Judy Hopper, our *valiant* guests."

Pearce put on his best poker face, but guileless Judy frowned with confusion. The captain was clearly frustrated and off her game, but she caught Judy's expression. It only added to her suspicion. Sotero glanced at her clipboard. "I just received these orders twenty minutes ago from a Colonel Ian Sanders, out of AFRICOM's offices in Stuttgart. I've been instructed to give you full logistical support for your mission."

Colonel Sanders? Pearce stifled a laugh. It was a funny way for Ian to let him know he was the one who made the arrangements.

"I've been instructed by my superiors to offer any assistance I can as well," Holliday added.

"But these orders are highly irregular," Sotero insisted. "And I've never heard of this Colonel Sanders."

"Did you try calling him?" Pearce asked. "We're doing this on the fly, so a lot of things won't be regular." The late-night arrival meant a junior officer was in charge of the base, and Pearce intended to take full advantage of Sotero's inexperience.

"I called Stuttgart immediately. But, unfortunately, the direct line to his office is out of service."

Good move, Ian, Pearce thought.

"Did you try Washington? Someone in the Pentagon?" Pearce asked.

"It's four in the morning there, sir. I'd just get some other poor OOD slob like me."

"Base commander?" Pearce asked.

"Not picking up his cell phone. Left a voice mail."

"What's the problem, Captain?" Holliday stiffened. "This is an emergency medical evacuation of an American citizen in a hostile environment. These two people are risking their lives to save another, so let's loosen up a few buttons and get to work for these people."

"I'll need to see some ID, please," Sotero said.

"There's no need. I'll vouch for them," Holliday said.

"SOP, sir," Sotero insisted.

"Not a problem," Pearce said. He and Judy both pulled current passports from their pockets and handed them to her. She verified names and photographs.

"I'll need to make photocopies," Sotero said.

"There's time for all of that later," Holliday insisted. "Let them get some chow and some shut-eye."

"What time will you be departing?" Sotero asked Judy.

"What time?" Judy glanced at Pearce.

Holliday jumped in. "We're still waiting for a shipment of medical supplies. It should be here in four hours."

"Destination?" Sotero asked.

"That's 'Need to Know,' Captain," Holliday said.

He turned to Pearce. "How soon until you're ready to leave?"

"Soon as we can refuel and run a brief maintenance inspection," Judy said. She yawned.

Sotero caught the hint. "I'll assign ground crew to take care of the refuel, maybe have them check systems, too, if you like."

"That would be great." Judy was happy to get extra hands on the job, but after they were done she would still do her own walkaround, the way her father trained her.

The captain stepped past Judy and stuck her head in the cargo door. "Mind if I take a look around?"

"Never seen a plane before?" Pearce said. "The Air Force used to have a bunch of them back in the day."

"Need to check for contraband."

"Captain Sotero, please," Holliday insisted. "This is a humanitarian mission."

"And this is a United States Air Force base. We have protocols, Mr. Holliday, and it's my ass if I don't follow them."

"Not a problem," Judy said. "Feel free to look around."

Judy wasn't concerned. Pearce's special-delivery cargo to South Africa was carefully hidden and stowed away in a secret locked compartment.

"Before you get started, Captain, how about some food and drink for our guests?"

"Of course. Let's load back up and I'll run you two over to the mess hall. I've got a couple of BOQ trailers open if you want to shower and catch some sleep." She eyed Pearce, then Judy. "Do you folks want one bed or two?"

"One," Troy said, serious as a heart attack. He wanted to tease his way out of Judy's doghouse.

"Two beds," Judy corrected. She punched Pearce in the shoulder. "Two *trailers*, now that I think about it."

J udy had only planned to shower, but as soon as she toweled off and re-dressed in her dirty clothes, she got the bright idea to lie down on the bed for a few minutes to rest her aching back. She passed out immediately.

Three hours later, a soft knock on the door startled her awake.

"Ms. Hopper? Are you decent?" Holliday whispered.

Judy bolted upright, dazed and groggy. "Uh, yeah. Come in."

The door pushed slightly open and Holliday slipped in, shutting it swiftly behind him as if he were sneaking between barracks in a prison camp. The bachelor officers' quarters were little more than a motel room—a bedroom with a desk and TV set and a bathroom.

"Sorry to wake you, but we have a situation," Holliday said.

"What situation?" Judy swung her legs off the bed and reached for her boots.

Holliday touched a finger to his lips as he removed a handheld scanner from his pocket. He waved it back and forth as he moved toward the bathroom, then thrust the bug scanner through the bathroom door and checked the readings. "We're clear here."

"So what's the situation?" Judy asked again.

"It's your friend Pearce. He's gone."

"What do you mean he's gone? Is the plane still here?"

"Yes, and fueled and ready to go, and your package arrived from our friend in Colorado."

"'Our friend'? How do you know her?"

"Margaret and I go back a long way. We actually dated in college for a few months. But she thought I was a flake because I wanted to join the Peace Corps after graduation, so we broke up. But we remained good friends ever since. She even nominated me to be the ambassador to Morocco, but when she resigned, Diele had me replaced and I was shitcanned to this backwater. Turns out this place is getting more interesting by the day. Here." Holliday handed her a slip of paper.

"GPS coordinates."

"Your new destination, just over the border in Mali. Got them thirty minutes ago."

"Why isn't she communicating with us directly anymore?"

"Margaret thinks her communications are being monitored, so she had to backdoor this through your man Ian."

"Who's monitoring her?"

"Not sure. That's probably why she's going dark for a while. You and your team will be on your own until further notice. Any idea where Pearce might have gone?"

"Without these coordinates? No. You're sure he's gone?"

"He's not at the plane, he's not at the hangar, and he's not in his quarters. I can't exactly tell Captain

Sotero he's gone missing. She's already cockeyed about this whole thing. The last thing we want is for her to unleash base security for a manhunt."

Judy stood up. "I'm going to grab some more coffee, then I'll head back over to the plane."

"If Pearce doesn't show up, will you still take the mission?"

She shrugged. "Of course. Mike Early is an American, isn't he?"

Holliday's voice took on a fatherly tone. "Couple of things. You're aware that this mission is strictly off the books, right? I know Margaret burned some bridges when she was in office, but now she's persona non grata all over D.C., like she's got the plague or something."

"She told me as much when she called me."

"That means you're not legally crossing into Mali airspace."

"Shouldn't be much of a problem."

"Not unless you get into trouble. If you do, the American government won't be able to help you, because you're breaking the law."

"We've never counted on anybody to help us. Especially the feds. No offense."

"The Air Force might also arrest you when you return, since you're originating your flight from one of their air bases. They'll track your plane to and from Mali using your IFF transponder."

"Still not a problem. I can shut it off from the cockpit before we enter Mali airspace." That was illegal under international air traffic regulations, but Judy believed it was better to ask for forgiveness than permission when it came to operational security.

"Right, and you'll need to. But once you do, any military aircraft that encounters you will assume you're either hostile or criminal and will likely shoot you down." Worry framed his kindly face.

"This ain't my first rodeo, Mr. Holliday." Judy tried to comfort him with a smile.

"You're a very brave young woman."

"I'm a pilot for Pearce Systems. It's what I do."

"And what is Pearce Systems, if I may ask?"

Judy had to think about that. She'd been away for several months now. Heard through the grapevine it had changed a lot.

"It's a private security and technology firm. Drones, mostly. Air, sea, and land."

Holliday frowned, curious. "And here you are on a drone base. That's quite a coincidence."

"Gee, it is, isn't it? I hadn't thought about that until now."

He tried to read her guileless face. "Are you a drone pilot, too?"

"Me? No, I'm terrible at it. Even with haptics. I fly by feel, not numbers."

"But a drone is safer, isn't it?"

"Sure, at least for the pilot. But I don't fly to feel safe. I fly because I love it. It's what I was born to do."

"Well, I'll say it again. You're a very brave young woman. Best of luck to you."

"Thanks. We're gonna need it."

= 16 =

Glory Box Café
Driggs, Idaho
7 May

I t was 3 a.m. when the blond woman with a French-
braided ponytail and a Colorado Buffalos ball cap
slipped into a padded booth. A few locals lingered in
the main lounge. Sleeve tattoos and pierced noses, mostly.
Dusty moose heads, snowshoes, and salmon trophies
adorned the rough-timbered walls. A performance space
in the corner was empty save for a mic stand and an empty
stool. She could smell the sweet tang of pot in the air.

A heavy Hispanic kid with a mop of curly hair and a
pencil-thin beard ringing his jawline dropped a large plastic tumbler of ice water and a menu in front of her. His
black T-shirt was stained. Pink letters read GLORY BOX.
She asked for coffee and he asked what kind, they had a
bunch. "Strong," was all she said. But he was slurring his

words, probably stoned, so she added, "Caffeinated," and as an afterthought, "two eggs, fried hard."

She sipped the coffee and waited. It was all she could do. Ian had managed to get her the address safely. She used every trick in the book to get here without being followed—cash only, no cell phone, and the blond wig being the three most important. Now she sat in the all-night café and waited for Ian to contact her again.

Margaret Myers took another sip. She guessed the coffee was Sumatra, but she wasn't sure. It was strong, all right, and a little burnt. But she wasn't here for the coffee.

The Hispanic kid and the cannabis aroma brought back memories. She was glad she had waged war on the drug lords. A lot of bad hombres got planted in the dirt, and drug violence had decreased dramatically on both sides of the border now that President Madero was in charge down there. The irony, of course, was that marijuana had been legalized in several states since then, including her home state of Colorado. There was much further to go in the drug war, but President Greyhill wasn't the man for the job. Maybe her critics were right. Maybe the nation would never have the wherewithal to fight it like a real war. If that was true, legalization was inevitable, and it wouldn't end with marijuana.

How would history judge her? She'd asked herself that question a thousand times in recent weeks, then pushed it away before she could answer. It was a vain, stupid question, and the answer would only come long after she was dead, past her caring. But the question kept coming back nonetheless.

So many things hadn't gone the way she'd planned as president. Drone strikes, a showdown with the Russians, resignation. She had shown resolve, then quit. But that was the deal she had made. The alternative was a shooting war with the Russians and a showdown with Congress. But she couldn't fight the feeling that she had failed.

No matter how she justified it, she had quit her job, and she had never quit anything in her life. There were still so many things left undone that she might have been able to accomplish had she remained in office. And now she'd put the destiny of her country in the hands of Greyhill and Diele, exactly the kind of career politicians she'd always railed against.

But "What If?" was a fool's game and she needed to stop playing it. Now.

Myers's free-range eggs finally arrived, fried hard, along with four triangles of whole-wheat toast. The menu solemnly promised, "Non-GMO, soy-free, vegan, Kosher" foods. No mention of rubbery and burnt. It didn't matter. She wasn't hungry anyway.

The one good thing she'd taken away from last year was meeting Pearce. She'd lost the ability to trust very many people, especially after entering politics. But Pearce was definitely one of the good guys, good as his word. That was hard to come by in politics or anywhere else these days.

She'd once felt the same way about Vin Tanner, too.

The only people she knew she could trust with her life were Pearce and, by extension, Ian. As soon as she fled her home, she bought a burner phone with cash, called Ian on the road, told him she needed a perfectly secure method of communicating with him. An hour later, he made the arrangements.

Once secure, Myers explained her situation. Told Ian cryptically she needed some alone time, her first use of coded language in this new adventure. He understood. They decided to go old-school. He sent her a package, indirectly, through third and fourth parties. The package directed her here, to the Glory Box.

Now she was waiting for the next link in the chain. She felt like she was in a cheap spy novel. Felt foolish sitting in this hippie dive at three in the morning with a six-hundred-dollar wig on her head and picking at a plate of rubbery free-range eggs. What was she doing?

She was hiding, of course. And running for her life. At one time, she was the most famous woman in the world. She couldn't exactly walk around in broad daylight without attracting some attention. But the wig and the tortoiseshell glasses and a dark café full of alternative lifestyles allowed her to hide in plain sight. At least long enough to hear from Ian.

A rusted Subaru Outback with dented door panels and a bent roof rack pulled up to the sidewalk. A tall, thin woman with a buzz cut and neck tattoos pushed through the door. She glanced around the room, looking for somebody, her head on a swivel until her eyes locked on Myers. She marched over to Myers's booth.

"Are you Margo Denver?"

Ian had given Myers a different name on the previous delivery, but the same pattern. The first letter of the first name had been an *M*, too.

"Yes."

The woman's long, thin fingers fished a padded envelope out of a fringed paisley shoulder bag. Myers noted the black fingernail polish and the sad, large eyes highlighted with blue eye shadow. She handed the envelope to Myers.

"Thank you. Do I owe you anything?"

"Nah. I'm doing this as a favor for Troy."

"You know Troy Pearce?" Myers asked. Her curiosity got the better of her.

"Yeah. But I haven't seen him around in a while. He used to come in here at least once a month. Is he okay?"

"He's been away. On a business trip."

"For a whole damn year?"

"Something like that."

"If you talk to him, tell him Sadie said 'Thanks.'"

"For what? If I may ask."

"Paid my rent for the year. He's been a real good friend to me and my kid."

Myers motioned to the booth. "Have a seat. Let me buy you breakfast."

Sadie shook her shaved head. "Can't. My boy's asleep in the car. I just ran over here to give you that. I was told I had to deliver it in person exactly at 3:15 a.m. But thanks anyway." She looked at Myers's plate and the half-eaten eggs. "You should try the veggie empanada next time. It's real good." She nodded, turned on her boot heel, and left.

Myers watched her climb back into the Subaru and pull away from the curb before opening the envelope.

It was from Ian. Keys. Codes. Instructions.

Relief flooded over her. She was almost there.

$=$ 17 $=$

Harry Fowler wanted her. Always had, ever since he'd first laid eyes on her twenty years before. Fiero knew it, too. Didn't matter. They could still work together, even be friends, which they were. But she was immune to his charms as few women were. That made her all the more desirable to him, of course. But business was business. He poured them each two fingers of his favorite, Bushmills twenty-one-year-old single malt.

As her national campaign manager, Fowler's job was to consummate her greatest political desire. The next best thing to bedding her, he supposed. Hated telling her today that she wasn't going to be the next president of the United States, at least not next year. Ruined all kinds of prospects. He handed her a glass.

"Why not wait for 2020?" he asked. He sat in a chair across from her, getting out from behind his desk. The walls were lined with photos of him and all of the politicians he helped get elected over the years, including Fiero.

"I'm not getting any younger. And Greyhill is weak. He can be taken out."

"He's bulletproof, I'm telling you. If the election were held today—"

"—he'd win. Yes, yes, I've heard it before. Poll after poll. I don't believe in polls. Opinions can be changed. Look at Bush 41. He had an approval rating of over ninety percent at one time. He couldn't be beaten either, until he was."

"Greyhill's invulnerable right now. He's continuing everything Myers initiated. The economy's picking up, thanks to her energy policy. That means the deficit's inching down without raising taxes, thanks to her budget freeze. And for the first time in a long while we aren't gearing up for a new ground war. Just exactly where do you expect to find the key to his chastity belt?"

"That's just it. He isn't invulnerable. He's Calvin Coolidge. The do-nothing president."

"What's your bumper sticker going to say? 'Trust Me, Not Your Lying Eyes?' Everything getting better feels like he's doing something right to most people."

Fiero shook her head. "No, that's not my point. I think I've found the issue."

"Domestic or foreign? You're perfectly positioned for both."

"China."

"Are you kidding? You of all people." Fowler was

referring to a sweetheart deal she helped broker for a Chinese shipping company to lease valuable warehouse space at the Port of Los Angeles last year despite the fact that two of its ships had been seized for smuggling illegal aliens into the country. The Department of Homeland Security had originally blocked the deal, but Fiero had rammed it through with help from across the aisle. Her husband's offshore business partners were grateful, and showed it. California news media remained characteristically uninterested in these kinds of unpleasant affairs, as far as Fiero was concerned. It was partly due to the fact that she always brought home the bacon. But Fowler suspected there were other reasons, too, and he wasn't sure he wanted to know what they were.

"Who better to raise the warning flag? I've championed trade and commerce with China from the beginning. I've headed up three trade junkets to the mainland in the last five years. I'm the most pro-China senator on the Hill, so if I sound the alarm, people will listen."

"How will Anthony feel about that?" Fiero's husband did a lot of business with the Chinese.

"He'll be fine with it. So will the Chinese. They understand the concept of optics. They probably invented it."

"So what's the issue with China? Yellow Peril and all of that?"

"Don't be racist. I was just in a briefing two days ago. China is all over Africa now. All we need to do is provide the public a color-coded map showing African nations falling like dominoes to Chinese influence."

"Who cares about Africa?"

"Seven of the ten fastest-growing economies of the world are on the African continent. And it has the most arable land in the world—over sixty percent. It's eventually going to be the world's food basket. And it's also a treasure trove of rare minerals. We're going to lose all of it to the Chinese, thanks to Greyhill. I can beat him over the head with that all day long."

"And what about your base? I can't see the Sierra Club getting wet over your plan to exploit Africa's natural resources."

"We can gin up the NAACP types, get them focused on China's miserable human rights record on the continent. Get the Greens ranting about the Chinese record on environmental issues over there, and raise hell with the aid organizations—show China robbing food from starving African children to feed themselves. C'mon, Harry, this is all low-hanging fruit." She held up her glass, signaling a refill.

He took his time picking up the bottle and bringing it back over to her. Gave him time to think. Could she be right? She had amazing instincts. Or was there something else going on she wasn't telling him about? He tipped in two more fingers for her, then two for himself.

"Maybe" was all he would give her for now.

"Do you know the real reason why Clinton beat Bush in '92?"

"You mean besides the dirty tricks, the media bias, and the Bush team's tone-deaf incompetence?"

"It was because Clinton had the balls to get in the race. Sam Nunn, George Mitchell, even Al Gore were better suited to make a run at it, but they were afraid they couldn't take down a sitting president with high approval ratings, so they bailed. I hate that kind of weakness. I'm not saying it's going to be easy, but nothing worth having ever is. Fortune is a woman, right? *E con più audacia la comandano.*" Fiero winked and took another sip.

Fowler laughed. Who the hell else in this godforsaken town would have the audacity to quote Machiavelli anymore?

What a woman.

"Maybe we can even get him to invade," Fiero said.

Fowler laughed again. "Are you kidding?"

"No."

Fowler shook his head. "You know Greyhill won't invade. He's riding high in the polls on the 'no new boots on the ground' stuff."

"Maybe he won't invade. But if I call for military intervention, I'll get the neocons on my side and he'll look like a weak sister. Besides, they're still blaming him for the budget freeze and the damage that's been done to the DoD. He needs their support, and this would be an easy way to get it."

"And if he does invade?"

She chuckled, then did her best Dana Carvey–does–George Bush impersonation: "Read my lips—no new boots on the ground."

Fowler smiled at her joke. Back in 1990, the congressional Democrats engineered a budget crisis, then demanded President George H. W. Bush raise taxes to solve it. He foolishly complied, and Bill Clinton's campaign staff blasted the former war hero president for breaking his "no new taxes" pledge and essentially called him a liar for doing so. No matter that Clinton himself promised to not raise taxes on the middle class and then broke that vow as soon as he took office, it would always be the hapless moderate Republican who was remembered as losing a presidency for breaking his promise.

"If I can goad Greyhill into a Mali invasion of any kind, we can beat him with it like a club and ride his broken promise all the way to the White House in 2016."

Fowler smiled with admiration. "It's still a great play, even if he doesn't bite. You have to prove that 'women are from Mars, too,' if you want to be the next commander in chief. If Greyhill doesn't invade, he'll just be proving your point that you're stronger on defense than he is and that you take the Chinese and al-Qaeda threats more seriously than he does."

She nodded. The pieces fell into place. "Either way, Greyhill loses. He invades, he breaks his promise and he's a liar. He doesn't invade, he's weak on defense and can't be trusted with our national security. That's a win-win for me."

Karem Air Force Base
Niamey, Niger

The sun hadn't risen yet, but the lights were on inside the hangar.

Judy admired the new paint job on the Aviocar's tail.

The sergeant who'd painted the Red Crescent logo beamed with pride. Red paint stained his long black fingers.

"The Air Force almost didn't let me enlist because I got busted for tagging when I was a kid. Now look at me."

"Looks fantastic, Sergeant. You did a great job. The logo is spot-on."

"You can find anything on the Internet. Just hope it works."

"I'm sure it will," Pearce said, suddenly appearing out of nowhere. He patted the young man on the back. "Go grab yourself some breakfast. We'll take it from here."

"Thank you, sir. Will do. Don't have to ask me twice when it comes to grub." The airman snatched up the improvised stencil off the ground and tossed it into the trash can on his way out the door.

"Where've you been?" Judy asked. "And what's that you're carrying?" She nodded at the duffel slung over one shoulder.

"This? It's that thing I brought with us from Moz. Don't you remember?"

"No."

"Sure you do. And by the way, I've been here the whole time."

"But—"

"The *whole* time." Pearce forced a smile.

"Do I need to know why you've been here the whole time?"

"In case you're ever called to testify."

Judy shook her head. She can only imagine what Pearce had stolen, or whom he'd stolen it from.

"Sunrise at 6:47 a.m.," Judy said. "We need to be in the air well before then. You should grab a shower before we leave."

"I'm fine."

Judy sniffed, turned up her nose. "Hope you've got cologne in that bag, chief, or you're walking."

Showered but not shaved, Pearce sat in the copilot's seat as usual, studying a map. They were at cruising altitude. The steady thrum of the engines filled the cabin, muted by the noise-canceling headsets he and Judy wore.

"You want to talk about what happened back in Maputo?"

Pearce left three men on the floor of the Elephant Bar, broken and bleeding. He was lucky to get the two of them out of there alive with the title to the Aviocar without having to kill anyone. But Judy was the most nonviolent person he knew, and the incident had really upset her. She still hadn't opened up to him about it. He was worried for her.

"Soon as you tell me why you've turned into a drunken sad sack. And what's with the long hair?"

"I should've thanked you earlier."

"You should've done a lot of things earlier. What's in the bag?"

"Stuff."

"Booze?"

He shot her a look. "No booze."

"First you stole from God, and now the federal government. You're not exactly racking up good karma."

"I figure the government owes me."

"What did Myers send?" Judy was referring to the sealed aluminum case with the Red Crescent logos marked *Équipement médical d'urgence* Holliday delivered to the hangar just before they left.

"Plasma, bandages, and antibiotics."

"That doesn't make any sense. We could've gotten that stuff from the base clinic."

"And thirty thousand euros. Guess Mikey ran up a helluva medical bill over there."

"Holliday said something about Myers's security situation."

"She might have kicked a hornet's nest when she reached out earlier on Mikey's behalf. I think she's just being careful."

"So what's the plan?"

"Easy as pie. In and out. Mikey's supposed to be waiting for us at 0700. Put him on, drop the case, and we're out of there."

Their headsets both rang, three short beeps. Judy opened the line. "This is Hotel, over." They agreed to use the NATO phonetic alphabet for security reasons, even though their line was quite secure.

"Hotel, this is India, over. Is Papa with you? Over." Ian stressed the second syllable correctly. His Scottish brogue rumbled on the headsets, like a drunken Ewan McGregor whispering in her ears.

"I'm here. What's shaking?"

"The situation on the ground is changing rapidly. Looks like a convoy is heading your way. ETA 0720 at current speed."

"What are the particulars?"

"I've got eyes on one APC, five trucks. I'd estimate fifty combatants, maybe less."

"How do you know this?" Judy asked. Pearce Systems didn't have any drones in the area.

"The International Space Station is passing overhead right now. They've an optical camera on board for geological surveys they aren't using at the moment." Ian chuckled. "Or think they aren't using. Unfortunately, it's passing out of range. I'll lose my link in two minutes."

"Military?" Pearce asked.

"Malian army. I can see the flag."

Judy shook her head. Gave Pearce the stink eye. "Yup. Easy as pie."

"Repeat that, Juliette?"

"Never mind," Judy said.

"You're in contact with Mike-Mike, correct?" Pearce asked. Margaret Myers's code name, not to be confused with Mike Early, code name Echo.

"Correct."

"Have her communicate with her intel source. Echo's got to be there on time or we're all dead."

"Roger that, Papa. One more thing. Intel source now has a name. 'Female, unknown' has been identified as

Cella Paolini. Mike-Mike thought you might know her. Take care, you two." Ian logged off.

"What?" Pearce shook his head, dope-slapped.

Judy caught Pearce's stunned expression. "Who's Cella Paolini?"

"She's my wife."

CELLA & TROY
2003

= 18 =

Afghanistan–Pakistan border

6 January

Troy Pearce scanned the village down below him through his binoculars. He was perched five hundred meters higher up on the mountain in the snow-covered trees, looking down, half hidden by a fallen log. The village was a poor excuse for human habitation, even by Afghan standards. A squalid collection of mud-brick buildings with pens attached for goats and chicken coops. A small boy, naked from the waist down, peed against the wall of his house, steam rising from the piss. The Pakistan border was just five klicks away.

"Wyoming is just like here?" Daud whispered. A bright, incredulous smile poked out of the thick, woolly beard of the twenty-five-year-old Afghani. His dark eyes sparkled beneath his dark brown *pakol*, a flat woolen cap with a thick round bottom made famous by the *mujahideen* martyr Ahmed Shah Masood. Daud popped another piece of snow into his mouth to keep his breath cold so as not to make a vapor.

"Maybe not as many Pashtuns, but yeah, where I come from is a lot like here. Pine trees, too. Here." Pearce handed his friend the binoculars. The Afghani's trusted AK-47 was slung across his back.

"I should like to visit Wyoming someday."

"My grandfather built a cabin near the Snake River. I'm going to fix it up if I ever make it back there."

"If? Don't speak like that, my friend."

"*Inshallah*, then. And you're more than welcome to come."

"*Inshallah*? You are Muslim now?" Daud's smile was infectious. He handed Pearce back the binoculars.

"Not exactly."

"If I came to the States, I would finish my engineering degree. America has the best engineering schools. Everyone knows this."

"What kind of engineering?"

"Civil. My country needs more roads and bridges if it is going to develop properly."

I admire your enthusiasm, Pearce thought to himself. You're going to need a helluva lot more than roads and bridges to drag this dump into the twenty-first century.

"I have an uncle in Texas. Perhaps a school there."

Pearce shook his head. "Stanford is the ticket."

"It is difficult to enter, yes?"

"Maybe I can pull some strings for you there." Like

someone once did for me, he thought. Changed his life. Without Stanford, he wouldn't be here.

"You like to fish, Daud?"

"I don't know. I have never fished."

"What? How is that even possible?" Pearce took a rod and reel with him everywhere he could.

"We eat goats around here, mostly. They cannot swim."

Pearce scanned the village again, then the thick trees around it. "You think Khalid's still coming?"

"Where else would he go? His wives are here and it is cold, is it not, and nearly night?"

Pearce nodded. He and Daud had led a small band of fighters to observe the village below on a rumor that the local chieftain, Asadullah Khalid, a Taliban commander, was returning from Pakistan today with a load of RPGs, traded for heroin bricks cultivated in the valley. Their goal was to capture him, but failing that, he was authorized to terminate the bastard. The trick for Pearce would be to keep Daud from killing him first.

The wind gusted. Pearce shivered despite the government-issue polypropylene thermals beneath his eclectic mix of local garb. Daud was clad in little more than woolen pants, a Canadian army surplus sweater, and a knitted scarf, but after six hours out here in the snow it was Pearce's teeth that were chattering. He never ceased to admire the endurance of these mountain villagers.

Daud's village was ten kilometers away. He was the son of the village chief and had studied English and engineering in Peshawar. He volunteered as a translator with the U.S. government, which is how Pearce found out about him. Daud's village hated the Taliban almost as much as they hated Khalid's village. It was easy enough for Pearce to recruit Daud and his men into the CIA's war on the Taliban in this part of the country. He'd been embedded with them for the last two weeks.

"Why do your people hate the people in this village so much?" Pearce asked in bad Pashto.

Daud spit. "They are worse than *kafir*s, with no honor or loyalty except to themselves. In the last war they made alliances with the Russian pigs. Two of my uncles were killed by the Russians, and other men, too, and our women raped because of those dogs."

"And now the Taliban," Pearce added.

"And the Devil, too." Daud spit again.

A branch cracked behind them. Both men whipped around.

"Ahmed!" Daud whispered loudly.

Nothing.

Daud raised his AK-47 in the direction of the sound. "Ahmed!"

"What?" a voice whispered back.

Thump.

A grenade landed in the snow at Pearce's feet.

Daud shoved Pearce backward over the log. Troy tumbled ass-over-teakettle with a yelp, and on his first rotation caught a glimpse of Daud tossing something back up the hill. Automatic-rifle fire split the air above. Pearce spread his arms wide to slow his roll, then dug his boot toes into the snow on the next tumble. He was facedown in the powder when he heard the *whoomph* of the grenade explosion. He leaped to his feet, snapping the M4 butt stock against his cheek and aiming at the tree line. Caught a glimpse of Daud racing straight up the hill and dashing into the pines.

Pearce called after him. Stupid, he knew.

"DAUD!"

Savage cries and more gunfire. Pearce's brain registered AKs, for sure. But also the high snapping crack of HKs. Strange.

One of Daud's men, Hamid, dashed parallel across the ridgeline, firing his weapon above where Daud had entered the trees. Pearce charged up the mountain, legs burning with every step, like hundred-pound weights were clamped on his boots. A burst of bullets chopped the snow around him. He wheeled to the right and put three rounds in the chest of a black-turbaned fighter. The man's mouth opened in a silent cry as he toppled backward, rifle flying through the air.

Pearce turned back uphill and stormed toward Daud's position in the trees. It felt like sprinting in molasses. He finally reached the trees. Hamid was there, kneeling down, Daud grimacing and holding his bleeding thigh with both hands, blood pooling in the snow.

Pearce broke open a med kit. Hamid ripped open Daud's trouser leg and wrapped his weathered hands around the thigh above the wound to stanch the bleed. The wiry Afghan was the same age as Pearce, but with his milky left eye and leathery skin, Hamid appeared to be ten years older, maybe more.

"You looked very funny falling over that log," Daud said through gritted teeth.

"Idiot," Pearce said, quickly examining the wound. "You're lucky it went clean through. Missed the bone." But Troy wasn't sure the artery wasn't nicked. He was bleeding fast.

"You should see the other guy." Daud grimaced. "Not so lucky."

Hamid jabbered in Pashto as Pearce dumped Quik-Clot into both the entry and exit points of the wound, then quickly wrapped the double-padded "Israeli bandage" around Daud's thigh and secured it tightly on the pressure applicator clip.

"Hamid says the cowards ran away but we lost Ahmed. Ahhh! It burns!"

"That's the QuikClot. Good news, you'll stop bleeding. Bad news, you'll never be a lingerie model."

"Don't forget Ahmed. His father . . ." But Daud passed out.

Rage and despair overwhelmed Pearce. His first solo mission in country and it had gone to shit.

"Let's get him out of here," Pearce said to Hamid, not bothering to use his broken Pashto.

Hamid didn't speak a word of English but understood Pearce perfectly. He clapped Pearce on the shoulder with a leathery hand. "It has already been written."

Pearce hoped that wasn't true. He wanted to write Khalid's last chapter himself, in the bastard's own blood.

= 19 =

Hamid and three other fighters held the corners of the heavy woolen blanket that carried Daud like a stretcher. Pearce was on point, but his night-vision goggles were useless. The moon had fled and the stars had turned to falling snow. The infrared scope on his rifle lit the way.

Pearce first led them farther down the hill, then back around and higher up, suspecting an ambush. He was right. Pearce took out two of Khalid's men with single shots to the head before they knew what hit them. When the other bad guys opened up in the night, their flashing barrels made them targets, and Daud's men took out two more with Pearce providing covering fire. The air rang with automatic-rifle fire, muzzle flashes sparking between the trees like strobe lights. Then it stopped.

The black night returned, and the sound was swallowed up in the gauze of thick, wet flakes blanketing the mountain.

Pearce kicked the bodies over and flashed a light in their faces, giving Hamid a clear look. Hamid nodded with recognition at each face, spitting heavily in the snow at the last.

"Khalid?" Pearce asked.

Hamid shook his head no. The other fighters rifled through the pockets of the dead men. They pulled out wadded rupee notes, cigarettes, stale rounds of naan. No contraband.

Pearce went back on point. Hamid and the others followed silently behind at a distance, carrying their precious cargo through the frigid air.

Pearce trudged ahead, exhausted. A headache raged. Hours of concentration and physical exertion had taken their toll. No matter. He had to push on. There was still another kilometer to the village, maybe more. He checked his watch. It was just past two a.m. on the illuminated dial. He heard the rush of feet tramping in snow up ahead. Flashlights swept through the trees. Pearce signaled the men behind him to halt and drop, and he raised his weapon to fire. A ghostly gray head walked into the target reticle and Pearce laid a sure finger on the trigger. He hesitated.

It was Daud's father.

Six other fighters from the village were with him. The

new men took up the stretcher and the band raced back to the village, carrying Daud into his father's house and laying him on the rug-covered dirt floor in front of the fire.

In the dim, flickering firelight, Daud looked bad, pale and beaded with sweat. His lips moved, but he wasn't conscious. They stripped his snowy garments off and his mother covered him back up with a couple of dry blankets. Pearce checked the green Israeli bandage. There was a bloodstain, but it was small and dry. The wound must be infected. Why else the fever? Pearce had only oral antibiotics, but Daud was in no condition to swallow them now.

"Doctor," Daud's father said. He motioned with his hands and added, "Helicopter."

Pearce told him in his clumsy Pashto that the snowstorm wouldn't allow it.

"Cella, Cella," his mother said, pointing at the doorway. Two teenage boys standing in the doorway shouted something Pearce didn't catch and bolted away into the dark.

"'Cella'?" Pearce asked.

The old man flashed a toothless smile.

= 20 =

Pearce's teeth chattered. He'd never been so cold in his life. He'd grown up in the snowcapped Rockies bow-hunting mule deer and cutting timber. Knew all about cold weather, but nothing like this.

Pearce shook his head. His mind was wandering again. It was still two hours before dawn and every able-bodied man from Daud's village was posted on guard, including Pearce, watching the road. After the ambush, they could only expect a counterattack from Khalid and his Taliban fighters. The two villages had exchanged potshots for years, but now the war had come with a vengeance.

Pearce thought about the gunfight earlier that night. At least three kinds of automatic rifles had fired in the dark. Every kind of rifle had its own distinct sound, even if it fired the same caliber of round. He was firing an

M4 loaded with 5.56mm, and Daud's men all had AKs firing 7.62mm. But Pearce had heard the distinct retort of Heckler & Koch G3s. They shot the longer 7.62mm NATO round. He used to own one. Recognized the sound instantly.

Since when did Taliban fire G3s?

The sound of grinding gears slapped him back to reality.

Down the hill, in the distance, a pair of headlights threw two wide cones of light through the falling snow. A faint engine roar finally made its way up to him, most of the sound absorbed in the blankets of white powder.

Pearce raised his M4 and tracked the vehicle through his infrared scope, but at this distance in the heavy snowfall he couldn't make out more than the shape of the car, the blazing heat signature from the engine, and the headlights.

The vehicle bounced and fishtailed unsteadily up the hill until he could make out the shape of an old UAZ, the Soviet army's version of an American jeep. Pearce counted a driver and two heads in the shadow of the cab. It flashed its lights and honked the horn. The engine rattled like a high-speed whisk scraping the inside of a stainless-steel bowl.

"Cella! Cella!" a voice rang out behind him, then another. Pearce turned around. Light spilled out of open doors, bodies outlined in the frames.

Since he could hardly feel his hands, he decided to head back to Daud's house and get warmed back up and maybe try and figure out who Cella was. In the two weeks he'd been embedded with Daud's men, he hadn't once heard the name mentioned.

By the time Pearce reached Daud's house the UAZ was parked and empty. Pearce stepped through the door and was greeted by a blast of heat from the roaring fire and a hot cup of tea from Daud's mother.

She smiled, flashing her three good front teeth, and pointed over to a figure kneeling down next to Daud's bed, low on the floor in the far corner. Cargo pants, military boots, and a heavy parka hood hid the form.

"Cella." The old woman muttered something else in Pashto that Pearce didn't quite catch, but he gathered it was good, judging by the laugh lines bunched around her eyes.

"You must be the *Amrikaa*," a woman's voice said. The accent was distinctly Italian. A canvas bag with medical supplies was open by her side.

"That's what the passport says," Pearce said, wishing he hadn't set his M4 down. "You?"

She pulled her hood down and faced him. A lick of light honey-brown hair peeked out from beneath a heavy woolen scarf wrapped around her head, no doubt a nod to Muslim customs but also to the frigid conditions. Her high cheekbones, long jawline, and perfect teeth smiling through full lips belonged to a runway model. The Italian accent only added to the effect. But it was her topaz-blue eyes that captured him. Pearce guessed she must be from the north, maybe from the Italian Alps.

"Dr. Cella Paolini."

"Pearce."

"You did this?" She pointed at Daud's bandages, dried blood on the edges. He was sound asleep. His breathing was shallow and rasping.

"Yeah."

"Not bad. You probably saved his life." She eyed him up and down, dressed like a local over his heavy-weather gear. His *pakol* was still flaked with snow. "CIA?" She turned back to Daud and touched his face with the back of her hand, checking for fever.

He shrugged, ignoring the question. "What brings you to this part of the world, Doc?"

"I'm with Medicia Oltre Frontiere. We're a medical aid society. My clinic is not far from here."

"Never heard of it."

"Like you, we try to keep a low profile." She pulled a hypodermic needle from her bag, along with an injection vial of clear liquid. Cipro, Pearce guessed by the purple label.

"What's your prognosis, Doctor?" Pearce asked.

"He's a little warm, which isn't surprising. But his father says he hasn't made any urine since he's been here. That could be oliguria. And his breathing. Do you hear it? A classic sign of lactic acidosis. Those three symptoms alone tell me he's suffering a case of sepsis. Of course, I can't be sure without lab work."

"I only had oral antibiotics, but he was knocked out with morphine. Couldn't swallow."

"Doesn't matter. Antibiotics aren't enough anyway. He needs intravenous fluids. But we must hurry. Every hour he's not treated increases his mortality by almost eight percent."

"Can't we treat him here?"

"I didn't bring enough supplies. He'll have to come back to the clinic with me. Now, or he'll die soon." She stood and pulled the bag strap over her head and onto her far shoulder.

"You can't go back now. We're expecting an attack," Pearce said.

Cella gave instructions to Daud's father. He rose to his feet and approached his son's bed.

"If we don't take him now, he'll probably die," Cella said. "I'm not worried. I'm known around here. Only medicine. No politics."

Daud's father grabbed the ends of the blanket by his son's head in his gnarled fists, preparing to lift him.

"Then I'm going with you," Pearce said. He grabbed the blanket ends at Daud's feet, then glanced at the old man and the two of them lifted simultaneously. Daud was cocooned in the folds.

"You fight your battles, I fight mine. Alone."

"Seriously, it's dangerous out there. I won't let you go."

She shook her head and sneered. "If you try to stop me," she said, nodding at the old man, "he'll shoot you between the eyes. Or his mother will. Besides, I have other patients at the clinic and they are alone back there. Very dangerous for them."

Pearce asked the old man permission to escort Daud back to the clinic. He agreed.

"Now I have his permission to go. Do I have yours?"

Cella shrugged. "Like you Americans say, 'It's your *funerale*.'"

Cella's compound was technically in Pakistan, about five kilometers from Daud's village on the other side of the border. Pearce marveled that the two teenagers had been able to run so far through the heavy snow in the frozen night to fetch her. Most American kids their age couldn't have done it. Too much time planted on the couch playing World of Warcraft until their eyes bled.

The UAZ pulled up in front of a cinder-block building, a utilitarian rectangle with a steep roof, square windows, and two steel doors. One door posted the sign MEN'S CLINIC, and the other WOMEN'S CLINIC, in English with international male and female symbols for each.

Cella ran over to the men's door and unlocked it, then came back to the jeep to help Pearce wrestle Daud through the snow and into the warm clinic.

"Two clinics?" Pearce asked.

"Strict separation of the sexes. The mullahs insisted. Otherwise, no clinic at all."

Inside the building, Cella led them to an empty bed. The air was warm. He smelled the kerosene heater on the far wall. There were two other occupied gurneys on the clinic floor. A boy's voice called out from one.

"Cella? Is that you?" The voice was slurred as if slightly drugged, and panicked. Pearce saw a torso propped up on elbows on one of the cots. The voice was in shadows.

"Yes, it's me, love. Go back to sleep. It's early."

"Who is that with you?"

"A friend. Go back to sleep."

"And that's why you lock the doors on the outside."
Pearce lowered Daud's head and shoulders to the bed.

Cella lowered Daud's feet. "Thieves will steal the medicine and rape any women they find. Boys, too." She pointed at a storage rack. Told Pearce, "Two blankets, quick."

Cella opened a locked steel cabinet and pulled out a 1,000mm saline bag and a sealed IV kit, then rolled over an old-fashioned stainless-steel IV stand. She hung the bag on the hook and opened the kit. Pearce watched her snap on a pair of surgical gloves, then quickly and expertly set up the IV and insert the needle into the back of Daud's hand. "No pump?" Pearce asked.

"No. Gravity-fed is best. Especially with antibiotic. Pushing the antibiotic too quickly can cause problems."

Pearce was impressed. IVs were deceptively complicated and even fatal, if not handled properly.

He fought back a yawn. Checked his watch. Still another forty minutes until sunrise. He glanced around the room. Beds, cabinets, sink, a small office desk. Simple, but clean, organized, and well supplied.

"Quite a little place you have here, Doctor."

"I have a very generous donor base." Cella pulled on a stethoscope.

"The women's side is occupied, too?"

"Yes. Quiet, please." She listened to Daud's heartbeat

and breathing, then held his wrist for a pulse count. She sniffed the air.

"You stink," Cella said to Pearce. "You need to shower."

"That's not funny."

"I'm not being funny. You smell like stale urine and shit. If you've been drinking the water around here, you have diarrhea. Correct?"

"That's life in the field."

"But not in my sterile clinic. Unless you want to go back outside, you need to get cleaned up. Soap, hot water. You remember how to shower, don't you?"

"Where?"

"There's a shower through that door. And throw away your soiled clothes. I have others you can use."

"We're in a combat zone. I can't—"

"Fine, then go back outside and smell. The stink alone will keep the Taliban away."

Pearce seriously considered going back outside to keep an eye on things. But he was finally getting warm again. And he did smell like an outhouse. What the hell.

Pearce headed to a small bathroom. He peeled off his clothes and undergarments, tossing everything soaked in sweat, shit, or pee into a pile in the corner. He stacked the body armor on a chair and stepped into the small shower and pulled the plastic curtain shut. The water flow wasn't strong, but it was stinging hot on his filthy, chilled skin and it felt good.

It took him a solid ten minutes to scrape off the crusted grime with a stiff plastic brush, and he spent another ten washing out crevices and cracks that hadn't seen clean water or soap in almost a month. Even he was grossed out. He pushed chunks of whatever into the drain hole with his big toe, then swept the rest of the hairs and whatnot into the drain with his size-14 foot before turning off the water.

Pearce pulled aside the plastic curtain, thankful that the small bathroom had kept the steam. He was almost hot now, another sensation he hadn't felt in a lifetime or two. He instantly noticed that his filthy clothes had disappeared and a pile of fresh clothes was neatly stacked on the now open chair, the body armor carefully placed underneath the seat.

Pearce dressed. Thermal underwear, heavy boot socks. Civilian, Italian labels. And beneath them, local woolen pants and a green hospital scrub shirt. There was a name stenciled on the front: "PAOLINI." A pair of Nike running shoes, clean but used.

Pearce emerged dressed in his new clothes, but in his stocking feet.

"What's wrong with the shoes?" Cella asked without looking up. She sat at the small desk, making notes. A pair of wire-rimmed reading glasses were perched on her nose.

She finished her notes and smiled at him. Could she be any more beautiful?

"Too small. Especially with the socks." Pearce wiggled his toes. "I'll clean my boots instead, if that's okay."

"They're by the heater, getting dry." She looked him up and down, clearly pleased. "Everything else seems to fit."

Pearce looked down at the name stenciled on his shirt. "He and I are about the same size, looks like."

"Looks like," she repeated, not taking the bait.

"I miss anything?" Pearce asked.

"It stopped snowing. The sun is up. And there's a pot of tea steeping. Pour us some, will you, while I finish these notes?"

"Sure." Pearce padded over to the sink area. A pot sat on a hot plate, steam curling up from the spout. Two thick ceramic cups with Italian navy logos were next to the pot. He poured.

"How's Daud?"

"His IV will finish in about thirty minutes, then he gets another one. I want to give him four more after that."

"That's a lot of fluid." Pearce set a cup in front of Cella.

"But the latest protocols for sepsis call for it." She picked it up and blew on it. Pearce tried to ignore the shape of her mouth when she did it.

"You must be exhausted. I know how to hang an IV bag. Go get some rack time," Pearce offered.

"I'm fine for now. Maybe later. I must make my rounds in a few minutes. The others will wake up soon."

"How many patients do you have now?" Pearce asked.

"Two women and two girls, next door. One late-term pregnancy, one anemia, and two bladder infections. On this side, Tariq is the old man over there, Ghaazi is the boy you met earlier, and you know Daud."

"Where are they all from?" Pearce took a sip of tea.

"Some are from across the border, some from this side. All different villages. Tariq was the chief of his village years ago, wiped out by the Russians. He is the last survivor of his clan."

"And the boy?"

"Ghaazi's father is a *talib* who fled to the Tribal Areas."

"You know Italy is at war with the Taliban, right?"

"My war is in here. The only enemy I fight is death and disease. What you idiots do out there is your business."

"But you're helping the enemy of your country."

"I'm taking care of his child, who lost a foot to a mine planted by the Afghan army. I suppose you think it is my patriotic duty to let the boy die for the sins of his father?" Cella took another sip of tea.

"No. But the boy will probably grow up and become a killer like his father. Doesn't that bother you?"

"I can't know for sure if he will grow up to be a killer. He probably will. There is killing all around him. What else does he know? Right now, I know he needs my help. I also know that the mine that took his foot was probably American. A lot of American mines have killed a lot of innocent people around here. Doesn't that bother you?"

"I hate it. But that's war. The sooner it ends, the better."

"And your job is to help end it, yes?"

"Yes."

"And you enjoy this work? Killing the enemy?" Her blue eyes bored into his.

"No, but it's necessary."

"Necessary. Yes, of course. Then perhaps it is necessary for you to finish the job the mine began. Where is your gun? Or would you prefer to simply strangle the child while he sleeps?" A devilish smile creased her mouth. She took another sip of tea.

"I wish I had your moral clarity. It's a luxury I can't afford right now."

"I think you are a good man, despite what you do."

"You don't know what I've done."

"Stay here with me for a month. You will be surprised how clear things become when you start saving lives instead of taking them."

Her words were fingers pulling on a string deep within him. He felt light-headed. Needed to change the subject. He pointed at the name stenciled on his chest. "This guy. Brother? Or husband?"

"Neither." Her face soured. "Bodyguard. My father insisted."

"Who just happened to have your same last name?"

"A legal fiction. It would be too scandalous for an unmarried man and woman to be living under the same roof here in this place. So Vittorio came as my fake husband. Passport, clothes, everything."

"Where is he now?"

"Dead, a month ago."

"How?"

"A local army commander named Marwat. Runs drugs and guns. They ambushed Vittorio. Thought he was Interpol."

"Then you're in danger, too."

"No. I have lots of friends around here, remember? They kill me, they have a civil war on their hands."

"That won't save you."

"It has so far."

"And does your father know that Vittorio is dead?"

"No."

"Because if you told him, he'd just send another, right?"

"Yes."

Pearce rummaged around in his memory for a moment. "Paolini. Aerospace manufacturing. Helicopters, right?"

She sighed. "And other things."

Pearce glanced around the clinic again. Very well stocked. "And he's your 'donor base.'"

"He makes money killing people, so it is only right that his money should save them, too." She pulled off her glasses. "How would you like some food?"

"Very much, thank you. I'm starving."

"Then make us something. There are some fresh eggs and bread in that refrigerator, and a pan in the bottom drawer. I must go next door and check on the women."

Pearce's mouth watered at the thought of fried eggs. "Sounds like a plan." He headed for the refrigerator and pulled out a bowl of eggs. Started to relax.

Until the explosion.

= 21 =

Afghanistan–Pakistan border

7 January

Pearce grabbed his M4 and a parka before diving into the UAZ. The distant explosion he'd heard was in the direction of Daud's village. Distant jet engines split the air like rolling thunder, and black smoke smudged the crystalline blue sky above the mountain.

Pearce had given Daud's radio to Hamid and told him to keep it close. "Hamid! Hamid! What is happening?" Pearce yelled in Pashto.

No response.

The snowstorm had passed, but the clear sky had only dropped the temperature. Pearce shivered in the cab, waiting for the motor heat to kick in. He slammed the gearshift through its paces, clutching as fast as he could to get up to speed. The ancient Russian jeep slipped and yawed in the snow as he gunned the throttle, but its four-wheel drive kept him moving generally forward.

Pearce called on the radio again, over and over. Nothing.

He wound his way back up the hill toward the village. Somewhere along the way he'd crossed back over the border from Pakistan. It was hardly a road, more like a clearing between trees. He followed Cella's tire tracks from last night, hoping they were, in fact, hers. But he remembered a hairpin turn that he now took that brought him to a steep incline. Daud's village would be about three kilometers up the road. He slammed the brakes and listened. Over the idling motor he could make out the heavy *whump-whump-whump* of rotor blades beating the air.

The road leveled out for a short stretch. As best he could remember this little patch was about three hundred meters from the village. He pulled off the road and hid the vehicle in the trees, killed the motor, and grabbed his rifle. The helicopter engine thundered overhead and voices shouted at the top of the hill.

Pearce checked his only mag, then squeezed the release latch, pulled back the T handle, and charged a round into the receiver. He wished like hell now he hadn't left his fighting pack at Daud's house. The only gear he had with him was his rifle, combat knife, and boots. He didn't have time to pull on his body armor.

Pearce picked his way up the hill through the trees, keeping cover, careful to stay as far away from the road as possible. His face burned in the cold air that carried the smell of burnt wood and flesh. He crested the hill and dropped into the snow, which was covered in fine dust and ash.

He used his rifle scope to scan the smoldering village, a hundred meters to his right, across the road. His heart sank. Houses were flattened, and craters smoldered. Broken bodies, or pieces of them, were scattered on the ground. He counted twenty Taliban fighters laughing and joking as they picked through the smoldering ruins, nudging the corpses of Daud's men. A few carried AKs, but most carried HK G3s, just like he'd heard last night. In the distance, a UH-60 Black Hawk helicopter circled on over watch.

Pearce swung the scope around again. There. Khalid himself. The black-bearded *muj* was sharing a smoke with a U.S. Army captain wearing an Airborne unit patch.

Pearce tried to put the puzzle pieces together. Why would the Air Force level this village with JDAMs? That Army captain must have called it in. But why? Maybe Khalid told that captain that this was an AQ village. Shit. But Daud and his village were registered with the CIA as allies, and Pearce's command knew he was hunting Khalid for running drugs and guns across the border. Hell, his command had authorized the mission. So who FUBAR'd?

He'd figure that out later. Pearce centered the target reticle on Khalid's upper lip just below the nose, aiming for the "apricot," the medulla oblongata. He slowed his breathing, preparing to pull between heartbeats.

He hesitated. Shooting Khalid now would be suicide.

It wouldn't bring Hamid or Daud's father and mother back to life. Wouldn't fix anything. If he wasn't lucky, he might accidentally shoot the captain. It was a really bad idea.

Pearce's rifle barked. Khalid's face erupted in a cloud of pink mist and broken teeth.

That's for you, Daud.

Pearce rolled to his left, then stood and ran in a half-crouch back down the hill through the trees. Angry voices shouted behind him. Rifles cracked. Bullets *zoop*ed in the air just above his head, snipping branches and spitting snow in front of him. Pearce's lungs burned as he gulped down the frozen air, his legs pumping high through the thick cotton candy of loose snow until he reached the UAZ.

He yanked open the door, fired up the engine, and spun the jeep back out onto the road. He shoved the stick into first gear and leaped out, hoping the Black Hawk would take the bait and chase the UAZ while he dove through the trees down the perilous slope back to Cella's compound. If the helicopter didn't kill him, the run down the side of the mountain probably would.

= 22 =

Two hours later, Pearce stumbled out of the steep tree line, back on the Pakistani side of the border. Bathed in sweat, thighs burning, breathless, he scanned the snowy path just beyond the clinic entrance.

Not good.

The blue steel gate was battered and twisted on the lock side, rammed open by something heavy and hostile.

Pearce dropped to the deck in a puff of snow just as a Pakistani soldier stepped into the open gate area. He wore heavy-weather camouflage gear and carried a G3 rifle.

Just like the rifles that Khalid's men carried.

That was enough confirmation for Pearce. The Pakistanis, or at least some of them, were helping the Taliban.

With allies like that, how could we possibly fail to win this war? he thought.

Assholes.

The soldier scanned the road carelessly, then stepped back inside the gate, out of view. Pearce dashed across the road, as far away from the sight line of the gate entrance as he could get. A stand of pine trees marched up to the high stone walls of the compound. Pearce used them as cover. When he reached the wall, he listened. He counted three voices in the little courtyard, but heard more voices shouting from inside the clinic.

Pearce slung his rifle over his back, pulled himself up silently onto a low-hanging branch, then climbed to another just above. He could barely feel his hands. His gloves were still in the clinic. Up in the second branch he had a view just clearing the wall. He saw three men directly below him, sheltering themselves against the chilling breeze behind a heavy-duty truck parked near the wall, shivering and smoking cigarettes.

Pearce considered his tactical disadvantages. He was outnumbered and outgunned here in the courtyard, an unknown number of bogeys were in the clinic, and Cella was nowhere in sight. No grenades, no flash bangs. Could he evade detection and make his way into the clinic without endangering Cella's life, or Daud's? He tried to formulate a plan, but his mind was numb with fatigue and clouded by an agonizing headache brought on by the frozen air and lack of food.

A gunshot burst inside the clinic. Cella screamed.

Pearce pulled his knife and leaped over the wall.

So much for planning.

The Pakistani officer held a fistful of Cella's hair in his powerful grip and pointed a pistol in her face, inches from his.

"CIA! WHERE IS CIA?!" he screamed in broken English.

"I . . . don't . . . know!" Cella cried.

"Here," Pearce said.

The officer whirled around, still clutching Cella by the hair, the other hand pointing the gun toward Pearce. He fired.

Too late, by a breath. Pearce had fired first, kneeling.

The pistol round cracked on the doorframe just above Pearce's head as the Pakistani's throat blossomed in petals of blood and meat. His hands went limp as his spinal cord severed from the base of his skull, freeing Cella, dropping the gun, dead before he crashed to the floor.

Cella stood frozen in a half crouch, trembling.

Pearce ran to her and threw an arm around her. She wrapped both arms around his neck, clinging to him like a life raft.

"The others?" he whispered.

She raised her face. It was smeared in tears and snot. Her left eye was blue and swollen shut. She pointed at the women's clinic. "Five of them." She noticed that Pearce was bathed in wet blood.

She gasped. "Where are you hit?"

He shook his head: I'm not.

He shoved her against the far wall, trying to get her out of sight of the doorway, just in case. "Wait here," he whispered.

"Stay with me. They will be waiting for you."

He shook his head again. "They think their buddy just shot you."

Pearce ducked back out the door in a low crouch as Cella raced over to Daud's bed. The Afghani's brains were spattered against the far wall and he was bled out all over his pillow. Too late, she knew. But something in her had hoped.

She suddenly realized she was sticky with blood, too. The blood that was on Pearce.

Panicked shouts rang out on the other side of the wall. So did five muffled gunshots. Cella flinched.

Seconds later, Pearce raced back through the doorway.

"The women were all dead. I'm sorry," Pearce said.

Cella buried her swollen face in her hands and sobbed.

Pearce glanced at Daud's bed, then at the other two. The boy and the old man were shot through the head as well.

"Was that the asshole that killed Vittorio? Marwat?" He nodded at the corpse on the floor lying in the spreading pool of blood.

All Cella could do was nod.

"We need to scoot."

"Where will we go?"

"The only place we can."

= 23 =

They changed out of their bloody clothes and lay-
ered up as warmly as possible, careful to avoid any
military-supplied gear, Italian or otherwise. Over
Cella's protests, Pearce allowed her just one backpack
stuffed with whatever she could fit in it, along with her
passport. She tossed him Vittorio's.

"What's this for?"

"It might prove useful."

Pearce opened it, examined the photo. "I hardly look
like him, and I don't speak Italian."

"With that beard, who can tell? I can always vouch
for you." She forced a grim smile. "Just keep your mouth
shut."

The only real food Cella had on hand was a loaf of

bread and two chocolate bars. Pearce thought about doing the Rocky thing and cracking open the eggs into a glass and swallowing them whole, but he thought the consistency would be like snot so he passed. But while Cella was pulling together her papers, Pearce found a cabinet full of plastic bags labeled *Razione Viveri Speciale da Combattimento.* It wasn't hard for him to figure out what they were, but he was glad the Italian combat rations were also dual labeled in English—probably a NATO requirement. He pulled out several bags with the most appealing contents, including ones marked *Cordiale/Bevanda Alcolica,* because Pearce knew that every now and then a good belt might come in handy.

God bless the Italians.

The last thing Pearce asked Cella to do was the worst, but to his surprise, she agreed without protest. They dragged the dead bodies from outside into the clinic and flooded the floors of both clinics with kerosene from the heaters. He then bundled her up into the Pakistani army truck. The vehicle was clearly marked with Pakistani flags on the hood and the sides. The U.S. Army wouldn't dare fire on it if they came on this side of the border, which, as far as Pearce knew, they wouldn't. After pulling the vehicle out past the broken gate, he ran back in and set fire to stacks of blankets soaked in kerosene, but not before snagging one of the dead soldier's field caps. By the time the truck lumbered away from the clinic it was engulfed in flames.

"Now what?" Cella asked.

"We head south."

Kabul was less than two hundred miles directly north of the clinic, but Pearce knew he couldn't drive straight there. Khalid's men, the U.S. Army, and God knows who else were likely still searching for him up the road just over the border. His first concern was Cella's safety, and the best he could do was get her to the Italian embassy in Islamabad. But how?

"Samira was the wife of a chief in a village about four kilometers from here." Cella sighed. "She was pregnant with her third. He would help."

"He might already be dead. Obviously, Marwat and Khalid were connected. Marwat knew about you and your clinic. Khalid must have tipped him off about me being here."

"How?"

"Maybe they captured one of Daud's people. Tortured him for information. Told him about you and I evacuating Daud to the clinic."

"Would they have had the time?"

"Maybe, maybe not. Maybe they had planned to take you out all along and it was a coincidence that Daud's village was hit at the same time. I don't know. But either way, if we're being hunted, the first place they would look for us is any village that has a connection to you. And if they aren't already there, there's no point in leading them there. You've seen how they handle business in these parts."

"Then what do we do?"

"Ditch this truck as soon as we can. If we can get to a phone, I can call somebody."

"A phone? Are you joking? The CIA can't afford to give you your own cell phone?"

"I have a sat phone. But I left it at Daud's place. I fucked up."

An hour later, they made their way into the flatlands where the temperature had warmed up enough to turn the snow to slush. Pearce was dark enough to pass for a local, especially with his beard and army field cap pulled over his head. Cella lay flat on the bench seat whenever traffic passed in the opposite direction, which was seldom and, thankfully, always civilian—and they were too afraid of the army to dare cast a glance into the windshield.

They parked the truck in a stand of trees off the road when they saw the first power lines. Pearce knew they would lead to a place requiring electricity. But it took them another two hours of walking until they came to a collection of walled houses, shops, and even a gas station. Cella covered her entire head and face with her knit scarf. She'd also had enough sense to grab a heavy woolen shawl back at the clinic and wrapped it around her shoulders and torso to hide her figure, hunching over a little as she walked to try to conceal her height. The place was a little larger than a village, but hardly a town, let alone a city. One of the shops advertised telephone services in both Pashto and English, so they made their way there.

They entered the shop without incident, and Cella asked for the telephone service since her Pashto was far better than Pearce's. But the man behind the counter smiled beneath a pair of thick lenses and a bad comb-over and replied in faultless English that they were more than welcome to use the phone so long as they could pay. Pearce got the sense from the proprietor that he was sympathetic to Westerners, so he offered him a stashed one-ounce gold coin for both the phone service and his silence. The man's smile only got bigger, and he swore secrecy.

Pearce reached a senior CIA field agent in Peshawar, a base of U.S. undercover operations since the days of the Soviet occupation of Afghanistan.

"Can you sit tight where you are for two hours?" the agent asked.

Pearce asked the proprietor if he could accommodate them with a flash of two more gold coins and the keys to their abandoned truck. The shopkeeper nodded violently.

"Yeah, no problem. But don't drag your feet, either."

An hour and forty-five minutes later, Pearce and Cella were in an armored Chevy Suburban heading back to Peshawar. When they reached the CIA station, Cella was met by an Italian diplomat who choppered in from Islamabad as soon as her embassy had learned that a Paolini was in need of assistance. Before she left, Pearce asked for a private moment with Cella.

"I'm sorry about everything that happened. I feel responsible somehow."

"It's this stupid war. It's crazy. It will kill you before it's all over. You should leave. Come with me. Now."

"Don't tempt me. I'm probably due for a firing squad as it is."

"You already have an Italian passport with your name on it. You're my husband, remember?" She tried to charm him with a smile.

"If I can ever make it up to you—"

"You can. Stay alive. And come find me when this is all over."

"It's a deal."

"And thank you for saving my life." She threw her arms around his neck and hugged him tight, then leaned back and kissed him lightly on the mouth.

And with that, she left.

P earce spent the next two days in Peshawar recovering from dehydration and fatigue before he was debriefed and reprimanded, first by the local station's senior supervisor and then by his unit commander back in Kabul, who ordered him to report back immediately.

Pearce caught the next available Air Force transport flight from Peshawar to Kabul, where he submitted to another two hours of debriefing and another sharp reprimand before a brand-new bottle of Maker's Mark was cracked open and the two men drank until midnight. Pearce stumbled out of the door with a thirty-day pass in his hip pocket and two big ideas in his head.

Pearce chased down the first big idea the next night, making his way to FOB Salerno in Khost, Afghanistan. He broke into the compound, searching for the private quarters of Colonel J. Armstrong, the unit commander of the airborne outfit responsible for the massacre of Daud's village.

Pearce's heavy boot smashed open the bathroom door, where he found the bull-necked officer on his commode with his BDUs around his ankles, savoring a Marlboro while relieving himself. Before the startled officer could react, Pearce shoved the colonel's own vintage Colt M1911 .45 pistol against his forehead, widening the older man's eyes with shock.

"Are you out of your mind, soldier?"

"There was a village on the map called Dogar until just a couple of days ago, when your unit burned it to the ground and killed about a hundred friends of mine. I'm going to kill you for that."

"Then why are we talking?"

"Because I'm going to give you a choice. Tell me how much Khalid was paying you and then I'll kill you fast and easy with a bullet to the brain. But if you lie to me, I'll gut you and let you bleed to death in a puddle of your own excrement. Which will it be?"

"Khalid is one of our agents. I was paying him."

"Why did you attack the village?"

"Khalid said Dogar was a Taliban stronghold, responsible for the gun trafficking in the area. Named a *talib* called Daud as the number one bandit."

"You stupid fuck. Khalid is the *talib* shitting all over us up there. Dogar was on our side. Daud and I were hunting Khalid. That was all on the books months ago."

"Who is 'we,' son?"

"CIA."

"How the hell are we supposed to know what you spooks are doing down there? We're Army."

"Don't you high-level pricks talk to each other before pulling this kind of shit?"

"As a matter of fact, we don't. My people don't talk to yours, and yours don't talk to mine. Still too much territorial pissing going on between commands. The whole war effort's turning into a goddamned goat rodeo." The colonel gestured at his trousers. "You mind?"

Pearce stepped back but didn't lower the gun. His instincts said the colonel wasn't lying. Killing a man wasn't an issue for him, but killing an innocent man was.

The colonel yanked up his pants. "I'm real sorry about your friends, son. Truly I am. And I would've put a gun to your head, too, if the shoe had been on the other foot. The only difference is, I would've pulled it without jawboning beforehand."

"Yeah. I'm kind of liberal that way," Pearce said. He tossed the colonel's antique pistol into the unflushed toilet, splashing slop onto the linoleum. "But I'm working on it."

The colonel's skull flushed red. "My granddaddy carried that Colt from Bastogne to the Remagen bridge."

"Like I give a shit. Next time, pick up a fucking phone and call somebody before you decide to slaughter an entire village, especially a friendly one."

Pearce backed out of the door and disappeared into the night without being followed by the colonel, still cursing in his bungalow. That completed his first big idea.

His second big idea was going to be a whole lot more interesting.

= 24 =

The second big idea Pearce had the night he left
Kabul was definitely better than the first.

It took him two days to make the haul from
Khost to Islamabad, where he boarded a Qatar Airlines
flight to Milan. He slept for the entire thirteen-hour
flight, even during the layover in Dohar.

He was awake and refreshed when he deplaned at one
o'clock in the afternoon at Aeroporto Milano Malpensa.
To his surprise, Pearce was greeted at the gate by name
by a short, barrel-chested man in a turtleneck and sport
coat too small for his bulging arms and shoulders. His
bald scalp, broad nose, and deep-set eyes reminded him
of the famous Italian dictator—if Mussolini had been a
cage fighter.

"Welcome to Italia, Mr. Pearce. My name is Renzo

Sforza." The man shook Pearce's hand. "I am the Paolini estate manager. Ms. Paolini has put you in my care."

Judging by the crushing grip, Pearce thought maybe "custody" was a better word than "care."

Sforza escorted Pearce to a waiting convoy of three silver Maserati Levante SUVs. Three men stood by each of the vehicles, chiseled and handsome as fashion models in après-ski jackets and cargo pants. Relaxed and smiling, Pearce thought they looked like they were posing for a sports magazine cover photo rather than conducting a security transport operation. Only the Beretta pistols tucked into their shoulder harnesses suggested otherwise.

When Pearce approached the lead vehicle, he was greeted with the affable swagger of fellow operators—friendly, confident, and lethal. He offered his backpack for inspection, but it was declined with a smile. He climbed into the rear passenger compartment and the mini convoy sped north on the Strada Provinciale 52 to begin the journey to Lake Como.

The window separating the driver's compartment from his lowered and Sforza handed Pearce a cell phone. The window slid back up, and a moment later it rang.

"I wasn't expecting a reception," Pearce said.

"I couldn't take any chances," Cella said. "How was your flight?"

"How did you know I was coming?"

She laughed.

"I mean, how did you know what flight I would be on?" Pearce asked.

"We have computers in Italy, too."

"Exactly where are you taking me?"

"We have an old family villa at the lake. Just a little place for you to rest and recuperate. Doctor's orders."

"I'm looking forward to seeing you again."

"Me, too. Unfortunately, I won't be there when you arrive."

The convoy whisked along State Road 583 up into the mountains past Como, winding along the steep grade through a dozen postcard villages and towns perched on the mountain or swooping toward the water. Pearce marveled at the deep-blue color of the lake and the giant snowcapped peaks towering over it. Even taller mountains in the Swiss Alps loomed in the distance. The Maseratis made their way along the narrow lane, which seemed barely able to accommodate two cars, particularly in the little towns. An hour and a half later, Pearce's vehicle came to the town of Bellagio, sitting at the end of a point of land that bisected this end of the lake. Pearce checked his Google maps. It looked like the Bellagio peninsula pointed at the crotch of a running woman, the lake forming two legs running down either side of the peninsula, with the much broader trunk of the northern lake forming her torso.

The SUVs climbed up the hill toward a massive stone-walled villa occupying the top of the wooded hill at the farther point on the peninsula.

That's when he knew Cella had lied to him.

Just a little place for you to rest and recuperate, she had said, Pearce reminded himself.

The big iron gates at the end of the winding driveway opened electronically and the three-vehicle convoy sped into a courtyard, where they were greeted by uniformed house servants and more bodyguards.

Sforza opened Pearce's door. Pearce got out, stretched.

"Welcome to Villa Paolini, Mr. Pearce. Let me show you to your room. Any special requests?"

"Hot shower. And I might toss my clothes into a washer. Long trip."

"Very good. Follow me, please." Sforza motioned for Pearce to follow as he pulled out a cell phone and barked an order.

Sforza marched up the grand marble staircase and opened the broad wooden double doors at the top of the landing, pointing Pearce the way in. The room was actually a suite with floor-to-ceiling windows and a stunning 270-degree view of the deep-blue lakes and towering mountains. It looked more like an IMAX theater screen than an actual room with a view. The room itself was easy on the eyes, too, featuring polished white marble, granite, and light wood complementing the natural view. Pearce could hardly take it in.

"I trust you find the room acceptable, *signore,*" Sforza grunted.

"If this is all you have, I suppose it will do." Pearce

scratched his ratty beard. "I didn't bring my GPS. You wanna point me in the direction of the bathroom?"

"Of course."

Sforza led him to a marble quarry posing as a bathroom. Larger than many homes he'd stood in, the bathroom was a vast expanse of stone, glass, and silver fixtures, but it was the antique barber's chair and the sturdy woman in a white barber's coat that caught his attention. She was mercilessly beating a cup of shaving soap into a frothy lather with a badger hairbrush. Pearce unconsciously tugged on his beard.

"Perhaps you require a shave, *signore*?" the woman asked. Her accent was Italian, but her blue eyes and sharp features were definitely Germanic. Pearce knew far northern Italy had been Austrian territory before the First World War.

"Yeah, maybe so."

"Call if you need anything else, *signore*," Sforza said, turned on his heel, and left.

Pearce enjoyed the best shave of his life as the barber deftly removed his beard, yielding a baby-bottom-smooth finish with a pearl-handled straight razor and generous helpings of eucalyptus-scented lather.

Pearce took a long shower in a huge walk-in enclosure with six showerheads that also featured a view of the lake. When he emerged from the shower, open suitcases of new clothes were already laid out on the king-sized bed, all in his size, of course. He feasted on a platter of antipasto, cheeses and fruit, and washed it all down with a bottle of Pellegrino sparkling water. He pulled on casual clothes, a vest, and hiking boots and made his way outside. The air was crystal clear and fragrant with pine. The sun was out, and the air was relatively warm despite the higher altitude—certainly nothing like Afghanistan, which, he could hardly believe, was just a few days behind him. He'd stepped out of hell and fallen into heaven in such a short period of time that he felt disoriented.

Under Sforza's watchful eye, Pearce toured the grounds around the villa and took in the stunning views of the mountains and lake all over again. The clean air alone was enough to revive his spirits, and the gentle hiking was working out all of the kinks in his muscles after so many hours of sitting on planes and in cars. But another wave of fatigue washed over him and he headed back to his suite. He called down for beer and soon received a half dozen bottles of chilled Tipo Pils in a silver bucket brimming with ice. The tasty local craft beer brewed in Como was citrusy and sweet. Pearce downed two while watching a stunning sunset purple a jagged mountain sky, and he was suddenly homesick for the Rockies, the first time in years. He shrugged off a wave of bad childhood memories about his father that suddenly flooded in, brushed his teeth, and hit the sack. He passed out almost as soon as his head touched the pillow.

He dreamed of Cella. Her hungry mouth teased its way up his hard stomach until it found his neck and then his mouth. His rough hands cupped her breasts as she grasped him with her long fingers and thrust him into her, wet and eager as he was hard, and she gasped again.

And that's when he realized it wasn't a dream.

Their sex was feral, greedy, frenzied. A HALO free fall, waiting for the chute that never opened. The Tingle, he called it. The sheer loss of control, the inevitability of death. Until the chute opened, and then, release.

He marveled at the strength in her long, athletic limbs and hard torso, muscled after a year in the high mountains feeding on animal protein. Her energy built as the night drove on, rising, cresting, then rising again until something deep within him broke, and he gave in to the thing inside, primal and unknowing. Beyond. They devoured each other until sheer exhaustion stole them both away. They awoke, tangled in the sheets and wrapped around each other, the morning light heavy in their eyes.

And then they started all over again.

Pearce woke again with the afternoon sun high in the windows. He pulled on a new set of clothes and sped down the wide marble stairs to the kitchen.

Cella smiled at him over a glass of wine. She was frying fish and green beans in olive oil in a pan over the stove. She wore a tight sweater and formfitting jeans. He tried not to stare at the sheer beauty of her, but failed. He approached her. She kissed him. He could taste the wine.

"Hungry?"

"Yeah."

"Good. We'll eat, and then I'm taking you somewhere."

"I think you already did."

She blushed.

That surprised him.

They walked hand in hand along the waterfront promenade of Bellagio. The buildings were ablaze in afternoon sunlight, each painted in glowing yellow, or ocher, or blue beneath red clay-tiled roofs. The buildings ascended from the water to the side of the forested mountain powdered with snow. Tall cypress stood guard like sentries over the sleepy winter harbor, mostly empty save for the few white sailboats of the intrepid locals.

Troy and Cella strolled past the high-end stores and shops tucked beneath the awnings, then turned up the narrow alleys, climbing the worn stone steps past more shops and an auberge. Cella led them higher up and then to a stone gate overlooking the town. With the mountains in the background and the red-roofed steeple in the middle, Pearce thought he might have been looking at a painting.

"I wish it were spring." Cella sighed. "You should see the colors with all of the flowers, all along the harbor, and up here, too, in the hotel gardens, and spilling out of every house garden, too." She touched a twisting vine climbing the stone wall. "This wisteria hangs like a thick cluster of purple grapes."

Pearce tried to imagine the splashes of color. He'd seen pictures of this place but never imagined he'd ever visit. He glanced past Cella's shoulder and caught the eye of one of her bodyguards trying to remain inconspicuous in the distance. In the summer it would be easy to hide in the crowd, but now the village was nearly empty. Even some of the shops had closed for the winter.

At sunset she took him to her favorite restaurant. She was greeted by the owner with a kiss on each cheek and offered a private balcony overlooking the lake. They feasted on lake mussels bathed in butter and garlic, peppered beef filets, and risotto. They took dessert, cognac, and coffee, too, and waved away Sforza's silver Levante for the long walk back to the villa.

The evening ended the way the day had begun, and they fell asleep in each other's arms again, wordlessly.

Cella took Troy out on her private boat the next day and they visited a few of the other lake villages, as picturesque as Bellagio, though smaller and less well known. The day after, Sforza arranged a ski trip at Madesimo, near the Swiss border. Cella and Troy insisted, however, that the bodyguards join them on the slopes. What was the point of trying to remain hidden on a downhill run? The snow was powdery and wet, and neither gave ground to the other as they carved their way down the long runs. When the sun finally fell, they drank buttered rum in the lodge by a roaring fire. After a long, hard day of skiing, Troy and Cella were both exhausted, but hot showers and mulled wine revived them and they wrestled the night away again.

"Do you have religion?" Cella asked, standing in the Duomo di Milano, Milan's famous soaring Gothic cathedral. They stood at the left of the altar beneath the feet of San Bartolomeo, towering over them.

"You mean, like this guy?" Pearce pointed at the Renaissance statue, perfect in its rendition of a man flayed alive, his skin hung about his shoulders like a shawl. The forlorn saint looked like an illustration for musculature in *Gray's Anatomy*.

"He is the patron saint of tanners. Men with knives. He would be a good saint for you. He is a martyr."

"No, but thanks. I've seen what martyrs can do." He admired the artistry of the work, but grimaced at the horror of it.

"San Bartolomeo was a man turned inside out by the world that hated him. You could use an intercessor like that."

He glanced at his feet. The red, white, and black marble was cut and shaped in the form of flowers. The soaring columns were forests of stone that climbed high into the arched vault above. Brilliant stained glass filled the long window frames. Pearce had never been in a church this large or ancient before. It was overwhelming. He felt small in there. He supposed that was the point.

"Let's go."

Cella showed Troy the best of Milano, her hometown. She was proud of it, the way Italians are, especially Milanese. She showed him Leonardo's famous *Last Supper* fresco at the convent of Santa Maria delle Grazie, and took him shopping at the Galleria Vittorio Emanuele II, which with its beautiful glass dome and carved marble floors seemed to Pearce to be another kind of cathedral. She made him spin on the testicles of the

Torino bull for luck, and bought them both formal evening wear on her account at Biffi, then took him to the magnificent Teatro degli Arcimboldi to see *Otello*, apologizing profusely that she couldn't take him to La Scala because it was closed for renovations, as if she and Milano had somehow sinned against him. Pearce loved the opera, his first, and the evening they spent together at the Grand Hotel. She slept in his arms as he stared at the ceiling with images of the flayed Christian martyr standing in the center of Daud's ruined village, beckoning him with skinless fingers and a lipless smile. Or maybe it was Daud.

W hy?" Cella asked. She was confused. They had spent a perfect week together. Heaven.

Pearce folded his favorite shirt and tucked it neatly into his pack. He wouldn't need the others, or the suitcases.

"Orders. I don't have a choice."

She sat on the bed. "That's a lie you tell yourself. You choose to obey orders. You can also choose to disobey them."

"If I disobey them, they might shoot me."

"If you obey them, someone else might shoot you."

"That's the life I chose."

"Then choose another."

"I would if I could. But I'm a soldier. I have a duty to my country."

She took his hand. "Let me be your country."

Pearce smiled. "Don't tempt me."

"I will tempt you." She kissed his hand, then pointed at the magnificent view of the lake. "All of this will be yours. And more. This is nothing, believe me. My father has houses all over the world. Stay with me, and we'll see them all."

Pearce sat on the bed next to her and took her hand in his.

"Tell me, why did you leave all of this? My whole house growing up would fit inside just this bedroom, with room to spare."

"These are just things. People are what matter most, don't you think?"

"And that's why you came to the same place I did."

"We weren't in the same place, you and I. Not really. I went to heal. You went to kill."

"And if I stay here with you? How many more operas will you take me to before you're bored? Before you decide you have to go back to Afghanistan?"

"I will never go back to that place."

"At least we have that in common."

"What do you mean?"

Pearce stood. "I just got the call. I'm heading somewhere else."

"Where?"

"I can't say. It's classified."

"It's Iraq, isn't it?"

Pearce tried not to convey his surprise. How did she know?

"What? You think I'm stupid? You think I don't read the papers?"

"I don't make the call. I just answer it."

Cella stood. "What call? To topple Hussein? Why him? Why now? Because he supports al-Qaeda? But most of the 9/11 assholes on the planes were from Saudi Arabia. Bin Laden is from Saudi Arabia. Why aren't you invading them?"

"Hussein's a war criminal. He used chemical weapons against his own people."

"Do you mean the chemical weapons you Americans gave him? The ones you helped him use against the Iranians?"

"I'm a soldier, not a politician." Pearce zipped up the pack. "I want to stay here with you, I really do. But I have a job to do first. When I'm done, I'll come back."

Her eyes raged, wet with tears.

"To hell with your war, and to hell with you. If you leave, don't call, don't write, don't ever come back."

Cella ran out of the room. Everything in him wanted to chase her.

But he didn't.

Duty called.

= 25 =

The Tuareg driver flashed the lights of his Toyota Hilux pickup three times. The sun had risen ten minutes earlier and the sky was pinking, but the great silver disk was still hidden behind the hills five kilometers to the east.

"Again." Mossa scanned the sky for a speck coming from the southwest, binoculars held to his turbaned face.

The driver flashed his lights three more times.

"There." The plane was ten miles out. Mossa recognized the make. He'd seen Aviocars all over the Middle East, one of the workhorses of the skies. At its current speed it would be landing in about two minutes.

"One more time, Moctar."

Three more flashes.

Mossa brought the glasses back up. The plane's wings waggled three times. "They see us," he said.

J udy finished the last waggle and leveled the plane again.

"Two minutes, boss."

Pearce pulled out the small duffel he'd snatched from AFB Karem and unzipped it. He removed an Air Force M4 carbine with an HK M320 grenade launcher slung underneath. He checked the magazine and safety.

"Where'd you get that?"

"Won it in a card game."

"I've seen you play cards, remember?"

"Let's just say there's an Air Force Security Forces sergeant who's gonna be embarrassed as hell when they do weapons inventory this morning."

"I thought you weren't expecting any trouble."

"You heard Ian."

"You stole that before Ian gave us the heads-up."

"Can't be too careful."

"That's great. You're pissing in everybody's soup today, aren't you?"

"Just so long as you and I are okay," Pearce said.

"Jury's still out on that one. Keep your belt on. It's going to be a bumpy ride."

M ossa watched the pilot flare the wings as the plane
approached. Sand and rock kicked up behind the
aircraft but the wheels landed softly, without a bounce.
Impressive.

He tapped his driver on the shoulder and the Hilux
jumped.

Time to get the American.

J udy feathered the rumbling engines and the props
slowed enough that she could release the foot brakes.
She unbuckled her safety harness in the pilot seat and
joined Pearce in the back.

Pearce stood at the open cargo door. He'd already
secured the emergency stretcher to the deck in case Mike
had to lie prone. Otherwise, he'd put Early in the more
comfortable copilot's seat and he'd take one of the folding jump seats back in the cargo area.

Pearce had his rifle slung over his back. He didn't want
to appear threatening to whoever was driving up, but he
wanted the gun handy in case trouble pulled up instead.
Both the rifle and the grenade launcher were racked. Safe-
ties off.

The Hilux raced up to the cargo door. Three men. All
wore desert camouflage fatigues and indigo blue turbans
that hid everything but their eyes. The Blue Men, Pearce
reminded himself. He half expected robes and camels.

One manned the machine gun mounted in back, one drove, and now one stood in the passenger seat. All Pearce could see of the standing man's face were his dark eyes, sharp and suspicious. The other two stared daggers at him.

"You are Pearce?" the standing one said.

Pearce nodded. "Where's Early?"

The man motioned with his hand. "Come. We don't have much time."

Pearce didn't like the way this was setting up. "Who are you?"

"I am Mossa Ag Alla."

"Chief of all the Imohar!" the gunner shouted, careful not to point the weapon at Pearce.

Mossa waved a hand to silence the younger man.

"You were supposed to bring Early," Pearce said.

"Yes, Early. Hurry. There isn't much time."

"You know about the Army convoy heading your way?"

"Of course."

If Early was badly wounded, it might make sense that they wouldn't have brought him out here, just in case Pearce didn't arrive.

Or it was a trap.

Pearce said to Judy, "Mind the fort. I'll be back."

"And miss the chance to meet the missus? No way."

Pearce's icy gaze said otherwise. He yanked a comms link out of his vest pocket and put it in his ear.

"Fine," Judy said. "At least snap a photo for me."

"I'll stay in touch."

"Be careful," Judy said, and headed back for the cockpit.

Pearce grabbed the small aluminum attaché case, then

jumped down into the rocky sand. He scrambled into the back of the Toyota, and Mossa gave the order to drive with a wave of his hand. The driver mashed the gas pedal and the Toyota leaned hard into a steep 180-degree turn, then sprung upright as it rocketed for the village.

The pickup skidded to a halt in front of the well. Mossa stepped out of the Toyota and motioned for Pearce to follow. The other two stayed behind on alert. Pearce kept his weapon slung over his shoulder and gripped the aluminum attaché case in one hand.

Mossa marched to a nearby house and stopped. Bullet holes scarred the mud-brick walls. He motioned to the doorway illuminated in early-morning light. It was already warming up.

"Your friend is in here."

Pearce nodded and marched past Mossa into the little house. This close he could see the lines around the older man's eyes. The Tuareg fighter was five feet ten and powerfully built, but still four inches shorter than Pearce.

Mike Early sat at a small table drinking hot tea. The kettle still steamed where it sat on the hot coals in the fireplace. His left arm was in a sling, and an olive-drab *shemagh* was draped around his neck, the U.S. Army's version of a *keffiyeh*.

"Troy? What are you doing here?" He stood. A wide, toothy grin spread across his bearded face.

"Came to get you out of here." Pearce crossed to

Early and bear-hugged his old friend. "Heard you were wounded and needed an evac."

Early held up his slinged arm. "This? I've had cases of clap worse than this. It's just a sprain."

"That's not what we were told."

"Don't blame him. I made the call." The woman's heavy Italian accent gave her away.

Pearce turned around. Cella stood in the doorway. He'd steeled himself for the moment but still nearly lost it. It had been years since he'd seen her. She was clearly exhausted and undernourished, but even in her faded camouflage she was stunning.

"Why?" Pearce asked. His voice was even. "And why me?"

She wore her hair pulled into a ponytail, revealing the proud cheekbones and angular jaw he remembered so vividly. Her blue eyes bored into his. "I knew you would come for your friend." She stepped closer. At six feet even, she was nearly as tall as he was. A ray of golden sunlight struck her face, softening it. "It's been a long time, hasn't it?"

"Yes," Pearce said. He had a million questions, but now was not the time.

"You two know each other?" Early asked.

One of the corners of Cella's mouth tugged slightly. Almost a smile. "Yes, we know each other."

"I'll be damned. It's a small world."

"And getting smaller. There's a convoy on the way." Pearce motioned to Early. "We need to haul ass."

"Me? I'm not going anywhere," Mike said. "I've got a job to do."

"What job?"

Early nodded at Cella. "Her. I'm her security."

Cella rolled her eyes. "My father's watchdog."

"It's complicated. Like an arranged marriage," Early said.

"So what am I doing here?" Pearce asked. He glanced at Cella. "I take it you want a lift?"

"Not for me."

Pearce nodded at Mossa. "Him?"

"No," he said. "My place is here, with my people."

Cella brushed past Pearce, close enough that he could smell the sweat in her hair. A memory flooded him. He pushed it away. She stooped a little as she entered a low doorway toward another room. Pearce followed.

Cella pointed toward a bed. A young girl lay on it. Motionless. Eyes closed.

"I need you to take her."

"A body?"

"Asleep. I gave her a sedative for the journey."

"Who is she?" Pearce asked.

"My granddaughter," Mossa said. His fierce black eyes softened beneath the indigo veil.

"My father in Milan is expecting her," Cella said.

"I'm not running a taxi service. Call somebody else."

"We can't. Everybody else would use her to get to Mossa. The only person I trust to help us is you."

"And you knew about this?" Pearce asked Early.

"First I'm hearing about it. But it makes sense. We're in the shit out here."

"You trust me," Pearce said to Cella. "But you lied to me."

"You were my last hope. My only hope," Cella said.

"I don't understand. What is the girl to you?" Pearce asked.

Cella searched Pearce's blue eyes, a question weighing heavily in her own. A moment passed. She found her answer.

"She's my daughter."

$$= 26 =$$

Myers buried her nose in Pearce's shirt and breathed it in again. It smelled just like him. A combination of sweat and testosterone, mingled with wood smoke and bacon. It brought back fond memories. She hadn't seen him in over a year, but the olfactory sense was the most powerful of them all and, when triggered, elicited strong emotions, too. Something stirred inside of her, but she felt guilty as hell, sitting in Pearce's cabin, wearing his shirt while her clothes were in the wash. She was invading his privacy in the worst way, though technically she'd been invited to do so.

She had never depended upon anyone since she was a young girl putting herself through college. But she was afraid and alone, and without sufficient resources for the job at hand. She ran a software company, not a security firm, and was persona non grata with the Greyhill administration, so she turned to Pearce, the only man she truly trusted for help. First for Mike Early, then herself.

There was something indescribably male about Pearce. She'd thought about him often since her resignation. She called on him to take out the Mexican cartel killers who had murdered those poor teenagers, along with her only son. Pearce did as he was asked, and more. She owed him everything. So did the nation. They had all let him down, it seemed. She hoped he had found Mike Early in time and gotten him out of Mali in one piece. Mike was a good guy. So was Pearce. She trusted him completely. He didn't let her down when she needed him. And now she needed him again.

It was impossible to be around Pearce and not feel like a *man* was in the room. Solid, dependable, masculine. The kind of man who would fight and die for his country, a rare breed these days. The kind of man who would defend a woman's honor and her life, whether in a bar fight or a firefight. There weren't many of those left, either. Video games and boy bands and androgynous movie actors were feminizing everything. In the current culture, the masculine was pitifully obsolete, testosterone an environmental hazard.

Myers poured herself another cup of coffee and gathered her wits. Enough dawdling. Time to get to work. Ian's package that had been delivered to her at the Glory Box café by Sadie contained all of the necessary keys for Pearce's cabin and vehicles, along with the alarm code passwords she needed. Pearce had left instructions with Ian that he was to give Myers any and all support she needed should she ever require it. Myers had offered Pearce and his team much the same, though in her capacity as a hands-off owner of a private software company, there wasn't much she could bring to the table compared with the resources available to Pearce Systems.

She began the terminal session on Pearce's Linus desktop by plugging in the flash drive Ian sent her and followed his script exactly. Moments later she was tunneling on Ian's encrypted virtual private network (VPN). Ian's VPN operated in the Dark Net where 97 percent of all Web content was located and yet was mostly inaccessible to the billions of online users. The Surface Web where people used Google and Facebook was only a tiny fraction of the online world. While some black market vendors hid in the netherworld of the Dark Net in order to sell illegal or contraband items, legitimate users, like Ian, just didn't want to be found.

Myers established a secure videoconferencing connection to Ian, who was located in the renovated Mercury auto plant in Dearborn, Michigan, that served as Pearce Systems' headquarters and primary research facility.

"Hello, Ian. It's nice to finally meet you in person, sort of."

"Same here, Madame President. I'm glad you made it safely."

"Please, call me Margaret. We're going to be working together."

"Of course. Are you comfortable?"

Myers saw herself in the smaller conferencing window wearing Pearce's shirt. It must have seemed presumptuous. Maybe even Freudian.

"I'm quite comfortable, thank you. The cabin is rustic but charming."

"I believe his grandfather built it."

"It has a lot of character. And good coffee."

"I have you under surveillance on my end. You might care to activate the local security monitors as well, just to be safe."

Myers scanned the bank of monitors over the desk. Security camera images covering the entire compound filled the screens. There were also cameras rotating shots room to room inside the cabin. "Already did."

"Very good. Have you had a chance to inspect the motor home?"

"Briefly. It looks like something out of Star Wars." She had already checked out Pearce's mobile command center. She knew Pearce had run many of his ops remotely from the retrofitted vehicle.

"You may need to access it later, but for now the terminal you're on will suffice. Perhaps we should begin at the beginning. Please tell me why you needed a secure location."

Myers gave a brief explanation of her visit to Justice Tanner and his subsequent suicide, along with the strong suspicion that she was being watched by whoever had blackmailed him.

"What evidence do you have of blackmail?"

"I knew the man for twenty years. His suicide was both an apology and, I think, a clue."

"Clue?"

"He was very nervous and hostile when I met with him. I've never known him to be either. Whoever had the power to blackmail him probably had the ability to keep him under surveillance. I think that's why he was nervous and hostile. Probably trying to protect me, though I didn't see it at the time. If he had been blackmailed he couldn't say anything to me if he was under surveillance, so I believe he might have killed himself in order to invite an investigation."

"If you don't mind my saying, that's a bit of a stretch."

"Maybe. But he seemed to bear the weight of an enormous amount of guilt for violating his own principles. The weight of history, too. His controversial opinion will be read and criticized for as long as there are law books."

"So his death could be the result of guilt, but the basis of a clue. That makes sense, though it would hardly stand up in a court of law."

"I initiated a few search queries two days ago. My own security measures indicated that I was being monitored. Without question, I know I'm on the right path. I'm determined to find out who is behind his death."

"Do you have a course of action in mind?"

"Yes, and I'm going to need your help. We need to start digging, but we need to do it in a very secure way; otherwise, I'm afraid we'll both be targeted by the same people who came after Vin. I'm willing to take the risk, but I won't put you or Pearce Systems in jeopardy."

"No worries there. This is what we do. Where do we start?"

"I always start with a simple question. Who benefits?" Myers knew the K Street game well enough to know that changes in legislation and regulation could be even more profitable than just simple cash transfers. Politicians and lobbyists—many of whom were former politicians—were obvious candidates.

Wall Street banksters and hedge fund managers would have also benefitted from the ruling, and that would be another place to start. But something told Myers that was too obvious. The sophistication of the malware that tried to infect her motherboard's BIOS suggested more advanced software abilities than the average stockbroker usually possessed.

On the other hand, a few Wall Street firms hired the best mathematicians and software engineers to create and execute blindingly fast investing algorithms—"robo-traders" or "algos"—that made faster, better, and emotionless computer-generated trades in milliseconds throughout global markets. Often utilizing high-speed data (HSD) sold to them by the exchanges themselves, institutional investors made billions in high-frequency trading. HFT was responsible for at least half if not more of all Wall Street transactions these days, turning massive profits on fractional stock movements, or legally "front-running" trades made by slower investors. Profits, like war, depended on beating opponents to the punch.

Speed was everything, and no human trader could ever hope to keep up with the automated systems. The same would be true in war, Myers feared. Automated generals and admirals could eliminate future conflicts by displaying their drone squadrons and rebotic fleets more swiftly and decisively than their human counterparts.

Of course, all of that data harvesting and processing relied heavily on hardware and software systems. When the algorithms failed, "flash crashes" and other high-speed-data train wrecks occurred. But billions of dollars in profits were being harvested by these "drone" trading systems. They also had to be protected by sophisticated hardware and software security systems in order to safely conduct billions of financial transactions every day, accurately and securely. So, yes, there were Wall Street suspects, too, along with the politicians and lobbyists. Come to think of it, a number of Wall Street figures were also former politicians and lobbyists. In fact, they were all interchangeable parts of the same vast machine. This would be a difficult knot to try to untangle.

"Let's talk about this for a moment," Myers said. She drummed her fingers on the desktop. "Tanner made an *outrageous* legal decision. Thousands, if not millions, of people stand to profit in some way from it—some more than others. A few of those would have benefitted the most, so they would have had the most to gain. But the outrageousness of the decision tells me that the leverage they had over him must have been unbelievable. Big decision, big threat, big payoff. Make sense?"

"Impeccable logic."

"But what could the deep, dark secret have been? Tanner would have been vetted for every significant position he ever held, including the Colorado Supreme Court, but even before he was formally nominated to the United States Supreme Court, we had the FBI conduct a standard background check. So either Tanner did something terribly wrong after he was confirmed to his appointment, or something he had done was very ancient and very well hidden. The first scenario speaks to ongoing surveillance, and the latter to extreme research capabilities, don't you agree?"

"Agreed. In either scenario, government resources most likely would be needed."

"Or a government contractor."

"Or it could have been a stroke of bad luck that someone happened to stumble across something."

"That's like saying someone stumbled across buried treasure. No, you have to dig for buried treasure, and the bigger the treasure, the deeper you hide it. Besides, I don't know how to write an algorithm for luck. If I did, I'd use it to play Powerball, wouldn't you?"

"Another possibility would be faked evidence of some sort."

"You didn't know Vin Tanner," Myers said. "If someone had ginned up fake evidence, he'd fight tooth and nail against it."

"Unless the false evidence was so well documented that he knew he couldn't fight against it, or worse, maybe he even believed it."

"I'm not following you."

"You know, something like 'Here is a picture of you with this person when you were drunk. You just don't remember doing this terrible thing with them because you were so drunk.' Most people believe visual evidence, even if it contradicts their beliefs. It's so easy to fake photographs these days. It's very difficult to trust anything digital."

"I agree. Faked evidence is a possibility. But I still believe we're talking about a government agency or government contractor. But you know government people. They all talk. So if the word never got out about this, then it must have been a very small operation."

"Rogue perhaps?"

"Not authorized, for sure. At least, not legally."

"Where does that leave us?" Ian asked.

"A few people who stood to most benefit from a single, outrageous decision utilized one or a few highly capable research and/or surveillance people to find or create blackmail data on Justice Tanner. So at least the numbers of actual participants seems to be shrinking. But the number of candidates is still huge, counting just high-ranking politicians and Wall Street CEOs. Let's try two tacks. First, can you put together some sort of search query about outrageous decisions?"

"That's a rather indefinable and unquantifiable search parameter, don't you think?"

"We can attack it in two ways. First, we can tackle this from a political angle. We can look at all committee and subcommittee hearings, selecting out those focused on big-budget items like defense or regulations that affect big financial institutions."

"I am a stranger in a strange land, but I believe there are many such committees and subcommittees in your Congress."

"Okay, I'll make it easy on you. The Ways and Means Committees in both the House and Senate are responsible for the tax laws. They also happen to be the most powerful and coveted of all committee appointments. Those are the two biggest fish to catch as far as lobbyists are concerned. Finance, Banking, Commerce, Energy, and Defense would be the other big ones—all of their subcommittees, too. Those committee votes are all legal documents that are in the public domain and easily pulled down. In the case of legal decisions, limit the pool to federal appellate and Supreme Court decisions. And let's limit our search to just the last three years."

"Just?" Ian laughed.

"The second way to attack this is to define 'outrageous decisions' as those that have resonated strongly with the attentive public. So we'll conduct high-frequency word searches limited to a distinct vocabulary—words like 'inexplicable,' 'indefensible,' et cetera—and look for those on the top twenty political, financial, and military blogs, Twitter feeds, and what have you, to see what decisions have most outraged the attentive public that uses those sites."

"We are still dealing with tens of thousands of decisions."

"Not really. Remember, we're only looking for the most outrageous. The real outliers. I think we're talking hundreds, or maybe just dozens, of such extremely controversial votes. Of course, if we don't come up with anything, we can widen the search. Unfortunately, federal bureaucracies write thousands of administrative laws every year that are every bit as binding as any piece of congressional legislation. But let's not go there yet."

"Thank heavens."

"So the idea is this. If we can find the most outrageous political decisions and then find out which person or persons most benefitted from most of those decisions, I think we'll have a pretty good pool of suspects to look into."

"Most benefitted?"

"Let's quantify that, and let's just focus on money for now. Let's set a figure of ten million dollars. If someone didn't profit at least ten million, don't keep them in our pool. The kind of hostile surveillance and research operations we're theorizing about would cost a lot of money. Anything less than ten million is chump change in Washington."

"I should think that any politician that suddenly increased their net worth by ten million dollars in a few years would make headlines."

"You'd be surprised. There are more millionaires in Congress than nonmillionaires these days. And some of them are worth far, far more. But I take your point. We're probably talking about corporations, private trusts, hedge funds. But just in case a political person is behind this, we should target those financial institutions with C-level managers married to the members of committees or courts we talked about."

"Good thing I don't have a private life," Ian said.

"I'm terribly sorry. I know I'm asking a lot, but whoever drove Tanner to kill himself is now out for me. And if they can take out a Supreme Court justice and possibly a former U.S. president, I have to believe they are a threat to other members of the government, and maybe not just this government."

"Quite right. It is an honor and a privilege to work with you on this. I really wasn't whinging, I promise."

"Thank you."

They worked out the specifics in the arcane and mysterious language of computer programmers, then divided up the responsibilities. Myers would work from the safety of Pearce's cabin and Ian would do his part from Pearce Systems headquarters, so long as Troy didn't require his services. Myers agreed, secretly hoping that Pearce wouldn't need Ian's assistance, because if he did, that meant Troy was in trouble and she was in no position to do anything about it, and that infuriated her.

= 27 =

I don't understand. Why didn't you just haul out of here?"

"We're out of fuel. We wouldn't get twenty kilometers," Mossa said.

"You should've thought about that before you—"

"You arrogant bastard. What do you know about our situation?" Cella's eyes were blue coals.

"We planned on refueling here, but the Ganda Koy drained the tanks into the sand," Mike said. "So we're stuck."

"With the army on the way?" Pearce said. "You guys aren't stuck. You're fucked."

"Save my daughter. Please," Cella said.

Pearce ran his fingers through his long hair, thinking.

He hated being lied to. Hated being in the middle of another war on a piece of ground that wasn't worth pissing on. Hated the whole situation. But it is what it is, he finally concluded.

"All right, fine. We'll take the girl," Pearce said.

Mossa nodded his thanks.

"We can crowd a dozen of your men on the plane," he added.

"No. Our fight is here. And even if we came with you, the minute we landed in Niger we would be arrested. Better to die as free men than live as slaves in a Nigerian salt mine."

"Then let's quit jawboning and roll," Pearce said.

"Thank you," Cella said, her eyes brimming with tears. "I'll get her now."

Pearce tapped his comms. "Judy, we're on the way. ETA in ten. Fire up the engines."

Pearce drove and Mike stood in the pickup bed, manning the Russian PK machine gun. Early wore his *shemagh* around his face, Tuareg style, and a pair of Ray-Bans against the choking sand billowing up around him. His personal weapon was an FN SCAR-H CQC, a close-quarters modular battle rifle. Early loved it because it was short, light, deadly accurate, easy to strip and clean, and fired the hard-hitting 7.62mm NATO round.

Cella wedged into the passenger seat with her daughter on her lap, still groggy. The child was long but thin, with a mop of thick black hair. Cella folded her up in her arms as best as she could.

"You can keep the ransom," Pearce said. Thirty-thousand euros was a lot of money, but it wasn't his.

"It's not ransom. It's my trust fund money. My father sends it to me when there is a need among the people."

"How is your father these days?"

She ignored the question. "Did you bring the medical supplies as well?"

"It's all there."

The girl moaned.

"She okay?"

Cella brushed the girl's hair away from her face. Pearce glanced at her. She was a pretty young girl on the verge of a ferocious beauty. In a few years she'd be her mother's twin.

"She's waking up a little, which is good. But I don't want her to be completely awake, at least not until you're in the air."

"Why not?"

"She is . . . *ostinato*. Like a mule." Cella grinned. "Like you."

"Me? More like you."

The Toyota bounced along. Pearce checked the fuel gauge. Nearly empty. The Aviocar filled the windshield.

"What's her name?"

"Dorotea, after my mother."

"How old is she?"

Pearce thought she looked six years old, maybe seven. He wasn't sure.

He tapped the brakes and brought the Hilux to an easy stop next to the open cargo door. The motors were loud even though the props were barely spinning. Early jumped off the back and opened Cella's door as Pearce climbed up into the Aviocar.

Early took the girl in his big arms and easily lifted her up, even with the sling on. She was still mostly passed out, but her eyebrows knitted into a frown. He carried her to Pearce and raised her up. "Careful with this sack of potatoes."

Pearce took her up, careful not to bang her head on the door. Cella climbed in after her. Early followed.

"Put her next to me so I can keep an eye on her," Judy said.

Pearce carried the girl to the cockpit and set her in the copilot's seat, then kneeled down and strapped her in. She yawned. Her eyes fluttered open for a moment. Something about them. Beautiful.

The little girl was clearly confused by her surroundings. Maybe even thought she was in a dream. She looked around. Saw Pearce's face. She gazed at him, smiled a little, then passed back out.

"Here is how you can reach my father," Cella said, handing Judy an envelope.

"Is he expecting her?" Judy asked.

"All her life," Cella said. "Now he gets his wish."

Pearce stood. "Call ahead to Bert Holliday and give him a heads-up on the new situation. She's going to need papers at the very least. He'll help you with the girl's grandfather, too, I'm sure."

"Will do, boss. Soon as I'm in the air."

"No. Maintain radio silence until you land, then radio us a thumbs-up so we know you're okay," Pearce said. "Don't forget, you're a target with that IFF disabled."

"What are you talking about? Aren't you coming with me?" Judy asked, but she heard the resolve in his voice.

"Brother, we're a lost cause out here," Early said.

"Is there any other kind?" Pearce clapped Early on his good shoulder. "Besides, weren't you the one who always used to ask me, 'Who wants to live forever?'?"

"I was young and stupid back then."

"Well, you're not young anymore."

"Troy, this is serious. There's no reason for you to risk your life for Mossa," Cella said. She laid her fine-boned hand on his forearm.

"I'm not risking anything for Mossa," Pearce said. "I don't even know who the hell he is. But I'm not leaving my friends high and dry."

Early's shoulder mic crackled. "We have company coming, Mr. Early." It was Mossa, calling from the village.

Early responded. "Heading back your way now."

"Good luck, you guys," Judy said. She started to turn for the cockpit door, but stopped and threw her arms around Pearce's neck. "You and Mike keep your heads down, okay?"

"You know it."

Judy nodded and headed for the cockpit.

Mike jumped out of the cargo door and Cella scrambled out right behind him, but Pearce headed to the back of the cargo area. He fished a key out of his pocket and unlocked a hidden door in the floor plate, then snatched up two large black Pelican storage cases by the handles. It was the South African load he couldn't drop off earlier. Nothing like real-world testing, he thought to himself. Might have to charge them extra for the service.

Pearce tossed the cases out the door and dropped to the ground. He shut the cargo door behind him as sand kicked up in their faces from the revving engines, louder by the second. Early was already back in the pickup bed and wrapping the olive-drab veil back around his face for the ride back.

"Don't worry. Judy's the best pilot I know," Pearce said to Cella, shouting above the rising noise as he tossed the cases into the back of the truck.

Cella wiped her eyes with the flat of her hand and fell into the passenger seat.

Pearce yanked open the driver's door, and then it hit him. He glanced back at the plane, gaining speed.

The girl's eyes were blue, like clear topaz. Just like Cella's.

Blue. Just like his.

CELLA & TROY
2009

= 28 =

Altis Belém Hotel
Lisbon, Portugal
21 August

The sun warmed Pearce's face as he savored the last sip of vintage Porto on the terrace after dinner. He normally didn't take sweet liquor, but the waiter swore it was from the finest Port house in the country from the best grapes and choice *aguardente*. It was a nice way to watch the sunset as fingers of light glinted through the sails of the yachts anchored across the promenade. It was his first trip to Portugal, so he indulged in the local menu as was his custom. Dinner consisted of *caldo verde* soup and a plate of char-grilled sardines, fresh from the Atlantic.

The meeting with the Irishman had gone well. It would be a lucrative contract with a UN-certified NGO, a first for his company. Pearce wanted to build up the non-security side of his business, and this was the next logical step in that direction. Aerial survey work over Indonesia would be relatively easy and virtually riskless. Both the Indonesian government and UN climate-change scientists were interested in cataloguing biomass burnings and drought conditions on the island of Sumatra. It would be a five-year renewable contract, with additional drone flight training and supervisory services fees tacked on for a bonus.

"Troy?"

Pearce turned around. He couldn't believe it. He stood.

"Cella."

Her face broke into a brilliant smile. She threw her arms around him and hugged him hard. Pearce hesitated. The last time he'd seen her was six years ago in Milan, bolting angrily out the door. His joy at seeing her now overwhelmed the bitter memory. He hugged her back.

"You're alive," she whispered in his ear. She finally let go, and held him at arm's length. "It's so good to see you." She touched the side of his face. "No beard. Good. You have such a nice face." She squinted. "A few more scars, I see. But small."

"Please, sit," Pearce said, gesturing at his table.

A waiter appeared. "Vodka martini, stirred, straight up with a lime twist," Cella ordered with a smile.

"Right away." The waiter glanced at Pearce's empty glass. "You, sir?"

"Make it two. And make it doubles."

"Very good, sir."

Cella grasped his hand. "I can't believe you're here.

What are you doing in Lisbon?" Her large blue eyes sparkled intently. Pearce's heart raced. She still had the same effect on him, six years later. She hadn't aged a day. In fact, she looked more beautiful than ever. She wore a simple silk blouse, gray slacks, and flats. Stunning.

"Business. You?"

She looked him up and down. Slacks, shirt, sport coat. "Very stylish. You actually look like a business-man." Her tone suggested conspiracy.

He laughed. "I really am a businessman."

She frowned, incredulous. She'd only known him as a CIA operative. Thought he'd never leave the agency. "What kind of business do you do these days?"

Pearce shrugged. "Nothing interesting, I promise. But what about you? What brings you to Lisbon?"

She hesitated. The drinks arrived. They lifted glasses. The last rays of sunlight danced in the vodka.

"To . . . ?" Cella asked. It was a loaded question.

"To now."

They touched glasses. Took sips. Cella set her glass down.

"I'm here at a UN conference for medical relief work-ers. I run a small women's clinic in Libya. I was asked to speak about the role of women in the medical pro-fessions in the Middle East. And networking, of course." She took another sip. So did Pearce.

"That's great to hear. How long are you in Lisbon?"

"I leave tomorrow. You?"

"Same."

They sat in silence for a while, sipping their martinis, watching the sailboats in their docks, bobbing in the gentle current of the Tagus River, flowing into the great Atlantic. They were both lost in memories of each other, though neither would admit it. Their glasses drained. The waiter appeared, as if on cue.

"Another round?" he asked.

Pearce looked at Cella. There was nothing holding her here, was there?

"Sure."

"Very good, sir." He left.

Cella's eyes teared up. "I thought you were dead."

"Why?"

"Because I never heard from you. No letters. No calls. I used to dream that you would come and visit me, at least."

Pearce was confused. "I thought you made it pretty clear that you never wanted to see me again."

Cella jerked, as if shocked by an electrical current. "Why would you say that?"

"Oh, I dunno. Telling me to go to hell seemed like a pretty good clue." He softened his sarcasm with a smile.

She laughed. "You don't know women, do you? Or maybe it's just Italian women you don't know. I was scared, that was all. Scared for you. Scared for me. What we had . . ."

She laid her hand on the table. Pearce laid his hand on hers.

"I guess I'm an idiot."

"There's no guessing about it."

Pearce felt the heat on his face.

So did she.

The waiter returned five minutes later with the drinks. There was a hundred-euro note tucked under one of the empty glasses. The American and his woman were gone.

Pearce's suite overlooked the Targus. The modernist design featured black woods, white marble, and gleaming fixtures. From the king-sized bed he watched a sailboat tack into the early-morning wind. Cella did, too, as Troy ran his fingers through her thick, lustrous hair. They were both naked beneath the white linens. Happy, exhausted.

They had picked up where they left off six years earlier. Incredibly, it was more intense. Years of nurtured memories had created an insatiable longing. Now they found each other again. And then there was the ticking clock. Only one night to be together. They hardly slept, stealing brief moments of rest until one of them revived and started all over again.

And again.

And again.

"What time is your flight?" he asked. The digital clock flashed 5:22 a.m.

"Not until ten. You?"

"Eleven thirty. We have time for coffee. I'll order room service."

Cella shook her head. "Not yet," she said as she crawled on top and pulled him inside of her again.

————

They lounged in reclining chairs on the south-facing balcony in sumptuous bathrobes, finishing off a pot of strong black Brazilian coffee and a tray of chocolate biscotti and fresh fruit. They both stared at the river, mesmerized by the morning sunlight dappling the water.

"Don't leave," Troy said.

She laughed. "You can't be serious. Even you must be exhausted by now."

"No. I mean, *stay* with me."

"I can't. I have work to do. A life to go back to. So do you."

Pearce crossed over to her chair and sat in it. He took her by the hands. "What do you want me to say? I screwed up. Maybe I should've stayed with you before, but I didn't. I thought about finding you later—like, a million times I thought about it. But the way you ended it—"

"The way I ended it? No, my love. I offered you everything. You turned me down. You ended it."

"But you know why I had to leave."

"Yes, I remember well. You said you had a duty. Well, now, so do I." She sat up and kissed him on the cheek. "This time together was a wonderful gift, but it ends here. You made your choice years ago, and then I made mine." She stood.

"Do you love someone else?"

She looked at him, puzzled, as if he'd asked her a question in Urdu. "I loved you from the moment I set eyes on you. I know I sound like a silly schoolgirl, but it's true."

"Then why not stay with me?"

"Life is more than love, Troy. You taught me that. You made your commitments then, now I've made mine. I'm sorry."

She bent over and kissed him again. They held each other's face in their hands, kissing gently, without lust.

Gently, good-bye.

2015

= 29 =

The village of Anou

Kidal Region, Northwest Mali

7 May

Pearce's truck skidded to a halt by the well. Mossa knelt in the dirt, his men circled around him, the other Toyotas parked nearby. Early climbed down from the truck bed as Pearce and Cella opened their doors.

Mossa stood. "Mr. Pearce? Why aren't you on the plane?"

"Heard you were shorthanded. Mind if I hang around?"

"It's your life. Spend it as you will."

"What's the plan?" Pearce stepped closer to the group.

Mossa kneeled back down. He'd drawn a crude sketch of the village. Pearce had caught a glimpse of it from the air before they landed earlier. Anou was roughly a square, a ragged three hundred yards on each side, bordered by a low sand-brick wall. A one-lane hard-packed road led into the town from the southwest, linking it to Gao. The land on either side of the road was mostly loose sand and scrub juniper. Vehicles would have to stay on that road if they needed sure footing. On the western and northern sides of the wall there were clumps of jagged rock thrusting up through the harder-packed sand and loose rock, and even a few trees, twisted and barren. There were also remnants of older houses that had long since been broken down by years of wind and neglect. Soldiers on foot could easily traverse the area, but wheeled vehicles would have a harder time of it.

"There is an old Soviet BTR-60 armored personnel carrier at the head of a convoy of five trucks," Mossa said. He drew a road in the dust with a long finger. "As you can see, there is only one road coming into the village. They will advance as far as the wall but no further, then dismount, the BTR leading the way. The commander will be in the BTR. We have an RPG that can take out the BTR, then—"

"Permission to speak?" Pearce asked.

Mossa glanced at Early, asking an unspoken question.

"I heard you once say that a piece of salt doesn't call itself salty. Troy here is the best warfighter I know."

"Speak, then, Mr. Pearce."

"You need fuel if you want to get out of here. That BTR carries at least seventy, eighty gallons of diesel. You need to capture it, not blow it up."

"What do you propose?"

"Depends. What else do you have in your inventory?"

Mossa gave him the rundown. It wasn't much, but it had possibilities.

Pearce had a few toys, too. They made a plan.

"You think like an Imohar," Mossa said. "You may not live long, but at least you will die well." Cella translated. The other Tuaregs chuckled in agreement.

T he eight-wheeled BTR slowed to a crawl one hundred meters out from the entrance to the village. The front and side hatches were shut against gunfire, but the top ones were left open because the heat was unbearable even at this early hour in the morning. It rolled along for another thirty meters, but still there was no firing from the village. The commander signaled a halt to the convoy and the BTR braked. The five trucks a hundred meters behind him did the same.

The side hatches popped open and eight Red Beret soldiers in camouflage spilled out and ran in a low crouch toward the wall. They hit the wall and hunkered down on either side of the road, out of breath and sweating, and surprised that they hadn't been fired upon. The squad leader glanced back, taking comfort in the big 14.5mm KPV heavy machine gun on top of the BTR keeping watch over them. It would pour out liquid lead at the first sign of trouble.

The squad leader, a sergeant, gave the hand signal to his men and then rushed through the gate, guns up, building to building, up the narrow road toward the town square—old-school "cover and maneuver." The old buildings were mostly one and two stories tall. No sounds, no movement in the windows, so they pushed on toward the well in the center of the village.

And that's when he saw the girl. She was Tuareg and beautiful. She stood at the well with a clay water pot. She sensed something and glanced up. Saw the squad leader, dropped her pot, and ran for a darkened doorway.

The squad leader signaled his team and advanced for the house. His men followed. Four men circled around back, but the squad leader and three others stayed out front, backs pressed against the wall.

"Tuareg! Come out!" he shouted in French.

"Non!" the girl shrieked.

His corporal pulled a grenade.

"No. Wait," the squad leader said in Songhai, and pushed the grenade back down.

"Come out! We won't hurt you. We're only looking for bandits, not little girls."

A moment passed, and the girl appeared in the doorway, trembling. Her pale brown eyes were wet with fear, but it didn't diminish the beauty of her long, angular face.

"Who else is in there?"

She shook her head. "No one. Only my sisters."

"How many?" he asked.

"Two. Both younger."

"No one else?"

She shook her head. "All dead, or gone. We're the last. We had nowhere else to go."

The squad leader couldn't believe his good fortune.

He turned to his corporal with a feral grin and said in Songhai, "See?"

The corporal grinned back. "Such a beauty."

"We have time, if we're quick about it."

The sergeant lowered his weapon. He towered over the trembling girl. "Show us," he said, nodding at the house. He pulled out a chocolate-flavored PowerBar from a pocket and held it up to her. She snatched it out of his hand. He laughed. "If you are telling the truth, there will be more."

"I am telling the truth," she said, leading the way in.

True to her word, two other teenage girls were in the room, both sitting on the bed, clutching each other in fear. The sergeant, the corporal, and another soldier stepped into the cool of the house.

"Look around. There is only one other room," the girl said, pointing at the doorway. "My bedroom. I'm the oldest now."

"Show me," he said, barely able to contain himself.

She nodded and stepped into her bedroom. She turned around. "See? I—"

The sergeant clapped a heavy hand on her mouth and wrapped his other arm around her back, forcing her onto the bed. He heard a commotion in the other room. His men, no doubt, having their way with the younger ones.

The sergeant's broad nose nearly touched the girl's face. Her eyes flared with fear.

"I'm gentle, I promise. I don't like to hurt girls. Don't scream, don't bite. I'll be quick, and then we'll be on our way. Okay?"

She nodded yes beneath his hand, and he felt her body relax a little.

"Good. Quick and gentle. I promise," he said again with a brotherly smile. He stood back up and unbuckled his belt, dropping his trousers. She saw the hardness of his manhood beneath his boxers. He pulled them down, then fell back on top of her, grabbing her shoulders.

"Here, let me help you," she said, reaching one hand to the back of his neck as if to kiss him.

"Yes, good," he grunted as she guided him toward her face.

The knife blade in her other hand plunged straight into his ear. His scream lasted until the tip of the thin steel blade plowed through his ear canal and into his brain stem. His body flew up and away from her in a violent spasm, then crashed to the floor.

Mossa stood in the doorway, his eyes smiling beneath the veil. He wiped his own bloody dagger on his trouser leg.

"You did well, little sister."

"My sisters?"

"Untouched. We killed the others before they could harm them." He sheathed his blade.

The girl leaped out of bed and kicked the sergeant's corpse in the head, then spat on it.

"Bring me a hundred more of them, Mossa, I beg you!"

= 30 =

The village of Anou
Kidal Region, Northwest Mali
7 May

Early and Pearce scrambled up to the third floor of the only three-story building in the village. It was fifty meters back from the wall, but it had the best view. Pearce and Early shouldered their rifles and muscled the big Pelican cases up the narrow stairs.

Inside the house was a horror show, not unlike the many poor houses Pearce had cleared out in Iraqi and Afghan villages after the *haji*s had been inside. Blood, bullet holes, busted furniture. And the requisite pile of human feces in the corner. Predators marking their territory. They climbed a rickety wooden ladder through the hole in the roof and took up their position.

Pearce lay flat as possible on the roof to keep out of sight of the army troops who would be scanning the rooflines for trouble. He couldn't see the street below him from his position, but the roar of the BTR's big diesel in the road near his building told him it was almost showtime. A two-foot-long firing tube lay by his side, extracted from an opened Pelican case.

The BTR slammed to a stop at the well, as expected. The hatches were still open. Mossa was sorely tempted to toss the grenades inside, but Pearce had authority in his voice when he spoke, the kind of authority that comes only from men who have commanded in battle and lived to tell about it. So Mossa kept to the plan, and he and Moctar rolled four grenades beneath the BTR just as it skidded to a stop. Even the thin bottom-plate armor was too thick for the grenades to penetrate. But that was the point. They didn't want to take any chances and destroy the vehicle.

Moments later, the grenades exploded, shredding all eight tires.

The exploding grenades were Pearce's signal. He stood with the tube launcher and fired, throwing a Switch-blade UAV into the sky. The electric-motored aircraft carried a high-definition video camera, laser target designator, and Wi-Fi transmitter.

Red Berets piled out of the trucks as fast as they could dismount, NCOs shouting orders in their ears. The soldiers fanned out and raced for the sand-brick wall for cover. Out on the road, they were completely exposed. The wall was their only protection outside of the village. Without it, they'd be sitting ducks.

The big transport trucks revved their diesels, belching black smoke out of the exhaust pipes as they raced backward out of harm's way.

Pearce was still standing on the roof. The BTR's machine gun opened up, pulverizing the mud-brick buildings in the square. The building shuddered under the soles of his boots, as the BTR had turned its massive gun in his direction.

Moctar and Mossa charged the BTR. The side hatches slammed shut as the two Free Men clambered up the back of the vehicle and onto the top, emptying their AK-47s into the open roof hatches. The 14.5mm gun silenced. Mossa listened. Nothing. He peered in. Blood and brains were splattered all over the compartment filled with gun smoke.

haven't flown one of these for a while," Early said. "You should let me work that thing." He nodded at the weapon at Pearce's feet, a specially modified M-25 grenade launcher with a high-capacity magazine.

"No worries. The Switchblade's on autopilot. You're just the backup."

Pearce pulled on a pair of what looked like old-school mountaineering sunglasses. They were actually a mil-spec version of MetaPro holographic glasses loaded with Pearce Systems proprietary targeting software. The MetaPro glasses were mirrored to the Switchblade's onboard camera that broadcast a 3-D stereoscopic image of the battlefield inside the MetaPro's HD lenses, giving Pearce a holographic bird's-eye view of the Red Berets crouching behind the wall.

Early watched incredulously as Pearce's fingers danced in the empty air in front of his face, swiping, sizing, and tapping a giant invisible touchscreen.

"What the hell are you doing?"

"Selecting targets."

Once the targets were selected, the Switchblade's computer transmitted data to the programmable "smart" laser-guided 25mm grenades in the M-25 launcher for a firing solution.

Pearce snatched up the bull-pup-styled grenade launcher, pulling the M-25 buttstock tightly into his shoulder.

He fired, putting all twenty rounds in the air.

———————

The Mali soldiers hugging the wall had nowhere to hide. Airbursting grenade rounds exploded just a meter above their heads. Pure carnage. It was as if Pearce jammed a twelve-gauge shotgun against the back of each man's skull and pulled the trigger.

The Tuareg Hiluxes leaped across the sandy moon-scape. Two raced for the fleeing trucks, stuck running backward in a single line of retreat along the hard-packed road. The three other Toyotas flew across the sand and rounded the wall, firing in enfilade at the few surviving soldiers, limping away as fast as their wounded bodies could manage or cowering by the wall clutching their unfired weapons. A half dozen Red Berets who screwed up enough courage to race through the gate toward the well before the grenade attack were cut down by the 14.5mm gun in the immobilized BTR. Mossa had turned the gun around and stood in the turret firing the big weapon, his feet slipping in blood.

The first two Toyotas quickly caught up with the trucks. Like ships o' the line in the age of sail, the pickups came along broadside the five trucks, brandishing their machine guns. The trucks didn't stop. The first Toyota fired short bursts and blew out the tires of the rearmost truck, the first in the line of retreat. The tires shredded, wrapping around the rear axles and flipping the big truck over. The next truck in line slammed its brakes, slowing its crash into the toppled vehicle. The remaining three trucks slammed their brakes in time, avoiding a crash altogether. As tempting as it was to open fire on the vehicles, Mossa gave strict orders to capture the fuel in their tanks. Of course, he gave no orders when it came to the surrender of the drivers. None was needed.

In the desert, the Free Men took no prisoners.

= 31 =

The village of Anou

Kidal Region, Northwest Mali

7 May

Another gunshot beyond the wall ended someone's misery. It was a kind of mercy, Pearce knew. If a wounded man were left out here beneath the blazing sun, his death would come eventually, but only after insufferable pain over many hours—if he was lucky. Wild dogs might finish the job, too. War was a bloody business, and suddenly he was up to his neck in the crimson tide all over again. But today was different. It wasn't cold-blooded revenge. He'd picked up a gun again to protect his friends. That was different from butchering a ruthless foe to even a score. His soul was still reeling from Johnny's death, but he needed to keep that dark memory locked up inside for now.

The Tuareg fighters were draining the army trucks and the BTR of their last drops of fuel so they could fill their Hilux fuel tanks to the brim. Jerry cans were recovered from the trucks, too, and a few more rounded up in the village. Those would get filled with diesel next and loaded into the pickups for transport. Fuel was harder to come by than water in the desert.

Pearce repacked the Switchblade UAV into the firing tube. The spring-loaded wings, tail, and ailerons folded up easily. There were two more compressed-air firing chargers left in case Pearce needed to relaunch in the near future. The rest of the South African UAV combat system was already packed up in separate smaller storage cases and all of them placed back in the big Pelican, a completely self-contained unit. Unfortunately, Pearce had fired all of the programmable X-25 grenades, but at least the little UAV's camera could still be of use. And there was still his M4 carbine with the 40mm grenade launcher, and Early's vicious SCAR-H.

"Never even got a shot off, thanks to you and your model airplane. Speaking of which, that new rig of yours is something else. Love the modification." The M-25 grenade launcher was designed for line-of-sight operation, meaning that the operator had to see the enemy location in order to aim it. With the aerial surveillance modification, not only was there almost nowhere for a bogey to hide, but the operator could "fire and forget" since the UAV remained locked on each target.

"You would've been more impressed if you'd seen anybody get inside a building. When the bad guys play hide-and-go-seek, the M-25 always wins."

"Can I keep this?" Early asked, tapping the M4.

"I have to give it back to the owner, otherwise I lose my five-dollar deposit. So tell me about this Mossa guy."

"He's a pretty big deal."

"Then what's he doing out here?" Pearce waved a hand at the tiny village.

"The Tuaregs are like the Kurds. Big enough to be located in several countries, but not strong enough to carve out their own nation for themselves. Well, maybe until now. Tribes and clans from Algeria, Niger, Libya, and Mali are gathering around him, or at least the idea of him."

"What's so special about him?"

Early shook his head. "Hard to explain. But he has the same effect on his people that Richard the Lion-Hearted had on the English when they were waiting for him to come home."

"Sounds like you've gone native. Dreams of *Lawrence of Arabia*?"

"No, nothing like that. I'm only here as long as Cella's here, and now that her daughter's out, I'm hoping she'll follow soon."

Pearce set the firing tube into its molded slot inside the case. "Last I heard, you were grouse hunting in Argentina, living the life of a retired country gentleman."

"Grouse hunting gets boring after a while. They don't shoot back."

"I'd consider that an advantage myself." Pearce shut the lid of the Pelican case and snapped the throw latches.

"I'm not exactly crazy about it either, but for the money Cella's father is paying me, I can put up with it a while longer."

"How much is getting killed worth these days?"

"It was a one-off. Ten thousand a week, tax-free. But it was only supposed to be for three weeks, not three months."

"Why'd you step back into it? I mean, really?"

Another gunshot rang in the distance.

"You know how it is," Early said. He glanced over the village. "I know there's something wrong with me, but I love this shit."

Pearce frowned. "Killing poor stupid bastards in uniforms?"

"No. That's the worst part of it. But you know as well as I do there are bad guys out there. Someone has to stop them."

"We did. About fifty of them. And every one of those dead mutts out there thought *we* were the bad guys."

"So who's gone native?"

"Not me, Mikey. I hate the bad guys, too. I'm just saying, let the Tuaregs and the Kurds and all the others fight their own damn battles and get your ass back to that beautiful wife of yours and those two gorgeous kids."

"That's the plan, brother," Early said with a groan as he stood. "And it may even happen, thanks to you."

Pearce and Early made their way back to the well, looking for Mossa. Early called ahead on his shoulder mic. Mossa was in Ibrahim's little storefront, studying the ancient French military map still hanging on the wall.

"I'm going to check on Cella. Holler if you need me," Early said to Pearce. He left for another house. That left Pearce alone with Mossa.

"What is your plan now?" Pearce asked.

"How well do you know the history of the Sahara, Mr. Pearce?" Mossa still stared at the map.

"It's a big pile of sand. I hear armies get lost in it pretty often."

"Yes, they do, since at least the ancient Romans who crossed over here two millennia ago. The bones of many invaders are covered in the shifting sands. But it wasn't always desert. There are cave paintings in the Tassili N'Ajjer that date to 6000 B.C. Do you know what they depict?"

Pearce shrugged. "No idea."

"Grass, rivers, antelope, buffalo, cattle, elephants, giraffes. Even hippos. But so much has changed, has it not?"

"The world is always changing."

Mossa ran his fingers over the expanse of paper desert. "And men must change with it. Even my people. But the Sahara is still our home, the land Allah himself has given us." He turned to face Pearce, his own face still hidden by the indigo *tagelmust*.

"So you want to defend this place?" Pearce asked.

"Why not?"

"Because it's a shit hole, if you'll pardon the expression."

"But it's our shit hole."

"It's not defensible, especially if the government decides to bring in any kind of long-range ordnance or aircraft. They'll pound this place to dust."

Mossa nodded. "I agree. But letting go of things is becoming harder in my advancing years. If we leave, then the Ganda Koy win."

"And if you stay, you die."

Mossa stepped to the doorway and watched his men prepping their vehicles. "The way you fight is not our way. But it was . . . impressive."

"War is changing, too."

"You stayed to fight for your friend?"

"Yes."

"And Cella?" Mossa turned to face Pearce again.

"No." But Pearce thought about it. "And yes."

"You knew her before?"

"She was a doctor. Saved the life of a friend. But that was a long time ago, in a different war."

"I understand."

"Dorotea is your granddaughter. Cella must have been with one of your sons."

"She was the woman of my oldest son, Rassoul. He was also a doctor. He entered Paradise three years ago." Mossa's eyes bored into Pearce's. "If we stay, you will stay?"

"If Mike stays, yes. He is my friend."

"Mr. Early is a good man. A good fighter."

"Better than you know, on both counts. Don't waste him."

Mossa laughed. "I have no intention of wasting him. Or you. No, you are correct. This place is indefensible. Let the sand have it." Mossa crossed back over to the map and jabbed a finger into it. "We'll retreat to here, in the mountains."

"Do you have other men who can join us?"

"Not yet. The Malians have struck here, here, and here." Mossa touched the map at each battle site. "And there is trouble throughout the region. The chiefs and elders asked permission to defend themselves as they see best, which is the best strategy now. We are like grains of sand in the wind. The best we can hope to do is keep stinging the eyes of the lions. We are still not yet strong enough to offer a pitched battle to a standing army."

"Will the Mali army follow us into the mountains?"

"They will follow wherever I go. It seems that I am the prize. But we can hold them off quite well there."

"Then we're off to the mountains."

"And soon. There are no survivors today, but perhaps one of their officers was able to get off an emergency message during the attack, quick as it was."

"Even if they didn't get off a message, the fact that none of them will be calling in a report will alert their command. Are there other army units in the area?"

"None more than a day's journey away."

"Then you're right. We need to get rolling."

"Any word from your pilot?"

"Not yet." Pearce checked his watch. "She won't be landing for another twenty minutes. I told her to maintain radio silence for security."

"That is wise. Please be sure to inform me when you have news of my granddaughter."

"Of course. But don't worry, Judy is a great pilot."

Pearce smiled to comfort the old man. He was telling the truth. Judy was a great pilot, but he was still worried. Murphy's Law FUBAR'd more ops than he cared to remember. He wouldn't relax until Judy and the girl were safe on the ground.

= 32 =

Judy was still five minutes from the Niger border when the alarm blared. An air-to-air missile had locked onto the Aviocar. Her scope indicated the attack plane was some thirty miles behind her and closing fast. A military aircraft, no doubt.

She had no information at all about the Mali air force, but Ian had mentioned something about the Soviets earlier so she hoped that the jet behind her was just as antiquated, even if it was lethal. But even old, the jet behind her was still a heck of a lot faster than her two turboprops. She wondered how much time she'd have before it would launch its missiles. She guessed the military pilot probably required a visual confirmation. In her mind, that gave her thirty seconds, max.

Judy glanced over at the girl in the copilot seat. She was still out cold, which was good. Judy didn't want the child awake, especially if things went sideways.

Judy stomped on the right rudder control and slammed the yoke into the firewall, banking the plane hard into a steep turning dive, hoping beyond hope that she could shake the radar lock. The negative g's tingled in her gut and her rear end lifted out of the chair, pressing her small torso against the seat harness. Three seconds later, she reversed, stomping on the left rudder control and yanking the yoke as hard as she could toward her chest, lifting the plane in a steep left climb, pressing her hard against the chair at the same time her body rolled against the belts. She was riding the roller coaster from hell. Judy glanced over at the sleeping girl, her head pressed against the bulkhead. The alarm kept blaring. Not good. Maybe she deserved it, but the girl didn't.

One last shot.

The Aviocar was a flying truck, nothing more. No weapons, and slow as molasses. Electronic countermeasures and chaff would be a waste. Any jet jock worth his salt would get a look at the old girl, flip on his gun switch, and have some target practice. A flying fish in a barrel. But Ian had devised a trick. He removed the active homing radar unit from a decommissioned AIM-54 Phoenix antiaircraft missile and installed it in the Aviocar. Maybe the old transport plane couldn't carry a long-range antiaircraft missile like the Phoenix, but it had the wherewithal to carry a small, secondary radar, didn't it?

Here goes nothing, Lord, was the best Judy could pray under the circumstances. She punched a button on her console, painting the jet behind her with her own air-to-air missile radar signal, just like the one she was experiencing. Now, as far as the pilot behind her was concerned, a U.S. Navy Hornet just locked on him with a Phoenix missile. There was only one thing he could do if he wanted to survive the engagement.

Run.

And that's just what he did. The radar blip on Judy's scope angled hard off her tail and reversed course, dropping altitude and picking up speed, racing away like a scalded cat, silencing the shrieking missile alarm in her cockpit ten seconds later.

Thanks, Ian, I owe you one, she thought. It had been a long time since she'd last seen him. Time to fix that. Maybe she'd even buy him a beer.

The village of Anou
Kidal Region, Northwest Mali

Pearce, Early, Mossa, and his fighters gathered up several cans of ammo and five machine guns from the dead Malian troops and loaded them into the Toyotas. But there were too many AK-47s to haul, so they spiked the barrels by bending them into right angles. Any pistols they didn't take they disassembled, ruining the firing springs and tossing the rest of the gun parts in all directions. Anything else lethal or of use to the Mali army was loaded into the trucks and the trucks set on fire. The BTR was left intact, but Moctar rigged a booby-trap grenade beneath the driver's seat. The first man who sat in it would trigger the spring-loaded mechanism.

Mossa dismissed Early and Pearce for the last bit of business. As non-Muslims, they were forbidden to touch Muslim corpses, and Mossa assumed that most or all of the dead Red Berets were Muslim. Besides, Westerners already had a grim view of his people, perhaps especially of Tuaregs, so he didn't want the two Americans around to watch. Mossa and his men gathered up each of the Red Berets and sat them up against the wall, facing away from the city. Then they placed the spiked AK-47s in each of their laps. Now the Red Berets formed a gruesome palace guard for the massacred village. If nothing else, Mossa hoped the image would strike dread into the next column of Mali soldiers who dared approach.

Pearce and Early found Cella in one of the houses tending to one of the raped girls lying on a bed. Cella rung out a wet cloth and set it on the girl's forehead, then motioned for the two men to follow her.

"How is she doing?" Early asked.

"Not well. She lost a lot of blood." Cella pulled out a pack of cigarettes and offered them. Early took one, and Pearce passed. Cella flicked a Zippo and lit Early's, then hers.

"Judy called in. They landed fine, no problems. Holliday will be picking up your daughter soon."

"Who is Holliday?"

"A friend. The chargé d'affaires at the American embassy in Niamey. He's making all of the legal arrangements, and he's already contacted your father."

"Please thank him for me." Cella took another drag.

"Why don't you thank him yourself? Let's get out of here."

Cella shook her head. Her thick honey brown hair was shiny with oil. Pearce could only imagine the last time she'd bathed. "I'm needed here. These are my people now."

Pearce glanced at Early. *Help me out here.*

"Don't look at me. I came here to bring her home. That was three months ago."

"You're running around in the middle of a civil war. You've got no business being here, especially now that your daughter is gone."

"My husband is dead, but Mossa remains my father-in-law. He is good to me and good to his people. But they have no access to medical care, and that is what I can give them. You of all people should know this."

"And your daughter? Doesn't she deserve a mother?"

Cella's blue eyes flared. "She deserves a father, too." She took a last drag, dropped the cigarette, and crushed it under her boot. "Look what happened to him."

Thirty minutes later, Mossa, Cella, Early, and Pearce gathered at Ibrahim's store. The boy was carefully folding his grandfather's map into a square for safekeeping.

"We'll leave very soon. It will be crowded in the jeeps with you two new men, and the five women—"

"Four. We just lost one," Cella said. She turned to Pearce. "The one you asked about."

"Daughter, you decide where the women ride. It will be a long journey and with few stops."

"What about me?" the boy asked. He kept folding the yellowed paper.

"You will ride with Humaydi. He has two sons your age."

The boy shook his head. "I will ride with you." His fingertips carefully pressed the ancient map creases.

Mossa stared at the boy, unused to such defiance. He gave orders in battle, men obeyed, men died. But this child?

The boy looked up at him, his eyes wounds.

Mossa nodded. "You will ride with me."

The boy made the last fold, forming a neat square, not saying a word. It was settled, then.

Pearce's phone rang. It was Judy. They chatted briefly, but his phone died. No charge.

"My daughter?" Cella asked.

"She's fine. With the ambassador now, heading back to the American embassy."

"Thank God," Mossa said, shutting his eyes briefly.

"Your father is scheduled to arrive late tonight on a chartered flight. If everything goes well, he'll depart again with her back to Italy in the morning. Judy will only call back if there's a problem. That is, if I can get this charged up."

"They've got universals in the trucks. You can charge it up on the way out," Early said.

Mossa turned to Pearce. "Thank you, Mr. Pearce. For everything." He extended his hand.

"Glad it all worked out." They shook. "Now we need to get you to your mountain."

= 33 =

T he French Foreign Legion patrolled the barren stretch of desert with the permission of a reluctant Algerian national government. Cocaine shipments from Bolivia had been making their way into Europe through the porous sands of the Algerian Sahara, an ironic twist to the Americans' War on Drugs. The Algerians appeared helpless to stop it, though the French government suspected that certain corrupt officials in Algiers profited by the venture. The French decided to take matters into their own hands.

The French government generally, and the French army in particular, had been stretched beyond the breaking point since the Great Recession began in 2008. But the French Foreign Legion had a long history in this desert and, despite their limited resources, volunteered a section of their best. Working from incomplete Interpol reports and questionable intelligence from Algeria's security service, the Département du Renseignement et de la Sécurité, today's patrol was heading for a stretch of remote highway that was reportedly used as a temporary airfield for drug shipments.

First Lieutenant Pyotr Krasnov rode at the head of his small column of five Renault Sherpa 3As, low-profile trucks that looked like aerodynamic Humvees. A Russian national, he previously served with distinction in the 98th Guard Airborne Division as a sergeant in the South Ossetian War, but he was put under house arrest pending a court-martial after assaulting an officer he considered cowardly. He avoided prosecution only by escaping the camp and fleeing the country.

Now Krasnov proudly wore the *kepi* of the French Foreign Legion. A tattoo of huge block letters ran the length of his muscular right forearm that read LEGIO PATRIA NOSTRA—"the Legion is my Fatherland." He was willing to fight and die for France because the Legion had given him a home, no questions asked. Bald and thick like a power lifter, the two-meter-tall ex-paratrooper was as tough as they came in one of the world's toughest fighting units. He was one of the few foreign nationals to fight his way up into the officer corps, making him an even rarer breed of elite warrior.

Lieutenant Krasnov hated the jihadists. He had had a bellyful of them on his tour in southern Afghanistan, and he'd seen the carnage they wrought over the years in suicide bombings in his former country, particularly the fanatical Chechens and their murderous assaults against hospitals, theaters, and even schools. He was happy to be chasing the scum today, but if the intel wasn't any better than what he'd received over the last several weeks, he expected this to be another waste of time and fuel. His column raced along the flat paved road at 120 kph just in case any IEDs were deployed and his Sherpas blasted out electronic jamming signals to prevent remote IED detonations. A large IED could tear even armored vehicles like his in half like a soft baguette.

"Lieutenant, do you see that?" His driver, a lanky American kid, pointed at a man in the road far up ahead waving a white cloth vigorously over his head.

Krasnov pulled up a pair of field glasses. The man in the road was obviously an American or European. His long blond hair was matted with sweat and tucked under a salt-stained ball cap. His big, bushy beard made him look like a Viking, even from this distance, and he wore a civilian uniform of some sort, but Krasnov couldn't quite make out the logo. A Nissan pickup was parked near him on the side of the road in the sand, its hood up.

Krasnov radioed the rest of the convoy to prepare to stop. His driver tapped the brakes and began to slow, downshifting as the tachometer drifted toward zero. The driver eventually stopped, pulling even with the broken-down truck. Krasnov radioed to the other troopers to remain in their Sherpas, but he dismounted along with the two privates riding in his command vehicle, a

dour blue-eyed Pole and a hawk-faced Spaniard. The
American driver remained seated, engine idling.

"Hey! Thank God! You speak English?" the man
said. His white teeth smiled through his wild beard. His
name was stitched on the sweat-soaked shirt of the faded
British Petroleum uniform: "Magnus Karlsen." The
accent sounded Nordic to Krasnov. The man certainly
looked the part.

"Yes, I speak English. What are you doing out here?"
Krasnov smiled behind his dark wraparound sunglasses,
but his suspicious eyes darted all around the scene.

The Pole and the Spaniard kept their automatic rifles
slung low as they casually circled around the truck,
checking for weapons and drugs.

"Stupid GPS! It sent me the wrong way. And then
this piece of shit"—Karlsen kicked the Nissan's fender
hard—"decided to run out of petrol on me."

"Swedish?" Krasnov asked.

"Norwegian. I think we are both far away from home."

"You think so?" Krasnov pulled his glasses off and
wiped the sweat off his face with his gloved hand. He
glanced up at the Spaniard, who shook his head no,
indicating nothing unusual about the truck.

"You need some water, Mr. Karlsen?"

"Yes, please. I ran out." He pointed at half a dozen
small empty bottles littering the sand around him.

Krasnov reached into the Sherpa cab and pulled out
an unopened liter bottle of water. He tossed it to the
big Norwegian.

"Thank you." He cracked it open and drained it in

one long chug, the water dribbling down the sides of his mouth onto his beard and shirt. He finished and grunted like a sated Viking would, then crushed the bottle in his thick fist and tossed it. "How about some petrol? Can you spare any?"

Krasnov nodded. "A little. Ten liters should be enough to get you back to town."

"Perfect. Thank you."

Krasnov nodded wordlessly to the Pole, who crossed to the Sherpa and reached for the jerry can.

"You want me to call you in?" Krasnov asked. "Your bosses must be worried."

Karlsen grinned again. He pulled out an old cell phone from his pocket and waved it at Krasnov. "Called in two hours ago, before the battery died. They should have been here by now. You didn't pass them on the way here?"

Krasnov shook his head and said, "No," still scanning the horizon. In the far distance, high in the hazing blue sky, a plane. The Russian shielded his eyes with his gloved hand but couldn't make it out. Too high up. Probably nothing. The windless air stank of diesel fuel now.

The Pole set the jerry can down after filling the Nissan's tank. "Finished, Lieutenant," he muttered.

"Secure that can, and the two of you load back in."

"Yes, sir."

The Norwegian folded himself into the cramped pickup cab and turned the key. The engine coughed for a couple of revolutions and then sputtered to life. "Excellent!" The bearded man threw a big thumbs-up at Krasnov.

"Better get going," Krasnov said. He shut the Nissan's door, leaving his hands on the sill.

Karlsen held out a big, sweaty hand. "You saved my life. I can't thank you enough."

Krasnov hesitated, then shook his hand.

Karlsen nodded his thanks again, slammed the truck into first gear, and sped away past the convoy of Sherpas. Krasnov watched him for a few moments, then keyed the radio mic on his shoulder. "Time to get back to work, gentlemen. And keep the music off. I want everybody on high alert."

The big Russian tapped on the driver's window. It rolled down. "I want you to call that guy in. Have someone run a check on those plates, too."

"Already did, Lieutenant."

Seven hundred meters away, Karlsen slammed the brakes. The rubber squealed on the asphalt.

Krasnov glanced toward the noise. He raised himself up on the Sherpa's step to get a better vantage. Saw Karlsen's truck parked on the road, driver's door open. Where did he go?

Krasnov glanced down at the road beneath his feet, then the sand by the side of the road. He saw it. There.

Too late.

One hundred feet of C4 erupted. Even half a mile away, Karlsen felt the pressure wave. It rocked his truck and spattered sand in his face like buckshot. The earplugs hardly helped, but he covered his ears with his hands, too, and opened his mouth. The air sucked out of his lungs so hard he thought they'd come up through his mouth.

But a second passed and he gasped for air and knew he'd survived. His nose was runny. He pinched it with his fingers. Blood. His ears rang and his head ached. His pagan forefathers would have said that Ragnarök had begun—the end of the world. But, *inshallah*, not yet. At least not for him. Not for Al Rus. Not for the Viking.

The big Norwegian muttered a prayer of thanksgiving to Allah, then stood and brushed himself off. He crawled back into his Nissan and sped back to the scene. Smoke and dust boiled over the explosion site like a fog of doom. On the far side of the road, the Sherpas were gone. A debris field of twisted steel littered the sand. Clearly, no one had survived.

He stopped the truck where the MICLIC had been planted. The mine-clearing line charge was a hundred feet of C4 block assemblies strung together by nylon rope. The deadly charge was given to him by brothers from Fallujah who had retaken that city in 2014. The city was full of U.S. Marine Corps ordnance left behind for the worthless Iraqi army and police—tons of it. Guns, grenades, radios, claymore mines, and even MICLIC.

Al Rus knew that the French would use electronic jammers—that was standard operating procedure against wireless remote IED detonators. But the jammers couldn't stop an old-fashioned hand-cranked generator connected to copper wire. Primitive, but effective, especially in the hands of a trained engineer like Al Rus. The former BP employee had converted to the true Islamic faith, Salafism, when he was stationed in Saudi Arabia. Before he joined AQS, white German jihadi brothers in a Waziristan village taught him how to handle weapons and explosives and took him on their raids into Afghanistan against NATO forces, where he killed his first European infidels. He had a talent for it.

Al Rus stepped back over to his truck and dug around under the seat. He pulled out a radio and called his second-in-command, informing him it was now safe for the plane on the far horizon to land on the road ahead. In an hour, the cocaine would be loaded onto Algerian trucks and shipped north, making its way to the heart of the land of the Crusaders. If depraved Europeans wanted to pay good money for the poison he sold to them, so much the better. That money was used to wage jihad and help the poor and widows, and so it was blessed.

= 34 =

Jasmine Bath's paranoia knew no bounds. She was determined to live long enough to enjoy the wealth she had accumulated over the last few years, and even more determined to enjoy a long and happy retirement, which, according to her schedule, would begin in precisely seven months, given current revenue streams.

It was probably time to get out by then anyway. Computer security was about to make a great leap forward with DARPA's PROCEED initiative, exploring methods that would allow the computation of encrypted data without first decrypting it, even in the cloud, making it virtually impossible for hackers like her to write malware code to break it. Worse, security operations themselves would become automated, just like future combat.

Advanced machine learning algorithms would soon become the security gatekeepers, not only preventing but even anticipating human-designed attacks.

Bath's first line of defense was to remain hidden from the NSA. The easiest trick was to leak NSA training documents to various media outlets under the names of known whistle-blowers. That kept the NSA in a constant state of paranoia and self-limiting defenses as media and congressional inquiries escalated. The NSA simply didn't have time to look for someone like Jasmine, especially not even knowing she was there to begin with.

The most effective tool in Bath's defense arsenal was the alliances she created with other unwitting players in the field. Posing as an anonymous member of various hacktivist groups, Jasmine would empower them with resources that both distracted the NSA and created new targets of national interest. In the last few years, the anarchist hacker group ALGO.RYTHM had made frequent headlines by breaking into DoD computer bases, stealing embarrassing State Department cables, and disabling the LANs of the big national laboratories, then publishing their exploits. Of course, ALGO.RYTHM hackers managed to complete these missions only by following the guided maps through agency software defenses fed to them by Jasmine Bath. If ALGO.RYTHM hackers got sloppy with their opsec, CIOS would dispatch a specialized field operative to pinch off the potential leak, usually with a small-caliber bullet to the brain.

The closest anyone had ever come to identifying Jasmine occurred just weeks after the Utah Data Center at

Bluffdale had gone online. She still wasn't quite sure how he'd picked up her digital scent, but he did, and his abilities were far superior to those of anyone else she'd ever encountered at the Q Group, the NSA's security and counterintelligence directorate. She finally evaded him by destroying his career, falsely linking him to the most recent Utah Data Center catastrophe. It was one of her best ops.

Jasmine knew the security protocols at the UDC because she'd designed half of them while in the NSA's employ. The UDC was NSA's vast, multibillion-dollar server farm, and the crown jewel in its burgeoning intelligence-gathering empire. It was deemed impossible to infect the computers there with any kind of virus thanks to the external firewalls, which suffered tens of thousands of automated attempted hacks daily.

But the internal security procedures were equally important. Those protocols kept any devices from being smuggled in that might carry infectious malware. The NSA knew that it was a USB thumb drive infected with the Stuxnet virus smuggled into the Natanz nuclear facility that wiped out over a thousand Iranian centrifuges. The NSA took every precaution to avoid a similar attack on the UDC.

Every precaution but one, Jasmine determined.

A search of UDC employees uncovered the medical records of a senior programmer at the facility. The fifty-eight-year-old woman had recently had one of the new wirelessly programmed heart pacemakers implanted. The wireless pacemaker was monitored and updated via a cell phone call. All Bath did was hack into the poorly secured mainframe of the medical device manufacturer and install a Stuxnet-like worm on the woman's pacemaker via the cell phone. Once the infected programmer was at her computer station, the self-propagating worm used the pacemaker's wireless capabilities to infect the SCADA system Wi-Fi routers. Those SCADA computers, in turn, controlled the air handler units that cooled the 1.2 million square feet of the vast server farm. Once the air handler units failed—along with the warning alarms and software monitoring the failure, disabled by the same worm—acres of servers overheated and eventually caught fire, destroying 400 terabytes of collected foreign intelligence. While this represented only a small fraction of the total amount of data stored at the UDC, it was an amount of data equal to all of the books ever written in the history of the world.

Internal security inspections investigating the multimillion-dollar catastrophe located the worm, and it was traced back to the home computer of the Q Group investigator who had nearly uncovered CIOS and its operations. His hard drive also contained encrypted links to offshore bank accounts affiliated with the anarchist hacker group ALGO.RYTHM.

The innocent Q Group investigator was swiftly arrested, tried, and convicted. A life ruined, a family bankrupted, all thanks to falsified evidence created and planted by Jasmine Bath.

= 35 =

Adrar des Ifoghas
Kidal Region, Northeastern Mali
7 May

The convoy of five Toyota pickups sped through the desert toward the mountains in a long, steady line, spread out enough that the sand kicked up by the truck in front didn't spatter the windshield of the one behind. Overladen with extra ammo, weapons, gear, and people, they couldn't do top speed for fear of hitting the soft patches of sand and either busting shocks or, worse, spilling the trucks over and tossing their human cargo onto the ground. The ride was hardly smooth, though. The extra weight caused the trucks to rise and fall like a ship on a heavy ocean swell, especially in back where Pearce and Early rode in Mossa's truck. They'd suffered far worse in years gone by, but hours of sweltering heat and stinging sand in an open truck bed wasn't exactly a Disneyland ride, either.

"I'm getting too old for this shit," Early complained through his *shemagh* and aviator glasses. "Bring any Dramamine with you?" Early was on the verge of puking from motion sickness.

"Beats working for a living, doesn't it?" Pearce shouted back.

As they neared the mountains, the sand began to give way to small rocks, then hundreds of larger rounded stones as large as soccer balls as they approached the mountain range. They slowed. The steep hills in front of them were covered with piles of eroded granite blocks, some over five meters tall, like broken teeth thrusting out of a sandy jaw. Impassable by vehicles.

At the first steep incline Mossa signaled a stop and the convoy halted. Early and Pearce jumped out. It felt good to stretch their limbs after hours of riding folded up in the back, crowded in with two other fighters and Pearce's gear. Pearce was the only man without a *tagelmust*. He pulled off his boonie hat and glasses and shook the sand out of his long hair and shaggy beard.

"Didn't exactly come prepared, did you?" Early asked.

"It was supposed to be an extraction, not an insertion," Pearce said.

"There's a dirty joke in there somewhere, but my brain is too rattled to find it."

Mossa had stepped out of the cab and was calling on a handheld walkie-talkie. The boy stood close by him.

Pearce didn't understand the lingo. It certainly wasn't Arabic or Pashto.

"What's he saying?" Pearce asked Early.

Early shrugged. "Beats me. I never picked up on the patois."

"He's calling ahead to his men, though they surely have watched us all the way here. He wants to be sure they don't fire on us on the way up," Cella said. She took a drink out of her canteen and held it out to Early.

"Thanks." Early took a swallow as Pearce glanced up the rising chain of ragged mountains. The tallest peaks in the far distance rose some eight hundred meters.

"On the maps they call this the Adrar des Ifoghas— the mountains of the Ifogha clan," Cella said. "The Imohar have fought many battles here. Algerians, Chadians, the French, and, lately, al-Qaeda Sahara. And yet they still remain."

"How do they survive?" Pearce asked. "There's nothing but rock and sand here."

"The massif has many shallow valleys and wadis, and villages are scattered here and there." She rolled away one of the larger stones with the toe of her boot. A yellow scorpion flared its stinging tail, then fled for the cover of another. "And a few surprises."

Pearce nodded at the top of the hill in front of them. "The welcoming committee."

A dozen Tuareg fighters stood on top of the big granite blocks, faces shrouded in indigo, rifles perched on their hips.

"Now we climb," Mossa said.

"What about those?" Early asked, pointing at the Toyotas.

"They have another purpose," Mossa said. "Grab your boxes, Mr. Pearce."

Pearce pulled the two big Pelican cases out and shouldered his rifle. Early slung his SCAR over his good shoulder.

Mossa barked orders and the trucks sped away back toward Anou, each with a driver and gunner. The rest of his men and everybody else remained, including the four women and the boy.

"Follow my path exactly," Mossa called over his shoulder. Mossa led the way up, snaking his way through the field of stones.

They climbed the mountain in silence, never following a straight line. Sand and rocks crunched beneath Pearce's boots. Some of Mossa's men wore sandals. The women and the boy did, too. Pearce assumed the mountain must be mined. He kept looking for trip wires or other triggers but never spotted any, so they must have all been buried. His practiced eye couldn't spot any of those, either. Every now and then he saw a spent shell casing, the brass sometimes gleaming, sometimes tarnished. Depending on how long ago they'd been fired, he assumed. He counted five different calibers he recognized, and a couple more he wasn't sure of.

The sun was kneeling down toward the far horizon behind them, but the heat was still miserable, though perceptibly less miserable than before. Pearce felt like the slacker in the group, struggling to keep up the pace on the rising grade. His thighs burned and his clothes were drenched. He realized how badly he'd let himself go. It had been six months since he'd done any serious running or any other kind of regular workout. The Tuaregs moved easily through the stony field and the heat. Even Early seemed immune to it. Halfway up they picked their way through a steep trench, whether natural or man-made Pearce wasn't sure. The entire approach up the mountain was a natural barrier to all kinds of vehicles, wheeled or tracked. A great defensive position. No wonder the Tuaregs had been able to stand their ground here.

A few minutes later they were close to the summit of granite boulders. Mossa's fighters dropped down from the rocks and came down to greet them. Pearce couldn't understand a word of what they said, but the laughter, backslapping, and hand gestures were universal. Comrades greeting comrades after a harrowing, successful mission, recounting the action, moment by moment. Pearce knew when they reached the part about the Switchblade UAV and grenade launcher, because the entire group turned nearly in unison toward him in stunned silence.

"Mr. Pearce, come meet my commanders," Mossa said, gesturing with his hand.

Pearce ambled over to the knot of indigo turbans and combat fatigues. He felt strong hands clapping his back now, too, as he pressed in closer. Strange that the men still didn't uncover their faces, he thought.

Mossa introduced him to the local commanders, each the head of his own small clan, and a fighting leader in his own right. Fierce, sharp eyes shined beneath the headdresses as Mossa named each man and listed his particular prowess in battle or recent victory. Many had fought for Gaddafi in the Libyan army. The old dictator had recruited hundreds of Tuareg fighters over the years and were considered some of the best soldiers under his command. When the regime fell, most Tuaregs fled back to their native homelands with as many weapons as they could carry. Too closely identified with the murderous Gaddafi regime and hated by ethnic Libyans, the Tuaregs knew the wrath of the foreign rebels leading the Libyan revolution—many of whom were radical Islamic jihadists—would soon turn on them as well.

Pearce nodded his head slightly to each in deference, and nodded further as he acknowledged each man's honorific.

"And what of you, Mr. Pearce? I know nothing of you, except that you are friends with Mr. Early and my daughter-in-law. But first, explain to my men the nature of the weapon you unleashed on the dogs in Anou."

Pearce hesitated. Since he was a kid growing up in the wilds of Wyoming he'd been a loner. The only son of a drunken, angry father, he took solace fishing and hunting in the mountains by himself, or lost himself in books by the fire at night. Even when he served with the CIA he'd mostly been alone behind enemy lines or in very small groups of fighters. Both his nature and his training drove him to stay in the background, unseen, unnoticed—until he struck. He hated being the center of attention of anything, whether it was a toast at a wedding or a sales pitch to a group of potential clients. He was uncomfortable even now, though it only involved explaining to a curious group of Tuareg warriors the technical aspects of a new weapons system. But Pearce knew the cultures of the East. He dared not embarrass or shame Mossa by refusing his invitation to share his exploits.

So Pearce relented, explaining the basics of the modified M-25 system. But he didn't break open the Pelican case and pull out the gear to show them.

"And you are American military?" Mossa asked. He was translating for one of his men.

"No."

"CIA?" Mossa asked. A wave of murmuring swept through the group. None of them apparently spoke any English, but the dreaded three-letter word was universally recognized.

"No." Technically, true. Pearce had been out of the service for a decade.

"Then how do you come by such weapons?" another man asked through Mossa.

"I own a company that develops these weapons. We train others for money, and sometimes we sell the drones, too."

Drones! The Tuaregs muttered the hated word to themselves over and over. Another American word understood and feared the world over. Some of them were clearly agitated. Pearce knew that the American government had sent drones to help the Libyan rebels. Tuareg soldiers in the Libyan army must have died because of that decision.

"You've come to fight for us?" a man called out in Tamasheq. Mossa translated.

"No. I came to help my friend." He patted Early on the back. "Now he is safe. Now I must leave," Pearce said.

Pearce saw the disappointment in their eyes. A few even glared at him. Did they think he was a coward?

"Come. We need to make plans for your departure," Mossa said. He clapped an arm around Pearce's shoulder, a sign of his favor to the dissemblers, and led the way.

"Mossa!" A man high up on the rocks pointed just moments before Pearce heard the *whump-whump-whump* of rotor blades hammering the air.

An attack helicopter roared in the distance, a thousand feet off the deck, barreling straight for their position. Pearce had to shield his eyes to see it. The chopper was framed by the blinding circle of the sun, but its huge, ugly frame was familiar. He'd seen them before, up close and personal, but he also knew their history. In the 1980s, the Soviets hunted Afghan *mujahideen* with the big armored Hinds to great effect until the CIA smuggled Stinger missiles into the country. The *mujahideen* feared and hated the big ugly air machines. Ironically, the modern Afghan air force flew them, too. It pissed Pearce off that Afghans were allowed to buy military equipment from their former enemies instead of from the allies who saved their asses. And they bought them with U.S. taxpayer dollars, too.

Down on the plain, four of Mossa's trucks sped four abreast, bouncing and slewing in the sand, racing back for the mountain.

"Where's the fifth truck?" Early asked, then cursed himself. In the far distance he saw a black, oily smudge.

"The Devil's Chariot," Mossa said, binoculars to his eyes. "Mali air force."

That's what the *mujahideen* had called them, too, Pearce remembered. At least when the Hinds were hunting them.

Mossa kept his eyes glued to his binoculars. Spoke an order to Balla. His lieutenant turned and disappeared behind the towering rocks behind them.

The trucks were three, maybe four miles from the mountain, the big chopper half that distance behind them. Didn't have to be an air force general to figure out the math wasn't good for the slower-running Toyotas. The nose of the Hind flashed as its four-barrel Gatling gun opened up. A second later, the air cracked with echoes of machine-gun fire.

Geysers of sand spit up around the speeding trucks.

"They're fucked," Early whispered.

"Not yet, Mr. Early," Mossa said, eyes still glued to his binoculars.

The four trucks suddenly split up, the two on the far ends turning at forty-five-degree angles, the middle two at twenty-seven degrees. Now the pilot had to focus, pick a target.

Balla thundered up with a shoulder-fired SA-24 missile launcher, pulling it onto his shoulder, putting his eye to the scope. He asked Mossa a question with a single word. Pearce could guess the meaning.

"Five kilometers and closing," Mossa said in English, for the Americans' sake.

Early and Pearce exchanged a glance. That missile launcher was a Soviet weapon, nicknamed Grinch in military circles. It was the functional equivalent of the American Stinger missile.

The Hind banked hard left to chase one of the trucks on the far end. The gimbaled machine gun roared again. Sand sprayed around the truck. The other Toyotas turned, chasing the Hind, firing their machine guns. Bullets sparked on the helicopter's heavy armor. No effect.

"Now," Mossa said.

The Grinch puffed, blowing the missile out of the tube, then the missile engine kicked in with a roar. It raced toward the turning Hind, a trail of crooked white smoke marking its path.

The Hind knew a missile had locked on it. The pilot juked hard just as the Grinch missile launched, and dropped antimissile flares.

Too late.

The Hind erupted in a fireball as the finger of smoke slammed into the hull. The top rotor separated from the chopper, pinwheeling away as the rest of the wreckage rained toward the sand.

The Tuaregs cheered and clapped Balla on the back.

"Built in Russia, killed by Russians," Early joked.

"Serves them right," Pearce said.

Mossa turned to Pearce. "That should buy us some time."

= 36 =

Adrar des Ifoghas
Kidal Region, Northeastern Mali
7 May

Mossa led the way.

The boy hovered close to the Tuareg chief. Cella was next, shepherding the four women. Pearce and Early were behind them. Moctar, Balla, and the rest of the fighters took up positions among the rocks, hidden from view. Pearce assumed they were left behind to watch for signs of Mali troops.

Mossa wended his way between two tall pillars of granite split like a V, opening a dark chasm in the mountain. He stepped over the inverted apex of the V and disappeared. The others followed suit. Pearce found himself in a broad, low-ceilinged passageway. He had to duck several inches in order to avoid hitting his head, but the dark air felt like a cool water bath compared to the heat outside. Mossa's LED flashlight washed on the path in front of him. Enough light bounced off the ground that Pearce could make out dim scratchings on the rock walls. An alphabet he didn't recognize. Pearce couldn't tell if they were a hundred years old or a hundred thousand. Didn't care. His pulse was quickening and his legs ached. He was grateful that Moctar and Balla had volunteered to carry his cases.

Pearce wasn't part of the 2001 assault on Tora Bora or Operation Anaconda in 2002, but he'd seen some of the classified after-action photos when he was at The Farm. Al-Qaeda made great use of natural caves like this one in Afghanistan. The Russians had bombed the hell out of the underground sanctuaries but never did the damage that American B-52s were able to inflict. The idea of being buried under tons of rock had never appealed to him, especially after the stories his dad told him about the North Vietnamese and their tunnel complexes. His dad had volunteered a few times to crawl down those holes with nothing but a Smith & Wesson revolver and a flashlight. And those tunnels were made only of dirt. His dad was a helluva storyteller, even when he was drunk, which was most of the time. But the way he'd describe slithering on his belly through the dark underground, twisting around ninety-degree bends, waiting for bayonets or grenades or poisonous snakes to strike out at him from the dark, had made him cry as a child. As a small boy, they sounded like monster stories, but they were true—and they had happened to his father. Crying, of course, meant an ugly sneer from his old man and the back of his thick, gnarly hand, but young Troy was as scared for his father inside of those tunnels as if he had been there himself.

And now he was. Or so it seemed. His heart raced.

No, he reminded himself, you're not under the dirt and on your belly and there aren't any Charlies just around the corner waiting to shoot you in the pitch-black.

A few steps later he emerged out of the short passageway into a tall, spacious cave big enough to fit a house in, and light poured in from a kind of natural chimney that led up to the surface. The light would be dimming any minute when the sun finally set, but for now it was a relief, like when the movie projector finally kicked on inside of a dark theater. Beneath the open chimney hole was a fire pit, smoldering with coals that filled the room with a smoky haze.

Circling the fire pit were several small woven rugs. In a far corner, another collection of rugs. But what really caught Pearce's attention was the collection of ammo boxes, stenciled crates, and stacks of bottled water. Moctar and Balla set Pearce's cases next to them.

Mossa gestured for Pearce to take the rug next to him on his right. The boy immediately plopped down on the rug to Mossa's left. Moctar and Balla headed for the supplies while Cella took the women to the far corner.

Pearce sat down, glad to finally take a load off of his weary legs. It had been a long day. What began as a short flight across the border to pick up Early had turned into an all-day gunfight. No food and little water in the last eighteen hours only added to his fatigue.

"You look tired, Mr. Pearce," Mossa said.

"You're not?"

"Exhausted!" Mossa laughed. "It has been a long day, but a good day. A day of days." He glanced at Early. "How is your arm?"

Early held up his salt-stained arm sling. "Who wants to arm wrestle?"

Mossa chuckled beneath the folds of his *tagelmust*. "We should rest. We have much to talk about later." Mossa clapped Pearce on the knee, then reached up to the end of the indigo cloth and unwrapped his headdress, exposing his face for the first time.

Pearce sensed something in Mossa's gesture. He had imagined what might be underneath all of that cloth. But that was the point, wasn't it? The Tuareg's handsome face was long, with a narrow jaw and medium lips, and his light brown skin was mottled with blue indigo, no doubt sweated off of his garment. His nose was narrow and high-bridged, almost aquiline—maybe Pearce imagined a Roman general somewhere far back in his bloodline. His dark hair was long and straight, but shot through with gray, as was his thick mustache, the only hint of his true age. He had to be at least sixty years old, maybe seventy, Pearce reasoned, if his son was the same age as Cella.

Pearce stole a glance at Early. The big former Army Ranger winked at him. What did the unveiling mean?

Mossa lay down on his side, his head resting on the ten meters of indigo cloth bunched up like a pillow. The boy lay down, too. He wouldn't get his own *tagelmust* until he reached adulthood. With the Mali army on its way, Pearce wasn't sure the boy would get to live that long.

Pearce dreamed of curry stew. Dreamed he was scooping up giant spoonfuls of it into his mouth, tangy and sweet. The dream was so vivid he could smell it. His eyes fluttered open. Battered aluminum pots steamed on bright orange coals, burn marks etched on their sides. A blue metal teapot, too. Clearly, the fire had been built up while he was asleep. The warmth of it actually felt good here in the cave.

Pearce sat up, groggy. He didn't remember falling asleep. He rubbed his eyes, yawned.

"Just in time for chow," Early said. He nodded at the plastic bottle near Pearce's knee. "Drink up."

The cave was black now, illuminated by a half dozen solar-powered lanterns.

Cella and two of the women arrived with small aluminum bowls and spoons. Cella ladled up the contents in the pots into the bowls and the women passed them out. After the men were served, the women got their own food and returned to their corner of the cave to eat.

It was strange for Pearce to see Cella like this, so quiet and unassuming, but yet not subservient. More like an actor playing a role, earnestly. Yes, she was definitely playing a role, he decided, obeying the rules of the clan that had adopted her. But she was also their doctor, and Mossa's daughter-in-law, which gave her an exalted status. She seemed happy, straddling two worlds.

Pearce took a bite. It was hot. Chicken and curry. Not bad.

"Where did this come from?"

"Turkish rations, courtesy of Colonel Gaddafi," Mossa said.

"The curry's good," Early said with his mouth full.

Pearce checked his watch. It was just past nine. He looked at the boy. He was greedily spooning food into his mouth as fast as he could. Mossa rubbed the boy's head with his hand and said something. The boy smiled, and curry dripped down his chin. It was good to see the kid finally smile.

Balla and Moctar were slurping their curry and chatting with each other between hot bites.

Early leaned in close. Whispered. "These guys, taking off the veil? That's a big deal. Means they trust you. It was a month before I ever saw their faces."

"He's righteous?" Pearce whispered, nodding at Mossa.

"Yeah. Good leader, out on point. His people love him. So does *she*." Early nodded over at Cella, not wanting to mention her name.

"What's the story there?"

"Have to ask her."

Cella approached with a tarnished silver tray with small, thick glasses and a box of sugar cubes. She set it down in front of Mossa. She turned to leave.

"Stay, daughter, and drink tea with us."

She nodded her thanks. The boy scooted over, and Cella kneeled next to Mossa.

Steam flumed out of the blue teapot's long open

spout. Mossa leaned over with a rag and picked it up by the handle.

"Black Chinese tea is first brought to a boil," Cella explained.

Mossa lifted the teapot and set the spout near the first glass, then raised the pot dramatically into the air. A long stream of steaming tea poured into the small glass, frothing it up from that height. He lowered the pot just as dramatically, perfectly timing the fall with the filling of the glass, tipping the pot up at the last second, not spilling a drop. He repeated the practiced ritual, one glass after another.

The boy's eyes were wide with excitement. He said something in French.

"What did he say?" Early asked.

"He said, 'Just like my grandfather used to do,'" Cella answered.

Pearce fidgeted, impatient.

Cella laughed. "He's only getting started."

Early nudged Pearce. "You're on Tuareg time now, buddy. Sit back and relax. This will take a while."

Early was right. When Mossa had filled the last glass he set the blue pot down, opened the lid, poured each frothy glass back into the pot, and repeated the process all over again. The old chieftain was completely absorbed in the ritual.

"Guess he never heard of K cups," Pearce said.

"It's their way of processing the tea, blending it and cooling it, until it's just right," Cella said. "But it's really about something more than tea, isn't it?"

"And this is just the first round. There's two more afterwards," Early added.

Mossa spoke as he continued to pour and process with flourish. "The first glass we drink is strong and bitter, like life. The second glass is mixed with sugar, and so is sweeter. Like love."

Mossa lowered the pouring pot, frothing the last glass. He set the pot down, finished with pouring. He picked up the tray and held it toward Pearce. Pearce picked up a glass. It was, indeed, cool to the touch. Mossa passed the tray around and everyone but Cella took one.

"By the third glass, the tea is thin, almost like water, and more sugar is added, and so it is very, very sweet, like candy. And do you know what we call this third glass, Mr. Pearce?"

Pearce shook his head.

Mossa lifted his small glass as he would for a toast, and grinned. "We call that last, sweet glass 'Death.'"

After the last glass of tea, Mossa, Moctar, and Balla rolled cigarettes with fine Egyptian tobacco, filling the room with thick, oily smoke. Pearce declined the generous offer to join them but was surprised to see Early indulge. "When in Rome" was his response, but he seemed to really enjoy it. Confessed he'd taken up the habit again after joining Cella out here in the desert.

"You going native, Mikey?"

"This place grows on you, that's for sure," he said. "Sand, sun, stars. Nice to get off the carousel."

Pearce looked up through the vent hole. A veil of stars and a waning crescent moon. He imagined a band of cavemen sitting in this very spot ten thousand years ago when the ground outside was lush with grass and the hunting was good. He understood what Early was saying. Wondered about Early's wife and kids back in the States, though. He'd get the story later.

Mossa finished his cigarette, savoring the last tendrils of smoke curling up out of his mouth and into his mustache before stabbing it out in the sand. "Time to walk the perimeter. Join me," he said, motioning to Pearce and Early. Balla stayed behind to clean up. Moctar, Mossa's most devout commander, had already left for evening prayers.

The trip back through the low tunnel still bothered Pearce, but it didn't seem as long as the first time, and they soon emerged into the warm night air. More stars. Mossa relieved himself against a rock. Pearce and Early joined him.

The towering stones formed shadows of jagged teeth in the thin moonlight. Pearce felt like he'd been swallowed. Mossa led them station to station, checking on the men at their posts. Three of them had night-vision binoculars—Russian, German, and French.

"Nothing," they each reported. All quiet.

"The Malians hate night fighting, despite all of the training you Americans have given them over the years," Mossa said.

Mossa led them to a perch overlooking the desert floor below.

"What are your plans now, Mr. Pearce?"

"I need to contact my people. Arrange for a flight out of here. I'm guessing I can't leave from the same place I arrived."

"The army will be here in the morning at the latest. There won't be any place for that plane of yours to land."

Pearce turned around. Pinpoints of campfires and firelight all across the mountains. In the distance, a small valley.

"What about over there?"

"The army is like a tide. It can't wash away this rock, but it will crash against it. They will bring in their jets, also. Shoot down any plane they see."

"Any suggestions?"

Mossa thought about that. "The army won't cross into Algeria, not even for me. There is an airfield not far from here on the other side of the border. It should be safe to land your plane there."

"Can you show me on a map?"

"Of course," Mossa said. "But who needs a map?"

"I do. Better yet, GPS coordinates."

"As you wish."

Mossa showed Pearce the journey they would take. Turned out, "not far" meant a six-day journey. Distance, like time, had a different meaning out here. He wondered how many bones were buried in the sand.

= 37 =

Adrar des Ifoghas
Kidal Region, Northeastern Mali
8 May

A megaphone barked in French in his dream. Distant, echoing. Strong mint tea made his mouth water. He woke. Pearce was on his feet before his eyes were fully open. It was dark in the cave, save for the fire pit and one lantern. He glanced up at the chimney hole. Still dark outside. Checked his watch. An hour until sunrise.

"No worries, Mr. Pearce. Just our friends announcing their arrival," Mossa said. He was pouring tea. "Still time to eat."

"What is he saying?"

"An invitation to surrender peacefully. If I refuse, he will come and seize me by force."

Early was rummaging through the food crate. "How

in the hell am I supposed to know what's in these things?" He pulled out a black plastic bag. "It's all in Turkish."

"Think of it as a box of Cracker Jack." Mossa laughed. "Take what you can get."

Early grabbed three bags and hustled back over to the fire. "How do you know about Cracker Jack?"

Mossa feigned personal injury. "I may be a desert brigand and a feared terrorist, but I am not uncivilized."

Pearce scanned the darkened corners of the cave. "Where are the others?"

The electronic voice echoed again. Pearce didn't need to know French to hear the anger and fear.

"Balla and Moctar are out there, preparing to greet our friends. The women were moved to another cave further back for safety, along with the boy. When this is all over, there is a village that will take them in until they can return to their families."

"How did you convince the boy to go with the women?"

"I gave him my pistol and told him to guard the women with his life. The best way to cure a young boy's fears is to give him a man's duty. Even at his age he feels the power of caring for those he loves." Mossa nodded, agreeing with himself. "Yes. He will be a fine warrior someday."

"And Cella?"

"Worried about your 'friend,' Mr. Pearce? Don't. Early has his eye on her. So do I."

"She's doing one last check on the women before we haul out of here," Early said. "Then she'll come with us."

"Us? It's just me, remember?" Pearce had called Judy earlier with the map coordinates for the Algerian airstrip.

"It's a dangerous journey alone," Mossa said. "I will take you myself."

An explosion in the distance.

Pearce knew the sound all too well. "Mortars."

"And so it begins." Mossa smiled, holding out a glass of tea to Pearce.

"And where he goes, I go," Cella said, dashing into the cave, breathless. She dropped down next to Mossa, threw an arm around him in a brief hug. He patted her hand, handed her a tea.

Another explosion.

Pearce felt the earth tremble slightly under his ass. Medium mortar round, a hundred yards downslope. Closer. Still finding the range.

Early cut open the pouches. "Bingo. Looks like crackers, a bag of apricots . . . and chocolate."

Three more explosions walked up the mountain, each closer than the last.

Mossa laughed. "You see? Just like Cracker Jack."

The mortar rounds fell like hailstones on a tin roof. Lots of noise, little effect. Sheltered by tons of granite, most of Mossa's people were hidden in mountain caves or natural spider holes. Heavy weapons opened up below. Diesel engines raced. The symphony of death. Pearce knew the tune well.

"What about aircraft?" Pearce asked. His stolen M4 was slung over his shoulder.

"They know we have missiles, so they will stay above twenty thousand feet. If they drop bombs from that height, they are more likely to hit their own troops. Useless." Mossa burped, checked his watch. "They will begin their advance any minute now." He glanced up at the cave ceiling, listening. The mortars stopped. So did the machine guns. The last echo of gunfire faded into silence.

"This won't take long," Mossa said. "You are welcome to remain in here and have some more tea."

Pearce held out a hand. "After you."

Mossa snatched up his automatic rifle and dashed through the low-ceilinged entrance, Pearce close behind and Early in the rear. They had all helped themselves to ammo and hand grenade stores in the caves. For the first time since he had arrived in Mali, Pearce felt ready to go.

Mossa led them to a covered lookout nestled in tall stones and pointed out the battlefield, then the sky. Vultures circled overhead in the early-morning light. He pointed them out. "They always know, even before the first shots." Three lines of black Malian soldiers in camo threaded their way up the hill behind three BTRs just like the one back in Anou, each line about a hundred yards apart. They met no resistance.

The southernmost APC was the first to broach the deep trench, taking a steep angle of attack to minimize the downward slope. When the front wheels crested the far end of the trench, the nose of the vehicle pointed nearly skyward, like a whale breaching the surface of the ocean.

Shhhhttt—BOOM! An RPG slammed into the bottom deck of the personnel carrier, easily penetrating the thin armor. The vehicle erupted in flames. Even up here, Pearce could hear the screams. The soldiers who followed too closely behind were killed by the explosion or burned, too, and the others farther back driven away from the intense heat. A few still had their wits and fired in the direction of the RPG smoke trail. The other two columns fired wildly at the rocks in front of them, too, hoping to hit something.

The big 14.5mm machine guns on the surviving BTRs opened fire. They stopped short of the trench line, waiting for their accompanying troops to clear the way for other RPG teams hiding up ahead. Officers and sergeants shouted at the cowering troops, who finally pressed on, pushing through the trench first, then up into the steeper inclines, throwing grenades, firing rifles.

Meeting no resistance, they advanced more confidently up the hill, but the BTRs stayed put, offering covering fire with their heavy weapons.

Mossa let the soldiers climb farther up the hill. Towering piles of granite and basketball-sized stones broke up the neat columns, and the geologic formation of the mountain face gradually funneled the Malians into a paralyzed mass in the middle of the slope.

This was the moment Mossa had been waiting for. He radioed Balla and Moctar as he activated a remote-control switch.

The ridgeline opened up in a volley of machine-gun fire, tearing into the front rank of troops, dropping them. The others hit the deck or stepped back.

The ground erupted behind them as an electronically activated land mine exploded, mowing down a half dozen men in the rear. The mass of soldiers instinctively surged forward. Another explosion tore into the squad in front.

They were trapped.

Panicked shouts as bullets tore into their ranks. The big diesels on the BTRs roared to life, belching smoke as drivers threw them into reverse.

A Mali soldier jumped up and ran back down the hill with long, determined strides, bullets spanging on the rocks around him. Miraculously, he didn't hit a mine. Another soldier leaped up without his rifle and followed suit, but bullets stitched across his back and he tumbled into the sand, triggering an explosion.

Mindless panic erupted as the soldiers leaped up and scattered, mines exploding, bullets flying. One by one they dropped as they fled, or were ripped apart by the explosions at their feet. Shards of granite swept their ranks like shrapnel.

Mossa watched the carnage unfold, emotionless. Like killing a goat for supper.

CRACK! A bullet exploded against the rock just above his head.

Pearce knocked the Tuareg down and covered him with his body.

"Where?" Pearce asked Early.

"Eight o'clock, about five hundred yards up on the ledge." Early hunkered down behind a boulder, signaling the direction with a stab of his finger.

"You all right?" Pearce asked Mossa.

"Still alive."

Now Tuareg mortars opened up. Sand geysered on either side of the fleeing BTRs. Gunfire raked the sand and rocks around the few remaining soldiers still able to run, fleeing for their lives. Corpses littered the mountainside along with the wounded.

Another sniper round smashed into the stone above their heads. They were out of his sights now, but he was still on the hunt, hoping for a random strike.

Malian soldiers down the hill who had found enough cover feebly fired back up at the rocks. Enough fire, though, to keep everyone's head down.

Pearce had only one 40mm grenade for the M4 in his hand, but it had only a four-hundred-meter range. And there was no way he was going to get into a pissing match with a trained sniper, swapping five-hundred-yard shots with a gun ill-suited for the purpose.

"Sit tight," Pearce told Early, then dashed back into the cave where he'd spent the night. A minute later, he emerged with the unopened Pelican case he'd been hauling around since he'd arrived in Anou. He popped open the lid.

More rounds cracked into the rocks above Early and Mossa.

"What new toy do you have now?" Mossa called out.

Pearce uncrated an electrically powered Hybrid Quadrotor, modified for the South African Recces. With four rotors for vertical lift and one for pushing like a plane propeller, the HQ didn't need a runway. Pearce pulled out the controller tablet and hit the auto-launch button. The vertical rotors fired up, kicking up sand like a leaf blower, blasting the drone into the sky. It hit the preprogrammed altitude of five hundred feet in seconds. The onboard camera automatically activated and streamed a live image onto the controller tablet. Pearce quickly found the sniper on the ridge and tapped his image. A red box overlay indicated that the target had been acquired.

"Here goes nothing," Pearce muttered, and tapped the strike button.

The HQ didn't hesitate. It raced another thousand feet higher, paused at the apex, then dove headlong toward the clueless sniper, exploding on impact. Five pounds of ultra-high-explosive material vaporized the shooter. The "suicide" drone had worked perfectly.

Pearce scooted back over to Mossa and Early. "All clear, but keep covered up. There might be another one."

"Not likely," Mossa said. "Look."

The three men surveyed the battlefield. The two BTRs were long gone, while the third still roared with flames, black smoke boiling into the morning sky. The few survivors on the mountainside were badly wounded, clutching their guts, moaning, bleeding, dying.

Another goddamned killing floor, Pearce thought, and there he stood in the middle of it. Again.

Pearce glanced up into the sky. Those birds circling high up on the thermals had seen it all before, too. Thrived on it. He'd seen them everywhere he'd ever been in a fight. Maybe they were following him, like gulls after a fishing boat.

Pearce had no idea how right he was.

= 38 =

What Pearce failed to notice was that not all of those birds circling overhead were the same.

One of them belonged to Guo. It was a hawk drone, covered in lifelike plastic feathers. An amazing example of bio-mimicry at its best. The hawk drone's high-resolution cameras had captured the entire battle, as well as the men who had fought it. The Tuaregs, of course, had their faces covered by their distinctive indigo *tagelmust*s, but the hawk's cameras had captured parts of the faces of two *guǐlǎo*s. The images were being fed into JANUS, DARPA's latest facial-recognition software, recently stolen from the Americans. JANUS focused on facial and skull morphology—pieces of faces, or faces contorted by smiles, shadows, frowns, et cetera—rather than on perfect full-face captures. It took only a few moments for the software in Weng's computer to identify Troy Pearce and Mike Early.

Suddenly, Guo's mission had become exceptionally interesting. He called in the failed battle and the discovery of the two Americans to Zhao, still in Bamako.

Zhao residence
Bamako, Mali

Zhao thanked Guo for his report and the two formulated a revised plan. With any luck, it just might work.

Unfortunately, Zhao didn't believe in luck and he couldn't afford to take any more chances. Failure was not an option. An avid martial artist, Zhao studied the greats. One of his favorite fighters, Mike Tyson, once said, "Everyone has a plan until they get punched in the face." Zhao felt like he'd been punched by Mossa in the face now. Twice.

He picked up his secure phone and called an old friend in the United States, a very well-connected man who could help him solve his problem—for a price. A man who was in desperate need of something Zhao could offer him. A man who preferred to be called The Angel.

L'Argent Bar
Washington, D.C.

Jasmine Bath played dumb. Funny how easy it was to do. A change of tone, a furrowed brow. A lie becomes the truth. And the truthfulness of the liar, once established, never questioned. People wanted to trust her, to believe she was on their side always. She was happy to oblige.

No, of course I will never monitor your calls. Your privacy is important to me. Trust is important in this business. You know that. Without it, we're both dead.

That's how the first meeting always went with a new client, even one as powerful and savvy as The Angel. But that had been a while ago. They hadn't had a face-to-face since then, so when he called and asked for a meeting, she obliged. It would go one of two ways, and one of them might prove fatal to her.

The Georgetown bar he picked was one of the oldest in town, and one of her favorites. Low light, high-backed leather chairs, wood walls, and superb yet unobtrusive service. It was a public meeting in an intimate, exclusive setting. That was a good sign.

Jasmine sipped her WhistlePig straight rye on the rocks, listening attentively. She pretended she hadn't parsed every syllable of Zhao's recorded phone call to him demanding to know why Americans were protecting the Tuareg terrorist Mossa. Pretended that she hadn't recorded his postcoital bedroom chat with his wife, asking her who Troy Pearce was, what Pearce Systems was all about, and why Pearce was in Mali. Bath just smiled and nodded and sipped and listened. Waited before asking the obvious questions.

"And what did your wife say about Pearce? I mean, who is he, really?"

"She pled ignorance because she really doesn't know

anything about him. She tried to explain Pearce's connection to Myers, which, frankly, I never fully understood."

Neither did Jasmine. Pearce was an open secret, hiding in plain sight. The few times she tried to access data on him, she was either shut down or sidetracked. At the time, it was interesting but not important.

"It's a damn shame we never got to those impeachment hearings on Myers. Probably a lot of things got swept under that rug," he said.

"No doubt."

"Do we know if Myers has any interests or concerns in Mali?"

"Part of my contract with you is to monitor all of President Myers's communications—"

"Just 'Myers.'" The Angel visibly stiffened, took another sip of his Old Fashioned. "She's a former president who quit the office. She doesn't deserve the title."

"It's funny you should ask me about Myers and Mali. She made a recent phone call that seemed harmless enough." Bath had run a search of all of Myers's e-mails, calls, and texts, sniffing out references to Pearce and Mali after The Angel's little bedroom chat with his powerful wife. It paid to be on top of these things, to appear omniscient when really one needed only to be proficient. Only one reference popped up a few days ago.

"A call to whom?" he asked.

"Pearce. He was in Mozambique when he took it. Sounded like he was in the cockpit of a plane when he spoke with her. Myers was sending him to exfil Mike Early out of Mali. That's quite a coincidence, don't you think?"

"Nothing about Mossa?"

"No."

The Angel jiggled the ice in his glass, thinking. "The call makes sense. Myers would send Pearce to Mali to fetch Early, because Early worked for Myers, too. One of her security advisors, as I recall. But Pearce never left Mali."

"How do you know he's still there?" Bath knew the answer was Zhao. She had to feign ignorance; otherwise, The Angel might suspect she'd listened in on his call.

The Angel smiled. "I have my sources."

Bath frowned, thinking. "Maybe Myers was speaking in code. Maybe she wasn't really sending Pearce in to rescue Early, but was really sending him in to *help* Early."

"Help Early with what?"

"Mossa."

"If that's the case, then they're both in Mali at Myers's behest and now they've both been seen helping Mossa. That means she must have ties to Mossa, too. When you find out what those ties are, let me know. But for now, at least, I've got Myers connected to Mali and to Mossa. That's all the ammunition I need. One more thing: I want you to begin seeding the blogosphere with stories and pictures about Mossa, the Tuaregs, terrorism, Africa— you get it. I want to push the themes the senator will raise on Finch's gawd-awful show tomorrow. In fact, here—"

The Angel forwarded a video from his phone sent by Zhao. It was an edited version of the video shot by Guo's hawk drone, showing Tuaregs shooting helpless, wounded Mali soldiers.

Bath pulled it up. "Oh my God. This is terrible." Of

course, she didn't tell him she had already seen it, having captured it from his phone earlier.

"Use it. Turn it viral."

"No problem." Bath wasn't kidding. She ran one of the world's largest virtual click farms. Her operation could generate up to three million fake "likes" per day on any given YouTube or Facebook page by deploying malware that hijacked legitimate IP addresses and using them to "like" the page, thus making the fake "likes" look real to the site managers. She justified her actions, in part because she didn't resort to the click-farm "sweatshops" in Third World countries like Bangladesh, where human drones pounded away for hours at keyboards registering thousands of "likes" per night for a dollar or two. Thanks to The Angel, the Department of State recently paid her $630,000 to get over two million automated fake "likes" on its Facebook pages.

For a hefty fee, Bath could turn almost anything into a viral hit. It was well known that Twitter and Facebook had millions of fake users, so she clearly wasn't the only one doing this kind of thing, but nobody did it better. Her malware programs could also boost the "star" ratings of products offered by online vendors like Amazon or iTunes, blasting her clients' sales through the roof and tanking their competition with equally bad reviews. Two best-selling authors and one Grammy-nominated musician had hired her in just the last year. For wary consumers of all stripes, it was becoming increasingly difficult to trust the ratings systems.

"You saw my e-mail about Myers?" Bath asked. "That

she's still sniffing around the Tanner issue?" Bath saw Myers's pursuit of Tanner's suicide as a far greater threat to both of them than the sideshow in far-flung Mali.

"Yes. That's a problem."

"What do you want to do about it?"

Bath wanted Myers dealt with, soon. She wondered if The Angel had the guts to pull the trigger if it came to that. If killing an ex-president had to be done, she preferred his fingerprints be on the corpse, not hers. But then again, it might provide CIOS with a very lucrative billing opportunity.

"I want you to dirty the water," he said. "Let's roll out a campaign against Myers and her lapdog Pearce. Link them to Mossa and AQS, but discreetly. That should keep her distracted, and keep her away from Tanner."

"Audience?"

"The national security establishment, of course. The usual suspects. CIA, NSA, FBI. But do that thing you do. Make it look like legitimate chatter from the bad guys."

Bath hid her rage. She knew damn well how to plant false information on the web to impugn people. She'd practically invented the NSA's handbook on the subject.

The Angel smiled. "I want to put Pearce and the others on Greyhill's radar, too. I need Greyhill sweating every second that he doesn't do something about this new 'threat' we've just uncovered."

"Not a problem." Bath was happy to oblige. People might get killed if Greyhill overreacted, but that was on him, not her. She was just the messenger. In her line of work, morality was a fiction she could ill afford.

= 39 =

Adrar des Ifoghas
Kidal Region, Northeastern Mali
9 May

The small band picked their way down through the shadows of the eastern slope while on the other side of the mountain the Mali army lay dead under the merciless afternoon sun.

After the battle that morning, Cella tended the few wounded Tuaregs while Mossa and his men dispatched the suffering survivors. They returned to the cool of the caves, ate again and drank, then Mossa led his men in the noonday prayers while Pearce and Early waited outside.

Pearce raised Ian on his recharged sat phone. Didn't tell him about the battle, just that everything was on schedule. Got updates on Judy, who was comfortable but now restricted in her air base quarters. Cella's daughter was already on a chartered flight to Rome.

He thought about Lisbon. Counted the years. Dorotea was a beautiful little girl. It was certainly possible. And those eyes.

First chance he got, he needed to talk to Cella.

After prayers, Mossa briefed Pearce. Mossa assured him that two devastating defeats in two days would send the Malians reeling back to Bamako. There'd be nothing to fear from them for a month, at least, and he'd be back well before then. But Mossa was no fool. He still posted guards, and rotated them frequently out of the scorching sun and back into the caves for rest, water, and food, waiting for the worst of the heat to pass before they began the next leg of their journey.

Mossa was wearing his indigo *tagelmust*, of course, but had swapped out his combat camouflage fatigues for a traditional blue kaftan and cloth pants, all in royal blue. Leather sandals had replaced his boots, too. Pearce wondered why the change.

Moctar and Balla volunteered to carry Pearce's remaining Pelican case containing the M-25, Switchblade UAV, and firing tube. He couldn't imagine them hauling his load on foot for the next six days, but then again, he didn't know how he'd manage it by himself, either. But he couldn't leave that technology behind. Too expensive, and too dangerous if the wrong people ever got ahold of it. He'd proven that already back in Anou. And, technically, it was still the property of the South African army, even if they hadn't taken possession of it yet. He'd have to refund the Hybrid Quadrotor, of course, but at least he could truthfully report on its combat effectiveness.

Like Mossa, Moctar and Balla had rewrapped themselves in their *tagelmust*s. It was the Tuareg way. Both men were a decade younger than Pearce, but he knew that only because they had uncovered their faces the night before. Wrapped up again, they were ageless, mysterious, and fearsome.

"Moctar, a question."

"Yes?" The young Tuareg had good English.

"Most Muslim women cover themselves, but not the Imohar women. Why is that?"

"Why would I want to cover my daughters' heads? I want them to feel the wind in their hair and the sun on their faces, the way Allah intends."

"Western women feel the same way. They refuse to be covered."

Moctar laughed. "That is the difference between your people and mine. If I tell my women they shall be covered, then they shall be covered. But I give them the freedom to be uncovered because it pleases me. Your women don't cover because it pleases them. Your women rule you. All your women wore hats before, yes?"

"Yes, quite often. Until the 1960s."

"Women's Liberation," Moctar said. He pronounced it like a judgment rather than a fact. Pearce let it go.

Balla called out, pointing ahead. An RPG was slung over his shoulder, along with a pack carrying more HEAT rounds.

"And there is our transportation." Mossa nodded at a small caravan of fourteen camels marching toward them, shimmering in the heat of the sand. Seven camels carried Tuareg gunmen, AKs slung on their laps. Seven other saddles were empty.

"Do you have a mechanical one of those?" Mossa joked, pointing at the camels.

"Actually, yes. It's called an LS3—a Legged Squad Support System. It looks like a headless, skinless horse."

"Truly? That would seem to be both a marvel and a nightmare," Mossa said.

"I grew up mucking rich people's horse barns. The LS3 has some advantages."

"Mucking?"

"Shoveling shit."

"The problem is the putting of the horse in a barn, not the shitting of the horse," Moctar observed.

By the time they made it all the way down the mountain, the camels had arrived and were already kneeling. The camel driver saw Mossa and raced over. The two men embraced like old friends. Balla and Moctar began securing the Pelican case to a camel.

"Have you ever ridden one of these beasties?" Early asked.

"No," Pearce said.

"You're in for a treat."

"That's what you said to me that time you tried to hook me up with that WNBA power forward."

"Excuse me? I'd like to hear that story," Cella said, chuckling.

"She was on a USO tour in Iraq. A big girl, let me tell you," Early said, lifting his hand a foot above his head like a measuring stick. "About yea tall, and a French braid like a hawser, down all the way to the middle of her back. You know, from behind you could—"

"Forget it," Pearce barked.

"Pearce! Early! Come!" Mossa beckoned them with his hand.

The six kneeling camels were still four-foot-tall mounds of muscle and very light brown hair, almost white. On top of each were wooden saddles with high slanted backs and elongated three-pronged forks where a stubby saddle horn should be. Each of the saddles was elaborately decorated with goat leather and brass cutouts in bright geometric patterns in bold colors, especially red and turquoise. The animals were further adorned with trappings of long leather strips and woven fabrics. The other Tuaregs remained mounted. Their hands were coal black, as were the small part of their faces he could see behind their veils.

Moctar pointed at Pearce's camel. "Your ship of the desert, for a sea of sand," he said. He laughed. "I heard that in a movie once."

Pearce had ridden plenty of horses growing up in Wyoming. He'd even broken a few broncs in his youth—or at least tried to. He knew the key to riding an animal was to exude confidence. Nervous riders made nervous mounts. Pearce marched up to his camel, grabbed the fork, and hauled himself up on the stirrup, like he'd done it a thousand times before. The camel never flinched. None of them did. They were a serene bunch. The Zen masters of the Sahara. Pearce knew that a group of horses would have been far more skittish, especially around strangers.

"You've ridden camels before?" Mossa asked.

"Horses."

"I rode an elephant once, in a circus near Tupelo," Early said. "Cost me five dollars."

"I should like to ride an elephant someday," Mossa said as he mounted his own animal.

The camel driver and Mossa exchanged words. Mossa nodded, turned to Pearce.

"He would like to trade you for your rifle." Mossa pointed at Pearce's M4 slung over his shoulder.

"What's wrong with his AK?" Pearce asked. "This thing is a little finicky in the sand anyways."

"Mano likes the new M320 grenade launcher on it. He feels the side-loaded breech is superior to the previous model."

Pearce smiled. "Man knows his stuff."

"Mano Dayak is a dealer in such things. He can fetch a great price for that weapon back in Niger."

"What would he give me for it?"

Mossa chattered a question. The driver answered.

"Two AKs and a camel of your choice."

"Very tempting. Tell him I'll think about it."

The camel driver tapped Pearce's camel with a crop and the animal's rear end rose up. It felt like he was in the front seat of a downhill roller coaster. Pearce clutched the saddle with every ounce of strength in his thighs to keep from pitching forward, even though he was gripping the fork. A moment later, the camel stood on its front legs and leveled out. Pearce's butt was nearly ten feet in the air. It seemed like twenty. He liked the view up there. But it also made him feel like a target.

The other riders all mounted their camels, and the animals rose on command. Mossa's animal was blazingly white and the tallest by far, and the most ornately decorated. He prodded his camel with a commanding "Het-het" and took the lead. Pearce's fell in line automatically, no doubt by force of habit. The small caravan was headed for the endless yellow horizon. As strange as the last twenty-four hours had been, he couldn't begin to imagine what the night might bring.

$$= 40 =$$

Three a.m.

The bodies lay where they fell during the day, cut down by gunfire, grenades, or land mines. Most had bloated, baking beneath the scorching sun all day. The burned-out hulk of a six-wheeled BTR stood upended where it had died, a hole blown in the bottom deck by an RPG as the vehicle crested the trench line, the crew turned to ash.

In all, Guo counted seventy corpses on his way up the mountain. The Mali troops were brave enough but poorly deployed, and even more dismally led. As far as he was concerned, they had been useful for mine clearing at best. The hard way.

The veil of moonlight and the blanket of stars provided

more than enough ambient light for this new generation of night-vision equipment. Two of Guo's best men advanced to either side of him, quiet as butterfly wings. They were all kitted out in the same black tactical uniforms and fully enclosed helmets. The uniforms were temperature controlled and the headgear completely covered their faces, ears, and mouths, much like a high-tech motorcycle helmet. Black flexible "smart glass" wrapped across their faces, fronted by double-barreled night-vision goggles. Each helmet's enhanced audio provided another tactical advantage over their opponents in the dark. Guo's command helmet also featured POV windows from the other two operators' cameras, giving him additional tactical information.

The three operators easily located the four Tuareg lookouts on the ridge above, two men dozing off and two others whispering in low tones. Telling stories, judging by the way they laughed and smoked. From their distant observation post, Guo and his team had counted fifteen Tuareg fighters in the battle. That left eleven not visually confirmed. He was certain Mossa was still alive. Why else would the other brigands remain behind?

His orders were clear. Kill Mossa, capture Pearce. That wouldn't be easy, but glory was only glorious because it was hard-won. Thankfully, Guo had another tactical advantage to deploy. He blinked an order in his command window and the other two men halted, then took cover. They were just a hundred meters from the ridge.

Guo pulled a cylinder from a vest pocket and emptied the contents on the ground. Pulled a controller from another pocket. A hundred Madagascar hissing roaches scurried up the hill. Each of the giant cockroaches was fitted with cameras and sensors and steered with controls wired to their abdominal sensory organs and antennae. Software auto-piloted the bio-bots to find the warm Tuareg bodies hiding up above. Guo and his team tracked their movements and location on the helmeted smart glass.

Originally developed for search and rescue in collapsed buildings, the bio-bot roaches were excellent surveillance tools in war. Dr. Weng's lab found that using living insects offered numerous advantages over manufactured ones. They had been designed, perfected, and field-tested over millions of years by Nature herself. The best humans could do was mimic natural systems. Weng found that the problems of propulsion, fuel, and load bearing were still overwhelming for miniature human-manufactured insects like mosquitoes and spiders. Even when they were successfully built, their range and payload capabilities were negligible. Retrofitted cockroaches provided a naturally selected, high-tech solution. It was only a matter of time before the hawk drones would be replaced with real ones controlled remotely, too.

Thirty minutes later, the bio-bots had located fifteen warm bodies. It was too dark in most of the caves for the roach cameras to function properly, so it wasn't clear where Mossa and Pearce were located. Mossa's death was imperative. Pearce's capture was secondary. The three operators separated, moving into positions, dividing up targets. Guo gave the signal.

Suppressors muted the bark of their automatic rifles. Single shots took down the first three Tuaregs. Grenades tossed behind boulders took out four others. The team advanced up the hill. Guo fired a grenade launcher throwing flash bangs. Two more Tuaregs dropped, clutching their ears, until Chinese bullets shattered their brainpans. Guo and his men finally crested the hill. The remaining Tuaregs were clustered in two caves. No easy way to get them out. Guo pulled a white phosphorus grenade and tossed it into the first cave. When the phosphorus was exposed to the air, it flashed a brilliant white light and caught fire. A Tuareg leaped out of the cave enveloped in unquenchable flames, screaming. Guo's men let him pass. A second came out, clothes ablaze, gun firing. He was cut down, but not before putting a round into the smart glass of one of his men. The operator's POV video image on Guo's command screen went black.

According to Guo's display, there were still three people left in the first cave, and six more in the next, ten meters ahead. Guo dashed for the second cave and tossed another WP grenade. More screams.

WHOOSH! An RPG screamed out of the black maw of the cave and roared over Guo's head. He dropped to the ground reflexively. Good thing. Bullets spanged into the rock just behind him. Had he remained standing, he would have been cut in half. His comrade called, two more down.

BOOM! A grenade went off ten meters behind him. His second video screen went blank. His last comrade down. Guo laughed, battle-crazed. This is how heroes died, he told himself. He tossed another flash bang into the cave, waited for two seconds for the flash to pass, then tossed in a conventional grenade. It thudded. Guo dashed in, gun blazing. Bullets tore high into the chest of a man against the far cave wall trying to raise a rifle. The other four were already dead.

Guo heard the crack of a rifle. A sledgehammer slammed into his back, square in the center of his body armor. Guo dropped to the ground and rolled hard to the left, drawing his pistol. He emptied the mag into the man's chest. The Tuareg spilled to the ground, grasping sand in his fists until a last breath escaped his lungs.

Guo stood up unsteadily and surveyed the rest of the carnage. Five dead in here. But not Mossa or Pearce. Just a boy and four women, burned to death. Disappointing.

No glory in that.

He stumbled back out into the warm night air and loaded a new mag in his pistol. He approached the prone body of his man by the cave and checked for a pulse, but there was none. Blood soaked the sand around the corpse. Too bad. Guo edged his way as quietly as he could into the other cave. He crept along a broad, low-ceilinged passageway for several meters until he came to a large natural cave. There were two bodies on the ground. One moaned. Guo ran over to the one moaning. Not Mossa, not Pearce. He checked the other body. Dead. Not Mossa, not Pearce.

Guo kneeled down next to the bleeding Tuareg. He pulled a knife. The Tuareg's eyes widened with terror.

"Where did Mossa go?" he asked in French.

Five minutes later, after much blood and pain, the Tuareg died. And Guo had his answer.

= 41 =

Meet the Nation was the oldest of the Sunday-morning news shows, and its anchor, Howard Finch, the most ancient and venerable of the bunch.

"Senator Fiero, thank you so much for being here today. Presidential candidates are even busier than sitting senators, so I appreciate your taking the time to join us this morning. My sources in the know say that you have the Democratic nomination all but sewn up for 2016. That must feel pretty good."

"As you well know, there's nothing ever 'all sewn up' in politics, especially in the Democratic Party. We're listening to the American people, and they're concerned about the direction this nation's headed."

"My polling data suggests that the majority of Americans are pretty happy with the way things are going now under President Greyhill. For the first time in a long time, we seem to be fighting in fewer places, fighting fewer political battles over things like debt ceilings, and experiencing something of an energy renaissance, thanks to the new federal policies on oil and natural gas extraction."

You're a smug old bastard, Fiero thought. "There's no doubt that our economy has enjoyed a temporary boost from the oil and gas industry, but of course, all of that began under former president Myers, not President Greyhill."

"So you don't give President Greyhill any credit for the peace and prosperity this country is currently enjoying?"

"Well, I certainly give him credit for not undoing the hard work that we in the Congress accomplished along with President Myers in helping right the fiscal ship, particularly in regard to the budget freeze. But there are still millions of people in this country, Howard, who haven't been able to dig out from the wreckage of the financial crisis of 2008, and this country faces significant strategic threats that are ill-served by our current foreign policy."

"What threats are you referring to?" Finch asked.

"There's a new 'Scramble for Africa' now under way. China in particular is making tremendous headway all over the continent, securing significant reserves of natural resources in the forests, waters, and mines of that great continent. They're also establishing strategic relationships with African governments along the way."

"No offense, Madame Senator, but help me out here. Why do we care a fig if China is growing rice in Angola or fishing in the Gulf of Guinea?"

"The West owes a particular moral debt to the African continent for our centuries of exploitation, particularly our own sordid history regarding the slave trade. It's our responsibility to see that Africa develops in a way that benefits all Africans, not just the wealthy dictators and oligarchs, and certainly we shouldn't allow the continent to once again be reexploited by the mercantilist policies of the Chinese government. That being said, the Chinese are playing a very smart geopolitical game. The greatest opportunity for Chinese influence today—Chinese money, Chinese trade contracts, and even Chinese weapons—is Africa. If there's ever going to be a shooting war between our two great nations in the future, the Chinese warships, tanks, and planes used against us will be built and fueled from the natural resources they harvested out of African soil."

"Are you proposing we put American boots on the ground in Africa to stop the Chinese?"

"We already have boots on the ground over there. The reason why AFRICOM was created back in 2007—and by the way, I voted for that spending authorization—was to take on the al-Qaeda threat in Africa. But it's been horribly neglected under President Greyhill. I'm drawing up a bill to strengthen and expand those forces to meet the rising tide of militant Islam that's exploding across the continent, particularly in places where Chinese influence has taken hold. Mali, for example. I'd hate for that poor nation to become another staging base for al-Qaeda, the way they used Afghanistan."

"I thought the French took care of the Islamic threat in Mali back a few years ago," Finch said.

"The French managed to push back the threats briefly, but the al-Qaeda presence is on the rise. Jihadists all over the region have engaged in terrorist acts against pipelines, tourists, and local police forces. But, of course, not against Chinese facilities, at least not in Mali."

"Are you implying a Chinese connection to terrorists in Mali?"

"There's a natural alliance of interests, don't you think? At least, if your goal is to push out Western influence. And isn't that the stated goal of both the Chinese Politburo and the jihadist terror organizations?"

Finch shook his head. "I'm sorry, but I just think Americans have had a bellyful of foreign wars these days. As you've rightly pointed out, this nation still faces severe crises at home. Why get involved in a country like Mali? I'm willing to bet that half of Americans can't even find it on a map." He laughed. "I'm willing to bet that half of Congress can't find it on a map."

Fiero flashed her megawatt smile, hiding the rising rage boiling up inside of her. "I assure you, Howard, that those of us on the Senate Intelligence Committee are well aware of the location and significance of the nation of Mali. And let me give you an example of why the American people should care about what's going on over there. Most Americans agree that we need to be moving forward as quickly as possible on green energy.

We're all too painfully aware of the effects of carbon dioxide and other greenhouse gases created by burning carbon fuels. Green energy is the future, and the future of green energy is energy storage in the form of batteries, and batteries aren't possible without what scientists call rare earth elements. Mali is a potential new source of REEs, and the Chinese are locking them up even as we speak—the same way they did other resources, like lithium in Afghanistan after we pulled out. It's clear to those of us on the Intelligence Committee that the Chinese are following a very deliberate resource strategy. And yet President Greyhill seems content to do nothing about this. So no one should be surprised if, in a few years from now, all of the batteries in our electric cars are all manufactured in China. Or, worse yet, maybe all of our electric cars themselves will have to be made over there because they won't sell us the batteries."

"So it's your opinion that the United States needs to act on this matter? To secure what you term 'REEs'?"

"What I'm saying is this. There's no question that the American people are tired of war, but the American people are also very practical. As you suggested, Howard, most Americans simply aren't aware of what's going on in Africa, and I've decided to sound the alarm—even if it costs me an election. That's what real leadership is all about. But President Greyhill seems to be more interested in winning an election than in protecting the interests of the American people. I just hope it's not too late to act before then. And if I might quote President Myers, all it takes for evil to thrive is for good people to do nothing."

"Interesting," Finch said before turning to the camera. "We'll be back after these messages."

Fiero glanced over Finch's shoulder. Fowler was standing by camera number two. He had a thin smile on his face, and he nodded his approval, adding a wink as an exclamation point.

A home run, in Harry Fowler–speak.

She just wished she could see Greyhill's face when he finally watched the tape. It was her first shot fired in anger, and she'd aimed it right at Greyhill's nut sack.

= 42 =

Adrar Province
Southwestern Algeria
10 May

The sand in front of them was mostly flat, dotted with the occasional juniper bush. Pearce had no idea how those plants could possibly thrive out here, but there they were. Just like the Tuaregs, he supposed. These nomads had managed to survive out here for two thousand years as well, despite the heat and seeming lack of water. Thrive, in fact, trading in spices, salt, gold, and slaves, purchased or stolen between empires.

Taking his cue from the Tuaregs, Pearce had pulled off his combat boots. Not only was this cooler, but now it was his soft feet resting on the camel's neck rather than the hard soles. No point in making the camel suffer.

After an hour in the wooden saddle, his backside was already getting sore even with the cloth padding added.

It didn't bother him too much. Saddle sore was a rite of passage where he grew up. The soreness was even a kind of comfort. Not everything about his childhood had been miserable. Life in the mountains working for his dad's failing sawmill was always hard, but a whole lot better than growing up in a slum or refugee camp. There were days he missed Big Sky Country. But today wasn't one of them.

The ride on the one-humped camel was remarkably comfortable, better than on most horses he'd ridden over long distances. Maybe it was the soft sand, too, and their big padded feet. They hardly seemed to leave an impression. The camel's gait was long and graceful, like a slow-drifting creek. The effect was hypnotic. Their elongated shadows rode just ahead of them and to the right, gliding across the sand. Pearce had let the rope rein drop from his hand. His camel was so docile that it followed the animal in front without any guidance from the loop of rope tied around its lower jaw.

What struck him most about the journey now was the utter silence, save for the swishing sound of the camel's soft pads on the sand. If he hadn't heard that he might have thought he'd gone deaf. As a Westerner, he was accustomed to the constant bombardment of big-city noise, as true in the Third World these days as anywhere. This was a welcome respite. But soon he found himself battling his demons again. "Like a house swept clean," the silence soon gave way to bad memories. Memories he'd tried to bury, but always returned. Johnny Paloma, especially. He nudged his camel on, even managing to get him to pick up speed. Caught up with Early's.

"How's the arm?" Pearce asked.

"This? Fine. In fact—" Early slipped the sling off, tossed it in the sand. He flexed his arm, grimacing a little. "Feels good."

"How about your head wound?"

"Head wound? There's nothing wrong with my head."

"Really? Then why in God's name are you out here instead of at home with Kate and the kids?"

Early's handsome face darkened.

"Last time I saw you was on a Facebook post in Santorini with the family," Pearce added. "You look better without a beard and the olive-drab bandage wrapped around your noggin, too, by the way."

"Santorini. Yeah, that was a great trip," Early finally said. "We always have great trips."

"So?"

"You know how it is. Kind of hard to ride the bench once you've played in the game."

"An adrenaline junkie? Fine, I get it. So take up hang gliding."

"Not the same. Besides, hang gliding doesn't pay as well."

"You don't need any money. Kate's dad is loaded."

"I'm no freeloader. And after the Myers thing, well, let's just say I wasn't getting a lot of offers. The K Street cats want access, and I was persona non grata on the Hill, even with the blanket immunity."

"And Kate's okay with this?" Pearce pointed at the wilderness. "Shouldn't you be coaching a Little League team or cutting the grass?"

"This was supposed to be temporary. Then I was promised a replacement."

"But Cella's father never found one?"

"Sure he did. Problem is, I found him, too. With his throat cut ear to ear, bled out in the sand a half mile east of Timbuktu. I called it in. 'Another guy's on the way,' he said. Until then, I sit tight. At twice my rate, too. That buys a lot of Little League uniforms."

Pearce thought about that. "You're worth it. Cella's lucky to have you."

Early laughed. "Tell her that. She wants me gone so bad she can taste it."

"What's the story with her?"

Early eyed him. "You tell me, partner. You have a longer history with her than I do."

"What did she tell you?"

"Nothing. Which tells me a whole lot."

"Her dad has always had someone around to protect her. I'm just surprised it's you, that's all."

"It was a gig. I took it. I'm home as soon as I can get there."

"I'm flying out in five days. Come with. Trust me, Cella will be fine. Especially with Mossa and his men around."

"You sure? The noose is tightening around his neck, in case you haven't noticed. That's why she sent her kid away."

"What kind of mother does that?"

"The kind that loves her kid."

"Then why didn't she go with her?"

"If you know Cella, you know how fierce she is. She's devoted to the old man."

"How did she ever decide to raise a family out here? You'd think she'd move back to Italy just for the sake of her daughter."

"She's a complicated lady. You'd have to ask her."

"That means the noose is tightening around your neck, too, you know."

"I got a big neck. Stiff one, too."

"Seriously. You might not walk away from this one."

"Can't help that. I've been hired to do a job. I'm going to see it through. So would you, if you were me. I think."

"What's that supposed to mean?"

"Unlike me, a handsome Army Ranger on a grand adventure in the Sahara, you look like a steaming turd recently shat out of a cat's anus, a dim shadow of the CIA stud I used to know. What the hell happened to you?"

"After the Myers thing, I kinda lost it. Did some shit I probably shouldn't have done, but had to. You know how it is."

"Yeah, I do."

Words like "duty," "honor," and "loyalty" were more than just slogans for men like Pearce and Early. Early heard rumors that Pearce had gotten his revenge on the Russian responsible for the death of Myers's son.

"But it was more than that. You were right about her, Mikey. She was the real deal. I actually started to believe again. And then she was forced to resign. Politics as usual."

"And then what?"

Pearce blew out a long breath. "I ran, I guess. Hid in the work. At least, the humanitarian stuff."

"How was that working for you?"

"Okay, until a few days ago."

"What happened?"

"The last job went sideways. One of my guys got killed."

"I thought you weren't working security anymore."

"That's the hell of it. We weren't. For just that reason. We were trying to track a few rhinos. Johnny got killed anyway." Pearce didn't describe the condition of Johnny's corpse when he found it. "I wasn't there when Johnny needed me. He paid the price."

"He signed on. He knew what he was in for, working for you."

"Should've been me, not him."

"Someday, it will be. You know that. So do I. It's just that his ticket got punched before yours did. You've got to let that go."

Pearce thought about that for a while. "If Cella left, though, you'd leave, right?"

"I'm a huge fan of Mossa, but I'm a bigger fan of my wife and kids. If you can convince her to vamoose, I'm on the next flight out of here with the two of you."

"I'll see what I can do."

Early laughed. "Good luck with that."

$$= 43 =$$

Pearce's cabin
Near the Snake River, Wyoming
10 May

Myers's body craved a good run, but her common
sense told her to stay put and out of sight.
Heaven only knew what kind of resources may
have been deployed to find her. Even George Clooney
owned his own spy satellite these days, but at least he
was putting it to good use keeping tabs on African
warlords. By now her disappearance had raised alarms
with whoever was behind the Tanner suicide. She had
to assume they were still looking for her.

Neither she nor Ian had slept in the last few days as
they applied digital brute force to the vast data sets she
had proposed in their search for the identity of Tanner's
blackmailers. In lieu of sleep, Myers resorted to periodic
yoga stretches and body-weight exercises to keep the

blood flowing and her muscles taut, fighting the inertia of countless hours of software writing and data analysis. She found a couple of crates and rigged up a crude standing desk to do her computer work. She'd read recently that sitting for more than three hours per day increased heart disease by sixty-four percent, among other pathologies. Sitting, apparently, was the new smoking.

Myers checked the clock on her computer. It was almost time for Ian to check in. She'd passed on her assigned analyses as they were completed over the last two days, but she still kept crunching data sets, following other leads that popped up. There was no question in her mind that the person or persons behind Tanner's death were political, and most likely American, though international criminal syndicates had been known to play powerful roles in American political life, especially at the state and local levels both in the past and recently.

The one solid conclusion she had reached was that her old friend was as clean as she thought he had been. She'd known Tanner and his family for years and knew him to be an honorable judge and wonderful father and husband. But Myers was after his killer or killers, so she went after his records hammer and tongs, pulling out all of the stops, digging down to the subatomic level. To her great relief, she found absolutely nothing. With Ian's help, she had been able to secure Tanner's FBI background checks—as president, she'd only been briefed on the glowing summaries— and discovered that the FBI couldn't believe his pristine personal and professional life. More than one of the FBI's interviewees had referred to him as "Saint Vincent."

Myers had even managed to find one of Tanner's fourth-grade report cards posted on the Internet—someone had found it at a garage sale and put it up, inappropriately, on Pinterest. Even then, according to his teacher, Tanner was an outstanding young gentleman with impeccable manners, social skills, and high academic potential. Taken together, her inability to find any dirt likely meant that the blackmail "evidence" used against the esteemed jurist had to have been manufactured out of whole cloth.

For a brief period of time she began to wonder if Tanner's death was somehow pointed at her, some kind of payback for a slight—real or imagined—committed by her while in office; but she'd been out of office and out of the political loop long enough that she eventually dismissed the idea. What would be the point now? Besides, if these people were powerful enough to get a man of Tanner's character to put a gun in his mouth and blow his own brains out, she knew that they could have just as easily come after her with whatever "evidence" they had concocted against him.

Her monitor dinged. Ian was checking in. "Here, Margaret."

"Good to see you, Ian." Myers saw that he looked as tired and baggy-eyed as she did. The two of them had hardly slept the last two days as they sorted through the mountains of data they had compiled. "What do we have?" Myers asked. She had forwarded her findings to Ian and he had spent the last two hours cross-referencing their results.

"There is a lot of outrage in American politics, isn't there?"

"Yes, unfortunately. Some of that is ginned up by the politicians themselves to rally votes, but mostly it's bad policies by a failed government that's hurting millions of Americans fueling that rage."

"I don't know if this is the right list or not, but based upon everything we discussed and the search results we have generated, there are four congressmen, three senators, and five corporate CEOs that rise to the top of the outrage list. These are some very hated people."

"Then those are our targets. Any connections between them?"

"Funny you should ask that. There is one senator and one CEO that are very closely connected. Both go by the surname Fiero."

"As in, Senator Barbara Fiero?"

"Précisément. Her husband's name is Anthony. These are very rich people, by the way."

"I've met Senator Fiero. She is many things, including extremely intelligent, ambitious, and beautiful, but the one thing she is not is a computer programmer. She isn't our super hacker."

"Maybe she has her own private Edward Snowden in the NSA," Ian joked.

"Edward Snowden wasn't in the NSA. He worked as a private contractor for the NSA. That's a big difference. What do you know about the senator's husband?"

"A little mysterious, that one. He's a private hedge fund manager with many international connections."

"Is he a computer guy? Or does he have access to one?"

"He's not a computer guy, but he appears to be

connected to a very savvy data outfit known as CIOS. It's a first-rate shop. The best, really, run by the best software engineer in the business. Answers to the name of Jasmine Bath."

"Better than you? That's hard to believe, given what I've seen you do and what Troy has told me about you."

"I'm no slacker, but I don't have the background and experience she's had in the TAO. She is to computer spying what Peyton Manning is to your American football."

"So CIOS and this Jasmine Bath computer genius could mount an operation like the kind we're talking about?"

"With the kind of cash the Fieros have? Absolutely. And if they really are using her to turn the kinds of decisions we've talked about, then they're even richer than what we think, I'm sure."

"How so?"

"This isn't about blackmailing individuals. They're extorting whole industries. Imagine how much money they could solicit from the entire banking industry, or the entire oil industry, if they could deliver legislation that would save those industries tens of billions of dollars in taxes and regulatory expenses. And then imagine the stock picking they could do, knowing months in advance that these sectors were about to benefit from huge changes in favorable legislation or court rulings."

"I'm still not buying it. You're talking about the next Democratic nominee for the presidency. The senator is already quite wealthy thanks to her husband, and she's already one of the most powerful politicians in Washington. Why would she play these kinds of games?"

"When is anyone ever satisfied with the money and power they already have?"

Myers didn't have an answer for that. Time wasn't their friend and they had limited resources. They could start digging into the six other candidates they had generated as well, but that would only put them further behind. She'd gotten as far as she had in life by learning to trust the people around her, and Ian clearly thought the Fieros were the two best suspects to pursue.

"Okay, then. Those are our targets. The Fieros and CIOS."

"Targets? Are we talking wet work?"

"No, but they'll wish it was wet work when we're through with them."

"Best be careful with CIOS. Bath will have every security precaution in place, as well as the means to retaliate against us if she thinks we're coming after her in any way, wet work included."

"Agreed." Myers frowned.

"Problem?"

"It's hard to imagine Barbara Fiero would be caught up in something like this. But as I think about it, maybe it's not so far-fetched. She has a reputation for being the luckiest woman on the Hill. She always seemed to know exactly the right place to be or the right vote to cast or the right person to meet at just the right time. If she has the kind of extreme insider information we're talking about, that would explain a lot."

"Knowledge is power, Margaret. You of all people should know that."

"They say genius is seeing the obvious. Clearly, I'm no genius or I would have seen through her earlier."

Myers remembered Fiero during the NSA hearings held by her committee in the Senate. She was one of the few Democrats on that committee adamantly in favor of the NSA's domestic spying program. One of the Democrats asked the NSA straight up, "Are you spying on Congress?" Fiero interrupted the question and said, "That's a national security question that shouldn't be asked in a public forum. But I, for one, support the NSA's security programs both here and abroad, and I for one wouldn't care if they were listening in on my telephone conversations, because I have nothing to hide."

The gall of the woman, especially if what they now believed about her actually turned out to be true. She should have seen it.

"Ian, now we have to go on the offense. Are you still with me?"

"To the bloody end."

"Thank you."

Myers hoped that Ian's words weren't prophetic. They divided up tasks and went back to work.

$= 44 =$

Maersk Oil Pumping Station
Tamanghasset Province, Southern Algeria
10 May

The sobbing Algerian was twenty-three years old, clean-shaven and close-cropped. The knees of his Maersk oil coveralls were soaking up the Danish engineer's blood on the cement floor, seeping from the headless corpse a few feet away.

"Are you a woman? Quit crying!" Al Rus shouted in Arabic. He slapped the young man's face.

The Algerian fought back his desperate tears, gasping for breath, trying to stem the tide.

Al Rus hit him again.

"Are you a Muslim?"

The boy's eyes sparked with hope. "Yes! Yes!"

"Then why are you helping these Crusader dogs rape your country?"

"My father. He is not well. We needed the money—"

"Thieves steal because they need money."

"I am no thief. I was only an apprentice to that man."

"You are no Muslim."

"I am of the faithful!"

"You swear it?"

"I swear it!"

"Why should I believe you?"

"I repent!" The young man turned his head and spit on the corpse of his dead Danish friend.

"You will stop helping the Crusaders?"

"Yes, yes, a thousand times, yes! Mercy. In the name of Allah," the boy whimpered.

Finally, Al Rus nodded. "Yes, I believe you have repented of your thievery. But I think you are weak in your faith. You are no Salafi. I think you will turn back to your thievery and burn in the fires of hell in the next life."

"No! I am strong in my faith. You will see."

Al Rus nodded again. "Yes, we will see."

He stepped over to an interior door and pushed it open. On the floor, a woman. Naked, bruised, bloodied. But still very much alive.

Al Rus held out the knife handle. The Algerian glanced at the woman, a friend, and then at the knife.

Salvation.

The young Algerian stood up unsteadily on trembling legs and took the knife. It shook in his hand. He glanced back up into the Norwegian's merciless face.

Al Rus's satellite phone rang. He pulled it from his belt. Saw the number. Nodded to the Algerian, then to his men, and stepped outside into the burning sun to take the call.

It was already hot, and not yet noon.

"Yes, of course. I have been waiting for your call," Al Rus said in English. It was Guo.

The woman's screams echoed from the pump room. He ignored them, focusing on Guo's detailed instructions. Didn't notice her screaming suddenly choking off, like a needle lifted from a record. Guo provided him with GPS coordinates, time estimates, and a final word of warning.

"I understand." Al Rus snapped off the phone. One of his fighters, a Chechen, approached him. "Here's your knife."

Al Rus took it, wiped the bloody blade on his pant leg.

"Did you take a video?"

"Yes. Of course," the Chechen said. "It will be posted shortly."

"Good. There is still one more lesson for the others. No one is fooled. 'A dog always returns to its own vomit.'" Al Rus hated secularized Muslims worse than devout Jews, or even Christians.

The Chechen glanced back at the pump house, nodding in agreement.

Al Rus smiled. "And then we have a new mission."

= 45 =

Ian's task was clear: spy on Jasmine Bath and Senator Fiero. The risks were equally clear: decades in a federal penitentiary—or worse. The trick was coming up with a strategy that would accomplish the former and avoid the latter.

Jasmine Bath was the best in the business. Period. Her cyberdefenses were impeccable, but her ability to counterattack was fearsome indeed. On the other hand, Senator Fiero and her husband would be more vulnerable and less able to retaliate in the digital realm, so they were the better targets to pursue. Undoubtedly, there would be some sort of exploitable link between Bath and the Fieros. Ian knew if he could break through the Fieros' defenses, he might have a good shot at breaching Bath's.

The problem with that strategy, though, was that Bath and CIOS would undoubtedly be keeping a watchful eye on the Fieros. Ian had to find a way to disable CIOS without being detected so that he could exploit any breaches in the Fiero firewalls. But how?

Ian wasn't confident he had the resources to deal with Bath. It reminded him of an exam he was once given in computational semiotics at Oxford. The tutor came into the lecture hall and demanded that each student come up with a question too difficult to answer—and then answer it. The entire room groaned with frustration and anger. It took Ian a few moments to realize the purpose of the exercise. People prefer the path of least resistance. People tend to work on problems they already know they can solve, thereby limiting intellectual growth. But avoiding problems that seemingly can't be solved also limits intellectual growth because it means that people become increasingly unaware of what it is they don't know. Science, in the end, is about knowing, and the beginning of "knowing" is finding out what you don't know. Only by becoming aware of the impossibility of a problem—insufficient knowledge or skill—would possibilities for solutions begin to suggest themselves. And that's when the first solution to Ian's insoluble problem suggested itself.

Ian knew he wasn't smart enough to overcome Bath, so he needed to draw on others for help. The international hacktivist community had been under assault by the national security agencies of Western governments throughout the world in the last two years. Whether through DDOS attacks, counterhacking, or just old-fashioned spycraft—honey traps, bribes, break-ins—agencies like the NSA and Britain's GCHQ had crushed the backbone of many autonomous hacker groups. The surviving members were both afraid and eager for payback. Ian knew how to tap into their collective talent and rage.

He reached out to an old contact in the GCHQ who provided him with the necessary info. Carefully hidden behind a series of hijacked computers, Ian faked a new Edward Snowden leak, distributing the explosive "secret" that CIOS corporation and Bath had been the primary architects of the most recent antihacktivist campaign, along with a few IP addresses. This tiny nick put enough blood in the water to draw in the hacktivist sharks, and within hours a digital feeding frenzy had begun.

Within twenty-four hours of Ian's launch, CIOS was fighting for its digital life, with Jasmine Bath leading the defenses. If Ian couldn't disable CIOS and Bath, he could at least distract them long enough so that he could accomplish his second strategic objective—going after the Fieros.

Ian attacked the Fieros on two fronts with Myers's help. First, he deployed one of Pearce Systems' most reliable human assets, a redheaded Kiwi named Fiona York. As a former JTRIG operative specializing in physical operations, she was perfectly suited for what he had in mind.

York and an assistant picked up sixteen specially fitted miniature air and ground vehicles from Rao's lab. Some of the MAVs deployed the same high-speed miniature cameras swallowed in pill form to photograph colons.

The MGVs were fitted with gecko-inspired microfiber pads that allowed them to climb walls or other vertical objects. Their primary objective was building and car windows. They were equipped with low-powered infrared beams that could "hear" the vibrations on glass caused by people speaking on the other side of them—a surveillance technique invented in the 1940s by the Russian Leon Theremin, inventor of the Theremin music synthesizer.

York deployed the miniatures with the help of a SmartBird drone, dropping them near the Fieros' personal residences and vehicles in California and D.C.

But Ian's main attack was cyber. It was only logical that CIOS would have put better security on the senator since she was their primary client and her home was geographically proximate to CIOS headquarters. Ian further surmised that Anthony Fiero didn't want his vast financial empire exposed to Bath's probing queries, which was yet another reason Ian decided to focus his efforts on him. That focus paid off quickly.

Ian knew that Fiero's private company would have its own IT resources, separate from CIOS. A frontal assault on mainframes or hard drives was possible, but time-consuming. Better to attack on the periphery. Fortunately, that kind of attack was easier than ever these days, thanks to the "Internet of Things," the machine-to-machine communication that facilitated more and more of modern life. Ten billion devices were connected now. By 2020, that number would rise to fifty billion.

Ian began by downloading the latest hacker list of known back doors to the top ten business software apps. Through one of those back doors, he gained access into an older version of Microsoft Outlook on the tablet of Anthony Fiero's personal assistant. From that infection vector, Ian was able to make the leap into a variety of other Microsoft software programs, which then spread into the assistant's laptop, then other devices and apps connecting the assistant's laptop to Fiero's laptop. Then the infection really spread.

Once inside Fiero's laptop, Ian's malware infected Fiero's tablet, iPod, and even his Xbox One game system. The Xbox One Kinect feature provided Ian with voice and video images inside of Fiero's home, which activated whenever the motion-activated Kinect system was triggered by his presence, recording everything he did or said in front of the gaming machine.

Automated software and data synching between machines and cell phone then spread the virus to Fiero's phone, a treasure trove of data unto itself. A side benefit was that the phone infection spread to Fiero's wireless Bluetooth connection, which, in turn, gave Ian access to Fiero's car and its "smart" radio and GPS apps. Now Ian could listen in on or record any conversation Fiero had in his car through the radio and speakers, and geolocate him even if Fiero's phone wasn't there.

The other significant penetration Ian achieved through Fiero's phone was to invade the "smart" thermostat system Fiero deployed to remotely control his utilities when he was away from his home. Unfortunately for Fiero, the apps that controlled the smart thermostat also sent wireless data to the utility company, which in

turn had access to Fiero's bank accounts for automatic
bill pay. Once Ian was inside Fiero's bank account, he
downloaded copies of all his financial transactions and
acquired the personal data needed to find and penetrate
other bank accounts, domestic and offshore, including
those of his wife, who was also linked to those accounts.
Those financial holdings were so vast, however, that Ian
had to bring in a trusted consultant, a former Europol
bank examiner who specialized in tracking down illicit
Russian mafia drug money around the globe.

Ian also created several botnets exploiting the viral
pathways now infecting almost all of the Fieros' computer
and computer-controlled devices, including Anthony's
newly installed "robo-toilet." The botnets all went to
work copying, downloading, or recording every sliver of
data they could get their digital hands on. Like the NSA
and its massive data-collection capabilities, however, Ian
was overwhelmed with the sheer volume of data pouring
in. It would take several days, maybe even weeks, for them
to sort through it all and connect the dots. Myers had set
about the analysis task immediately, while Ian kept
expanding the data-collection nets. She was happy to let
him take the lead on this operation. She had always been
smart enough to delegate the hardest work to the most
talented members of her team.

For all of their success, Ian thought the best news
was that they had managed to slip their noses under the
tent without Bath even knowing they were there. In a
long string of personal achievements in the digital world,
Ian couldn't think of anything to top that.

= 46 =

Adrar Province
Southwestern Algeria
10 May

They rode until late evening, arriving at a wadi to rest and feed the camels. The sun had long before dropped below the jagged horizon of the Adrar miles behind them. The flat sands shimmered like a silvery sea beneath a high, blazing moon.

Balla stood watch in the distance over the camp while Moctar prayed the last prayer of the day. The camels stretched their long necks, grunting as they munched on the salty green leaves of the tamarisk trees. There was no water, but the camels had drunk their fill before they'd arrived at the Adrar. The Nigerian camel driver was baking bread in a shallow desert oven he'd dug with a trenching tool. That left Pearce, Mossa, Early, and Cella to sit and relax around the small campfire where the teapot was heating up. It was still near eighty degrees Fahrenheit, but that was thirty degrees less than the hottest part of the day, so the evening felt almost cool.

Mossa had unwrapped the *tagelmust* from his face and smoked a cigarette. He sat cross-legged, sharpening the *takouba* resting on his knees with a whetstone. The traditional Tuareg sword was about three feet long and almost two inches wide at the base near the leather-wrapped hilt. The sound of the stone scraping on the ancient steel was the only sound in the air, save for the munching jaws of the camels.

"I want to thank you for saving my life today, Mr. Pearce. Twice."

"I was just trying to save my own neck. And please, call me Troy."

Mossa held his *takouba* up, examining the fine edge he'd just put on it. "You have amazing weapons in your arsenal. Did you invent them yourself?"

"No. I have a research team that sometimes creates new systems, but mostly we take existing technologies and modify or combine them. The grenade launcher you saw me use in the village was off-the-shelf technology, and so were the MetaPro glasses. We just wrote a piece of targeting software to link the two, and to make them function better together."

"You saved many lives today," Mossa said. He laid the blade back down across his knees, put the whetstone away.

"And took many more," Cella added.

"Hardly seems kosher," Early said. "All this new

technology has too many advantages over us mere mortals. Might even make wars obsolete someday." Early recalled the slaughter at the village, but he'd seen plenty of other examples of technology-induced carnage on too many other battlefields.

"From your lips to God's ears," Cella said. "It can't happen soon enough."

"Your machines will change wars, but not the men who fight them. There will always be wars, until there are no men," Mossa said. "When all men are dead, then their machines will still keep fighting for them, because they will have been programmed by the men who made them."

"It's *Terminator* and Skynet," Early mused.

"I loved that movie," Mossa said.

Early burst out laughing. Cella and Pearce did, too, infected by Early's loss of control.

"I said something funny?" Mossa said.

When Early finally recovered, he wiped the tears from his eyes. "No, I'm sorry. I meant no offense. But you look like an ancient warrior from the distant past. The thought of you sitting in a movie theater with your sword, watching a futuristic sci-fi movie, well, it just seemed funny."

"I watched it on a DVD, actually. At my son's home in Tripoli, years ago." Mossa's eyes misted into a memory. Cella took one of his hands in hers, squeezed it. The others stared into the crackling fire.

Pearce wanted to know more about Cella's husband. How they met, how he died, and how Cella of all people would be caught up in a genocidal war like this. But now was not the time.

Mossa returned to the present, to his guests. "You two met in your war, yes?"

Pearce nodded.

"In Afghanistan, or Iraq?"

"Iraq," Early blurted after an uncomfortable silence. "A joint mission, helping the Kurds in the north."

"You were both CIA?"

"Me? Hell no. U.S. Army Ranger." Early threw a thumb at Pearce. "He was the spook."

"A spy. Interesting. I don't think of spies as fighters." Mossa flicked his cigarette into the fire.

"I was with the Special Operations Group, part of the CIA's Special Activities Division. Sort of like their own little army."

Mossa brightened. "So you were a soldier?"

"Yes."

"But not now?"

"No."

"And yet here you are, fighting."

"That's different." Pearce pounded Early on the shoulder. "I came for this knucklehead. But now, no more wars."

"What did you learn about war in Iraq?"

"He also fought in Afghanistan," Cella said. "That is where we met. A long time ago."

"What did I learn? I learned that war is too important to be left to the politicians."

"And yet they are the ones who want them. But it has always been that way. What else?"

"I know that I fought with good men, mostly." Thoughts of Annie washed over Pearce. "And women."

"Women fighters?" Mossa was incredulous. "What a waste."

"Yes, a few women back then. More now, these days."

"Why did you fight in Iraq?"

"For my country."

"What changed?"

"What do you mean?"

"Why did you stop fighting? Did you stop being an American?"

"The war was voluntary. Most Americans didn't fight in the war. Almost none of the politicians did—neither did their children."

"You got that damn straight," Early said. His face soured. "Funny how the guys that never fought are the first to want to fight."

"That is true everywhere," Cella said. "Politicians want the votes. They get votes when they bomb other people."

"We call them 'chicken hawks' back home," Early said.

Mossa lit another cigarette. Pointed at Pearce. "But I asked about you, not about the chickens. Why did you stop fighting?"

"We started two wars we didn't know how to finish. Too many people I knew got killed waiting for my government to figure that out."

"We have a saying: 'It's easier to fall into a well than to climb out of one.'"

"We jumped into two of them," Early said. "Now look at them, now that we're gone."

"But you had the best weapons. Did your technology fail you?" Mossa asked.

Pearce shook his head. "No. The technology worked fine. We killed many, many more of them than they killed of us."

"And yet you are the ones who quit the war. You, yourself, left. So your technology did fail." Mossa pointed at Moctar, head devoutly touching his prayer rug. Mossa whispered, "Moctar loves his people, but he loves Allah even more. Such men are more dangerous than drones."

"Even to you?" Pearce asked.

"Yes. Even to me. He is al-Qaeda Sahara."

"What?" Early couldn't believe it. "Then why is he here?"

"Keep your friends close and your enemies closer." Mossa winked. "He will only put a bullet in me if he is ordered to. He loves me like a father, and his people. He is a good man, as well as devout. Besides, even the prophet Jesus had his Judas, did he not? Not that I am a prophet or even the son of a prophet."

"The *muj* always knew that they would win simply by not losing," Pearce said, using the pejorative slang word for *mujahideen*. "They were willing to die by the tens of thousands. They bought time with their blood. But I agree. Technology is never a substitute for the will to win."

"So many needless deaths," Cella added. "On both sides."

"They started it," Early said. "I'm just sorry we didn't finish it."

"And how would you finish it?" Cella demanded.

"Kill every last motherfucking one of them," Early said.

"'Them'?" she asked.

Early's eyes narrowed. "The *muj*. The crazy bastards. The terrorists."

"They call us terrorists," Cella said. She meant Mossa and her adopted family.

"I don't know who 'they' are. But I know you. You're the good guys."

"And if you didn't know us?"

"But I do. I'm here, aren't I?"

"Imbecilli!" She flipped a dismissive hand in the air.

"Daughter, please." Mossa raised his head. "These are our guests."

"I'm sorry." Cella wrapped her arms around her raised knees and buried her face, hiding from the conversation.

Mossa turned back to Pearce. "So you stopped fighting the war, and yet you are still a warrior. Both of you."

"Not for America."

"Why not?"

"You don't understand. Our politicians are corrupt."

"You Americans. You are so quick to change everyone else's government. Perhaps you should change your own."

"That's called treason where we come from," Early said.

Mossa smiled. "Truth is always treason to the wicked. Was not George Washington a traitor to the British Crown?"

"I'm no politician," Pearce said. "And the country is divided."

"Ha!" Mossa laughed. "You don't know the Imohar, do you? We have a little unity now because everyone else is trying to kill us. When the outside threat is gone, watch what my people will do to each other again."

"What do you mean?"

"The MNLA wants Azawad—a separate Tuareg nation. But Ansar Dine wants sharia law, not Tuareg law, al-Murabitoun wants to wage jihad against foreigners, and AQS wants a West African caliphate. But worst of all, most of our people have settled in the cities driving trucks or in the villages raising sheep and selling tires and tobacco, and are forgetting our ways altogether."

"So why do you still fight? Every government around here wants the Tuareg fighters to surrender, and want you dead."

Mossa ran his fingers along the *takouba* blade, his fingertips gliding over carved images in the metal.

"The men who make our swords are called Ineden. Do you know this term?"

"Blacksmith?" Pearce offered.

"Yes, that is what they do, but Ineden are also a separate caste of people. They have their own special language and, it is said, their own magical powers, which they breathe into these swords as they make them. Do you understand?"

"No."

"The Ineden are forged, by God, to make swords. I am Ihaggaren, forged in God's furnace to wield the sword. Like you, I am a warrior. Do you not see? The warrior is given by God to serve his people. I win my war by being faithful to God and to my people. What they do with their victory, *inshallah*, is up to them. That is why you are miserable, Troy. You are a *ronin*, a masterless warrior. You know this term?"

"I'm surprised you do, but I don't know why I'm surprised by anything you say anymore," Early said.

"When a samurai no longer had a master, he sold his services or turned to crime," Pearce said. "Or killed himself."

"No. When a samurai no longer had a master, he was no longer a samurai. He lost his purpose." Mossa turned to Early. "A samurai is devoted to his master, not to war. Serving his master was his true purpose. Did you know this? Or have you not read *The Hagakure*?"

"When did you read it?" Pearce asked. He had been assigned it as a text at The Farm years ago.

"When I was a young man, younger than you. It meant nothing to me at the time. But my Russian instructor had insisted on it, despite its being a 'remnant of bourgeois classism,' or some such nonsense."

Pearce couldn't help but smile. Had the Soviets copied the CIA curriculum, or the other way around?

"How long were you in the Soviet Union?" Pearce asked.

"Not the Soviet Union. Benghazi, at the military

academy, for six months. We had several Russian instruc-
tors. Gaddafi was a socialist, besides being a Pan-Arabist."

"You fought for Gaddafi?"

"I was recruited into the Islamic Legion in 1971. He
recruited many poor fighters, but especially Tuaregs. He
favored us, and gave us the chance to fight. Good money,
homes. My two sons were born there." He nodded at
Cella. "Her husband. He became a doctor."

"And your other son?"

"A fighter, like me. With his brother, in Paradise. I
hope to see them both soon."

"Don't say such things," Cella said.

Mossa ignored her. "Libya was good to me. But it all
came at a very high price. A price I was willing to pay
for too long."

"What was the price?"

"To forget my people, my fathers, my tribe, my chief,
in order to serve Libya and the Pan-Arab movement. But
Gaddafi forgot that Tuaregs are not Arabs. We are Ber-
bers, and we were here in the Sahara before the Arabs.
And, *inshallah*, we shall be here long after they are gone."

Mossa drew a big circle in the sand with his finger, then
split the circle into parts and named them. "Libya here,
Niger here, Mali here, Algeria here, Burkina Faso here.
Do you see what these nations all have in common?"

"Sand," Early said. He never missed the obvious.

Mossa laughed. "No. Not even that." Mossa wiped
the borders away with his hand. "They are merely *lines*
in the sand. Meaningless. The Sahara is the Sahara, and
the Imohar are its masters, without borders."

Mossa turned to Pearce. "I was miserable when I came home. I thought it was because I was a warrior without a war. But in truth, I had become a *ronin*, like you. It wasn't until I took up the rifle on behalf of my people that I became human again." He slipped his *takouba* into its leather sheath. "If you don't mind my saying, you are like a sword without a sheath. You, too, Early. Do you understand my meaning?"

"No," Early said.

"The best sword remains in its sheath so that it is ready when it is needed. A sword outside of its place will rust and break and become worthless, only to be tossed into the fire."

Cella shook her head. "You men and your talk of war and borders and killing. If you made life inside of you instead of taking the lives of others around you, you would hear how foolish you sound."

Mossa laughed. "You should talk, daughter! You are the fiercest warrior of us all. You fight for those you love, too. Only not with bullets."

The camel driver called out, lifting the great round wheel of bread out of the hot sand.

"You see? All your talk of war, and you should have been making tea!" Cella stood up and headed over to the camel driver to help.

"She is worse than two generals," Mossa said. "But she has a good heart." The Tuareg glanced at Pearce. "But you already know this."

"She saved many lives in Afghanistan, including mine, I think."

"And yesterday you came here. Perhaps she is the one I should thank for our lives." Mossa stood. "But first I shall make the tea."

Pearce scanned the wide horizon. If the Malian army decided to come after them here, nothing could save them. He was all out of tricks now and there was nowhere to hide.

= 47 =

Maersk Oil Pumping Station
Tamanghasset Province, Southern Algeria
11 May

Lieutenant Beaujolais kneeled down to get a better photo on his cell phone. The Danish woman was beautiful. Such a waste. He pressed the button. The cell phone camera flashed. The woman's face appeared on the small screen. Blond hair, brown eyes, a mouth twisted in a rictus of terror.

He pressed SEND. The message was addressed to the French Foreign Legion command. He stood. The rubber soles of his boots made a crackling sound as he moved. The floor was sticky with blood. He took a photo of the Danish woman's twisted body, three feet away from her head.

"Lieutenant!" The shout came from outside.

The lieutenant pulled his pistol and dashed outside. The corporal's voice came from around back.

"Lieutenant! Here!"

Beaujolais ran to the far side of the building. The corporal, a wiry Haitian, pointed in the distance. A man stumbled around in the distance on a low dune, like a drunk.

"You! Stop!" the lieutenant called. But the man stumbled on.

Beaujolais fired his pistol in the air. "STOP!" But the drunk plodded on.

The lieutenant and the corporal ran the distance, their boots marching a straight line through his wobbly footprints. They were both in fantastic shape, but sprinting uphill a hundred meters in the hot sand left them both exhausted, thighs and calves throbbing.

The lieutenant's eyes stung with sweat. He wiped it away with his free hand, afraid he was seeing things.

Mon Dieu.

The wide-eyed Haitian corporal saw the same thing.

The two soldiers raced the last few meters, shouting for the man to stop in French, English, and Arabic. He didn't.

The Haitian dropped his rifle and tackled the man from behind. He didn't resist. They rolled him over. The drunken man held up his two arms, raising blackened stumps to heaven, crying out, *I am no thief!* in Arabic, blood and tears streaming down his lidless eyes. He wasn't drunk.

He was out of his mind.

No question. This was the man on the AQS video beheading the Danish woman in the pump house posted just hours before.

The Haitian opened his canteen and tried to give the

man water, but he spit it out. The corporal dumped it on his face to cool him and relieve his sun-scorched eyes.

The lieutenant shot a cell phone picture of the man's blistered face for confirmation from HQ, but he was certain it was him, the killer in the video. But this wretch wasn't AQ Sahara. They wouldn't do this to their own kind. Besides, he had no beard, no weapon, and they left him behind—unlike the other two masked butchers in the video holding the girl. Maybe they forced this man to behead her?

"Who did this to you?" the lieutenant asked in Arabic.

The man wept and burbled.

"I can't understand you."

"Al Rus," the man finally muttered.

The lieutenant cursed. They had just missed him. But at least they knew he was in the area. Maybe headquarters could do something with that.

The Oval Office, the White House
Washington, D.C.

Diele poured himself another scotch. Without asking.

Again.

President Greyhill was coming to regret his arranged marriage with the esteemed former senator from Nevada. Diele had helped broker the deal that got Myers to resign her office in exchange for blanket pardons for Pearce and his friends. The broker's fee Diele charged was the vice presidency. The exchange gave Greyhill the big desk in the Oval Office, but he could never shake the feeling that Diele had one hand on the doorknob, ready to shove him back out.

But Diele had his uses. He was a formidable ally to have in his corner—the kind of bare-knuckled street fighter who would gleefully kick an unsuspecting opponent in the balls before the fight even began. The kind of fighter that would rather kick an opponent in the head when he was down on the ground clutching his scrotum than actually get in a ring and prance around for ten rounds. That made Diele extremely valuable to Greyhill.

But the vice president was a pain in the ass, too. Didn't know his place. Stomped around the Oval Office like he owned it. Drank up Greyhill's best liquor. Didn't even have the courtesy to ask Greyhill if he wanted one of his own, which he did.

"Quit pissing your pantaloons. It's a nonstarter," Diele said over the top of his glass. "Fiero can't touch us."

Greyhill shifted in his chair behind the famous desk. The pronoun "us" grated on him. "You've seen the head-lines today, haven't you? Seems Fiero is awfully prescient."

Today's below-the-fold front-page article in the *New York Times* featured a map of Africa and the spreading influence of the Chinese. A *Washington Post* op-ed had picked up on the Fiero Sunday-morning interview, too, and echoed her concerns.

"Slow news day at the fish wrapper, that's all. And who watches those tired old news shows anyway?" Diele fell onto the couch, put his feet up on the heirloom coffee table. Greyhill clenched his jaw. Diele was a primitive.

"But what about her point? China and REEs and all of that? And, of course, the terrorist connection."

"What terrorist connection? She didn't offer any proof. Just some damn hearsay speculation. Don't you see? She's throwing everything out on the stoop, see what the dog'll lick up. Or in this case, the reporters. You can smell her desperation. Don't you think if any of this was legit, it would've popped up on the PDB?" Diele was referring to the Presidential Daily Brief, a document provided each morning by the director of national intelligence. Greyhill preferred an oral presentation by someone from the DNI's office with just bullet points. He seldom read the actual documents. Diele pored over them.

"Our national intelligence community hasn't always batted a thousand. Remember Benghazi? A dead ambassador and three brave Americans murdered by our 'allies.' Just because something isn't in the PDB doesn't mean it isn't happening."

Diele drained the last of his drink. The ice rattled in the glass. "Worst-case scenario? The terror threat turns out to be real. Then we send in the drones. But don't even think about getting sucked up in that quicksand over there. It's all a damn mess. The first Marine boot you put on the ground over there will be marching on your political grave."

Greyhill frowned. Diele might be right. His instincts usually were. But Greyhill had taken note of the vice president's grammatical shift. Suddenly, it was "your" political grave. Another irritating pronoun. He took the change as both a warning and a threat.

= 48 =

The raccoon rings beneath Captain Sotero's eyes spoke volumes to Judy. Clearly, the woman hadn't slept in days. No doubt because of her and Pearce's arrival four nights before.

The captain sat at the small table in Judy's dining/living room in the spartan visiting BOQ trailer where she'd been largely confined by AF Security Forces guards since her return from Mali.

"You have everything you need here, Ms. Hopper? Any personal items you need sent over?"

"No, everything's fine. Just a little cramped, that's all. But I'm used to that." Judy had grown up in even more austere environments as a missionary kid in Africa.

"Wouldn't mind being able to stretch my legs every now and then."

"Sure, no problem. Just help me clear up a few things, will you?"

Judy smiled. "If I can. I mean, I've told you everything I know already."

"You see, that's what I'm not so sure about. I think there's a lot more to you and this humanitarian mission you're supposedly on. For starters, where is the American you were supposed to be evacuating?"

"Like I said before, he decided not to come."

"And you said his name was?"

"I didn't say." Judy didn't know if Mike Early was in trouble or not for being there. Her dad had raised her with the maxim "Better to keep your mouth shut and appear the fool than open your mouth and confirm it."

Sotero's weary eyes narrowed. "His name is Mike Early. Your friend Mr. Holliday just confirmed that for me."

"Okay."

"But your friend"—Sotero checked her notes on a tablet—"Pearce, he decided to stay?"

"Something like that."

"In Mali?"

"Yes."

"You see, that's what's confusing to me. Do you remember Sergeant Wolfit? The man who was with me the night we first met?"

"Vaguely."

"Square-jawed? Broad across the chest?" She mimed his torso with her hands. "Always looks pissed off?"

"What's your point?"

Sotero pulled up a map on her tablet, turned it around. Pointed at a winking dot. "See that? That's an RFID chip. The one that was attached to Sergeant Wolfit's weapon. The weapon he believes your friend Pearce stole from him that night, an M4 carbine."

"Do you always plant RFID chips in your guns?"

"We inventory everything, especially weapons. It's easier to chip and scan them than do the paperwork. The Air Force is pretty good at technology these days."

"Makes sense."

"So you know anything about that? I mean, Pearce stealing his weapon?"

"You'd have to ask Troy when you see him."

"If you'll look closely at the map, you'll see the chip is now located in Algeria. What's Pearce doing in Algeria?"

Judy shrugged. "Maybe it's just the gun that's in Algeria."

"Why would the weapon be in Algeria without Pearce?"

"You'd have to ask Troy when you see him."

"So you're saying Pearce is not in Algeria right now?"

"I have no idea where he is exactly."

"But he's probably still in Mali?"

"Like I said, I have no idea."

Sotero spun her tablet back around. "Is Pearce really on a humanitarian mission?"

"He went in to get Mike Early, yes."

"That's kind of strange, too. We checked with the State Department as well as with the Mali government. We have no record of Mike Early entering the country of Mali, at least not legally. What is Mike Early doing in Mali?"

"I don't know. You'd have to ask Mike when you see him."

"Is this Early guy still in Mali? Or is he with Pearce in Algeria?"

"I'm sorry. I'm not trying to be difficult. I really don't know."

"Okay, let's try another tack. Do you have any idea why my base commander has been detained in Frankfurt?"

"No."

"Funny thing is, he was dispatched to Bonn–Bad Godesberg for what was apparently a bogus meeting the same day you arrived here, and when the meeting didn't occur, he was flagged by the NSA as a possible terror suspect on the way back. He's still in custody."

"That's unfortunate."

"You don't understand. Colonel Kavanagh is the most squared-away officer I ever knew, and a real straight arrow. He's a ring knocker—academy grad, third-generation Air Force. No way he's AQ-affiliated. I think someone's messed with his data profile. You have any idea who that might be?"

"No."

"Or why they would want him detained while you and your friends are operating out of this base?"

"No."

"Of course you don't." Sotero took a deep breath. "Let me ask you something else. Do you know who Mossa Ag Alla is?"

"No, I don't."

"Never heard of him?"

"Not that I can recall."

"He's an AQ affiliate. A real bad-ass. Just got bumped up to number one dickhead on our extensive list of dickheads."

"I believe you."

Sotero sighed with frustration. "Okay, one last try. When you flew out of here on the tenth, your IFF signal stopped broadcasting when you crossed into Mali airspace, and then you dropped off the radar. What was that all about?"

Judy wasn't a missionary anymore, but she couldn't bring herself to lie about anything. It just wasn't in her nature. "Security precautions."

"Failure to broadcast an IFF signal is highly irregular and dangerous, which is why it's also illegal."

"Illegal in Mali, technically, since that's where the violation occurred. I don't suppose you have jurisdiction over there, do you?"

"And did you make any unauthorized or unscheduled stops on the return flight?"

Judy had to think about that. Technically, her flight to the Niamey civilian airfield was both authorized and scheduled, just not with the United States Air Force. "No."

"Look, Ms. Hopper, I'm not trying to disrupt or interfere with your CIA op or whatever it is you guys are actually trying to do, but all I have to stand on is an extremely thin paper trail—basically, a one-paragraph order from this mysterious Colonel Sanders whom I still can't reach—and nothing else to show for it. You were supposed to bop in and out and then bounce out of here in twenty-four hours with your man Early. Instead, there are now two Americans missing, presumably at least one of them is in Algeria, and he's carrying a weapon stolen from a very pissed-off SF sergeant who's about to be busted to corporal if that rifle doesn't show up in the next twenty-four hours." Sotero caught herself rambling. She rubbed her face to help her focus.

"So this is all about a missing rifle?"

"No, it's not about a missing rifle. It's about you people clearly lying about what your real mission is, and about me not being able to get independent verification that authorizes your fake humanitarian mission. I need to be very, very sure that I haven't let a couple of bad guys onto my base. If I have, there's a cell in Leavenworth with my name on it."

"I promise, Captain, you haven't."

"This Pearce guy, he's a friend of yours?"

Judy wanted to call him a first-class jerk for the way he'd been acting lately, but now was not the time for a Dr. Phil moment. "Yes, he's a friend. A very good friend. A decorated veteran, too."

"I'm glad to hear that. So you'd vouch for him?"

"Of course."

"And you wouldn't want anything bad to happen to him, right?"

"Not at all."

"Straight up?"

"Word of honor."

"Well, since you're being perfectly honest with me, let me be perfectly honest with you. I just got word that a strike mission has been set for that dickhead I was telling you about, that Mossa character? Reaper, missile, you get the picture. If your friend Pearce is with Mossa, your friend Pearce is going to die."

"Oh my word. When?"

"You tell me where Pearce is, I'll tell you when the strike is."

"I told you, I don't know."

"Do you know somebody who does? Because if you do, you'd better give me his name."

Judy knew somebody, all right. Ian could still locate the tracker in Troy's body. She also knew Ian had just eavesdropped on their entire conversation. She just prayed that he could do something about it.

He couldn't.

CIOS Corporate Offices
Rockville, Maryland

Jasmine Bath listened in on the entire interrogation, too. She already knew Mike Early was a former close associate of Margaret Myers. When Sotero had initiated a query on Early and his status in Mali earlier, two of Bath's algorithms tripped and he was flagged. She traced back the query to Sotero's tablet and immediately hacked it.

Bath had always admired Pearce, if for no other reason than she had been able to acquire so little information about him. Either he or someone working for him was very good at keeping him out of all of the known databases and obliterating his digital shadow. There were thousands of "Pearce-shaped holes" everywhere she looked, as if someone was going in after Pearce whenever he popped up anywhere and erased any data relative to him and his company, Pearce Systems—one of the few organizations in the world she'd never been able to hack. This all just confirmed what she learned earlier from her hacked phone call between Zhao and Anthony Fiero.

Today's interrogation now also confirmed for Bath that Pearce and Early were both in Mali at the same time as Mossa, and Myers had initiated Pearce's mission into Mali, presumably to rescue Early. And yet Early was never rescued, nor did Pearce return. In fact, thanks to the RFID chip tracking on Captain Sotero's hacked tablet and its ridiculously childish security system, Bath now knew where both Pearce and Mossa were located in Algeria.

That was all information that Fiero would desperately want in light of the concerns raised by Zhao. Information that Bath passed on immediately to Fiero before she herself succumbed to the pressure to torpedo it. Bath hated the idea of Pearce getting killed before she could meet him and figure out how he had managed to remain such a mystery to her. But Fiero was still paying the bills. Her curiosity about Pearce would have to remain unsatisfied.

No matter. Bath knew she would find greater satisfaction in her newfound knowledge that connected Zhao Yi, the Fieros, Pearce, and Mali. Knowledge she could use to finally untangle herself from the violent web she had been spinning all these years.

Bath decided it was time to make her move. She couldn't afford to wait seven more months to retire, despite her plans. She'd been riding the tiger too long. Staying on would prove fatal. But if she wasn't careful, so would the dismount.

= 49 =

Senator Fiero picked up a photograph from the fireplace mantel. It was a picture of Vice President Diele leaning against the Oval Office desk, talking down to President Greyhill seated on the couch. Very telling.

"You're confusing the hell out of me, Barbara. Yesterday, you were busting our balls on national television about our failure to address the terrorism threat, and now you're here asking us for a favor."

Diele poured himself a scotch from a crystal decanter. The cold ice cracked beneath the warm liquor. He didn't offer her one.

"I'm sorry. I'm not sure why that's confusing to you. You've read the same reports I have. This terrorist Mossa is a dangerous new threat in the region. I want him stopped. So do you." She set the photo back on the mantel. "I know you, Gary. You want this guy's scalp as badly as I do." Diele and Fiero had served together in the Senate for years.

Diele took a thoughtful sip of scotch. "You're right, I do. He's Asshole Numero Uno, as far as I'm concerned."

Jasmine Bath had done a brilliant job seeding the various jihadi websites—legit and NSA-managed—with the uploaded war footage supplied by Zhao. Dead bodies, flaming vehicles, Tuaregs firing machine guns. A real horror show. Her automated systems also planted hundreds of fake comments on those sites in support of Mossa, linking him and the Tuaregs with al-Qaeda, *jihad*, and every other hot-button word flags that lit up the NSA algorithms. Within forty-eight hours of the first upload, Bath had transformed the obscure Tuareg chieftain into a worldwide villain. Carefully leaked "anonymous government sources" also put Mossa and his "AQ-affiliated terror group" on the front pages of the leading mainstream media sites, always scrambling to fill the insatiable twenty-four-hour news cycle.

"Terrorists like this Mossa character are Whac-A-Moles. You smash one down, three more jump up." Diele took a sip. He was starting to look his age, Fiero thought. His famous mane of silver hair had receded in recent years and his pinkish-gray scalp was really starting to show. He needed a good set of hair plugs if he ever hoped to make a presidential run.

"Who said 'The cost of freedom is eternal vigilance'?"

"Does it matter?" Diele asked.

"No, I suppose it doesn't."

"And you probably know the answer anyway. You always did like to show off." Diele fell into an upholstered chair. He pointed at the empty one next to him. "Take a seat."

"Thank you." She sat.

"You still haven't answered my question. Why not go running to another talk show this Sunday and decry this administration's failure to deal with the Tuareg threat? Isn't that your strategy? I bet Fowler is behind all of that."

Just like Diele to give credit to a man, Fiero thought. She bit her tongue.

"I did answer you. I really do think this Mossa sonofabitch needs to be taken out, quickly, before he causes real damage over there—or over here." She smiled demurely. "You and I have worked together well in the past on the issues that mattered most, wouldn't you agree?"

Diele nodded thoughtfully. Fiero had always voted the right way when it came to the War on Terror. She'd supported all of the NSA spying stuff that even he felt a little uncomfortable with, at least privately. Diele loved crossing the aisle and cutting good deals with reasonable people. What most voters didn't understand was that mainstream Republicans and Democrats in Congress shared nearly identical values. They only kicked up a big stink about the other side to keep their voters in line. But the truth of the matter was that Washington was perfectly content with itself, even if the American public loathed it.

Diele's father had taught him years before that every system was perfectly designed to get the results it achieves.

Congress was no different. Congress wasn't broken. Congress was perfect, as far as most congressmen were concerned. It gave them wealth, power, and privilege.

"Yes, I'd agree with that. You've always been reasonable on the issues that mattered most."

"This one matters, Gary. You know it does. I don't want another 9/11 on my conscience. Do you?"

"God knows I'm not opposed to a drone strike. You know my record on that. It's just that Greyhill is scared shitless to pull the trigger. He's enjoying the highest approval ratings he's ever had. He won't want to rock the boat."

"Why does it have to be public knowledge?"

Diele leaned forward, raised a silver eyebrow. "You're telling me you'd keep quiet about this? It would be a helluva feather in your cap to claim you provoked us into a drone strike. At the very least, you could say Greyhill had broken his promise to keep us out of any new wars."

"A drone strike isn't 'boots on the ground,' and it's hardly a war. Presidents Bush, Obama, and Myers all saw to that. But, yes, formally I am promising you, Scout's honor, that I will keep my mouth shut." She ran two slender fingers across her chest, then held them high, like a Boy Scout pledge. "That's how serious I am about this." She wasn't kidding.

After Guo's report of the failed battle, Zhao contacted Anthony Fiero and made an offer. If his wife would help take out Mossa, then he could make arrangements to supply his consortium with rare earth elements. If she couldn't show Zhao at least a good-faith effort with a drone strike, there was no way he'd keep his promise and she and her husband would go bankrupt. Worse, a bankruptcy would be a financial scandal that would ruin her chances in the election.

"And if Greyhill refuses to launch the drone strike?"

"Then it will be one more albatross I'll hang around his neck come election time. Don't forget how JFK beat Nixon like a drum by mocking the Republicans for being weak on defense."

Fiero saw the calculations spinning in Diele's eyes. Her threat to campaign against Greyhill made the unlikely promise that she wouldn't blow the whistle on this meeting seem more credible to the old fox. The best lies always contained the most truth.

"One last thing, Barbara. How is it you came by this intel? Thirteen intelligence agencies have tried and failed to find this guy, and you waltz into this office with the goods quicker than a hooker at a Shriners convention."

"I happen to believe that the private sector is almost always more efficient than the public sector, even when it comes to intelligence gathering. After all, look how heavily dependent the NSA has been on the good graces of Google, Verizon, and all of the other big data corporations."

"Your source?"

Fiero didn't dare tell Diele that her source was a Chinese operative who had eyes on Mossa in the desert. Of course, neither had Zhao told her it was actually an AQS operative by the name of Al Rus who was actually conveying the intel.

"My husband does quite a bit of work with a private

security company called CIOS. They specialize in searches like this. They're rather lean and nimble, not some ossified government bureaucracy. They've located Mossa with an RFID chip."

"Who managed to plant that on him?"

"No telling. But the intel is good."

"You're absolutely certain?"

"Yes." That was only half true. She was certain that Troy Pearce carried a rifle embedded with an RFID chip. She just assumed he'd be standing next to Mossa when a Hellfire missile came crashing down.

"Worse-case scenario? It's a signature strike. You take out a few bad guys, even if it's not the right bad guy."

Fiero was referring to the latest iteration of drone strike policy. Originally, the president or some member of the national security staff targeted specific individuals after some kind of official vetting. President Obama was famous for his regular "Terror Tuesday" meetings where he personally selected individuals for death by drone, weighing carefully the evidence presented to him by various agencies.

But such procedures became ponderous and time-consuming. By the time a target was vetted they often had already disappeared. Also, the "evidence" presented was sometimes of dubious origin anyway. The current policy was far more efficient. Anonymous individuals—no names, no discernible identification—who fit the "signature" of a terrorist—for example, a young man armed with a rifle on the road to a known terrorist village—could be killed under the presumption that he was probably a terrorist anyway. After all, if it walked like a duck and quacked like a duck, it must be a duck.

"Easy enough to confirm," Fiero said. "Dispatch a Reaper out of Niamey. Put him on camera, run it through your database, and if he's the target, pull the trigger." She smile-frowned. "Gee, Gary, do you want me to go over there and do it myself?"

Diele laughed, standing. "You're something else, you know that?"

"So I've been told." Fiero locked eyes with Diele. Saw the bolt of electricity that coursed through him. Better than Viagra for most of these old guys, she'd been told.

"Can I get you something to drink?"

"That would be delightful. Bourbon, neat, if you don't mind." She didn't want Diele's grubby hands touching her ice.

"Lime or lemon?"

"Neither, thank you."

Diele splashed a couple of fingers of Maker's Mark into a glass.

"Now that we're being so chummy, let me throw you a couple of bones," Fiero said. "First of all, Myers is tied up in this somehow."

Diele twisted a lemon slice and hung it on the rim of the glass. "How?"

"Remember Mike Early? He was one of her special assistants for security."

"Vaguely." He refilled his own glass.

"He's over there with this Mossa character. She also dispatched Troy Pearce over there to be with him." Fiero was careful to leave out the fact that Pearce was sent to get Early out of there. "You do remember Troy Pearce?"

She knew, of course, that he did. Diele hated Myers's guts and had learned after the fact the vital role Pearce had played in the drone counterterror operations she had launched against the Mexican drug cartels. That put Pearce on Diele's shit list, too. But since Greyhill had extended blanket immunities to Myers and anyone she named in exchange for her resignation, Diele was never able to get even with Myers or Pearce.

Diele handed Fiero her drink, his face flushed with anger.

"Thank you, Gary."

"Pearce, eh?"

"And Myers."

"How is Myers connected to all of this?"

Fiero was careful with her answer. She'd seen a copy of that morning's PDB. She knew Diele had seen it, too. Thanks to CIOS, Myers and Pearce had been effectively linked to Mossa and AQS, but not in any concrete manner. It wasn't conclusive, but it was good enough to raise eyebrows around the room, she was certain.

"Not sure, but does it really matter?" Fiero said. "She clearly wants something over there. For all I know, she's cooking up some sort of deal with the Chinese. Mossa is key to the whole region. Take him out and likely you'll be screwing Myers in the process. How's that for a bonus?"

Fiero had chosen her words carefully. Diele had been a famous cocksman in his day, and his lust knew no bounds. She'd seen the way Diele had leered at the first female president whenever they were in the room together, much the same way he leered at her when he thought she wasn't looking.

"Greyhill is still smarting from the ass-whipping she gave him in the primaries," Diele said, which was true enough, but getting even with that bitch Myers was okay by him, too. "I'm sure he'll be on board with this."

"How sure?"

"He's got his head so far up his ass he doesn't have a clue what's going on around here. He's more interested in playing golf with some ambassador or sitting in on policy briefings than actually running things. I do most of the day-to-day around here. I'll give the order, and if he ever gets wind of it, I'll sell it to him." He took a long sip of scotch. The ice tinkled as he drained the glass. His eyes brightened. "Myers will seal the deal."

"One more thing, Gary, in the spirit of full disclosure."

"What?"

"If Pearce and Early are running around with Mossa in the desert, they're going to be collateral damage in a drone strike."

"Fuck 'em. If they don't want to get blistered, they shouldn't put their dicks in the toaster."

"They're American citizens."

"They're enemy combatants, as far as I'm concerned."

"You would've made one helluva president, Gary," Fiero said. She raised her glass in a mock toast. "Or maybe you already are." She finally took a sip of her drink.

The old man's ego swelled. He knew she was piling

it on, but he didn't care. She was right. In many respects, he was the acting president.

"One more thing, Barbara, while we're being so chummy. I need you to promise you'll back us up on this should it ever come to a committee hearing or, God forbid, a full Senate inquiry."

"You have my word. And I can keep my people in line. You also have the chair of my committee in your pocket, along with the other neocon Republicans to back you up. You won't have any trouble from us."

"Good. One last thing. I want you to back off of Greyhill on this whole 'soft on terrorism' angle your campaign is running."

"Why should I? It's true, isn't it?"

Diele darkened. "Doesn't matter. Technically, he's my boss and the head of my party. I'm supposed to watch out for him."

"Technically, you are. Taking out Mossa takes one arrow out of my quiver, as per our agreement. But the truth of the matter is, you want Greyhill to get reelected so you can keep your job. I get that. But I want his job, too. So how about this? I keep hammering on this, and if he wakes up and finally sees the threats and starts to take action, we'll all be better off. But if he doesn't and the American public still supports him, he'll still get reelected and you'll still have your job. There's a third possibility, of course."

"What?"

"That I keep hammering, that it costs him the election, and in the spirit of bipartisan cooperation, I nominate you as SecDef or any other damn position you'd want in my administration."

"Sounds like a step down to me."

"Okay, then here's a step up. I keep hammering at Greyhill from the outside while you pull your levers on the party on the inside, eroding confidence in his leadership. If my campaign is successful, Greyhill's numbers will plummet before the convention, and you can ride in to rescue the nomination for your party."

Diele's face turned positively postcoital, brimming with satisfaction. "You and I always did work well together, didn't we?"

"We're the smart ones, Gary. We're the ones that run the whole damn town."

= 50 =

After the wadi they traveled east two more days deeper into the desert, riding in the mornings, resting in the heat of the day, then pushing on past sunset. They were making good time. Mossa explained that they weren't riding traditional pack camels, but smaller and faster Arabian war camels that could cover over a hundred miles per day if needed, but for now their pace was more relaxed. Pearce and the others rode most of the day but walked the last few miles in the cool of the evening to spare the animals, tied nose to tail by ropes slack with indifference.

The desert had changed since the wadi. Now they traversed gently sloping dunes gradually rising toward the jagged teeth of the Hoggar Mountains in the distance.

This was more like the Sahara of his imagination, though still not quite as grand as he'd pictured.

They all walked in silence. The desert seemed to require it. Pearce felt humbled by it, the way a student waits for the master to speak. The setting sun behind the caravan threw long shadows in front of Pearce, the head of his image stretching past the Tuareg walking in front of him. It would be night soon. He was lost in the rhythms of the camel's unusual gait. Right rear, right front, left rear, left front, step after silent step. Every horse he'd ever known walked just the opposite: right front, left rear, left front, right rear. There was something graceful, even hypnotic, in the strange, silent padding of the great white animals.

Troy had made no efforts to speak with Cella privately since they'd left the village. It was impossible to do so with her father-in-law hovering over her, and she had shown no interest in a private conversation. She seldom strayed more than a few yards from Mossa, especially now that there were no wounds or injuries to treat among the others. They seemed deeply connected, though they hardly spoke, either, except in the company of others. He'd noticed over the years that most Middle Eastern men seldom spoke to women, at least the older, traditional men, even when women were around, which was seldom. But Pearce suspected that their mutual silence was consensual rather than cultural. Cella probably felt very safe around Mossa. Perhaps their common grief had bound them together as well.

"What are you thinking?"

Pearce startled at Cella's whispered voice. She had somehow managed to slip into step next to him without his noticing. Maybe he really had been hypnotized by his camel's gait.

"Not much, really."

"I love the desert this time of day."

"It's amazing," Pearce agreed. The darkening blue sky was giving way to purple, and a swath of stars glittered in the vast expanse overhead. In the distance, a great rock arch towered over the sand, like a portal to another world.

"The Tuaregs are matrilineal. Did you know this?"

"Hadn't really thought about it."

Cella pointed at the jagged teeth of granite mountains looming far ahead. "Tin Hinan is the mother of all Tuaregs. She lived in the fourth century B.C. At one time she was buried out there."

"But not now?"

"An American archaeologist stole her body in the 1920s with the help of the French army. Or so it is believed by some."

"Sounds like an Indiana Jones movie."

"I liked those movies. Especially the first one. I liked the woman in it, especially his woman. What was her name?"

"I don't remember."

"It doesn't matter. I liked her."

"Why did you like her?"

Cella's face lit up. "Because when Indy accidentally found her in Tibet, she punched him in the face instead of kissing him."

Pearce laughed. He jutted his chin out and thrust it toward her. "Knock yourself out."

"Don't tempt me."

"I probably deserve it."

"You definitely deserve it."

They walked along in silence for a while.

"I always thought you would come back to Milan," she finally said.

"I did, too."

"What happened. A woman?"

"A war." He took a few steps. "And a woman. Later."

"You leave her, too?"

He shook his head. "She died." It was hard for him to say that, even now, a decade later. He thought of Annie often, but strangely, not so much on this trip.

"Oh. I'm sorry."

"You lost someone, too. Your husband."

"Yes." Now it was Cella's turn to be flooded with painful memories.

"How?"

"He came back here to be with his father when the war broke out a few years ago in Mali."

"He was a doctor?"

"Yes."

"Killed?"

"Yes. A week after Dorotea and I arrived in Bamako."

"I'm sorry. He must have been a good man."

"He was. He deserved better."

"Your daughter is beautiful. At least he lives in her."

Cella's eyes searched his. Pearce grew uncomfort-

able. What did she want to know? That he knew Dorotea's eyes were the same color as his? That he hadn't
stopped thinking about it since the moment he put the
girl on the plane? He looked away. They walked in
silence for a while. Pearce wanted to catch up with Early,
anything to get away.

"Have you been back to Lisbon?" she asked.

She said Lisbon casually, as if it meant nothing to her.
Or him. After all, it had been six years before.

"Once. Business. You?"

"No."

"No more UN work?"

"No. The clinic kept my husband and me busy enough."

"How did you meet him?"

"He was a cultural attaché in Roma. We met at the
opera, actually."

"A cultured man." Pearce hadn't been to an opera
since Milan.

"You almost met him. He would have come to Lisbon, but he had other business."

Pearce thought he'd been slapped across the face.

"I didn't know you were married when you were in
Lisbon."

"To my shame, I forgot I was married when I saw
you again."

Six years. It seemed like an eternity ago, until now.
Memories of Lisbon washed over him. Now he knew
why she didn't stay with him. But what did that mean
now? He didn't know what to say to her. He fell back
on his combat training. Fail forward.

"Your daughter is beautiful."

"She will be spoiled rotten by the time I see her again. My father is a maniac. He has probably already bought her a horse, and maybe even a castle in the Tyrol to hide her from me."

Low Tuareg voices called out. The camels stopped.

"What is happening?" Cella asked.

Early jogged toward them from the front. His sling was gone, but he clearly favored his injured arm.

"The boss wants to see you."

"Problem?"

"Could be. Scout just came back."

Pearce, Early, and Mossa lay flat on the crest of a dune next to the scout, a young Nigerian Tuareg named Iskaw. Towering chimneys of granite loomed a half mile ahead. The dunes were like waves of a rolling sea of sand washing up against the rocks.

Mossa held a pair of mil-spec binoculars to his eyes. He conferred with the scout in whispered Tamasheq, then handed the binoculars to Pearce. "Take a look. Just inside the rocks."

Pearce glanced through the glass, but he hardly needed to. The small flickering campfire was easily seen by the naked eye. The firelight danced off of the tall stone columns above, almost like a strobe.

"Do you see him?" Mossa asked.

Pearce adjusted the focus. Now a shadow came into view. It stood in front of the fire, its back to Pearce.

Couldn't see his face. He wore Western clothes. Definitely not a Tuareg.

"A European," Mossa said.

"I can't make him out." Pearce thought he saw a beard on the man's face.

"The scout saw him clearly earlier. Swears he is a European. Tall, bearded."

"Anyone with him?"

"No. By himself, out here. Very strange."

Pearce handed the glasses back. "Can we go around him?"

"No, our camp for the night is just past his position."

"Why there?"

"Water."

"We can take him out," Early said.

"But he may be innocent," Mossa said.

"Out here? Maybe." The big former Ranger wasn't into taking chances these days.

"Only one way to find out." Pearce rose. "You three wait here. If he cuts my head off, he's probably a bad guy."

= 51 =

Pearce crept to within ten feet of the man by the campfire, his back still toward him. The air was sweet with the tang of burnt camel dung crackling in the flames.

"I thought you were a cautious man," Pearce said. "I'm surprised you let me sneak up on you like that."

August Mann turned around, a cell-phone-sized monitor in his hand and a grin on his dark, bearded face.

"No surprises. I've been tracking you with this SPAN. You can tell all of your friends to come out now." Mann's German accent punctuated his faultless English.

SPAN was a self-powered wireless ground sensor network. Mann had scattered the tiny sensors like seeds all around the area. Anyone who came near enough to one of the sensors lit up on his monitor, which was linked to a portable sUAV Mann had deployed overhead.

"Just you?" Pearce asked.

"One war, one German. What else do you need?"

Pearce laughed. The two old friends shook hands, grinning, warriors in the field together again. A brilliant engineer and a fearless fighter, Mann was Pearce Systems' very first hire and now headed up their nuclear deconstruction operations in Europe deploying unmanned ground vehicles (UGVs). It was good to have him here. The lanky German came from a long, proud line of military men. His grandfather had commanded a PZKW IV in Rommel's Afrika Korps. Mann served briefly as a tanker with the Federal Republic's Bundeswehr, too, before helping to develop their first combat UGVs.

"I assumed you'd bring some friends along," Pearce said.

"I did."

"Where are they?"

Mann pointed in the distance. "Out there, lurking in the gloom, keeping an eye on things."

Like Pearce, Mann preferred the civilian side of drone operations these days, but when wet work was necessary he was the first to answer the call, usually relying on a cadre of trusted East European operators to assist him.

"How many?"

"Six."

"How good?"

"Untested. But reliable." Mann glanced at his monitor again. "How many with you?"

"Thirteen, plus one extra camel. Yours, as per your request."

Mann showed him the monitor. "There are fourteen persons out there." One blip was far from the others.

"Looks like we have company."

"Problem?" Mann asked.

"Nothing but."

Mann tapped his screen. A moment later, a shotgun blast echoed in the night. Mann smiled. "No more problems."

"Reliable, and now tested."

"Yes."

"Thanks for coming, August. No telling what's waiting for us up ahead."

After Mossa had laid out the route from the Adrar des Ifoghas to the airstrip, Pearce was able to pass along the GPS coordinates to Ian, Mann, and Judy along with an estimated schedule of arrival times—just in case they lost radio communications. Mann had promised to arrive here at the Tassili du Hoggar with whatever reinforcements he could bring. He and his team had parachuted in just hours before. Judy was still scheduled to pick them all up in the Aviocar three days from now.

Pearce whistled in Early and the others out of the dark. Mann was introduced to Mossa and the rest of the caravan, along with the unburdened camel that had been brought along for him. One of Mossa's men checked the corpse in the sand. He brought back an assault rifle and a pair of night-vision goggles smeared with blood to Mossa.

"He says it was an Arab," Mossa said. "No stone."

"What does that mean?" Mann asked.

"Shi'a pray with a stone," Pearce said. "Sunnis don't. Neither do Salafists. AQS is Salafist."

They all pushed on toward the oasis farther into the narrow granite canyons, their tall spires scraping against a luminous moon. Soon there would be food and water, and then they could all bed down for the night. Mann's aerial drone and ground team would keep watch over the caravan.

Pearce was exhausted, mostly from the heat. For the first time in his life he felt like he was getting too old for the field, but there was nowhere else he'd rather be, trudging through the desert beneath a canopy of stars in the company of brave companions.

$=52=$

he kneeling camels were bedded down for the
night, as were the weary Tuaregs. A small campfire had burned itself down to red embers, but
the air was still warm in this part of the desert. They
were far enough out in the wilderness that there wasn't
much chance of encountering anyone else. Only someone who knew exactly where they were could possibly
find them.

Unfortunately, someone had.

Karem Air Force Base
Niamey, Niger

The ground control station was a windowless air-conditioned trailer parked near the hangar where Judy's Aviocar was secured.

Inside the GCS, an Air Force captain sat in the pilot's seat scanning six separate video monitors. In the seat next to her, a sensor operator. Together, the two of them were flying an MQ-9 Reaper twenty thousand feet above the Sahara Desert, silent as the stars.

The drone's onboard sensor had located the RFID tracking unit embedded in the M4 rifle Pearce had stolen earlier from AFB Karem, where this Reaper had been dispatched from.

"Confirmed?" the pilot asked.

"Confirmed." The twenty-year-old sensor operator was an airman just out of training at Holloman AFB. It was, in fact, his first combat mission in the field. In addition to the RFID signal, he had an infrared visual on the sleeping camels and Tuaregs.

The pilot confirmed with the CIA deputy director at Langley in charge of the mission. Diele's hand-picked appointee had access to the Reaper's video feeds, too.

"Cook them all, Captain. We want to be sure."

"Yes, sir," the captain said. She'd been trained to avoid collateral damage wherever possible, but these were all tangos as far as they could tell. She looked at her sensor operator. Saw the look in his face. A flicker of doubt. Suddenly this shit was real, not a video-game simulator like he'd been training on back in New Mexico. Today he would play God, tossing lightning bolts out of the blue, dealing fiery death.

"Light 'em up, son."

"Yes, ma'am."

Four Hellfire missiles were loosed, guided by the airman's hand.

Tamanghasset Province
Southern Algeria

The Hellfire II AGM-114N was designed to kill human beings in confined spaces like tunnels, caves, and buildings, but it was also an effective antipersonnel weapon in open areas. Each AGM-114N carried a thermobaric warhead combining PBXN-112 explosive fill and fluorinated aluminum powder. The bursting fill container created a cloud of oxidized fuel ignited by an explosive charge, resulting in a massive, fiery blast. The fiery blast, in turn, created an enormous vacuum that produced a crushing and sustained high-pressure wave.

The first Hellfire exploded three feet above Pearce's weapon just before the other three lit up their targets as well, all perfectly aimed. The resulting pressure waves ripped camels and men apart like claws from an invisible monster. Those not immediately atomized or incinerated had their lungs crushed by the vacuum and their internal organs liquefied by the force of the pressure blast.

Death for the entire caravan was instantaneous, or nearly so.

The Reaper's infrared camera recorded the explosions as brilliant flashes of light, and picked up the glowing heat signature of the white-hot craters and smoldering fragments of bone and metal scattered across the cooler sands a thousand feet away. The Reaper's video camera verified that there were no survivors. The deputy CIA director voiced his approval and commended the operators, promising a unit citation along with a solemn reminder to immediately erase all video and audio recordings of the mission. The hard drives were wiped before the deputy director ended his call.

Pearce Systems Headquarters
Dearborn, Michigan

Ian wanted to scream. He'd never been so frustrated in his life. Pearce had told him not to intervene under any circumstances—even if it meant Pearce's own death.

Ian complied.

But that didn't mean he couldn't keep an eye on things. Thanks to Judy's quick thinking during her interrogation by Captain Sotero, he knew a Reaper strike against Pearce was imminent. Ian broke into Karem AFB's mainframe and was able to monitor and record the Reaper's mission.

Ian hated terrorists. He'd lost both of his legs in the infamous London 7/7 bombing years before and had dedicated his life to fighting them. He understood the need for drone strikes and antiterror operations, but he'd also seen the mistakes that could be made, and the wrong lives taken, just like on this mission. That didn't help win the war on terror. Far from it.

The only consolation was that he now had another link in the chain of damning evidence against Senator Fiero.

Tassili du Hoggar, Tamanghasset Province
Southern Algeria

Pearce checked his watch. Just an hour before sunrise.

It had been hours since he awoke from a dream of distant thunder. Only, it hadn't been a dream.

The camels bleated nervously, too, as he glanced around. They quickly settled back down. He tried to go back to sleep, but couldn't despite his exhaustion, or maybe because of it. He never slept well in the field anyway, but even within the confines of the tall rock walls of the oasis he still felt naked and vulnerable, especially to an air strike. He remembered the sound now. Muted but echoed in the narrow chamber of rock where they camped. There had been several, nearly simultaneous claps. No telling how far away. Might as well get up.

Pearce reached for his M4 carbine but remembered he'd traded it with the Nigerien camel driver before they parted ways. Mano and his men were radioed by friends that a Niger army unit was harassing a Tuareg village on the other side of the border. He asked Pearce again for a trade. Pearce understood. Mano wanted a good weapon if he was going into battle. Pearce explained he had only one mag for the M4 and one grenade for the launcher, but Mano didn't care. He traded Pearce his good Russian-made AK-47 and five full mags. The trade made for good diplomacy. When the Nigerian Tuaregs departed for home, Mossa thanked Pearce for relenting. Pearce knew it was impolite in many Mideast cultures to refuse an offer of trade. The gun really wasn't his to begin with, but the Air Force had plenty more of them so he was glad to do it. He hoped it gave Mano an advantage.

Pearce finally rose and quietly stepped over to the cool green waters of the narrow oasis farther into the canyon. The sharp moonlight lit the wavy gray and brown rocks ringing the small pool of greenish water. He was afraid to drink it but glad to splash it on his face and the back of his neck. He probably stunk to high heaven, but he couldn't smell it anymore. Soldiers in the field got used to their own stench and the rank odors of their comrades. Sweat, urine, cigarettes, cordite, diarrhea, and wood smoke wrecked any possibility of olfactory sensitivity. Men at war reeked, but if everybody and everything did, who noticed? He checked his watch again. It was around midnight tomorrow where Ian was. Might as well see if he was awake and get a sitrep.

Pearce's cabin
Near the Snake River, Wyoming

Myers woke with a start. Someone was definitely outside.

She threw back the heavy green woolen blanket and

stepped onto the wood floor in one seamless move. She picked up the old .410 double-barreled bird gun she'd found in Pearce's bedroom closet and made her way toward the kitchen without turning the lights on. She'd been in his cabin long enough to have a good sense of the layout. The only thing she'd ever shot with a .410 before was white-winged dove in Uvalde, Texas, one hot September, but she figured the small-gauge rounds were good enough to at least scare the hell out of her would-be assailant, and maybe even kill them outright with a shot to the face. She wasn't scared so much as angry. How had they managed to find her?

She heard another noise in the kitchen. The sound of a closing door. Coming in or going out? Didn't matter. Had to find out who was wandering around out there.

Myers let the shotgun barrel lead her into the kitchen, when the lights suddenly popped on. She remembered what her father taught her years ago—keep your finger off the trigger until you're ready to shoot. The lights startled her and she mashed the trigger, but thankfully her finger only pulled on the trigger guard.

"Sorry, ma'am. Didn't mean to wake you." An athletically built young Asian woman stood next to the light switch. She wore Nike printed tights and a top, along with a Windbreaker that barely covered her shoulder-holstered pistol.

Myers lowered her shotgun, relieved. "You're one of Pearce's people, aren't you?"

"Yes, ma'am. Stella Kang." She extended her hand. "It's a pleasure to finally meet you." Stella was a Korean-

American from Los Angeles who picked a career in the Army over jail time for a crime she committed while attending USC. She accidentally chose the Army's drone program and learned to fly Ravens. After one tour over in the Sand Box she returned home and eventually wound up at Pearce Systems as one of his field operatives specializing in drone ops.

"What on earth are you doing here?" Myers checked her watch. "And at this ungodly hour?"

"Ian sent me."

"What for?"

"He's a big believer in backup systems. I guess I'm your backup, especially since you ditched your Secret Service detail after you resigned."

"Ian is a worrywart."

"He thinks you're being monitored out here. He's concerned about your security situation." She nodded at the small-gauge shotgun. "No offense."

Myers patted her gun. "If I'm attacked by a flock of pigeons, I'll be fine. You hungry? All I have is Spam around here."

Kang brightened. "Are you kidding? I grew up on Spam. Some tea would be great, too. We still have time."

Myers propped the shotgun in the corner. "Time for what?"

"Ian wouldn't give me all of the details, but he wants to put some other pieces into play. We've got to roll."

"Where to?"

Stella shrugged. "No telling, but I'd pack light if I were you."

Tassili du Hoggar, Tamanghasset Province
Southern Algeria

The camels drank their fill again while the rest of camp packed up their few belongings. They had all dined on the cold Turkish army rations Mossa and his men had hauled from the caves in Adrar. They wanted to get moving fast before the heat stole away the better part of the day.

Mossa approached Pearce, a small leather bag slung over his shoulder. His *tagelmust* hadn't been wrapped around his face yet. Pinpoints of silver dotted his unshaved skin.

"Today you will enter the Sahara as you Westerners imagine it. It is more beautiful and more terrible than you know. I should like to give you something to help you survive the journey." Mossa reached into his leather bag and set something into Pearce's hand.

"A date?" Pearce asked. The fruit was small and hard.

"It is God's survival pack. If you get lost out there, this date will allow you to survive for three days. The first day you eat the skin, the second day you eat the meat of it, and the third day you suck on the seed to generate water in your mouth."

"And the fourth day?"

"If you have not found water by the fourth day, you are dead." Mossa reached into his leather bag and tossed Pearce another date, laughing. "Here's three more days."

Pearce smiled, examining the dates. "Better than MREs, probably."

"One more thing. Give me your hat. It's ridiculous."

Pearce had been wearing his sweat-stained floppy boonie hat since Mozambique. It had done a pretty good job keeping the sun off of his face and neck, but it screamed to the world he was a Westerner, probably a soldier. He handed Mossa his hat. Mossa tossed it to the ground and pulled something else out of his pack.

"I would be honored if you would wear this," Mossa said. It was ten feet of indigo cloth. A *tagelmust*.

"I don't deserve it."

"You have fought well. I suspect you will have to fight again before we reach our destination. Since you fight like a brother, you might as well look like one." Mossa looked at the pile of folded cloth in his hand. "Pretty cool, eh?"

"Damn straight," Pearce said. He took it and unfolded it, obviously pleased. "Better show me how to put it on."

= 53 =

Tamanghasset Province
Southern Algeria
14 May

The huge transverse sand dunes rolled in great, granular waves. Mossa was right. This was the Sahara of Pearce's imagination. Straight out of *Lawrence of Arabia*. As thrilling as any seascape he'd ever seen, but silent as the blinding sunlight glinting on the billions of microscopic bits of quartz.

"Yes, rolling. A good description. These barchans really do move," Mann said, using the technical term for the huge dunes. "Up to a hundred meters per year." The German wore a white towel on his head secured with a bungee cord. A primitive *keffiyeh*. His long nose was painted with zinc oxide. The caravan snaked between the dunes, careful to avoid the steep slip faces, which could avalanche down.

"Nice hat," Pearce said.

"Not as authentic as yours, but it works."

"How are the girls?"

Mann had recently settled down with a younger wife. The union had produced beautiful twin girls. They lived in England where most of the nuclear power plant demolition work he supervised was taking place.

"They're becoming too English. I only speak to them *auf Deutsch* anymore."

Pearce hadn't seen the dark-haired German since the Mexico operation. Missed his company.

"Seems like you and I are always around the sand, one way or another." They first met years before while windsurfing off the coast of California, not far from Pearce's beachfront condo in Coronado.

"I forgot to bring my board. You?" The German grinned.

"Didn't even bring my shorts."

Truth was, Pearce was in heaven. He'd seen plenty of sand before, especially in Iraq. But somehow there it was a nuisance, a constant grit that got in his teeth and eyes. Sometimes it was so fine it was like talcum powder. And there was no shortage of heat over there, either. But out here, on the dunes of the Sahara, it all felt so clean. Purified. Now he understood, at least a little, why the ancient monks had fled to the desert. But maybe it felt clean because there weren't any people around. People had a way of ruining things.

———————

S ix hundred and thirteen meters now," Salah said.
His Chinese-made military binoculars featured a
laser range finder. The AQS fighter was perched just
below the crest of the dune, his body carefully hidden.
Only his head and binoculars were on the crest line—
barely—and the tinted lenses were designed to not
reflect the harsh sunlight. There was nowhere to hide
in the desert once you were seen.

"How many?" Al Rus asked. He was standing in the
bed of his Nissan pickup next to the big machine gun,
his short-barreled AK still strapped to his chest. Four
other armed pickups were next to him, engines off. They
were in the flattest part of the trough between two big
rollers. Beige camouflage webbing tented over their
vehicles, partly to hide, partly for shade. Not nearly as
efficient as camels and far louder, the trucks still made
the journey easily enough after his men lowered the air
pressure in the oversize tires to improve traction.

"Seven." Salah was still winded from the long, hard
crawl up the far slope of the dune. "Six Tuaregs. And
one fool wearing a dish towel on his head."

Al Rus's men laughed. The oldest, Abdelmalek, said,
"That must be Pearce."

"Quiet! Do you want them to hear us?"

The men hushed.

Al Rus checked his watch. His scout never reported
back. No matter. The scout had confirmed Mossa's
arrival at the oasis, and Guo's intel had been correct.

These dogs really were heading for the abandoned Aéropostale airfield. Al Rus had put his team between the oasis and the airfield. What else could he do? The desert was too vast to find a man who didn't want to be found. Perhaps someday he would acquire one of those devil drones. The Shi'a Persians had them and the Crusader infidels had them, so why shouldn't he?

"Vehicles?" Al Rus asked.

"None. Only camels."

Allah be praised, Al Rus thought. He has delivered them into my hands. "Come down, Salah. Carefully."

The young man slid slowly backward down the dune so as not to attract attention by his movement. Once his head cleared the crest line, he turned around and belly-crawled a few feet in the scalding sand, then leaped to his feet and ran the rest of the way, thudding into the side of a truck.

"Idiot!"

"I am sorry, lord," Salah whimpered. He was the youngest of the group.

"Clear the nets. On my signal, start your engines."

The men pulled down the nets and stored them in the truck beds as quietly as possible. Sound carried out here. Drivers took their positions, as did the gunners.

Al Rus took the gunner position on his truck, told his other man to drive. "Kill the infidels!"

The engines roared to life and the trucks jumped forward, throwing sand and exhaust as they raced between dunes. The plan was for two of the trucks to break off and attack from the rear, while the other three trucks would charge straight into the single file of camels heading toward them. The animals would break and run, and it would be an easy matter to chase them down.

Just as they passed the first dune, a shadow flickered in the corner of Al Rus's eye. He whipped around to see a four-wheeled vehicle no more than a meter tall pacing with them a kilometer away. Its cowling was ungodly, the shape of a demon's head, or an alien, long and smooth and black. His spine tingled. Something was wrong. Al Rus turned around in the bouncing truck bed. Another one of the vehicles was following them, also a kilometer back.

Mann showed Pearce his screen. He had just tapped on each truck image on the screen, then assigned a Wraith UGV attack drone to each.

"Ready on your command."

"Now," Pearce said.

Mann tapped the automated attack toggle while Pearce signaled Mossa and the others to retreat. Two electric-powered Wraiths sped past the feet of his camel. This was the "team" that Mann had assembled, literally, on short notice. They were the latest example of LARs—lethal autonomous robotics. Each solar-powered vehicle was capable of up to sixty-five miles per hour and each carried a drum-fed twelve-gauge shotgun capable of firing 250 rounds per minute. Mann had loaded each Wraith with 180 shells, alternating between explosive rounds, armor-piercing slugs, and antipersonnel 000 buckshot.

"This should be interesting," Mann said, clinically.

"The first real world test for the new software." He urged his camel to the crest of the dune where, perched high in the air, he could grab a commanding view of the action.

"Careful you don't get your head blown off," Pearce said.

Mann ignored him, intensely studying the action unfolding through his binoculars.

Pearce nudged his camel, joining him at the top. Mossa's camel trotted up beside the two of them.

"This is what you call war?" Mossa asked.

"This is what we call hell," Mann said.

The six Wraiths swarmed toward the speeding trucks, vainly firing their machine guns at the speeding UGVs. Fistfuls of sand spat near the Wraiths' tracked rubber wheels as they rocketed toward the pickups. When they had closed within range the Wraiths opened up. Heavy slugs tore into the thin steel door panel of the lead truck, splintering the driver's ribs before they plowed into his lungs. Screaming in pain and terror, the driver panicked and flipped the Nissan. The gunner was tossed high in the air, then thudded into the sand just seconds before the spinning truck crashed into him, snapping his spine. The Wraith continued to fire, emptying its ammo box in seconds, exploding the upturned Nissan and incinerating the men trapped beneath it. It then sped off to find a secondary target, as instructed by its swarming software program.

Three other trucks broke off and sped in different

directions, one racing for the shadowed slip face of the next dune. Big mistake. The front tires dug into the liquid sand as the vehicle tried to climb the steep face heading for the crest, triggering a mini avalanche that quickly swamped the truck's hood, smothering the engine and trapping the driver inside. The machine gun was fixed to a pivot point that gave the gunner a 180-degree sweep over the front of the truck, but not enough play to turn it completely around. The Wraith tracking it raced up to the bed and spat twenty-five rounds in a second, shredding the gunner along with the rest of the truck. It then sped around to the side, crashed into the truck cab, and detonated.

P earce watched the second Wraith explode, taking out the half-buried Nissan.

"What was the point of that?" he asked Mann.

"They're rigged to self-destruct. I assumed I wouldn't have the means to transport them back home and I didn't want them to be captured. Besides, I may have just invented the first automated drone suicide bomber."

"I hope you built seventy-two robot virgins to go with it."

T he other two surviving trucks spun in desperate circles and fired their weapons, but Al Rus commanded his truck to turn around and stop. Hitting a fast-moving target like the Wraiths while driving was a nearly impossible task. But the drones weren't engaged in serious tactical driving. They just came on hard and fast. With his truck stopped and facing down the approaching Wraith, Al Rus easily drew a bead on it with his machine gun. The Wraith sped directly toward him. He opened up with his machine gun. The large-caliber slugs threw up a wall of lead in front of the Wraith that it ran into blindly. Its thin cowling shattered just seconds before the unit exploded in a ball of fire. His driver shouted *"Alla-huakbar!"* as Al Rus gave the order to race away past the wreckage and toward safety, away from his dying friends and the fiendish robots cutting them to ribbons.

Three more explosions rocked the desert.

Al Rus watched the two Nissans explode in fireballs as the Wraiths detonated next to them. His command was dead, but at least he was alive—for now.

The two surviving Wraiths spun around, throwing rooster tails of sand into the air. Their ammo completely expended, they were only rolling bombs now.

Al Rus didn't know that. All he knew was that the two drones were gaining on him fast and his machine gun couldn't swing around. He unstrapped his AK-47, braced himself, and fired a series of controlled bursts. Steel-jacketed rounds tore into the Wraiths' thin cowlings.

Direct hits. The Wraiths exploded. He was home free.

Pearce, Mossa, and Mann watched the surviving pickup race away into the desert.

"What happened?" Pearce asked. "You let that one get away."

"I'll have to analyze the data later. But all in all, not a bad result," Mann said.

"We could chase him," Mossa offered. "At that speed, he will blow a radiator or a head gasket, especially in this heat."

"He could be leading us into a trap," Pearce said. "Let him go."

An angry finger of smoke rocketed out of the sky. It crashed into the pickup truck in the distance, ripping it apart like a fiery fist.

Pearce glanced at Mann.

"Don't look at me."

Pearce pulled out his sat phone and hit the speed dial. "Must have been Ian." The phone rang. Ian wasn't picking up.

Base Aérienne Arlit
Arlit, Niger

Lieutenant Beaujolais stood in the air-conditioned ground control center, cheering with the French Air Force Reaper pilot and the rest of the operations crew. He had provided the final visual confirmation the commanding officer required before launching the missile. Beaujolais gladly confirmed The Viking's identity. The Hellfire had just vaporized Al Rus. The AQS scourge of the Sahara was finally dead. Operation Dress Down Six was a success.

The purchase and deployment of American Reaper drones had already paid off handsomely for the French military, especially now that resources for their Africa operations were dwindling. But this new technology had just proven its value in spades. The ability to loiter for hours, identify suspects, and execute them with the push of a button heralded a new era in French antiterror operations in the region.

Corks popped. The commander poured the champagne himself. They raised glasses and the entire command shouted in unison, *"Vive la France!"*

= 54 =

Judy was still confined to her quarters. She couldn't sleep. She paced nervously in the cramped little room. She checked her watch again, as if that mattered. She was due to pick up Pearce in the Aviocar in less than twelve hours and she was still locked up in here with a twenty-four-hour armed guard stationed outside her door.

Ian had promised to call her last night but didn't. She couldn't stand it anymore. She fingered the copper-colored carabiner latched to her belt loop. The Security Forces guards didn't think twice about confiscating it. They couldn't possibly know it fired aerosolized super glue and pepper oil. Pearce had Rao make it for her, since she refused to carry a gun for self-protection. She could easily use it to disable the lone guard at the door, a really nice kid who was kind of sweet on her. But she couldn't do it, especially to a soldier just doing his duty.

The SF guards had given her cell phone back after her interrogation. Of course, they'd bugged it, or so Judy had to assume. She'd pulled the battery and the SIM card out and stored them. Besides getting tapped, Ian had taught her that a smartphone could also be remotely activated and used for both audio and video surveillance. But the SFs hadn't taken her analogue aviator watch, which actually wasn't just a watch. She flipped up the face and tapped the touch screen. It was meant only for extreme emergencies. This felt like one.

Ian answered.

Judy dashed into the bathroom and turned on the shower to mask her voice from the guard outside her door. "Thank God, Ian. Where have you been? You were supposed to call me."

"Busy, love. What do you need?"

"What do I need? I need you to get me out of here. I'm trapped."

"I know. I'm working on it. Working on lots of things. Sit tight."

"What about Troy?"

"Working on that, too. Bye." Ian ended the call.

"Ian! Ian!"

Judy growled, frustrated. She thought a very, very bad word but couldn't bring herself to say it. Her dad would have been ashamed if she had.

One of the smallest members of the European Union, Malta was a strategic three-island archipelago south of Sicily, some two hundred miles east of the Tunisian coast, in the heart of the Mediterranean Sea. The Armed Forces of Malta (AFM) was a very small volunteer force comprising land, sea, and air elements whose primary task was defense of the islands and safe-passage guarantees for the high-traffic commercial shipping lanes passing through its waters.

With a minuscule budget and few human resources, the AFM recently turned to drone technologies to enhance its capabilities. With the aid of an EU grant, the AFM engaged the services of Dr. T. J. Ashley, the former head of Drone Command during the Myers administration but now the CEO of her own private consulting firm. With the assistance of Dr. Rao and Pearce Systems, she had put together an air-sea rescue drone system package based on a highly modified Boeing A-160T Hummingbird VTOL aircraft and fitted with four external covered litters, like one of the old M.A.S.H. helicopters, just without a pilot.

Ashley's improved thirty-five-foot-long A-160X airframe could carry a 2,500-pound payload over 2,200 nautical miles at a speed of up to 165 knots. With a rotor diameter of just six feet, it was perfectly suited to land on flat decks and helipads, where wounded sailors or injured merchant mariners in the Mediterranean Sea could be loaded on—in theory—and transported back to almost any hospital in Europe, even London.

Ashley's initial field tests were encouraging. She'd managed to fly seven consecutive Hummingbird missions fully loaded with life-sized dummies on missions over five hundred miles without incident. The AFM wanted only a three-hundred-mile mission capability, but Ashley wanted to push the performance envelope as far as possible. The United States Marine Corps had successfully tested the Hummingbird as a supply vehicle over much shorter distances. If human cargo was going to be put at risk, she wanted to be damn sure that the machine was capable of transporting them safely. As a former Navy officer, Ashley knew how important air-sea rescue operations were and she was proud to be pioneering one of the first drone programs that could save sailors' lives at sea.

Ashley's short-cropped hair was buffeted by the strong predawn coastal winds, but she didn't mind. It was going to be another warm day beneath a brilliant blue Maltese sky, and the Hummingbird had just been prepped for its last test mission. If her luck held, she'd be heading back to Texas next week.

"Dr. Ashley?"

Ashley turned around. "Yes?"

"My name is Stella Kang. Ian sent me."

Aéropostale Station 11

Tamanghasset Province, Southern Algeria

Pearce, Mossa, and the rest of the caravan crested the last of the small dunes. A decrepit air station shimmered in the heat down below them. It looked more like an abandoned Howard Hawks movie set than a failed airport. A two-story-tall cement tower was flanked by two squat buildings, a pump house, and a generator room. A third building, the largest, was the hangar. The three buildings all faced the cracked but serviceable concrete runway and stood on the north side of it. A rusted pulley clutching a shredded halyard *tink*ed against the flagpole on top of the tower, buffeted by a nearly imperceptible breeze. Sun-bleached painted letters on the dusty hangar wall read "Aéropostale."

"I wonder if he ever flew here," Pearce said to himself.

"Who?" Early asked.

"Antoine de Saint-Exupéry."

"Say again?"

"The writer. You know, *The Little Prince*? He flew airmail routes for this outfit between the wars."

"Sorry, buddy. I skipped the Lit courses. But I can tell you all about my aunt Bertie's goiter."

"What happened to this place?" Mann asked.

Mossa pointed to the crumbling pump house. "The French dug a well there, but it was shallow and dried up after the first summer, so they had to leave this place. My father saw his first airplane here, when he was a boy. But that was a long time ago."

"Mossa gave you an airport, as promised. Where is your plane?" Cella asked.

Pearce checked his watch. "Still another hour. Judy will be here, guaranteed."

Mann raised a pair of binoculars to his face. "Not a

bad location, if you wanted to open up postal routes into central Africa."

"Drug smugglers fly their planes into here sometimes," Mossa said.

He ordered Balla and Moctar to scout ahead. They nudged their camels forward down the slope toward the airport, guns up, while the others waited and sweated in the late-morning heat.

The tower and the hangar were empty of drug runners, but decades of human detritus—crushed food tins, cigarette butts, empty paper oil cans—littered the hangar. The well in the pump room was dry as dust and the pump was long since removed from its bolted perch, as was the generator and any piece of valuable metal that might have been attached to it.

The tower building was no better. The first floor had served as some sort of lobby and office complex. The porcelain and plumbing in the two restrooms had been ripped out, save for the pan in the Turkish toilet, stained and vile.

The second story served as the observation tower. Whatever electronic equipment had been there had long been removed, and anything of value spirited away. The tower windows offered a 360-degree view, but they were wide open to the sky. Small shards of yellowed glass crunched beneath their boots, and the back wall was pocked with bullet holes.

"How's the arm?" Pearce asked.

Early shrugged. "Never better."

"Then you're here on overwatch." Pearce knew Early was lying, of course. If they were attacked, his friend would be in the safest position.

"You got it, chief."

"You want one of the RPGs?"

"Nah, I'm fine with this." Early charged his SCAR-H and flipped the firing-mode switch to automatic. The rifle had no burst mode.

"Stay frosty up here."

Pearce and Mossa worked their way back down the crumbling cement stairs to the skid-marked tarmac. They made their way over to the hangar where the rest had gathered. The rolling hangar doors had long since disappeared, burned for firewood, Pearce guessed. Even the metal tracks to guide the wheels had been ripped out of the floor for scrap. At least the corrugated steel roof panels were still in place, though sunlight leaked through the scattered gunshot holes, shot from inside judging by the shape of them.

The camels and the others were all inside the cavernous building, hiding from the sun. The cracked floor was strewn with dried chestnuts of camel dung of indeterminable age. Clearly, they weren't the first visitors to park their animals in here.

Mossa approached his men, sitting cross-legged in front of their kneeling camels. Pearce found Cella near the hangar entrance, smoking a cigarette, staring at the sand.

"We never finished that conversation we had the other day," Pearce said. "Borrow one of those?" He pointed at her cigarette.

"I thought you quit." She held out a pack. He pulled one out.

"I quit a lot of things."

She flicked her lighter. He lit up. They smoked in silence for a while. Pearce thought she would take the bait, talk about her daughter. Something was wrong about that situation. But it really wasn't any of his business.

"What's next for you?" Cella finally asked.

"Work."

"Where?"

"Wherever."

"Must be lonely for you."

"I was never much of a people person." Pearce saw movement in the sand. "What's that?"

Cella shielded her eyes. "Looks like a snake." The long, thin shape *S*'d down the dune toward them. She called over her shoulder to Mossa in Tamasheq.

Mossa came over to them. She pointed at the snake, now stopped on the dune. "What kind of snake is that?"

"I have never seen such a snake."

Pearce threw down his cigarette and bolted for the dune.

The snake suddenly reversed direction, *S*-ing backward up the dune, tail first.

Pearce was faster. He snatched up the snake around its neck. The snake flopped and twisted in his fist. He felt the tiny servos grinding in his grip as the rubbery snake body flailed. Pearce wrapped his other fist around the snake's neck and tried to twist off the head, as he'd done to a hundred other snakes in his life. But the metal spine wouldn't give way that easily. When he reached the tarmac, he put the flailing snake under his boot and cut the head off with his combat knife. He picked up the severed head. He lifted his boot and the body flopped around on the tarmac. He examined the head more closely as he marched back to the hangar. Video and audio sensors inside the unit. No question.

"What is it?" Cella asked.

"Surveillance drone." He tossed the head to Mann, now standing at the door along with Balla and Moctar.

"Excellent craftsmanship," Mann said. "Israeli or Chinese?"

"I'm betting Chinese." Pearce turned to Mossa. "Get your men ready. We're going to have company."

Pearce tapped his ear mic. "You see anything up there, Mikey?"

"A plane. Two, maybe three klicks away. Due west."

Pearce pulled his sat phone out of his pocket, speed-dialed Ian. "How soon?"

"ETA ten minutes." It was four in the morning where Ian was, and he hadn't slept in twenty-four hours. Pearce heard the fatigue in his voice.

"From what direction?"

"East."

Pearce cursed again. "I need eyes on the ground, and backup, if you can swing it. We've got company on the way, maybe already here."

"How many?"

"Don't know yet."

"Troy?" Early said.

"Yeah?"

"Chutes."

"How many?"

"Looks like . . . oh, shit. Six, seven, eight, nine—"

Ian interrupted. "I only have the one option if you want assistance."

"Do it. Now."

"Will do, but it will take longer than ten minutes to reach you. And there's been a slight change in plan."

"What change?"

= 55 =

Karem Air Force Base
Niamey, Niger
15 May

Same trailer, same ground control station, different crew.

There were only two Reapers on the base and two GCS trailers. The original DoD plan was to deploy four five-person crews, each working twelve-hour shifts in the two trailers, keeping both Reapers in the air twenty-four hours per day. But budget cuts and crew shortages meant they could only field two full crews at any given time, and that meant keeping only one Reaper aloft for twenty-four hours at a time. Until they were fully staffed and funded, the second GCS trailer would remain shut down in reserve.

This morning's crew, known as Blue One, was flying

a fully armed Reaper on a surveillance mission along the Algeria–Niger border. Technically, the computer was flying the machine on a preprogrammed flight pattern. Intelligence sources on the ground reported possible AQS traffic in the region. The Reaper mission was tasked with monitoring the border traffic and recording any suspicious movement.

Red One team had launched the aircraft sixteen hours earlier. Blue One had just relieved them four hours ago. The pilot, sensor operator, and GCS controller were bored out of their minds. The pilot wasn't even in her seat. She was doing yoga stretches, trying to work out a knot in her lower back. The mission monitor was in the clinic on IVs, fighting a bout of dysentery, so the flight engineer, Captain Pringle, was doing double duty. His feet were up on the desk and his eyes were shut, because he was pulling a double shift as a favor to the Red One flight engineer, who'd just taken a three-day emergency pass to be with his pregnant wife in Landstuhl, Germany, giving birth to their third son.

In other words, it was a typical workday. Until the sensor operator shouted, "Shit."

Pearce Systems Headquarters
Dearborn, Michigan

Ian easily took control of the Reaper. The night Pearce stole the M4 carbine was also spent installing a remote wireless override for the Reapers' ground control station. Just one of the many useful toys Ian insisted Pearce keep on hand at all times.

He radioed Pearce. "Help is on the way."

Karem Air Force Base
Niamey, Niger

Lieutenant Colonel Kavanagh examined the latest aerial surveillance photos, which Red One had produced the day before. A thick Cuvana e-cigar was parked in a pristine crystal ashtray on the desk, a gift from his forbearing wife. He loved the big flavor and vapor; she loved the fact that there wasn't any smoke or stink. A military marriage required many compromises. The e-cigar was an easy one for both of them.

Kavanagh was lean and hard for his age, despite his new career piloting a desk. He'd flown tank-busting A-10 Thunderbolts up until the year before, including Operation Iraqi Freedom, when a rapid decline in his visual acuity pushed him out of the cockpit. It wasn't too bad, though. Two more years and he could retire, and working with the latest drone technology had been a challenge in the best sense of the word. And as it turned out, he was a damn fine base commander, too. His wife even thought he looked handsome in glasses.

He zoomed in on the Reaper surveillance photo on his big desktop screen and highlighted the image anomalies. He hoped the poindexters back at Langley could make something out of them. If this was, indeed, an AQS border crossing, the terrorists must be wearing first-rate camouflage, because he hadn't seen anything more than rocks and camels in weeks. He didn't bother to look up when there was a knock on his door.

"Enter."

His administrative assistant, a young airman first class, entered. Her ABU name tag read "BEEBY." Her young face frowned with confusion. "You have a visitor, sir."

Kavanagh kept zooming and highlighting. "Who?"

"You won't believe it."

Kavanagh looked up. "Try me."

Kavanagh was still in a foul mood after the FUBAR over his credentials back in Germany. How or why anybody had put him on a terrorist watch list was beyond all reasoning. He'd only managed to get back to Karem last night after a long and uncomfortable ride in a rock-hard jump seat in the back of an unheated cargo transport.

The airman smiled. "Okay." She turned in the doorway and spoke to someone in the cramped waiting room. "The colonel will see you now."

Beeby stepped aside, and Margaret Myers marched into Kavanagh's office.

Kavanagh's jaw dropped. He rose. "Madame President?" He began to raise his hand in a salute, but checked himself.

"Former president. But please, call me Margaret." She extended her hand. He shook it.

The airman stifled a giggle.

"That'll be all," Kavanagh said, dismissing her. She left, closing the door behind her.

"Please, have a seat," he said, pointing at the only other chair in the tiny room.

"No, thank you. I've had quite enough of sitting for a while."

"Long flight?"

"Is there a short flight to this godforsaken place?"

Kavanagh smiled. "Good point. To what do I owe the pleasure?"

"I need a favor, Colonel."

"Favors are hard to come by on an Air Force base. We tend to function on the basis of SOPs."

Myers glanced around the spartan room. The large computer monitor dominated the tiny steel desk. A framed photo of Kavanagh's wife and children stood next to a picture of him as a younger man in the cockpit of an airplane. She knew it was an A-10 Thunderbolt, the same plane as the model airplane on the shelf behind his head. The Air Force Academy in Colorado Springs was one of her favorite places to visit as governor. She'd tried to convince her son to apply there, but he didn't have any interest.

"Even for your former commander in chief?"

"Depends on the favor, I suppose."

"I'd like you to release a young woman in your custody named Judy Hopper."

"May I ask why?"

"I suppose that's the second favor I'd ask you. I'd rather you didn't."

Kavanagh leaned carefully against his desk, folding his arms across his chest, thinking.

"I'm sorry, but Air Force regulations clearly state: only one favor per ex-president. I can grant you one or the other, but not both."

"Okay, then release Judy and allow us to proceed on our way."

"For what purpose? And please, don't tell me that cockamamie story about a rescue mission."

"It's about a cockamamie rescue mission. Can we leave now?"

"Seriously, ma'am. What is this all about?"

"It's about two American heroes who are stuck on the wrong side of the world that need a lift back home, badly. Right now."

"I can't authorize an illegal border crossing, even if it is for a spy mission. That kind of operation needs a much higher clearance than my pay grade allows."

"I'm not asking you to authorize anything. I'm asking you to let Judy go, release her airplane, and wish us luck. What we do when we lift off the tarmac isn't any of your concern."

Kavanagh scratched his silver hair, thinking, as he sat back down in his chair. The springs squeaked.

"If you got hurt or captured or, God forbid, shot down, it puts my ass in a sling and the U.S. government on the hook. I'm sorry." Kavanagh folded his hands on the desk.

Myers leaned on his desk, her face nearly in his. "If I got hurt or shot down or captured, technically, it would be my ass in the sling, not yours. And since when does an American military officer worry about his ass? Is that how you qualified to fly one of those?" She pointed at the A-10, affectionately known as the Warthog.

"No, ma'am."

"I know it takes a lot of guts to fly one of those. I know a lot of brave young men and women who graduated from the Academy. Just like you." She nodded at his Air Force Academy ring. "I'm not asking you to get out of your chair or out from behind your desk. I just need you to sign whatever paper you need to sign and let us go. I'll take full responsibility. I'll sign any document you put in front of me to that effect."

"I can't believe the CIA or the DoD or whoever has recruited you to run some special op into hostile territory. No offense."

"None taken. There are better-trained men and women than me for that sort of thing."

"So, then, you admit this is personal?"

She banged the desk. "You're damn right it's personal. These are friends of mine and their lives are at risk, and I'm not going to stand around and do nothing about it." She picked up the photo of the colonel's wife and kids. "Would you let some pencil-pushing bureaucrat stand between you and your family if you knew their lives were in danger?"

"Hell no."

"Then you understand."

"Who are these people you're going after?"

"Two of the finest men I've ever known. They risked

everything for me, and for our country, time and time again. They deserve better than what they're getting from our government, which is nothing."

"Why not call the White House? I'm sure the president would listen to you."

"Don't you think I've tried? The administration quoted me chapter and verse on the 'no new boots on the ground' doctrine. Can you imagine it?"

"But that was your policy, ma'am."

"Nonsense. My policy was to not start new wars that don't advance American national interests. But when American lives were at stake? I would've unleashed hell to save just one. That was my job as president. And that's my reasonable expectation as a citizen. President Greyhill won't send troops in order to protect *his* interests."

"You're putting me in a helluva position."

"What kind of position do you think my friends are in over there?"

Kavanagh's neck flushed red. "I wish to God you were still the president."

T he plane is already fueled and ready to go, according to the colonel," Myers said.

"I still don't think you should come. It's risky," Judy said. "And Troy would kill me if something happened to you." She was working a piece of gum hard in her jaw.

"If something happens to me it'll probably happen to you, so Troy will be the least of your worries."

The two of them headed for the Aviocar, which had

already been wheeled out onto the tarmac. They approached the plane. A square-jawed slab of meat in civilian clothes blocked the entrance to the Aviocar's cargo door. Judy recognized him. It was Sergeant Wolfit, the man from whom Pearce had stolen the M4 carbine. Judy noticed that a new M4 carbine was slung across the sergeant's broad chest, filling out a bright orange Tennessee Vols T-shirt. His narrow eyes bored a hole into Judy.

"We have permission to take this plane," Myers said. "Colonel Kavanagh authorized it."

Wolfit shifted his gaze to Myers. "I know, ma'am. I'm here to ask permission to join you."

"Why?" Judy asked.

He tapped his rifle. "Sometimes men are handier than drones."

"Permission granted. And please, call me Margaret."

Wolfit's flinty face broke into a wide grin. "Thank you, ma'am."

Judy pushed past Wolfit and into the cargo door, turning left for the cockpit. Someone else was in the copilot's seat, also in civilian clothes.

"Who are you?"

The silver-haired man smiled. "I'm a friend of Margaret's. Name's Kavanagh." The colonel extended his hand. Judy shook it.

"Hopper." She fell into the pilot's seat.

"We already ran the preflight check. You're good to go."

"Thanks." Judy reached into an oversize shirt pocket. Pulled out an old Polaroid photo.

"Hope you don't mind the company, Hopper."

"Not as long as you keep your hands off the yoke."

Kavanagh laughed. "I like your moxie, kid. But I probably have a few more years in the pilot seat than you."

"Don't bet on it." Judy pulled the gum out of her mouth and stuck it on the instrument panel, then fixed the Polaroid on the gum. Her good-luck charm. It was a faded picture of her as a young girl on her father's lap flying an airplane for the first time. Seemed especially appropriate now. There was a very good chance this flight would be her last.

= 56 =

Pearce ran to his camel and pulled off the Pelican case, flung it open, and grabbed the firing tube, already loaded with the fully charged Switchblade UAV. He wished like hell he had grenades for the M-25, but he'd already used them all back at Anou. But at least he could use the Switchblade for surveillance.

Pearce ran to the hangar entrance, pulled the launch tube over his shoulder, and fired. The pneumatic *whump* spit the five-and-a-half-pound drone into the air high enough for its electric motor to kick in. The small plane sped into the hazy blue sky. If there were any bad guys out there, the Switchblade should be able to see them.

"I have an image," Mann said, holding the tablet in his hands that served as both a flight controller and view screen. Pearce cross-trained all of his people to handle all kinds of vehicles for emergency situations like this. Even though Mann was a UGV specialist, he could pilot a UAV when the occasion called for it. Mann used the tablet only because he hadn't practiced with the MetaPro glasses yet.

Pearce cursed himself for not thinking about the UAV earlier. He should've been more cautious. He packed the tube back into the case and crossed back over to Mann. Mossa and the other Tuaregs were peering around the German's shoulders, too, trying to see what was going on. These hardened desert fighters had never seen such technology.

"Troy!"

Pearce whipped around. Cella pointed northeast, toward the horizon. He ran over to her.

"Look!

Pearce saw it. A white speck running low and fast, racing toward them. Looked like a chopper. Might be Ian's backup ride.

Or not.

"Troy!"

Pearce ran back to Mann. Wished his friend had brought his comm set.

"I'm counting six vehicles. Due west of our position, about two kilometers, and closing fast." He handed Pearce the tablet. Mann was right. They were screaming across the desert floor. He tried to zoom in, but when he did, he lost them—they'd race right out of the frame. When he zoomed back, he could see them but not really make them out. Looked like desert patrol vehicles, militarized versions of dune buggies. Two men each. Full-faced helmets. Fixed weapons on the platforms.

"Hostiles?"

"Identification unclear. But they don't look like taco trucks to me."

Pearce couldn't help but grin. The last time Mann had visited him in San Diego, he had feasted on every Asian-fusion taco truck in town. Swore he'd buy himself his own truck when he got back home to Germany.

The noise volume in the hangar rose. The familiar echo of beating rotor blades. That chopper was suddenly closer.

"Keep me posted," Pearce said, handing the tablet back to Mann. He ran back to Cella. Moctar and Balla followed him. Mossa stayed with Mann, fascinated by the technology in the German's hand.

The helicopter was less than a thousand yards away now. It kicked up sandy dust in spinning vortices as it raced toward the hangar.

"You see the bird?" Early asked in Pearce's earpiece.

"Yeah."

"And the vehicles with guns heading our way?"

"Noted."

"Any bets on who gets here first?"

A kilometer past the northeast end of the Aéropostale runway, Guo lay prone on the far side of a dune, hidden beneath a sand-colored sheet woven with reflective materials impervious to infrared sensors. He would be invisible to any optical camera overhead, and on an infrared monitor he would likely appear, if at all, as a glitch in the sensor.

His eye tracked back and forth through the high-powered scope. What made the modified rifle and scope special was the bullet it fired, developed by Dr. Weng especially for him. It was, in effect, a miniature guided missile. Based upon a design stolen from Sandia Labs, the bullet contained a miniature CPU, actuated fins, an optical sensor, and a power supply. The rifle scope contained a laser. All Guo had to do was paint the target with the laser and fire the bullet. The bullet's CPU would instantly course-correct against variables such as wind speed, friction, and even the Coriolis effect.

Guo had observed Al Rus's clumsy attack on Mossa's caravan from a safe distance and the ease with which the AQS fighters had been dispatched by the fast-running UGV drones Pearce deployed. What wasn't clear was the aerial strike against Al Rus directly. Was that UAV deployed by Pearce or someone else? Until he was sure, he would remain as invisible as possible.

Once again, Mossa and Pearce had escaped, but Guo knew exactly where they were headed for an extraction. The Aéropostale runway was the only logical choice out here. The best chance Guo now had to capture Pearce and kill Mossa was to intercept them there. He reported back to Zhao and explained the desperate tactical situation. Zhao authorized the deployment of Guo's specially trained team of handpicked fighters from the PLA's famed "Fierce Falcons" airborne assault unit. Guo kept them in reserve in Bamako, hoping never to deploy them. Now they were on the ground, racing for the airfield, two men each in fast-attack desert patrol vehicles equipped with Type 87 automatic grenade launcher rifles and 7.62mm machine guns. If they couldn't kill Mossa, Guo would, and if necessary, Pearce too—along with his entire team.

T hose DPVs are about a minute out," Early reported. "Permission to fire."

"Not until we know who they are." Pearce stood at the hangar entrance again, next to Cella. Balla and Moctar had joined him as well. Pearce had a clear visual on the copter now. The noise volume in the hangar had cranked up to eleven as Dr. Ashley's A-160 Hummingbird approached for landing on the far end of the runway. Ian had instructed Ashley to program the Hummingbird's AI navigation system to home in on Pearce's internal tracking device and to land at least one hundred yards away for safety. It had worked perfectly.

Moctar and Balla laughed, shielding their eyes from the dust, marveling at the pilotless Hummingbird flaring as it touched down on the tarmac.

Pearce had only seen photos of the pilotless air-rescue vehicle and the four coffin-shaped litters attached to the bottom like missiles on a rail. At least they were clear plastic. Maybe his claustrophobia wouldn't get the better of him.

"Get out of that tower, Mikey," Pearce said. "Let's scoot out of here while we can."

Early ignored Pearce's offer, tempting as it was. "Permission to fire on the vehicles?"

"Hold your fire. We still don't know if they're friendlies."

The hangar noise was deafening. The Hummingbird's Pratt & Whitney turboshaft engine had barely slowed, just enough to not take off again. Pearce could barely hear Ian shouting in his earpiece.

"What's the holdup?" Ian said. "You need to leave—now!"

Mann ran up to him, followed by Mossa. Pearce was blind to the advancing DPVs inside the hangar. The German pointed at the tablet. Leaned in close to Pearce's ear. Screamed to be heard.

"Six vehicles! Two split north, two south, two holding!"

Mossa slapped Pearce's shoulder. "Go! Get on! We will cover you!"

Pearce's eyes pleaded with Cella. He grabbed her arm. "That thing can carry four of us, including you."

She shook her head, nodded at Mossa: I'm not leaving without him.

"They're right on top of us, boss!" Early shouted.

"Switchblade down!" Mann shouted.

"Hold your fire, Mikey—"

BOOOOOM!

The Hummingbird erupted in a fireball. Flaming

debris scattered like a shotgun blast. A rotor blade shot through the hangar door over their heads with a *shraaang!*, spearing into the back wall, then crashing to the floor.

The camels leaped up, bellowing. The Tuaregs grabbed the rope bridles, trying to keep the huge animals from bolting out of the hangar.

"Guess we know they're not friendlies!" Early's SCAR opened up overhead, roaring in Pearce's earpiece. So did Early, shouting his war cry.

BAM! BAM! BAM!

Grenade explosions pounded the hangar walls. Dust rose like a low fog off of the floor even as it descended from the rafters. Pearce grabbed Cella by the arm and ran with her for cover in the hangar. The camels bellowed louder and shat.

Pearce shouted in Mossa's ear. "Take your men! Take cover! They're coming!"

More grenade rounds crashed into the walls. Still no one wounded. In the corner the floor was slick with piss and camel dung.

And then it was quiet. Not even Early's gun was firing.

"Mikey! You all right?"

"Reloading, that's all. Got my head down."

"Stay down!"

Pearce tapped his comm link. "Ian! Where the hell is my backup?"

"Thirty seconds away," Ian said.

Two desert patrol vehicles whipped around the burning Hummingbird wreck and slammed to a halt a hundred yards in front of Early's position. Two more DPVs whipped around the far side of the hangar and stopped a hundred yards opposite Pearce's position, guns manned and pointed directly at them.

Everybody pressed against the far wall, trying to keep out of the line of sight of the DPVs.

"Mr. Pearce. Can you hear me?"

It was Guo, in Pearce's earpiece.

Pearce didn't recognize the voice. How did he break into his comm link?

"Mr. Pearce?"

"Who the fuck is this?"

"Put down your weapons. You are surrounded."

"Ian, you hearing this?" Pearce asked.

"Hearing what?"

"Someone else on my comm link."

"Can't hear him on my end."

"Change channels anyway."

"Will do."

"Mr. Pearce?"

"You broke my helicopter, asshole. Who's gonna pay for that?"

"Put down your weapons. You and the bandit Mossa must come out. Your friends will not be harmed. Do it now, or my men will open fire."

"Give me one minute to talk to my people first."

"You have thirty seconds."

Pearce told Mossa what the voice had just said. Cella translated for Balla and Moctar. The two Tuaregs protested. Mossa calmed them down.

"They would rather die than see me surrender," Mossa told Pearce.

"They're about to get their chance."

"What time is it?" Mossa asked.

Pearce checked his watch. "Noon, give or take. Why?"

Mossa sighed. "The cavalry does not always arrive in time, do they?"

"Inshallah," Pearce said.

Piloting the stolen Reaper from Dearborn was less than easy. Ian's control signals were bounced off of a satellite Pearce Systems leased from the Israelis three hundred miles into space, but the overall distance between Ian and the Reaper's location over Algeria was several thousand miles. This created a four-second transmission delay, which meant that anything Ian was seeing was four seconds old. That made hitting moving targets a real challenge. The Air Force forward-located their drone base in Niger to avoid that very problem.

With the burning Hummingbird wreckage on the tarmac and six unknown vehicles surrounding the airfield, it wasn't hard to determine that Pearce and his team were facing hostiles. Ian's Presbyterian father had taught him it was always better to ask forgiveness than permission, so when the DPVs stopped moving, Ian fired at the two vehicles closest to Pearce.

The two DPVs nearest Pearce exploded, shredding them instantly. The sound of the missile strikes erupted inside the hangar like grenades going off inside of an elevator. The Tuaregs instinctively grabbed at their ringing ears, pounding with pain.

Pearce's ears had been damaged by combat over the years, which at the moment was a blessing, because the explosions didn't shock him as much. Early's SCAR opened up again.

Pearce ducked around the corner just in time to see Early's rounds walking up the hood of one of the DPVs, then plowing into the driver's torso. The standing gunner opened up on Early, but too late. Fingers of blood spurted out of the gunner's thigh, doubling him over, exposing his head to Early's withering fire. The helmet erupted in a gout of blood and the gunner tumbled to the tarmac.

Pearce fired his weapon at the second DPV near Early, but it was already rocketing away to a safer position beyond the reach of Early's gun. Mike had always been the better shot. Any rational observer would have bet that the DPV with the automatic grenade launcher and machine gun would win a duel against a lone man with a sprained arm and a rifle, but that only meant they had never seen Mike Early in battle in full berserker mode or heard his bloodcurdling war cry.

"Good shooting, Mikey. Now duck your ass back down," Pearce ordered.

Early wolf-howled. "The party's just getting started!"

"Save your ammo, cowboy. It's going to be a long day."

G uo raged.

Two vehicles destroyed by a UAV, and another disabled by the *guǐlǎo* gunman in the tower. Where did the UAV come from? If Pearce had a UAV at his disposal, surely he would have used it earlier.

No matter. He would solve the UAV issue later. The *guǐlǎo* problem he could solve now.

"Second positions," Guo whispered in his headset. The DPV nearest Early sped away instantly, and the two in reserve behind the hangar retreated back several hundred meters. They knew to keep moving in broad, irregular patterns to avoid the same fate as their comrades.

Guo painted Early with his laser scope, fixing the red crosshairs on the big American's head.

P earce turned around, shouted back into the hangar, "Everybody stay put. I'll be right back."

He scanned the tarmac. It was clear. The DPV he'd fired at was too far away to worry about. Pearce ran in a crouch out the hangar opening and toward the tower entrance, expecting a hail of machine-gun and grenade fire to cut him down before he got three feet. But his adrenaline had kicked in and his luck held, and moments later he sped up the crumbling cement stairs to the observation tower, shouting in his mic, "Mikey! Get covered up!"

Pearce reached the top of the stairs, greeted by Early's toothy grin plastered on his huge, sweaty face. "God I miss this shit!"

Early's head exploded. Blood and brain matter splattered on Pearce's face and torso. Instinctively, he dropped to the deck. Early's headless corpse thudded onto his back. Pearce rolled out from beneath the heavy body and sprung into a crouch, desperate to get away from his dead friend without exposing himself to the killing fire.

"Mikey . . ."

The ragged neck wound pumped hot blood onto the floor with the last beats of Early's dying heart, the blood surging over broken glass, spent casings, cigarette butts.

"GOD DAMN IT!" Pearce's face twisted with rage and grief.

Cella crested the stairs. Saw Early on the floor. She gasped. "Mike!" She ran to his corpse.

Pearce crashed into her, wrapping his arms around her waist, putting his back to the shooter to cover her, driving both of them back down the staircase just as another bullet smashed into the wall above their heads.

Cella screamed and cried and beat Pearce's shoulders with her fists, grieving and hating all at the same time as he forced her back down the stairwell.

= 57 =

Pearce vise-gripped Cella's wrist and dragged her in a dead run back to the hangar entrance, slinging her inside and into Mossa's arms. She buried her head in his chest and wept like a child. Mossa patted her head but locked eyes with Pearce, his face dark with grief.

Pearce shook his head. Mike's dead.

Mossa led Cella over to a corner and sat her down, then returned to Pearce. Mann stood next to him.

"A sniper, but I did not see where the shot came from," Mossa said.

Mann cursed. "They shot down the Switchblade earlier, so I didn't spot him, either."

"Ian? You see anything?" Pearce asked in his mic.

"Sorry, nothing."

"Can you take the others out?"

"I can try. But I only have two shots left. Good chance I'll miss them while they're on the move."

"You saw the Hummingbird wreckage?"

"I'm afraid so."

"Do you have a backup plan?"

"That was the backup plan."

"It's turning into a Hungarian cluster fuck down here."

"Fortunately," Ian said, "I have a backup plan for the backup plan."

T he sky flashed like lightning.

A second later, a thundering boom vibrated the air.

Pearce felt it in his chest. A flower of smoke petaled high in the sky, like a Fourth of July firework.

"Ian! Did you see that? Ian? Ian?"

Karem Air Force Base
Niamey, Niger

"Log the incident."

The Blue One flight engineer, Captain Pringle, had given the self-destruct order. Having lost control of the Reaper thirty minutes earlier and unable to regain control or force a return to base, the operational protocol was to hit the self-destruct switch. He knew he hadn't done anything wrong, but he'd get blamed for it anyway. The Air Force was funny in that regard. Destroying a fourteen-

million-dollar airframe, no matter the justification, was
generally frowned upon by the comptrollers in blue suits.

It was a lousy way to end a lousy mission, but better
than letting the MQ-9 get hijacked and parted out. If
Pringle was lucky, he'd only get a reprimand and a nota-
tion in his service jacket. If he had let that Reaper fall
into enemy hands, he would've been busted out of the
service for sure. Maybe even court-martialed. Too many
American RPVs had been stolen in recent years. Several
nations had built their drone programs primarily from
stolen American and Israeli technology.

Pringle wished to God he hadn't pulled this second
shift. He knew better than to do favors for anyone, let
alone volunteer. Life had proven to him once again: No
good deed goes unpunished.

Oh well, he said to himself, and shrugged. He'd been
thinking about separating from the service anyway. Try to
land some cushy civilian contractor job back in the States.

Didn't see it, exactly." Ian's brogue got thicker with
his growing fatigue. "My screen went blank. Near
as I can tell, they hit a self-destruct switch."

"I bet the bad guys saw it, too," Pearce said.

"Count on it."

Pearce worried. He figured the only reason the DPVs
hadn't attacked again was that they were afraid of the
Reaper overhead. If they knew it was out of action, he
could expect trouble soon.

"I need eyes on the ground, Ian."

"What about your Switchblade?"

"Shot down earlier."

"Then you're fecked."

"You just figured that out?"

CRACK!

The sound exploded in Pearce's earpiece.

"Ian! You there?"

Pearce Systems Headquarters

Dearborn, Michigan

The flash bang burst two feet from Ian's workstation. The exploding light stabbed his eyes and the concussive blast knocked him out a second later, blood pouring out of both of his ears.

The FBI SWAT team had disabled the building's security system with a chemical EMP grenade detonation and easily disarmed the three lightly armed security guards on the property, not at their sharpest just after four in the morning.

Earlier that morning, the special agent in charge of the Detroit FBI field office had received an emergency request from Washington to immediately assault Pearce Systems headquarters and seize all evidence and persons. Credible intelligence indicated that an AQ-affiliated cell located there was about to commit a terrorist act with a weapon of mass destruction.

The all-volunteer SWAT team, headed by an assistant SAIC, deployed to Dearborn within thirty minutes of the request. Thirteen minutes later, Dr. Rao, Ian McTavish, and a half dozen other Pearce Systems employees on the premises were in plasti-cuffs, hooded and loaded into security vans and whisked away to a secure location while other specialist teams began searching for hazardous materials and WMDs. Once the all clear was given, an intel team seized computers, phones, hard drives, and other storage devices. Before the sun rose at 6:07 a.m. that morning, Pearce Systems would be completely shut down and its personnel quarantined, all thanks to a bogus emergency command issued by Jasmine Bath through a back door in the FBI's Washington Bureau server.

Troy Pearce was on his own now.

Pearce's cabin, near the Snake River
Wyoming

Skeets received the go signal from Jasmine Bath at exactly 2:13 a.m. local. He knew that meant the FBI had just launched its assault on the Dearborn facility. His mission was to take out Myers and anybody else he might find in the cabin. The two attacks had to be perfectly coordinated. Bath couldn't afford for Myers to warn McTavish or vice versa.

"Skeets" was a nickname, of course, one of the ridiculous monikers that soldiers picked up while in service, especially in special forces units. A fourth-generation coal miner, the steely West Virginian had escaped black lung and double-wide-trailer payments by enlisting in the U.S.

Army. He tested off the charts and could run for miles without winding. But what brought him to the attention of the NCOs was his preternatural sharpshooter's eye and dull moral conscience. Killing came easy for Skeets, and without regrets. PTSD was for pussies.

The Army had been good to him. Fed him well, trained him better, even knocked some of the hillbilly out of him. He traded his thick regional accent for the clipped staccato cadence of Army patois. The war had been fun, and getting paid to hunt people even more so. But three tours of *yessir*s and *nossir*s and bullshit regs and ROEs were quite enough, thank you. He had the good sense to take online college courses in business in his downtime. Discovered he was a laissez-faire capitalist. Decided he wanted to be an entrepreneur.

So he quit Uncle Sam's Army and joined the ranks of private security contractors at five times his annual salary as a sergeant. He quickly earned a fearsome rep in the merc community and was soon invited to join the CIOS corporation.

CIOS was generous with its cash offer, and selective in the targets he would be sent to assassinate. Jasmine Bath, the corporation president, had personally assured him that only America's worst enemies would ever be targeted, and only those that could not be legally arrested or killed but otherwise posed an immediate security threat. Skeets told her she was lying and that he didn't give a rat's ass who the targets were, guilty or not. Bath hired him on the spot and his income doubled.

Skeets had kept the cabin under surveillance from a

distance for the last four hours but hadn't seen or heard anyone on the property.

He disabled the surveillance cameras mounted high in the trees with a silenced .22 semiauto firing subsonics, then burst into the cabin, 9mm pistol drawn. Found nobody. As instructed, he searched for computers, phones, and storage devices—anything that might identify more links in Pearce's network. But the place had been cleaned out. Skeets called it in to Bath. She told him simply, "Burn it down."

He did. The old cabin went up faster than dry kindling, the fire ignited by a timed charge. He watched the towering flames lick the early-morning sky in his rearview mirror as he sped away.

Skeets felt no remorse. Pearce was a target. So was the former president. It was a job. Nothing more.

Aéropostale Station 11
Tamanghasset, Southern Algeria

The situation was static, which was fine by Pearce, because that meant he was still alive to know the situation was static, and that the rest of the caravan wasn't dead, at least not yet.

Ian was offline, Judy was incarcerated, and the tangos out there hadn't opened fire since Early's death. Ian's stolen Reaper had pushed them way back, but the DPVs were still in control of the field with three of them remaining. The DPVs mounted automatic grenade launchers that could fire five hundred rounds a minute up to six hundred meters effective range, and the 7.62mm machine guns were almost as lethal.

If Pearce and the others tried to make a run for it on the camels they'd be run down and cut to pieces. But staying in the sweltering hangar reeking of camel piss indefinitely probably wasn't a viable option, either. It would only be a matter of time before the DPVs lined up across the hangar and unloaded their arsenal into them. At least the big animals had calmed down and were kneeling quietly in the back again.

"The explosion. Your drone?" Mossa asked.

"Not my drone, exactly. My man stole it. But it looks like it was destroyed."

"Too bad. It was useful." Mossa was staring at the burning wreckage of the two DPVs blasted by the Reaper.

"That sniper out there might be on the move, too. I didn't see the shot, but given the angle I'd say he was somewhere in that direction." Pearce pointed toward the northeast.

"If I were him, I would move," Mossa confirmed. "We could hunt him, but then his friends would hunt us." He looked up into the sky. "Without your friend up there, they will attack soon."

"You said something about the cavalry not arriving in time?"

"I radioed one of the local chieftains. He said he was on the way."

"Any idea when he will arrive?"

Mossa shrugged. "Abdallah Ag Matta is a good man, but he is an Imohar, and our sense of time is not like yours. He will get here as soon as he can."

"Let's hope it's soon enough."

= 58 =

"Phoenix-Zero, this is Juliette Niner-Niner. Come in, please."

It was Judy's third attempt to reach Pearce. He wasn't responding on this channel. She was worried sick. She was an hour late for the pickup. Was Pearce lying dead in the sand somewhere because of her?

The three DPVs skidded to a halt on the far side of the runway some five hundred yards opposite Pearce's position. The loose sand south and east beyond the cracked tarmac was flat for as far as the eye could see. They had a clear line of sight if they wanted to lob grenades and hot lead into the hangar.

Pearce's earpiece crackled again. "It appears as if you've lost your drone protection, Pearce. I should kill you all right now, but I have orders. I will make the offer one last time. You and bandit Mossa surrender, and I will let your other friends live."

"You still haven't told me who you are, asshole, or how you're gonna pay for my broken helicopter."

Guo laughed. "Your friend's head exploded like a balloon."

"You motherfu—"

"Yours will, too."

Machine guns opened up. An RPG rocket whooshed past the DPVs, its crooked plume trailing behind it. The big bulbous HEAT round exploded in the sand thirty feet behind the vehicles.

Mossa laughed and slapped Pearce on the back. "You see! Abdallah Ag Matta has come!"

Mossa's walkie-talkie crackled. A Tamasheq voice shouted over the tinny speaker.

Pearce shook his head. "Tell them to back off. Those DPVs will cut them to ribbons."

"Too late."

The DPVs gunned their engines, wheels throwing sand. They spun hard right in a synchronous turn, racing back toward the advancing Algerian Tuaregs.

"Troy!" Mann pointed at the sky. "Look!"

It was the Aviocar, about a mile distant.

"Is that our ride?" the German asked.

"I don't know." Then he remembered. "Shit!" He'd switched channels when his line was tapped by the shit-bird with the sniper rifle. Pearce switched back to Judy's channel.

"Judy, that you?"

"Yes! I've been trying to reach you. Are you all right?"

"Switch to the other channel. Hurry."

The DPVs opened up, firing their machine guns and grenade launchers at the Tuareg fighters.

Judy came back on. "What's the situation down there?"

Mossa ran back to the camels, shouting orders to his men.

"It's a Class Five shitstorm down here. Hold off. I'll get back to you."

Pearce ran back to Mossa and his men. "You can't go out there."

"I must. My people will die." Mossa mounted his camel. So did the others. Mossa and Moctar held their rifles high; Balla gripped an RPG.

"You'll die," Pearce said.

"Inshallah!" Mossa laughed. He yanked his camel's bridle, and the big beast rose, as did the others.

Pearce's camel began to rise out of habit, even though its saddle was empty. Pearce knew it would quickly follow the others.

He leaped on.

Mossa shouted his own war cry and sped out of the hangar, Balla and Moctar right behind him. Mann was throwing a long leg into his saddle. Pearce barked at him. "No! I need you here." He pointed at Cella.

The German gritted his teeth. He wanted to fight. But he understood authority, knew the woman wasn't safe by herself. He nodded curtly and dismounted.

"Thanks," Pearce said, urging his camel out the door and into the harsh light. Pearce's animal caught up to the others quickly. The four men galloped abreast, racing for the battle raging ahead.

Thirty camel-mounted Algerian Tuaregs charged in a line toward the airstrip, desperate to save their Tuareg headman, Mossa, cursing the devils and firing their rifles. They'd managed to close quietly within a hundred yards before opening up, completely surprising the DPVs. Abdallah Ag Matta waved his *takouba* high above his head. If he was going to die, he wanted to die like his fathers of old.

He did. An armor-piercing round tore out his throat and threw him from the saddle.

Several more Algerian RPGs were loosed, smoke trails twisting in their wake. Exploding warheads rocked the speeding DPVs, but the Chinese sped onward, closing the gap. They opened fire.

The first 35mm grenades exploded, throwing murderous shrapnel. Camels screamed as hot steel shards ripped into their hides. Torrents of lead ripped open their bellies, spilling their guts, spewing blood and fat. The wounded animals tumbled forward on their crumbling legs, tossing their riders, some already dead in the saddle. The smaller, faster war camels Pearce and the others rode had recovered their nerve now that they were out in the open and charging into battle. Pearce couldn't believe how fast they moved and how smooth their gait was. It was easy for him to fire his rifle—far easier than if he had been on a horse at full gallop. Six long days on the back of his animal had produced both a bond and a knowing skill—good enough that riding the camel felt like second nature now.

The four of them closed the gap on the unsuspecting Chinese from behind. As Pearce had predicted, the charging Algerian Tuaregs were getting mowed down by the automatic-weapons fire, especially the grenade launchers. One of the DPVs peeled off to chase a knot of Algerians in full retreat—but Pearce guessed the Tuaregs were just trying to lead the vehicle into a trap. Pearce followed behind the Chinese, putting the gunstock to his cheek and firing controlled bursts. The DPV gunner's helmet cracked open and the man tumbled out of the speeding vehicle and into the sand.

Pearce shifted his aim and fired again. Armor-piercing rounds tore into the hood, causing the driver to twist the wheel violently—too violently—cartwheeling the DPV in the softer sand where the Tuaregs had led him. The driver was tossed in the air but fell clear of the tumbling vehicle, only to catch a hundred rounds of volleying fire in his chest as the cluster of Tuaregs wheeled their animals around and emptied their guns into him.

The blue-turbaned Tuaregs glanced up at Pearce and waved their rifles high in the air. It suddenly occurred to Pearce he was wearing a *tagelmust*, too, and must have looked just like them. All warriors share a bond, even enemies, but at that moment Pearce was a Tuareg. He shouted his war cry and urged his camel after the other DPVs still chasing the few remaining Algerians, now in full retreat, turning in their saddles and firing their guns in vain.

WHOOSH! Balla fired his RPV in full gallop. It smashed into the rear of the nearest DPV, blasting it into a cloud of fiery metal. Pearce cheered along with the others riding beside him. But their joy was premature. The final DPV's launcher erupted, still chasing the other Algerians. Dozens of grenades exploded beneath the feet of the fleeing camels, breaking them open, spilling their intestines, snapping their legs in half. The last Algerian Tuaregs and their animals died screaming in the reddening sand.

And then the DPV wheeled around, machine gun blazing.

Pearce felt the slugs pounding into his camel's chest and the great beast lunging downward. Pearce jerked as hard as he could out of the saddle to leap clear, but the fifteen-hundred-pound animal collapsed, landing on top of Pearce's leg. Searing pain jolted through his knee and up his thigh.

Instinctively, he knew it wasn't broken. The soft sand had saved him. So had the dead camel as more rounds pummeled into its corpse, now shielding Pearce from the DPV. Pearce glanced up just in time to watch Moctar and Balla charge.

Moctar's belly crimsoned and his upper body fell away. The lower half stayed in the saddle, hot blood geysering onto his galloping camel.

Balla shouted and fired his weapon, but he aimed too high and missed. Bullets pounded his chest like angry fists and threw him to the ground.

Mossa charged madly at the DPV, flinging his AK aside and raising his *takouba* high in the air. The faceless gunner turned his gun but held his fire—waiting until Mossa had closed within inches. The gun erupted. Mossa's upper body disintegrated in a hail of fragmenting grenades. The DPV gunned its engine and sped away toward the north.

Pearce leveraged his free foot against the saddle and pulled on his pinned thigh with his hands. His luck held. His leg was trapped beneath the dead camel's shoulder, near the neck. Otherwise, he might have been trapped for good. A few moments later, he worked his injured leg free. It was sore like a bad sprain, but he tested it and it was still mostly functional. He suddenly realized Judy was screaming in his earpiece.

"Troy! Troy!"

"Judy?"

"Thank God! You're alive!"

"Apparently."

"Where are you? Are you okay?"

"I'm south-southeast of the airstrip, about two hundred meters, about even with the hangar." Pearce limped over to Mossa's camel. It knelt down next to its master's corpse like a grieving dog.

"Yes, I see you now. I'm coming in."

"No! It's too dangerous. There's a fast-attack vehicle down here."

"I see it. It's heading north, about three hundred meters north of you. Plenty of room."

"Don't argue with me, damn it. I said wave off."

"Sorry, Troy, but she's following my orders," Myers

said. "Hope your bags are packed. How soon can you be at the hangar?"

"Two minutes."

"We'll be there."

Pearce approached Mossa's camel. It opened its huge mouth and growled.

"Shut up and ride!" Pearce threw his good leg over the beast and it complied, rising up quickly. Pearce grunted "Het-het" and got the camel galloping back toward the hangar.

The bullet-wrecked DPV flew over the crest of the dune and slid to a halt on the far side about a kilometer north of Guo's position, out of sight of the hangar as per Guo's instructions. Guo remained in his sniper hide beneath the reflective cover, waiting for the Americans to clear the area. He didn't want to give Pearce the satisfaction of a last-minute Hellfire missile strike with victory in his hand. Guo had killed Mossa, so his primary objective was achieved. Capturing Pearce was only a desired outcome, not a mission priority.

There was one more mission objective to be achieved. There were several options to achieve it. With Zhao's permission, he'd initiate the most necessary one.

Judy surveyed the wreckage in her windscreen. She was still five hundred feet off the deck. Three smoldering DPVs were to her right, and the smashed Hummingbird airframe blocked the end of the runway. Judy would have to get up a good head of steam if she hoped to clear that wreck on takeoff. The Aviocar needed four hundred meters of runway to get airborne. That would be cutting it darn close, but that was the least of her worries at the moment.

"There he is," Myers said, pointing to the east. Pearce was up ahead, a hundred yards from the tarmac, galloping toward the hangar, his head still wrapped in the indigo *tagelmust*. Myers called in her headset, "We see you, Troy."

His voice crackled back. "Last one to the hangar buys the beer."

"He looks friggin' cool. I want one of those," Kavanagh said.

"The camel or the turban, Colonel?" Myers asked.

"Both."

Judy set the Aviocar down smooth as silk on the cracked runway but couldn't avoid the debris scattered on the tarmac from the smashed Hummingbird. The Aviocar's heavy rubber wheels threw chunks of metal against the fuselage. She prayed the wheels hadn't been punctured or the airframe damaged. She'd have to check before they tried to take off again.

"Nice landing," Kavanagh said into the headphone mic, grinning behind his aviators. "Your dad would be proud."

"If our luck doesn't hold, we'll both find out how proud he is. In person."

She taxied past the burning wreckage of the two DPVs taken out by Ian's Reaper. Judy ordered Kavanagh to feather down the engines while she braked the plane, parking in front of the hangar, leaving the two motors running at low RPMs.

Judy waved at Mann crouching in the shade of the hangar. He smiled and waved back, his other arm draped protectively over the Italian woman Pearce had described earlier as his wife. She looked like she'd been through hell and back after six days of desert travel and the nightmare that had just transpired here, but she still looked gorgeous. It wasn't fair, Judy thought.

The Red One team sensor operator called in. "Colonel, you've got company heading your way." He was patched into everyone's headset. Kavanagh had ordered the second Reaper at Karem AFB into the air and both teams on duty. If he was going to go out in a blaze of glory, he wanted all hands on deck to witness the folly.

"What is it?"

"Three bogies coming in hot and low on the deck—about ten meters."

"Fighters?"

"Cruise missiles."

"ETA?"

"Three minutes, tops."

"You heard it, people," Kavanagh said. "Let's get this train loaded and rolling."

"Troy? Did you catch that?" Myers asked.

"Yeah." He was breathless in the headphones.

Wolfit pushed the cargo door open and jumped out, M4 at the ready, just as Pearce's camel thundered past the plane's rudder.

Myers, Kavanagh, and Judy scrambled out after Wolfit.

Everybody ran for the hangar except Judy, who ducked beneath the plane to check for damage.

Pearce halted the camel at the hangar entrance and slipped off before the camel had a chance to kneel. He slapped its flank and it bellowed in protest, then trotted into the hangar where the two remaining camels knelt.

Cella ran up and threw her arms around Pearce's neck. Myers ran up, too, with Wolfit and Kavanagh at her side.

"Troy, we've got to go," Myers said.

"Mossa?" Cella asked. "The others?"

Pearce shook his head. "I'm sorry."

Cella swore bitterly.

"You're coming with us," Pearce ordered.

Cella glared at him, then softened, nodding yes.

"Good." He turned to Myers. "Take her, please."

"What about you?"

"Not without Mikey."

"Where is he?" Myers asked.

Pearce ran as fast as his limp allowed back toward the tower, Mann beside him.

"There's no time," Myers said.

"You two get back to the plane. We'll hustle him back, I promise."

Kavanagh nodded at Wolfit, and the two of them chased after Pearce and Mann while Myers and Cella dashed for the plane.

Judy was still underneath the Aviocar. She didn't find any damage in the fuselage, but the starboard wheel was leaking air fast. "C'mon, you guys!" she barked in her headset.

Pearce was the last one up the tower thanks to his limp. The colonel knelt by Early's corpse and was covering his bloody neck stump with his own civilian shirt. The staircase was narrow. Wolfit handed Pearce his weapon and took Early's feet, Kavanagh the shoulders. Pearce noticed the colonel's knees were soaked in blood. Everybody's boots were slick with it, too. Mann led the way down, and Pearce followed the rest.

They cleared the stairs and dashed for the plane.

"ETA one minute, Colonel," Red One reported. "Advise you leave now."

"Working on it, son. Thanks for the tip."

Judy had already strapped back into her seat and revved the engines, keeping her feet pressed hard against the brakes. The plane shuddered in protest.

Mann ran and leaped into the cargo area as Wolfit approached. Wolfit stepped up into the bay effortlessly and swung around, the two of them pulling Early's heavy corpse in behind them, deep into the cargo area. Kavanagh walked Early's broad shoulders in, then jumped in behind him.

Pearce limped as fast as he could. Myers shouted at him. "Looks like you're buying the beer!"

The air cracked.

Pearce spun like a top, then dropped to the tarmac, blood spraying from his head.

= 59 =

As soon as he saw Pearce drop, Guo called the DPV for a pickup. He had to evacuate quickly—no time to savor the killing of the two Americans today. The cruise missiles would be arriving within moments to sterilize the battlefield. He was under strict orders to leave no evidence of Chinese presence behind, and with five smashed vehicles and ten dead operators in the field, there was only one way to burn away the evidence. The mobile missile launch platform in Mali had already fired on his command. He designated the COMPASS locators in three of the DPVs as the targets.

The surviving DPV slowed just enough for Guo to leap into the passenger seat. He shouted, "GO!" but it was hardly necessary. The driver smashed the gas pedal to the floor. The rail threw big sand and fishtailed as the Chinese raced due north, away from the coming holocaust.

Three ground-hugging Chinese cruise missiles streaked across the Algerian desert, flying just meters above the terrain to avoid radar detection and air defense systems. Onboard TERCOM and COMPASS navigation systems maneuvered autonomously around obstacles while keeping the missiles zeroed in on their targets. They had been launched just minutes before from a single portable launcher now deployed in Mali by Dr. Weng and Zhao, with more missiles for reloads stored in a Chinese-secured Bamako warehouse.

The CJ-10 "Long Sword" cruise missile had been largely designed from reverse-engineered American Tomahawk cruise missiles salvaged by the Pakistanis from failed cruise missile strikes against the Taliban in the late 1990s. Like the Tomahawk, these weapons were designed for surgical strikes. Tomahawks were the weapons of choice for many American presidents before the advent of drone technologies like the Predator, and sometimes after. President Obama launched over two hundred Tomahawks against Gaddafi's military in 2011, helping to topple his murderous regime. In fact, the Americans had launched two *thousand* Tomahawk strikes against other nations without declaration of war since 1983—ample precedent for today's action, as far as the Chinese were concerned.

The Long Swords locked onto their respective targets

just one kilometer away, their 500 kg warheads set to ignite with devastating precision.

Sergeant Wolfit slammed the cargo door shut as the plane lurched forward.

Cella hovered over Pearce's unconscious body, medical bag open, cutting away at the *tagelmust* still wrapped around his head. Myers straddled his legs to steady him against the shuddering fuselage streaking down the runway.

The *tagelmust* finally gave way. Myers gasped. Pearce's face was slathered in a mask of indigo and surging blood.

"It's just a scalp wound," Cella shouted. She smiled at Myers. "He's alive."

"Thank God," Myers whispered.

Judy slammed the Aviocar's throttles as far forward as they could go, but the boxy little plane still wasn't hitting maximum speed, thanks to the deflating starboard tire. The smoldering ruins of the Hummingbird loomed large in the windscreen. They weren't going to make it—

"Now!" she barked.

She and Kavanagh yanked back on the yokes together, pulling them hard into their guts. The Aviocar leaped into the air like a thrashing marlin.

The plane shuddered as metal screamed against metal, the belly of the fuselage scraping hard against the twisted remains of the A-160. Judy felt the Aviocar twist—and for a fleeting second she was sure they were going to crash. But the rugged transport plane corrected under Judy's deft rudder and yoke work, and seconds later they were in a steep-banked climb with nothing but hazy blue sky filling her windscreen.

"Yee-haw, baby!" Kavanagh shouted. He flashed a huge grin at Judy. "You wanna fly A-10s sometime, you look me up, you hear?" His voice boomed in Judy's headset. She was glad for the distraction and grateful nobody else in the cargo area was online. Early was back there, dead, and Pearce shot in the head. Kavanagh's caterwauling was all she could handle for now.

The three cruise missiles each struck within half a meter of their designated targets, guided by the COMPASS locators on the DPVs. The fuel-air explosions produced a massive concussive blast followed by a boiling cloud of searing fire hot enough to melt the desert floor. Anything not vaporized by the initial pressure wave was consumed by the engulfing flames. One square kilometer of the Earth's surface had just been wiped clean of organic life and any evidence that it ever existed.

The force of the blast waves rocked the Aviocar as it clawed its way past two thousand feet, shaking everything inside that wasn't strapped down.

"Jimminy Christmas!" Judy shouted as she white-knuckled the yoke for a second time, wrestling the plane back into line. How the Aviocar managed to keep flying was beyond her.

"You must be living a clean life, Hopper. That was damn near miraculous."

"I'd say it was good engineering."

"I was talking about the flying, not the plane."

Judy allowed herself a smile. "Thanks."

"I can't wait to see how you handle an Algerian fighter."

"Why do you say that?"

Kavanagh pointed high in the windscreen. "Take a look."

A MiG-25 jet fighter streaked across the sky. She guessed fifteen thousand feet. Its flight path perpendicular to their own. She glanced at her warning switches. No antiaircraft missile lock.

"He must be texting his girlfriend. He doesn't see us." Judy nudged the Aviocar lower to the ground. At least make it harder for the MiG pilot to see them if he changed his mind after all.

"And if he does see us?"

"Hope you're a praying man, Colonel. This Aviocar has the speed and firepower of a postal truck."

Fiero residence
Washington, D.C.

The small manila envelope arrived at the Fieros' home late in the evening by private courier. She glanced at the return address. Part of a prearranged code. She tried not to panic. Fiero thanked the mysterious young man in golden dreadlocks, tossing him a fifty-dollar bill to get him quickly off the porch and on his way. Her husband was at their home in California. She would have preferred to open this in his presence. He liked to face bad news head-on. She hated it, but avoided the temptation to Skype him as she tore the envelope open.

Inside, a three-by-five index card. A wafer-thin 32-gig flash memory card was taped to it, along with the phrase "1 of 2" constructed from multiple magazine cutouts, like an old-school kidnapper's ransom demand.

This was bad. The double entendre clear, as per their arrangement. *Previous arrangement*, Fiero corrected herself. This card meant that her relationship with Jasmine Bath was over. She had worked with Bath for years, using her husband, Anthony—The Angel—as an intermediary.

The intel on this flash card was a double-edged knife. On the one hand, it would contain information Fiero could use to protect herself against her enemies. The republic was founded on the principle of checks and balances. "Ambition must be made to counteract ambition," Madison said. But Madison was only half right. Greed and ambition were the two sides of the scale that kept things in balance, but fear was the fulcrum. Bath's data was like a thumb Fiero could press on either side of the scale to tip things her way. Greed and ambition were her best protections with Bath on her side.

But the other flash card, still in Bath's hands, contained intel that could also ruin Fiero and her husband if Bath was feeling threatened by her. Bath was saying that the memory card was one of two, but also that Fiero was one of two—both of them held weapons that could destroy their enemies, as well as each other. Bath was allowing Fiero to protect herself but was smart enough to protect herself against Fiero.

It was a smart play. Bath had been inaccessible for the last forty-eight hours. Fiero's first assumption was that she had bailed out, and her first impulse was to find the bitch and kill her. Bath was the only person in Washington with the kind of inside information that could put her in a steel cage to die of old age. That made Bath a threat, and Bath knew it. But Bath also knew that keeping those secrets secret were her last, best defense in the event Fiero ever found her. Keeping Fiero safe was Bath's best guarantee of remaining safe. So it was a stalemate.

The only problem was, Fiero hated stalemates. She only wanted to win. But this time she'd have to live with her frustration. She could imagine a life behind bars far more frustrating than this turn of events. At least she still had her power, her money, and her freedom. She could still even win the White House. And who knows? She might yet get the better of Jasmine Bath, whether in this life or the next.

Karem Air Force Base
Niamey, Niger

Pearce awoke two days later. His body had needed the rest as much as his brain needed the time to heal itself.

Myers hadn't left his bedside. His eyes fluttered open.

Saw her smiling face. She wore camouflaged Air Force ABUs.

"Welcome back."

"How long?"

"Two days. You had us worried there for a while."

Pearce smiled. "Sorry about that."

"Did you go toward the light?"

"Yeah. And it was a train." He winced with pain. "A damn big one. Where are we?"

"Back at Karem."

"Arrested?"

"Anything but. Colonel Kavanagh is taking good care of us. No one in D.C. knows we're here and the base is on full alert. We're safe, for now."

She raised his bed. He saw himself in the full-length mirror on the opposite wall. Lightly touched the white gauze bandage wrapped around his head.

"I thought you looked more dashing in the blue one," Myers joked.

Pearce rubbed his shaved face. "I seem to be missing a beard."

"Came free with the haircut. Dr. Paolini said it was medically necessary."

"She always hated my beard."

"Can't say I disagree with her."

Pearce glanced around the room. Mossa's prized gift, the *tagelmust*, was nowhere to be found.

"I'm sorry. It was bloody and one of the techs tossed it into a biohazard burn bag before anyone noticed."

Pearce shrugged. *"Inshallah."*

"Do you know what happened to you?"

"The last thing I remember was picking up Early."

"You took a pretty good lick on that noggin of yours."

"What's the verdict?"

"Full recovery expected. But you might have to start parting your hair on the other side of your head once it all grows back in."

"You're assuming I actually comb my hair."

Myers explained what had happened to him. How the bullet had only grazed his head but opened up his scalp, which bled furiously. The best guess was that the speeding bullet had hit him just hard enough to knock him down, but slamming his head on the tarmac had knocked him out cold.

Myers described in great detail Judy's masterful handling of the Aviocar and saving all of their lives. She didn't tell him the ride in back was like sitting inside of a tumbling clothes dryer.

She went on to describe how Cella stanched the bleeding with a pressure bandage and cradled Pearce's head in her lap in the back of the plane as Judy fought to maintain control of the Aviocar. How Cella's clothes were soaked in blood by the time they landed at Karem, and how Cella had pushed the base medic aside and sewed Pearce up herself, cleaning and dressing the wound with skill.

The door knocked lightly and swung open. It was Cella. She saw Pearce was awake. She beamed. Approached the bed. She wore clean Air Force hospital scrubs. She leaned over and kissed his cheek. "Back from the dead, I see."

"Call me Lazarus." He pointed at her scrubs. "You get drafted?"

"The Versace store was closed when we got here." Cella pinched Pearce's wrist, feeling for his pulse, counting the seconds on her watch. "How are you feeling?"

"Fine."

"Liar."

"Okay, I feel shitty, but not too shitty. Headache. Vision a little blurry."

"That's to be expected. You have suffered a severe concussion, but fortunately no brain bleeding."

"We have to get you out of here. You need better medical attention than the base can provide," Myers said.

"Where am I going?"

Cella grinned. "With me."

Pearce stood by the floor-to-ceiling picture window, watching Ian and Dorotea play soccer. The Scotsman and the girl laughed and jostled like two old friends.

"Both are artificial legs?" Cella asked.

"Yes. Robotic legs, technically." Pearce tapped his skull. "He has a wireless BMI implant that drives them."

"He moves quite well."

"The legs feature miniature gyroscopes and accelerometers embedded on semiconductor chips, rare earth magnets, brushless electric motors, advanced software, you name it. He's the project manager for it, so it only seemed fair to let him have the first pair."

"Fantastico."

Ian bounced the soccer ball on his forehead like a

trained seal, barking like one, too. Dorotea howled with laughter.

Pearce squeezed Cella's hand. "Thank you."

"For what?"

"For the last month. You gave me back my health. And more."

After Pearce woke up in the clinic at Karem AFB, Myers and Holliday arranged for Cella's father to charter another jet and secretly bring the two of them back to Italy, where Cella could tend to Pearce's medical needs and her father could provide them both security.

At first, Pearce continued to suffer blurred vision and nausea, along with frequent headaches. But a consulting neurologist prescribed medications, and over the course of the following weeks Pearce went from bed rest to walking and then finally light exercise.

But the best part of his recovery had been learning how to play again. Under the watchful eye of Renzo Sforza and his security team, the three of them hiked and rode horses around the estate and, later, sailed and swam around the less populated areas of the lake. Pearce and Dorotea formed an instant bond, despite the fact the child spoke virtually no English and Pearce spoke neither Italian nor Tamasheq. Within days, the precocious little girl had taught herself a few phrases in English from an online language program. She also insisted on cooking for him, brushing aside the kitchen's gourmet chef with a flurry of hands and florid Italian. Dorotea's culinary repertoire was limited to scrambled eggs and butter pasta, which Pearce ate lustily in her presence to her squealing delight, and that made her love him all the more.

She had Pearce's eyes, no doubt. But Pearce hadn't raised the issue of the girl's paternity. Pearce didn't think it was fair to the child, nor to Mossa's son, nor Mossa, either, who had protected both Cella and Dorotea with his life. Dorotea was who she was no matter who the biological father might be, and Pearce loved her for that. If the girl wasn't his, would she be any less beautiful or brilliant?

Cella leaned against Pearce, happier than she'd ever been.

Pearce whispered in her ear, "We need to talk."

Cella glanced at him. What was in his eyes? She couldn't tell. She didn't dare hope, but still. A future together. Maybe more.

"What is it?"

"I'm heading back home," Pearce said.

Cella paled. "For how long?"

He shrugged. "Forever, I guess."

"That's a long time."

"I belong there. It's who I am."

"I don't understand. You belong with us."

"I know. Just not here. Come with me."

Cella's eyes flared. "Why should we? Our home is here. My father is here."

"But this isn't my country. These aren't my people."

"Dorotea and I, we are your people."

"It's not the same. You heard Mossa. I am what I am, an American and a soldier. My job is to defend my country."

"You know how I feel about war."

"I know. I hate it, too. So does every thinking person who has ever fought in one. I hope I never have to fight another one again."

"You're a liar. You love it. Why else choose it over us?"

"You know how I feel about you and Dorotea. That's why I want you to come with me."

Cella's face hardened. She turned away from him, arms crossed. She stared at her daughter outside, playing with Ian.

"Her blue eyes are mine, not yours."

"Blue is blue."

"She is not your daughter."

"I don't believe you. Not that it matters."

"She was born ten months after Lisbon. I can show you the birth certificate. She is Rassoul's."

"You knew all along?"

"Of course."

"Why didn't you tell me?"

"You wanted to believe it, so I let you."

"Why tell me now?"

"I wanted you to know the truth. Now you are free."

"How does that make me free?"

"I won't go with you, not for war. But I can't have you stay for a lie, either."

He wrapped his arms around her. "I don't care that she isn't minc."

She softened, turned around. "I know. You are a good man. But you are determined to leave. If you left and thought she was yours, you would feel guilty for being away, perhaps come back. Now you can go with a clear conscience."

"I hate leaving without the two of you."

She touched his face. Searched his eyes. "And yet, you choose it."

"So do you."

"I am who I am as well." She wrapped her arms around his neck.

He held her close, whispered in her ear, "If you ever change your mind, you know where to find me."

She nodded. "And you as well, you fool."

Pearce held her tightly. He smelled the summer in her hair. The last light of the sun was falling behind the jagged ridgeline, throwing shadows on the lake.

It would be night soon.

= 61 =

Cayo Grande
Los Roques Archipelago, Venezuela
1 July

Jasmine dug her toes into the blinding white sand, admiring the intense clarity of the blue Caribbean. The warm sun caressed her skin, darkening it nicely. Even the mint in her *mojito* was particularly sweet. The weekend trip to the idyllic Venezuelan island was a first little present to herself, the promise of still better things to come.

She wished she could have seen Fiero's face when the senator received the envelope. Fiero always knew the time would come, but foolishly assumed that Bath would telegraph her departure date. Events had spun out of control. Myers and her team had gotten too close and knew Bath was after them—otherwise, why would

Myers have fled the cabin? That left too many loose ends. Loose ends that could be twisted into a noose to hang her with.

CIOS had been the source of Jasmine's strength, but on the run, it posed her greatest threat. The only way her enemies could ever find her is if they pointed it back in her direction. She'd been exceedingly careful to minimize her digital footprint while still at CIOS, and then obliterated what little there was of it when she bolted.

The humans in her network posed the biggest risk. An automated kill switch wiped them away, too. Skeets was the last. Yesterday's coded notice in *El Nacional* confirmed it. Jasmine's last contract killer was dead.

She'd gone completely off the grid, of course, and dove deep into the analogue weeds. Paid for everything in cash, living a modest, prearranged fictional life in Caracas, unnoticed in its large Afro-Latin population. Hid her marvelous hair in braids, and her stunning almond eyes behind a pair of Ray-Bans.

Venezuela suited her perfectly. The anti-Yanqui Maduro government would never honor an American extradition request for her were one ever made. Frequent blackouts, street protests, and other social ills were a tolerable nuisance in the otherwise modern capital, but they were also a benefit, keeping the failing socialist government too busy to attempt finding someone like her, were they so inclined.

It suddenly occurred to her that the greatest crimes ever committed were the ones never discovered. Jasmine wondered where her achievements would rank on that infamous, unknowable list. She smiled. Took another sip of her *mojito*. No one could touch her now.

She was free.

Aviation Mission Fellowship Station
near Mwinilunga, Zambia

Pearce tossed Whit Bissel the keys to the brand-new Cessna bush plane parked on the grassy apron in front of the hangar. The motor ticked, still hot from its recent flight. They stood next to it, admiring its lines.

"I don't know what to say." The beefy blond missionary still wore his oily coveralls and the same wire-rimmed glasses.

"Don't say anything. It was easier to buy you this than telling you I'm sorry for the way I acted, which I am."

"That plane's worth a lot more than the avgas you borrowed from me before."

"You mean stole from you, not borrowed," Pearce said. "I bought the plane in Jo'Berg. There's a Cessna dealer down there."

"I heard about your friend. I'm sorry for your loss."

"His name was Mike Early," Judy said. "He was my friend, too." She was walking up from Whit's house carrying a tray with glasses of tea. "How does she fly?"

"Better than the pilot," Pearce said.

"But you're the pilot. That's not saying much." Judy grinned. She'd taught him how to fly. He was actually pretty good at it, just not as good as she was. "What's wrong with your hand?" She nodded at the bandage wrapped around his left hand.

"This? Nothing. Just a little cut."

"Those are the worst," Whit said, sipping his tea. "Especially paper cuts. They really sting."

Judy gave Pearce the stink eye. "You know lying's a sin, right?"

"I'm a sinner, all right. But I'm not lying."

He wasn't. It really was a cut—from Guo's combat knife. Pearce had used it to open up the Asian's belly, then plunge it through his throat and pin him to a tree. Pearce could still hear the frenzied hyenas whining and yelping as they fed on the dying operator.

Pearce reached for a glass of tea. "Thanks. Cheers."

Judy set the tray down on a workbench just inside the hangar. She walked back past the Cessna. Saw something in the tail's vertical stabilizer.

"Hey, there's a bullet hole."

Pearce and Whit got closer.

Whit nodded. "Sure looks like one."

Judy and Whit turned to Pearce. He shrugged. "Yes, it is."

"And?" Judy asked.

"I'll call Comair. They can fly someone up from Jo'Berg and fix it."

"No need. That's an easy patch job," Whit said. He headed back to the far end of the hangar to grab some tools.

Judy leaned in close. Whispered, "What aren't you telling me?"

"What you don't need to worry about. Everything's fine."

"You sure? You're okay?"

"Better than okay. I promise."

Pearce really was feeling pretty damn good. Ian's intel, as usual, had been dead-on. He found Guo and his men in the DR Congo aiding a regional warlord in exchange for a diamond mine contract. Pearce took out Guo's men with single shots to the head before turning Guo to dog food. A twofer, as far as Pearce was concerned.

"How about you?"

Judy smiled. "It's good here."

"Any chance you coming back?"

"Do you know why I left the first time?"

"I have an idea."

"I lost faith in a lot of things, including humanity. People suck."

"Tell me about it."

"But when I walked into that bar? I knew I wasn't supposed to be there. I don't regret doing it, because you're my friend and Mike was in trouble. But after he died and you nearly got killed, I woke up."

"To what?"

"I've been running for a long time. Especially when I was working for you. Don't get me wrong, it was great, but it was still running. It's time to stop running."

"The God stuff?"

She smiled. "Something like that."

"Still friends, though. Right?"

Judy threw her arms around his neck. "You'll always be my friend. I just can't do what you do anymore."

Pearce held on tight. "You ever need anything, you call, you hear?"

A truck horn blasted in the distance.

"'Bout dang time." Pearce checked his watch.

"Africa time." Whit laughed, walking up. He tossed a toolbox in the grass.

A big diesel fuel truck pulled onto the long grassy airstrip, followed by a flatbed truck carrying a huge empty plastic storage tank.

"Two thousand gallons ought to keep you for a while, Rev. Thought you could use a proper storage tank, too."

Whit shook his head. "You're too generous, Troy."

"You did me a favor by not knocking me on my ass when I told you I was taking your avgas."

"How could I resist? You were quoting scripture."

Judy laughed. "Yeah. What's the story with that?"

"Some other time." Pearce turned to Whit. "And I've prepaid for another two thousand gallons. Just call the distributor when you need it."

"I'm embarrassed. How can I ever thank you?"

"First thing, take care of this woman. She's the best."

The big towheaded missionary blushed. "You don't have to worry about that."

"Second, I need a favor."

"Anything."

The big diesel tanker rumbled to a stop near the hangar, its big hydraulic brakes blowing air. Whit jumped up on the running board and showed the driver where he wanted the storage tank placed. The driver nodded, released the brake, and pushed on. Whit jumped back down and returned to Pearce.

"Now, what can I do for you?"

"I need a ride back to Jo'Berg in that brand-new Cessna of yours in the morning. Need to catch a flight home."

Whit laid a strong hand on Pearce's shoulder. "Africa can use a good man like you. Plenty of honest work to do just around here."

You wouldn't be saying that if you knew what I've done, Pearce thought.

"Thanks, but I'm done with Africa for now."

Judy threw her arms around Troy's neck again. "You'll always have a place here if you need it."

"Hey, Pearce. You can steal my gas, but not my girl." Whit's big, toothy smile flashed just a hint of menace.

Pearce shook the big missionary's hand. "One more favor, Whit. Make damn sure I get an invitation to the wedding, okay?"

= 62 =

Sino-Sahara Oil Corporation Building
Bamako, Mali
7 July

The Chinese had picked the location for the new Sino-Sahara Oil corporate high-rise to annoy the Americans. The newly completed forty-story building stood on the banks of the Niger River, but more important, towered over the lowly American embassy just a half mile away.

To Zhao's dismay, the building replicated the garish modernist designs he loathed. That was because Zhao's uncle, the chairman of CNPC, hired an unimaginative Beijing architectural firm owned by Zhao's cousin, who provided the chairman with the appropriate kickback.

The building's sole design virtue, in Zhao's opinion, was that it was now the tallest building in the city by far. With any luck, the sunlight gleaming off of the soaring mirrored-glass skyscraper would blind the American ambassador or, at the very least, annoy him to distraction, reminding him daily of China's rising dominance on the continent.

Zhao's luxury suite on the top floor was proof of his dominance as the new head of the corporation. Mossa's death and the resulting collapse of the Tuareg rebellion had guaranteed China's acquisition of the new REE deposits and cemented Zhao's reputation as the man who could always be counted on to complete the most difficult missions. Vast new economic and military resources were now flowing into Mali and the region. Zhao's political future was assured and his family wealth enlarged, thanks to his success.

Zhao ordered his voluptuous Ukrainian secretary to alert his limousine driver to start the vehicle. His private jet would be leaving from Bamako Airport shortly. Zhao entered his private express elevator, one of the fastest in the world, built by the Japanese firm Toshiba. By virtue of its computerized lift and braking system, it rocketed him directly between his penthouse suite and his exclusive parking area in the subbasement at nearly forty miles per hour. It took only 7.27 seconds to travel the forty floors—a distance of four hundred feet.

Zhao was scheduled for a meeting in Beijing tomorrow with the president of China himself, first among equals on the ruling Standing Committee. It was the greatest honor of Zhao's life. A new, broader Africa initiative was under way and Zhao was rumored to be the man to head it up. No doubt this was the next logical step in his progression toward leadership in the CPC. His meteoric rise to the pinnacle of national power might soon make him the youngest president in China's history. The elevator doors shut as Zhao's spirits soared.

Just 7.27 seconds later, the entire building shook with an explosion as the elevator doors in the subbasement smashed open. It sounded like a plane had crashed in the elevator shaft.

The limo driver ran to the wreckage and tried to pry open the bent stainless-steel doors. He couldn't. The concrete structure surrounding the elevator shaft had cracked on impact. Tons of concrete wedged the crushed doors in the frame. All the driver could do was peer inside. The flickering LEDs flashed like strobe lights on the blood-drenched interior. Zhao's body had been pulverized by the high-speed impact, then shredded by the shards of shattered glass that had lined the elevator walls.

Ian's virus had worked perfectly. Penetrating the Toshiba mainframe had been relatively easy, putting the elevator completely in Pearce's control. He recorded Zhao's brutal demise on the elevator cameras.

Pearce watched the video on his transatlantic flight. He only wished Mossa could have seen it, too.

= 63 =

t was the party of the year. If you weren't there, you weren't anybody.

Senator Fiero was practically the president-elect, or so it seemed, though the election was still over a year away. Greyhill's "do nothing" governing style was wearing thin, while Fiero rode higher and higher in the polls thanks to a carefully orchestrated and well-funded advertising campaign, aided by the willing compliance of a Democrat-dominated media.

Early on, Fiero had amassed so much cash in her campaign coffers from all of the big donors that no serious challenger within her party rose up to campaign against her. The only other Democrat in the primary race that was registered in all fifty states was Congressman Lane.

He may have been rising in the polls, too, but he was woefully underfunded and lacked any credible endorsements from party leadership. Thirteen members of the Kennedy family denounced his use of JFK's inaugural *Ask not* phrase as unbecoming and, possibly, actionable in a court of law. Five Kennedys had publicly announced their support of Fiero's candidacy, and the three most powerful among them were here at the party tonight.

Pearce centered the crosshairs squarely on Fiero's upper lip. She had floated like a butterfly between guests all night—foreign ambassadors, Hollywood celebrities, hip-hop artists, and media pundits had all passed through the glass in his scope as he tracked the senator from room to room. Fiero hadn't stood still long enough to take a clear shot.

Until now.

Pearce's fingertip rested lightly on the trigger. It required less than two pounds of pull to fire. He slowed his breath, counted his heartbeats. Sent the signal from his brain to his finger to begin the smallest contraction, building pressure slowly, not allowing a jerked finger or a ragged breath to alter the shot trajectory. The pressure in his fingertip built. It was nearly sexual. The climax would be a solid thud from the tip of the suppressed sniper rifle; the release a spiderwebbed windowpane three hundred yards away and a spray of blood pluming from Fiero's Botoxed face.

The expectation tingled the length of his arm all the way down to his index finger. Any moment now.

And then a woman stepped into view.

Margaret Myers.

The former president stood in front of Fiero, completely blocking his shot. The hand-loaded .300 Winchester Magnum round was powerful enough to tear through Myers's skull and plow into Fiero's. But that wasn't an option.

He and Myers hadn't spoken in over a month, but she had communicated her opposition to his killing spree through Ian. Myers knew Fiero was on his list. *You can't just go around murdering politicians you don't like. The rule of law protects all of us. If you shoot Fiero, who'll shoot me?*

He ignored her. Johnny, Early, Mossa, Balla, Moctar, Mano. The rule of law didn't do them any good. Why should a lawbreaker like Fiero benefit from the law?

Damn it.

He withdrew his fingertip from the trigger completely, glanced away from the scope. He nearly vomited. Myers had escaped death by the slimmest possible margin. One more heartbeat and she could have been Jackson Pollocked all over Fiero's stainless-steel Sub-Zero refrigerator.

"Ian," he whispered in his mic.

"She made me do it," Ian replied.

"Who made you do what?"

"Don't blame him," Myers said. Her voice was in his earpiece.

Pearce put his eye to his scope again. She wasn't in the kitchen. He moved the scope around, window to window. Found her in the second-story bathroom glancing out of the window, searching, but not in his direction. He watched her lips move. Her voice arrived a split second later, the briefest of time delays.

"I can't see you out there, Troy, but I know you can hear me."

"How?"

"Sorry, old man. But I owed her one," Ian said. Clearly, he had told Myers what Pearce planned to do that night.

"You're fired," Pearce said.

"You're hired, Ian," Myers countered. "And I'll double your salary."

"You think this will stop me?"

"No, Troy, I don't. But I've notified the Secret Service that there might be a problem. They'll be on you as soon as I give the order."

"Give it."

"I'd rather not."

"What do you want?"

"A word."

"Shoot."

"Nice punning, former employer."

"Shut up, Ian."

"I understand you want justice, Troy. I can give it to you. But not at the end of a gun."

"I'm listening, but I'm also aiming." Fiero had wandered back into his scope. She stood in the living room now, laughing too hard at something Alec Baldwin was saying.

"A bullet through the brain would be far too painless of a death, and far too quick, for someone as loathsome as Barbara Fiero," Myers said.

"I like the way this is sounding."

"I have a better way to make her suffer. She'll be tormented every waking breath."

"Tell me what to do."

"Stand down. Do nothing. I'll take care of it," Myers said. "You have to trust me on this."

Silence.

"Troy?"

"Trust issues, remember?"

"If I'm not telling the truth, you can always kill her later, right?"

More silence.

"How soon?"

"It begins tomorrow."

"How will I know you've done it?"

"You won't be able to miss it, I promise."

"I'll hold you to it. Otherwise, Fiero's dead. Diele, too."

"There's a bigger picture here, Troy. And killing those two dirt bags will only ruin it."

"If you start lecturing me about political compromise, I'll start shooting."

"We're beyond compromise. But violence isn't the answer, either. You'll only be helping them in the long run."

Myers explained her plan, filled in the big picture.

Pearce was stunned. He wanted bloody revenge, but she was right.

Her plan was better.

= 64 =

Pearce didn't pull the trigger on Fiero, but Myers did. Pulled it on Diele, too. She released Bath's secret audio of them plotting the illegal drone strike against Mossa and Pearce, which would have resulted in Pearce's death, an innocent American citizen and a war hero.

The story first leaked on Fox News, a network Fiero had targeted for punishment over the years. Payback was a real bitch. So was Fiero. Fox News was happy to toss her into the wood chipper of public opinion.

Bath had recorded virtually everything Fiero had ever done as a form of protection against her wily employer. It was also a form of leverage. Fiero was one of the most powerful politicians on the Hill. If any law-enforcement agency ever decided to take Bath on, she knew Fiero would be forced to protect her in order to protect herself.

What Bath hadn't counted on was Ian McTavish, the hacking genius that penetrated her defenses and stole everything she had before she destroyed it. Of course, what Bath possessed wasn't limited to Fiero. CIOS held the entire Hill hostage, whether they knew it or not. Bath had hacked everybody, never realizing that Ian had hacked her. Now Myers and Ian had all of Bath's data at their disposal.

The first recording they released was Fiero's conversation with Diele, suggesting an illegal drone strike on Mossa and Pearce. To any political insider, there was hardly anything startling about the audio. It was a typical closed-door conversation, cold-blooded and calculating—standard Washington fare. But the Fox News morning anchors ate it up. So did the public. It was *House of Cards* for real. By noon, the talk-radio personalities were running with the scandal. By the end of the day, most evening news shows—local, national, broadcast, cable—led with it.

Harry Fowler, Fiero's campaign manager, was in damage-control mode the minute the story first broke that morning, calmly placing a few phone calls to network presidents on his speed dial to quell things down and keep the contagion from spreading. It didn't work.

The Fiero scandal had serious legs, and the dying broadcast networks couldn't afford to be left holding Fiero's bag. Audience share was everything. Like the Great Powers in World War I, the networks and cable news outlets were willing to shed buckets of blood for a scant few percentage points of gain. By the end of the day, Fowler and his team were in full panic mode, leaping into raging news infernos everywhere on the horizon, smoke jumping without parachutes. And that was just the first day.

Now that Fiero and Diele were a major news item, the networks were hungry for more revelations. Ian chummed the waters carefully, ladling out the juicy chunks in digestible, quotable bites, not only to the media but to party organizations as well. Why not turn the sharks on each other?

The Sunday-morning talk shows were crammed with Republican and Democratic legislators jockeying for position, trying to seize the moral high ground from their opponents, each concentrating their verbal volleys on either Fiero or Diele according to party affiliation. Neither had any true defenders. The best either party could hope for was that the other party would get the most blame.

But the public was outraged at both parties. Even the venerable Howard Finch, an old ally of Fiero and a life-long Democrat, gave an impassioned plea at the end of his show, *Meet the Nation*, urging Fiero to reconsider her decision to seek the presidential nomination.

Fiero's election hopes evaporated, and Diele's future was suddenly questioned. Greyhill pushed him off of the ticket, fearing the vice president's scandals would ruin his own reelection chances, hoping to hide behind the paper-thin shield of plausible deniability.

Myers felt no guilt breaking her agreement with Diele and Greyhill to keep the incriminating audio under wraps in exchange for the pardon and release of Ian, Rao, and the others. Both men had committed a federal crime by agreeing to the deal in the first place. It would only add to Diele's time in prison and put Greyhill in the center of the firestorm. Her calculation was dead-on. Both men kept their mouths shut. And they didn't renege on the pardons—*You can't unring the bell*, Diele told Greyhill—because Myers would release that audio conversation, too.

Myers reveled in the ruin of Diele and Fiero. But as far as she was concerned, it was only the beginning.

Myers feared for her country. It had been seized decades before by career politicians, an entrenched class of professional extortionists skilled in the art of the shakedown, and worse, of stealing money from future generations to buy votes. They enriched themselves and their families at the expense of the country. The greater crime was that their self-serving policies contributed to America's rapid decline. Chronic unemployment, failing schools, endless wars, massive trade deficits, and crumbling infrastructure could all be laid at their feet, and yet, they were never held accountable.

Knowledge was power, but secret knowledge was the most powerful. The permanent political class continued to rule virtually unopposed despite the fact that the majority of Americans held them in contempt, as every public opinion poll confirmed year after year. What voters lacked were specifics. Regarding flagrant violations of the law, prosecutors lacked evidence. Myers was determined to change all of that.

Every member of the House was up for reelection in 2016, and one-third of the Senate. The Fiero and Diele exposures were an earthquake, but Myers wanted to create a political tsunami that would wreck the permanent political class that had bankrupted the nation and betrayed the Constitution.

Fiero and Diele were quickly pushed off the front-page headlines as fresh sacrificial goats fell victim to the media knives. The new revelations were bigger than WikiLeaks, the Watergate tapes, and the Pentagon Papers combined. Dozens of veteran politicians suddenly found the urge to "be with their families" rather than continue in public service before any incriminating data was released against them, hoping to avoid expulsion or conviction in order to maintain their lucrative, full-salaried retirement packages.

The ones that didn't quit were clean, because they had nothing to hide. Men like Rep. David Lane, the only Democratic presidential candidate still qualified to run in all fifty states.

The data dump continued. So much quality information was released that newsrooms had to rehire entire staffs previously let go. Those newsrooms and editorial boards that tried to protect political favorites were quickly bypassed by the New Media outlets willing to tell the truth. Federal, state, and local prosecutors geared up for a series of high-profile trials.

Myers couldn't be certain where all of it would lead, only that the power of entrenched incumbents might soon be broken.

Everything was about to change.

= 65 =

Galápagos Islands
Pacific Ocean
18 October

J asmine Bath had a long bucket list. That was part of the reason she had needed to amass so much cash for her permanent retirement. She hadn't quite reached her ultimate goal, but twenty-eight million dollars would go a long way, particularly the way she had invested it, spread out over twenty hedge funds in ten countries under as many different aliases.

She arrived in Ecuador under one of her many false identities, in this case a Swiss passport, and paid for everything in cash, including the hotel where she was staying, the air flight out to the islands, and the private Galápagos snorkeling tour—item number one on her list.

———————

The October water around the archipelago was brisk but more than manageable in her wet suit. She had snorkeled and dived on numerous occasions in Hawaii, the Caribbean, and Fiji, but these ancient, pristine islands in the middle of the vast Pacific held a particular allure for her, thanks to Darwin. In her mind, this place was *the* origin of species. That wasn't true, but no matter. It was her dream, and she was finally here.

Jasmine knew all about the wide variety of marine species she was likely to encounter. Seafaring iguanas, gentle whale sharks, and eagle rays were particularly interesting to her, but she was most excited about the sea turtles. She had a lifelong love of the magnificent, gentle creatures. She had swum with green turtles all over the world, and had recently donated a large monetary gift to a Florida turtle habitat—anonymously, of course. Swimming with the turtles in the Galápagos would be the ultimate experience.

Her private guide boat took her out to a favorite turtle haunt off of Roca Redonda, one of the smallest islands that made up the volcanic archipelago. The tiny western island was actually the top of a volcano. Deepwater marine life as well as mammals flourished in the nutrient-dense dark blue waters on this side of the archipelago thanks to the Humboldt Current. Captain Girondo—a young, muscular Argentine—would remain on the yacht to fix a gourmet lunch and, if her plans worked out, take a deep plunging dive into her unexplored regions later in the afternoon. There was one other boat in the area. Captain Girondo said it was a research vessel. No fishermen were allowed in these waters.

Today she decided to free dive without benefit of tanks. She'd take more time tomorrow and go deep. Thirty minutes into her paddling Bath managed to encounter several schools of harlequin wrasse, steel pompanos, bumpheads, surgeonfish, and sea horses among the coral. She swam with a red-mottled underwater iguana for a while and watched a yellow-bellied sea snake swim past. A dozen dolphins rocketed by her, and two curious sea lions came right up to her and played with her for a while. She'd read that the animals in these waters had no genetic memory of humans and were naturally fearless of visitors like her. She was utterly delighted. But she was also growing disappointed. Where were the turtles?

She continued swimming in lazy circles, bobbing on the surface until something caught her eye. In the distant murkiness of the deeper waters to the north she saw a cluster of movement, slow and deliberate. She took a deep breath in her snorkel and dived deep into the water to get a better view. She felt her ears pop as she descended twelve feet or so. No question. A bale of green sea turtles was stroking its way in her direction. She was thrilled. They were moving deceptively fast. They were less than three hundred feet away. She was tempted to surface again and catch another deep breath, but she was afraid her movements might be too jerky and send them off in another direction. She decided to sit tight and remain motionless, knowing she could easily hold her breath for another thirty seconds. On their current path they would swim right past her. With any luck, she'd be in the middle of them. Maybe even catch a ride.

The first great parrot-faced turtle approached. It cast a wary eye at her but decided she was no threat and swam past. A strong eddy brushed against her from the force of his powerful flippers.

A wall of enormous green turtles zoomed in right behind the first, dropping below her feet, passing to either side of her, skimming above her head, flippers stroking. Glorious.

The largest turtle of the bale approached, probably the oldest, she guessed, certainly the most graceful. As it pushed gently by, Bath reached out and grasped the top ridge of its shell, near the neck. Her air was thin and her lungs burned a little, but she didn't dare let go. She couldn't believe how swiftly and smoothly the big animal moved in the water. The ancient turtle clearly sensed she was holding on to him and it seemed to paddle faster, either to compensate for her weight or to shake her off. But it swam straight and didn't seem distressed, so she held on. She felt such freedom. It was a dream come true, the chance to be at one with the—

Pain stabbed her ankle, like a knife cut. She wanted to scream but resisted, lest she drown. She released her grip on the turtle's shell. Twisted around to see what had struck her.

It was another turtle, its beak clamped around her bleeding ankle. She couldn't believe it.

But this turtle was different. The colors were right. So was the size. But the eyes.

Lifeless glass.

It wasn't a turtle.

It was a machine, built exactly like a sea turtle.

The drone turtle began paddling in reverse, pulling her down.

Bath felt the water from its powerful strokes brush against her face. They were falling fast.

She kicked her seized leg, but the metal beak only cut deeper into her flesh. Blood clouded the water. The drone's flippers paddled faster, the machine now pointing directly down into the inky black of the abyss. Stroke by stroke she was being pulled down, faster and faster. She heard the drone's restless servos grinding in the water.

Bath glanced back up at the surface. The dappling sunlight was falling away fast. Searing pain exploded in her ears, like knitting needles stabbed into her eardrums. Her beating heart pounded inside her skull.

She kicked hard with her free leg, thrusting the big dive fin with all of her strength, clawing at the water above her head—anything to reverse direction. But the turtle was far too powerful and heavy. She felt the last of her air evaporate with the extra, futile effort.

Her lungs burned as if filled with acid. She looked back down at the turtle mindlessly plunging into the sunless void. Blood from her ankle streamed past her face. The freezing water burned her ungloved hands. She strained every muscle to bend forward and grasp her calf. She pulled with all of her strength. Nothing.

The water turned from blue to black. She wanted to scream.

She couldn't scream.

Had to scream.

Wasn't fair.

Not this.

The turtle dived relentlessly, dragging Jasmine down with it, the two disappearing into the black, trailing bubbles and blood and the echoes of her wordless screams.

I n the cabin of the boat, Dr. Kenji Yamada asked, "How much deeper?"

Pearce's peace-loving whale researcher and UUV expert didn't have much stomach for killing, but he understood its ecological necessity, especially in this case. Diseased animals had to be culled. The ponytailed scientist just couldn't do it himself.

Pearce wouldn't let him anyway. Pearce controlled the turtle drone. Had to.

Pearce had funded Yamada's Honu project. Yamada used the funds to modify a Naro-Tortuga drone so that it looked exactly like a green sea turtle, enabling it to swim with and study the ones populating the Hawaiian Islands. Yamada never imagined the unit would be deployed like this.

Early's death still haunted Pearce. He woke up some nights slapping at his face, certain that Early's brains and blood were clinging to his skin. The days weren't much better, haunted by the faces of Early's small children streaked with tears, his sobbing widow, the folded American flag placed in her hands, the lowering casket. Mike was a true warrior and a true friend, and now he was truly gone.

Pearce had to make it right. Had to make the last person pay in full.

Jasmine Bath had to die.

But she'd been too clever. Covered all of her tracks, burned all of the bridges. Couldn't be found.

Until now. Because Ian was better than Bath.

Ian called, said he had found Bath, gave him the details. Pearce worked out a plan, but not just to kill her. That was too easy. Wanted her to suffer, and worse. He knew that was wrong. He didn't care, or couldn't. The rage consumed him.

Hi-def and infrared cameras along with audio mics embedded in the drone's head recorded every moment of Jasmine Bath's raging, terrified misery. Pearce wanted her dead, but he needed to see her die. Badly.

She didn't disappoint. She put on quite a show the deeper she went. Thrashing and screaming in a hail of bubbles until the last one dribbled away, the light dimming in her panicked, bloodshot eyes until she finally let go.

But the drone didn't. It swam deeper still.

Bath's limp arms trailed above her head, hair braids pluming in the frigid water as the blackening deep swallowed her up in silence.

"She's dead, Troy," Yamada said. "You can release her now."

Pearce wanted to, but couldn't. Couldn't shake the image of Early's head exploding in front of his eyes.

Drowning Bath wasn't enough, terrible as that was. He wanted to drag her down to crush depth, watch her body erupt in a pink, gory cloud.

Wanted to drag her down to hell.

But Yamada was right. The woman was dead. The debt paid.

Pearce released his grip on the controller. Let her go. Watched her corpse drift away into the fathomless dark.

His rage, too.

He was free.

= 66 =

The night was cold and clear, the Milky Way a vast gauzy film across a moonless, blue-black expanse. Snow-heavy pines creaked in a light breeze.

Pearce stood on the porch, pistol on his hip, coffee in hand. He thought about Daud.

He'd rebuilt the cabin all by himself. Taken him months, but it was worth it. Time to get sober again. Time to process everything, especially what Mossa had said back in the desert. The old man was right. Pearce was a masterless warrior. Useless.

The bright halogen lights of an SUV bounced into the tree line, inching its way along an unlit path in the snow. Pearce couldn't be sure who it was from here. Bath had a network of wet-work operators. Even dead, she could get her revenge if she was vindictive enough and had signed the right kind of contracts.

After Ian had filled him in on all the details of his hacking op against Bath and the others, Pearce decided it was time to go back to basics, at least out here. Fireplaces, axes, well water, dried fish. He went completely off the grid at the cabin, no electronics of any kind, including surveillance. Connectivity meant vulnerability. He preferred the sound of chopping wood to laser printing anyway. He had all of the electronic gear he needed in the RV, and at his condo in Coronado, not to mention Pearce Systems headquarters in Dearborn. But out here was his solitude and silence. This was his desert.

The SUV cleared the tree line and approached the cabin. Pearce squinted in the harsh lights. Tossed his coffee and set the cup down on the rough-hewn table. The SUV lights snapped off.

Heavy doors slammed shut. Two figures in hooded parkas exited the SUV. Dark shadows crunched in the snow, trudging toward him. A figure emerged into the firelight from the window flickering in the snow. She pulled down her hood.

"Troy."

Pearce nodded. "Glad you made it."

Myers looked good. Radiant, actually.

Pearce stepped off the porch and gave her a hug. Myers pointed at the man standing next to her.

"Troy, this is Congressman David Lane."

"Just Dave," Lane said, shaking Pearce's hand.

Myers trusted Lane. That was good enough for him.

It was time to serve again.

Time to get back in the fight.

ABBREVIATIONS AND ACRONYMS

ABU	Airman Battle Uniform (Air Force "fatigues")
AFB	Air Force Base
AFRICOM	Africa Command
AMF	Aviation Mission Fellowship (fictional)
Ansar Dine	"Defenders of the Faith"
ANT	Advanced Network Technology (a division of the NSA's TAO)
AQS	al-Qaeda Sahara (fictional)
BDU	Battle Dress Uniform (Army "fatigues")
BMI	Brain Machine Interface
BOQ	Bachelor Officer Quarters
COMPASS	Chinese version of GPS
CTD	Counterterrorism Division (FBI)
CXS	Communications Exploitation Section (FBI CTD)
DARPA	Defense Advanced Research Projects Agency (US)
DDoS	Denial-of-Service attacks
DNI	Director of National Intelligence
DPV	Desert Patrol Vehicle
FAE	Fuel-Air Explosive
FAV	Fast-Attack Vehicle
GAD	General Armament Department (a PRC/PLA version of DARPA)
GCHQ	Government Communications Headquarters (the British version of the NSA)
GCS	Ground Control Station (drones)

GPS	Global Positioning System
HFT	High Frequency Trading
HSD	High Speed Data
JDAM	Joint Direct Attack Munition
JTRIG	Joint Threat Research and Intelligence Group, the GCHQ's anti-hacktivist division
LARs	Lethal Autonomous Robotics
LS³	Legged Squad Support System
MAST	Micro Autonomous Systems and Technology
MAV	Miniature Air Vehicle
MGV	Miniature Ground Vehicle
Mil-Spec	Military Specifications
MNLA	National Movement for the Liberation of Azawad
MSS	Ministry of State Security
NSA	National Security Administration
OPSEC	Operational Security
PDB	Presidential Daily Brief
PLA	People's Liberation Army
PRC	People's Republic of China
PROCEED	Programming Computation on Encrypted Data
REE	Rare Earth Element
RPV	Remotely Piloted Vehicle
SAD/SOG	Special Activities Division/Special Operations Group [the CIA's special forces unit]
SCADA	Supervisory Control and Data Acquisition
SPAN	Self-Powered Ad-hoc Network
STOL	Short Take Off and Landing
sUAV	Small Unmanned Aerial Vehicle
SVR	Sluzhba Vneshney Razvedki (Russian Foreign Intelligence Service)
TAO	Office of Tailored Operations (NSA)
TERCOM	Terrain Contour Matching
UAV	Unmanned Aerial Vehicle

UDC	Utah Data Center
UGV	Unmanned Ground Vehicle
USAFE-AFAFRICA	U.S. Air Forces in Europe-Air Forces Africa
VPN	Virtual Private Network
VTOL	Vertical Takeoff and Landing

DRONE AND OTHER SYSTEMS

DRONE SYSTEMS	TYPE	MANUFACTURER, AGENCY, OR COUNTRY OF ORIGIN
A-160T Hummingbird	UAV (transport)	Boeing Advance Systems
Bio-Bot	Living organisms fitted with hardware and software for automated control	North Carolina State University
Hybrid Quadrotor	UAV (attack)	Latitude Engineering
LS³	Legged Squad Support System (transport—for now)	Boston Dynamics
Naro-tartaruga	UUV (research)	ETH (prototype)
Silent Falcon	sUAS (surveillance)	UAS Technologies
SmartBird	UAV (surveillance)	Festo
Snake	UGV (surveillance)	Tohoku University (prototype)
Switchblade	UAV (surveillance)	AeroVironment
Wraith	UGV (attack)	United Drones

OTHER SYSTEMS	DESCRIPTION	MANUFACTURER, AGENCY, OR COUNTRY OF ORIGIN
AGM-114N Hellfire II	Air-to-ground missile, thermobaric munitions	Lockheed Martin
Botnet	A network of hijacked computers used to perform automated tests over the Internet without the owners' knowledge or consent	Worldwide

BTR-60PB	Personnel carrier	USSR
DROPMIRE	Surveillance hardware	NSA
FN SCAR-H CQC	Special Forces Combat Assault Rifle (Heavy, 7.62mm NATO) Close Quarters Combat version	FN Herstal
HEADWATER	Software backdoors	NSA
JANUS	Facial recognition software	DARPA
JETPLOW	Firewall firmware	NSA
LOUDAUTO	Surveillance hardware	NSA
M-25 grenade launcher, "the Punisher" (formerly XM-25)	Laser-guided, programmable, automatic air burst grenade launcher	Heckler & Koch, Alliant Technologies, L-3 IOS Brashear
M58/59/MICLIC	Mine Clearing Line Charge	American Ordinance
MC-130 Talon	STOL special operations military transport aircraft	Lockheed Martin
PHOTOANGLO	Surveillance hardware	NSA
Satis	Bluetooth-activated robo-toilet with automated flush, spray, music, fragrance release, and data record features	Lixil Group
SOMBERKNAVE	Wireless Internet traffic rerouting software	NSA
SPAN	Self-Powered Ad-hoc Network, a wireless ground sensor	Lockheed Martin
WP	White Phosphorus	Worldwide
XKEYSCORE	Surveillance software	NSA

AUTHOR'S NOTE

While many of the drone and related systems described in this novel are currently deployed, others are based on patent filings, prototypes and research proposals. In some cases I modified or simplified their performance characteristics for the sake of the story. However, I'm confident that some variants of what I've imagined could soon be a reality.

ACKNOWLEDGMENTS

Once again I am gratefully indebted to the entire team at G. P. Putnam's Sons, especially my amazing editor Nita Taublib and her invaluable assistant editor Meaghan Wagner, along with Kelly W. Rudolph, Ashley E. Hewlett, Mary Stone, Christopher Nelson, and the indefatigable sales crew who all support me and the series so well.

I remain well represented by the deep bench at Ink-Well Management, including my savvy agent, David Hale Smith, his gifted assistant, Lizz Blaise, and the social media savant, Lisa Vanterpool.

My very first book tour was an unexpected delight. It was a privilege to meet some of my fantastic readers face-to-face as well as the booksellers who make all of this possible. I owe a special shout-out to Barbara Peters and John Goodwin at The Poisoned Pen bookstore in Scottsdale, Arizona, for hosting my very first public appearance with *Drone*. Amy Harper at Barnes & Noble in Lewisville, Texas, couldn't have been more supportive, and it was an honor to visit with McKenna Jordan and John Kwiatkowski at Murder by the Book in Houston. Sundog Books in Seaside, Florida, was always one of my favorite indie bookstores but seeing *Drone* next to Tom Clancy's latest was an unexpected thrill. Can't wait to see you all again next time.

Thanks to all of you who support Troy & Co. in print, digital, and audio formats. It's been a real pleasure connecting with those of you who have reached out through Twitter, Facebook, and e-mail—keep it coming. Finally, special thanks to Dr. Tim Gottleber who was my go-to resource for questions digital and dangerous in this novel. Mistakes in the manuscript, fictional or otherwise, remain my own.